AUSTRALIAN OUTBACK

Four Journeys to a New Country
Ride on the Wings of Faith and Love

MARY HAWKINS

BARBOUR
PUBLISHING

Faith in the Great Southland ©1999 by Barbour Publishing, Inc.
Hope in the Great Southland ©1999 by Barbour Publishing, Inc.
Love in the Great Southland ©1999 by Barbour Publishing, Inc.
Great Southland Gold ©2002 by Mary Hawkins

Cover image © GettyOne

ISBN 1-58660-968-8

All Scripture quotations, unless otherwise noted, are taken from the King James Version of the Bible.

Published by Barbour Publishing, Inc., P.O. Box 719, Uhrichsville, Ohio 44683, www.barbourbooks.com.

Our mission is to publish and distribute inspirational products offering exceptional value and biblical encouragement to the masses.

ecpa Member of the
Evangelical Christian
Publishers Association

Printed in the United States of America.
5 4 3 2 1

Australian
Outback

MARY HAWKINS is an Australian married to a minister. They have two married sons, a daughter, and one grandson. Their ministry has taken them to many interesting places over the years. Besides almost forty years throughout Australia, these include Africa and even a few years in England, trying to get used to those upside-down seasons in a much colder climate!

FAITH IN THE
GREAT SOUTHLAND

For my dear sister, Shirley Rylance,
who over the years has shared my love for books,
as well as history—and above all,
the love of Christ.

Prologue

England, April 1835

The excited shouts of the crowd squeezed into the public gallery died away. A stillness descended on the courtroom as the judge impressively drew his gown around him at last and rapped his gavel again and again. He looked down at the papers on his desk briefly before staring again at the white-faced young man standing in the dock.

"John Martin, you have just been found guilty of the felonious slaying of Lord Farnley's gamekeeper, Jock Macallister."

A murmur swept through the people. The heavily veiled woman at the farthest corner of the room unsuccessfully tried to stifle a desperate sob. A few heads of the curious swung toward her. She shrank back on her hard wooden bench, one dainty, black-gloved hand pressing the veil to her lips. They stared, but then Judge Wedgewood's ponderous tones brought every eye back to him.

"Do you have anything to say before I pronounce your sentence?"

Every head swung to the condemned man. His tall, strong figure stiffened. He raised his head even higher. As they had many times during his trial, his dark eyes desperately searched the room.

"As God is my witness, I declare once more that I am not guilty!" His slightly accented voice rang with desperate conviction. "The guilty person knows this, and one day. . ." His voice choked with rage and despair. "One day he will have to face an eternal Judge greater than you, Your Honor."

An angry murmur swept through the people at the fellow's effrontery.

The judge adjusted his wig, picked up his gavel, and brought it crashing down in front of him. He stared back at the man before him from beneath his beetling eyebrows and waited until all was dead quiet again.

"Indeed, young man," he replied at last in his impressive tones, "that will be all our lot one day."

Judge Wedgewood picked up the pile of papers before him and shuffled them neatly together. When he had laid them down carefully, he raised his head and said angrily, "I find that you are an arrogant liar who, in a final act of desperation to try and escape conviction for your dastardly crime, dared to declare himself to be the son and heir of my old friend, Lord Farnley."

"I am his son!"

Angry shouts erupted from the crowd. "There's no way old righteous 'Arry would ever 'ave a Frenchy foreigner for a son," someone shouted.

A discreetly clad gentleman in dark clothes bowed his head to hide a delighted smile as Judge Wedgewood banged his gavel until order was restored once again.

The prisoner only glared at the spectator for a moment. Several times already he had protested his mother was Spanish, not French.

"Lord Farnley could not be here in person to refute your preposterous claim because of the desperate illness of his dear wife, but unfortunately for you he has sent the court a sworn statement that you are nothing more than a stranger he kindly took into his employ some months ago."

The prisoner stared back at him defiantly for a moment, but then his shoulders drooped in sudden defeat.

Satisfied, the judge paused and drew something black from the receptacle buried deep in his robes. A hushed murmur raced through the crowd. It was the black cap.

"Prisoner at the bar! Have you anything to urge why sentence of death should not be passed upon you?"

John Martin raised his head and looked steadily at the judge. Then his gaze again swept the room. It caught and held the pale eyes of the gentleman in the front row. The gentleman's eyes dropped first.

The slightest frown twitched the prisoner's ash white face. Then he suddenly straightened his shoulders and stood to his full height as he turned calmly to the judge.

"I have said all I can, Your Honor, except to declare once again my complete innocence and pray that one day the guilty man will be found."

The experienced judge stared back intently for a long moment as though impressed despite himself. "It is in my power to sentence you to hang by the neck until you are dead for such a heinous crime."

The man before him did not flinch. This he had known throughout the trial.

"Oh, no, no, not that!" a woman's despairing voice cried out.

John Martin's head swung sharply around, searching the crowd eagerly.

The gavel thundered again.

"Instead, I will have mercy on you. John Martin, I sentence you to be transported to the great southland of Australia for the term of your natural life!"

Chapter 1

September 1835

The large traveling coach lurched on the uneven surface as it turned and slowly approached the wharf. Elizabeth Waverley leaned eagerly out the window for her first glimpse of the ship that would eventually reunite her with her father.

"For goodness sake, Child, do show some decorum," wailed the stout woman beside her as she pressed a handkerchief daintily to her nose. "And how you can be so pleased to leave me so suddenly like this after all I've done for you I'll never know. You know Lord Weldon's son was on the verge of proposing."

"Oh, Aunt Sophia," Elizabeth began impatiently as she subsided. Then she paused, swallowing back for the hundredth time all she would like to have told her aunt and chaperone about the highly esteemed Frederick Weldon and his sly ways. After holding her tongue for so long about their last encounter, now was not the time to upset her dear aunt any more.

She glanced at the other wide-eyed occupant of the carriage and then shrugged. In the close confines of the ship, poor, frightened Betsy, whom her uncle had somehow persuaded to be her maid for the next few months, would undoubtedly get to know most of her business—already did in the way servants always seemed to.

More gently she said to her aunt, "There has never been the least chance I would ever marry anyone here so far from home. Dear Aunt, you know I always intended to return to Australia as soon as Father would let me."

Sophia Lantry straightened. "But that's just it, Child. He hasn't asked for your return. Couldn't you at least have waited until you heard from him?"

"No, I finished at St. Peter's Lady's Academy last year. As far as I'm concerned, my education was the only reason I let him persuade me to come to England."

Elizabeth's voice had remained quiet, but her aunt had heard that implacable note in her voice too many times over the last three years to do more than sigh and say peevishly, "Well, after all I've done for you, the least you could do is show some sorrow at saying good-bye so suddenly to us all."

The older woman was suddenly enveloped in strong young arms and kissed soundly. "Oh, Aunt, you know I'm sad at leaving you and Uncle Harry and all the friends I've made here. It's just. . .just. . .with Father's old friends returning on this ship it was just too good an opportunity to miss."

11

Sophia returned her embrace and then pushed her away. "Oh, I know, Elizabeth, I know." She sighed again. "I should—you've told me enough over the years. You were born in New South Wales; that dreadful place is your home, and despite all the attractions of England you've been homesick for the smell of eucalyptus ever since you got here—or some such nonsense."

Elizabeth's laugh rang out. "And for the freedom of the open spaces. And it's not a dreadful place," she protested vigorously. "It has the most beautiful harbor, wonderful beaches, and the wildlife—" She stopped abruptly and laughed softly at her aunt's genteel snort before once again turning eagerly to the window as the coach came slowly to a halt.

In a few moments the two women had descended with the help of her aunt's groom. They stared around at all the hustle and bustle of a busy wharf just prior to a ship leaving port. Miss Betsy Bent stumbled slowly out behind them to gaze in fascination at the tall masted ship at the center of furious activity.

"Elizabeth!"

The absolute horror in her aunt's voice made Elizabeth catch her bottom lip firmly with her teeth. When her aunt had insisted on accompanying her to the *Royal Lady* in place of her uncle, who had succumbed to a severe episode of gout, she had hoped fervently that the other "passengers" would have been on board the ship and out of sight by the time they arrived.

Now the moment of truth had come, and she braced herself, knowing that her aunt had also seen the long line of poor wretches in drab gray prison clothes stumbling up the gangplank onto the ship.

Before she could respond, her aunt cried out, "Elizabeth, oh, my dear girl, it's a convict transport ship! You can't go all that way with criminals on board!"

Betsy Bent suddenly wailed in a shrill voice, "Convicts! Criminals. . .no, no! Madam. . .I can't go. No matter what the master says, I won't go!" With that, she burst into tears and climbed back into the coach, slamming the door behind her.

Aunt Sophia wrung her hands, looked at Elizabeth's face, and then went back to the coach to beg the servant not to fail them.

Elizabeth was silent. When Dr. Richmond had warned her he was traveling back as the surgeon on board a transport vessel, she had only hesitated for a moment and then insisted that made no difference to her.

Her father had endured this journey as a convict more than forty years ago. It was something the now-wealthy Australian pastoralist never talked about. Oh, over the years she had pieced together some of the torture he had endured on that voyage, but something deep inside her had made her want to understand more about the hard, solitary man who was her father.

Aunt Sophia grabbed her arm and actually shook it. "I can't talk any sense into that stupid woman. Elizabeth, you can't possibly go on that ship, especially not without a maid!"

Elizabeth opened her mouth to respond, to tell her she would share Mrs.

Richmond's maid or do for herself, but nothing was going to stop her from going on this ship. Before she could utter a word, a loud commotion made them both swing around. A small detachment of mounted soldiers approached. In their wake came a large coach. As it lumbered to a stop not far from them, the horsemen immediately surrounded the vehicle in a wide circle, noisily forcing back the crowd of curious people.

There was a chill wind blowing off the water, but the men crammed miserably together on the top of the coach had not a coat nor blanket between them. All was confusion, noise, and dust for a few moments. Several loud orders were shouted, and the men stood. A few clutched their miserable bundles and began to scramble to the ground. They weren't moving fast enough, and some were seized and dragged roughly down by their guards to sprawl in the dirt.

Simultaneously the doors of the coach were swung open, and other men stumbled their way out to stand shivering on the wharf. The poor wretches' movements were accompanied by the rattle and clash of metal on metal, and Elizabeth drew in a quick breath. However, she quickly noticed that unlike the long line of other convicts already boarding the ship, at least these poor creatures wore individual fetters on their hands and feet.

An officer approached rapidly from the ship, calling out, "This the consignment from York?"

Her gaze still riveted on the group of prisoners, Elizabeth heard a harsh voice respond, "Aye, and a long, hard journey it's been."

"Elizabeth, you can't go on that ship with those dreadful men!"

At her aunt's loud, now almost-hysterical cry, Elizabeth saw one of the prisoners, an erect man who stood head and shoulders taller than those around him, swing his head toward them. For one long, piercing moment, dark eyes from beneath thick, black eyebrows swept over her tall figure from her red gold curls peeping out around the hood of her traveling cloak to her sensibly shod feet.

Then his eyes met hers. For one piercing moment he studied her intently as though committing her face to memory. Then he scowled before turning sharply away and shuffling forward toward the ship.

Elizabeth shivered. Hardly hearing her aunt's continuing protests, she stared after the convict. Despite not being able to take more than a small step because of his chains, he carried himself erectly. His clothes might be as filthy as the others, but they had once been of good cut and quality.

For one brief moment there had been eager anticipation in the dark gaze. Then there had been only the deepest anger, even hatred. As he had swung away, his shoulders stiff and unyielding, some other expression had touched his face, something that could have been utter despair.

❧

A woman called Elizabeth. How ironic.

For one brief, insane moment, John Martin had wondered if Beth Farnley had come at last to insist he was innocent, to stop this madness that had left him rotting in prison all those dreary winter months since his arrest and mockery of a trial. He was sure it had been her voice that day. . . .

"Move along there!"

The hard prod in his back forced John to stumble against the short, thin man in front of him. That poor man had unwittingly fallen foul of the guards on the long journey to London and was in much heavier chains than the rest of them. He almost fell, but John managed to grab him and pull him upright. Blank, empty eyes turned toward him.

"Sorry," John muttered.

It cost him another blow to his back. "No talking, there! Come on, you scum, the sooner you're on board, the sooner you'll all be snug."

As the harsh, sarcastic voice cursed them, frozen limbs made them slip and stumble toward the long gangway. Someone behind John cried out in pain.

Then a boy's voice rang out. "Father—where's my father?"

The man in front of John swung around again. His eyes flared to life. "Tim!" he cried in a great shout. "Here, Son, I'm here!"

His last words were drowned out by the shouting of the guards as they tried to stop the darting, twisting figure rushing toward the convicts.

The boy was close. He never took his eyes off the man in front of John. Then, as the boy's father gave a desperate shout of warning, John too saw the danger. In trying to dodge a burly soldier, the child had moved too close to the edge of the wharf. He stumbled, tried to gain his balance, and then disappeared. Seconds later, they heard the splash of water.

For a fraction of a second Tim's father froze; then with a loud wail, the man stumbled forward. With horror John knew he was about to follow his son into the cold, dark water. Neither father nor son would have a chance. Those heavy iron fetters would drag them down.

John grabbed the man as he tried to push his way past him. "I'll get him, you fool," he muttered, and despite the sudden uproar of the crowd and the shouted orders of the guards, he dived into the dark water.

Almost as soon as he could walk, John had learned how to swim in the river on his grandfather's property in Spain. Normally it would have been no great task to scoop the dazed boy out of the freezing water, but the light chains on his own arms and legs pulled him down.

Months of prison food and lack of exercise had weakened him more than he had realized. It took every ounce of energy he could muster to grab the dazed, floundering boy, cling to him with one hand, and hang on to a moss-covered pier with the other to prevent them both from slipping back under the black, filthy water. It seemed forever before rough hands hauled them out. John collapsed in a heap onto the wharf.

As he lay gasping for breath, he was vaguely conscious of a loud woman's voice in the crowd above them demanding to be let through. A rustle of petticoats drew closer. A gentle hand was using a delicate, perfumed handkerchief to wipe away some of the debris and slime that clung to his face.

He opened his eyes and stared directly into the greenest eyes he had ever seen.

"Are you all right, Sir?"

Her cultured voice was soft, like the whisper of a breeze through the fields of corn in the paddocks at home. Her hood had been thrust back. Those red gold curls had escaped the ribbons tying them back from her beautiful face. They tumbled in glorious profusion to her shoulders.

She was staring at him anxiously, as though she really cared that he should have come to no harm.

And she had called him "Sir."

That first gentle courtesy he had received since he had been arrested in a Yorkshire wood was worth a dunking in the foul, freezing Thames.

"I'll be fine, and. . .and thank you, Madam."

For a timeless moment after his breathless whisper, their gazes locked. His hand moved instinctively up toward her face. The irresistible velvet texture of her glowing skin felt as soft as it looked. Suddenly a soldier thrust her aside. Even so, something deep inside him suddenly exulted. She had made no attempt to flinch away from the touch of his large, wet hand.

"That'll be all, Madam," the harsh voice of the officer in charge ordered. "We'll get him on board with the others now."

Rough hands hauled John to his feet and shoved him forward. He heard the woman called Elizabeth give a sharp protest, but then he was stumbling up the gangplank, even colder now in his soaking wet clothes. Despair once again settled over him like a cloak as he at last descended into the dark hold of the ship and away from the goodness and sweetness of her face.

❧

Elizabeth stood frozen to the spot, watching as the man was half dragged, half pushed up the gangplank to at last disappear after his fellow convicts.

Then one gloved hand crept to the cheek he had touched. . .had touched almost reverently. That desperate, hungry look in his eyes. . .eyes that weren't brown after all, but the darkest blue.

"Oh, Tim, Tim, you foolish boy! I told you and told you they'd never let you near him."

"But I prayed so hard, Ma!"

The weary hopelessness in the woman's low voice and the boy's sad cry captured Elizabeth's attention. She swung around to see a neatly clad young woman a few years older than herself bending over the shivering, wet boy.

Elizabeth ignored her aunt's even louder gasp of horrified protest and crouched down beside them, relieved to see the sobbing boy seemed little worse for his dunking.

She straightened and said briskly to the gaping groom, "The child's freezing. Quickly, that rug from the carriage."

The convict must be even colder in his wet clothes. She forced her thoughts away from him to concentrate on the boy whose life he had saved. Taking the rug from the groom, she wrapped the boy carefully in its warmth.

His mother put her arms around him tightly and said in a shaking voice, "Thank you, Miss."

Elizabeth hesitated and then asked softly, "Your husband is being transported to Australia?"

Pain-filled eyes looked at her. "Ten years they're sending him away for. Ten years! All because he was foolish enough to get involved with some political agitators trying to make a better life for me and his family. He's a good man, not. . . not a criminal! I've been trying and trying to get someone to listen to me, to even let me and the boys go to New South Wales to be near him. Otherwise. . ."

Her voice broke, and tears began rolling down her cheeks. She looked toward the ship. "I don't know if my Timothy will survive ten years out there." Her voice dropped to a choked whisper. "We'll never see him again."

Had it had been like this for her father's family?

Elizabeth doubted it. Instead of coming from such an obviously educated and no doubt respectable background as this woman did, her father had been spawned in the black slums of London, not knowing anything but a life of misery and despair, trying to survive by petty thieving until fate in the guise of a harsh magistrate had sent him to the then-new penal colony far across the seas.

"Things. . .things aren't as bad for the convicts now as they were years ago, especially if he doesn't re-offend," Elizabeth said softly.

The woman straightened and studied Elizabeth for a moment. A bitter light filled her eyes. "Not as bad? Did you see how thin he was, how cold? Why there wasn't a coat amongst the lot of them, and I even sent a special warm one to the prison for him. Goodness knows what happened to it—probably on the back of some guard who thought it too good for a convict to own!" She shuddered. "And those horrible chains. . ."

Elizabeth's aunt pulled at her arm. "Elizabeth, we have to talk while there's still time to change your mind about going on this ship!"

The woman's eyes widened. "You're going on the ship?" she asked eagerly. "All the way to Australia?"

Elizabeth nodded briefly, resisting the insistent tug on her arm. "What is your husband's name?"

"Timothy Hardy." She drew in a quick breath. "If. . .if you could see your way clear to find out how he goes, and even. . .perhaps. . ."

Elizabeth turned to her aunt and said firmly, "Why don't you start up the gangway, Aunt Sophia? I'll only be a moment more."

Aunt Sophia searched her charge's eyes for a long moment and then shrugged resignedly. "I do hope your boy is no worse for his accident, Mrs. Hardy," she said stiffly before nodding to her and moving away.

Elizabeth scrabbled for writing materials in her large reticule. "Perhaps I could send a note to you about the voyage, Mrs. Hardy," she offered gently and was amply rewarded by the look of profound gratitude in the mother's and son's faces as she carefully wrote down their address.

Elizabeth smiled, said her farewells, and went to follow her aunt. Then she paused. "I don't suppose by any chance you know the name of the man who rescued your son?" she asked hesitantly.

"While. . .while he was making me hang on to him, he told me his name was John," the small boy said in a choked voice. "He. . .he said not to fret—he'd look out for my father."

"John!" exclaimed his mother. "I wonder if that's the John Martin my Timothy mentioned in his letter telling me when they were sailing. Why, he's a murderer, just escaped hanging, he did. Transported for life instead."

Elizabeth was motionless for a moment. Suddenly a vivid picture of angry, hatred-filled eyes transformed to a wondering, bemused gaze searching out her very soul.

"He was still a very brave man," she said quietly, and then impulsively kissed the tearful Mrs. Hardy before smiling gently and turning away toward the ship.

She reached the bottom of the gangplank and paused. Closing her eyes, she whispered under her breath, "Oh, God, keep us all safe. Watch over those poor men and always give me Your strength and compassion to do what is right. And. . . and comfort John Martin and. . .and bring him faith and. . .and. . ."

Her eyes flew open. Now, where had that thought come from? She had nearly added the words "someone to love him."

Taking a deep breath, she straightened and continued forward onto the ship that would be her home for the next few months.

Chapter 2

"All settled in, Elizabeth?"

"As best I can, I guess, Dr. Richmond." Elizabeth surveyed her tiny cabin a little ruefully and then smiled at the gray-haired man in its doorway. "It's even smaller than the one three years ago."

He smiled back sympathetically, and then he frowned. "I am so dreadfully sorry that neither you nor my wife have a woman to wait on you."

Elizabeth chuckled. "But neither of us could know the other's maid would let her down. At least Mrs. Richmond's had the excuse of a sudden illness, whereas mine. . ." She grimaced.

"That may be so," he said severely, "but you would certainly have been more comfortable with help, and more comfortable on pretty well any other ship except one specially fitted out to hold as much human cargo as possible." He hesitated and then added dryly, "I gained the impression that your esteemed aunt was unaware this was a transport vessel?"

As Aunt Sophia had been very vocal about that fact during her brief time on board before they had sailed, Elizabeth's eyes twinkled at him. "I'm only glad Mrs. Richmond was kind enough not to mention the fact we would be the only two women on board. Somehow there never seemed to be a right time to actually inform my aunt of what type of cargo was on this ship once she decided early this morning she had to say her farewells from the wharf."

He smiled a little reluctantly back at her. "Well, I'm sure the cabin boy will do all he can so you don't miss your maid too much, and perhaps later on we may find a suitable convict to help." He paused and then added slowly, "It isn't going to be an easy voyage, Elizabeth."

She sobered immediately. "I know." She hesitated and then asked slowly, "Did you find out if that convict who rescued the boy is all right?"

He frowned. "He was still freezing cold in his wet clothes. I found him as soon as I could after we left the wharf and insisted he be given a change of clothes. But it'll be a miracle if he doesn't get at least a cold or sore throat for his efforts."

A few days later the surgeon was sadly proved right.

For security reasons the convicts were kept chained and locked below deck until the ship had been at sea several days. Elizabeth was one of the few people who did not suffer from the heaving of the ocean, but she felt deeply for those like the doctor's wife who were prostrated within hours of the ship reaching open sea. Several of the soldiers had also succumbed, but the ones she felt the most for

18

were the wretched convicts below the hatches where she knew the ventilation was very poor.

Dr. Richmond had been kept extremely busy trying to help those afflicted with seasickness, and she saw little of him. Then one morning he knocked on her cabin door. She was shocked at his weary, drawn face.

"Oh, my dear sir, you look exhausted! Do come in."

He shook his head. "No time, my dear," he said abruptly. "I'm afraid I have to take you up on the offers of help for others besides my wife that you've persisted in making, Elizabeth."

"Of course, I'd be only too happy, but what about your poor wife?" Elizabeth asked anxiously. "I visited her before breakfast, and she told me all she wanted to do was sleep."

"Yes, yes, she's improving every hour. It's one of the convicts, that man John Martin you've asked after several times. I've been up with him all night trying to get his fever down. I'm afraid he developed a chill which went to his lungs. Now he's very ill."

The memory of those anguish-filled eyes had haunted Elizabeth, and she gave a distressed cry. Suddenly the doctor swayed. She grabbed his arm and pushed him onto a chair.

"I have wished all along you'd let me help others besides Mrs. Richmond," she exclaimed. "You've worn yourself out." She hesitated and then asked swiftly, dread filling her, "Is. . .is Mr. Martin going to die?"

"Not if I can help it," Dr. Richmond said grimly. "He's earned my utmost esteem for his assistance the last few days. Why, he's cleaned up and ministered to those poor wretches without a murmur of complaint, as tender as any woman could have—and most of them only cursed him for his efforts. And he hasn't been well himself—he's had a bit of a cough ever since his swim."

He sighed and continued wearily. "I should have kept a closer eye on him, I'm afraid, but that storm a couple nights ago caused havoc among the crew as well as the soldiers. Not until he went down like a log did I realize how ill he was. I've been up with him most of the night, but this morning his lungs are very congested, and he's delirious with a very high fever."

Elizabeth straightened. "You should be in bed yourself, Dr. Richmond," she said firmly. "As you may remember, I helped look after my mother before she died. Just tell me what you want me to do."

The doctor smiled slightly and murmured, "I remember very well. You were so young, but. . ."

He stopped abruptly, and she flushed and looked away from the admiration in his tired eyes.

"I've insisted the captain have our patient removed to a small cabin next to mine so you do not have to go below to the convict quarters," the doctor said briskly. "One of the cabin boys will assist you. I'll be there when I can, but as though I didn't have enough to do, two of the sailors managed to get into a fight last night. One has a cut that requires stitching."

He hesitated, and then said gruffly, "I then have to attend a flogging. The captain has ordered each man to have twenty lashes. You might like to avoid the deck later today."

There was silence for a long moment. "I've seen a man flogged once before, Dr. Richmond," Elizabeth said softly at last. "It was many more than twenty strokes, but it was not an experience I have ever wished to repeat."

Dr. Richmond frowned at her. "My dear young lady, whoever allowed you near such a thing? Surely your father. . ."

Elizabeth grimaced at his sudden discomfort. "No one. I slipped away from my father on a trip to Sydney. He was very angry with me," she added sadly.

And that was an understatement. Her father had been white-faced and more furious than she had ever seen him in all of her sixteen years.

She had often wondered if her rebellion that day had been the last straw for him and the reason he had made all the arrangements for her to go to England without even telling her. It had been only six months later that they had again made the long trip across the plains of western New South Wales and then over the Blue Mountains to Sydney for her to board the ship for the long sea voyage to England and the exclusive academy.

Well, thankfully that was all now behind her. She was on her way home at last, and she refused to think of her father's anger with her for not obtaining his permission for her to return. Instead, she would concentrate on doing all she could for the convict who had been in her thoughts constantly since she'd waved a slightly tearful farewell to Aunt Sophia and thankfully watched the shores of England recede into the distance.

❧

John felt as though he were floating in a burning sea. Then vaguely he realized he was being carried somewhere. Something banged painfully against his side. A rough voice began cursing and then stopped in midstream. A woman's sharp voice told someone to be more careful; then he slipped back again into that welcome land of darkness.

When he surfaced again, all he could hear was that sharp voice again. It was inclined to fade in and out, but he thought it was saying something about removing those chains.

"Very good idea," he heard a strange voice croak.

There was a faint rustling, and then he smelled perfume. Forcing his eyes open, he saw an angel bending over him. Or was it? Were angels' eyes such a glorious green? Certainly no angel's eyes should be filled with such worry.

"Oh, Sir, you are awake. How do you feel?"

The voice was no longer sharp but filled with tenderness. . .compassion. . .for him? Yes, only an angel would. . .

He opened his mouth and heard that strange voice croak again. "Green. . . thought. . .would be. . ." Then it was all too much effort, and he closed his eyes again and drifted back into that gray world waiting for him.

❦

"The convicts are still far too restless to have their chains removed. Furthermore, Captain Longman agrees with me, Miss Waverley. He claims it's not worth the safety of all on board his ship."

Elizabeth forced back the furious words she longed to fling at this pompous officer. She glanced anxiously at the convict lying motionless on the narrow bunk. His eyes were closed again, and his face had a waxen hue that worried her immensely.

Drawing a deep breath, she said quietly, "I have been told that the usual practice is, or used to be, that all the chains are struck off once the ship is in blue water."

She did not consider it necessary to tell him that an old friend of her father, also an ex-convict, had told her this years before when she had tried to find out all she could about the treatment of the convicts, trying to fathom what had made her father the stern man he was.

Instead she added angrily, "But I repeat, I am not asking for the chains of all the convicts to be removed, just those of this unfortunate man whom I am convinced is far too ill to be of danger to anyone."

Lieutenant Edwards stared doubtfully down once again at the large body on the narrow bunk. Elizabeth followed his gaze.

John Martin stirred, tossing his head from side to side for a moment, and then was still again. His hands moved restlessly, and the chains between his wrists tinkled slightly. Elizabeth forced herself not to wince as she had each time her attention had been drawn to the metal bands on his arms and ankles, especially the bruises and cuts caused by the irons.

"Look, Lieutenant, Dr. Richmond left me with express instructions. This man must be sitting propped up at all times, and he has to be rolled from side to side regularly as his body is sponged down to try and keep his fever controlled. His fetters make this extremely difficult, and they have actually hurt my arm. Look here, Sir."

Elizabeth thrust the long sleeve on her dress back from her arm. Her forearm certainly did have a red mark on it, but it had not been caused when her patient had moved unexpectedly. Instead she had almost lost her balance from a roll of the ship and bumped into the iron on his leg. Her statement wasn't really an untruth. The patient had certainly nearly hit her a few times when he had thrashed around in his delirium.

The lieutenant had been looking at her arm intently—a little too intently, she suddenly realized. She did not at all like the sudden gleam in the slim young man's eyes.

Hastily she pulled the sleeve down and glanced around the cabin. "And where is that cabin boy I was promised would be helping me?"

The smirk disappeared. He scowled and said haughtily, "Still being sick like the rest of them, I should imagine, Miss Waverley."

Elizabeth had already discovered that she would need help with John Martin to get even a few sips of water past the dry, cracked lips when he was very restless. He was such a large man that she most certainly needed help to move him. In his delirium he had resisted her so much that she had indeed been afraid of being harmed by his chains, so instead she had commenced sponging his hot face and arms.

Then Lieutenant Edwards had burst into the cabin without so much as a tap on the door. The scowl on his face had made it obvious that the removal of one of his charges to this small but clean and tidy cabin had been against his will.

"Unfortunately, Mrs. Richmond is still not well enough herself to help me." Elizabeth chewed her top lip for a moment. Then she opened her eyes wide and smiled appealingly at the soldier. "Sir, I've been wondering if perhaps one of the other convicts might help me for awhile. As you're probably aware, the whole ship's crew has to be on deck this afternoon for. . .for the punishment session."

The man's scowl deepened. She conjured up the sweetest smile she could and was rewarded by the slightly dazed look that replaced the scowl.

"I really do need help, Sir," she pleaded prettily. "Dr. Richmond has been so good to me, letting me travel under his and his wife's chaperonage, and I do want to look after this patient of his the very best I can. The poor man's already worn himself out looking after us all during these rough seas."

She was rewarded by the softening of the lieutenant's face and the smile that tilted his slightly too full lips. One long finger tapped on his chin. Her patient moved restlessly again, and she was glad of the excuse to break eye contact as she hastened to try to restrain his arms as they again moved jerkily.

This time the chain lying across his chest did fly against her hand. Her hand stung only slightly, but it was too good an opportunity to miss. She gave a little scream and let the tears that had been threatening ever since she had seen the bruised and bloodied wrists and ankles flood her eyes. She turned beseechingly toward the hapless Lieutenant Edwards.

He immediately sprang to her assistance and tried to restrain the man he was ultimately responsible for. "I. . .I see that you do indeed need help, Miss Waverley," he said reluctantly at last. "But I'm not sure if there's a decent enough man among the convicts I'd trust to assist you."

It was on the tip of her tongue to angrily demand why he or one of the soldiers under his command could not show some charity toward this poor ill creature, but then she remembered her plan.

"There was one man," she said very slowly.

He frowned, and she added hastily, "I was on the wharf when John Martin saved this convict's son from drowning." It was on the tip of her tongue to blurt out Timothy Hardy's name but realized her knowledge would be frowned upon by this small-minded man. "Surely even a hardened criminal would know he owed this man some debt," she added instead.

The lieutenant looked thoughtful. "You may be right, at that." He beamed at her, suddenly all affability. "I'll look into it at once." He bowed and hurried away.

It was still a good hour later, however, before Elizabeth heard the heavy clomp of footsteps outside and hastened to open the door.

The officer who had greeted the coach of convicts on the wharf and who had helped drag John Martin away up the gangplank stood in front of her. He pushed forward a small man and said harshly, "Here's another bit of scum to help you with that bigger one, but why you and the good doctor would go to all this bother I'm sure I don't know, Madam."

Elizabeth stood aside for Timothy Hardy to enter but then slipped between him and the burly soldier. "Thank you, Officer; I'll manage fine now."

The sergeant scowled at her and then moved aside to reveal another behind him. "Thought you insisted on the irons coming off, Miss."

"Oh. . .oh, yes, of course," she said hastily and gestured for them to enter. She beamed up at him. "How kind! Do thank your lieutenant for me, please. I know God will bless you both for your compassion."

Not even this hardened soldier was immune to her sunny smile. He relaxed and smiled back at her. "Well, reckon they'll all come off soon as the floggin's over today. It kinda unsettles them all, knowing they could be next when they step out of line. There'll be a guard in the corridor at all times," he added with a warning frown at the still figure of Timothy Hardy.

Elizabeth smiled back as pleasantly as she could and, as soon as the fetters had been removed from both of the convicts, thankfully ushered the two men out. Only then did she turn and speak to the small man staring wonderingly from her to John Martin.

"Now, Sir," she said briskly, "this brave man is very ill because he saved your son. We have work to do to make sure he survives for you to thank him."

"Oh, I've already done that, Madam." The man's voice was soft and cultured like his wife's. "And I've countless times already thanked God for this man."

She smiled approvingly at him. "Good. I have certainly been praying for you both as well as your wife and small son ever since I met them on the wharf, Mr. Hardy."

He stiffened as though shot. "My wife, Madam? She was there to see me off?"

The sudden pleading light and dawning hope in his eyes made her smile a little mistily at him. "Yes, she most certainly was there. She told me what a good man you were and how she'd been trying to get permission to say good-bye and even to travel on the ship with you."

Tears filled his eyes. A harsh sob shook his slight frame. "Not a word have

I had in weeks. I. . .I thought. . ."

"Your wife spoke very fondly of you, Sir."

Despite his tattered appearance, the man seemed to grow in stature before Elizabeth's eyes. It was not just the chains and the journey that had brought him to despair, Elizabeth suddenly realized, but the thought that his wife had turned her back on him.

"Thank you, Madam," he said in a much stronger voice. "They dragged me away with all the others when John here went into the water after young Tim. We think they must have been afraid others would jump overboard to try and escape. I didn't even know if my son and John were safe until they threw him down the hold after us. But not a letter, not even a message, have I had from my dear wife since I wrote and told her I would be transported on this ship."

What an inhumane system this was to not even pass on letters or messages! Compassion raced through Elizabeth. She reached out her hand and touched his shoulder. "She told me she had sent you a coat, so I'm sure she must have written to you. I can assure you that she still cares for you very much—even asked me to write to her about how you get on while I'm with you on this ship."

"No!"

Elizabeth removed her hand as though stung.

"Please," Timothy said hoarsely, "you mustn't tell her all the horror. She will only be even more devastated. I. . ." He bowed his head. "I'm too ashamed."

Elizabeth stared at him sadly. Obviously even these first few days on board had been a nightmare to this man, and he expected much worse to come.

"I'll be very careful," she assured him softly.

A harsh cough brought both their heads around to the bunk crowded against the wall.

"Now," she said steadily, "let's make John more comfortable."

Timothy moved swiftly forward as John mumbled and moved restlessly. He stopped short as the sick man opened his eyes and cried out, "Beth, where are you? Beth, I need you desperately! Father! Father, where are you. . . ?"

His voice faded away into incoherent muttering, and Timothy and Elizabeth looked at each other.

Then Elizabeth brushed angrily at the tears that had flooded her eyes at the utter despair that had been in the weak, croaky voice. "We have much work to do, Mr. Hardy. And as we work, we must pray. He must live!"

"Aye," responded Timothy softly. "They say he's a murderer, but whatever he's done, he's still deep down a good man. I've already been praying for him." He hesitated and then looked directly at Elizabeth. "He's a soul in dreadful torment and despair, but he still. . .he still cares about others."

Elizabeth stared back at him for a moment and then turned swiftly away. "And now we must care for him," she whispered.

There were many times during the following long hours that Elizabeth was grateful it was Timothy Hardy alone who was there to hear more of the tortured ramblings. Many of his words were in a foreign language Timothy thought was Spanish.

At one stage, it was obvious John Martin was reliving his trial. Then he shouted something out that made Timothy and Elizabeth look at each other. Her eyes were wide, filled with questions.

Timothy nodded slowly at last. "I. . .I've been wondering. . . ," he began to say and then had to leap forward as their patient started trying to sit up and was at risk of toppling over.

They didn't speak again. It seemed an intrusion to be forced to listen to the private life and mind of this man, even more so to discuss what he said. Most of it they could make little sense of anyway, but he did rave on and on about a woman called Beth.

The first time he called out, "Elizabeth!" she thought he was calling her, but then he muttered, "No, no, not her. Beth. . .why?" She guessed the woman he called had the same name as herself. He didn't mention his father again but muttered angry words about someone called Percival and a Lord Farnley. Then even his voice ceased, and he lay deeply unconscious. The exhausted doctor paid a quick visit later on in the day. He shook his head, commended their efforts, and then stumbled away for some well-earned sleep himself.

All through that day and far into the night, death hovered very close in the small cabin. Elizabeth and Timothy fought it with everything they could. When Elizabeth discovered that Timothy's faith in God was, like hers, a deep personal relationship with Him, they even prayed together for the ill convict.

Sometimes the large body shivered and shook. They piled blankets on, but it wasn't long before the fever would return worse than ever. Then they sponged the large body down with cool water. Elizabeth was glad of Timothy's help as they forced down the many sips of water and then the medicines the doctor had left for them.

As early morning light at last filtered through the small porthole, they were both exhausted. Timothy was dozing on the other bunk at Elizabeth's insistence. She had already taken her turn to rest only briefly, more to stop Timothy's fussing over her than anything. But she had been unable to sleep and very quickly had resumed her vigil beside John Martin.

She left her hand on the man's hand so she would feel him stir and wearily leaned her head back against the wall. Closing her eyes she whispered, "Oh, Lord, we've done everything we can for this brave man. Please save him."

She hesitated and then added urgently, "Timothy said this man's very angry at You for letting him be imprisoned when he says he's not guilty of any wrong and swore at him every time he tried to mention You. I don't know if he knows about You loving him so much You sent Jesus to die for him."

Tired tears seeped from her closed eyes. Her own relationship with God was still very new. "Please don't let him die before he believes in You," she added simply.

The hand beneath hers jerked, and her eyes swung down to her patient. Blue eyes were watching her. For the first time they were really seeing her, and for a moment she was speechless as she stared back at him.

Then the tears started streaming down her face. There were large beads of perspiration on his forehead. Dr. Richmond had told them if that happened it would be a very good sign that his body was fighting the infection in his lungs.

Besides all that, and despite the dazed look that now entered those incredible blue eyes, she knew that for the first time he was truly conscious of her and his surroundings.

Chapter 3

The angel was still there. She was praying, and she also sounded as though she was. . .was crying!

John frowned. Angels weren't supposed to cry. Angels were supposed to. . . Well, he wasn't quite sure what angels were supposed to do, but certainly crying wasn't one of them. He must be dreaming again.

He started to let his eyes drift shut once more, but they flew open as a soft voice exclaimed, "Oh, you're awake."

This time the beautiful face was transfigured by the most glorious smile he had ever seen. He stared at her, drinking his fill. Then something gently touched him, and he realized she was wiping his forehead.

"Where? What?" Was that croak really his voice?

"Shh," he was told as he felt the feather touch of a finger on his sore lips. "Don't try to talk yet. You've been very sick, but. . ."

The voice faltered and stopped, and he wished it wouldn't. It was filled with warmth and loving care. There had been so little of that in his life so far. Only Beth. . .

Beth!

He struggled to sit up and hardly felt the firm hands that tried to prevent him. Was that horror all a dream, or was this the dream? Suddenly he couldn't breath and started to cough.

"Timothy!"

There was distress in the angel's voice. Vaguely he knew he'd met someone recently called by that name, and then a familiar face loomed over him.

"It's okay, my friend," deep tones told him from a thin face filled with a wide smile. "Don't try and move yet."

John tried to relax at the firm command, and the coughing fit gradually subsided. He continued to stare unbelievingly at the woman beside Timothy.

"Hold him up a little, please, Timothy, and I'll give him another pillow so he can have a drink."

Angrily he gritted his teeth and tried to sit up, but he discovered it took too much effort and was glad of the strong arm that came around him.

Then the woman's delicate perfume was all around him again. This time he knew it was no dream. A cup was held to his lips, and he gulped down the fluid thirstily. It cleared the last fog from his mind, and when he rested his head back on the soft pillow, he allowed his gaze to sweep around the room. He wished it would stop moving up and down.

Then he remembered.

He was on board a ship taking him to the Great Southland for the rest of his miserable life. Bitterness, anger, and despair had been his constant companions since he had walked stiffly from that friendless, crowded courtroom. They crashed in on him again, stronger than ever.

"I've been sick, you say? Then why didn't you let me die?"

The eyes of the woman widened. A flash of anger filled them. "I thought you were a very brave man, John Martin, but only cowards wish they were dead!"

Then he knew he'd seen her before. That old woman had called her Elizabeth. She had been looking at them with such a wondering look on her face, as though convicts were some different kind of species from the rest of the human race.

He had been angry that his pulse had taken a great leap at the sound of the name Elizabeth. That had been her full name. Then, when he had known he was wrong, he had sunk to even greater depths of despair. For one ridiculous moment he had thought that at last Beth had come to say good-bye, to perhaps give him some hope that this was all a nightmare he would one day be able to wake from.

He stared back at Elizabeth and said harshly, "When a man has nothing left in life to hope for or have faith in, isn't it time he be allowed to die, Madam?"

She gave a very distressed sound, but a wave of exhaustion was closing his eyes. Just as sleep claimed him, he muttered, "Besides, angels should be waiting at heaven's gate, not crying."

🦋

Elizabeth stared at him. He was delirious again. She looked worriedly up at Timothy and was immensely relieved when he chuckled.

"When a man recognizes a beautiful woman, he's certainly on the mend." Then his smile faded. "I'd say it's going to be a lot harder to bring healing to his soul than his body."

For a moment she wasn't sure whether to laugh or cry as she stared down at the still form of John Martin. She had the weirdest feeling that such a state of mind could become quite common around this man. He stirred something to life in her that had never been touched by all the gentlemen her aunt had begun parading past her these last few months, in an attempt, so Elizabeth had shrewdly suspected, to fasten her interest and stop her desire to return to Australia.

John slept deeply the rest of that day, only rousing a little at various intervals when they insisted he swallow the tea and broth the ship's cook had been cajoled by Elizabeth into providing.

Dr. Richmond called late that evening and examined his patient. "You're right, Elizabeth. I do believe he is starting to improve at last."

Elizabeth had been worried by the long periods during which the once-strong body had been so motionless. Timothy had tried to assure her that John

Martin had exhausted himself caring for other convicts before becoming so ill himself. He had not added that no doubt there had been little enough sleep in the cold depths of the prison in Yorkshire, but looking at his own drawn, thin face she gained some inkling of that.

Now she exchanged a delighted smile with Timothy as she asked the doctor, "He is just asleep then, Sir, and not still lapsing into unconsciousness?"

She hardly needed to ask, for their patient had stirred briefly while he was being checked, even mumbled about cold hands, before rolling on his side away from them.

The doctor nodded. "His breathing is certainly much better, but there is still considerable congestion in his lungs. It will take several days before he regains much strength."

But the very next day her patient was well enough to try Elizabeth's patience to the limit. He growled at her when she tried to persuade him the doctor had said he was to only have very soft food and was not to be allowed out of bed at all.

"Stop fussing, Woman," he snapped at her when she tried to make him more comfortable by shaking up the pillows and the bedclothes.

Woman! Elizabeth opened her mouth to tell him how rude and ungrateful he was, but then something clutched at her heart as she glared into his dark eyes. More than a touch of pain and vulnerability reached through to her before he scowled and looked quickly away.

Suddenly she remembered a time not long after her mother had died. Her father had been confined to the house with a broken leg after a horse had thrown him. He had been a difficult patient too, frustrated and angry at finding himself so helpless.

Adam Stevens, one of her father's stockmen, had seen her tears one day after her father had roared at her to leave him alone.

"A strong man like your father hates to be reminded he can become as helpless physically as anyone," he had told her gently. "He feels humiliated, and it makes him remember other. . .other unpleasant times as well."

Adam was a young convict who had been assigned as a laborer to her father. He had been serving a ten-year sentence for fraud, but her father trusted him, and she had grown very fond of him. It had been the first time she was aware that Adam had known about her father's background.

In case the flood of sympathy that swept through her became visible, Elizabeth turned her back on John. Later that evening she was not so successful in hiding her feelings.

She had briefly left the cabin and on her return found John Martin struggling to stand up. Scowling at him, Timothy was standing with his hands on his hips.

She gave a startled gasp of protest, and Timothy said grimly, "He wouldn't listen to me when I told him Dr. Richmond said he was to stay in bed at least another couple of days—even swore at me."

Elizabeth hesitated uncertainly. Then the large figure swayed and, even as Timothy reached out to steady him, started to cough. It was one of the worst bouts he'd had. Quickly she moved and plumped up the pile of pillows. The moment the coughing subsided, she ordered briskly, "Swing his legs back up, Timothy."

By that time the dark head was leaning on Timothy as though the last scrap of strength had been drained from him. He was beyond protesting as they helped him to lie back once more. As his head flopped back on the pillows and his eyes closed, Elizabeth was distressed at how much his large frame was trembling.

It had been a long, exhausting night and day. Tears welled up in her eyes. She stiffened and fought them back, but a sob broke from her. She swiftly started to turn away, but his eyes had flown open and a trembling hand reached out and grabbed her shoulder.

Elizabeth wasn't quite sure why she couldn't stop the tears from flowing, but she raised her chin defiantly when she realized he was staring at her with absolute amazement.

She dashed away the tears angrily. "So, Sir, you so despise the care I. . .we have taken of you that you are in a hurry to return to your luxury quarters in the hold!"

Then she was ashamed of taking refuge in her anger as his face lost every bit of color it had gained the last few hours.

"That's the second time you've cried." His voice was barely audible. "I'm. . . I'm sorry, Elizabeth. . .Miss Waverley. . . ."

His face had softened. Gone was that cold, hard look that always somehow hurt something deep inside her. She felt herself softening toward him but shrugged off his hand and turned toward Timothy.

"It's been perfectly obvious for hours that our patient is going to behave exactly as he pleases. I'm tired," she added abruptly. "I believe I'll have my meal in the dining room after all. It's quite clear you don't need me here."

As she swept toward the door, Elizabeth was proud that her voice had held not the slightest tremor.

🦋

Silence filled the cabin after the door had snapped closed behind Elizabeth. Neither man moved.

Then Timothy grunted, picked up a plate from the tray, and plonked it down next to John. "Well, guess that gives the two of us three meals," he snapped.

John stared down at the food. A few moments ago he had been hungry. Now he felt too sick at heart to be bothered eating. Elizabeth could not have given him more tender care if she had been his sister—or his wife.

He shook his head. How had that thought crept past the guard he had been trying to keep in place all day? But the touch, the sweetness of her had been inescapable from that first moment he had opened his eyes.

John stared at the food. He looked up at the little man who had proved over and over how much he cared about him. Timothy was looking down so miserably at his own plate that at last John started to eat. Then his appetite kicked in again, and it wasn't long before both men were finished.

"I suppose we'd better enjoy this luxury while we can," Timothy sighed, expressing the thought on both men's minds.

John looked around the room. "It's amazing that we've even been allowed in here at all."

"Dr. Richmond insisted, said he didn't want to lose your help with the other men," Timothy said quietly. He hesitated and then added firmly, "But the least you can do is treat Elizabeth with more courtesy and respect. She's a good woman."

John was silent for a long moment. "I became too friendly once with a 'good woman.'" His low voice was filled with bitterness. "If she'd been a woman straight from the gutter, it couldn't have ended up any worse."

"You've mentioned this Beth a couple times," Timothy said encouragingly. "Was she the woman who caused such problems?"

🦋

Elizabeth had discovered that everyone who was capable of eating in the dining room had already done so by the time she arrived. Her anger had faded, but her appetite had been very poor. After forcing herself to eat a few mouthfuls, she slowly made her way back to the cabin.

The cabin door was slightly open, and she stood still in the passageway as she heard Timothy's question. She held her breath as she waited for John's answer.

🦋

John's laugh was harsh. "Yes. Not that she seemed so terrible. She was always going on about the church and the local minister and how wonderful he was."

He was silent for a long moment. "I met Beth Rivers one day when her horse had cast a shoe. I had been in England for several weeks but had only a few days before managed to get a job on the Farnley estate working with Jock, the gamekeeper. I was feeling especially lonely that beautiful spring morning, and she was the most beautiful woman. . . ."

He paused and swallowed. "We became good friends in the next few weeks. I thought she was my only real friend in all of England. She said her mother was sick, and she was worried and lonely too. We. . ." He flushed slightly but lifted his head proudly.

"One day in the woods we. . .I. . .my feelings became too much for me and we. . .I kissed her, and she kissed me back."

He looked swiftly up at Timothy. When he merely raised an inquiring eyebrow, John smiled slightly. "I know," he said softly. "It was just one kiss, but Beth did not think so." He sighed. "Perhaps it was then I fully realized just how young and inexperienced she was."

Timothy did not move. After taking a deep breath, John continued in a low voice. "I know now I was just reaching out because I felt so alone, but then I thought our friendship might be turning into something deeper. Her reaction shook me. She. . .she was shocked, horrified. She felt that if anyone had seen us she would be compromised. She was so upset that I. . .I very foolishly burst out that if that had happened, I'd marry her."

He was silent for a moment and then sighed. "I know now I did not love her, and it was a very foolish thing to do for just one kiss, but. . .but it was then I found out who she really was. She was scared someone might have seen Lord Farnley's stepdaughter kissing the offsider to his lordship's gamekeeper. Apparently she had kept her own father's name when her mother had married Lord Farnley, the man I had come all the way from Spain to find. He. . .he. . ."

John looked up wearily at Timothy. "It's a long story, but he is my father, and by that time I had almost decided to approach him and show him the Bible, my mother's letters, and tell him I was his son. But I had been stupid enough to compromise his stepdaughter with secret meetings and then that kiss."

"Your father's a lord!"

At the stunned look on Timothy's face, John gave a harsh laugh. "Hard to believe? Yes, it was for me too when I found out. I don't want to talk about him."

Timothy looked very troubled but kept silent. John stirred restlessly and then continued.

"Of course Beth wanted to know why I was so upset, and I couldn't tell her. I mumbled some excuse and left her there in the wood. A few minutes later I found Jock's body. He had been killed sometime beforehand, while I was with Beth."

Timothy raised his head sharply. "So she could have testified you were with her?"

John nodded grimly. "At first I didn't say anything about her. It didn't seem right to involve her, but then when I realized how serious it all was, I wrote to her several times. I begged her, pleaded with her to come forward and verify my story, but she never did. The prosecution just read out a note from her saying she had not seen me that day and asking to be excused from personal testimony as her mother was very ill."

He laughed harshly again. "Perhaps I may have been starting to fall in love with her; perhaps I was only beginning to hope I was lovable—that there was someone in the world who could love me. She was so sweet and had told me she really liked me and wanted to be my friend, you see, and I had believed her. I have acknow-ledged she was very young, but I believed she cared for me and that we were good enough friends for her to at the very least do what she could to save my life. But apparently her precious honor was more important to her than saving a humble workman from the hangman's noose."

Neither man spoke for awhile, and then Timothy said quietly, "I'd say Elizabeth Waverley is a woman straight from heaven." His voice held reverence.

John raised his head and stared bleakly at the man who was fast becoming his friend. "She was praying for me when I was sick, wasn't she?"

Timothy hesitated and then said directly, "We were both praying for you, separately as well as together, and God has partly answered our prayer."

As he stared back at him, John felt something cold and hard deep inside him ease. During all these miserable months he had thought there was no one left in the whole world who cared whether he lived or died. And now here was this little man telling him. . .

"We believed you were very close to not waking up again," Timothy added very softly, "and despite your wish that you had died, I for one am very glad you're on the mend, and I know she really cares also."

John swallowed rapidly. "I. . .I can't afford to let anyone care for me, and I certainly can't let myself love. . .care for anyone, especially a woman." Suddenly he looked directly at Timothy and asked quietly, "How long is your sentence?"

Timothy scowled. "I told you that first day. Ten years." He added abruptly, "It does no good dwelling on it. What about you?"

"Life."

John saw Timothy wince and close his eyes briefly. John gave a harsh laugh and looked at the ceiling. "So, you see, there's not much point in anyone caring what happens to me. I've been told numerous times by various guards, soldiers, and even other prisoners that I was lucky not to have been hung. Instead, I'm at the mercy of England's penal system until the day I die, and we've both already had a taste of that. From what we've heard and seen, it can only get worse."

There was silence for a long moment. Weariness washed over John again. "No one believes me when I tell them I've never killed anybody, and no one is ever likely to now."

"Are you a murderer, John Martin?"

The soft voice startled both men. She was standing in the open doorway, watching them. Elizabeth moved forward slowly, not once taking her eyes from John.

John savored her beauty, from the healthy color on her serious face to her dainty feet. Speechless, he looked into her clear, direct eyes as she stopped close to him. *Surely no one could lie to an angel,* he thought helplessly.

"Well, John Martin, do you swear before my Lord Jesus Christ that you have not killed anyone and are undeserving of this incarceration?"

His mind flashed back to the time he had desperately shouted out his innocence in that crowded courtroom. So many times he had already protested his innocence.

He felt as though he could hardly breathe as he returned her gaze. "I swear before God that I am innocent of murder."

He could hear the hopelessness that swept through him echoing in his voice, and he closed his eyes, not wanting to see the disbelief in her beautiful ones.

"Then, John Martin, somehow we are going to have to prove it to the authorities, aren't we?"

His eyes flew open.

A tender smile shone at him.

As he stared unbelievingly at her, the smile widened to a mischievous grin. "I don't believe a delirious man is a good liar. It was a long night, and you told us quite a lot about yourself."

John glanced wildly at Timothy. He also was smiling gently at him. Then John's eyes locked with Elizabeth's, and for the first time a flicker of hope lightened his heart.

🦋

As she saw his face lighten, Elizabeth's heart went out to him. She had stood outside the cabin's partly opened door listening, battling tears at his words and heartache. Now she looked away, not willing to let him see her own reaction, and then bustled forward, removed the dinner tray, and placed it out in the corridor before carefully closing the door.

"Let us hope we do not have any unnecessary interruptions." She pulled a chair closer to the bed and looked at both men, who still had not moved. "Now, my father is not a man without some influence in New South Wales, and he may be able to help," she said briskly. "But the first thing we have to do is find out what happened to land you here."

John closed his eyes tightly and then opened them again to stare unbelievingly first at her and then at Timothy.

After a long moment, Timothy made a helpless gesture with his hands. "We have nothing else to do. Can it do any harm to tell us all about it? What happened after you found the murdered man?"

John's gaze darkened. "I've done nothing but tell what happened over and over again, but no one has believed me. Why should you two?"

Elizabeth looked at him steadily. "Because when you were delirious you called and called someone named Jock, then you said, 'What are you doing there? He's cold, so cold. Dead! No, no! My knife? No, no, I didn't kill him.' "

Her voice had echoed only some of the expression that had been in the voice that had shocked both his listeners in the dark hours of the night. When he merely stared at her, she continued calmly, "There was a lot more, most of it mumbled words we couldn't make head nor tail of, but you called for your father and. . .and Beth."

Astonishment filled his dark eyes. He gave an unbelieving snort and fell back on the pillows. "Now I know you're insane. There's no way I would have called for my father."

The bitter, angry tone was filled with hate and caused Elizabeth's heart to ache even more. At the same time, a little voice inside her acknowledged that he had not refuted calling for the woman named Beth, the woman she had just overheard him say he had kissed. Suddenly she wondered if that kiss had been so hungry, so passionate from a love-starved man that it had frightened the inexperienced girl he had portrayed Beth to be. Perhaps that had been another reason the young woman would have been so upset.

Timothy and Elizabeth glanced at each other. She saw her own sadness reflected in his face before she turned back to the large figure on the bed. Timothy had a son whom he loved dearly and who loved him. Her own father was a silent, taciturn man, but she had never doubted his great love for her. Yet for some reason, John hated his father.

She said gently, "Sir, I'm not sure how long we have before we are interrupted or even before you must return to. . .to. . ." She bit her lip, hating to think of the conditions both men would be returned to eventually. Hastily she added, "Could you at least tell us where you come from? Your voice has an accent neither of us has been able to place."

❦

John opened his eyes and stared blindly in front of him. Suddenly he could see the bright sunshine of the corner of Spain he had grown up in and longed passionately to be back there in its warmth and light. He heard his grandmother's gentle voice insisting to her angry husband that with all his other studies, their only daughter's son must learn to speak and read English properly, "like she would have wished."

How glad he had been that the old lady had lived until he was old enough to understand that she had insisted on those lessons because his father had been an English soldier, an important man, an officer. Then she had died, and there had only been the bitter old man who had always hated him, as well as the uncles and cousins who had made his life as miserable as they could.

The memories flooded back. "My mother was Spanish, and I lived in Spain all my life until my grandfather died a few weeks before I went to England," he said abruptly at last. "To my utter amazement he left me a very large amount of money. Of all his grandsons, I was the only one who had worked hard beside him on his prosperous farm. He had always treated me harshly, but in his will he did what he thought was fair. He left all the property to my uncles and cousins. The very day of the funeral they made it clear I no longer had a home.

"That same night, while I was wondering where to go and what I should do, my mother's sister crept into my room and gave me a small box. She told me she had kept the contents hidden for her beloved sister. All my life she had been afraid her father would only burn them as he had destroyed everything else belonging to the daughter who had dared to marry an English soldier and then died giving birth to his son.

"And. . .and she told me that my father had not been killed at Waterloo as I had always been told. He had returned, but he left me with them. She clammed up after that and raced off as though she regretted giving me even that information."

John gave a harsh sound that could have been a laugh. "All my life the old man had led me to believe my parents had never married. Suddenly I was told my mother and father had been married after all, but he had not wanted me and had left me with that awful family."

"What was in the box?" Elizabeth asked quietly after he had been silent for some time.

"Letters from my father to my mother and a small English family Bible."

"A family Bible!" exclaimed the fascinated Elizabeth. "But. . .but surely that would have had your father's family tree in it and would have been a treasured possession for a soldier to give away."

Surprise crossed his face, and then he looked thoughtful. "You English do seem to put great honor on your Bible. Even in your courts—"

Suddenly he started to cough again. They managed to get him to sip more of the medicine, but it was awhile before the paroxysm passed.

"Perhaps you should rest now, John, and tell us more later," Elizabeth said gently.

"No," he gasped. "Be. . .right. . .soon."

Elizabeth insisted he have more of the medicine the good doctor had left to soothe the coughing attacks. When his breathing had returned to normal and he was resting quietly at last, she asked, "Was there anything in the letters that could prove you were his son?"

"He called her Sophia, his beloved wife, and was so thrilled John Harold had arrived safely."

His voice was harsh, and Elizabeth clenched her fists at the pain in his face.

"All those years I had been called Martinez, my mother's name, but here was proof that he had married my mother. My first instinct was to wave it in front of all those who had despised me for so many years. But then I knew the money and the letters were like a ticket to freedom. They had always hated me, and I didn't want to have anything to do with any of them anymore."

He stopped and looked angrily at Elizabeth and Timothy. "Freedom! It led to pain I never dreamed could exist!"

Elizabeth swallowed, trying to get rid of the lump that had lodged in her throat. As he had been talking, she had pictured the boy he must have been, growing up in such an unloving atmosphere. Those brilliant blue eyes alone must have made him stand out amongst his dark-eyed cousins and been a constant reminder to his family of his origins.

She wanted passionately to assure him that one day he would be free, that there must be some way the real murderer could be found. She put her hand on his, but he flung it aside. She felt a humiliating blush spread swiftly up her cheeks before she realized that he wasn't even looking at her, his tormented thoughts in another place, another time.

"At first when I arrived in England it was all so exciting," he continued in a weary voice. "It was easy enough to find out the name of the regiment that had been stationed in my family's village near Salamanca during the Peninsula War against Napoleon. Even finding out someone who had known this man called Harold Farnley was easy, but that's when it all became so impossible. He wasn't just an ordinary soldier. My aunt had been right. He was an officer, but even more than that, he was now Lord Farnley, a wealthy landowner, married with another family.

"Tell me, how can you bounce up to someone like that and tell him you're the son he abandoned more than twenty years before?" John lifted his head and glared once again at his two intent listeners.

Neither moved. After a long pause Elizabeth said in a low, choked voice, "Some hurt, angry men would have no problem at all doing that."

"And where would it have got me?" He subsided again onto the pillow. Suddenly he hammered his fist on the mattress furiously. His voice rose. "Tell me, what kind of man would turn his back on his own son and never try to contact him? I had to find out what kind of man my father was. I managed to get a job on the estate. I had to get to know this Lord Farnley and see if I wanted to have anything to do with such a one!"

Elizabeth sprang anxiously to her feet to hush him, but it was too late. The door flew open. Lieutenant Edwards strode angrily into the room.

Chapter 4

The next morning Elizabeth wasted no time in having a sketchy wash, dressing, and hurrying back to the cabin next to the doctor's. There had been no time for further talking among the three friends the previous night. Dr. Richmond had entered the room just as they were trying to make light of John's outburst to the suspicious officer.

He had succeeded in getting rid of the lieutenant for them, but he had also ordered Elizabeth to her own cabin with the firm words, "There is no need for you to stay any longer this evening. I'll give our patient something to help him sleep, and if there are any problems, Mr. Hardy will be able to send word to me."

In truth, she was very tired and had been glad of the privacy of her own cabin. She had prayed fervently and then fallen into a deep sleep the moment her head had touched the pillow.

Now she was eager for John to tell them the rest of his story so that somehow they could work out how to go about proving his innocence.

"Ah, Elizabeth, up early, I see."

She paused as the doctor's voice greeted her from his open doorway. "Have you seen your patient this morning, Sir?" she asked eagerly.

He looked at her a little strangely and then said quietly, "Come in and say good morning to Mrs. Richmond, my dear. I'm pleased to say she is much better now."

Elizabeth hesitated for a moment and then said with a slight smile, "I'm very glad to hear that, Sir, but I was actually referring to John Martin."

"Come in, and I'll tell you how he is."

Elizabeth found herself being escorted firmly into the doctor's cabin. Something about the doctor's demeanor frightened her.

"Is. . .is something wrong?"

"No, no," he hastened to reassure her.

"So there you are, young lady. I do think you could have spent some time with me yesterday."

The querulous voice was filled with indignation, and Elizabeth hurried to greet Mrs. Richmond.

Elizabeth's rather flustered protestations were interrupted by the doctor, who said briskly, "I've already told you, my dear, that this kind young lady has been good enough to help me with a convict who was very close to death."

"And very unsuitable that was. Truly, Dr. Richmond, I don't know what you could have been thinking of to allow a gently nurtured young lady like Elizabeth anywhere near one of those dreadful men. I don't know what her father will have to say of our care of her!"

"Oh, but they weren't—"

"The man would have died without her, Madam." Dr. Richmond threw Elizabeth a warning glance.

Reluctantly she subsided, knowing only too well the damage her reputation would receive in many circles if she were known to have befriended a convict, let alone two of them. More importantly, any gossip could hurt her dear father.

"Now," he continued with a warm smile, "I called you in to say a big thank-you for your help and to tell you that our patient is well enough to have been returned to his own bunk."

Elizabeth stared at him in absolute dismay. Then she realized his smile did not reach his eyes and that he was watching her closely.

With a tremendous effort she forced a smile. "Good news, indeed, Sir, but last night he was still very sick with the most dreadful cough. I must confess I do believe a couple more days' care would have been most beneficial."

"Well, your patient didn't agree with you in the least," Mrs. Richmond snapped. "Apparently he agreed to go quite readily. Rather surprised the lieutenant this morning, I must say. He said he thought the fellow would protest most vigorously. That other strange little man said he'd look after him. Now, do let's stop talking about those poor creatures. We wanted to talk to you about various activities that are organized on this ship from time to time to help the journey pass as quickly as possible."

Elizabeth tried her best to join in the older woman's chatter. The depth of her disappointment stunned her, but she valiantly tried not to let it show. Once or twice she saw the good doctor watching her and managed to smile at him brightly.

He soon showed her that she had not succeeded in fooling him. When he at last ushered her from the cabin, informing her abruptly that they could both do with some exercise on deck, he said directly, "Your patient will certainly not be as comfortable in those cramped quarters in the hold as he was under your care, Elizabeth, but you need not worry unnecessarily about the convicts. This may be only a converted merchant ship fitted out with the necessary berths and security devices to ship convicts instead of cargo, but I make sure all convicts under my care receive the best treatment I can obtain for them."

He paused and frowned as he studied her face. "You really must forget about the convicts, my dear Elizabeth. Your father would not like to know you have had any contact with them at all."

She stiffened proudly and stared steadily back at him. "John Martin is a good man, Sir. He has sworn he is innocent, and I believe him."

Alarm filled the older man's face. "Do not be so foolish, Madam!" he said angrily. "All convicts protest their innocence."

She was silent for a long moment, then asked quietly, "Did my father, Sir?"

Shock widened his eyes. Then they narrowed, and he said softly, "Be very careful, Elizabeth. My friend believes you are unaware of his past and would be most upset if he knew. I have never spoken of it even to my wife."

Elizabeth's mother had told her that her father had been imprisoned at Port Arthur in Van Dieman's Land for most of his ten-year sentence. Then he had worked on properties west of Sydney before managing to obtain a grant of land for himself when he had completed his sentence. Her mother had been the daughter of an important, wealthy family he had worked for and from the start had been intrigued by the stern but kind young man. Against her family's wishes she had married the still-young, hardworking emancipist.

"He had been so hurt by life and yet could still smile at the world. I fell in love with him," her mother had told her simply, but with such a soft glow of love in her eyes that the young Elizabeth had vowed then and there never to marry anyone she could not love like that.

And it was obvious to all that the rather stern man adored the woman who in his eyes had deigned to love someone so far beneath her. Shortly after they married, they had moved west of the ranges. The few people in that vast land did not know about his past. Then the surgeon had taken up land bordering his property.

According to her mother, Dr. Richmond had recognized Elizabeth's father from his own brief time at Port Arthur and had at first kept his distance. Fortunately the good doctor had believed that everyone should have an opportunity to put his past behind him.

Over the years as they battled the harsh land to establish their properties, a deep trust and friendship had grown between the two men from such different backgrounds. Perhaps it was because each knew the horrors of the convict system even though that knowledge had been from such different perspectives.

"Sometimes I think both men need each other to talk to about those days," her mother had told her daughter with a sad look. "There are times when the nightmares return. He will never speak of them to me, but he has been so much better since knowing Dr. Richmond."

Dr. Richmond had turned away, staring across the rolling deep blue waves for a long moment. "To answer your question, Elizabeth," he said at last, "no, I've never once heard him protest his innocence, but he has been punished for what he did as a very young man. He was born and bred in some of the worst slums in London, where men do anything they must in order to survive. I have always admired tremendously the way he has so successfully made a new life for himself."

He looked back at her steadily. "Australia has been the land of opportunity for many a convict who has been brave enough to work hard and put the past behind him. I honor your father for the man he has become, and I am proud to call him my friend."

Elizabeth's eyes moistened. "And I am very proud he is my father, Sir. I love him dearly."

"Then I know you'll do naught to hurt him, my dear." With that, the doctor smiled at her, bowed, and strode swiftly away.

Elizabeth looked after him, her eyes blinded with tears. Then she turned and grasped the rail and stared out across the water to the endless horizon.

The doctor was right; her father would be angry if she told him of her association and growing regard for the two convicts, especially John. The way her father had tried to stop her from becoming too friendly with any of the assigned convicts who had worked for him from time to time, the way he had hurried her past any chain gang they had been unable to avoid passing, his reluctance to even mention the penal system in her presence had been a part of her life as long as she could remember.

As she had grown older, she had not been able to understand what had amounted almost to an obsession on his part at times. She had defied him on several occasions, causing friction between them until her worried mother had disclosed her father's convict past, making Elizabeth solemnly promise never to mention to him that she knew.

"Foolishly, he is so bitterly ashamed of what living in the London slums made him. He was only a boy when he was sentenced as a pickpocket, but he has never been a bad man. He only wants to protect you from all evil," the gentle voice had told her. But it had been the unfailing love, respect, and admiration her mother had always shown for him, as well as Elizabeth's own respect for her big, loving father that had made her try to keep her promise all these years.

Deep in thought Elizabeth began to pace slowly along the deck, only vaguely aware of the attention she was attracting from several of the crew and soldiers. Surely her father would be sympathetic to someone who had been wrongly convicted. Perhaps he too had met someone over the years whom he had believed could have been innocent. *But how can I gain his support for John Martin—or Martinez or Farnley or whatever the man's name is,* she wondered a little crossly.

Someone nearby delicately cleared his throat. "Ah, my dear Miss Waverley."

She started and turned her head. "Lieutenant Edwards," she acknowledged with a dignified nod.

"I'm. . .er. . .glad your reprehensible task is at an end and we can now see you taking the air."

Elizabeth looked quickly around her and was made aware that several people were now within earshot. A toothless old man in the convicts' gray uniform was swabbing the deck nearby.

As the surgeon-superintendent of the *Royal Lady,* Dr. Richmond had ensured as many convicts as possible were given work, knowing that besides the usual privations of food and fresh air on a long sea voyage, the main problem was boredom. Much unrest was prevented when the convicts were given something to do. The convicts swabbed, scrubbed, and laundered, taking as much menial work off the crew's shoulders as possible.

The old man gave Elizabeth a furtive, toothless smile. He had so greeted her cheerfully—yet respectfully—several times before, and she smiled back before returning her gaze to the lieutenant.

He was glaring at the old man. Afraid the man would suffer for her friendliness, Elizabeth quickly moved forward so that her body hid him from view. "It is certainly a beautiful day, Lieutenant," she said brightly with a gurgle of laughter, "and do you think my father's old friend would really give me a difficult task? He was merely saving me from boredom so early on our voyage. But thank you for your concern," she added demurely.

To her amusement his chest seemed to literally puff up. He affectedly tugged at the cuff of his scarlet uniform jacket and held out his arm, which was bent at the elbow. "Shall we promenade, Miss Waverley?"

She managed not to smile at his pomposity. Did one "promenade" on board a ship? Thoughtfully she looked at him. It was obvious that Dr. Richmond would not take at all kindly to being quizzed from time to time about the convicts. Quickly she decided this slight young man would be as good a source of information as any during the long sea voyage, so she only hesitated briefly before taking the proffered arm.

In the days and weeks that followed, Elizabeth often regretted her impulse to accept the lieutenant's friendly overtures during the walk around the deck that morning. Unfortunately Lieutenant Edwards was the kind of man who believed that no woman of good taste and breeding could fail to be enamored with him.

There were times when she could have screamed with boredom as he talked on about himself and his future aspirations. She bore it all for the snippets of information about the convicts that he at times let slip after light encouragement.

It wasn't until Mrs. Richmond spoke to her one evening that Elizabeth imagined she might have a more serious problem.

"Oh, how exciting it must be for you, my dear Elizabeth," that good lady said soulfully.

Since Elizabeth had just spent the past hour listening to the lieutenant telling her for what seemed the hundredth time about his family's wonderful mansion in beautiful Devon, she was completely at sea.

"Madam?"

The ship had sailed to the Tropics, and both ladies used their fans in the midday heat. Mrs. Richmond paused, looked at Elizabeth keenly for a moment, and then laughed. She tapped her on the wrist with her fan before vigorously waving it again to try and make the hot, humid air more bearable.

"Oh, don't think I'm too old to remember how it was when a handsome young man was courting me."

Elizabeth had become quite fond of Mrs. Richmond despite her talkative nature. She smiled at her gently. "Oh, I'm sure you must remember quite a few beaus before you met your husband."

Faint color touched the lined face. "For sure, my dear, for sure, but until my dear Dr. Richmond, none courted me as earnestly as your young man."

"My young man!" Elizabeth stared in horror.

A picture flew into her mind of a broad-shouldered, tall man with jet-black, curly hair who gazed at her so directly from deep blue eyes. Surely Mrs. Richmond did not know of the times she had been able not only to catch glimpses of John doing the various tasks assigned to him, but also stopped to speak to him! Even that morning she had been thrilled to see that he had a much better color.

"It's very obvious that Lieutenant Edwards will seek out your father as soon as he can to—"

"Lieutenant Edwards! You think that he. . .I. . . ? Mrs. Richmond! No, no, you are sadly mistaken," she said sharply. "Besides, he must know that I have not encouraged him in the least."

Mrs. Richmond let her fan drop and frowned. "Well, I don't know how you could say that when you spend so much time with him each day, and I must say it does you no credit to raise false hopes in him."

"But. . .but I haven't raised false hopes. Why, surely I have spent no more time with him than. . .than with you or Dr. Richmond," Elizabeth protested rapidly. "Surely you realize that the captain and his officers have been too busy to spend time with any of us, and on a ship how can we avoid anyone when there are so few. . .well, so few we are allowed to associate with," she added. "Especially since your husband is so adamant about no longer having me help him with the convicts."

Mrs. Richmond sniffed and stared at her disapprovingly, but to the embarrassed Elizabeth's relief, the woman did not refer to the matter again.

However, Elizabeth was sufficiently alarmed by the conversation that she made sure she was more reserved with the lieutenant from that moment on. While remaining polite, she spoke briefly and rather coldly to him. Several times she saw chagrin, and once such a dreadful flare of anger burned in his cold eyes that for a brief moment she was afraid. She suddenly realized how mistaken she had been in thinking this man was delicate. There was a dark, cold side to him that he usually kept well hidden beneath his soft, flattering exterior. She prayed much about the whole matter, but something deep within her withdrew even further from the man.

Then she found out that when the lieutenant was not happy, those under his command were made miserable also.

The ship stopped only briefly at Cape Town on the coast of Africa to replenish supplies and fresh food and water. It was a delight to see Table Mountain gradually come out of hiding as the clouds around it dispersed, to see the forests and brilliant blooms of geraniums and roses after all the weeks of staring across the expanse of the empty sea.

Elizabeth thoroughly enjoyed her first trip ashore, even though once she put foot to solid ground the earth seemed to heave and move. After weeks of the constantly rolling motion of the ship, it suddenly seemed as though the hard ground was unstable and the ship so firm. It did not take her long to gain her land legs again, and she and Mrs. Richmond gladly went off to see all they could of the bustling port town.

However, on returning to the ship they were dismayed to find a very angry doctor. Despite all Dr. Richmond's protests, the captain insisted on keeping the convicts locked below deck while in port.

"Captain Longman's hands are tied," he angrily confided to Elizabeth and his wife. "Lieutenant Edwards has given shore leave to most of the men under his command and left too few to guard the convicts above deck. The ship's crew are frantically busy securing and loading the ship. The conditions below deck are dreadful. It's too hot, not enough fresh air, and I'm afraid—"

He stopped abruptly, apparently realizing he should not be alarming the two women, but Elizabeth was consumed with worry. She hastened to her cabin and threw herself on her knees.

"Oh, Lord, protect John and Timothy from evil. Keep them strong and. . .and safe. Help Dr. Richmond and. . .and help me. . . ."

Her voice died away, but she spent much time on her knees until she gained a measure of peace that God was in control of all their lives.

The doctor became busier and busier the next couple days as many convicts succumbed to fever once again in the hot, airless, and foul atmosphere of the hold. A few fights had broken out among the miserable men, and Elizabeth's anxiety increased for John and Timothy. Dr. Richmond steadfastly refused Elizabeth's offers of assistance and instead arranged more excursions ashore for her and his wife to escape the increasing tension on board ship.

Elizabeth did enjoy seeing all she could of the strange sights and sounds of the bustling port, but the ladies found that tension in the town was also high. There was considerable unrest among the Boers. The law abolishing slavery that Britain had passed the previous year had ruined a number of their farmers, and many had decided to leave the cape colony. Thousands of them were planning a journey into the interior to start new lives away from British rule. There was much wild talk, but also fear of the native tribes they would encounter and no doubt upset—especially the fierce Bantu-speaking peoples.

As wonderful as it was to be on dry land again, both women acknowledged their relief by the time the ship sailed. However, there was no immediate relief for the convicts. Most of the soldiers, including Lieutenant Edwards, had unfortunate aftereffects from their nights ashore. Aching heads and bodies meant they were more intolerant than ever of the convicts.

As the ship plowed through the waters of the Indian Ocean toward the west Australian coast, the tension on board continued to mount. Despite both the captain and the doctor's pleas, Lieutenant Edwards remained adamant. The convicts had been behaving far too badly to be allowed out of their dark, dank conditions.

They were far easier to control below deck than above, he insisted.

But he was soon proven wrong.

Despite all Dr. Richmond's efforts, the third night out, an elderly convict died. At dawn, when they realized what had happened, the terrified convicts rioted.

Elizabeth was wakened by shouts of alarm and running feet outside her cabin. For a moment she froze. Then she heard a distant, escalating roar of hundreds of angry voices. She offered up frantic prayers for John and Timothy as she quickly flung on her clothes. No one was in sight when she cautiously opened her door and peered out. Suddenly a muffled shot rang out. She took a deep breath and raced to hammer on the door of the doctor's cabin.

"Mrs. Richmond, it's Elizabeth," she called loudly.

The door flew open, and Mrs. Richmond pulled her in, immediately slamming the door shut and locking it.

"Oh, my dear, we have been ordered to stay here until we are told it is safe to leave," she said a little hysterically. "It's as Dr. Richmond warned and warned that arrogant young man. The convicts would only bear so much."

Gradually the distant noise died away except for an occasional loud voice that sounded as though it were issuing orders. Elizabeth was on the verge of ignoring Mrs. Richmond's frantic pleas not to leave the safety of the cabin to find out what was happening when the doctor at last appeared.

His face was pale, his clothes disheveled and streaked with grime. "One convict shot dead and several to face severe penalties," he snapped grimly in response to their anxious faces. Then he hesitated and looked at Elizabeth.

Her heart nearly stopped at his expression of sympathy.

"Your two patients seem to have been in the thick of things. They are among those at this moment being hauled above deck before the captain and the lieutenant. No! Elizabeth—!"

But his anger and urgent call did not stop Elizabeth's headlong flight from the cabin. Her heart pounding, she scrambled up the gangway and onto the deck.

Chapter 5

I t seemed as though the whole ship's company was assembling on the deck. A stream of dazed, stumbling convicts were being herded together, guarded closely by grim-lipped soldiers with their rifles at the ready.

Elizabeth stared frantically around and could not stop the cry that burst from her lips. The bruised and bloodied figure of John Martin was swaying slightly amid a small group of convicts slightly apart from the others.

At her cry, Lieutenant Edwards swung around and stared haughtily at her. She stared back at him, not troubling to hide her anger and disgust, letting him see she blamed him for this whole mess.

It was a mistake.

His lips curled in a menacing smile before he turned away and stared thoughtfully at John Martin and Timothy Hardy.

The names of the convicts who were blamed for starting the riot were called out. They included those of Timothy and John. When those two names were read out, Elizabeth gasped and then realized that the lieutenant was watching her, waiting for her response.

However, it appeared that she was not the only one dismayed. She saw Sergeant Hobbs step forward, salute, and speak quietly to his superior officer.

Elizabeth slipped closer, in time to hear him protest a little louder in his rough voice, "But, Sir, several of my men said that the last few days they have several times managed to calm the others, and today those two helped our soldiers quell the riot."

Something deep inside Elizabeth relaxed. Somehow she had known the two men she still could not help but think of as friends could not have been among the leaders of the riot. Then she tensed at the lieutenant's icy response.

"That's enough, Sergeant! According to a couple convicts, they were among the leaders, and unfortunately for them the only man who could tell us either way is the one I shot dead."

The sergeant hesitated but then turned abruptly away. Elizabeth saw the anger on his flushed face even as the lieutenant roared out so all could hear, "A Botany Bay dozen to the lot of you! And may it be a lesson to the rest of you miserable scum!"

Groans and cries for mercy came from all quarters, but the tall figure supporting his slight companion said nothing. Elizabeth felt the doctor muffle an exclamation and turned to him, feeling a sense of relief.

"Surely a mere twelve strokes is a relatively mild punishment?" she whispered with some surprise.

He gave a harsh snort and said angrily, "A Botany Bay dozen is not twelve. It's twenty-five, and more than capable of exposing a man's backbone."

Twenty-five lashes! She stared at him and then swung around. "No, no, how could you?" she cried out furiously. "You. . .you. . ."

Impulsively she started forward, only to have her arm grasped firmly and pulled back. "Leave it, Elizabeth," the doctor whispered earnestly in her ear. "You'll only make it worse. If he won't change his mind on the word of his own man, he won't be seen to back down for a woman."

That he was right was made immediately apparent. The lieutenant stared her straight in the eye, and she saw something like triumph in his face as, without taking his eyes from her, he called out harshly, "And change that to fifty each for Timothy Hardy and John Martin as the main instigators."

The grip on her arm tightened, and Elizabeth bit back the horrified protest that sprang to her lips. Not taking her eyes from the lieutenant, she straightened, determined to stare him down, letting him see she knew this for what it was—petty vengeance on herself.

Still obviously afraid of what she may try to do, the doctor frantically whispered, "The sentences are still relatively light in comparison to those of earlier years. No longer are five hundred given out as in the earlier part of the century. Lashes of twenty-five to one hundred are quite normal. On rare occasions one hundred and fifty are still ordered by magistrates.

"He's probably only ordered such a small number because of the number of convicts involved. He may fear the strength of the scourger may not last the distance." Dr. Richmond added grimly, "Besides, he knows that I have to verify the conditions of the men as they are flogged. I just wish Captain Longman was not so weak as to allow this officer to behave as though he were the main authority on this ship!"

With that, the doctor hurried away to attend to some urgent duties before the floggings commenced. His place was taken by his pale-faced, distressed wife, who urged her charge to retire below deck until the whole miserable business was completed.

Elizabeth looked at her. After a long moment and with a measure of calm that she knew could only come from God, she said quietly, "Mrs. Richmond, I fervently believe that if we as the only two women on board were to stay and witness the events here, it may curb some of the. . .the ferocity of the strokes. But if you find you cannot stay, Madam, I must."

The two women had developed a good understanding over the weeks of enforced contact, but not until the older woman stared at her for a long moment and then said quietly, "I agree entirely, my dear," did Elizabeth know that they shared a common strength of purpose.

Only then did Elizabeth allow the tears pressing against her burning eyelids to run down her cheeks. She scrubbed them angrily aside, mentally and spiritually preparing to do battle with anyone who would seek to order her and Mrs. Richmond away. She also understood that she would need all her strength to be able to witness the horror of what was about to happen.

She saw Dr. Richmond refrain from trying to further persuade his wife, and she realized that he recognized that her quiet but adamant refusal was final. That Mrs. Richmond's strength of character was already known to her husband was evident by the respect and resignation in his eyes.

At last, when all was ready, Lieutenant Edwards gave a sharp command. A soldier shoved Timothy and John forward to the front of the rows of convicts. Timothy reeled, but John managed to stop him from falling to the ground. Elizabeth saw John's lips move, and then Timothy straightened a little. John moved slightly away, and once more his dark gaze swept over the watching crowd, not faltering as it passed over the two women.

The hours that followed were to sear Elizabeth's memory forever and made her a devout proponent of the abolition of the use of flogging as a punishment and deterrent for convicts. At one stage she remembered the thick, mottled scars on her father's back and understood as never before what he must have endured.

She decided that flogging had to be one of the most humiliating invasions of the body that could befall a prisoner. Surely for the majority of people the emotional damage inflicted by the lash must be even worse than the physical. And yet it was the physical that she found so horrifying that several times she felt she must lose her senses.

Only once did Captain Longman try to order the two women below. Elizabeth did not try to hide her scorn of him as they refused. Color rose on his lined cheeks, and he dropped his eyes before hurrying away.

Lieutenant Edwards did not approach them, but his chest seemed to stick out more prominently as he barked orders to his men.

Elizabeth gritted her teeth, suddenly realizing as one poor wretch stumbled away and he barked an order for another to take his turn that the lieutenant seemed to actually be enjoying his power over those men. Then another thought struck her. *Surely he can not think that watching his power over others would somehow heighten my regard for him!*

Only once more did Elizabeth see John Martin look toward her. For one fleeting moment his dark gaze lingered on her before he stared woodenly away, his expression shuttered.

Timothy seemed in much worse shape than his tall, well-built companion. He seemed to be in a daze, and only his friend's strong arm around him kept him from falling. His clothes were heavily bloodstained and hanging in strips from him, his face swollen and smeared with blood from a cut on his forehead.

The other convicts were flogged first, and every time Timothy or John dared to look away, the soldier guarding them cuffed them with the butt of his rifle. Obviously part of their punishment was to watch their fellow prisoners suffering.

And suffer they did.

Some men cried out from the first lash of the vicious thongs of leather. A few older, tougher men somehow managed to stifle their pain and received murmurs of approval from watching sailors, soldiers, and convicts. One older salt even called out, "You're a real Pebble, man," as one short, stockily built man, his harsh face lined, his hair streaked with gray, never uttered a murmur as his back became slowly crisscrossed with weals and trickles of blood.

Elizabeth glanced inquiringly at Dr. Richmond, who had stood between the two women after acknowledging their adamant refusals to go below.

"A 'Sandstone' is a man who is soft under the lash, a 'Pebble' is much harder, and an 'Iron man'. . ." He stopped abruptly as Elizabeth could not prevent the shudder that shook her.

When each trembling figure stumbled away, Elizabeth's mind numbly wondered what fifty lashes would be like.

Then Timothy was prodded forward.

Elizabeth sucked in a deep breath and looked swiftly at John. His expression did not change, but Elizabeth noted his lips had thinned to a straight line.

Her heart shrieked out to God, *Where are You? Why don't You stop this horror, this suffering?*

Timothy stumbled. He was dragged upright and groaned loudly as his arms were bound around the mast. Then the remnants of the rags on his back were ripped away. He stiffened and suddenly sagged against the post.

A peculiar stillness fell over the watching convicts. Then a loud, mocking voice called out, "Where's your God now, Holy Joe?"

John's head whipped around, and he stared hard in the direction of the voice. He remained silent, but several indignant voices cursed the man until the soldiers barked out commands for silence.

The whip made its peculiar crackle. White marks appeared on the pale back. Ten more times it lashed down, turning the skin to a bright pink, then red as the skin was broken. Not once did Timothy cry out.

After the sergeant had called out the tenth stroke in his monotonous voice, Dr. Richmond's loud, angry voice cried out, "One moment, please."

Lieutenant Edwards moved swiftly to intercept him as he strode toward Timothy. "Dr. Richmond. . ."

The doctor interrupted him harshly. "It is my responsibility to determine if this man can stand any more punishment at this time."

"The law says you only should examine after fifty—"

"The law says many things, Lieutenant Edwards," interrupted the doctor loudly, "including that the health of these men is my responsibility. I also make out every one of my reports in *at least duplicate!*"

His voice held a definite threat on the last words. It was obvious his report on the lieutenant would already not be favorable. The two men eyed each other tensely, and then to Elizabeth's relief the officer moved back.

Unfortunately for Timothy, he gave a low groan and straightened slightly as Dr. Richmond swiftly examined him. After a lengthy pause, the doctor hesitated and then nodded briefly to the grim-faced man holding the cat-o'-nine-tails.

"Sir. . .Sir," Elizabeth protested in a low voice as he rejoined them. She stopped abruptly at the swift shake of the head the doctor gave her and the warning look in his eyes.

"I thought he was unconscious. If I stopped it now, it would only begin all over again at another time. Best to get it over with," he whispered softly in clipped words.

The next few strokes cut the skin in several more places until blood was trickling freely. Elizabeth closed her eyes tightly.

A loud, tormented voice with a slight accent rang out. "No more! Add the rest to my number!"

Every head swiveled toward John Martin. There was a sudden deathly silence. He shuffled forward a few paces toward Lieutenant Edwards, his chains ringing out loudly in the stillness.

For once the officer was disconcerted. He gaped at the man approaching him who was daring to show such friendship, such compassion. Lieutenant Edwards even fell back a step before collecting himself and looking a little frantically toward his sergeant. That worthy gentleman marched swiftly over to him, and whatever he said seemed to decide the matter.

Edwards backed farther away from the convict who towered over him both physically and mentally. He held a dainty handkerchief delicately to his nose. Suddenly he looked across the deck with narrowed eyes at Elizabeth. She stared directly back at him.

For a long moment he continued to hesitate. Then he glared up at the convict and suddenly screamed, "You'll not only have the rest of his cuts to your back but another ten for insolence, you dog!"

Elizabeth heard Dr. Richmond mutter softly under his breath. He started forward and assisted the soldier releasing the crumpled figure at the mast. Immediately it was obvious Timothy could not walk. The doctor glared defiantly at Lieutenant Edwards and summoned two convicts to carry Timothy below.

As if in some dreadful dream, Elizabeth was aware of all that was happening with Timothy, but not once did she remove her eyes from John Martin. He shuffled forward to take his punishment, and she drew in one swift, quivering breath.

After awhile, the sound of leather striking flesh and the sergeant's voice intoning the number of lashes blended together in a haze of pain. Her anguish for John was too deep for tears.

The doctor returned to examine the tall, once-strong figure at least twice, but each time he reluctantly stepped aside. The dreadful flogging went on. Only vaguely was she aware that Mrs. Richmond moved and put an arm around her.

Then at last the dreadful ordeal was over. Once again the doctor helped release the prisoner. But John pushed away those who would help him and stumbled and wove his way toward the hatch. For the last few minutes, the convicts had been still and quiet. A sudden shout of approval roared forth.

Elizabeth made to move forward, but the arm supporting her tightened its grip. "No, no," Mrs. Richmond murmured sharply. "You must stay here. It will only increase that monster's hatred for the poor. . .poor. . ."

It was the stifled sob in her friend's voice that stopped Elizabeth. She straightened and turned to find that Mrs. Richmond was right. Lieutenant Edwards was watching her avidly. Somehow she stifled the sobs that were struggling to take over her trembling body. She raised her head and stared back at him steadily, feeling nothing when it was he who looked away first.

Elizabeth stared dazedly at the sergeant who was waiting to speak to his commanding officer. Then her gaze wandered to the scourger who was leaning heavily against the ship's rail. Both men were drenched in sweat. The midday sun was extremely hot. Everyone on deck was feeling its effects, especially the convicts forced to stand still. Surely the horror must stop soon.

As she stared around, gradually her dazed mind became aware that the captain and his officers were hurrying away. Even as she watched, the ship's crew started to disperse. Suddenly she realized the rolling of the ship had increased. Even as she swung around to look seaward, the deck beneath their feet heaved up so sharply both women were almost flung off their feet.

"Man the topsail! Get those sails in! Get those convicts below deck!"

Captain Longman's voice roared out moments before the ship plunged down. There were loud cries of fright from both convicts and soldiers. Several were flung to the deck.

A low bank of dark clouds rolled toward them across the white-flecked ocean. The ship rose up on the crest of another huge wave. Several strong gusts of wind struck the ship, and then it plunged down again. Elizabeth and Mrs. Richmond hung on grimly to the rail and each other.

Suddenly there was a chorus of shouted commands. Captain Longman's voice roared again. "Clear that deck! Get those men below!"

Sailors had sprung into action everywhere. Many were climbing the riggings to furl the sails. The soldiers barely glanced toward their two officers before beginning to herd their charges below deck.

Elizabeth and Mrs. Richmond carefully made their way down the gangway. At the entrances to their cabins, they paused, looked at each other, and with one accord made their way farther along to the cabin that had been used several times now as a sick bay. Even as they reached it, they could hear Dr. Richmond's voice snapping out instructions.

Dr. Richmond glanced up briefly from the still body of Timothy and barked, "About time! Here, one of you hold this arm." His wife moved swiftly forward as he added angrily, "How could I have missed that broken arm and shoulder?"

Elizabeth's gaze swept swiftly around the cabin. Relief filled her when she saw the large body facedown in the other bunk.

Mrs. Richmond nodded toward John. "Do what you can for him, my dear."

Fearfully she started to wash the blood away from his torn back, wincing as a muffled groan was wrenched from him, wishing fervently that he was unconscious like his friend.

The squall struck in full force. Grimly they fought to care for their charges as the ship pitched and rolled. Once Elizabeth was almost flung across the room. A strong arm reached out and grabbed her. Dark eyes blazed at her for one brief moment before John let her go and closed his eyes again.

She was more careful after that, and it took a long time to cleanse his wounds. The movement of the ship made even standing upright very difficult.

Only once more did he open his eyes. In a soft voice filled with wonder he croaked out, "You shouldn't be doing this. You shouldn't have even been there."

She closed her eyes briefly and then stared earnestly at him. "Yes, I should," she whispered back in a choked voice. "I'm not sure if it did or not, but we hoped that our being there would. . .would help."

"Yes, it helped."

He didn't say anything more for a long time, and then she heard him murmur, his voice filled with wonder, "You. . .you didn't leave. You stayed and. . .and. . ."

Elizabeth saw a faint smile soften his whole face. Then to her relief the effect of the small dose of laudanum Dr. Richmond had given him from his precious supply took effect, and he even dozed off.

During the rest of that day and into the dark hours of the night, Mrs. Richmond showed she was no stranger to sickrooms as she bossed Elizabeth around. The two women spent the night in the cabin while the ship tossed and rolled its way through the storm. Dr. Richmond had many other patients from the riot as well as the storm, and when he returned late that evening, his concerned wife sternly insisted the red-eyed, exhausted man try to get some sleep.

"Go on, my dear," she urged him. "I'd be surprised if both these men escape having a fever the morrow, and who knows what other injuries you'll have to attend before the sea calms. The last thing we need is a sick doctor."

In the end he was forced to acknowledge she was right. After sternly admonishing the women to call him if they needed him, he left them to watch over the two men.

"Although I've been very thankful there have been no female convicts on board this ship, another woman's hand would have been welcome this night," Mrs. Richmond said grimly after he had gone.

The ship tossed and reeled its way through the dark night, but when dawn arrived the skies were still black, although the wind and the rain had eased some of their fury.

To both women's dismay, Timothy had not regained consciousness. John had spent a very restless night and was undoubtedly starting a fever. After she straightened from feeling his forehead and observing his flushed cheeks, Mrs. Richmond sighed. "Well, it's as I thought. We'll have a very busy day ahead of us with these two," she said grimly.

Turning to Elizabeth, she said in a voice that defied any argument, "Go at once and have a rest, change those clothes, and have something to eat. Then I'll take my turn as soon as my husband returns."

Elizabeth numbly did as she was told, even dozing briefly before coming awake with a start and rushing back to the makeshift hospital room.

Dr. Richmond was there alone. He surveyed her for a moment and then said briefly, "My wife is resting." He nodded toward Timothy. "He has stirred several times and is now in a natural sleep. The other one. . ."

He paused and shook his head wearily. "He never has fully recovered from his congestion of the lungs, and now infection of his back has set in as well."

Something had changed in Elizabeth during those horrifying events the previous day. Calmly she moved forward and felt John's burning forehead. He opened dazed eyes, stared at her with some undefinable expression, and turned his head away.

She steadily met the doctor's weary eyes. "Tell me what I must do, Dr. Richmond."

After rapping out instructions, he hurried away. Mrs. Richmond returned a little later and said grimly, "I've managed to convince Dr. Richmond to let me accompany him to check on the other convicts. There is far too much for him to do alone, and he doesn't completely trust the convicts, or soldiers, for that matter, to tend to the injured properly."

With that, she too disappeared. Elizabeth took a deep breath and returned to persuading John to swallow more fluids. A little later, with considerable relief, she welcomed the wide-eyed cabin boy, who shyly informed her he had been sent to help.

They were once again bathing the weeping wounds on John's poor back when a grim-faced Sergeant Hobbs flung the door open.

Elizabeth sprang defensively to her feet. Before she could speak, the sergeant dismissed the cabin boy with a nod. As he scurried away, Sergeant Hobbs barked, "How are they, Ma'am?"

She had been gritting her teeth, trying to stop the tears of outrage and grief at the pain she had just been forced to give John, and at the sergeant's words, she opened her mouth to furiously denounce him, Lieutenant Edwards, and every soldier on board. But he had moved to peer from one bunk to the other, and she read genuine concern in his exhausted, weathered face.

He gestured impatiently. "Is Hardy going to be all right? Doctor said he's broken some bones."

"See for yourself," she said curtly. "He only regained consciousness very briefly during the night and has not stirred since."

Sergeant Hobbs moved closer to examine the small man. "I told him he was hurt bad," he muttered angrily and then sighed. "Doubt if he felt anything after that first coupla strokes."

There was no need for Elizabeth to ask whom he meant. After a brief moment, she said feelingly, "He will when he wakes."

"He won't be as bad as he woulda been if this other fool here had not. . ."

The harsh voice stopped abruptly. He was still scowling as he turned and advanced toward John. Elizabeth drew in a quick breath. John was watching them.

Sergeant Hobbs stared at him silently. Then he shook his head slowly and said in a wondering voice, "Why would a murderin' scum like they say you are do a thing like that?"

Elizabeth looked at the sergeant in some surprise, first at the astonishment in his voice and then at the sudden realization that she had not felt any real surprise at all that John Martin was capable of acting in such a way. She had seen before the genuine affection he had for Timothy. Besides, she had already once seen him risk his own life in the dark water of the Thames.

Sergeant Hobbs muttered angrily, "And despite what Lieutenant Edwards said, several of my men insist you were trying to stop the riot, not start it, and even helped prevent us from being injured by the rest of them scum."

"Timothy tried to stop them too." John's voice was weak but still angry. He stirred and then caught his breath as pain clawed him. "They. . .they are not all scum—just very frightened, angry men deprived of their freedom in that hole."

He scowled at the sergeant and then glanced quickly at Elizabeth. "Are you sure Timothy's going to be all right? I knew he had been trampled, but I couldn't get to him quickly enough."

Elizabeth took a moment to swallow the sudden lump in her throat. This was the first time since those moments the night before that he had spoken to her.

"Besides his broken arm and shoulder, Timothy is all right. Dr. Richmond has assured us that the bump on his head does not seem too severe."

Relief flickered on John's face. He relaxed and closed his eyes. The sergeant had been watching them both. He suddenly scowled and put out a large hand toward John. Elizabeth moved swiftly forward, only to stop as the rough soldier's hand gently touched the wide forehead.

"He's burnin' up with fever," he exclaimed.

"Yes." She took a deep breath. "Dr. Richmond thinks it's a combination of some return of his previous lung trouble, shock, infection on his. . .his back, and the general debilitation all the convicts are suffering from."

John's eyes flew open again. He stared warily back at the sergeant. That gentleman turned slowly and studied her accusing face. She held his gaze steadily.

Suddenly he straightened and took a deep breath. "Well, at least I can now do somethin' about some of it." He hesitated and then said formally, "Until Lieutenant Edwards recovers, I am taking over his responsibilities."

"Lieutenant Edwards is ill?"

The man suddenly grinned at her, and Elizabeth was startled at the way it changed him from a stern soldier to an approachable man.

"Well," he drawled, "if bein' out like a light since banging his head falling down the gangway in his hurry to get down from topside when the storm started is ill, he's ill."

"Does Dr. Richmond know?"

To Elizabeth's utter amazement, the man winked at her. "Dr. Richmond has been run off his feet like, Miss Waverley, and we didn't like to bother him last night, like. That is," he added hurriedly, but still with a glint in his eyes, "not until we'd obeyed orders, like, and made sure all the convicts were safely locked away below deck. Besides, no one really knew the lieutenant was missing for a very long time. It's very dark in them passageways with no lights allowed because of the storm and all.

"Then when I did stumble over him. . .well. . .had no time with the storm and all to find the good doctor last night, you might say, Miss. Only had time to dump. . .er, put the lieutenant on his bed, like." He shrugged carelessly. "No one seems to know how long he laid there in the passageway before anyone noticed 'im, neither."

Elizabeth continued to stare at him, not sure whether to laugh or feel sorry for a man who had so dreadfully lost the loyalty and respect of his men. Then she silently wondered why the doctor had not mentioned the accident.

Suddenly the man in front of her stiffened as though remembering to whom he was speaking. All amusement disappeared, and he briefly saluted her and marched toward the door. There he turned.

"No sayin' how long the lieutenant'll be out of action, and I have me own as well as his duties. I'll send you what help I can," he finished abruptly. He hesitated a moment and then added warningly, "Only I don't know nothin' about it at all later on, if you understand me, Miss." Then he was gone.

Chapter 6

Lieutenant Edwards kept to his cabin. Only once did Dr. Richmond volunteer any information about him. "His head's hard enough to mend without any problems," he growled. "It'll ache for a good while, though."

Unfortunately he was not as optimistic about Timothy's recovery, and the first few days shook his head over the still-semiconscious man.

To their relief, John recovered quite rapidly from his fever, and his back started to slowly dry up. The dreadful wounds began to heal over, but Elizabeth knew he would carry the scars the rest of his life.

But as the days passed, Elizabeth privately worried about him. "Sometimes there's such a dreadful look in his eyes," she whispered to her friend. "He stares into the distance so and. . .I. . .I'm so afraid. . . ."

Mrs. Richmond nodded grimly. "My husband has told me many times that flogging can sometimes do something to a man's spirit that will take years to heal, if ever." After a moment she added quietly, "We must just continue to give him and Mr. Hardy all the care we can as well as pray for healing of their minds and hearts."

When John was well enough to be returned below deck, they appealed to the sergeant to permit John to stay and help with Timothy. That tough but compassionate soldier was more than willing to allow it.

The sergeant was already starting to improve the conditions among the convicts, following without any demur the doctor's suggestions. They were allowed on deck more often for various reasons, including extra work that was allocated to them to alleviate the boredom.

Elizabeth was surprised how quickly most of those who had been flogged recovered, and one day she earnestly complimented the sergeant.

His rugged features relaxed into a pleased smile and then he murmured, "Just followed the surgeon's instructions, Miss Waverley, Ma'am. Extra rations of rum were used on the backs to clean 'em and not poured down their mouths."

She smiled gently at him. "It certainly seemed to stop the infection on our patients." Hesitantly she said, "And your lieutenant is improving, so I am told?"

The man's face darkened. "Not well enough to be issuing orders yet. On other ships I've been on, it has been the captain who has been responsible for discipline and order. Even our officers have to obey the captain. If it had been so here. . ."

He paused and then continued gruffly. "Captain Longman has, and not before time, if you'll pardon me, Ma'am, insisted to 'im that 'e is in charge and

I am following his orders and. . .and so far Lieutenant Edwards 'as not summoned me to 'is cabin."

That rather pleasant state of affairs continued as the ship plowed across the empty ocean and ever closer to their destination. Mrs. Richmond gradually relaxed her vigil over her charge, seemingly willing to leave Elizabeth alone at times with the two convicts.

To everyone's relief, Timothy gradually regained his senses. He obediently took the nourishment offered to him, would smile his sweet smile, and then usually fell asleep again.

The atmosphere between Elizabeth and John after that first night became very tense. He was silent, not volunteering any conversation, and when forced to speak to her did so in sharp monosyllables. She had hoped they would quickly regain the easy rapport that had grown between them during his last confinement to this cabin, but she found that his continued silences began to agitate her more and more. Despite her anguish for what he had been through, she started to feel not only frustrated and a little angry, but also hurt that he persisted in practically ignoring her.

There was little she could do or say while under Mrs. Richmond's eagle eye, but one day she was sitting quietly reading when that lady was absent, and to her surprise and delight, John asked quietly, "Does that happen to be a Bible you're reading, Miss Waverley?"

She looked up and answered, "Why, yes, of course." She smiled gently at him and added, "But I thought I was Elizabeth, not that cold 'Miss Waverley' anymore."

He stared into her eyes for a long moment. Briefly she saw a flash of pain before he looked down again at the large, rather battered book in her hands. There was a long pause, and she found her heart lifting in prayer for him. She hesitated, wondering what he would say if she offered to lend the Bible to him or to read out loud.

While she was wondering what to do, he suddenly looked directly at her. For one more brief moment she saw a crack in the expressionless face and cold gaze that had been on his face since the flogging. There was such a look of longing, of vulnerability, that she held her breath, but then he turned his head sharply away to center his gaze once again on the still form of his friend.

"Would you like to borrow my Bible, John?" she asked quickly.

He was still for a moment, and then he turned very slowly and looked at her again. "No, thank you. I have been sharing the small one Timothy has managed to hang onto." He paused and then added grimly, "That is, if it has not been stolen again while we've been here."

Something thrilled inside her that at last he was talking to her. "Someone stole his Bible?" she asked a little breathlessly. "Who would ever steal a Bible?"

His lips twisted in a grimace, and he gave a harsh laugh. "It was taken when I was sick. We did get it back, minus a few pages used to roll their filthy tobacco in."

Elizabeth refrained from asking how he had managed to find it. "It's hard to understand how anyone could steal a Bible," she said quietly, "or to so misuse it."

She hated the harsh sound that he gave before he sneered, "All except a handful of those men below deck would steal anything if they thought they needed it, Miss Waverley."

"Oh, please," she burst out, "do call me Elizabeth like you used to."

His expression hardened. "That proved to be very foolish, Miss Waverley," he said in cold tones.

Tears sprang to her eyes, and she angrily dashed them away. "You do blame me for the severity of your. . .your punishment, but not anywhere near as much as I blame myself!"

He stood up so quickly the small chair he had been sitting on fell over. "Blame you! No, no," he said in a choked voice. "How could I blame you for. . .for being there, for staying! But I hated for you to be touched by any of that ghastly business, to be there to see me. . .see me. . .but you were so brave, so. . ."

He paused, swallowed, and added quickly, "I can assure you some of the old lags muttered that the scourger's arm was surprisingly weaker than it usually was. They gave you two women the credit." He stopped abruptly and turned away.

Elizabeth stood and went to him. It was as though she had no control over her feet or the hands that reached out to gently touch his clenched ones. "Oh, John, but you and Timothy paid in part for my foolishness in allowing. . .in letting that. . .that man think that I. . ."

She stumbled to a halt, tears running freely down her cheeks, and she lowered her head, hoping to hide them.

His hands turned and convulsively clutched her small, dainty ones. Then he placed a firm finger under her chin and raised her face and wiped at her wet cheeks so gently with the back of his hand that the tears flowed even faster and a small sob escaped.

Suddenly he let go of her hands only to wrap his arms gently around her until she was cradled against his strong body. Her own hands came up, but as she touched him he winced, and she let her hands fall helplessly beside her and just leaned all her weight onto him.

Never before had she experienced such a feeling of safety. . .of security, but suddenly he wrenched away from her and turned his back.

His rigid shoulders heaved once. Then he spat out a stream of furious words in a foreign language.

With a trembling hand, Elizabeth wiped her cheeks. She managed to give a small laugh, and it was one of the most difficult things she had ever done. "I'm afraid I don't speak any Spanish, my dear John. You will have to tell me all that again in English."

Neither of them moved. Then Elizabeth wrapped her arms around her waist. He sensed her slight movement and turned slowly toward her. For a long time he stared at her, and she bravely returned his look.

"I should not have touched you, Miss Waverley." His face had lost its hectic flush and was deathly pale. He gave her a slight, formal bow and said in the expressionless voice she hated, "Please accept my sincere apologies."

Elizabeth just stared at him. A violent shiver swept through her.

That seemed to shake him more than any words could. "Oh, my dear, don't you see, I am a man condemned to living imprisonment for the rest of my life!" The words burst from him in a torrent. "Someone so. . .so pure as you cannot have anything to do with such as I. Last time. . .last time being deprived of your brightness made the darkness seem even darker. . .more difficult."

Relief and sadness in equal measure swept through Elizabeth. "I am not foolish enough to think we can be anything more than friends, Sir." Even as the words left her lips she knew that some deep, inner part of her refused to believe them.

"We should not even be friends!"

Anger touched her. "No one tells me whom I can be friends with. Friendship just. . .just happens."

"Not if the 'friends' cannot see each other."

"True friendship withstands time and distance."

He was silent, then whispered, "But not a lifetime of imprisonment."

She too was quiet for a long moment. "Perhaps that is why I so much want to try and prove your innocence, John Martin."

Such a look of longing filled his face that she had to bite her lip to keep from crying out. Instead, she added rapidly, "I want you to finish telling me your story."

"But you cannot befriend a convict!"

"I already have." Her spirit lightened. His voice had held less conviction, and she smiled faintly at him. "In fact I believe I have now befriended perhaps three—no. . ." She cocked her head to one side. "I considered one of the convicts assigned to my father my friend, so I guess that makes four."

She laughed outright at his astonished face. "I am a currency lass, remember?" She chuckled again at the bewilderment in his face. "You haven't heard that expression before? Those of us born in Australia are called currency lads and lassies as opposed to people born in England called British sterling."

She became serious again. "It's different from England—especially out west where we have to rely so much on each other."

John stared at her, and their eyes studied each other carefully. Suddenly she did not know what to say. Instead of urging him again to tell her about himself, she sat staring down at her clenched hands. There had been a gleam in his eyes that had not been there before, and she bit her lip, wondering if perhaps he would prefer a woman who was not as bold, as willing to be friendly.

"Perhaps I should tell you a little more about myself," she blurted out at last.

He hesitated and then nodded. So she told him briefly about growing up on a small farm and then the upheaval of moving farther west. "Father took up land that he could graze thousands of sheep on. He did very well," she said simply. "Then my mother died, and it was as though a light inside him had been turned off. He gradually withdrew, even from me."

Her voice wobbled a little, but she smiled. "I never doubted he loved me, even when he insisted on sending me to England to learn how to be a lady, as he put it." She pulled a face. "I tried very hard there, but I seemed not to have much in common with the girls in England. Every time I wrote, I begged Father to let me come home, but he always put me off."

She fell silent, and at last he said softly, "You mentioned convicts assigned to your father when you moved. There has been talk among the men about the possibility of being assigned. No one seemed too sure what being assigned means, except they worry about it a great deal.

"One man told some of us about an old acquaintance of his, one of the Tolpuddle men transported for trade union activity last year. He was assigned to a magistrate on the Hunter River. James Brine was forced to dig postholes, even though he had bare feet that were so cut and sore that he could not put them to the spade. There were other stories. . . ." He stopped and then asked slowly, "Does your father still have some working for him?"

"Since I've been in England, I do not know. He has never mentioned them in his letters to me," she answered quietly. "A man called Adam Stevens was assigned to him before I left. He is serving a ten-year sentence for fraud. Anyone assigned to my father is treated very well if they work hard and do the right thing by him," she said with a proud tilt to her head.

"How does the system work?"

"In 1831 I believe there were 13,400 assigned convicts, but for some time now there has been a move to stop the practice," she continued rapidly. "From what I understand, anyone who wants a convict to work for them has to apply to the government. I remember once my father had to pay his convicts ten pounds a year, but Governor Darling changed that not long before I went to England. Now the master has only to issue essentials like blankets and clothes instead.

"There are all kinds of laws to try and protect convicts and the men who have them, but. . .but I heard my father say there are good and bad men among convicts and masters alike who abuse the whole system."

Still staring intently at her, John nodded thoughtfully. "My grandfather's farm in Spain had sheep—many sheep!"

"In his last short letter that arrived a few months ago, my father told me he was considering buying more sheep and moving even farther west."

They stared at each other. Her heart beating faster, Elizabeth looked away first.

After a moment she said a little breathlessly, "You. . .you worked on your father, Lord. . .Lord Farnley's estate also?"

"Yes." His voice was thick, more heavily accented.

She dared to glance quickly at him. Her eyes lingered on his pale, tense face as he went on to tell her about the long hours he had worked with Lord Farnley's gamekeeper.

"He was a good man, poor Jock Macallister, a good man. His granddaughter was very beautiful, and he had a hard job keeping an eye on her, he did."

Elizabeth's eyes narrowed.

He scowled and added, "He was right to. Why, even Lord Farnley's heir, Sir Percival, cast his eyes her way."

"Sir Percival?"

"Yes," he said briefly. "I did not like him. His father was my. . .Lord Farnley's only brother. I still sometimes wonder if—" He stopped abruptly, and Elizabeth saw his hands move convulsively.

"He would be your cousin then, John."

At her soft words, a dark look filled his face. "Oh, yes, treacherous Percival Farnley is my cousin."

He looked into the distance, and Elizabeth waited quietly, hoping he would continue. Her patience was rewarded when he uttered short, harsh words. "I first met him one day in the woods near Jock's cottage. He was with Jenny. A very haughty, angry young man I thought him." He gave a mirthless laugh. "He called me an insolent rogue when I offered to escort Jenny home."

"Jenny?"

John glanced at her sharply. "Jock's granddaughter. I didn't at all like the attention he was giving her, and neither would have her grandfather. Fortunately Beth arrived, and she walked back with us both. For some reason Jenny was very upset, and I was glad to let Beth talk to her."

Elizabeth clenched her hands and waited. She was not sure if he had guessed she had heard what he had told Timothy all those weeks ago, and she was not at all sure she wanted him to tell her any more about the woman he had called out for so many times when he had been out of his senses.

"Beth. . ." John took a deep breath. "Beth was the daughter of my. . .Lord Farnley's last wife. She was very beautiful, and everyone told me that he had always favored her more than Kate."

Another woman! Elizabeth was not sure she wanted to know about any more women in his life. A little sharply she asked, "Who is Kate?"

"Kate is my. . .my half sister. She is only a couple years younger than me. Apparently my father quickly found someone else to marry when he returned after the war with the French. Then when she died some years later, he married Beth's mother."

He paused for awhile, and Elizabeth could only look at him sadly and be thankful for the wonderful love that had always existed between her own mother and father.

"Beth is very beautiful, has such incredibly blue eyes. Even more than a beautiful face, she has such a caring heart—or that was what I thought for a long time."

Elizabeth looked up. His voice had thickened.

"I was with her when Jock was killed."

She could not bear the pain and hurt in his voice and said swiftly, "I heard you tell Timothy about her." What she really wanted to know was whether he loved Beth.

He stared at her, and a tinge of color crept up his high cheekbones. She looked down at the hands in her lap and realized they were tearing at her handkerchief.

"I also heard you tell him you found Jock Macallister," she blurted out.

His gaze darkened. Then he closed his eyes as though trying to block out the ghastly memories.

"He had been stabbed," he said shortly. "The knife was still in him. Instinctively I tried to remove it, but while I was trying to pull it out, Percival arrived with his servants. He accused me loudly and hauled me off to the magistrate."

The stark words ceased. Elizabeth knew there must be more, much more. She held her breath, waiting for him to continue, but he remained silent.

A soft voice beside them asked, "Did you hear him tell me Beth could have proved he was with her, but the fool was too honorable to mention her until it was too late?"

They turned to see Timothy watching them both. Elizabeth exclaimed, "Why, Sir, you are awake and looking so much better too!"

"Probably well enough to be returned to our other fancy quarters," Timothy said with a wry smile.

"Oh, I can't bear the thought of you down in that dreadful place," cried Elizabeth. "Mrs. Richmond won't let me go down there, but she has told me how dark and crowded and odorous it is."

Timothy gave a slight shrug and then winced. Although his back was no-where near as bad as John's, any unwary movement pulled on the scars starting to form. "I think you should tell Elizabeth all you can about what happened if she still is determined to help you, John."

John was silent, and Elizabeth's heart sank, wishing that Timothy had not spoken and broken the atmosphere between them.

Then, to her relief, John said shortly, "There's not much more to tell."

Timothy stared at him. "What about Beth's part?" he said indignantly at last. "Don't you still believe she should have vouched for you, spoken up at your trial?"

John shook his head.

Elizabeth looked from one grim face to the other. She wondered even more about this Beth. How could any woman turn her back when she might have saved an innocent man from the gallows?

John scowled at Timothy. "I really don't see much point in talking any more about it. I've been sentenced. I'm here. I'll be here for the rest of my miserable life, and that may not be too long if the events of a few days ago are repeated."

Elizabeth sprang to her feet. "That's a terrible thing to say! You can't give up!"

That cold, distant expression she hated so much—even feared—was back on John's face. "I don't see that it is really any of your business, Miss Waverley."

Elizabeth began to tremble. Then she felt a spark of anger. "You're right, Mr. Martin, your affairs are certainly none of my business," she snapped, "but I do believe a great wrong has been done to you. Any person with an ounce of decency or compassion in them would seek to right that wrong." With a swish of her long, full gown she rose, and a moment later was gone.

John stood very still. For a moment the sharp agony in his heart rivaled the lash of the cat-o'-nine-tails.

"That was not very well done, my friend," Timothy's quiet voice said behind him. "She is a good woman and considers you her friend."

"And that's the very reason I had to speak to her like that," John said in a low, passion-filled voice. "There is no future in it. . .a beautiful young woman like her getting too fond. . .too friendly with a convict. It could ruin her whole life. You saw yourself how that man treated her."

"Since you started praying with me, I hoped you might have wondered like I have if God's hand is not in all of this." Timothy's voice was very quiet. "How many times do you think a God-fearing, good woman like Elizabeth Waverley would just happen to be on any convict ship, let alone this particular one where a man like yourself was being sent to pay for a crime he has not committed?"

John stared at him, an arrested look on his face. "God's hand? You really think. . ." He suddenly shook his head sharply. "No. I might now believe that God loved me enough to send the Christ to save me from hell. But why would God trouble Himself more than that for someone like me? You, perhaps, a good person who has long ago committed his life to Christ, but not me."

"And that same person could no doubt have died under the lash without a tall, strong man to take his stripes on himself. How do I thank you for that? You took my place and. . ."

Timothy stopped and drew in a sharp breath.

"Stripes," he murmured after a pause. "Jesus took our stripes. He was whipped, scourged, but it was for sin—oh, not His own—for yours and mine. With His stripes we are healed," he finished with a smile.

John glared at him. "What's this about stripes? You told me about Him being crucified but not about a. . .a flogging."

"Didn't I? It was all part and parcel of the crucifixion scene, I guess." Timothy relaxed back on his pillows. "It was the Roman soldiers who did it, but it was like this. . ."

Chapter 7

Congratulations, Captain. Dr. Richmond has told me that your ship has made very good time."

Captain Longman acknowledged Elizabeth's civil words with a slight bow. "Just so, Miss Waverley, just so. It is only one hundred and twenty days since we left England," he boasted with a beaming smile. "The winds have on the whole been very favorable to us, especially this last part of our journey. We will be entering the heads of Port Jackson early tomorrow."

Elizabeth privately thought that the winds since leaving the fledgling colony at Fremantle on the western shores of Australia could have been a little kinder to them. It had blown a gale for days, certainly sending the *Royal Lady* flying over the water, but not giving its weary passengers a very pleasant time as it pitched and tossed. Still, it was wonderful to be close to the end of this harrowing journey.

"You must be very excited at the thought of soon seeing your father, Miss Waverley," said a voice near her elbow.

On the surface the words were pleasant, all that was polite, but Elizabeth stiffened slightly. She turned and saw the slight sneer on Lieutenant Cecil Edwards's face. Not once since he had at last left his cabin and rejoined their company had a word been said between them about the dreadful consequences of the convicts' poor treatment and the riot, but Elizabeth knew that she had made an enemy.

To everyone's relief, the lieutenant had not tried to assert himself above the captain again. Elizabeth had several times secretly wondered if that was more because of something Dr. Richmond may have said to him than the fact that the flogging incident or his accident may have changed him. But whatever the cause, except for a few minor skirmishes among a few convicts, there had been no other incidents to mar the rest of the journey.

"Of course, Lieutenant Edwards," she said briefly. She caught Mrs. Richmond's watchful eye and added reluctantly, "Are you all packed, Sir?"

He nodded and then to her relief turned away as Dr. Richmond hurried into the dining room.

"There you are, Sir," his wife said severely. "We are all waiting upon you to commence our last dinner together."

As the doctor apologized, Elizabeth saw the comfortable smile the two exchanged, and a pang raced through her. How pleasant it would be to have a marriage where each understood the other so well.

It was a festive evening. Not even the occasional sneering comments by the lieutenant could dampen the excitement that surrounded them at the thought that their long journey would conclude the very next day.

Elizabeth's own excitement was tempered by two things. One was how her father would welcome her, and the other the continual nagging concern she had for John and Timothy.

She had been thrilled when Dr. Richmond had managed to have John assigned to looking after the women's needs. This had often included cleaning out their cabins, and several times she had managed to spend some time with him to coax him to relax his cold, withdrawn manner toward her.

Then one day he had looked at her and said hurriedly, "Timothy said you would want to know that I now believe that Jesus has forgiven me. I'm. . .I'm a believer."

She had stiffened, but before she could comment he had hurried away. There had been a noticeable softening in his whole demeanor, a light in his eyes that had dispelled the pain. She was very happy for him, but she had thought the change in him was because his feelings for her had been growing even as hers were for him.

The two men had succeeded in gathering a few of their fellow convicts together for times of prayer and Bible reading. When trying to read her Bible and pray by herself in her cabin, she envied their fellowship, and a strange feeling of loneliness came over her at times, only dispelled when she saw John for precious few moments.

She had tried not to think of the horrible possibility of never seeing him again after they left the ship. She had determined shortly after the riot to petition her father to try to acquire both Timothy and John as assigned convicts, not that she'd mentioned the idea to Mrs. Richmond. She was sure the lady would be horrified.

But that last evening on board the *Royal Lady*, Elizabeth quietly asked Mrs. Richmond, "Do you know what happens to the convicts when we anchor in Sydney Cove tomorrow?"

Her friend looked at her for a moment and then replied as softly, "They have already been put in chains, ready to be marched ashore as soon as the appropriate government officials come aboard and do what they have to."

At the distressed sound Elizabeth made, her lips tightened. "You would be best to put all that has happened on this ship behind you, Elizabeth. Surely you always knew that any friendship with any of them was useless, quite useless, especially as your father. . ."

Elizabeth looked up quickly. "You know about his. . ." She paused, not sure whether to put her question into words, but her friend was nodding.

"You forget that your mother and I became very good friends. She told me that your father is an emancipist." She hesitated for a moment and then added gently, "And my husband and I both know that he never mentions those early years of his life here, unlike other prominent men who have served their time and seem to be proud of the fact they are emancipists."

"He has always been very busy establishing his property and putting its interests and his family first," Elizabeth said proudly.

"And that he has done very well, indeed," Mrs. Richmond added hastily. "But you would be advised to remember that, except for the necessity of having assigned convicts to work for him because good servants and workmen are difficult to persuade to go out into the bush, he has never had anything to do with the current politics—even the current strong move to abolish the transportation system altogether."

Elizabeth suddenly noticed that Lieutenant Edwards was watching them with considerable interest from across the room and hoped he had not heard their softly spoken words. For a fleeting moment a very unpleasant expression flickered across his face, but it was gone so quickly she thought she must have been mistaken. She watched his handsome face change completely as he suddenly smiled at something the captain was saying, and yet something made her feel very uneasy.

Oh, it would be good to go ashore the next day away from this ship, its horrible memories, and that man. If only she could be certain of John's well-being. And Timothy's also, she reminded herself quickly. But she knew that the welfare of the tall, dark man with the unforgettable smile was what burdened her heart the most.

After dinner that evening, Elizabeth was too excited to retire early and went for one last moonlit walk along the deck. A couple times during the afternoon they had seen a faint smudge on the horizon to the west and known they were drawing close to land as the southerly winds drove them up the coast of New South Wales. Now nothing could be seen except where the bright moonlight turned the dark waters to silver.

"Good evenin', Miss Waverley."

Startled, she spun around and then relaxed. "And a good evening it is, Sergeant Hobbs." She and the sergeant had become quite good friends away from Lieutenant Edwards's ever-watchful eyes, and now she asked, "Do you think your wife may be at the wharf tomorrow to welcome you back, Sir?"

"Oh, no, Miss, she knows better than that," he said cheerfully. "I'll be too busy tomorrow handing over our charges, and she wouldn't be able to be away so long from the children anyway."

Elizabeth was silent for a long moment. Quietly they shared the stillness of the night as the ship carried them ever closer to home. There wasn't even the murmur of a human voice, only the winds in the sails and the slap of the waves against the hull.

At last, in a low voice she asked, "What. . .what happens to the convicts tomorrow, Sir?"

He stared at her for a moment and then said, "Well, very soon after the ship's tied up nice and tight, I reckon it'll be swarming with officials and government men checking documents and whatnot. Then. . ." He paused before adding slowly, "After all the passengers have gone ashore, I reckon we'll probably march those poor men below to wherever they have to go. Then in the next day or so there'll undoubtedly be a reckoning for their behavior, especially. . ." The sergeant stopped abruptly.

For a moment Elizabeth was frozen in horror. Then she said rapidly, "But surely enough punishment has already been meted out for. . .for anything that has happened on the journey."

Sergeant Hobbs hesitated and then said heavily, "Lieutenant Edwards will put in his report. It will depend. . ." Once again he stopped, looked at her for a moment, and then said hurriedly, "Miss Waverley, I am afraid for the two men you cared for after the floggin's, especially John Martin. Ever since we left England, Lieutenant Edwards has shown an uncommon interest in the man."

A cold chill swept through Elizabeth.

"Lieutenant Edwards refuses to listen to our assurances and. . .and seems to have taken a set on him," he added hurriedly in a low voice. "I. . .I thought you should know, like, but please don't say that I said anythin', if you please. It's just that some offenses are hangin' matters."

Before Elizabeth could speak, he gave a hasty bow and moved quickly away.

Elizabeth turned back to stare blindly out across the dark ocean. Oh, she knew only too well how her compassion for the two convicts had drawn Lieutenant Edwards's attention to them. But what else could he be planning that so concerned Sergeant Hobbs?

Sudden resolve tightened her lips and made her raise her chin. Let the lieutenant put in his report. She would have something to report herself! Nothing more would happen to John if it lay in her power, no matter what her father might say to her for involving herself in convicts' affairs.

The next day she was on deck early with Dr. Richmond and his wife to watch the ship enter the heads of Port Jackson and sail slowly up the beautiful harbor. As they passed the small sandy inlets, cliffs, and heavily timbered shoreline, she was amazed to see how many more fine buildings had been built among the trees during the years she had been in England.

Determined not to miss a moment, Elizabeth stayed on deck until the ship at last docked. The usual flotilla of small boats met them with many a coarse joke and message called across the water. As she had many times before, she wondered how those unfortunate people on that first fleet of eight ships had felt that hot January day in 1788 as they had at last unloaded here. Their journey had taken eight long months from Portsmouth.

She felt a touch of sadness that her father would not be there to meet her. All the arrangements had been made to travel with the Richmonds to her home beyond the Blue Mountains. So, as they at long last walked on unsteady sea legs along the wharf, it was with quite a shock that she suddenly saw a familiar face from home.

With a startled cry, Elizabeth lifted the front of her long skirt and rushed forward through the crowd. "Adam! Oh, Adam, is it really you?"

The tall, handsome man, dressed more neatly in his city clothes than she had ever seen him, turned and stared at her. A puzzled expression filled his eyes. Then recognition flashed across his handsome face. For a moment he stared as though he could not believe what he saw, and then he moved gladly forward.

Impulsively she thrust her hands out. As he reached to clasp them, a myriad of emotions chased across his face.

"Elizabeth! Oh, I'm sorry, I mean, Miss Waverley. How did you get here so swiftly?" He let her hands go and then looked at Dr. Richmond and his wife as they joined them. "Dr. Richmond, Mrs. Richmond!"

"So swiftly?" Her merry laugh rang out. "Why, it seemed such a long, long journey." She looked eagerly around. "Oh, Adam, is my father here too? How is he? What wonderful chance has brought you to Sydney and to this ship?" Elizabeth continued to peer around at the bustling crowd, still searching for her father.

With another happy, excited laugh Elizabeth swung back to him again, but then she faltered. The expression on Adam Stevens's face had changed. She saw he had lost a little color. For one moment she thought he was looking, why, almost pleadingly at Dr. Richmond and his wife. Then he was shaking their hands enthusiastically, and she decided she must have imagined it.

"Elizabeth, you do not know that Adam is no longer a convict? He has been waiting for a grant of land," Dr. Richmond was saying with a keen look at the other man. "Did your father not tell you?"

"Why, no. How marvelous! I didn't know you were so close to completing your sentence, Adam. Are you not still working for my father then?"

Adam swallowed convulsively, then cleared his throat and said in a choked voice, "Well, in a manner of speaking, I guess I am still working. . . ." Then he said more firmly, "Yes, I am still working for your father, Miss Waverley."

"Oh, where is he then? Surely he would not have missed an opportunity to come to Sydney with you?"

Suddenly Mrs. Richmond tapped her on the arm and said quite sharply, "Really, Elizabeth, can't you wait until we get out of this dreadful sun before interrogating this poor man?"

Mrs. Richmond nodded shortly at Adam. "How are you, Adam? Well, I trust. Now, do you think you could get us out of this sad crush? I do declare I am feeling quite faint with the heat. All those months in England made me forget how hot it is here in December so close to Christmas," she added fussily and turned to continue along the wharf.

Elizabeth reluctantly followed her, still staring around, expecting any moment to see her father coming toward them. But she waited until Adam had led them to the shade of a huge warehouse.

Mrs. Richmond was fanning herself vigorously and then looked around haughtily. "My goodness, this place reeks of filth. Why the authorities don't clean this up I'll never know."

Elizabeth was beyond noticing her surroundings. "Now I do not need to bother you anymore, Mrs. Richmond. I will be able to travel home with Father. Oh, I do hope he does not have to stay in Sydney too long. I do so want to go home and see the sweeping plains beyond the ranges where he has taken up more land," she added longingly. "It was one of the reasons I was keen to come home when he told me in his last letter. I have always wondered what the country was like farther inland."

She glanced down at her friend, laughing at herself. Mrs. Richmond did not respond. She was staring back at her husband and Adam with a worried frown. Elizabeth followed her gaze and saw that Adam and Dr. Richmond were standing some little distance away. Adam was speaking rapidly in a low murmur. Whatever he was saying made the doctor start. Then they turned and looked at her.

Apprehension gripped Elizabeth. She watched their grave faces as they slowly started toward her, not taking their eyes from her. As she saw the doctor's face more closely, a lump of ice settled deep within her. They stopped in front of her. She looked wildly from the anxious face of the younger man to the shocked, pale face of Dr. Richmond.

"My dear Elizabeth. . ." His voice cracked.

And she knew—knew something had happened to her father.

She vaguely realized Mrs. Richmond murmured something in a distressed voice.

Dr. Richmond reached and took her icy hand. "You must be brave, my dear. Your father had an accident. Adam sent a message immediately to you. It would have passed us on our way here."

He took a deep breath, and his hold on her hands tightened.

"I'm so sorry to have to tell you your father died nearly two months ago."

Chapter 8

John had once thought nothing could be worse than being locked in the dark, damp, foul hold of the ship for days on end with chains on his feet. But at least there he and Timothy had at times been able to keep up each other's spirits, pray together, and even talk about Elizabeth in guarded words.

Now he had chains on his feet in a stinking, small cement cell crowded with far too many convicts, frightened men who could only wonder why they had been separated from the others so abruptly after a few days ashore in their new barracks. And he had not seen Timothy's cheerful, somehow peaceful face since the day Timothy had been marched off alone to some unknown destination.

None of them knew why the irons had been placed on their legs again or why they had been herded together in this small cell. Fear had grown as day after day passed with no information about what was to happen to them. There had been no contact at all with the outside world except for their tight-lipped guards.

John knew it was not what any of them had been told to expect. They had thought they would quickly be put to work on government tasks or even assigned to work for someone. As he'd studied the faces of his cell mates that first day together, he had suddenly realized it must have something to do with the riot aboard the ship. Each man there had been one of those flogged afterward. But if that was the case, he could not understand why Timothy was not with them.

It had been very hard in this place to continue to believe in the loving, caring God Timothy had been teaching him about. But the stories and words of Scripture they had shared for so many weeks were not easy to forget. When his spirits were particularly low, some verses would flash into his mind and somehow bring comfort and encouragement that God was indeed in control of his life, and that, above all, He would watch over him and work all things out for his good.

But there were still many demons of fear to face and conquer the morning his name was called out and he was roughly marched from the cell. The small room he was at last pushed into was furnished only with a table and chairs. Two men were in the room. One was seated before a pile of papers at one end of the roughly hewn wooden table. He briefly glanced up and returned to wielding his pen.

The other older, gray-haired man swung around from peering out a small, barred window and watched John's shuffling, clanging steps. From his meticulous clothes and haughty demeanor, he was obviously a man of some importance.

John came to a halt in the middle of the room, straightened to his full height, and calmly returned the man's stare. The two guards who had escorted

John saluted and withdrew. Then came the sounds of brisk, heavy boots as someone else entered the room behind him.

The well-dressed man did not pause in his careful survey of John's filthy, unkempt appearance and the tattered prison clothes that he had been wearing for far too long without an opportunity to wash either himself or them. Then he muttered something savagely under his breath and strode forward to lean both hands on the table.

"Are those fetters really necessary?" he barked.

"Lieutenant Edwards's orders, Sir."

At the short, abrupt words in a familiar voice, John stiffened, swung his head around, and looked straight into the expressionless face of Sergeant Hobbs.

"What's this all about, Sergeant?" he asked sharply. "Why—?"

"That's enough, you. You will speak only when spoken to!"

Despite his sharp words, John thought he saw a look of warning in the sergeant's eyes, and so he subsided. Warily he looked again at the other man, who was studying him closely.

"Mr. John Martin?" At John's abrupt nod, his expression tightened, but he said in the same brisk voice, "You would do well to answer me civilly. Have you not been told why you have been brought here, Sir?"

"I am a convict," John snarled. "Convicts are not told anything!"

The man raised his head haughtily and stared silently at John. John returned his stare, but something in the man's steady demeanor made him subside and say wearily, "I beg your pardon, Sir. I and several other convicts have been kept in a filthy small cell for nearly a week, and we have not been told why or what is to happen to us."

The expression on the man's face changed. A flush of anger rose in his cheeks, and he roared so suddenly that John jumped.

"Lieutenant Edwards again, Sergeant?"

"Yes, Sir!"

A fist was brought down heavily on the small table, sending documents flying. The smaller man frantically rescued his pot of ink and scrambled after the papers. His companion snatched the pen from his clerk's hand, grabbed a piece of paper, and wrote fiercely.

"See that gets to Lieutenant Edwards's superior officer immediately!"

Sergeant Hobbs saluted and swung on his heel. Before he opened the heavy door, he glanced at John and winked. John stared after him in astonishment. What was happening?

"I am Magistrate Hall, and this is my clerk." The man gestured for John to sit and then sat down himself.

He began to speak very swiftly, and John listened in ever-increasing amazement. "On receiving three differing reports, an inquiry is now under way about the conditions and subsequent behavior of all those aboard the *Royal Lady* relating to general treatment of the convicts leading to the riot and its aftermath."

The magistrate shuffled through the now-restored pile of documents and then peered at one as he continued. "The reports are from Lieutenant Edwards, Captain Longman, and an extremely interesting one from the well-known and esteemed Dr. Richmond. I see here one of the passengers—ah, yes, a Miss Elizabeth Waverley—has also written out her observations. Very clearly, I might add."

John's heart leaped. So she had not forgotten him after all.

Mr. Hall glared at John over the pair of glasses precariously perched on the tip of his nose. "I have been appointed by the board of inquiry to initially interview those involved and obtain their statements."

He paused, and his gaze was suddenly piercing. "Many have already told their stories, Mr. Martin, and you would do well to tell me the truth. Those in the cell with you will also be heard as soon as possible. Now, Sir," he said even more abruptly, "tell me your version of events from the time the *Royal Lady* docked at Cape Town."

John opened his mouth, but no words came out.

"Come, come, Mr. Martin. Please proceed to tell us your version of events!"

John started, realizing he was still staring in a daze at the man before him. He pushed away thoughts of Elizabeth writing for him, cleared his throat, and started to speak.

He was very cautious when asked for more details about the appalling conditions that developed in the hold of the *Royal Lady* at Cape Town and how their hope of relief once the ship had put to sea had gradually faded.

As he spoke, he relived the horror of those days. His voice became harsh, his slight accent more pronounced as he talked and talked. Several times he could not refrain from praising Timothy's attempts to try to calm the panic that began among the convicts as one after the other became very ill.

The clerk scribbled furiously. John only realized much later how cleverly the magistrate had framed his questions whenever John paused briefly, wondering what was wise to say and what to leave out.

When he at last stopped speaking, there was only the squeak of the clerk's pen. Magistrate Hall sat frowning down at his clasped hands. Then even the pen was still.

John felt suddenly very weary. Would he be believed? Was there a chance he could be hung as he had heard had happened to other convicts who had rebelled with violence?

The magistrate raised his head and searched John's face intently. "Can you name the leaders who actually started the attack on the guards and tried to seize their weapons?"

John stiffened. "I couldn't really name anyone specifically. I cannot even say that the man who was shot was a ringleader, even though he happened to be just in front of me when he was hit. Almost every man jack of them was ready to try anything. They were convinced they were going to die anyway and had worked themselves up to believe they may as well die trying to get out to the fresh air."

"But surely they knew they were out to sea, a long way from land, and they had no chance of taking over the ship!"

John closed his eyes for a moment. Once again he was back in the horror of the sweltering heat of the fetid, dark hold, his throat parched, his stomach churning at the revolting smells, trying desperately himself to hang onto his sanity.

He raised his head slowly and stared blindly in front of him. "Sir, you would have to realize how dark, how dreadful our situation was. The first few weeks after we left England had been hard enough but nothing like what we were experiencing then. The heat was stifling; men were falling sick everywhere. Then that man died, and despite the surgeon's efforts, others seemed close to death. They felt all hope was gone."

"And what about you and this Mr. Timothy Hardy you keep referring to?" There was a sneer in Mr. Hall's voice. "Are you trying to tell me either of you were any different? You use the word 'they.' Why should I believe you two were any different?"

John looked straight at the magistrate. He was watching John very closely, and strangely there was no hint of derision in his eyes.

"Because Timothy, a small, frail man, had such a strong personal faith in God, and somehow he helped me to have some too," John said simply.

Something flashed in the magistrate's eyes before he looked down at the table. For a moment John thought the long, tense hours since he had arrived in this strange land must be causing him to see things that could not possibly be there, like a gleam of respect in this magistrate for a convicted murderer.

John continued in an expressionless voice, explaining in more detail how Lieutenant Edwards had ordered his soldiers to put down the riot and had himself shot the convict. The soldiers had used their rifle butts ruthlessly, and it was still a marvel to John that they had not all opened fire. Perhaps they had seen how weak and helpless the desperate, emaciated men had been.

After John reached the end of his account, Mr. Hall sat strangely still. Then in a very low voice he observed, "You have not yet told me of your punishment."

John went still. He opened his mouth, but no words would come out. The memory of the pain and humiliation of the flogging would never leave him if he lived to be a hundred.

"At least tell me how many lashes you received, Mr. Martin." The voice was still low but nonetheless demanded a response.

John's mouth was strangely dry. He swallowed and at last said harshly, "It is not something I like to think about, Sir. I believe there were over sixty."

The man stared at him with a frown. "You only believe?"

John forced himself to smile slightly. "Others told me so. After awhile I did not hear the count."

There was silence for a long moment as Mr. Hall bent his head over his pen and paper. "Would you consider it too much of an intrusion to show me your back, Mr. Martin?"

John stared at him. After so many months of being ordered about as though he were mere dirt, to hear the man's soft, apologetic request sounded strange. Then Mr. Hall raised his eyes, and John saw compassion and sympathy. Suddenly his heart swelled with hope. It was the first time he had met anyone in authority besides Dr. Richmond who seemed to understand.

John rose slowly, turned around, and eased off his shirt. He had not seen his back, but the swiftly sucked-in breath of both men told him that the newly healed scars he could only touch must look even worse than he thought.

Not once during his interview had he mentioned Elizabeth. Now memories of a woman's tender hands ministering to those wounds scorched through him. He had been trying hard for many long weeks not to think of Elizabeth, so he would not go mad with longing.

Always he had to battle the bitterness that tried to overtake him when he thought of what might have been if he were not a convict. He saw no hope of ever proving his innocence now so far away from Yorkshire, and he looked on her sincere words as the wishful thinking of the sweet, inexperienced young woman she was.

The interview was abruptly terminated. Magistrate Hall rose and said shortly, "Thank you, Mr. Martin. You have been very helpful. I may need to speak to you again, but that will be all for now."

John found himself marched back to the cell by the same silent guards. He was not entirely surprised to find the other convicts in a ferment of excitement. Shortly after he had been taken away, all their leg irons had been removed and they had been allowed plenty of water to wash in and been issued new clothes. One of them had had the presence of mind to ask for a set for the man they now crowded around, clamoring to hear what had happened. But most of them greeted what he told them with expressions of dismay and sullen anger.

Later that night as he tossed restlessly, for the first time John let his iron will relax and thought about Elizabeth. Her sweet face and tender smile haunted him. He smiled as he pictured her glorious red gold hair that fell in ringlets when not tied back as she had leaned across him. He thought he smelled again her sweet perfume.

As he tried to shut out his grim surroundings by closing his eyes, he saw again those incredibly green eyes flashing with so many emotions. They had darkened when she had been bewildered or upset and blazed green fire when furiously angry, as they had when he had mentioned Beth.

Several times he had thought of Beth since he had begun his new relationship with God. Timothy had helped John to come to the point where he could genuinely ask for forgiveness for all his bitterness toward her. When at last he had been able to forgive Beth—even to pray for her—a tremendous burden had fallen from him.

And many times during these last few weeks he had prayed earnestly for Elizabeth. Now he prayed again for her until sleep freed him from his tumultuous thoughts. Then it was her eyes, softened, damp with tears, and filled with love for him that he dreamed of.

Events moved swiftly after that initial interview. A few days later the court hearing commenced before an impressive bench of magistrates, including Mr. Hall. To John's dismay and increasing concern, Timothy was not present. Except for the two women, all the other major participants were there.

Lieutenant Edwards crisply and haughtily gave his version of events, but his haughtiness swiftly changed to anger as first Sergeant Hobbs and then Captain Longman verified the convicts' statements, telling of his neglect of the convicts under his care. John watched the lieutenant's face twist into a sneer as Elizabeth's statement was read. The look of hatred he turned on John made him go suddenly cold. This man's nature was even more vicious than he had thought possible.

Then Lieutenant Edwards's anger turned to fear as he was completely humiliated by Dr. Richmond's version of events. Most of the magistrates on the bench treated Dr. Richmond as an old friend, and it was obvious to all that both the captain and the lieutenant had sadly underestimated Dr. Richmond's standing in the colony.

Within a couple weeks, John was visited by a jubilant Sergeant Hobbs, who had come to say farewell before taking an extended leave at his small farm at Parramatta.

"Lieutenant Edwards has been demoted to sergeant and transferred to Van Dieman's Land, so I hope we've seen the last of him," he told John. "I doubt too if Captain Longman will be given another convict transport contract."

"Have you heard what will happen to the rest of us? Do you know where Timothy Hardy is?" John asked urgently. Rumors had been flying thick and fast among the convicts, one of them that those who had started the riot might yet be hung.

The sergeant's lined faced became grave. "I believe Mr. Hardy has been assigned to a farmer," he said abruptly. "But some of them ringleaders have cause to be afraid. I've heard they may be shipped to the penal settlement of Norfolk Island, where last year conditions were so bad there was a dreadful mutiny and attempt to escape. Many were killed, and later thirteen convicts were hanged."

He paused, and then his face lightened. "Don't worry about you being one of them," he said hurriedly. "I think they believed my word about you saving my very own skin."

As foolish as he knew he was, John had kept hoping against hope that Elizabeth might find some way to visit him. Desperately he longed to ask the sergeant if he had heard anything of her, but he managed to keep silent.

It was another few days before he found out the sergeant's predictions had been correct. Several frightened and sullen convicts—those who had inflicted the worst injuries to some of the soldiers—were marched off to board a ship for dreaded Norfolk Island. Another day passed before John was curtly told he had been assigned and ordered to collect his belongings.

As he carefully rolled up his meager belongings, his mind was filled with turmoil. He lifted up his heavy heart in silent prayer. Despite his frequent requests for information, he had not been told one word of what was happening to Timothy, and he wondered if he would ever see him again.

"You've been assigned to a good master, so make sure you work hard and keep yourself out of trouble," he was warned roughly before at last being thrust outside into the bright sunlight.

A tall, handsome man about his own age and dressed in smart town clothes was waiting impatiently. Nearby was a well-laden dray drawn by two large, restless horses.

"There you are at last," the man said sharply. "Get aboard. We're late."

John threw his small pack behind the small, hunched-over driver, who was very busy trying to keep his two charges quiet. The driver's face was hidden beneath a large straw hat.

"Good morning, John. Glad you could join us."

At the quiet voice filled with a mixture of excitement and amusement, he froze. Then he turned slowly and stared at the neatly dressed driver. Bright eyes and a beaming face were observing him closely.

"Timothy? Why, Timothy. . ." Words failed him, but both his hands shot out to eagerly grasp the slim one being extended toward him.

"Well, are you going to stay here all day?" the stranger snapped. "For myself, the faster we leave this place behind us and smell the free, clean air of the bush, the better. Get those horses moving!"

John watched in a daze as Timothy loosened his grip on the reins and the horses started forward.

They were soon moving at a brisk pace, and as Timothy skillfully tooled the reins to dodge the traffic in the busy streets, he murmured, "Don't worry about Mr. Stevens's short tongue. He wanted to be well on the road by now. He has been all that is good and kind. A strange, silent man, he seems to really hate being near the jail. I believe he only finished serving his own sentence last year, and I guess prisons still make him a bit edgy."

"Do you know where we are headed?" John asked at last after the sheer wonder, surprise, and overwhelming relief at being with Timothy again had died away enough for him to have control of his voice.

Then suddenly he wondered, and by no means for the first time, just what it was about this small, insignificant-looking man that had drawn him to so want to be with him. Certainly Timothy had been almost overwhelming in his gratitude for saving his son, but that alone had not been the reason they had become friends.

And then as he watched the beaming smile flood Timothy's face, John realized it was because in the misery and suffering they had shared, this man had loved him. Even when he had cursed and sworn at the injustices done to him, even in his darkest hours, this little man had loved him.

As Jesus had? As Jesus did even now?

John sat a little straighter. The fact that God loved him seemed more real.

Timothy had not answered his question immediately. He was guiding the horses carefully to avoid a dust-covered stagecoach, and when John glanced again at his friend's face, his heart sank to see a frown creasing his forehead.

"No, I don't know where we're going, not really," Timothy said slowly, "except that Dr. Richmond assured me that this Adam Stevens is a good man and has a new property on the western plains of the other side of a place called Bathurst. Has some cattle, but mainly sheep, he said."

"You've spoken with Dr. Richmond?"

Timothy looked at him with some surprise. "Yes, of course. Why, didn't he come to see you?"

"No," John said shortly. "The only time I've seen him was in that court of inquiry one day. I was surprised you were not there, in fact. Haven't heard one word about what was happening to any of us."

Timothy's frown deepened. "Oh, I was there, all right, but obviously not at the same time as yourself. But that's strange, Dr. Richmond not seeing you. He did sound very concerned for you when he came and saw me both before and after that court of inquiry."

Elizabeth.

Pain swept through John. The wise old doctor in his own way was trying to protect Elizabeth from her concern for a convicted murderer with a life sentence.

After a short silence, John said abruptly, "Fill me in on what you know about the results of that inquiry."

"You mean you don't know?"

There was such amazement in Timothy's voice that John looked at him sharply. "Only that our friend Lieutenant Edwards has been demoted and transferred to Van Dieman's Land. Some of the men were sent to Norfolk Island."

A shadow crossed Timothy's face. Then a huge smile transformed him. But it faded abruptly, and he looked away.

Alarm flashed through John. "Timothy? What's wrong?"

"Nothing's wrong, but I don't know how to tell you that I. . .I've been given a ticket-of-leave."

A momentary pang of envy shot through John. All convicts knew what a ticket-of-leave meant. Timothy no longer had to work as an assigned man for a master and was free from the government claims of forced labor. He had to stay in the colony but could work for himself wherever he wanted to, earn money, start a new life, even if the knowledge hung over him that he had to live an exemplary life so the ticket-of-leave would be renewed every twelve months.

"Why, Timothy, that's absolutely marvelous." John shot out his hand and wrung Timothy's hand once more. "But I thought that if there was any chance of getting one it would not be until after several years of a sentence had been served."

Two spots of color rose in Timothy's usually pale face. "Dr. Richmond convinced them. Apparently he told them that he did not know what he would have done without the help of both of us throughout the whole voyage, and that instead of being thanked we had been so cruelly punished."

Timothy paused, and then he added in a rush, "I didn't know how to tell you. It doesn't seem fair that I was given one and not you when you were the one who tried so hard to prevent the soldiers from being hurt and were then punished so. . .so severely. Dr. Richmond told me there was considerable debate about you, but they decided that I had only been sent here on a short term for political infringements. You. . .you were a. . .a murderer."

John was silent while he tried to deal with the old pain once more. Even if somehow he were to prove his innocence, would that label follow him until he died?

"And with my size and strength I'm a danger to society," he said roughly at last and gave a bitter laugh.

"But this Adam fellow seemed quite happy to have you assigned to him," Timothy said quickly.

"Probably because he is taking us to the wilderness out west and he thinks there's little mischief to get up to there."

After a long pause, John asked softly, "Was Elizabeth ever mentioned?"

Timothy shook his head sadly. "Once I ventured to ask Dr. Richmond about her. He became very haughty, even angry. Said it was best if we forgot all about her."

John stared blindly ahead. Forget her? If only that were possible!

They were silent after that. John wondered wearily just what was ahead of them. There had been a lot of rumors and speculation about the country west of the ranges and the danger from savage aborigines. There were still vast tracts of land in the West that no white man had ever set foot on.

As they left Sydney and then Parramatta, John's heart was heavy. He was relieved and thankful to be with Timothy, to be out in the fresh air, and to be assigned to a master who was proving to be courteous and kindly.

He offered up even more thanks to a provident God when they passed a convict road gang working and repairing the dangerous, narrow road winding its way over the Blue Mountains. They were guarded by bored soldiers with fixed bayonets. With a shudder, John could only imagine the conditions they lived and worked under.

But every plodding step of the horses was taking him farther from the one person he longed so desperately to be with. He was feeling sad and hurt that, despite her earnest protestations of wanting to prove his innocence and even her written testimony in court, not once had Elizabeth sent him a message. It was no surprise she had not been allowed to visit him, but surely she could have found some way of contacting him.

By the time they had set up camp that first night, Adam Stevens had relaxed. "Ah, it is so good to be out of the city again," he said simply after he had shown them how he wanted things set up and how to build and light a safe campfire in the hot summer.

As he later told them about the bush and their destination out west, his new sheep station, he completely lost his reserve. He also warned them of some of the dangers of the bush.

"Always keep an eye out for snakes," he said finally, and then gave a bark of laughter as both Timothy and John intently surveyed their immediate surroundings.

They looked at each other a little sheepishly but then laughed with him. And it was so good to laugh again, especially out here with only the dark bush and the startled birds and wildlife to hear.

John was amazed at how quickly the light disappeared completely in comparison to the long evenings in Yorkshire. He said so, and Adam stopped poking at the small fire he had placed a blackened tin container on to make tea and looked at him steadily.

"It's not like home here," he said quietly. "No long summer days, but then no long winter nights either. When Mr.—" He stopped abruptly.

After a long pause, as he stared at the leaping flames, he said slowly, "Especially when I first went right out west, the land seemed so vast, so flat in comparison to England. The trees and bushes are not the same bright greens. Not many at all have leaves that change color and fall. But I hope you will find like I have that there is a beauty, a tranquillity, a healing in this vast land so different from England."

There was nostalgia in his voice, and all three were silent until the billy boiled and they were eating some of the bread and mutton from the food supplies. After awhile Adam continued telling them what they should expect in the months ahead.

Then John asked something that he had been wondering about off and on all day. "Mr. Stevens, from what you have said, it will be a hard life out on this new property of yours. Timothy said you finished serving your time a year or so ago. Have you no wish to return home to your family?"

Adam Stevens gave a harsh laugh. "Home? I no longer have a home or family who cares in England. There's nothing there for me anymore." He stood up and threw the last of his tea into the dying embers of the fire. "You'd better get some sleep," he snapped. "We break camp as soon as it's light. Oh, and don't call me 'Mister.' Adam will do."

The days and nights rolled by until at last they arrived and set up camp near the Gordon homestead on the Bathurst plains. Adam told them he had been able to purchase several hundred head of sheep from the friendly owner of the station, and that he had already purchased many more at another property in the area.

"They are being held for me there, and I'm leaving you here to mind this flock while I go and fetch them."

John had been looking at the bleating sheep and protested quickly, "We had sheep where I grew up in Spain, but I don't know anything about the care of sheep here."

Adam looked at him thoughtfully and then smiled grimly. "That's another reason to leave you here. I've made arrangements for my old friend, Will Gordon, to give you some lessons. Once we're out west, you'll be learning the hard way if I'm not around."

So, learn they did. And there was much to learn about finding the right pastures, crutching, detailing lambs, protecting the sheep from blowflies, learning how to use the blades that cut the greasy valuable fleece from the backs of belligerent sheep. They listened meekly, asking a few questions but realizing it could take them a lifetime to learn all there was to know.

Both men thought Adam had been strangely reticent about his movements, but by the time he returned several days later with more men and more sheep, both Timothy and John were too glad to be on the move again to ask too many questions. More supplies had also been obtained from wherever Adam had been, a place they were rather puzzled that the usually friendly man refused bluntly to talk about.

The supplies had been loaded on a long wagon pulled by a team of bullocks. The old, wizened bullock driver stared them up and down, spat out a clump of tobacco on the ground, mumbled a couple of words that included a swearword and "new chums" before ambling off to attend his charges.

"At least he didn't call us convicts," John said with amusement as he and Timothy looked at each other.

As they let the sheep graze on the journey west, day after day slipped slowly by. And gradually the long, quiet days did start to bring their own healing.

But try as he might, John could never completely banish the image of red gold hair framing the beautiful face of Elizabeth. Her soft voice and flashing green eyes continued to haunt his dreams.

Had her reunion with her father been as sweet as she had hoped? Was she enjoying the wide open spaces she had told them about? He often wished she had told him just where her home was. All he knew was that it was at least two or three hours on horseback from Parramatta.

Timothy often talked nostalgically about his wife and small son. Somehow John could not bring himself to speak out loud about Elizabeth. In his dreams she was his alone to admire, to dare to love. And sometimes when he awoke and knew he might never see her again, that reality was almost more than he could cope with.

Chapter 9

January 1837

M y dear Elizabeth, what a delightful surprise! How truly lovely to see you again after all this time. But how could you travel all this way without your companion? I trust that my dear cousin is well?"

Elizabeth nodded and returned Mrs. Richmond's embrace with enthusiasm. She forced a smile as that good woman held her by the shoulders, studied her carefully, and without waiting for an answer said, "There is still a shadow in those beautiful green eyes, my dear, but I'm glad that you have put away those dull mourning gowns of yours at last." Although she spoke in her usual forthright way, she smiled gently.

Elizabeth squeezed her hand once more before letting her lead the way into the cool shadows of the house. "Well, it is twelve months since. . .since we arrived home on the *Royal Lady,*" she said quietly.

Mrs. Richmond paused momentarily and then said quickly, "Would you like a cold drink or a cup of tea to refresh you?" She sank onto a chair and fanned herself vigorously.

"Oh, definitely a cold drink to start with."

"I declare this must be the hottest January we've had."

Elizabeth watched with some interest as Mrs. Richmond gave brisk, detailed instructions to the neatly uniformed servant who had been quietly waiting in the background.

When the servant had scurried away, Elizabeth said, "Yes, it has been hot. The river is getting dangerously low for the stock, although they do say there has been rain in the hills and the weather may improve. But enough of that," she added hastily. "All we seem to talk about lately is the weather. I am afraid your cousin is recovering from a slight fever, and I left in such haste she was unable to accompany me."

She smiled slightly at Mrs. Richmond's frown and added, "I was quite safe with one of my women, and a couple of my men escorted us. How is Dr. Richmond?"

"I'm sure he will be very happy to see you, but he does take his guardianship of you very seriously. I'm sure I don't know what he will say about your coming without Sarah."

"He must realize that in another few weeks I will be of age and can then do as I please."

Mrs. Richmond looked taken aback at the sharpness of her words.

Elizabeth forced a smile, and after swallowing rapidly, Mrs. Richmond said swiftly, "Dr. Richmond is quite well, although he too is worried about the lack of rain and keeps talking about visiting our property at Bathurst even though the manager is so excellent. But he has been very busy here on this small farm, and then of course there has been all this debate about self-government for New South Wales as well as the abolition of transportation." She stopped abruptly and bit her lip.

Elizabeth had stiffened but managed to keep the smile on her face as she said calmly, "I think that far too many landholders fear the shortage of labor in the bush if they can no longer get assigned convicts. One doubts if many newly arrived immigrants would be very willing to travel so far from Sydney and all their comforts."

She stopped speaking as the servant entered with a tray of refreshments and watched as Mrs. Richmond said, "Thank you, Mrs. Hughes. I trust you have settled well into your new quarters?"

The woman bobbed a curtsy. "Yes, thank ye, Ma'am. It be very beautiful."

She beamed at her mistress so worshipfully before bustling off about her duties that Elizabeth gave a low laugh. "Another woman from the Female Factory at Parramatta?"

Her friend handed her a glass of fresh orange juice and then looked at her serenely. "Of course, and as always, I had her thoroughly investigated. And how many convicts do you have working for you now, may I ask?"

Elizabeth smiled impishly at her. "As many reputable ones as I can find work for, of course." Her smile faded. "However, there are none that I can trust as we could Adam Stevens."

Mrs. Richmond had just lifted her glass to her lips, but suddenly she choked. "Oh dear, how clumsy of me," she said fussily as she dabbed at the juice that had spilled down her gown. "My new maid will be very cross at having to clean this again so soon. I do declare she only just finished repairing and cleaning it yesterday." A blush had stained Mrs. Richmond's cheeks.

It was not like Elizabeth's friend to be so upset by such a small incident. Elizabeth's heart leaped. *So she does know.*

She carefully put down her own glass. "Have you recently heard anything of Adam, Mrs. Richmond?" she asked brightly. "I was so disappointed last year when he had already left for the outback before our business in Sydney was completed." She paused and added, "Oh, by the way, I saw our mutual neighbor, Mrs. Gordon, two days ago."

Mrs. Richmond was still avoiding looking at her, but at that name she started.

Elizabeth smiled and added sweetly, "You do remember Mrs. Gordon, don't you? Their huge property runs down to our southern boundary. She has such a tribe of children that she very rarely leaves home. She asked after Adam and the two men he left with them while he came to Waverley Station for our sheep to take to my father's new property, or rather, Adam's new property now. Remember," she added sweetly, "the one Father left Adam in his will?"

With considerable interest, Elizabeth saw her friend give such a start her cup of tea tilted alarmingly. Elizabeth continued in her bright, conversational tones, saying, "Mrs. Gordon was all effusive cordiality. She assured me that at least we could feel comfortable that the two convicts he had with him seemed decent enough, had quite captured all with their pleasant ways, despite their appalling ignorance of how to cope in the bush. They were so newly arrived from England, you see."

To Elizabeth's immense satisfaction, Mrs. Richmond suddenly put down her cup with a rattle. In a suddenly sharp voice Elizabeth added, "How is it that no one told me about those two men Adam brought back from Sydney?"

Mrs. Richmond began tearing at a handkerchief in her lap.

"She couldn't remember their names," Elizabeth continued, "only having met them briefly before being brought to bed with her tenth child. Apparently one convict, a small, insignificant-looking man had a ticket-of-leave, but the other one. . ."

Elizabeth took a deep breath and stared challengingly at Mrs. Richmond, who was now watching her with a resigned expression.

"The other one was so handsome, so Spanish-looking with his black curly hair and unusual blue eyes, that all the ladies in the place were in a twitter."

Mrs. Richmond stared at her and then gave a deep sigh. "I told Dr. Richmond you would find out," she muttered.

"It was John Martin and Timothy Hardy, wasn't it?" Elizabeth's voice had risen.

Mrs. Richmond studied her carefully and nodded.

Elizabeth suddenly sprang to her feet. "Do you have any idea how often in the last twelve months I've tried to find out what happened to them? Beyond telling me about Timothy's ticket-of-leave and that John had been assigned, you. . .you knew nothing, you said. Nothing! You knew, and neither of you said a word. Not a word!" She wrung her hands together. "I suppose my notes to John were never delivered either?"

Mrs. Richmond shook her head reluctantly.

"Oh, what must he be thinking of me? Not even a message since we left the ship!" Elizabeth burst out. "All his life people have failed him, and now I have too!"

"Elizabeth, sit down!"

Her friend's voice was so forceful, Elizabeth stopped her pacing and stared.

"That attitude of yours is the very reason why Dr. Richmond forbade me to tell you he had arranged for John Martin to be assigned to Adam Stevens. It seemed providential that he was leaving immediately for the outback, too good an opportunity to miss."

Mrs. Richmond sighed. "Elizabeth," she continued in much gentler tones, "you must know that any fondness you may have for a man serving a life sentence has absolutely no hope of. . .of. . ."

She stopped, and Elizabeth felt the heat staining her cheeks. Very slowly she sank down into her chair, her head bowed. Suddenly a sob shook her, and then the tears started to trickle down her face.

Mrs. Richmond was on her feet in a flash. "My dear girl, I do feel for you, but this will not do; it really will not do."

When Elizabeth's pent-up tears had ceased and she had been petted and embraced by a very upset Mrs. Richmond, she at last lifted her chin and said firmly, "John Martin is a very fine man, and I have many times asked God to help me forget him, but instead, my longing to see him again continues to grow. I am not a fool; I know how impossible it all is, and yet. . ."

She paused, not sure how her friend would respond to her other news. "I immediately wanted to start making preparations to travel out to visit. . .visit Adam, but our neighbor had also brought some mail to me that had been delivered to them by mistake. One was from Timothy's wife. I have written to her a couple of times. This letter told me she had heard from Timothy at last. He had written just before leaving Sydney to work for a very kind man called Adam Stevens, but she was not sure if his address in the country meant it would be possible for her letter to reach him by the time she and her son arrived in Sydney.

"Her letter had even taken a long time to reach me, and I thought I should confront Dr. Richmond first and see if you had any more information. Also, it seems the *Royal Admiral* was to leave only a few days after she had posted this letter. I am worried about her and decided before I went to find John that I should talk to you first about him, and also to ask if you could look out for her."

Mrs. Richmond stared at her. To Elizabeth's relief she did not immediately comment on her proposed trip to the outback, but exclaimed, "Timothy Hardy's wife!" Then her eyes narrowed. "And how could she find the money for. . . ?" She paused and eyed Elizabeth thoughtfully. "You sent it to her, didn't you?" she asked bluntly.

Elizabeth hesitated and then said shortly, "It was nothing. You know that my father has left me quite a wealthy woman."

"That was very well done of you, Elizabeth." Mrs. Richmond's voice was full of admiration. "So, she should be arriving soon. How wonderful for Mr. Hardy." She stopped short and said slowly, "Now, just a moment; what did you say was the name of the ship?"

"The *Royal Admiral*."

"Why, I do believe that is the name of the ship that Dr. Richmond mentioned only this morning. He is expecting news from London about the push for self-government and was quite excited that the ship had been seen anchored off the heads last night, waiting to enter the harbor at first light."

Elizabeth's eyes widened. "Oh, that poor woman, imagine how bewildered she must be in all the hustle and bustle at the wharf." She jumped up. "I must go and meet her."

Mrs. Richmond insisted on accompanying her, but when they arrived, the passengers were already disembarking.

"Oh, I do hope we have not missed her," Elizabeth exclaimed as she craned her head to try and see through the crowd.

The back of a tall man with short, curly black hair caught her attention. He looked so much like John Martin that she stared at his neat, country clothes for a moment and then looked blindly away. So many times before she had thought she had seen him, even once in a long line of convicts being marched past her coach.

She continued searching the crowd, but her eyes were drawn back to the tall man. He turned his head and looked toward her. For one moment she thought that mentioning John Martin to someone for the first time in months was causing her to conjure him up. His gaze swept over her and then suddenly he started. His eyes widened in disbelief.

Their gazes clung.

She stood motionless, hardly daring to breathe. Then she saw him straighten his shoulders. He started pushing through the crowd toward her.

"Why, I do declare, isn't that Mr. Hardy over there?" Mrs. Richmond panted beside her.

Elizabeth hardly heard her. That other familiar face loomed ever closer. Then he was in front of her. She was vaguely aware that Mrs. Richmond gave a startled gasp of recognition, but not once did Elizabeth stop staring into John's blue eyes until he executed a very gentlemanly bow. But he said not a word, just stood there waiting for her to either turn away or acknowledge him.

She could not move; she just stared at him wildly. His face had filled out; his skin was even darker from being in the hot sun. He looked fit and well. He looked absolutely wonderful.

His eyes suddenly changed from startled pleasure and wonder to pools of pain. He moved a step back, and she was startled into extending her hand to him.

"John, why, John, it is you. For a moment I thought. . .I thought I must be dreaming." Her voice sounded as breathless and excited as she felt.

His face lit up. Her hand was enveloped by his strong, darkly tanned one. He lifted it to his lips. It was far from being a conventional gesture. His lips caressed her fingertips, and she began to tremble. His grip on her hand tightened convulsively.

"Elizabeth, Miss Waverley. . ." He paused, and she saw him swallow, realizing suddenly that he was as affected as she was.

"Oh, Miss Waverley, Miss Waverley," another emotion-filled voice intruded. "My wife. . .my wife's here, and Tim. They are actually here!"

John dropped her hand as though he had been stung and took a step back.

Elizabeth was still bereft of words. She stared at him until a tearful, excited voice behind her said, "Miss Waverley? Oh, Miss, how can I ever thank you?"

Elizabeth swung around and was suddenly enveloped by warm young arms.

"I was in the very depths of despair when your first letter arrived. There had been no word from my Timothy. Not a word, although his letters to me did arrive at last in one big heap," Mrs. Hardy babbled on. "And then when the money arrived. . .I. . .I. . ."

Her voice faded away as big tears started streaming down her cheeks. With a helpless gesture, she turned to her husband again, who immediately put his arm around her, saying in a voice as tearful as hers, "Now, now, Molly, my dear, now, now. Don't start the waterworks again. You'll upset young Tim."

Elizabeth, still unable to speak, stared at them for a moment, and then her gaze went back to John's strong, handsome features. He was staring at her but looked down as a small voice said loudly, "Why, aren't you the man who pulled me out of the water?"

As he bent to greet young Tim, his face lit up in such a breathtakingly beautiful smile that Elizabeth swallowed sharply and looked away. Her gaze encountered her friend's worried face, and she took a grip on herself.

"It's really lovely to see you arrived safely, Mrs. Hardy," she said huskily, "but do let me introduce you to my friend, Mrs. Richmond."

Mrs. Richmond raised an eyebrow. To Elizabeth's relief she said politely, "How do you do, Mrs. Hardy?"

Timothy's wife pulled away from his sheltering arm and finished using his large handkerchief to mop up her face. She beamed at Mrs. Richmond and bobbed a curtsy. "Oh, you are the wife of the doctor who was so kind to my husband. How can I ever. . .ever thank you all? I. . .I. . ."

Seeing the danger of more tears, Elizabeth said quickly, "And I'm sure there will be opportunities later to say all that has to be said."

She faltered for a brief moment as her gaze encountered John's unsmiling one. Then she straightened and asked in a firmer voice, "Where are you staying? I'm sure Adam would not mind if we joined you so we could enjoy a good talk." She looked around. "He is with you, isn't he?"

"Adam left on a ship for England not so very long ago." John's voice was harsh, his expression guarded. "We have been staying at an inn well on the way to Parramatta."

Elizabeth stared at him in astonishment. "England! But I thought he had vowed never to return there."

"His uncle has died. To Adam's utter astonishment he is joint heir with his brother of a considerable estate. His brother demanded his return to sort out their affairs. Adam has left us in charge of Stevens Downs until he returns," he added with a proud lift of his head.

"But I thought—" Elizabeth stopped short, realizing she was about to reveal information she had been told in confidence one lonely winter's night by the young convict suffering so badly from homesickness and despair.

It seemed that Adam was after all going to see the brother he had thought never to see again. But that was his business. This was a new country, a new life.

What did old history really matter to anyone else except the one concerned?

"This is neither the time nor place for a conversation about Adam's doings," Mrs. Richmond said briskly. "Now, why don't all of us return to my home for refreshments? It is also on the road to Parramatta. We all do have quite a bit to talk about."

Elizabeth looked at her with gratitude. It was so typical of her kindhearted friend. She gave most people the impression of being very proper and correct, but here she was, inviting two convicts to her home as though they were honored guests. Elizabeth risked another glance at John and saw the utter astonishment in his face. He at least realized the full import of the invitation.

It was obvious that Timothy Hardy did also. "Why, Mrs. Richmond, Ma'am, I. . .we—we could not impose on you," he stammered. He paused and then said with considerable dignity, "We do thank you for your condescension, but we yet have to see to the unloading of our belongings, and we will need to get settled at the inn before night falls."

Mrs. Richmond hesitated for only a moment before taking a deep breath and turning to the other man. "And what about you, Mr. Martin? Are you free to accept my invitation? I do believe Elizabeth wants to speak to you about something."

John's eyes widened in amazement, and then he glanced swiftly at Elizabeth. Once again her friend had taken her breath away. She felt the color rise in her cheeks.

"I promised Timothy to help him with their belongings, Ma'am," he said hesitantly.

"Of course," Mrs. Richmond said briskly, "but I'm sure that once they're settled they would prefer to spend some time alone. Perhaps you could visit with us this evening."

Still John hesitated, and Elizabeth said swiftly, "I believe you said that Dr. Richmond would not be home until late tonight, Mrs. Richmond?"

A flash of gratitude for her understanding crossed his face. Mrs. Richmond paused only momentarily before assuring him that was so.

"I'm sure we all have much to talk about," she added politely. "I'd very much like to hear firsthand how Adam's new station is going."

Elizabeth took much care with her appearance for the evening. Fortunately, she had packed one of her best dresses for the trip, knowing that the Richmonds lived such an active social life she might well need it, even for a brief visit.

All her unusual primping and fussing before her mirror was amply rewarded by the gleam of admiration and then delight that filled John's face as his gaze swept over the rich, green dress that emphasized the green of her eyes, and her artfully arranged red gold curls.

She felt heat sweep through her in a tide and knew by the smile that suddenly sparkled from his dark eyes that the color had risen into her cheeks.

Being the gracious hostess she was, Mrs. Richmond greeted John pleasantly. Not for a moment did she betray that all the way home from Sydney she had desperately tried to talk Elizabeth out of becoming involved again in his affairs and only yielded defeat when Elizabeth had said strongly, "There is naught you can say or do to change my mind. People have let John Martin down all his life. Before God, I refuse to be another."

After he had taken the seat indicated by their hostess, he said politely, "I trust your father is pleased to have you home, Miss Waverley?"

She had thought some months ago that she had shed so many tears for her father that she could have no tears left for him. Now she felt their sudden sting again at the unexpected question.

She bent her head and with gratitude heard Mrs. Richmond say softly, "Unfortunately, our dear friend was killed a couple months before we arrived from England. We only found out the day the ship arrived."

John gave an exclamation of distress.

Mrs. Richmond rose suddenly and said briskly, "I need to see our cook about tomorrow's menus, and you young people have much to speak of," and whisked herself from the room.

There was a tense silence for a long moment. Elizabeth sat staring down at her hands, still fighting the tears at the memory of her double grief at losing the two men she cared so much about. Then suddenly John moved and crossed the room to sit beside her on the brocade-covered couch.

"I'm so very sorry about your father, Elizabeth."

She slowly raised her head. "I so wanted him to meet you, John."

Surprise shone at her from his dark eyes. Then he scowled. "I hardly think your father would have been interested in meeting a convict."

"You're very wrong, John." She paused and then said steadily, "Do you remember that I once told you I was already friendly with four convicts?" After he had given a brief, reluctant nod, she said simply, "My father was very young when he was transported to Australia."

🦋

Shock held him rigid. At last he said slowly, "I would imagine that would be all the more reason he would not have wanted his own daughter to befriend convicts."

She hesitated before saying reluctantly, "I'm afraid you are probably right, but now we'll never know." After a pause she said thoughtfully, "But my father was a very shrewd judge of character. I think he would have wanted to help you if he had let himself get to know you."

"How can you possibly know what kind of a man I am?"

"I know."

John continued to stare at her. He shook his head in disbelief. How could this woman stand there looking at him from such steady, confident eyes? Never before had anyone except perhaps Timothy and, more recently, Adam Stevens demonstrated such faith in him.

"No dishonorable man risks his life to save a stranger's small child from drowning or earns the respect and admiration of a tough soldier like Sergeant Hobbs and hundreds of fellow convicts." She paused and then added softly, "And only a very good man will suffer as you did for his friend."

He was speechless, unable to tear his eyes from her as she rose and came closer.

"But I am so very sorry I couldn't find you all those months." Briefly she explained, and the sadness and regret that swept into her face as she spoke confounded him even more.

"You tried to find me?"

She nodded briefly. Tears moistened her eyes, and he held his breath, willing her silently not to cry. He couldn't bear to see her cry. Her tears threatened to melt the hard core that had been deep inside him for so long, despite his new relationship with God.

He was thankful when she brushed a hand almost angrily across her eyes and turned abruptly away.

"Everyone I approached confessed complete ignorance about the fate of the two convicts exonerated of bad behavior after the inquiry. All I could discover was that they had been assigned and moved out to work in the bush. That was what Dr. Richmond told me himself," she finished angrily. "My father made him my guardian. Now I know it was at his instigation that the information was kept from me. He even failed to deliver my letters to you."

She wrote to me!

"But Adam told us it was he who organized the whole thing." John stopped abruptly, wishing he had held his tongue as she swung back and he saw her flashing eyes.

"I know. I only found out a few days ago where you were."

She told him how she had found out, and when she at last fell silent, he said quietly, "I can well understand their desire to protect you. You would have been especially vulnerable at that time."

"Mrs. Richmond told me all about it this morning," she said sadly. "Apparently Adam was sworn to secrecy and has been faithfully reporting how you are to them."

"Adam has become a good friend." John hesitated for a moment, wondering if it was wise to get her hopes up, but he was still rather dazed and too full of wonder at God's workings in his life himself to keep it all bottled up any longer.

So he blurted out, "While he is in England he has promised to see if he can recover the Bible and the letters of my mother I tried to have delivered to my father during my trial. Adam will speak to my father, and even my cousin Percival if necessary." His face darkened. "We believe that my mother's letters may never have been given to my father by Percival as he assured me while I was in prison, and Adam is going to confront Beth."

🦋

Beth again. A pang stabbed through Elizabeth.

She stared at him and then pushed away the sharp taste of jealousy. He had never loved Beth. Then suddenly she realized what it meant. Joy flooded through her and she beamed at him. "Oh, John, he's going to prove your innocence!"

Her hands went out to him of their own volition. An answering gleam of excitement shone on his face as he grasped them tightly and drew her closer.

"He says that if he can prove that I am the legitimate heir to a peerage, my trial would be proved invalid and I would have to be tried by my peers. Oh, Elizabeth, how I have longed to see you, to tell you. . ."

And then their arms were around each other and they were clinging together. He looked into her bright eyes and groaned helplessly as his lips descended to plunder hers.

Mrs. Richmond entered the room and stopped dead. "Elizabeth!"

They sprang apart guiltily, but Elizabeth refused to let go of his hand as she turned to her friend. "Oh, Mrs. Richmond, Adam's going to see John's father to prove his innocence."

Mrs. Richmond looked from one to the other and shook her head helplessly. During one bad patch the previous year when Elizabeth had sobbed out her grief and loneliness onto her friend's shoulder, she had repeated to Mrs. Richmond all that John had told her. She had told Elizabeth today that after telling her husband he had said, "In no way must you encourage her in those wild fantasies, my dear."

Now she sighed and moved slowly forward to touch Elizabeth's flushed cheek lightly. "My dear, this is the first day since being told about your father that you have that old happy gleam back in your eyes." She looked up at John. There was censure in her direct look, but she merely said, "I do wish you all the best, Mr. Martin," and then gave them both a smile that to her credit only wavered for a moment.

"I earnestly hope Adam succeeds, my dear," she said gently to Elizabeth as she moved forward and took her hand so that she was forced to relinquish her grip on John's hand. "But I would urge you both not to get your hopes up too much."

Chapter 10

Despite an occasional tense moment between John and Elizabeth, the three of them had a most enjoyable evening. The two women were fascinated by the stories John told about Adam's sheep station. Both knew the difficulties of farming on the fertile Bathurst plains, but this country west of the Macquarie River and the small settlement at Wellington was something different again.

"When the explorer Captain Charles Sturt returned from exploring the Castlereagh and Bogan River areas out there only a couple years before Father sent me to England, he told about a large and sun-blasted plain with little vegetation," Elizabeth said eagerly. "Have you found there is sufficient pasture for the sheep?"

For a moment, John was so caught up staring into her excited, flashing eyes, she lost his train of thought. Then the color rose in her cheeks, and Mrs. Richmond coughed delicately. John glanced swiftly at her. She was looking at Elizabeth with some astonishment and then turned to him.

To his considerable relief, Mrs. Richmond suddenly beamed at him approvingly and said, "Do tell us what the country is like, John."

He smiled back at her and relaxed even more. "I believe where we are is not quite as arid as farther west, but this time of the year it is very hot."

The time flew by as he went on to tell them about the discovery that the size of the block of land Adam had leased was proving to be inadequate. The pastures could not sustain the same number of sheep per acre as the more eastern properties, and they were being forced to occupy a much larger area than expected to find enough grass for the sheep.

"That's been happening all over the country for many years," Mrs. Richmond said comfortably. "It was only last year that we were allowed to buy licenses to pasture stock beyond the authorized limit."

Elizabeth grinned happily at her but eagerly turned back to John as he went on to tell them about the huge mobs of kangaroos that also competed with the sheep for the grass.

"And you've had some contact with the aborigines, John," Elizabeth noted anxiously. "Are they dangerous?"

"The aborigines in the area had never seen white men before," John told them. "They are quite friendly, although very suspicious, and keep to themselves. They started helping themselves to several sheep not long after we arrived. We never saw them, and most of the men were scared and all for going after them, but Adam managed to make contact and eventually befriend them. He is a great man," he added, and they heard in his voice how much he had grown to love him.

He went on to tell them how Adam had managed to set up a system where he let the aborigines have a sheep every now and again as well as some flour and sugar, on condition they would not disturb the flocks. He had also promised not to venture on certain land that they seemed to hold as taboo or used for their huge corroborees.

Adam had insisted all his workmen treat them and their women with respect and dignity. So far there had not been as many problems with them as there had been in other areas where the white man had intruded on the aboriginal territory.

Then some of the sheep had lambed just as the worst of the freezing westerly winds had swept in, and there had been more losses than they had hoped. But on the whole, Adam had not been too displeased with their first cut and the bales of wool that had been hauled away by their bullock teams a couple months ago.

"Have you. . .have you been very lonely way out there, John?" Elizabeth asked softly at one point.

He looked at her for a long moment, and he knew she saw the answer in his eyes before he looked down.

"Yes, there were times I was lonely," he murmured at last, "but somehow lately it hasn't been too bad. There's a special charm about the country that I can't really explain." He smiled wryly. "A sense of absolute freedom is certainly perhaps its biggest attraction, but there is a timelessness about the land that so often puts life into its right perspective. I have felt very close to God out there on the flat plains as well as in the silence of the bush."

No one spoke for a few moments, and then John looked directly at Elizabeth and said quietly, "Your father must have been a great man. Adam told us just before he sailed that your father had given him those sheep and his rights to that property."

"Apparently my father had obtained that land just before he was killed. All the plans had been made and most of the provisions already organized. I'm just so glad he left it to Adam," Elizabeth told him proudly. "It was no real surprise to me. Before I went to England he told me he was making provision for Adam in his will. Adam had saved his life more than once. . . ." Her face clouded.

"And he would have again, if it had been in his power," Mrs. Richmond said briskly. She suddenly stood up. "I'm afraid my husband may be home soon. I know that he will want to speak to you, Mr. Martin, but perhaps it would be best if you called in the morning?"

As he too rose to his feet, John looked at her steadily. He understood her silent message that it would be best if that particular interview took place when Elizabeth was not present.

"Of course, Madam," he said quietly. "I must apologize if I have outstayed my welcome."

A hint of color touched the older woman's face, but she merely nodded and graciously allowed him to take her hand as he bowed his farewell. "Perhaps you would like to see Mr. Martin out, Elizabeth?" she relented enough to say.

Elizabeth slowly led the way to the front door and out onto the small front porch. She turned suddenly toward him and asked, "When were you intending to return to the station, John?"

"We promised Adam we would return as soon as possible." He smiled at her as she looked up at him with a slight frown. As though unable to resist touching her, he reached out and placed a finger on the creased, velvety skin of her forehead. "The men Adam has surrounded himself with know their jobs and seem pretty reliable, but I know Timothy is eager to show his wife and son the new house we have been working on."

Elizabeth thought of some of the settlers' rough bush cabins she had seen made of logs, bark, and mud, and shuddered. She hoped Mrs. Hardy was not too shocked by the primitive conditions.

"And are you sure you will both be all right while Adam is gone? Did he say how long he would be away?"

"He anticipated his business with his brother would be very brief. Apparently they have never got on, especially since his brother's marriage. He hoped to be well and truly back within twelve months, depending on his securing a passage home."

He gave a light laugh. "Adam made sure that Timothy's ticket-of-leave was renewed before he left and that my assignment to him was also endorsed while he was away. We both have all the documentation quite safely, including any passes he thought I might need to move from one district to another."

A sudden inexplicable sense of foreboding touched Elizabeth, and she reached out and clasped his hand. "You will be very careful, won't you, John?" She hesitated and then said boldly, "I really think it would be safer for you all if I accompanied you on the journey west."

He looked silently at her for a moment and then turned away and clutched at the rail near the steps while he stared out across the front yard. Accompany them to the outback! There was nothing more he could have desired at that moment than her continued presence in his life, but he closed his eyes briefly in despair. She was so precious to him, and it was up to him to protect her.

He turned and looked at her sweet face raised so trustingly to his. "I must apologize for putting you in such an embarrassing situation earlier when Mrs. Richmond entered the room," he managed to say at last when he knew he had control of his voice and face.

Her smile dimmed slightly, but she said mischievously, "I'm not a bit sorry. I . . ." She took a deep breath. "I had hoped you might repeat it."

Because he could not help himself, his hands went out to her. She clasped them firmly in her dainty ones, and he clung to her while he searched her face in the dim glow from the outside lighting.

"Elizabeth, you know we can't do this," he said desperately.

She just smiled at him with so much love and gentleness in her face that his good intentions began to weaken. So desperately had he longed to see that smile, breathe that fragrance that always surrounded her—was the very essence of her.

"I know nothing of the sort," she said crossly. "Whether you take me with you or not, I'm still coming. Besides, it would be much safer for me and my maid traveling with you than by ourselves," she said.

He guessed shrewdly that she would have had others with them on their journey but refrained from comment when he saw the stubborn tilt of her chin. Suddenly he knew he was lost and started to smile at her.

Her eyes shone even brighter. "You. . .you shouldn't smile at me like that," she said a little breathlessly. "It does strange things to me. It always has."

He smiled in sudden delight. It was nothing to what her smile did to him!

"Can you possibly be ready by tomorrow, though?" he said doubtfully. "We have already been here longer than we had thought because the *Royal Admiral* was delayed, and we can't really afford to stay at the inn any longer."

"Tomorrow!" She looked taken aback but then smiled a little grimly. "No doubt it is just as well. I should imagine I will be glad to get away from the Richmonds and their lectures."

His doubt and dismay increased. Before he could open his mouth to again argue against her going, she lifted her chin and added hurriedly, "Of course I can be ready, but you did say you would call on Dr. Richmond in the morning."

He hesitated for a long moment and then sighed. So be it.

His grip on her hand tightened. "Timothy wanted to show his wife and son a little of Sydney before we leave. I will come here instead of joining them. We thought we would have an early lunch before we head off and camp just this side of the pass through the Blue Mountains tonight. Then a full day tomorrow should bring us well on our journey. We will travel much faster on the last stretch than our first time," he mused.

She stared up at him with such starry eyes that John felt his heart swell and could no longer resist. He swept her into his arms and eagerly claimed the lips she raised willingly to him.

"Twelve months ago I determined this could never happen again," he murmured against her lips and then gave a soft moan as her hands tightened on his shoulders and he kissed her again.

They were both breathless when they at last drew a little apart and stared at each other in wonder.

"Elizabeth, you do know there is so much I am longing to say to you, but I cannot; I must not! Not while I am a convicted felon."

Elizabeth felt in a daze. The words seemed to burst from him, and she lifted a dainty hand and placed it firmly over his lips. He grasped it and held the palm to his lips.

"I know, John, I know. But surely you can tell me one thing. Do you. . . ?" She paused, remembering all the etiquette her poor aunt had tried to drill in her for dealing with members of the opposite sex.

So what? Surely it isn't "etiquette" to kiss a convict either!

She raised her head and said steadily, "I love you, John Martin, but I know any chance of our relationship going further depends on what Adam can accomplish in England."

She felt the strong, muscular body so close to hers tremble as he stared at her. A myriad of expressions chased themselves across his face. She thought she saw love and hope. . .and then doubt.

Doubt? Doubt of Adam's success? Doubt of her love for him? Or doubt about his own feelings for her?

The thought slammed into her and she stepped back, searching his face. After all, there had been someone else in England for him. Beth.

She slowly drew in a deep breath, knowing she had to ask the question that had been haunting her.

"It also depends on how much you. . .you love me and also your. . .your feelings about Beth. Do you still. . . ?" She gulped and finished in a rush. "Are your feelings for Beth still there in any way at all? If—when—you are proven innocent, will you want to see her again?"

"Beth?" Sheer amazement stared at her from his dark eyes. Then he frowned savagely. "My friendship with her could have perhaps grown into something deeper, but any chance of that died completely when she did not answer any of my letters after I had been arrested and then did not come to the trial."

Relief swept through Elizabeth.

"Oh, Elizabeth, Beth was certainly pretty and gentle, the first person I had met in England who seemed to really care about me, who offered me real friendship. Because of my accent and being a foreigner, everyone else treated me with some measure of suspicion. I was lonely, and I think for some reason she was going through a very rebellious stage," he finished slowly.

Elizabeth withdrew her hands from his and clenched them so tightly her nails cut into her palms. "And can you be sure what you feel for me is not caused from the same reasons?" she asked quietly.

He stared at her silently for a long moment. Then he lifted one finger and traced it so tenderly down her face that she shivered.

"Beth and I only knew each other properly a few weeks, whereas you and I lived in close proximity for months. Besides, Timothy and Adam are my very good friends now, so, with my relationship with God, I'm no longer alone like I was then, even out in the isolation of the outback. I've known you much longer, and the way I feel about you cannot begin to compare with my feelings for her."

She searched his face, wanting desperately to believe him. "But you haven't told me yet what those feelings are, John."

As though shutting out her irresistible, pleading face, he closed his eyes tightly. "Oh, Elizabeth, can't you see that until I am free I dare not? There is no future for us unless Adam succeeds with his efforts on my behalf!"

Then they stared at each other. Sudden fear pierced through Elizabeth, and with a low murmur of distress she reached out to him again. "And while we wait, John?"

John looked at her, aching to tell her how desperately he loved her. He drew on every ounce of strength and faith he had and said steadily, "We will pray and trust in God. We will remember that He is good, and His goodness and keeping power never fail."

Then he drew her into his arms again, and they held each other close for another delicious moment before Elizabeth slowly pulled away and stared earnestly up at him. "So you do really believe," she marveled, "even after all you have been through."

He nodded. "More and more each day," he said briefly, and she looked down.

"It's been so hard, so very hard for me to keep on believing, trusting in God this past year," she confessed in a small voice. "Ever since your. . .that bad time on board ship, I have been full of doubts. I prayed so hard God would stop it, and when He didn't. . . There have been many times since when I have doubted God's love, His care. . . ."

John took a deep breath. "When I feel like that—and Timothy assures me it is perfectly all right to doubt as long as we work through those times—those are the occasions I spend reading about the cross," he said in a whisper. "That's where we know beyond a shadow of a doubt that God loves and cares."

She searched his eyes longingly. "I do so long to have fellowship with you and Timothy again in spiritual things," she said so wistfully that he gave a low, delighted laugh and bent for one more swift kiss.

"It will happen, my dear Elizabeth, it will happen. Starting tomorrow, it will happen."

Then he turned reluctantly away before he weakened any further. With a determined set to his shoulders, he walked out into the night.

When he reached the first curve in the long driveway from the main road to the house, he looked back and waved one more time toward the outline of her figure in the light of the doorway. He saw her hand lift, and then she was gone.

Tomorrow. Tomorrow he would see her again. Would be traveling with her for days.

He took a deep breath of sheer joy, and there was a spring in his step as he strode away.

Fortunately the Richmonds' house was no great distance from the inn. He was not sorry he had refused Mrs. Richmond's polite offer of a coach even for that relatively short distance. He needed time to think, to ponder on all they had said, and what he had longed to say. His heart beat with wonder, but it also ached.

How he had longed to tell Elizabeth how precious she was to him. How he longed to be able to ask her to be his wife. Tonight at least he had been strong enough, but what about tomorrow and the days after that? Doubt slowed his steps. Was she wise to return with them? Of course not. But he doubted now if he could stop her.

A rustling in the bushes brought his thoughts back to his surroundings. He suddenly realized he had forgotten just how far it was along this drive to the main thoroughfare. It had still been light when he had arrived, and now, away from the entrance lights of the house, it was very dark.

He had spent many hours on the open plains after the sun had set, but for some reason the trees and low scrub pressing close to the edge of the single carriageway seemed menacing.

As his footsteps rang on the hard, rough stones, he shook his head at himself with a slight smile, but he hastened his stride. There came another rustling in the bushes. He thought he heard a step behind him and paused briefly to glance around.

There was no one there, but a strange sense of uneasiness crept over him along with the certainty that he was not alone. There were two-legged creatures of the night who preyed on others. He hastened his steps even more, only to stop dead as he turned a corner and a large figure moved from the shadows and loomed just in front of him.

"Well, well," a sneering voice said loudly, "what do we have here? If it isn't that fellow Martin!"

John froze. This was no common footpad. He recognized that high-pitched voice.

"Edwards?" He managed to keep his voice steady but glanced quickly behind him. His heart sank as two men walked from behind some nearby trees and advanced quickly. One was much taller than the other, but a gleam of moonlight flashed on steel in the smaller man's hand.

"Now what would a scum convict be doing out here, do you suppose, gentlemen?"

"Going about his lawful business," John said calmly, while his heart started to pound. He glanced quickly to both sides, wondering at his chance of giving them the slip.

Cecil Edwards gave a bray of laughter. "Lawful! Lawful, you say?"

He moved closer, and John's heart sank as he saw the pistol in his clenched fist. "I have all the papers I need to be allowed abroad," he said sharply.

"Do you now? Papers can go missing, Martin, but I'm so glad you informed me of that."

There was deadly menace in the rapid words. John's heart became a block of ice. The man intended to destroy his papers and haul him before a magistrate as an escaped convict. Any assigned convict moving out of his immediate area for any reason at all needed signed passes on him at all times. With Adam overseas, it would be nigh to impossible to prove that his master had written and signed such papers.

No. He was wrong. This man would not risk Dr. Richmond's interference again. He intended to kill him now as a convict trying to escape being apprehended. Being so far from his master's property with no passes on him would be all that was needed for Edwards to escape punishment.

There was another loud, mocking laugh. "What do you think, men? I'd say there's nothing lawful about a convict being out after dark." He paused, seeming to consider, then said with another sneer, "Unless of course there was a skirt involved."

John tensed even more. "You've been following me," he said flatly.

Now he knew for sure this was a premeditated attack, an ambush. Sergeant Hobbs had been right to warn him, but he had thought that with Edwards safely in Van Dieman's Land and after all this time. . .

He drew in a deep breath.

"Ever since I saw you meet up with our mutual friend on the wharf this morning, I've had you followed," the triumphant voice told him. "And how is our charming Miss Waverley?"

John thought rapidly, his eyes trying to pierce the darkness to find a way of escape. But suddenly the three men rushed him at once, and after a brief struggle he was held fast with the pistol held hard against his head. For a moment he thought it was the end and offered up a brief prayer.

Then the pistol was removed. A sharp command was given, and rough hands searched his coat. His heart sank even further as his pouch was found and its contents withdrawn.

"Well, well, what do we have here?" Edwards crowed. "Tut, tut, I'm sure these papers must have been stolen. Can be of no value at all."

John watched helplessly as a match suddenly flared. Soon the precious papers that guaranteed him safe passage were blazing brightly. In the brief light he saw that both men holding him were watching the fire. He thought he saw a brief flash of sympathy as the larger man looked from the burning papers toward him.

Suddenly, with some relief he knew these were not soldiers out of uniform as he had feared. They were probably convicts themselves or ex-convicts that Lieutenant Edwards had coerced or even paid to assist him. He had learned very quickly there was a special bond between convicts and ex-cons.

John made up his mind swiftly and drawled insolently, "I thought you had been transferred to Van Dieman's Land. Were you too brutal for even that dreadful place? What happened, Lieutenant—or should I say, *Sergeant* Edwards? I heard you were demoted for your unjust flogging and barbaric treatment of us aboard the *Royal Lady*."

As John had hoped, the men holding him loosened their hold somewhat and gaped at him. Obviously this was news to them. Then they looked uncertainly toward Edwards.

"You wouldn't be that Floggin' Sergeant Edwards that flogged me old mate to death a few months ago in Port Arthur just before I finished me time here, would you?" the tall man snarled suddenly.

Edwards laughed harshly. "And who would that be, do you suppose? There's been many a flogging of scum who needed to be reminded who was master."

The words had hardly left his lips when John felt the large man's hands let him go as he took a step toward Edwards. With a swift movement John brought his boot down on the other man's foot and slammed his elbow savagely into his ribs.

Even as his old enemy gave a howl of rage, John twisted away. He sprang swiftly to his right and made for the shelter offered by the dark shadows of the bush.

The men behind him hesitated for a moment, but Edwards screamed, "Get him! I'll double the money if you don't let him get away!"

They rushed after him. The smaller one flung something that for a brief moment caught a moonbeam on its blade. The knife caught John on his shoulder just as he leaped wildly across the wide ditch he had noticed beside the track.

There were loud curses behind him, and he knew his ploy had worked. They had blundered into the ditch. But it would not delay them long, and he had been cut enough for his shoulder to be aching badly. He felt a warm trickle down his arm as he tried to glide as swiftly and as quietly as he could through the trees, thankful for the many lessons the aborigines he had befriended had taught him about moving swiftly and silently when hunting.

After some time, he managed to elude them enough to at last scramble up a tall tree and hide among its branches. He listened to the sound of his pursuers fading away. Then his head sank down onto his arms in near despair.

He knew beyond doubt that with his papers gone, Edwards would successfully post him as an escaped convict. He could be shot on sight, well before Dr. Richmond or Elizabeth could intervene. Even aborigines often caught escaped convicts and dragged them back to their masters or to the soldiers. Some desperate men ended up as bushrangers, terrorizing travelers and isolated settlers.

Briefly he thought of making his way back to the Richmonds' house. After a few moments he shook his head. He was not sure where he was, only that he had run a long way into the bush. By the time he found the house, Edwards would probably already be watching it again. He'd no doubt also have someone watching the inn.

John sucked in a shuddering breath. Would the man, as crazy as he seemed to be, try to harm Timothy? Then he remembered the rage in Edwards's eyes on board the ship when he had looked from Elizabeth to himself. She had dared to favor a convict over and above the smart, successful lieutenant. After all, he had let Timothy off the lash even if it had really been an excuse to give John more punishment.

He shuddered. He very much doubted if Edwards would bother with the other man. But knowing Timothy, he could get caught up in any fight that threatened his friend and risk losing his ticket-of-leave. It wasn't worth that risk.

And that left Dr. Richmond. The man had been just and fair to his charges on board ship, and yet he had deliberately gone to considerable lengths to protect Elizabeth from any more contact with him.

In so many ways, he agreed that it was right that Dr. Richmond should try to protect his old friend's daughter, even more so when her only relatives lived a world away in England. John doubted very much if Dr. Richmond would want to help him again, especially after his wife told him what she had interrupted this evening.

Somehow he had to stay out of Edwards's clutches until Adam returned.

There was only one thing he knew he could do.

Chapter 11

After waving to John one last time, Elizabeth slowly entered the house. She hesitated for a moment, knowing she should join her hostess again in the drawing room. Instead, she turned and flew to her bedroom to pace and dwell on every word John had said. She half-expected Mrs. Richmond would follow her but was thankful when no knock came.

It had been a long time since she had attended a church service or even prayed, but suddenly she flung herself on her knees. "Oh, God, You've been watching out for John after all. I do thank You!"

Her voice was choked with tears as she thought of all the dangers he had been through. As she opened her heart again to God, the words tumbled out. She poured out all her personal anguish and doubts. After awhile peace came and that sense of warmth and love from God that she had been missing for a long time.

"I'm so sorry, Lord," she whispered at last. "I've been forgetting about You. Please help me to be stronger, more faithful. It's so hard out there so far from Christian fellowship. Help me to trust You all the time, and, oh, show me what I must do," she burst out.

A few tears were shed, but then she sat and thought long into the night. Then she started making plans.

When she did at last climb into bed, Elizabeth was too excited to sleep very well and was up early. The woman servant she had brought with her was not averse to packing and returning home immediately.

"Don't like the city no more," the woman born and bred in the bush said with such a relieved look on her face that Elizabeth laughed out loud in understanding and sympathy.

But as she made her way at last to the breakfast room, she braced herself. As fond as her friends were of their property in the country, she knew they did not share her love of the life. And as for returning with John. . .

She took a deep breath and entered the room. Dr. Richmond and his wife were already seated at the table, talking in low voices. They looked up as she entered, and her heart sank at their grave faces.

They became even more distressed when she told them bluntly she was returning with John and Timothy. "I want them to see Waverley Station and stay for a brief visit if they possibly can, and then I would like to accompany them to

Stevens Downs," she added firmly.

"Elizabeth, surely you cannot have thought this through. There just cannot be any future for you with a man serving a life sentence!" Dr. Richmond exploded at last.

Elizabeth could not refrain from looking at her friend with reproach.

"Of course Mrs. Richmond told me about the man having the nerve, the effrontery, to kiss you!" he added, correctly interpreting their exchange of glances.

Elizabeth grinned happily. "I do believe it may have been me who actually had the effrontery to kiss him. He is filled with the same foolish scruples you have, Sir."

She cocked her head mischievously to one side. "But then," she added thoughtfully, "I'm not absolutely positive who started to kiss whom, but I think it must have been me, because John was almost as concerned as you about it afterward."

"Elizabeth!"

Mrs. Richmond's rather shocked exclamation barely registered. Elizabeth was thinking of that kiss. Despite his concern, it had not stopped John from kissing her again later. The jubilant thought and the memory that accompanied it brought the heat to her cheeks. Mrs. Richmond was studying her thoughtfully, and Elizabeth had the uncomfortable feeling she knew about those other kisses as well.

To Elizabeth's immense relief, Mrs. Richmond's lips started to twitch, but she looked down quickly to hide her face. With renewed confidence Elizabeth answered all Dr. Richmond's arguments with a smile until he at last stopped and shook his head sadly at her.

"There's nothing I can say to change your mind, is there?"

Elizabeth smiled at him gently. "I love John Martin and if as my guardian you will not give me permission to marry him, then I will wait until I am of age."

She paused then and looked down at her hands. "But you may not have to worry," she added softly. "He has not even asked me to marry him yet." Her smile disappeared as she faced the truth. "And he will never ask me to marry him unless he can prove his innocence."

Sudden relief filled Dr. Richmond's face. "Then he is a man worthy of your love after all."

To Elizabeth's astonishment, Mrs. Richmond sprang to her feet. "Oh, my dear Elizabeth, I can't bear that deep anguish and hurt in you. I have seen it every time we have met these last twelve months, and I've known it wasn't only because of your poor father's death."

She turned on her husband. "You men are all alike," she spat out. "You think only of the noble, the honorable thing. No matter that we women break our hearts while knowing what is best for us!"

He murmured a startled disclaimer, and Elizabeth stared openmouthed at her friend. Not once had she ever heard her speak so to her husband.

"I saw in these two young people yesterday such love that I know is very rare. There was no doubting that young man's love for you, Elizabeth. He was suffering terribly because he could not confess that love openly. And you. . ."

She stopped, her voice wavering, and Elizabeth saw tears form in her eyes. "Can't you see the change in her this morning? You know as well as I that she has not been able to mention her father, but last night she did so naturally to John Martin. It's as though all these months she's been making all the outward motions of living, but look at the light in her face. She's alive again, and that man is responsible!"

She turned and strode over to Elizabeth and enveloped her in a huge, slightly tearful hug. "If he doesn't ask you to marry him, you ask him, Elizabeth Waverley—and don't take no for an answer. Men!"

"Agnes!"

Both women ignored the shocked doctor as they hugged each other.

"Excuse me, Ma'am, this man said he had to see someone."

All three turned toward the doorway and the worried voice. Mrs. Richmond's new serving woman was wringing her hands nervously. Suddenly Timothy Hardy appeared behind her and strode into the room.

Elizabeth sprang to her feet. "Why, Timothy, what—?"

"Is John still here?"

She put one hand to her lips to stifle her cry of dismay. Something had seriously upset the usually placid little man. It was Dr. Richmond who answered him.

"As you can see, Mr. Hardy, your friend is not here. Now, may we please hear your reason for bursting—"

"He didn't return to the inn last night, and I just found these on the road." He held out a handful of charred remnants of paper. "They look very much like John's passes."

Elizabeth looked wildly from one man to the other as Dr. Richmond examined the scraps of paper. "Something's happened to him," she whispered. "He was going straight back to the inn."

"That's what I fear, Miss Waverley. And there's something else. My wife told me the *Royal Admiral* called at Van Dieman's Land on the way here. That's why they were late arriving. A Sergeant Edwards joined them for the trip to Sydney."

Mrs. Richmond gave a distressed cry. Her husband said grimly, "I heard only yesterday that he had been transferred back here. I meant to warn you all this morning. We must start a search for Mr. Martin immediately."

Elizabeth desperately wanted to join the searchers that were quickly organized. She only agreed to stay home when Mrs. Richmond said, "I think you should stay with me. Perhaps John may be trying to find his way back here."

She glanced up at her husband's stern face as she spoke, and Elizabeth saw the glance they exchanged. "You don't hold out much hope of finding him, do you?" she asked dully.

Dr. Richmond finished pulling on his coat and said gently, "We can only pray he has gotten away from that evil man, Elizabeth, but without those papers on him, he is in grave danger. The mere fact he has not returned here if he was attacked is cause for concern."

After he had gone, his wife said thoughtfully, "I'm not sure if he would return here. He was apprehensive about speaking to Dr. Richmond and may have doubted whether he would help him."

"He would be more concerned about involving me," Elizabeth said flatly, "which is probably the same reason he did not go to the inn—because he wouldn't want to involve Timothy. Supposing of course that. . .that. . ." Her voice broke.

"Now, no thinking like that," Mrs. Richmond said sharply. "Timothy told us he searched the immediate area on both sides of the track where he found the burnt papers. It looked as though there had been a scuffle and signs that more than one person had forced a way through the bush. It's far more likely he managed to get away. He may still be hiding or even have become lost out there."

But a grim-faced search party returned several hours later.

"We followed the trail for quite some distance into the bush, but then we lost it," an exhausted Dr. Richmond reported to the two women as he marched up the front steps.

Elizabeth swayed and clung to a veranda post.

"One thing you may be sure of then," Mrs. Richmond said swiftly with a warning look at her husband. "Whatever happened, it would appear that John managed to get away."

There was a sudden sound of clattering hoofbeats. They swung around as a detachment of uniformed men swung into sight.

Elizabeth gasped as she recognized the man leading them.

"Careful now, ladies," Dr. Richmond said softly. "Leave this to me."

Fierce anger burned in Elizabeth as Cecil Edwards bowed mockingly toward them from his saddle. "Dr. Richmond. Ladies."

Dr. Richmond had moved swiftly and left the house to confront the men in the yard. With his hands on his hips he asked sharply, "What do you want, Edwards?"

The man's eyes widened, and he said maliciously, "An escaped convict." He relished hearing Elizabeth's small gasp, and his eyes mocked her as he added, "An old friend of yours, I believe, Miss Waverley. Mr. John Martin has been seen in this city far away from his assigned master's property, and, when confronted, ran into the bush. I have informed the magistrates, and he has been posted as an absconded convict."

Mrs. Richmond's warning touch on Elizabeth's arm was all that stopped her from racing down the steps and physically attacking the scoundrel. It was all so reminiscent of another place, another time when John's life had been in danger from this horrible man.

"And what makes you search for him here, Sir?" Dr. Richmond asked angrily.

Edwards's eyes glinted. "Why, he was last seen leaving this very house, my dear doctor. Is it not natural that we should commence our search and inquiries here?"

"I can assure you he is not here." Dr. Richmond's scornful glance raked over all the mounted men. They lingered for a moment on one man not in uniform. He raised his voice.

"I would strongly advise you to commence your search elsewhere and make sure you treat this man fairly when you capture him, or you will have me to deal with."

Elizabeth relaxed slightly as the soldiers stirred restlessly and watched their leader. All obviously knew of the influence Dr. Richmond held.

Cecil Edwards suddenly lost his false affability. "Oh, we'll find him. You can be sure of that. Dead or alive, we'll find him, and if it is in my power it will be dead!"

No one moved until the horsemen had disappeared in a cloud of dust as quickly as they had come.

Slowly Dr. Richmond turned and joined the two women. Angry tears blurred Elizabeth's vision, but she brushed them aside and stared at him as she heard him give a sudden laugh and say, "Well, that is a relief, my dears."

He saw her bewilderment and said quickly, "Don't you see? It is obvious that Edwards has most certainly had something to do with John's disappearance and those burnt papers, but somehow John has managed to elude him." He hesitated and then added, "I did not want to distress you further by telling you that Timothy found a trail of blood before he came here this morning. We were afraid. . ."

He broke off and Elizabeth said slowly, "You thought he might already have been killed?"

Dr. Richmond nodded abruptly. "But don't you see, if he were dead, Edwards would be gloating, not mounting a search. And don't be mistaken, he was one very angry and frustrated man!"

Elizabeth stared at him, suddenly filled with hope. "And I think I know where John will be heading," she said slowly, and then flung around and gave Mrs. Richmond a swift hug. "Timothy and I must leave immediately."

She looked up and saw Timothy Hardy watching them from the open doorway. "Oh, Timothy, what do you think? Do you think John will try and make his way back to Stevens Downs?"

He hesitated, his face stern. "I heard what was said, but I thought it best if that man did not know I was here. The only place John would be safe until Adam returns would be back on the property where he was assigned to work." He paused and then added grimly, "But if we know that, so does Lieutenant

Edwards, and he will be after him."

"Then Elizabeth is right, and there is no time to lose." Mrs. Richmond bustled forward. "I hope your things are packed, my dear. It should not take me long to do my own."

"Agnes!"

She rounded on her husband and glared at him. "Walter, you do not think for one moment I am going to allow this child to go into all kinds of dangers in a strange place without my support, do you?"

Dr. Richmond looked at her helplessly. "But, my dear, you know I cannot accompany you at such short notice. There are patients relying on me, and I must be here when the news arrives from London."

Elizabeth exchanged a glance with Timothy, and with one accord they turned and entered the house, leaving the husband and wife to fight it out between them.

🦋

Elizabeth had long since said good-bye to Timothy, with the promise of being at the inn as soon as possible, before Mrs. Richmond rejoined her. Her friend's face was solemn, her eyes gleaming with so much excitement, Elizabeth refrained from complaining at her tardiness.

"Elizabeth, I have decided it is much better if we delay leaving until at least tomorrow."

She opened her mouth for a sharp retort, but Mrs. Richmond raised her hand and said forcefully, "I have promised Dr. Richmond faithfully not to say a word, but do believe me when I say it is essential that we give him time to put a couple things in place before we head west. He says he may even be able to organize joining us in a few days."

Mrs. Richmond gave an excited laugh. "Oh, my dear, he really does only have your interest at heart and has come up with the most marvelous scheme. Indeed, I am sorry I promised not to reveal what he is planning, but I did, and you must trust us."

"I trusted you twelve months ago," Elizabeth said challengingly after studying her friend's smiling face for a long moment. "Why should I now?"

Mrs. Richmond's smile disappeared. "We are both truly sorry, Elizabeth, for the way we deceived you. After he returned last night and then again this morning, Dr. Richmond and I discussed everything that has happened in considerable depth. He agrees with me now that in our desire to protect you we made a grave error of judgment."

She hesitated and then added swiftly, "Adam has sent us very regular reports about John Martin these past twelve months. He has had nothing but praise for the man. Adam also visited us before he left for England."

She smiled at Elizabeth's exclamation and said, "Yes, we already knew about him making some attempt to prove John's innocence. He also told us that he truly believes him to be innocent, and we had to admit that after what you both have told us, we also hold out high hopes that he will succeed."

Elizabeth stared at her. Then tears of relief started trickling down her face. "Oh, if only he does. He must."

After indulging in a few more tears, she calmed down enough to say ruefully, "So I suppose that means we had better send a message to Timothy to delay our departure."

"No, not theirs, ours."

Elizabeth looked at her in some surprise.

"Timothy told Dr. Richmond that they have a couple heavy wagon loads containing supplies as well as his wife's things, so they will be traveling very slowly. It would be much better for them to camp somewhere on the road tonight, just in case Mr. Martin is waiting for them. If we travel light and leave tomorrow morning, we will have no problem catching up with them, probably before they have crossed the Blue Mountains. We'll send them a message to that effect."

But she was wrong. By evening the next day their carriage had still not overtaken them. Timothy must have made better time than expected, and Elizabeth became concerned as they started down through the rolling hills on the western slopes of the Great Dividing Range.

They were traveling as light as they could and had made good time, despite a later start than Elizabeth had hoped. All their luggage and camping equipment had been rushed over to the inn to accompany the Hardys. Dr. Richmond had also sent a couple of men with Timothy as well as sending some of his most trusted men with the three women.

But at last, just as the last rays of the sun were changing the sky to glorious shades of pink and gold, Elizabeth and Mrs. Richmond rounded a curve in the dusty road in their fast carriage and came up to the large wagons laden down with camping equipment, food, and building supplies.

"Mr. Hardy's taking his missus on ahead to set up camp," they were told by the two men handling the reins of the huge cart horses.

It wasn't long before a small figure suddenly appeared from behind the trunk of a majestic old gum tree and waved vigorously to them. "Miss Waverley, Miss Waverley, Father left me to show you the way!"

Elizabeth smiled wearily at young Tim's excited face and instructed one of their outriders to let Tim climb up behind him so he could show them the way.

A neat camp was in the throes of being set up in a grassy clearing amidst tall timber beside a small, swiftly flowing creek. A carefully prepared fire was already blazing cheerfully on the pebbles at the water's edge, with a blackened tin of water heating slowly.

Elizabeth looked quickly around, and her heart sank when no tall, black-haired man appeared. Timothy was studying their faces hopefully, and when

Elizabeth shook her head, his face darkened.

His wife bustled forward. "No word yet of Mr. Martin, then? Well that means at least he is most likely to be still at large," she said comfortingly. "Now, you must be tired after coming so far so quickly. The water should be boiled soon, and then we can all have a nice cup of tea."

Elizabeth did not manage a quiet word with Timothy until later that evening. "Timothy," she began hesitantly, "you saw the bloodstains. Do you think John could have been seriously injured?"

"Oh, no, Miss," he answered swiftly. "There were only a few smears of blood a little way into the bush, and then again later we found some on the bark of a tree as though he must have had some on his hand. I doubt very much if it he was hurt too badly."

Elizabeth relaxed a little. "Then why do you think he has not made contact with you? Surely he must know you would head straight for home."

"I thought he might be waiting for us last night." Timothy looked around at the shadows beyond the campfire that was slowly dying down. "But when he didn't turn up we got away at first light to make it here. This is where we stopped with Adam over twelve months ago. He told us then that it was a good place for camping overnight, and I hoped John would have remembered."

They were sitting on a large, flat rock near the water's edge. Elizabeth tossed a small twig into the water. They were silent for awhile, watching it drift slowly away, listening to the sounds of the bush all around them, the soft gurgles of the running water.

"How has he really been, Timothy?" Elizabeth asked softly after a long silence.

Timothy stirred restlessly. "He never forgets for a moment that he is a convict, or a government man, as most of the other assigned convicts seem to prefer calling us."

She nodded with a slight smile and waited.

After a long moment, Timothy said quietly, "He still wakes up with nightmares at times."

Her heart clenched. "Night. . .nightmares?"

"He usually starts thrashing around and mumbling; then he might shout. Sometimes. . ." He hesitated and then added softly, "Sometimes he calls out your name."

Elizabeth turned her head swiftly toward him. "Does he call 'Elizabeth' or 'Beth'?"

Timothy reached out a hand and touched her arm. "Elizabeth," he said swiftly. "Never have I heard him mention Beth since the night he told Adam all about what happened."

Warmth swept through her on a tide. "Oh, he has to be all right, Timothy.

He has had so much sadness in his life, so little love!"

"He will be," Timothy said fervently, "and even if he is never acknowledged by his father, he will manage. Even if he is never able to prove his innocence, he is a strong man and he will cope. Besides, his trust in God has grown wonderfully these past months."

Elizabeth smiled gratefully. They were both silent again, letting the peace of the bush settle their hearts.

"Did John tell you that Adam has been paying him as much as he has me?"

Elizabeth shook her head. She knew that ticket-of-leave men worked for wages, but except for their food and shelter, convicts did not have to be paid.

"It's not very much," Timothy continued, "but John has hardly touched his. Adam even bought our new clothes we were wearing to meet the ship. John says that perhaps when he is free he will be able to have his own farm. He. . .he often talks about when he'll be free."

Elizabeth was very tired but that night lay awake for hours staring up at the stars. It was a very warm night, even though they were still in the mountains, and she tossed and turned on her hard makeshift bed of a blanket over leaves and branches.

She wondered where John was. Had he found shelter? It was comforting to know he must have a little money with him, but would he risk being recognized to buy some food?

"Oh, Lord, do watch over him tonight," she whispered, "and thank You that he knows You love and care for him."

Just when had she realized she loved John Martin? She thought back to that dirty, soaking wet convict who had risked his life to save young Tim. There had been something fine in the eyes that had searched hers intently, his anxiety for the boy showing in his cold, pale face.

Every contact she had with him after that had reinforced that deep inner knowledge that here was a special person, a wonderful man. And then he had shown his capacity for loving by taking Timothy's punishment that dreadful day.

Elizabeth shuddered, quickly banishing that particular horror as she had often done so many times before. John Martin was a man she was proud to love, and she would be even prouder if he loved her as passionately.

As she had the previous night in her soft bed at the Richmonds', she smiled as she thought of asking John to marry her. Then she wistfully hoped that she would never need to, that he would so honor her. She tried to remember if she had ever heard what a convict had to do to be allowed to marry. She knew that some men working for her father had been allowed to bring their wives to work on the station.

Wishing she had been brave enough to ask Dr. Richmond, she then wondered again, as she had several times, just what business he had insisted had been so important as to delay their journey. His wife had remained tight-lipped, just patting her hand and saying she had promised not to talk about it until the time was right.

Elizabeth dozed off and on but had fallen sound asleep when she was rudely awakened. The first faint streaks of dawn were lighting the sky and beginning to filter through the tall trees when three horsemen clattered into the center of their camp, shouting and cursing. At first she feared they were bushrangers, but then she recognized the voice she had hoped never to hear again.

Cecil Edwards shouted, "John Martin, we have you! Search thoroughly, men."

Chapter 12

For one dreadful moment, Elizabeth froze. She looked wildly around at the piles of blankets near the wagons where the men had slept. Had John arrived during the night?

Timothy's voice rang out. "No one move or you will be shot!"

She swung around. Several of Dr. Richmond's men had appeared from behind the trees surrounding the campsite. Suddenly Elizabeth realized these men had been on watch all through the night. Their rifles were aimed directly at the three horsemen. Other men were scrambling from their bedrolls under the wagons and grabbing their guns.

Edwards gave a furious oath and then shouted, "Are you going to impede an officer in the execution of his lawful duties? We are here to search for an escaped convict."

He kicked his horse forward. There was the sharp crack of a rifle. A puff of dirt rose from in front of him, and the horse shied violently, almost unseating its rider.

"But you will not be an officer very much longer, will you, Mr. Edwards?" a cool voice called out loudly.

Elizabeth stared at Mrs. Richmond. The rifle in her hand was pointed directly at Edwards.

"You have already been advised not to move, Mr. Edwards. My husband warned me you would follow us and this could happen. He also told me he discovered yesterday that charges are being prepared against you for excessive cruelty to prisoners in your care."

Elizabeth stared around numbly at the grim-faced men confronting Edwards and his two companions. Timothy was the only one who was not armed. Suddenly she realized why Dr. Richmond had sent so many of his men to accompany them as well as Timothy. Convicts and ticket-of-leave man were not allowed to bear arms. These were trusted servants, probably ex-military men, even emancipists.

"You won't be no soldier no more?"

Elizabeth looked sharply at the tall, rough-looking horseman who had flung the furious question at Edwards. She saw him look at his companion and then give a significant jerk of his head. They turned their horses.

"No money's worth bein' with you, Edwards. You've done naught but tell us lies since we agreed to help you," he shouted furiously as they moved away. "An' that you never flogged me mate must be another of them lies. We heard that the bloke who done it was likely to be kicked out of the army."

The circle of silent, grim-faced men moved and let the two men through. In a moment they had disappeared as quickly as they had come.

"I strongly suggest you go peacefully on your way, too, Mr. Edwards, and never break into someone's camp like this again," Mrs. Richmond said coldly. "We would have been justified thinking we were being raided by bushrangers and shooting you. Next time we might just do that."

In a moment the white-faced, defeated Edwards was swallowed up by the bush. No one moved until the noise of his going had ceased.

"Now perhaps John will be able to join us," Timothy said grimly, "but we'll still keep a lookout for Edwards until we're back on Stevens Downs."

Was that why John had not shown up? Had he guessed that Edwards would undoubtedly follow Timothy or even herself? Elizabeth looked eagerly around, almost expecting him to step out of the bush. Then she forced a smile at Mrs. Richmond and shook her head at her friend. "You always manage to surprise me. I didn't realize you even knew how to shoot."

Mrs. Richmond snorted. "You forget that your mother and I were often left alone for long periods of time on our properties while our husbands were away. Both our husbands made very sure we knew how to use a gun."

🦋

The next few days, Elizabeth eagerly watched, but there was no sign of the man she loved. She knew Mrs. Richmond watched her anxiously, and she usually managed to smile reassuringly at the older woman. But that smile became harder and harder to find late on the afternoon when they neared her home. The heavily laden wagons had made it a very slow journey. Long before this they had thought John would either be waiting for them or would have caught up. Confidence that he was still safe was at a very low ebb.

They were nearing the turnoff to Waverley Station when Elizabeth suddenly said to Mrs. Richmond, "I think we should send someone on to the homestead to see if he is there but continue ourselves on to the Gordons' place."

"Why do you think John might go there and not to Waverley Station?"

"Why did he not return to your house?" Elizabeth answered her tartly. "The same reasons would send him to the Gordons'."

After a moment Elizabeth relented and said apologetically, "Apparently John has been there with Adam more than once this last year and been received very kindly. If he went anywhere, he would go there. Even though he now knows where my home is, none of my people know him."

She beckoned to Timothy, who was riding nearby. After she explained to him, he hesitated and then said, "From what you've told me, your place is closer. My Molly and young Tim are exhausted by the heat. Would you mind if I sent some of the other men with you and continued on with them?"

"Better still," Elizabeth said briskly, "why don't you let me have your horse? I can cut across country much faster. Mrs. Richmond is weary too and can accompany you up to the house. My people know her, where they would not recognize you."

Mrs. Richmond protested, "Why don't you just send a man over to the Gordons'?"

Elizabeth hesitated. How could she describe the burning conviction she should go? She even wondered about it herself. Was it God's direction or her own instinct? At last she shrugged. "I don't know. I just feel I should go myself."

Mrs. Richmond stared at her, but at last merely said, "If you think you must, you must. But take a couple men with you."

Fortunately Elizabeth had dressed in a long, divided skirt that morning. Quickly she mounted astride Timothy's horse and led the way swiftly through the scrub toward her neighbors'.

As they cantered at last up to her neighbors' long, low bush hut that housed their large family, it was almost dark. Anxiously Elizabeth looked around.

"Let's try the stables and barn first," she said briefly and led the way past the homestead to the cluster of buildings beyond it.

As they at last pulled to a stop, her neighbor strolled from the barn and waved to her. When she went to dismount, he held her horse and beamed at her. "Why, Miss Waverley, it has been a long time since your last visit."

She smiled wearily at him, but before she could speak, he grinned mischievously and drawled, "But somehow, I don't think it's us you have come to see this time either."

A soft voice from behind her said wonderingly, "Elizabeth?"

She swung around and stared unbelievingly at the tall figure that stood in the shadows of the stable.

"John? Oh, John, you're safe!" she cried out.

His arms opened instinctively and then closed around her as she hurled herself into them. She clasped him tightly, feeling again his strength, his tenderness, and then lifted her face and sighed as his lips closed passionately over hers.

"I've been so scared," she cried when she at last could speak. "How did you get here? We've been expecting to see you every day, every mile."

"I take it you know what happened," he said in a low voice. "And Timothy guessed I'd head for Stevens Downs, did he?"

"I think it was Dr. Richmond who first suggested it."

Elizabeth felt him stiffen. "Dr. Richmond?"

"Timothy found the charred remains of your papers and came to the house." Quickly she told him what had happened, including Cecil Edwards's appearance at their camp.

His face darkened. "So he is still chasing me." Then his expression changed again. "Did you say there were three of them?"

She nodded. "We haven't seen any sign of them since then, but we think he is so obsessed that he would not give up easily."

Then she was enfolded in his warm, strong arms again, and she was trembling and laughing even while the tears of relief flowed freely. "I was right; you are here. You're safe!"

"Well, blow me down, if this here geezer hasn't gone and got the prettiest girl in the West," a laughing voice exclaimed.

She had forgotten all about their audience, but when she turned quickly around, discovered to her relief that the men had taken the horses to unsaddle.

Blushing furiously, Elizabeth pulled away and beamed at Mr. Gordon. "Oh, Sir, we have been so worried." She turned back to John and then cried out in distress.

He had moved out into the quickly fading light and she saw his face clearly for the first time. He was very pale, his clothes torn and filthy. Dark circles ringed his eyes, and even as she examined him he swayed.

He was looking at her with dazed eyes. "You are here; you are really here. I never expected. . ."

"Here, Man, come and sit down before you fall down." Will Gordon pushed past Elizabeth and grabbed hold of John as he swayed again. She, too, grabbed at his arm, but he winced and groaned, and she let him go.

It was only then she saw the bloodstains on his shirt, and cried out, "Oh, John, you have been hurt!"

"Only arrived a few minutes before we saw your dust and knew someone was coming. He thought it might be the blokes what done this to him," Mr. Gordon said grimly, "so he stayed outta sight. Has only had time to tell us briefly someone's out to kill him. Destroyed his papers. He managed to get a ride in a bloke's carriage over the mountains and then bought an old nag. A couple of our men found him this afternoon on their rounds and brought him in. The old horse was nearly done."

All the time he had been firing his rapid words at Elizabeth, they were half-carrying John back into the barn. At last they set him down on a pile of fresh hay, and she anxiously crouched down beside him.

He managed to smile at her and gasped, "Just hungry and tired. Be all right soon. And hurt some." His shirt was already undone, and she pushed it back with trembling hands to expose his shoulder.

"Just got in the way of a knife. It's fine."

"Shush. Don't try and speak." Her hand lightly touched his cheek.

His hand came up and grabbed her wrist. "It was Edwards. I think he must be insane. Burnt my papers. Meant to kill me."

"Hush now," she soothed him. "We know. Don't try and talk just yet." She briefly told the other men about Cecil Edwards's visit to the house and then their camp.

Will Gordon scowled and muttered something under his breath she was glad she could not hear. "Right," he said sharply. "We'll keep a guard in case he is still following you, but be best to stay hidden here in the barn tonight, just in case. Now, Miss, would you like to go up to the missus at the house, and—?"

"No," Elizabeth said firmly. "I'm staying here with John. I'm not letting him out of my sight again," she added fiercely.

"Elizabeth," John began to protest but stopped when Mr. Gordon gave a hearty laugh.

"Still as stubborn as when you were a wee thing! Best not to argue, Man. She'll not listen. We'll bring everything you and your lady need down to you from the house."

With that, he left them, and while they stared at each other, they heard him yelling out crisp orders. Elizabeth crept closer. John gave a huge sigh and with his good arm gathered her close.

They were silent for a long time, just content to be close. Explanations could wait until they had both rested and been cared for.

And cared for they were with the wonderful hospitality John had already discovered existed in the bush. Visitors were rare, and they were treated royally to food and hot water to refresh themselves and tend to John's wound. Clean clothes were even supplied for him.

By the time their needs had been met, it was night. The dark shadows were dispelled by a bright, full moon that beamed happily down. As much as Elizabeth would have liked to snuggle up beside John and share his rough bed of straw for the night, common sense prevailed when she saw her hostess's disapproving face at the briefest mention of it.

So reluctantly she let herself be led away to spotless linen and a comfortable bed in a room shared by a couple of shy, round-eyed children. The long, harrowing journey suddenly took its toll. She smiled at the children briefly before changing into borrowed nightclothes and tumbling into bed. She fell instantly into a deep sleep, not stirring until the sun was shining brightly.

"My goodness, Child, you still look tired," Mrs. Gordon greeted her. "Do you really have to ride all the way over to your house today? I'm sure that young man needs to rest too. Why don't you stay awhile? I sure could do with another woman to talk to," she added so wistfully that Elizabeth refrained from the hasty refusal already on her lips.

Elizabeth heard the sound of children laughing when she at last entered the barn. It seemed as though all but the two eldest Gordon children were crowded around John. Over their heads he smiled up at her so welcomingly and with so much love that for a moment a mist was before her eyes as she returned his quiet "good morning."

As she asked him about staying another day or so, she saw that John was already much better after a good sleep. He hesitated for a long moment, studying her intently. Then he gave one of his peculiar hand gestures and shrugs she always attributed to his Spanish upbringing. Then he nodded.

The children gave a whoop of delight and then looked askance at her from their shy, dark eyes. She smiled gently back at them and was quite content to sit on an upturned bucket and watch with longing eyes John's interaction with them. As the children excitedly told him all about their lives since his last visit, he listened courteously, but his gaze often strayed to her.

He knew each of them by name, gently teasing them. He admired the various pets they brought to show him and listened intently to one long, involved story about a large brown snake that their mother had killed in the hen enclosure only the day before.

It was obvious that he was very good with the children, especially with the quietest, shyest ones. She wondered about his cousins' children in Spain that he had told her about once during one of their rare times completely alone aboard ship. It had been obvious that he had loved them, despite their parents' antipathy toward him. Were they ever sad that he had disappeared from their lives?

What a wonderful father he would make, she found herself thinking as he admired the yellow, fluffy little chicken the smallest child had presented him with. He stroked it with a gentle finger and looked up to give her one of his heart-shaking smiles.

She just looked at him.

The expression on his face changed. His eyes glowed like fire, and without taking his eyes from her, he said crisply, "All right, children, I need to speak with Miss Waverley for awhile. Why don't you come back later? We might be able then to go and see that new foal you're all so excited about."

Neither of them moved for some time after the last child had reluctantly run from the barn.

"How come you look more beautiful every time I see you?" John said huskily at last.

The accent in his voice was suddenly very pronounced, and she looked up from her clasped hands, feeling suddenly shy and uncertain.

🦋

John saw the flush on her face and the expression in her eyes. His heart swelled. This beautiful woman loved him, really loved him. He took a deep breath and moved closer to her. He held out his hands. She did not move, just studied his face for a long moment.

He caught his breath, wondering what she could be thinking. Then a tremendous feeling of thankfulness filled him as he saw all her hesitancy vanish. Her face became so radiant that it nearly blinded him with her beauty. Then she was in his arms, and their lips met and told each other far more than mere words could ever have managed.

It was a magical day. Never before had they been so free to spend so much time at once together. For John it was bittersweet. He knew that soon they would once again be separated. If only Adam could succeed. He closed his mind to thoughts of his future, whispered a desperate prayer, and set out to enjoy this bright, God-given day.

After spending the morning together, they enjoyed lunch with the talkative Mrs. Gordon and the whole family. Then the children showed them their world, tumbling around them as they escorted them down to the river paddock to admire the new foal. When the children were at last called back to the house and their assorted chores, John and Elizabeth wandered hand in hand beside the quiet water that sparkled and flowed between the tall river gums.

Neither mentioned the threat that hung over John. Mr. Gordon had promised that no one would be able to set foot on the property without the guards he had posted seeing them, and John and Elizabeth were too happy and content in each other's company to worry.

At his urging, Elizabeth told John more about her life. He asked her many questions about her father and how a convict could possibly become such a respected citizen in this vast country. She told him about her childhood growing up first on a small farm near the Hawkesbury River that had been granted to her father on completion of his sentence.

He could picture her excitement when her father at last achieved his dream of taking up a large tract of land in the newly opened, rich countryside. However, he had refused to bring his wife and small child with him. There was to be no camping rough under canvas for the woman who had lowered herself to marry him.

John thrilled at the gleam in her bright green eyes as Elizabeth laughed up at him and said, "But Mother had a mind of her own. She put up with not seeing him only for a few weeks. We were both so miserable without him, and one day we just packed up what we could and went to be with him. At first Father was angry, but Mother always told me that he was so happy to have us that he just finished building the bush hut as quickly as he could."

She was silent for awhile, and looking down at her shining hair, John knew just how lonely that man must have been without the woman he had loved and his beautiful daughter.

"But the sheep did very well, and it was only a few years before Father built us our lovely Waverley homestead," Elizabeth continued softly. "Oh, John, I do want you to see my home. It has not a large number of rooms, but it is so cozy and charming. I know it may not be as grand as you told me your mother's house was in Spain, or even Farnley Manor in Yorkshire, but it is made of special stone

Father had hauled from the nearby hills. When the sun shines on it in a certain way, it sparkles and gleams as though it is alive. It was so good to see it again after all those years in England."

A cold shiver swept through John. Suddenly the peace of the day was shattered. She was a young lady who had been to a finishing school, had mixed with aristocrats. His life for the foreseeable future was to be on the windswept plains of Stevens Downs. There was no way he could ever ask her to leave her home for a rough, lonely hut, with Molly Hardy the only woman for hundreds of miles.

Chapter 13

Elizabeth took great delight in telling John all about her life before she had met him, including those years in England. She refrained from telling him about her Aunt Sophia's attempts at matchmaking, especially about the Honorable Frederick. But in the midst of her happiness, she suddenly realized John had gone quiet.

She paused and studied his face. His teeth flashed white as he smiled briefly at her, but his eyes were grave. A tremor passed through her, but she smiled blithely back at him and continued telling him about the very difficult last twelve months.

"Fortunately Adam trained a reliable man to take his place as chief stockman so he could leave the property with an easier mind while he struck out on his own. But there were still tough decisions to make." She hesitated and then said quietly, "The biggest one still has not been made. Some people have been urging me to sell out."

John's head swung toward her.

"Everyone, including the Richmonds, keeps telling me it's too lonely a life for a young girl with no family; it's not suitable, fitting." She dared to glance up at John's thoughtful face. When she saw the slight frown on his face, she added hurriedly, "I told them I'm not really alone. There are good people in the bush. Everyone helps each other. And besides," she hesitated only slightly before adding firmly, "my heavenly Father is always with me wherever I am."

She smiled up at him and caught his dark glance. She saw him swallow and waited hopefully. Not once had he made any attempt to kiss her since that first moment in the barn. Yet she had been sure he had wanted to. Several times she had seen love for her darken his eyes, but each time he had turned sharply away.

Like he did now.

Perhaps she would have to take Mrs. Richmond's advice after all. Elizabeth scowled. It was all right listening and agreeing silently to Mrs. Richmond's idea about doing the proposing, but it was an entirely different thing plucking up the courage to be so forward!

"How long will it take to ride to your home?" John asked abruptly. "I think perhaps we should go there today after all."

Elizabeth stared up at him for a moment and then said in a flat voice, "Mrs. Gordon and the children will be disappointed."

"But we really should let Timothy and the others know I am all right.

Besides, he must be anxious to reach Stevens Downs."

As much as Elizabeth desired to prolong this time with him, she had to agree. However, neither were prepared for the extent of their hostess's concern.

"Deary, deary me," Mrs. Gordon said with a worried frown. "Himself's been fetched by one of his men to help get one of them stupid cows out of a bog. He won't be at all happy about your going alone, and there's no man here to go with you."

John did hesitate at that, but Elizabeth said easily, "But my men are still here, aren't they?"

"Yes," she was told reluctantly, "but I know he intended to send more with you."

"Oh, I'm sure our Mr. Edwards has returned to Sydney by now. If not, he must be very uncomfortable camping out," Elizabeth said with a smile.

By the time they had saddled up and departed, Elizabeth knew it would be nearly dark before they reached her home, but she said nothing, just set a quick pace over the paddocks. They would have made it before dark, too, if John's old horse had not put its foot in a hole. Fortunately he managed to keep his seat, but when they examined the limping horse, the verdict was it could not be ridden farther.

"Oh, well, it's fortunate we are so close to home," Elizabeth said cheerfully. "Timothy's horse is certainly the strongest. You can double up behind me, and one of the men can lead your horse. It will mean a slow ride, though."

She saw John sway suddenly as he moved toward her. Biting her lip, she kept her horse steady as he heaved himself up behind her. But she heard his grunt of pain and knew that he must have pulled hard on his sore shoulder when his horse had stumbled.

"Look, it will be dark soon. You ride ahead to the house and bring back a sulky," she said to one of the men. "John will be able to hold his horse's reins."

The man she had spoken to hesitated and glanced around. They were in a clearing, but the shadows were darkening very rapidly.

"I'm feeling very tired," Elizabeth said more wearily than she really felt.

To her relief, John snapped, "You heard Miss Waverley. Perhaps you'd better both go. There's safety in numbers. Keep your eyes open, and if you see anything or anyone suspicious, come back immediately."

The men nodded. The horse's reins were passed to John. They kicked their horses into a canter and were gone.

Neither John nor Elizabeth spoke. John's hands around her waist tightened, and she felt as though she could travel for miles like this with him.

After some time she stirred and said contentedly, "Well, this is the last thick patch of scrub before the home paddock. They should be back soon with the sulky, and then we'll be home before—"

She broke off as they both heard a horse's soft snort and jingling bridle. John suddenly let go of his horse and put both arms around Elizabeth's waist. He dug his heels into the sides of the horse, but even as the horse leaped forward, it was too late.

The other horse loomed in front of them and blocked their way. Light gleamed on the rifle held in Cecil Edwards's hand.

John saw it come up and yelled, "Look out!"

He felt Elizabeth jerk on the reins and gripped the horse tightly with his knees. The horse shied as the gun roared and a bullet whistled past their eyes.

"Hey, hey, you won't escape me this time," a crazy voice screamed at them.

Desperately John clung to Elizabeth as she hauled on the reins to turn her horse. He had already observed that she was a superb horsewoman, but the track was so narrow there was little room to maneuver.

He glanced back and saw the rifle come up again. Frantically he tried to shield her slender body with his own. Then another tall shadow slipped from the trees beside them, and he stared in despair. One they might have escaped, but two?

A harsh, grim voice roared, "You murderin' swine! So you'd even kill the lady, would you?"

A gun belched forth its fire. Cecil Edwards let out a scream of agony and toppled from his horse. Their horse reared violently at the noise so close to it. A strong arm flew out to grab the bridle and a strangely calm but rough voice spoke soothing words until it again stood still.

Then they heard the sound of men shouting, and several horsemen galloped around the bend in the track from the direction of the house.

The tall, filthy man holding their horse gave a sharp curse and let go. He made a grab for Edwards's horse and in a flash was in the saddle. For a brief moment, he stared at Elizabeth and John.

Then in a soft voice he said, "It were for me mate, Jimmy. I bin a followin' 'im, you see, Ma'am. He were a very bad man. I be glad 'e did you and yours no harm. You'll tell them it were for me mate."

Then he shook the horse's reins and was past them just as the first horseman arrived. It was Timothy, and then another voice behind him called out anxiously. A very unexpected voice.

"Elizabeth! Are you all right, my dear child?"

"Dr. Richmond?" she whispered shakily, and then she slipped from the horse and was clasping her guardian's hands in both of hers.

He peered into her face and then looked over her shoulder. "You are both all right? We heard the shots, and were afraid. . ."

Timothy shouted, "Dr. Richmond, Sir! Edwards is hurt bad but still alive."

Elizabeth turned to John and buried her face in his strong shoulder. After a long moment, when her trembling had eased, he put her gently aside and strode over to the men crouched around Cecil Edwards. Elizabeth followed him shakily.

As John knelt down, a weak, panting voice called out, "Martin? Did I get him for my old friend? Is he dead?"

John stared at him and then briefly across his body at Dr. Richmond. He saw him shake his head slightly and knew the man was dying.

"I'm still here, Edwards," he said sharply. "Your shot missed us."

Edwards stared up at him, while the dark stain spread deeper into the earth beneath him. "Like it did on the ship. Well, don't think you're safe. You'll never be safe while he. . .he's after you." He coughed once, and then his head fell back.

John crouched in a stupefied silence, his brain working furiously. Someone else wanted him dead?

It was Dr. Richmond who put his thought into a question. "Someone else is after Mr. Martin? Who is it, Edwards?"

The eyes were closed, and for a moment they thought he had gone. Then he opened them and said in a barely audible voice, "At first it was for Percy I made your life as miserable as I could. He. . .saved my life once, you know. He. . .found out I was on your ship. . .asked me to. . .to. . .see you didn't make it. Then. . .then I hated you for my own sake. Because of you I've lost everything. . .everything. . . ."

"No, Edwards, you've lost because of your own sinful nature," John said sternly. "Only God can save you now."

"God? Once I did think there was. . .God. . .but not. . .now. . . ." The faltering voice stopped and the head fell back.

Dr. Richmond examined him for a moment and then slowly stood up. Elizabeth gave a soft sob, and John sprang to his feet and led her away.

"Oh, how dreadful to die without God!" she sobbed quietly as he tried to comfort her.

John's brain was working furiously. Percy? Had he meant Percival Farnley, his father's heir? The man who had sat each day in that courtroom, who had seemed shaken at the transportation sentence? Had it been because he had hoped for the death penalty?

"What was it he said right at the end, John?" Elizabeth asked tearfully, and in that brief moment he made his decision.

"Just that he hated me, that once he had thought there was a God," he said softly. He must make sure Dr. Richmond did not tell her the rest. There was no point in worrying her now that the threat to them had gone. There was nothing more that Percival Farnley could do. He was fifteen thousand miles away across the ocean.

🦋

Later that evening after Elizabeth had at last gone to bed, John did have a chance to speak privately to Dr. Richmond. The moment they were alone, the older man fixed him with a piercing glance and asked, "Now, Mr. Martin, do you know who this Percy fellow is that wants to put a period to your life?"

John looked back at the doctor steadily and said, "The only man by that name I know of is my cousin Percival Farnley."

"Farnley?" The doctor frowned. "Is not that the name of the man you claim is your father?"

John knew Elizabeth had told the Richmonds his story, so he raised his chin and said firmly, "Lord Farnley is my father, but he has refused to acknowledge me. His heir is his brother's eldest child, Percival Farnley."

Dr. Richmond nodded slowly, not taking his eyes from John's face. "I do hope that Adam is extremely careful when he starts making inquiries for you in England," he said at long last.

John relaxed and smiled grimly. "Adam being the man he is, I know he will be. We have already discussed my cousin and his role in the whole thing." He drew a deep breath. "Besides, I no longer care about Percival or the Farnleys. If Adam's investigations are successful, so be it; if not. . ." He shrugged.

He hesitated only briefly and then raised his chin and looked at Dr. Richmond steadily. "You may not choose to believe me, Sir, but these last few days I have realized as never before that I am in a loving God's hands. He has promised me His joy, no matter what man does to me, whether I am John Martin or Lord Farnley, whether I am convict or free man, whether. . ."

His voice cracked, but his steady gaze did not waver. "Sir, I. . .I want to assure you that your ward is safe from my attentions."

To his surprise the doctor gave a sudden bark of a laugh and rolled his eyes heavenward. "My dear Sir, you can be assured you are not safe from Elizabeth Waverley's attentions!" He gave a helpless shrug. "She will be her own mistress in a few weeks, but for what it is worth, you do have my permission to pay your addresses to her. As a point of fact, you no longer even need permission from the authorities to marry."

Suddenly John could not move.

Dr. Richmond pulled out a couple sheets of paper from his coat pocket and thrust them at John. "For the past year I have felt exceedingly guilty at my part in separating our dear Elizabeth from you. For months now I have been petitioning the powers that be on your behalf, bombarding them with Adam Stevens's glowing reports of your exemplary conduct. They decided at last that after twelve months you did need some more recompense for what happened aboard the *Royal Lady*, as well as the cowardly attack on your person the other night."

He gave a very ungentlemanly snort. "Perhaps they also realized I was not going to stop asking, or perhaps with all the current turmoil about self-government and the abolition of transportation they did not want your story to reach our fledgling newspapers. For whatever reason, they at last granted my requests, even to rushing things through so I could try and catch up with you."

He shook the papers impatiently at John. "Here, take them. I can assure you they will be of great interest to you."

John glanced blindly down, and his hands closed around the papers.

Before he could speak, the doctor added wearily, "Now, I am too tired for more talk. I had not long arrived here when the word came that made us go out to escort you home. We have ridden hard, with only the hard ground to sleep on for a few hours last night."

John opened his mouth, but Dr. Richmond said testily, "Good night, Mr. Martin. We shall speak again in the morning." Then he bowed and walked out.

John stared after him in a daze and then down at the papers in his hand. He did not need permission to marry? That could only mean one thing. Was it possible? Was this more evidence of God's goodness and care?

Then he looked around at the luxurious room, and his heart sank. How could he possibly ask a woman like Elizabeth to give up all this and marry him?

He slowly spread open the documents and started to read.

❧

Elizabeth woke early. The morning sun streamed into her room and across her face. Memories of the previous day rushed into her mind. Before going to sleep, she had let the tears soak into her pillow for a life that had been so wasted.

Now the sunshine dispelled the shadows of the night. The danger to John was gone. He would be safely assigned to Adam.

Instead of calling for her maid, she dressed quickly and went out into the garden. Although it was still early, the dew had already dried on the flowers. She paused beside the rosebushes her mother had planted so carefully many years ago. The summer roses were in full bloom, and she bent and caressed a velvety dark red petal.

"They are very beautiful, like their mistress," a deep voice said behind her.

She whirled around. "Oh, John, is it not a splendid morning? Are you an early riser too?"

He nodded briefly, and she noted that he looked even better than he had last night after he had washed and changed into his clean clothes, but he stared at her as though he had never seen her before. She frowned slightly at the tense, strained look on his face and then smiled at him. "I am glad you and Timothy have decided to stay a couple more days. It will give me a chance to show you some of Waverley and to pack my things."

His head jerked up. "Pack your things?"

She beamed innocently up at him, clenched her hands tightly behind her back, and said firmly, "Did not Timothy tell you? I'm coming with you all. I'm dying to see Stevens Downs," she continued chattily, turning to stroll over to another rosebush and pull off a dead bud.

"Elizabeth, I . . ."

She carefully planted another smile on her face and turned toward him again, hoping that her trembling hands were not obvious to him.

He fixed her with a piercing glance. "Elizabeth, it is a very harsh place farther west." He looked around at the garden. "There is nothing like this. The dwellings are very basic, made from roughly hewn logs and bark with the insides lined in hessian and paper."

"Oh? I thought it would be like that," she said brightly. "It will remind me of our first house here when I was a child."

He did not move a muscle. She stared into his eyes and then moved toward him, hoping her legs would hold her up.

"There is something I have been meaning to ask you, John."

He still did not move as she came right up to him. Then she saw his eyes were deep, dark pools of excitement and. . .and something else.

Her heart leaped. Perhaps she may not have to take Mrs. Richmond's advice after all.

A little breathlessly she said, "Is there any chance they could manage without you at Stevens Downs? I am very much in need of a trustworthy man to manage Waverley Station for me, and I wondered if I could have you assigned here to me."

A muscle in his tense jaw twitched. "I'm afraid that is not possible."

Elizabeth's courage was starting to fade rapidly under that relentless gaze. "What. . .what do you mean?" she faltered. "Don't you want to be here with me?"

Suddenly he reached for her, and she was folded so tightly against him she could hardly breathe. She raised her head, and his lips claimed hers again and again until her senses went spinning off into space.

"Elizabeth!" he groaned at last. "I love you so desperately."

She was beyond words and put up a badly shaking hand and caressed his dark cheek. He turned his head and his lips kissed her palm fervently.

"You can't have me assigned to you, because last night. . ." The wonder and awe of it was in his voice, in his blazing eyes as he paused and then continued in a choked voice, "Last night Dr. Richmond gave me my ticket-of-leave papers."

She gave a joyful exclamation and hugged him tighter still. "Oh, John, I'm so pleased for you! That means you can live wherever you want to in New South Wales, work wherever you want to."

He returned her embrace fervently, but at last he said with a trace of sadness, "I can stay here or work for Adam if he still wants me. But he has been very good to me and is relying on me while he is away, so I must stay at Stevens Downs. Otherwise I could most certainly stay here with you."

"No wonder Mrs. Richmond was so excited! Did Dr. Richmond tell you how he managed to get it for you?"

"No, he just gave it to me with. . .with another piece of paper last night." The strained note was back in his beloved voice. He suddenly let his hands drop away from her and took a step back. He looked so serious that she stared up at him anxiously.

"Elizabeth, you do realize that even with a ticket-of-leave I could remain a convict for a long time, perhaps forever, don't you?"

She was silent. Was he about to say good-bye?

Fear swept through her. She offered up a fervent, silent prayer. Instantly God's love swept her fear away.

She tilted her head and said steadily, "Our God is faithful, John. He has been with us both through so much. He could have you proved innocent, or failing that, even a pardon from the governor. Or perhaps He would have you just stay as a convict. It is all in His control. It doesn't really matter. I love you," she finished simply.

He closed his eyes for a moment, swallowed, and then looked at her with so much love and tenderness in his eyes that she could not breathe.

"Then, would you do me the honor of marrying this convict, Miss Waverley?"

His voice cracked on her name. It brought her out of her stupor into vibrant, pulsating life.

"Oh, yes! Please, yes! It is what I have longed for above all else!"

Then he kissed her again.

This time it was a reverent, awe-inspiring embrace, as a man and a woman would kiss before the loving eyes of their heavenly Father. God's love and peace enveloped them both. It was He and He alone who had kept them, had worked out all things, and would continue to work all things out for good for the rest of their lives.

Hope in the Great Southland

To Jan Zambra,
with love for her practical help,
fellowship, and prayers.

Many thanks goes to my family researchers
and the information in their books
Pedlers of Australia 1838–1986
and *From the Borders to the Bush: A Telfer Family History.*

Prologue

England, April 1835

It was done. This John Martin, the man he hated so much, had finished his final protestation of being innocent of the murder of Jock Macallister. Neither that nor his passionate entreaties that he was the long-lost son of Lord Farnley had been believed.

The black cap now in the judge's hands said it all.

His racing heartbeats increased. Exultation swept through him, even as the hushed murmur in the courtroom faded to a deathly stillness. Soon. Soon this impostor, this threat to his whole future, would be gone.

"Prisoner at the bar! Have you anything to urge why sentence of death should not be passed upon you?"

More words. Why did not Judge Wedgewood just get on with it?

He frowned. The prisoner in the dock had raised his head and was looking steadily at the judge. Then suddenly John Martin turned and looked directly down at the front row. At him. A wave of apprehension swept through him as their glances locked.

He suddenly wondered a little frantically what the man was thinking. Surely he could not suspect. . .

He looked swiftly away, no longer daring to hold that pleading, desperate look from those so-familiar deep blue eyes set in that deathly pale face.

"I have said all I can, Your Honor, except to declare once again my complete innocence and pray that one day the guilty man will be found."

He raised his head again swiftly at the prisoner's surprisingly calm voice after his previous frantic appeals and looked quickly at the judge. Surely he would not be overly impressed. Surely he would not change his mind. Not now.

He tensed even more as the judge said, "It is in my power to sentence you to hang by the neck until you are dead for such a heinous crime."

From the public gallery a woman's voice rang out. "Oh, no, no, not that!"

For a moment he thought he knew that voice. But no, she would not be here. Not today of all days.

He saw John Martin's head raise swiftly. His eyes were searching for the owner of that voice.

The gavel thundered. The judge's pronouncement of sentence rang out. "Instead, I will have mercy on you. John Martin, I sentence you to be transported to the great southland of Australia for the term of your natural life!"

The courtroom erupted around him. He sat frozen. Not the death penalty! The man lived. Incarcerated for life to a land over fifteen thousand miles away, but he lived!

At last he slowly stood and quietly slipped through the excited crowd spilling out from the courthouse.

It was not finished. There was still more to do before his future was safe.

Chapter 1

"Almighty and merciful God, we commit this body back to its kindred elements. . . ."

An icy wind swept across the harsh Yorkshire moor and through the small graveyard. Kate Farnley's shivers increased, and she pulled her cloak tighter around her tall body. If only her brother-in-law, William, would hurry! But his preacher's voice intoning the burial service droned on and on.

Her soul felt even colder, icy from shock.

Why, oh, why had she let her distrust of her cousin Percival, heir to her father's entailed title and lands, make her start going through her father's private papers so early this morning? Why couldn't she have buried him in peace, if not in love, mourning for him because this remote, strict, and religious man had after all been her father?

Now instead of grief, fierce rage consumed her at the terrible injustice done by the father she had always honored and believed to have been at least a fair and honest man, if stern and cold toward herself.

There was a stir in the crowd standing behind her. The noise of feet shuffling on the rough, hard ground penetrated Kate's misery.

"What the—?"

At Percival's angry murmur, Kate glanced around. A tall, dark stranger brushed past her cousin and strode forward to stand beside her. Percival looked furious at the intrusion into the family circle, but Kate stared at the man for a moment, briefly wondering who he was before looking back at William. No doubt some business acquaintance of her father's. *Anyone standing between Percival and me is always welcome,* she thought bitterly, even though her father had never understood her deep aversion to his nephew when trying to promote a match between them.

A muffled sob came from the black-cloaked figure on the other side of her, but Kate had no comfort to give her stepsister. Grimly she noted that William must have heard Beth. His deep, steady tones faltered as he glanced swiftly at his wife. Then he hurried on, his voice becoming crisper and more urgent as he spoke the familiar words of Scripture about the hope of the resurrection and the life to come for the man that had been Lord Harold John Farnley.

Kate closed her own eyes tightly. She remembered how her father had solemnly held to the comfort of those words just over twelve months ago when he had buried Beth's mother, the woman he had loved even to the exclusion of herself, his only child. Had he perhaps thought of his own eternal destiny during his very brief return to consciousness a couple days ago?

She very much doubted it.

The memories of those last few days since she had found her father unconscious on his study floor welled up and dissolved some of her anger. The doctor had gravely shaken his head and proclaimed that her father had suffered a heart seizure. Lord Farnley's strong, once seemingly indestructible body had not stirred for forty-eight hours, and then only for those brief, traumatic moments.

She and Beth had barely left his bedside, nursing him, praying for him, and then. . .

Kate stared blindly across at the open grave. Sudden anguish swept through her as she remembered how thankful she had been when she had felt her father's hand at long last stir beneath hers. She had quickly stood up to peer down at him, ready to quickly summon Beth. Afterward Kate had been glad that her stepsister had left the room a few moments before to check on the welfare of her small son.

Her father had stared up at her blankly. She had caught her breath at the urgent expression that had filled the eyes so like her own deep blue ones. He had opened his mouth, but no words had come. She had urged him not to try and speak, but he had become very agitated.

At last she had managed to get him to swallow a few sips of water, but the words that he eventually spoke had been almost inaudible, and she had bent close to his gray lips.

"In the safe. . .papers. . . ." he had gasped. "Find him. . .quickly. . . . Put it right and tell. . .tell him I'm. . .I'm sorry. . .so sorry. . . ."

Then something like panic had filled his face. His hand had tightened convulsively on hers. "Beth. . .mustn't know. No, no, wrong. . .don't look at them! Burn. . .burn them. . .Percy. . ."

The effort had been too much. They had been his last and only words before he had lapsed into unconsciousness again.

A deep shudder shook Kate. There had not been one last thought, no last word of affection for herself. But then, she acknowledged sadly, why should she have expected something she had never had from him all her life?

She had accepted the fact years before that her father was indifferent to her. He had married her mother immediately after returning to England and leaving the army that had so soundly defeated Napoleon at Waterloo. His father had died during that war, and he had returned as Lord Farnley. But his rush into matrimony to secure an heir had failed miserably.

It had not been a happy marriage, and only Kate, a useless daughter, had arrived. Kate could barely remember her mother, Catherine. After Kate's birth, she had remained an invalid for years until her death. She had left her husband with no son to secure the title and prevent the estates from falling into the hands of his despised brother.

Almost an indecently short time afterward, Kate's father had married a widow who already had a beautiful, fairylike creature for a daughter. Kate had grown up knowing that he loved her stepmother deeply and accepting that he bestowed on the spoiled Beth love she had never been given.

Kate had known for many years that he had also desperately hoped for a son from his marriage to Beth's mother, only to be bitterly disappointed once again. Then his much-despised brother had died, and he had reluctantly turned his attention to his nephew, Percival, now his only heir. To Kate's horror, he had even tried to promote a match between his only daughter and his future heir.

Perhaps this morning if she had not been so desperately hurt that even on his deathbed her father had said no words of love to her, she would not have so blatantly disobeyed him one last time. Instead of burning the large package she had found in the secret safe in his study, she had studied it wonderingly, her curiosity piqued. It was wrinkled and dirty, tied up with a strip of thin leather. In one last act of angry defiance, she had spilled its contents on the desk.

Perhaps if that small, battered Bible had not been on top, perhaps if she had not read the inscription on its front page addressed to "my beloved Maria" in her father's handwriting, perhaps if she had not read that first bewildering letter before dropping it in horror and shocked unbelief, perhaps if none of that had happened today she could have at least buried her father with respect, if not the love a daughter should have.

Kate stiffened. It didn't make sense. None of what she had read made any sense.

She lifted her head and stared blindly across the bleak landscape sloping away from the village church and its graveyard.

All her life she had known that her father had been obsessed with his desire for a son so that his detested brother would not inherit his entailed title and lands. She had always known that he had blamed her for not being the son he had wanted, blamed her for the death of her mother and her inability afterward to bear him a son. And so why, why?

"Kate!"

How she wished now that she had acted the obedient, docile daughter trying to earn her father's favor one last time. If she had burned the package unread, she would have never found out the terrible thing her father had either been a party to or—she drew a sharp breath—the instigator of.

"Kate! What on earth's the matter with you, Woman!"

The angry, hissed words were accompanied by a sharp nudge in her back, and Kate spun around ready to do battle with her detested, officious cousin. But then she realized the ceremony was almost over. Beth had moved closer to the grave but was now staring back at her, waiting for her.

Kate glanced swiftly around and then realized everyone was watching her sympathetically.

Except one.

Her eyes swept back to the massive stranger who still stood beside her, and she wondered why he was scowling so ferociously down at her. Her brow creased. She realized now that he had also been frowning earlier when he had pushed past Percival.

Beth sobbed loudly, and Kate felt foolish as she realized it was time for them to throw their flowers into the grave. For a moment she hesitated, and then she moved slowly forward.

For one last bitter moment she stared down and then swiftly threw the red rose she had been clutching. She watched it land on top of the flower-draped coffin and then stepped back blindly, almost missing her footing on the rough ground. A strong hand reached out and briefly steadied her.

"Thank you," she murmured in a choked voice, glancing up at the man.

She caught her breath.

The stranger had followed her. He was staring down into her father's grave with a look of such violent anger and frustration on his face that she pulled her arm sharply away.

Or perhaps he just seemed angry because his harsh face was so deeply lined by life and tanned by a hot sun. But no. For a brief moment, hostile, furious dark eyes glared back at her, and then he moved aside to make way for Percival Farnley.

Kate frowned. Who was he? Why had he been staring down at her father's grave with such frustration and anger? She took a step toward him.

"Kate!" hissed Percy much louder this time.

She hesitated, but the tall stranger was already moving away with swift strides toward the long line of carriages and horses near the church, his black cloak billowing out in the wind.

"Kate, you and your sister are to walk beside me back to the carriages," Percival's imperious voice said behind her. "I will of course help you with our guests back at Fleetwood."

She raised her chin and stared angrily at him. "You have no jurisdiction over me, Cousin Percival! And you forget, Sir, that according to my solicitors, Fleetwood Manor is still my home for another month. My sister and I can manage quite well without your assistance."

His eyes narrowed malevolently. "But I don't believe you will be able to continue very long without my. . .er. . .assistance, my dear Kate," he murmured and swept his eyes insolently over her black-clad figure, lingering on the fiery, copper hair framing her face beneath a black bonnet.

The bold smile that twisted his dissipated face did not reach his narrow, cold eyes. Suddenly he frightened her, she who had fearlessly withstood her father's sudden rages all her life.

"My father has left me reasonably well provided for," she snapped. "You have nothing that I will ever need!"

The expression that flashed across his face frightened her even more, and she knew that he meant to have her. Several times when he had visited them, she had been made aware of his desire for her. She had repulsed him time after time, but since her stepmother Elizabeth's death the previous year and with her father hinting at marriage between them, his attentions had become increasingly persistent and arrogant.

Knowing how much her father had professed over the years to dislike his nephew, that had hurt deeply. It had been one more incident to prove that Lord Farnley always put the welfare of his properties and lineage, even his beloved stepdaughter, before his own daughter's best interests.

For her part, something dark, something almost evil in Percival Farnley had always made Kate recoil from him.

As she did now. She turned swiftly away and made sure after accepting the condolences of a few people that she walked between her sister and brother-in-law back to their black-draped carriage.

The stranger had already disappeared, and Kate hesitated. She took a couple steps toward the old family servant holding the horses' heads steady.

"Tom, do you happen to know who that tall man in the long black cloak was, the one who just rode off on the large roan?"

The wizened, gray-haired man shook his head. "Never seen him afore, Miss Kate."

The horse he was holding tossed its head and moved restlessly. He turned toward it, murmuring soothing words and then muttering crossly, "I knowed we shouldna used this youngin' as His Lordship insisted, even if he is black and matched the others 'n all."

With the familiarity of one who had known Kate since she was born, he tossed over his shoulder, "Now do hurry and get aboard, Miss Kate. These poor critters are nearly frozen already, they are."

"How dare you speak to Miss Farnley like that, you insolent cur," the new Lord Farnley's haughty voice snapped loudly.

"And how dare you speak to one of my servants like that, Percy," Kate hissed angrily.

His unpleasant sneer made her long to hit him as she had when they were children and she had found him tormenting her dog. His arrogant voice proclaimed, "But as you should remember, he is actually my servant now, but I can assure you he won't be much longer unless he changes his attitude considerably."

Kate stared at him in horror. Of course she had known there would be changes, but surely not even Percival would get rid of servants whose parents and grandparents before them had also faithfully served at Fleetwood. Her heart nosedived as she saw the malevolent gleam in his pale blue eyes and knew he was more than capable of being so cruel.

"Surely this is no place or time to be arguing. Kate, we really should be the first back at the house."

William's deep voice was a welcome relief. Kate hurriedly took his outstretched hand and let him assist her into the carriage. She was thankful for his sensitivity when he gestured to her to be seated beside Beth while he took the seat opposite and next to their cousin.

And during that silent, tense drive from the village church and its graveyard, Kate reached a decision.

"Beth, William," she said impulsively as the carriage swung through the large gateway entrance to Fleetwood, "are you sure you could put up with me if I accept your kind offer to go and live with you in York for awhile? At least until I can set up my own establishment," she added hastily.

Percival moved sharply, and she glanced briefly at him. He was staring at her and quickly lowered his gaze, but not before she had seen the absolute fury on his face.

Suddenly she knew she had been extremely foolish to bring up the matter of her future in his presence. She stiffened, waiting for an outburst from him, and when it did not come, she became even more concerned.

Beth's pale face had lit up. "Oh, Kate, of course we could. I would love it above all things." Her face sobered and she looked quite apprehensively at her husband. "You. . .you do agree, William, don't you?"

As she watched William solemnly study his wife's pretty face for a long moment, a feeling of uneasiness about Beth and William's relationship swept through Kate. Several times these past days she had noticed tension between the young married couple, but had she put it down to Beth trying to care for little Harold while grieving her stepfather. Suddenly she wished she could take back her hasty words. Something was not right between Beth and William, and a third person in their home would not help.

To her immense relief, her brother-in-law turned, smiled slightly at her, and said with a note of sincerity she could not mistake, "Be assured you are very welcome, my dear." His lips tightened slightly, and he added in an even tone, "Beth will enjoy your company."

She smiled back at him and nodded at them both before turning to stare out the window.

Percival stirred and then said petulantly, "I have told you repeatedly there is absolutely no reason why you cannot do as your dear father wished and live in the dowager house."

Somehow Kate managed to bite back the sharp words that she longed to utter and instead said crisply, "I would think, Cousin Percival, you would be glad for me not to be looking over your shoulder constantly while you are bringing about all the changes you intend to make and which you did not cease to inform us of the last few days while waiting for Father to die."

Despite her efforts, her voice had sharpened as she recalled the numerous times she had been sickened by his obvious gloating and excitement.

"Changes that should have been brought about years ago if Uncle had only listened to my own father," he snarled. He opened his mouth to say more, but fortunately the carriage was coming to a halt and he had to be content with adding pompously, "The matter is not closed. I have certain plans for you. We will discuss your circumstances again later."

"No, we will not," Kate fired up. "I am too old to need a guardian, and my circumstances, as you put it, have absolutely nothing to do with you!"

"We'll see about that!" he snapped.

The carriage door swung open, and thankfully Kate could at last put some distance between them. As she stalked into the house, she hoped her features did not portray her sudden fear. She knew very well that his plans included marrying her. Percival was devious and dangerous. There was no way she could ever stay anywhere near Fleetwood, certainly not in the small but adequate dowager house on the estate as her father's will had stipulated.

There had been several reasons she had hesitated to accept Beth's pleas to live with them. Besides not wanting to feel like a dependent on their charity, she'd had little patience or sympathy in the past with her brother-in-law's ministry to the poor and homeless that flocked to his church and even their manse.

She was glad that Beth had married a man who truly believed he was called to the ministry by God. William was a kind and loving man, but on her only visit to them, she had found that she had been forced to associate with and even assist the undesirables who flocked to the young minister for help. Why, they had even kept a spare bedroom to house the most indescribable people at times.

But if she stayed here, it appeared she would be forever fending off unwanted attentions from her cousin, as well as being forced to watch the havoc he would inevitably wreak on her beloved home and the people working on the estate she had known all her life.

The pain and anguish returned in full measure. She had not only lost her father; she had lost her home as well. Not that it had ever really been the warm, welcoming home she had secretly longed for. But she had known no other.

And besides all of that, ever since she had stared at that Bible and those bundle of old letters still to be investigated, she had known what she had to do. If it was not already too late, somehow she had to right a terrible wrong, and also. . .

She drew in her breath sharply.

Also save Fleetwood from being ravaged by Percival Farnley.

Chapter 2

His hands clenched on the reins, Adam Stevens let the large roan horse have its head along the lane leading back to the village inn. The horse seemed as eager as he to get away from the cold wind and the large group of mourners in that miserable graveyard.

After all this time, he had missed confronting Lord Farnley by just a few days. If only he'd come straight here instead of going to see his brother first. But it had been over ten years since they had last seen each other and the parting had been so bitter, so full of recriminations. Ten long years, but still. . .

"I'm sorry, John, my friend," he muttered as he eased back on the reins and the horse came to a prancing stop outside the inn. "It could mean a lifetime for you."

He dismounted and nodded curtly to the lad who ran forward to take the horse.

"You be wantin' 'im again today, Sir?"

Adam hesitated and then made up his mind. There was no way he could give up completely now. "Could you give me directions to Fleetwood?"

The stable lad grinned cheerfully and nodded. Then his face sobered. "But the old Lord's bein' buried this very day, an'. . ." He scratched his head. "Be you a friend o' Lord Farnley's daughter, Sir?"

"Lord Farnley's daughter?"

His sudden harsh laugh made the lad stare. He frowned, and Adam recovered himself swiftly. A friend? That woman who could have saved John months of incarceration and misery, a friend?

"Is everything all right here, Sir?"

Adam swung around and forced a smile at the innkeeper. "Yes, of course. Your son was about to tell me how to find Fleetwood."

The innkeeper's face cleared. He beamed up at Adam from his plump face. "Why didn't you say before you were here for the funeral, Sir? Lord Farnley was a good man, a hard man but a just one."

Adam swallowed back the words he would have liked to say to refute that.

A large hand was stroking the innkeeper's chin. He shook his head sadly. "He'll be sadly missed and no mistake, especially with that heir of his takin' over."

Adam went still. "His heir? Who would that be?"

The innkeeper scowled. "Why, his nephew, of course, Sir Percival Farnley. Even when his father, Lord Farnley's brother, was alive, he was always visiting here with his cousins, more's the pity." He stiffened as though realizing he was saying too much to a stranger and looked a little apprehensively up at Adam. "You don't know the family then, Sir? Be you one of His Lordship's business acquaintances?"

"Oh, I know the family, all right." Adam heard the harsh note in his voice and saw the frown deepen on the honest, open face of the man staring at him. "At least one member of the immediate family, you might say," he added crisply. And then his lips twisted slightly in semblance of a smile. "And I certainly intend to make myself known to Lord Farnley's daughter. Now, good sir, perhaps if you could give me directions to Fleetwood?"

"Certainly, Sir, but would you not be wanting a bite to eat first, it being midday and all? And perhaps you would prefer your own carriage made ready? Your horses have been rested since you arrived from London late last evening. Fleetwood is some distance, and that wind is very chilly today."

Adam reluctantly agreed. As it was, he would certainly not be creating a favorable impression visiting on this day, and he might especially not gain entry if it meant intruding on the family and their guests at mealtime. With a twisted smile, he remembered that appearances were very important in the aristocracy. Already having thrust his presence on the mourners at the funeral had been a mistake. But he had been so angry, so frustrated. Using his uncle's opulent yet comfortable carriage would certainly be more appropriate.

He tossed some coins to the beaming lad to look after his borrowed horse and have the carriage ready after he had partaken of some food.

Fleetwood was several miles from the village and looked just as John Martin had described it all those months ago in another land so different, so far away. Almost twelve months had passed since John Martin had stared into the crackling, leaping flames of their campfire in that vast, empty land of the outback of New South Wales and at long last told Adam his story.

As he surveyed the gracious old manor house, Adam remembered with a touch of shame how back in Australia he had watched and listened to his assigned convict in amazement and unbelief.

"The estate is in a wonderfully fertile valley, and Fleetwood is a beautiful, stately house, set in well-tended grounds with a wonderful garden." John had paused and added dreamily, "And yet it is not just a showplace for all the many rooms, the rich furnishings. I only ever managed to see inside a couple of times, but it had an air about it. It. . .it is a home," he had said quietly with a longing note in his voice, and then they had both been silent for a time.

A couple of sheep in the flock they had been guarding on the hot, dusty plains bleated, and John had at last looked up. A fleeting smile touched his face as he said harshly, "These poor animals would think it was heaven there, the grass so green, so much water handy without traipsing miles to a dried-out creek bed, hoping there might still be a small lagoon."

Fleetwood was indeed beautiful. It was surrounded by well-laid-out, lovingly attended gardens and manicured lawns. Huge oak trees lined the driveway leading to the main entrance. The lawns were every bit as green as Adam had imagined that night in the dusty wilderness. But suddenly Adam shivered with the chill wind that managed to creep into the carriage.

Rain and cold. It seemed as though that was all he had felt since arriving in England. He smiled slightly as he thought of the number of times during the last few years when he had nostalgically thought of England's coolness in contrast with the weeks and weeks of searing heat that sapped the energy during the hot summer months.

He felt a sharp, unexpected pang of homesickness for Australia and the sunlit plains of his sheep station. Everything there was so open, so vast, with a peculiar charm of its own. And it would be so good to see his friends again. If only he could return with good news. Surely there must be someone who would know, who would be willing to listen, to search.

He frowned and concentrated on what he could possibly do next to help the man who had so quickly become far more than his servant. Then, a little ashamed, he suddenly remembered his promise to John and Timothy, his other man who had also been transported to Australia but had so quickly been granted his ticket-of-leave. Adam had promised those two fine Christian men, who had led him to a personal faith in a loving God, that he would always pray for wisdom and help. Bowing his head, he did so silently and fervently, even as the carriage drew to a halt.

To Adam's relief, nearly all the mourners must have departed. Only one carriage was still standing near the impressive front entrance. Adam did not hesitate to warn his coachman that he did not know how long he would be and then moved purposefully up to the black-draped, massive door.

He gave his name to the elderly, but still very dignified, butler and asked to speak to Lord Farnley's daughter. The man hesitated and Adam was aware of shrewd eyes very quickly summing up his stylish top hat, the black cravat tied in the very latest style, and his fashionable, expensive frock coat.

Suddenly Adam was glad he had let his brother persuade him to go on a shopping spree, even though at the time he had known it was one more effort on his brother's part to ease his own guilt and be reconciled.

An approving smile momentarily touched the corners of the wrinkled face before the butler stood aside, bowed him into the front hall, and led the way to an elegant, small waiting room. He said majestically, "I'm not sure if Miss Farnley is receiving any more visitors today, Sir, but I shall inquire."

When he had disappeared, Adam swiftly studied his surroundings. Several paintings adorned the walls, and he inspected them curiously, wondering if these were portraits of ancestors of the present family. Then he drew a swift breath and moved to more closely inspect the one of a tall, slim young man in an army officer's uniform.

One beringed hand was resting arrogantly on his hip, the other fingers open as though ready at any moment to grasp the sword by his side. The vivid blue eyes were striking, the face grim, unsmiling, and yet his chin was tilted as though he were ready to challenge the world.

Adam smiled grimly. Even so had another pair of eyes calmly challenged him more than once.

Slowly he moved to the window next to the portrait. There was a movement outside. A tall woman with bright, copper hair artfully arranged around her pale, tense face was striding quickly across the lawn toward him, a small brown dog jumping around her. She raised her eyes, and he stepped back out of sight, not willing to be caught spying. It was the young woman he had stood next to in the graveyard.

Adam frowned. He had thought she was John's Beth, Lord Farnley's stepdaughter, but that glorious hair was now free of its black veil. . . . Surely John had described his Beth as a dainty blond woman.

"Now, Shaggy," he heard melodious tones admonish, "I know you have missed your walk, but there has been no time, and you must behave if I let you come inside to Father. . .Father's study."

There was a break in the low tones that brought a fleeting sympathy for her, but then Adam clenched his hands and scowled. He must be mistaken. He was sure she was the woman pointed out as Miss Farnley. Let her suffer. Let them all suffer. It was still nothing to the suffering John was being put through!

She disappeared from sight, and Adam heard a door open. He moved swiftly across the room, stepped back out into the hall, and hesitated only a moment before striding toward the nearest door which should open into the room she had entered.

As his hand went out to knock, he heard a furious voice say, "Percy, how dare you go through my father's private desk!"

Adam froze. Percival Farnley. John had also told him a great deal about that unpleasant young gentleman.

"Must I keep reminding you, Katie, that this is all now my responsibility, as indeed you are also my responsibility," a haughty, rather high-pitched voice complained.

"I am most certainly not your responsibility. My name is Kate, and I have never given you permission to call me Katie. Percy, you may be my father's heir; you may be Lord Farnley now, but you have absolutely no right to go through his private papers that have nothing to do with the estate."

There was a brief pause. Adam hesitated, not sure whether to interrupt as he heard heavy footsteps cross the room.

Then a sneering voice spoke so threateningly that Adam stiffened once again. "Soon, my dear *Katie*, soon, when we are married, you will have absolutely no say at all in your future if you are not very, very careful. Really, my dear, we can now make our plans for—"

"How many times must I tell you we have no plans!" the woman exclaimed angrily and then suddenly gave a frightened little cry. "What are you. . . ? Don't you dare touch me, you. . .you toad!"

Sounds of a scuffle carried through the door.

Adam swung the door open and moved swiftly into the room. The woman was struggling furiously in the man's arms, rolling her head from side to side trying to escape his thick lips. Even as Adam bounded across to them, one well-shod foot kicked out and Percival howled. The next moment his lordship measured his length on the floor from a well-directed blow to his face by Adam.

Adam flexed his fingers ruefully. He couldn't imagine a worse way of introducing himself to the family. He looked at the woman. Admiration stirred in him. Rather than fainting or cowering at her ordeal, she was busily straightening her gown while glaring furiously down at her cousin. Then she looked up. As they had beside Lord Farnley's grave, the brilliance of her blue eyes pierced through him.

He looked quickly away. Suddenly he was uncertain. Her name was not Beth, but those blue eyes. . .

🦋

"Oh, Sir, thank. . .thank you," Kate panted breathlessly.

She stared at the man looking angrily down from his great height at the dazed new Lord Farnley and recognized the stranger who had so disturbed her at the funeral.

The man flexed his right hand and bowed slightly in her direction. "Think nothing of it, Madam. Only a bully and a coward attacks a woman in such a manner."

"How. . .how dare you!"

Lord Farnley was scrambling to his feet, blood beginning to trickle from his battered nose and cut lip. Kate stepped farther back, instinctively putting the stranger's strong body between them.

Her champion said calmly, "Would you like me to remove this. . .this toad, I think you called him. . .from your presence, Miss Rivers?"

"Miss Rivers?" Kate said in a dazed voice, wondering why this stranger would call her by Beth's name. Then as Percival swayed and took a step forward, she swallowed and added hurriedly, "I don't think that will be necessary, Sir. My cousin was just about to leave. Were you not, Percival?" she said in a much stronger voice. "Or perhaps you would like my servants to help you to your carriage?"

"A month you have, Cousin, a month, and then they are all my servants! Mine! As you will be!"

His voice was choked and a little muffled as he applied a handkerchief to the blood flowing freely down his face, but there was no mistaking the furious anger. His glare was full of so much menace that for the first time in all the years of despising her cousin, Kate was really frightened of him.

Determined to hide that sudden weakness, she tilted her chin and looked at the tall stranger. He was closely watching the other man with a peculiar look on his face. Suddenly he took a threatening step forward, but the man he had already knocked down so effortlessly turned and flung himself from the room.

For a moment, neither of them moved. Then Kate realized she was trembling and her legs felt strangely weak. She looked helplessly into dark brown eyes that were surveying her with a deep, almost censorious frown in them. Surely he did not think she had invited her cousin's advances.

"I think perhaps you had better sit down before you fall down, Miss Rivers," his low voice growled.

Kate felt her elbow clasped in a strong grip and allowed herself to be guided to the large chair next to her father's desk.

"I want to thank you for your timely intervention, Sir," she collected herself enough to say, "but I am afraid I am not Miss Rivers."

Astonishment replaced the frown. "But are you not Lord Farnley's stepdaughter?" Something flashed across his face. "Oh, you called yourself Kate. I had almost forgotten about Kate," he murmured in a way that made her crease her brow in puzzlement.

She managed a slight smile. "Well, yes, I am Kate, and I am Lord Farnley's daughter. You have obviously mixed up my stepsister Beth and me. The man who just left is my cousin, the new Lord Farnley." A spasm of pain swept through her, and she added swiftly, "And my sister is no longer Miss Rivers but Mrs. Garrett. And you, Sir, who are you? You were at the funeral, were you not? Are you an acquaintance of my father?"

"No," he said so harshly, Kate stared. "I never met your father," he continued, "and it is very unfortunate I arrived too late to do so. My name is Adam Stevens. We have a mutual. . .er, friend."

Kate's concern mingled with increasing curiosity as the stranger turned abruptly away and looked with considerable interest around the room. To her surprise, he suddenly strode over to stare up at the very large portrait of her father and Beth's mother that dominated the room. It was a very good likeness, particularly of Lord Farnley. He had always been a very serious man, but in this painting the artist had captured the tender light and smile in his vivid blue eyes as he looked at his new bride.

As much as Kate had learned to love her stepmother, it had always hurt her that nowhere in the house was there a painting of her own mother, except the small medallion in her own room. It was as though her father had wanted to forget that the black-haired, frail woman had ever existed.

"That is my father and Beth's mother, my stepmother, Elizabeth," she said quietly. "They were very much in love."

He glanced at her, with that frown back on his face, and she bit her lip. She must be more shaken than she thought to make such a comment to a complete stranger. She suddenly remembered how angrily the stranger had stared down at her at her father's grave, and sudden apprehension made her stand up and say briskly, "Now, Sir, it is very fortuitous for me that you were nearby, but how may I help you? If you do not know any of us, how come you were at my. . .my father's funeral this morning?"

Adam studied her for a long moment, all the time thinking furiously. At last he decided he had nothing to lose by going ahead with the approach he had decided on before leaving London.

He gave a polite bow. "I am not sure if you can help me, Miss Farnley. I have been overseas the last few years, and a gentleman I have befriended there asked me to contact Lord Farnley for him. There was a matter of some importance I wished to discuss personally with Lord Farnley on his behalf, and I am devastated I am too late."

The clear blue eyes misted with tears. She lowered her head, and suddenly Adam had an insane desire to offer her comfort, to hold that delicious body of hers tightly in his arms, to. . .

He stiffened. "I am very sorry to have arrived today of all days, and to trouble you at such a time," he said swiftly, "but I am returning to Australia in a few weeks and must journey back to London as soon as possible."

She went dead-white and swayed. "Australia!"

She knew something! Adam thought rapidly and then decided he had nothing to lose. "Perhaps you may be able to help me after all, Madam. I am acquainted with a gentleman called John Martin. He told me he lived in this area awhile back."

She stared at him from confused, suddenly misty eyes. "Oh, Sir, Sir, you know him? You actually know John Martin? You know where I can find him?"

Adam had not thought it possible her face could go any whiter, but suddenly it was a horrible pasty gray. She seemed to crumble. He gave a sharp exclamation and just managed to catch her up in his arms before she hit the floor in a dead faint.

Chapter 3

Kate felt as though she was floating. Then she became aware that strong arms were carrying her and that there was a babble of voices she wished fervently would go away because her head was aching so much.

"Fetch Mrs. Garrett," a voice barked above her, and she opened her eyes to see familiar dark brown eyes frowning down at her.

"Why are you always frowning?" she muttered crossly.

A spark of humor mingled with relief in those dark eyes. Satisfied, she smiled and closed her own eyelids, only for them to fly open as she realized she was being carried in strong arms and surrounded by worried, protesting servants. Before she could object, she was placed gently down, and those strangely comforting arms were gone.

She tried to sit up, but a stabbing pain in her head made her groan.

A firm hand pushed her back down. "Lie still, you little fool," harsh tones admonished her.

"Katie! Oh, you poor dear, I knew you should have tried to get some rest instead of trying to deal with Father's desk today."

Beth's anxious face peered down at her, and then with relief Kate closed her eyes as her stepsister took charge, ordering everyone from the room. Only when she heard Beth say fiercely, "And you, Sir, if you have done anything to hurt my sister, you will regret it, I promise you!" did she remember.

"No! Mr. Stevens," she called and winced. Her head was pounding, and she knew she was going to pay for all the sleepless nights and the stress of this last horrible day.

His face loomed over her again.

"Please, Sir, I am sorry to be so stupid," she managed earnestly, "but please do not leave. I will be well soon, and we must talk."

For a moment he studied her face, and then some tension in him seemed to be released. "Be assured I am not going anywhere until we have indeed talked, Miss Farnley. This day has been too much for you, and I should have waited. I do sincerely apologize for adding to your suffering."

Her hand went out and grasped the sleeve of his coat as he turned away. She glanced a little desperately at Beth's anxious face and said rapidly, "And, Sir, you will please not mention that. . .that person to anyone else?"

He stared down at her as though trying to decide. Then he stared across at Beth, and his features hardened. He quickly looked away and stiffened as he saw something on the wall above Kate's bed. He stared at it for a long moment, and her weary mind was eased as she remembered what was there.

Then his gaze dropped again to her. He looked bemused, a little puzzled, as he studied her. The sharp angles on his strong face softened as the hint of a smile touched his lips. For a moment longer his gaze swept over her now severely tousled hair and down to linger momentarily on her capable hand still touching him.

She snatched her fingers away as through they had been burnt. Heat started to mount up in her at the suddenly arrested look in his eyes. They stared at each other, each searching out the other, *trying to find that hidden person, that hidden soul,* she suddenly thought fancifully.

Still holding her gaze, he slowly nodded. "Of course, I won't say anything," he said abruptly. His piercing eyes softened even further. "You rest now," he said in a much gentler voice and then walked quickly from the room.

"Katie, what is going on? Who is that man?" Beth exclaimed. Then as Kate shut her eyes, she heard Beth add hurriedly, "No, no, do not answer; just rest. You are a dreadful color. When did you last eat properly? I noticed you had nothing at lunch."

Before Kate could protest, Beth had sent Kate's maid scurrying away to the kitchen for a tea tray.

"Beth, please do not let Mr. Stevens leave until I can speak to him," Kate begged as soon as they were alone. "He may have some important information for us."

"Yes, yes," soothed Beth as she helped her sit up for a sip of water. "He seemed just as anxious to speak to you. Now, you just try and relax for awhile. What a year and more it has been for you. You were thoroughly exhausted after helping me nurse my dear mama all those weeks, and then coping with Father as well as arranging our wedding. Then being with me before and after Harold John was born, and now Father. . ."

Beth bit her lip and continued hurriedly, "It has been a dreadful time these past weeks. I do not know what I would have done without my dear William to support me, and you have had no one."

To Kate's immense relief, Beth abruptly stopped speaking and continued her silence while hovering over her until Kate had partaken of a hot cup of tea and forced a little food down. Then Beth insisted she get some rest.

Although her mind was whirling with a mixture of emotions and questions, Kate did at last slip into a deep sleep of utter exhaustion. When she awoke she knew by the pale light that filtered into the room despite the heavy window drapes that it was early morning.

She stared blindly at the window, going over in her mind all that had happened the previous day. The events of the funeral and dealing with the condolences of their guests afterward had seemed to pass in a blur. She had felt so exhausted just trying to control the myriad of emotions—the tears, the bewilderment, the anger.

A shudder of revulsion shook her as she remembered Percival's attempt to kiss her. Then she smiled as she remembered that wonderful feeling of protection and safety that the tall, broad-shouldered stranger had given her.

And Adam Stevens knew John Martin.

Taking a deep breath, she got out of bed. Suddenly anxious that he might not have stayed through the night, she quickly dressed herself. When she had finished, she looked up at the texts above her bed. A faint smile tilted her lips as she remembered Mr. Stevens's response to them, wondering what he had thought.

She bowed her head and uttered a brief, urgent prayer. Then she took a last hasty look in her mirror at her hair hanging in loose curls to her shoulders. Perhaps she should have rung for her maid after all. She shrugged. How she looked really did not matter.

She had a hand on the doorknob when she hesitated. Then she quickly unlocked the hidden drawer in which she kept her jewelry and private possessions away from prying eyes. Her hands trembled slightly as she withdrew the package she had removed from her father's safe. She hesitated, wanting to examine the contents again, and yet so fearful. . .so fearful that her father would be able to hurt her even yet again.

Was it just a bare twenty-four hours since she had found them? As much as she had wanted to examine them closely, there had been no time for more than that cursory, stunned initial look at them. Old William, the butler, had knocked and hastily entered to tell her in faltering, upset tones so unlike him that her cousin, Lord Farnley, had arrived early for the funeral.

Upset and shocked, she had immediately swept the contents back into the package and hastened to her room to avoid her cousin. Her maid had been waiting to fuss around her until she was dressed to her satisfaction. By then it had been time to leave for the church.

Afterward, once everyone had gone, she had intended to look in the safe for anything else, perhaps a letter of explanation from her father. Unfortunately, Percy had been home ahead of her.

"And it seems that perhaps you can help me find out what all this means, Adam Stevens," she murmured as she thrust the package deep into a reticule she carried with her as she hurried from the room.

When she entered the large kitchen, Kate was disappointed that the housekeeper was already there starting her preparations for breakfast. She knew she had been foolish yesterday not eating and had hoped to grab a quick drink and something to eat before continuing her search of her father's study.

Mrs. Cook smiled at her with some surprise and then gave her an anxious frown. "Should you be up so early, Miss?"

With a pang Katie realized this dear woman, like all the staff at Fleetwood who had known her all her life, would no doubt be another one to lose her position in a few weeks' time. Not only a position, but a home as well.

"Miss Beth thought you would be so exhausted you would want to stay quiet today," the woman who was used to Kate's early morning forays for food said reprovingly.

"I've almost slept the clock around, and I feel much better, Mrs. Cook, Dear," Kate said with forced cheerfulness. "But I am feeling a trifle hungry now since I missed supper last night."

The round face beamed at her with relief. "Hungry you are, eh? Well, that can be easily fixed."

The smile disappeared. With a trace of disapproval that a complete stranger had been given hospitality so soon after the funeral when other members of the family had delicately elected not to stay, she asked hesitantly, "Will that Mr. Stevens be here for lunch as well as breakfast, could you tell me, Miss Kate?"

Kate stared at her. "Mr. Stevens stayed the night?" she asked sharply. At the disapproving nod, relief swept through her. After a moment she said slowly, "I do not know how long he will be here, but I will let you know. However, I have little doubt Lord Percival will be back for lunch."

Mrs. Cook stiffened, and Kate heard the apprehension in her voice as she sniffed and said, "I'm sure the new Lord Farnley will have no need to think the kitchen's standards here are not good enough for him, I'm sure." Then she hurried off to produce the tastiest tray she could for Kate.

Kate sighed. It was very obvious that the staff knew they would not be in for an easy time with their new master.

It took longer than Kate had hoped before she could escape the kitchen and at last make her way to the study. As she entered the room, she looked down with a faint smile of satisfaction at the place where Percival had landed on the floor. It was always good for a bully to meet someone tougher and stronger than himself.

And Adam Stevens had certainly been that.

She went to open the French doors to let in some fresh air and help wipe out the memories. She shuddered as she dwelt on Percy's determination to kiss her. It was by no means his first attempt to force his attentions on her, but this time there had been a strength of purpose, a gloating arrogance about the man that had frightened her. Suddenly she wished Adam Stevens had been around before to deal with the man.

Now, if it had been Adam who had tried to kiss her. . .

Shocked at the wanton thought, Kate shook her head, trying to banish the image of a firm, well-shaped mouth and piercing dark eyes that had searched her face so intently. She sat quickly in her father's chair behind the desk and then hesitated. She longed to finish reading the letters in her reticule, but she knew that before Percy returned she had to finish sorting out her father's private papers. The first chance her cousin had, he would be poking and prying again.

He had already demonstrated there would be no waiting the month out, and she had to remove anything her father would not have liked him to see, especially if it had anything to do with the package he had locked away in his safe.

She pulled open the top drawer and gave an exclamation of anger. Its contents were in such disarray that she knew immediately Percival must have been searching through it very quickly indeed. A swift inspection of all the drawers showed them in similar state. He must have gone through them in considerable haste.

"What were you looking for, Percival?" she exclaimed angrily.

"I think perhaps I may know the answer to that."

The soft voice behind her made her jump, and she swung around to see an elegantly clad Adam Stevens standing in the doorway watching her.

"Mr. Stevens, you startled me! I had not thought to see you so early."

"The Reverend Garrett and his wife insisted I stay the night. I think they were afraid I would disappear before you had a chance to speak with me."

❧

Adam studied her face, relieved to see that the strained look of utter exhaustion had disappeared. There was still a faint shadow beneath those brilliant eyes, but her cheeks were now a healthy color. The color in them deepened, and he suddenly realized he was staring and looked swiftly back at the opened drawers with their rifled contents.

As he moved slowly into the room, she asked, "Why would you think you know what he was looking for, Mr. Stevens?" Her voice was steady, and as he studied her thoughtfully the color receded from her cheeks.

"Because I believe he may have been looking for what I also came to find."

She looked puzzled for a moment. Then comprehension flashed across her face, and she drew a deep breath. "Would that be something to do with the John Martin you mentioned?"

"It is something that belongs to him," he said tersely. "Tell me, Miss Farnley, what do you know about John Martin?"

"Tell me, Mr. Stevens, what do you know about him?" she shot back.

They stared at each other. Adam admired the stubborn tilt of her chin, but then he recognized the trace of fear and uncertainty in her wonderfully expressive eyes.

"I met him some weeks after he arrived in New South Wales, and now he is working for me," he said slowly.

Astonishment washed away the uncertainty. "Working for you? But the last I heard about him he was a. . ." She bit her lip and turned slightly away from him to go and stare out through the open doors to the freedom of the open air and the blue sky.

"He is still a prisoner—or rather, a convict transported by the British justice system to the justice system of New South Wales," he said bluntly. "He is one of my assigned convicts."

She took obvious exception to the stinging censor in his voice and swung back to say fiercely, "He's a convicted murderer! He killed a faithful old servant of ours who would not hurt a fly."

He was silent. They stared at each other for a long moment, and it was she who looked away first.

"If you believe that, then why did you react so strangely last night when I mentioned his name?"

She studied him intently. "Because I. . .only that morning I found something. . . . Oh, how can I know if I can trust you?" she cried out.

There was desperation in her voice and her face. She suddenly looked so young and frightened that something deep inside Adam longed to comfort her, to reassure her that everything would be all right.

"Perhaps I should tell you something about myself," he said slowly at last, thinking rapidly of those things in his past he dare not tell her if he wanted her to trust him.

"That is an excellent idea. You arrive here a complete stranger at a very sensitive family time and have been given the hospitality of my home, and yet we know nothing about you, Sir!"

There was asperity and a trace of sarcasm in her voice that made Adam raise his eyebrows. She flushed slightly but merely lifted her chin and imperiously indicated a chair. "Please be seated, if you will, Sir."

He hesitated, considering her thoughtfully before sitting in a comfortable leather chair. He studied his hands, trying to work out how much to tell her.

At last he looked directly across the desk at her and said crisply, "My father and his older brother built up a clothing manufacturing business called Classic Styles in London. When my younger brother and I were still at school, both our parents were killed and our Uncle Samuel Stevens became our guardian. He had never married and was not used to nor did he like having two boys in his home, but he did make it his responsibility to train us both in the business to take over our father's share."

Adam paused. For years he had refused to dwell on the more unpleasant aspects of his upbringing. His uncle had been a tyrant and a bully. While Adam had stood up to the man, trying to protect his younger brother Andrew as much as he could, it had still been Andrew who had been the most affected. And certainly during the last years of Uncle Samuel's life, Andrew had endured much while Adam had, in a sense, escaped.

Wry amusement touched him at the thought, but he suddenly found himself softening toward his brother. After all, Andrew had been so very, very young, so in love with the even younger Clarissa. Perhaps this was God's way to help him forgive Andrew what was really unforgivable.

Adam shook that grim thought off and said swiftly, "My uncle was never an easy man to live and work with, but my brother loved the business enough to stay. Then I had a. . .a major falling-out with them both roughly ten years ago, left the business, and have been in Australia ever since."

He had almost flung the abrupt words at her. Kate was watching him closely, and he guessed she could not miss how stiffly he was holding himself as the memories flooded back. He hoped she had not seen his flicker of pain, swiftly controlled, when he mentioned Australia.

"My brother sent word of our uncle's death, and I have returned to assist in the winding up of my late uncle's affairs. I can give you our lawyer's address if you wish to check up on me."

He refrained from mentioning his utter amazement that his uncle had not cut him out of his will after all as he had vowed to but had instead given him an equal share with Andrew of the immense fortune he had accumulated.

Adam relaxed a little when Kate nodded her head slowly and said, "I own at least one nightgown made by Classic Styles and I believe a couple of dresses in the past."

He had a sudden vision of the delicate nightwear garments his brother had proudly displayed when showing him through the huge showrooms. His hands clenched at the thought of her dressed in one, and he said shortly, "Well, yes, the business has expanded prosperously in recent years by going into more lines than when I was involved."

He paused and added even more abruptly, "I am now at the other end of it all." At her puzzled frown, he explained briefly, "I rear the sheep for the wool."

She smiled at him a little shyly, and the unexpected sweetness of that smile washed through him. "I have heard about the large sheep farms in Australia and the settlers who have not long been given certain rights to the land they have moved their sheep onto."

"Stations."

She stared at him, and he added swiftly, "We only call smaller properties that grow vegetables, grain, or have a dairy, 'farms.' The sheep and cattle runs west of the mountain ranges have to be vast acreages because of the sparse vegetation and low rainfall and are called 'stations.' "

❦

Kate had always been very interested in learning about other countries and listened intently as Adam went on to tell her a little more. Stevens Downs was in the outback of New South Wales, several hundred miles west of Sydney.

When he paused, she asked softly, "Did you leave your wife on your. . .your station, Mr. Stevens, or did she accompany you back to England?" Immediately she wished she had not voiced the question as the light that had briefly lit his dark eyes disappeared.

"I have no family, Miss Farnley." His voice was cold and distant as he added, "I am no longer close even to my brother and his wife and sons."

As he paused, Kate suddenly knew by the fleeting pain in his eyes that something had happened in the past between the two brothers as well as with his uncle, some tragedy that had separated them those many thousands of miles.

She tensed as he said harshly, "John Martin has become much closer to me than Andrew, and I intend to do all that I can for him."

They stared at each other for a long moment, each trying to read the other's face. At long last it was Adam who said, "What do you know about John, Miss Farnley?"

She took a deep breath. "To my deep regret, very little about him as a person," she said sadly. "I don't think that I ever spoke to him myself. He arrived in this area looking for work and was employed on the estate primarily to help our gamekeeper, Jock Macallister, who was getting on in years."

She raised her head proudly. "My father was loyal to loyal servants. He believed in letting them keep their pride in their work. Even though Jock was getting too old, John Martin was to be trained by him, but never to really replace him. Jock apparently even had John staying in his own home." Her voice hardened. "Although he was treated like a member of the family, he bitterly betrayed them."

"Despite a judge and jury who decided otherwise, John did not kill Jock Macallister, Miss Farnley."

She stared at him. His quiet voice was filled with absolute certainty, his gaze steady.

"Then that makes only two people who believe in him," she said just as quietly. Then she put a hand to her mouth and shut her eyes. If what she had read yesterday morning about John was true. . .

"Oh, I do hope you are right, Sir!" she said.

"Two people?"

He had spoken so sharply that she raised her head quickly and stared at him.

"You said two people believe him innocent," he said impatiently. "You too, then, believe so?"

Kate stared at him a moment longer and then slowly shook her head. How could she believe? "I. . .I wish I could say yes, but I cannot. When his trial was on, things were in great turmoil here with my stepmother close to death. I referred to my stepsister, Beth. She had struck up a friendship with the young foreigner."

The man's face hardened, and he looked swiftly away.

Kate suddenly made up her mind to trust him. After all, she did not know where else to start to try and make some sense of it all. She gestured toward the open drawers.

"I believe my cousin, whom you. . .you met here yesterday, knows much more than I do, Mr. Stevens. I believe he was looking for more information when he went through these drawers in such a hurry."

"You think he was looking for something involving John?"

She looked back at him steadily, still wondering how much he knew and how much she should tell him about the contents of her reticule. "Yes," she said briefly.

"But before we go into that, I want to assure you that until yesterday morning when I. . .I explored my father's safe, I really knew very little about John Martin."

His steady regard did not change, and his expression told her nothing of what he was thinking. *He's certainly a master at keeping his feelings hidden*, she thought a little crossly.

"I only saw him from a distance a couple times. Actually, if you want to know about his time here, it should be Beth you are speaking to."

Rather to her surprise that did bring a sharp response. But the flash of anger was quickly controlled. "And you think she believes he is innocent?"

As she nodded slowly, Kate frowned, wondering not for the first time about the extent of Beth's involvement with the man who had lived and worked beside their chief gamekeeper.

"I believe she met him several times because she was quite good friends with our gamekeeper's daughter, Jenny. Beth was devastated when we heard that he had been arrested and was being tried for murder, especially Jock Macallister's murder."

She continued hurriedly, "My sister was most adamant that he could never have done such a thing, but it was all about the time her mother's health had deteriorated to the point none of us could leave her."

Kate frowned. "In fact, I personally did not know that the matter had come to such a hasty trial until Percival told us John had been found guilty and was about to be sentenced."

Her guest was very still and then suddenly looked down at his hands. One long finger slowly removed a piece of thread from his immaculate black coat.

"Percival?"

She stared at him curiously and then nodded abruptly. "Jock had been employed here since he was a child and his father before him. Apparently my father had delegated Percival, as his heir of course, to represent the family in the whole dreadful business. Mama was so ill Father refused to leave her," she said a little impatiently.

He looked up at her and said quietly, "John told me he and Beth were. . .were very good friends indeed, and you are telling me she knew nothing of his trial? Surely one would have thought she may have been called upon to give evidence on his behalf?"

He was watching her carefully as he spoke, and Kate thought he was suddenly even more tense than before.

Surprised, she frowned and said, "I fail to see what Beth could possibly have contributed."

"Only an alibi for him. He says he was with her long before he found the man's body and was subsequently arrested on the spot. He believes she could have verified he was nowhere near the place when the man was murdered."

Her eyes widened. "Then why did his lawyers not ask her to testify?"

It was his turn to look uncertain. "From what he has said, I am sure he thought they had interviewed her and that she said she had not seen him at all that day or any other. In fact, John believes she refused to testify."

Kate raised her head angrily. "Then he lied or was mistaken, because I know that my sister did not even know it was he who had been arrested until the day. . . the day her mother died."

He regarded her steadily for a very long moment and then seemed to make up his mind about something.

"John is a devout Christian, Miss Farnley," he said softly. "We have spent much time alone facing all the dangers of the bush and talking for endless hours about many things, including his new faith in Christ. I am very certain he is not a liar."

There was no mistaking the quiet conviction in his voice. After looking at him intently for a long moment, Kate at last responded as softly, "My stepsister is a very religious woman also. Are you a devout Christian too, Mr. Stevens?"

🦋

Adam had already decided that this was a very unusual young woman, but he wondered that a woman in her position in society would think of asking such a very personal question. She was regarding him closely, an extra touch of color in her cheeks.

"I have made a personal commitment of my life to Jesus Christ," he replied, looking at her steadily. "But this happened only a very short while before returning to England, and I can say with certainty that I still have much to learn and experience before I come anywhere near John's steadfast faith. And you? I noticed those embroidered texts above your bed. Do they mean anything to you, or were they just an exercise in sewing and merely ornamental?"

To his surprise, utter relief flashed across her face. The sudden sweetness of her smile shook him even more. "I am so glad and relieved your faith means so much to you."

That endearing touch of shyness filled her brilliant blue eyes again before she looked away. "My own faith is so weak that I need those words constantly before me. 'My grace is sufficient for thee: for my strength is made perfect in weakness' and 'Forgive seventy times seven,'" she quoted softly, if a little sadly, "have helped me to cope and given me hope many times."

He wondered why she needed to be reminded to forgive. Surely if anyone needed to be reminded of that it was men like him and John.

Suddenly she straightened. A determined glint replaced the sadness and need. "Right, Mr. Stevens, if neither Beth nor Mr. Martin are liars, then they have either been lied to or been very badly mistaken. Or. . ."

She hesitated and bit her soft, bottom lip. "My father was very protective of Beth, and apparently Jock Macallister was killed the day my stepmother was taken very ill. She was very sick for many, many weeks. Everything was in utter turmoil, and I know he would have prevented anything else intruding. Although afterward I did think it a little strange that Percival had not mentioned anything of the whole matter to me personally."

"From what John and I now know, it is not at all strange. Were you aware that your cousin was very helpful to John before and during his trial? Or at least, John thought he was at the time. Now he knows differently."

"Percival was helpful?" she said with surprise. "Percival Farnley would not lift a finger to help anyone unless. . ." She stopped and after a moment said very slowly and thoughtfully, "Unless it meant that it was in his own best interests to do so."

And of course that was the explanation. Percy knew.

Suddenly Kate was convinced beyond any doubt that what she had found in her father's safe was true. Whether Percival had been a party to keeping it a secret or not did not matter. Obviously he must have been aware or suspected the truth to risk searching for those documents.

That alone meant that he believed the information in them to be true.

With wonder and increasing excitement, Kate reached for her reticule and withdrew the packet. "Is this what you needed to see my father about, Mr. Stevens?"

Carefully she removed the Bible and the letters. She hesitated for the briefest moment before placing them on the desk between them and murmuring softly, "These papers and the entry in this family Bible claim that John Martin is my half brother. Do you know if that could possibly be true, Mr. Stevens?"

Chapter 4

Adam stared unbelievingly at the Bible, the bundle of old, yellow letters that were tattered as though they had been read and reread.

After all he'd gone through, the end of his search for John's precious belongings and the proof of his identity was as easy as this. He breathed a silent prayer of thanks. His hand was a little unsteady as he reached out to pick them up.

But this also meant. . .

"John's evidence that Lord Farnley is indeed his father has been here all the time?"

Kate Farnley went white, and tears filled her eyes.

He instantly regretted the wave of anger that had swept through him and that he had allowed into his voice.

"All the time?" Kate repeated in a husky voice. "That I do not know, Sir. I only discovered the package yesterday morning in my father's safe."

Adam picked up the Bible and opened the first page. After a long moment he raised his head and looked at her.

"The Bible has the Farnley family tree," she said softly at last. "I recognize it to be the same as has always been kept here, except. . .except for the last entry of a John Harold. But it. . .it does not seem to be in my father's handwriting. And the. . .the letters. . .I haven't read them all, but. . .oh, are they what you are here for? It's true? Father was married to a Spanish woman during the war with the French and John is their son?"

He could hardly hear her choked words, but there was no mistaking her anguish, her utter bewilderment, and he nodded briefly. "This appears to be the very package my friend John asked me to recover for him that would prove his claim. It is a long story, but his mother's sister only gave the letters to him after his grandfather died."

Kate cried out, "But it doesn't make sense. Always. . .always, Father has longed for a son. Why would he not acknowledge him all these years?"

"According to John, he did not know," Adam said softly. "After Lord Farnley had moved on with Wellington's army to Waterloo, his Spanish bride died in childbirth. Her family had apparently always feared her marriage to an Englishman, especially to a member of the aristocracy, would take her away from them, and they blamed him and his son for her death."

Her tear-filled eyes wide and dazed, Kate pressed her clenched fist against her lips. "I. . .I really do have a. . .a brother?"

He hesitated and said swiftly, "John told me that all his life he had borne the stigma of illegitimacy. Just before he came to England, this aunt took him to the priest who had married his mother to her handsome English army officer. Before then, at his bitter grandfather's insistence, John had only been told his despised father had been killed at Waterloo. In amongst those things should be a signed, sworn statement the priest wrote for John.

"John did not have a happy time growing up in a family who hated him. It was not until after his autocratic grandfather's death that his aunt dared to tell him the truth. Not only had his parents been married, but his father had after all come back for his bride and the child he knew his wife had been expecting. The grandfather maliciously let him believe the baby had died also."

Kate was still staring at him with huge eyes. "Poor Father," she whispered. "He never would talk about his time in the army. He must have deeply loved John's mother to risk marrying a foreigner like that at such a dreadful time of war."

A solitary tear slid down one cheek as she added softly, "I do know that only a few weeks after he got out of the army he married my mother to secure his title and estates. Apparently he despised his brother, Percival's father, who had recently married, and dreaded the thought that he was his only heir. But my mother only had one child, and I was only a daughter. I always knew they were not happy together, not like he was later with Beth's mother."

Her lips quivered ever so slightly. There was a blind, lost look in her eyes, and Adam had a sudden urge to once again put his arms around her and hold her safe. Suddenly he realized John was not the only wounded child of Lord Farnley.

"He may not have minded marrying a Spanish señorita, but he most certainly did not want to acknowledge a son being tried for murder or to be bothered to visit him!" Fighting the sudden uncharacteristic feelings that were threatening to swamp him, Adam's voice was unusually harsh.

Kate cried out, "No, no! Father was not like that. He might have been a hard man, but he was always just. He always did what he thought to be right. He was a God-fearing man, and I am sure he could not have known."

"Then why did he have these in his possession and yet do nothing?"

A deep sob shook her. "I do not know; I do not know. It has been burdening me ever since I found them yesterday morning."

The tears had become a torrent, and she gave in and put her head in her hands and wept at long last for the father who had never expressed any real love for her, who had so longed for a son instead of a daughter. And all these years there had been a son, someone of his own blood to inherit all that he and his ancestors over so many centuries had held so dear.

Adam stared helplessly at the weeping woman. There had never been any soft, feminine influence in his life—no mother, no sister. His uncle had employed nurses, a nanny, but never allowed any of them to mollycoddle the lonely, frightened boys, believing they had to be reared to be tough and independent even as he had been.

Kate Farnley's tears were unnerving him, thawing even more of that hard core deep within him that had been there ever since his brother and his uncle had turned their backs on him all those years ago. It had started to dissolve only since finding out that there were people like George Waverley and his daughter, Elizabeth. They had taken him in, given him his first chance in Australia, and given him hope that despite all that had happened to him he could make a new life for himself.

And more recently, not long after George had been killed, John Martin and his friend Timothy Hardy had arrived. Despite their convict chains of servitude, their faith in God was intact, and they had offered him friendship and trust. But above all they had given him news of a Living Hope, rekindling his own faith that there was a God who loved him and who had never abandoned him after all.

It suddenly seemed the most natural thing in the world to kneel beside this weeping woman and offer her all the comfort that was suddenly pounding desperately within him to give her. Adam wrapped his arms around her and let her sob out on his shoulder all her anguish and pain.

🦋

Kate found his strong masculine arms immeasurably comforting. Instinctively she snuggled into their warmth. Always these last few weeks she had been the one to offer comfort to others. Now, one large hand was smoothing her hair. A soft voice, no longer harsh, but filled with emotion, with comfort, murmured soothingly to her until her sobs died away.

She was reluctant to leave their haven and moved closer as an occasional shudder shook her. But then he stirred. The arms were removed, and she felt chilled.

A large handkerchief was thrust into her hand. She straightened, embarrassment suddenly sweeping through her in a hot tide.

"I. . .I am so sorry," she whispered, after mopping up the last of the moisture and unconsciously wringing the damp piece of cloth with her hands.

He did not answer her, and when she at last ventured to raise her head he was standing with his back to her, looking out through the outside door. His hands were clasped tightly behind him, his back rigid.

She looked hastily away again, but the image of his grave, tense figure was burnt on her mind. Instinctively she knew there was much more to the story about why he had gone to Australia and how he had met John Martin. His face alone told her he must have endured much. Who knew what dangers he had faced in that harsh land so far from England, a land that had often fascinated her with its stories of strange animals and the carving out of a convict colony on the other side of the world.

Taking a deep breath, she was relieved her voice was only slightly husky from her tears as she said, "Mr. Stevens, please, we should examine these letters. Despite what happened yesterday, I am afraid that Percival may descend on us again this morning, and we need to know what to tell him."

He spun around. "No, no! We must tell him nothing. Nothing!"

Stunned, she gaped at him. "But surely, this is evidence enough? As he believes he is the new heir. . ."

"Precisely!" He closed his eyes for a moment; then he studied her piercingly. "It would not be safe for John."

Her eyes widened at the blunt words.

He continued swiftly, advancing closer to her as he did so. "Do pardon me, Miss Farnley, but from what you and John have said about your cousin in this affair and what I saw of his behavior yesterday, I am convinced he is the last person to whom we should mention any of this business. It could be very dangerous for John if Percival had the slightest hint that we had these papers in our possession."

He hesitated and then said slowly, "Don't you think it highly likely that at least Percy's father would have known about the marriage, and would he not have mentioned that to his only son and heir to the estate?"

Kate looked down at the papers in her hands. Had he known? Of course the family would have been notified of the marriage!

Percy had known these papers existed. Undoubtedly that could explain why her cousin had been searching the office. But how would he have suspected that they were here? She sucked in a breath.

Had her father told him?

All her life, Kate had dismissed her cousin as an insignificant, unpleasant person to be pitied for the loss of his father and being left to the mercies of a doting and foolish mother. In recent years, she had despised him for his profligate lifestyle and, more recently, his determined pursuit of her.

She gestured to the pile on the desk. "So you think he could know that these exist?"

Adam nodded grimly. "Yes, I know he does. When it became evident at his trial that he would be convicted, John tried to convince anyone who would listen that he had evidence to prove Lord Farnley was his father. Although your cousin had purported that he wanted to help, John did not trust him sufficiently to tell him where the papers were. He did send his solicitor to where he claimed he had hidden them in his room.

"That gentleman apparently initiated a search, but when the authorities lifted the loose floorboard in his room at the Macallisters, they were adamant they were not there. Apparently, then his claims were dismissed."

"Because they must have been here in my father's safe all along," Kate said in a tearful whisper.

They were both silent. Kate wracked her brains, trying to think back to those weeks when her stepmother had been dying, the time John would have been imprisoned and had his trial. Her father had spent all the hours he could at his wife's bedside. Not for any emergency on the estate had he left the house in those weeks, ever wanting to be near when she called for him, which she had done often through many bouts of pain and suffering. Although she had been ailing for some time, he had refused to give up, to accept the doctors' sad shake of their heads at her deteriorating condition.

Once she had heard him murmur in an anguished voice, "I can't lose you too," and her heart had ached for him, thinking that he had meant her own mother, thinking that she had been too young after all to recognize his real grief then.

Now those words had new significance. He had lost a wife and child, and that must have ripped his heart out. The couple of letters she had haphazardly picked up and read had contained passionate protestations of his love for "my beautiful raven-haired Maria."

"There's something else."

Kate looked up at Adam. A look of sympathy filled his steady gaze, and she braced herself.

"At his trial, the judge said he had received a signed statement from your father dismissing all John's claims."

She stiffened. It made no sense. If he had loved like that, surely he would have at least wanted to meet the man who claimed to be his son.

"I don't. . .I can't believe that," she said with a calmness that surprised even herself. "We've got to read these letters," she said tersely and reluctantly reached out and picked one up. "The answer may be here. If nothing else, we must find the priest's statement."

When Adam Stevens did not speak, she glanced quickly across at him. He was watching her. "I don't think your father would like a stranger reading something so intimate," he said quietly. "Perhaps you could go through them and only show me those sections you think absolutely necessary to prove John's claims."

His sensitivity reached out to her. He understood how hard this was for her, and even more important, he was trusting her.

She smiled mistily at him. "Thank you, Adam." Hesitating for a moment at the strange feelings invading her, she at last added softly, "But, please, could you. . .would you. . . ?"

"Yes, I'll stay, if you want me to."

The sudden, unexpected sweetness of his smile was full of understanding at her need for company. Her heart lurched violently.

Swiftly looking away, she picked up the letter on the top of the pile and then paused again. "Would you perhaps like to look through the Bible?"

"It would be my pleasure."

❦

Relaxing again in the leather lounge chair, Adam tore his eyes away from the woman unfolding the first letter and opened the Bible.

He studied the impressive family tree at the front of the Bible and smiled slightly, thinking of John, wondering if he had any comprehension of what a long line of aristocracy he descended from. Certainly there had been times when flashes of arrogance and pride had been exhibited in the tall, black-haired, blue-eyed man. They had seemed incongruous, unbefitting a lowly assigned convict, but certainly not so for a man with such an illustrious ancestry.

And then Adam suddenly realized this too was Kate Farnley's heritage. He raised his head and studied her. She was absorbed in a letter. A solitary tear slid down one creamy, silken cheek. Her elegant hand impatiently flicked it away, and she turned the closely written page over.

She was incredibly beautiful, the most ravishing woman he had ever met, a woman a man could crave to look at, be with, for the rest of his life.

A tight fist clenched around his heart.

But not for him. Never for him.

He hastily looked back down at the Bible and began almost unconsciously to turn the pages. Then he realized just what he was handling. This was the Word of God.

Slowly, reverently he turned over the fragile, thin pages. The print was very small, but here and there he noticed various passages were marked. Adam wished his own Bible was as well read. He had been able to purchase it just before his ship left Sydney, and although he had spent many hours reading it on the long voyage, he had rarely opened it since arriving in England and while being an unwelcome guest in his brother's home.

To Adam's shame, there had been no Bible at all on Stevens Downs until Timothy had arrived with his treasured but battered small Bible. It had been guarded as best it could by he and John, and somehow, except for a few pages ripped from it once when it had been stolen by other convicts on their transport ship, had survived the long sea journey intact.

Timothy Hardy had willingly let Adam and John borrow it. Then, after Adam had told the two men that he too had come to believe, to have faith and hope in Christ, Timothy had invited him to join them when they took it in turns to read out loud from it.

Adam turned to the Psalms. Being at times himself a shepherd, the Twenty-third Psalm had very special meaning. The page of the Shepherd's Psalm was particularly marked and the edges damaged as though it had been turned to many times. Heavily underlined were the words, "Thou preparest a table before me in the presence of mine enemies."

Had John's father underlined them before going to face the soldier's enemies, or had it been his lonely, pregnant Spanish bride trying to live among her dis-approving family?

Kate gave a sudden loud exclamation.

Adam looked up at her quickly. Her eyes were riveted to the sheet in front of her, and then she slowly lifted her head and turned to him.

"It's all here, Adam. In my father's handwriting, he said how proud and thrilled he was to get her letter that John Harold had arrived safely and how he was longing. . .longing to see his beloved wife and. . .and son." She looked back down at the absolute proof in her hands, and then quickly through the remaining letters. "It is the very last one she received."

She slowly put it down and picked up another sheet of paper. "And this is the priest's statement."

Adam rose and walked eagerly across to her. Slowly she handed the relevant pages to him. While he swiftly read the outpourings of a proud husband and new father, she very carefully refolded the rest of the letters and restored them to their tattered envelopes.

"That's it, then," he said quietly. "John will have his inheritance at last, perhaps even his freedom."

They looked at each other. He saw the shadows in her eyes and could only guess at the heartache of reading the protestations of love of the man who had been her father.

When she nodded but still did not speak, he slowly folded the letter and gently put it with the others and then placed the Bible on top. Still without a word, she tenderly returned them to the large packet and carefully tied it up again.

"What. . .what should we do now?"

The quiet, pain-filled whisper and the way her head and shoulders were bowed hurt something deep inside him.

"Can you completely trust your father's solicitors?" he asked crisply, trying to dispel the sadness from her.

She looked up at him, with that half-blind look on her still face.

"Well?" he said harshly. "Yes or no?"

Her face cleared. She straightened and then stood up. "Yes, of course I can."

He was relieved to hear the usual decisiveness back in her voice as she said, "The firm has served the Farnleys for generations. Besides, they were as worried as I was at the estate going to Percival. They were completely aware of his profligate lifestyle, his gambling habits, and were trying to find ways to prevent him from squandering the lot."

"Then we must turn this whole matter over to their capable hands as soon as possible."

She nodded briefly and then was silent. At last she took a deep breath. "And I must do as Father said. Find John. . .my brother John. . ." Her voice broke and trailed away.

Then she straightened her shoulders and looked directly at Adam. "Will you help me find the real Lord Farnley, Mr. Stevens, and make sure he recovers his rightful inheritance?"

Something flared through Adam, leaving him with a hunger he had never before known. There was much strength of purpose in her beautiful, steady gaze. More than that, there was an earnest pleading mingled with a direct challenge

him as a man that he could not resist. He could not let this woman go out of
s life.

"Even if it means you have to travel to Australia with me?"

Her eyes widened. They flashed with wonder, with dawning excitement, with
ch courage it weakened him even further, while at the same time a feeling of
ld exultation swept through him, consuming him.

Kate nodded almost fiercely. "Even if it means I have to travel to Australia
ith you, Mr. Stevens."

Chapter 5

Late December, 1837

The elusive breeze teased the listless topsails of the weary ship. It al gently lifted a wayward strand of copper hair on the solitary figure starir out across the gentle swell of the blue waters of the Gulf of Saint Vincer on the southern coast of the great southland of Australia.

Kate rubbed her hand across the perspiration on her forehead. The man qu etly approaching her frowned slightly. It was hot with no sea breeze, but this wa cool in comparison to the inland heat of Australia at this time of the year. H smiled gently at her as she peered up at the limp sails.

He stifled a sigh and said, "Will not be long now, Miss Farnley."

She jumped and swung around swiftly with a slight frown. Then one of he radiant smiles nearly dazzled him.

"Oh, Adam, is it not exciting? But it is also so frustrating. So close, and no the wind has dropped!"

For a moment Adam stared at her, drinking in her beauty. He could not te her that he was a mixture of churning, contradictory emotions. One moment h wanted this journey to go on forever that he might always be near her. At othe times the torment of being with her without the intimacies his soul craved, know ing she could never be his, was an agony beyond description.

Her own smile faltered slightly, and he shook himself, forcing himself to smi gently at her sparkling face.

The familiar sharp pang of anguish that always came when she smiled at hir just so had an added strength this day. Their cozy times together aboard shi would so soon be finished.

Once the passengers bound for South Australia had disembarked and fres supplies were brought aboard, they would sail once again and be on their last le of this long voyage to Sydney. Once there, he would no longer sit across from he at every meal, enjoying her bright mind, her low melodious tones.

It had not taken many days all those weeks ago before they had become quit good friends, and she had a little diffidently asked him to call her by her first nam He had dared not, only calling her so in his daydreams. She had been puzzled a first and then resigned.

However, that had not stopped her calling him "Adam" and saying firmly few weeks after that first day in her father's study, "After all, it is ludicrous to de formally together when you are party to such deep secrets of my family and also a friend of my. . .my brother, Sir."

And since those first couple days at Fleetwood and then later in London at the Garretts' residence, she had treated him like a brother, a member of her family.

He had never become such good friends with a woman before, not even the youthful Elizabeth Waverley. The increasing closeness between Kate and himself, the way he could so often know what she was thinking, scared him to no end. But although he knew it increasingly annoyed and really upset her, he had steadfastly refused to call her by her Christian name.

That had been only one of the many ways he had determined to somehow keep his distance, to somehow save himself from throwing all caution to the winds and hauling her into his arms and telling her he loved her beyond life itself.

Her father had been a lord. Her place in society was so above his own. Even if the last years in Australia had never been, even if he had met her in England, any liaison with him would ostracize her from society. His family was in trade. She was heiress to a great estate and name.

And he. . .he was only the coward who had told her nothing of the horror and pain of the last years that had contributed finally and without question to his unworthiness.

So much had happened during the last few weeks before they had sailed over four months ago in the *Royal Duke*. Kate had insisted Adam go with her to hand over John's papers to her father's amazed, excited, yet highly perturbed lawyers. They had been relieved that there was such a good chance that Percival Farnley might no longer inherit and bring ruin to the estate. However, they were very upset and anxious about the good name of the family with the new Lord Farnley a convicted murderer and serving a life sentence in the antipodes.

That concern had been somewhat relieved after being assured of Kate and Adam's belief that the new heir was undoubtedly innocent. Apparently, they had also made some discreet inquiries of their own of the sentencing judge. He had admitted he had taken the unusual step of commuting the death penalty for murder to life transportation in case the impassioned claims of the young man had been true.

After that, they had very quickly set things in motion. Trusted envoys had been immediately dispatched to Spain to prove the identity of the said John Martin as the child of the late lord. "For if he is proved indeed to be that infant, John Harold Farnley," the most senior partner had loftily explained to the young couple, "then he could lay claim to a trial of his peers, which could be a very different thing from a district court."

He had sniffed disdainfully, but Adam and Kate had stared at each other with bright hope in their eyes.

As a result of these visits and the assurances heaped on them about the strong possibility of a satisfactory outcome, Adam had held his peace and refrained from repeating anything his friend John had said about Beth Garrett's failure to come forward with the alibi that might have caused a jury to change their verdict. There would be time enough for that if any new evidence was needed at a new trial.

Besides, when at last the whole matter had been confided to both the Garretts, Beth had looked so stricken, turned so pale, and trembled so violently that he had even felt a twinge of sympathy for her and not really been more than momentarily surprised when she had so vehemently insisted on accompanying her sister to Australia.

Adam had tried to persuade the two sisters that the long, tedious, and dangerous journey was not necessary, and that as soon as possible John Martin, or John Farnley, as he should be called, would be returned to England. But when the lawyers had told them it could take many months, even longer than a year before anything could be resolved, both women had been adamant. They had to meet John and be assured of his welfare.

"Besides," Kate had added so painfully that it had for the moment silenced Adam's protests, "the very last thing my father requested of me was to find him and tell him how sorry he was. The least I can do is go to my brother and personally tell him that. And. . .and how dreadful if something should happen to John before I could tell him."

Adam had silently agreed with her, knowing only too well the dangers that were faced each day on those vast, dusty plains.

Then the Reverend William Garrett had astounded them all by mentioning that he had heard much of Australia and their need for more ministers. Apparently he had several times thought of exchanging the fogs and cold of England for the sunshine of that great land.

Adam had studied the man of God for a long moment, then looked so swiftly at his wife that he had captured the amazed, almost frightened look on Beth Garrett's face as she stared at her husband before she had swiftly lowered her eyes. He had frowned and sharply looked again at the Reverend Garrett. The minister was watching his wife with such an expression of tenderness and concern that Adam had felt a twinge of envy that a man could so openly love a woman and call her his wife.

Despite his reservations about Beth, Adam had found his own attitude had softened considerably toward the young woman as a result of that good Christian man's regard for her. After all, she had obviously been highly indulged by her mother and then her stepfather and had been so very young and sheltered when she had met the handsome young man, John Martin.

During the many hours since, especially on the long three month's voyage, he had become very close to her husband. He had spent much time discussing spiritual things with William Garrett, realizing very quickly that here he had found a true man of God who cared greatly for his fellowman and sought to minister the Scriptures faithfully. He not only preached to others, but he also did his utmost to put those principles into practice himself.

Adam knew there was so much more that William Garrett could teach him, and perhaps, God willing, one day in the near future John and Timothy would have the opportunity of learning from William's superior knowledge of the Word of God gained from his many years of study.

"After all these weeks, Captain Lewis says he expects to anchor off Port Misery well before nightfall."

Adam blinked as those soft tones intruded on his thoughts. "Indeed, it is to be hoped that we do not have to spend even one more night on board this poor benighted vessel," he replied after taking a moment to bring his thoughts back from the past. "Although I'm not too sure I like the name of our landing place."

"Port Misery? Oh, Captain Lewis said that was just a nickname given it by the first migrants and not to worry about that," Kate told him cheerfully. "Apparently it is really Holdfast Bay where the ship anchors, even though it is some seven miles from the settlement of Adelaide, still being surveyed, I understand, on the River Torrens."

Adam gave an involuntary smile. That did not comfort him in the least.

Even as she spoke, the wind quickened and the sails filled and sent the ship hurrying toward its journey's end as though it agreed with him and would also be glad to finally put behind the dangers and traumas of the long journey.

❦

Kate watched Adam as he leaned on the rail and stared down at the gentle swell, so different from the huge waves of the last few days that had made them all so uncomfortable. She had slept little the night just past. Beth had once again been so seasick that Kate had insisted on taking care of young Harold so both Beth and William could sleep. But the small boy had not disturbed her. It had been her own troubled thoughts that had kept her long awake. And it was this man beside her who so constantly occupied those thoughts.

In many ways, he was still an enigma. It was obvious that a special bond existed between him and his friend John Martin—*Farnley*, she swiftly corrected herself. She knew there was much about his own time in Australia that Adam had not explained, especially how that bond between landholder and convict had grown.

At first she had thought it had just been because Timothy and John had led him to a personal faith in Jesus Christ, but from other things Adam had said, she strongly suspected there was some other reason that he never mentioned.

All she really knew about Adam Stevens was that after an irreconcilable falling-out with his brother and uncle, he had gone to Australia more than ten years ago and now owned a sheep station some three hundred miles west of Sydney.

"It was a shame we were delayed by that storm and had to spend Christmas Day on board." As Adam spoke, he turned and smiled gently at her.

Kate's own smile disappeared and she looked quickly away, but not before she knew he had seen her sad expression. The whole ship's company had done their best to celebrate the birth of the infant Jesus and Savior, but it had been a halfhearted effort at best. Everyone had still been so upset by the death of the small son of one of the migrant families. The turbulence of the surging seas had at long last proved too much for his frail body, and despite all their efforts, his small body had been committed to the ocean only a few days before Christmas.

Kate had often fervently thanked God that Harold Garrett was such a healthy child and had withstood the journey so well. Not like that other poor little mite. The day they had buried the tiny child at sea had been the saddest time of the whole voyage. His poor mother still crept around the ship in a daze of grief.

Beth and William had guarded their precious son even more, but Harold was now thin and miserable from the poor food that even those traveling first-class had endured now that their supplies were so low. William also had become drawn and lost weight this last week. Kate strongly suspected he was giving most of his meager rations to his wife and child, but when challenged, he had simply smiled gently at her and turned away.

"It has not been an easy voyage," Adam added quickly in a low voice. "Is your sister well this day?"

It was a moment before Kate replied in a husky voice, "She seems much brighter but has never completely recovered from that fever she developed a few weeks ago. I still cannot understand why she kept from us the fact that she was expecting another child until we were so many days into the journey," she added in a stronger, exasperated voice.

"No doubt so that her husband would not forbid her to travel," Adam replied dryly.

Kate glanced at him swiftly. "You do not like my sister, do you, Adam?" she asked in an accusing voice. "It puzzles me, for never was there a sweeter person than Beth, nor a better wife and mother. Besides, although she tries not to let it show, I know it upsets her greatly."

He stiffened, staring out across the waters of the gulf. She saw his strong jaw tighten and knew with a sinking heart that her fears must be right. The only explanation she had been able to think of for his coolness to Beth had been that John Martin must have told him something to her sister's discredit.

While she herself had been so preoccupied in caring for her stepmother and joining in the conspiracy not to let Beth know just how ill her mother was, there had been little, if any, time to spend with Beth herself. It was only later that she had suspected the rebellion which had stirred in the young woman who was barely out of the care of her governess had caused her to run wild for a few weeks after her mother's last collapse.

Who would know what Beth had foolishly done in that time! Then she had been married so young, because, as Kate had once confided to Adam briefly, "It was her mother's dearest wish to see her daughter married before she died."

Now she wished she had asked him before about Beth, even as he said a little sharply, "I am sorry if my attitude has concerned you, and I can give you no explanation."

"Cannot, or will not, I wonder."

At her censorious tone he glanced at her quickly, but before he could reply there was a loud shout of, "Land ho!" from the lookout.

Obviously relieved at the interruption, he said swiftly, "It would seem that we are indeed soon to set foot on shore. Are all your belongings packed that you will need in Adelaide while the ship is taking on supplies?"

"Yes, of course."

Suddenly all her hopes and fears rose up and almost overwhelmed her. She impulsively swung around and reached out to him. His hands automatically went to meet hers, and suddenly she was clinging to them.

"Oh, Adam, I could hardly sleep last night, and all day I have been in such a fidget. Besides being so concerned about Beth, I am worried about John. I so long to meet my. . .my half brother, but now that we are so much closer, I have been wondering even more how he will respond to me—to us. This journey has been so fraught with discomfort and danger, and I dare not try to imagine what it must have been like for him as a convict."

Staring a little desperately into eyes that had gone very dark again, Kate suddenly longed to have Adam put his arms around her, comfort her, keep her safe forever.

It was a long moment before he spoke, and then it was hesitantly, as though wondering just how much to tell her.

"Perhaps you *should* know," he said quietly at last. "It may help you to understand him when you meet. John rarely speaks of that journey. Most of what happened I have heard from others, mainly his friend and fellow convict Timothy Hardy. Also, the surgeon on board the ship, Dr. Richmond, and his wife who befriended John were very impressed with his courage and fortitude."

"The surgeon? Was John ill?"

That hesitation again, and then, as though he had made up his mind, Adam's hand tightened on hers until his grip was painful, but she did not wince.

In an expressionless voice, he said, "The convicts nowadays may not have as harsh conditions as even ten years ago, but apparently it was a dreadful journey."

Kate had heard rumors about the conditions aboard most transportation vessels, but she listened with increasing horror as Adam told her briefly about conditions the convicts had endured, especially on the ship that had transported John to Sydney.

Besides the severely cramped quarters, the sickness, and the refusal of the soldiers' commanding officer, Lieutenant Edwards, to remove the convicts' shackles for several days after leaving Cape Town, there had been the dreadful riot.

John and Timothy's desperate efforts to prevent the convicts rioting had been futile. Then they had been unjustly accused and punished. While Timothy had been let off some of his flogging due to his injuries and John's appeal on his behalf, John himself had received well over sixty lashes with the dreaded cat-o'-nine-tails. His body already weakened by illness, his life had only been spared by the dedicated care of the surgeon on the ship, the surgeon's wife, and their young friend, Elizabeth Waverley.

Adam recited the bare facts in a quiet, expressionless voice, staring motionlessly out across the blue water. As Kate watched him, his face became remote, the harsh lines even more pronounced.

She suspected that if she asked for details he would not tell her more, and she shuddered, not even wanting to know more of the horror. As it was, when he at last fell silent, she was trembling. Tears burnt her eyes and started trickling down her face.

"Will John ever be able to forgive us for all he has suffered, for our own neglect of him?" she whispered at last. "Even though we did not realize his trial was going on, the lowliest servant of my father's in the past received more consideration than he. And how can I ever explain that my father had those papers and did nothing? Nothing!"

She dashed a hand across her eyes. Adam came out of his silent reverie and turned toward her. His hand reached out, and a thumb smoothed away the moisture on one cheek. Then his hands enfolded hers in their strong, comforting grasp. For one blissful moment, Kate felt Adam draw her closer.

He stared at her, his eyes filled with molten, dark liquid passion. He opened his mouth, and she held her breath. But then an excited, girlish squeal intruded, breaking the tense moment. They glanced around, suddenly aware that others had joined them on deck to watch for the first sight of land.

His hands tightened convulsively on hers. He looked down at them, drew a deep breath, and slowly, almost reluctantly, let her go. When he at last looked back at her, she was disappointed to see that his reserve was again well in place.

"I have told you before that John helped me to give my life into our Lord's hands," he murmured. "He has suffered so much, but through it all he found, through Timothy's faithful witness, a God who shared his suffering, who loves him. He has been exercising the forgiveness that he believes God would have him give to all those who have wronged him."

He turned away and stared again across the blue waters. When he spoke again, his words were so soft that she strained to hear him above the increasing noise on deck.

"He will not be able to help loving you, my dear Kate," she thought she heard him say, and her heart leaped within her.

Before she could be sure she had heard correctly, he gave her a slightly twisted smile and moved away to acknowledge the excited comments of a fellow passenger.

Chapter 6

To everyone's relief, the strength of the breeze did not abate, and it was not long before the *Royal Duke* had anchored in Holdfast Bay. To the dismay of the passengers, they were informed the ship had to anchor so far offshore because it was over three hundred tons and was too large to navigate the mouth of the Patawalonga River. Smaller boats would take them and their be-longings the rest of the way to the beach.

On December 28, 1836, just over two years earlier, the *Buffalo* carrying the first governor to the new colonial settlement had anchored in the same place. Several of their fellow passengers enjoyed telling what they knew about the beginnings of what was to be these migrants' new homeland.

Way back in 1802, only fourteen years after the First Fleet had landed at Botany Bay, the wonderful navigator and early explorer Matthew Flinders had charted the southern coast of the newly settled land of New South Wales, as it was then called. As well as Gulf Saint Vincent, he had named Spencer Gulf; Port Lincoln on its western shore; Kangaroo Island, which the ship had sailed past before entering this gulf; as well as Mount Lofty, which was several miles inland.

As early as the 1820s, Edward Gibbon Wakefield had put forward his new ideas for selling land to free settlers at a fixed price, rather than merely giving out grants. The money raised could then be used to transport free emigrants to the colony. But it was not until 1834 that the British Parliament passed the South Australian Colonization Act and 1836 before a London banker and shipowner, George Angas, set up the South Australian Company, bought a large tract of land, and encouraged migration.

At first, attempts were made to settle on Kangaroo Island, but because of its poor soil and lack of water, other sites were considered. At last they decided that Colonel William Light should survey a site east of Holdfast Bay on Gulf Saint Vincent for the capital, Adelaide.

"And no convicts have or ever will, God willing, be transported to that new land," Adam heard Kate repeat at the end of one particular recital.

They had looked at each other, and it was Adam who had looked away first. He was thinking of that incident while standing beside Kate and William, watching a boat being rowed out to the ship. How different this was from the deep, sheltered harbor of Sydney Cove. All they could see of the land was what looked like a flat plain stretching to a faint line of low hills. A very few rough sheds and temporary-looking dwellings were scattered beyond the sand hills among the low scrub and grass.

He remembered the stories of old Sydney in the first couple years of settlement, of the first governor, Sir Arthur Phillip, and the hardships, the near starvation that had been experienced by convicts and freemen alike.

This looked far less friendly than Sydney's beautiful blue harbor with its tree-lined slopes and rocky cliffs. Suddenly, although they were going ashore while the ship was repaired and restocked, Adam was glad they were not disembarking to live here with the other subdued passengers.

Unexpectedly, the usually quiet William Garrett murmured, "A virgin land, a land of opportunity, of hope for hardworking, honest, God-fearing men."

Adam glanced at the man's rapt face and then around at the other passengers. It was a long moment before he drawled as softly, "For some it will be so, for others. . .I wonder."

His perturbation increased when, a little while after the first welcoming rowboat had left, Captain Lewis sought him out.

"A word with you in private, Mr. Stevens," the rather pompous little man intoned.

After they had withdrawn from the others and after a few delicate coughs and clearings of his throat, Captain Lewis said, "I am very sorry to inform you, Sir, that the *Royal Duke* will not be continuing on to Sydney as we had originally planned."

Adam's heart sank even as wrath began to fill him. "Sir, I understood us to have paid our passage all the way to Sydney and that you naturally would honor that arrangement."

The captain raised an imperious hand. "Of course, of course," he said a little too rapidly. "I am sure any outstanding monies will be refunded to you eventually, but circumstances have occurred beyond my control. As you know, we suffered considerable damage during that last storm. I have just been informed that the captain of a ship that arrived here from Sydney this morning and then almost immediately resumed its voyage to England said that the weather has been atrocious down the eastern coast. There is a huge swell from storms in the Pacific, and it is expected to worsen. So much so that they fear for the last ship that left here only a week ago bound for Sydney. I simply will not risk my vessel unnecessarily."

He drew himself up to the fullness of his short height to deliver his final blow. "Besides, this anchorage is noted for the way anchors drag through the sand." He snorted. "Perhaps that is why someone so inappropriately named it Holdfast.

"But as soon as temporary repairs have been completed I have been instructed to return immediately to England with urgent papers from Governor Hindmarsh. The rumor is that he may be replaced. He was apparently extremely annoyed this other ship left without waiting for him and his family. Indeed, I find it very fortunate that it is only your party who were continuing on to Sydney."

Before Adam could protest further, Captain Lewis swung sharply away, beginning to bark orders to his scurrying crew.

Adam was left with no choice but to convey the news to the others. William looked thoughtful but said nothing, while Beth's pale, thin face looked almost relieved as she glanced swiftly at her husband and hugged their son a little tighter.

Kate gave an exclamation of dismay. "But how and when will we get to New South Wales?"

Adam shrugged wearily. "We will just have to wait for the next ship, I would suppose."

"Could not we travel overland?" she queried eagerly.

He looked at her, aware as never before that anyone who had never traveled in the vastness of the Australian inland could have no idea of its distances, its inherent dangers.

"Although the explorers are penetrating farther into the interior, to my knowledge there has not so far been any such journeys through to the east from Adelaide. But I will certainly ask around," he said gently. "We will have to continue to rely on God to lead us where He wants us to go."

Then they realized they had to rush to pack everything they had brought and arrange for their belongings in the hold to be unloaded. Adam was particularly dismayed about the special equipment and furnishings he had shipped in the hold for the new homestead he hoped one day to build on Stevens Downs. At last he was able to make arrangements for these to be kept for the time being in one of the few storage huts at the bay. Finally they were ready to join the stream of passengers disembarking.

As their boat neared the beach, Kate and Beth watched rather anxiously as they saw that the women and children, even a few of the older gentlemen, had to be carried ashore on the backs of the sailors.

"Well, I'm not trusting you to anyone else but me," William declared in an unusually stern tone to Beth. Without argument, she let a young sailor take Harold and then allowed William to heave her into his arms and head off through the clear, shallow water and white sand to where the baggage was being dumped in a huge pile on the fine, dry white sand.

All the others had gone. Without a word, Adam and Kate sat watching William and Beth. Then they looked at each other.

"Your turn," Adam said a little hoarsely and busied himself taking off his boots and handing them to her to carry before rolling up the sleeves of his shirt and then the bottoms of his trousers as far as their snug fit would permit.

❧

A little breathless, Kate stared at him. She already knew how strong he was, had seen how he had heaved around heavy trunks as easily as any of the brawny seamen, but never before had she seen his smooth, brown arms and his strong wrists and ankles exposed.

Her gaze traveled over him slowly, down to those strong, capable hands she had seen so tenderly soothe Harold. Once his hands had very tenderly smoothed a wayward strand of her own hair behind her ear before he had abruptly turned away with a muttered apology, leaving her strangely shaken and trembling.

Then, only this morning, his thumb had wiped away her tears.

Suddenly, as he rolled up his sleeves, Kate noticed white, raised scars on his wrists. She frowned. At some time he must have suffered some injury to them. Then as he lifted his leg over the side of the boat she saw similar marks on his ankles. They were obviously scars from old cuts, old wounds.

She felt as if a knife pierced through her.

There had once been a conversation she had overheard on board the ship about the added sufferings caused by the iron fetters on prisoners. Only a few hours before, Adam had told her about the manacles and chains on the convicts on John's ship being left on far too long and contributing to the riot in the hot tropical sun.

His ankles and wrists had also once known cruel irons. She closed her eyes. Emotions tumbled through her. Pain and anguish mingled with appalled astonishment. Adam had been transported to Australia. He was a criminal and had done something so dreadful that a court had considered it necessary to sentence him to a land far from his brother, his family. No wonder he was estranged from them.

But what could a fine man like him have done? He was a Christian. But then he had told her himself he had only become a Christian after meeting the two convicts assigned to him.

Her eyes flew open. So he must have finished his sentence and decided to start a new life in a new country. But whatever changes had been wrought in his life in recent years, he would bear the marks and stigma of a convict for the rest of his life.

"Miss Farnley?" Adam had stepped into the water and was watching her, uncertainty in his usual decisive, direct gaze. "Will you trust yourself to me?"

Would she? Could she really trust an ex-convict? What had he once told her they were called now in Australia? Emancipists?

She thought of all they had experienced together since they had met, his protection of her against Percival, whom she had not seen since the day Adam had knocked him down, his loyalty to his friend and her half brother, John.

And she loved him. Love for this strong, silent man had so sweetly grown. She caught her breath. For the first time, she acknowledged it. She loved him. Had perhaps from those first days they'd spent together at Fleetwood.

As she stared at him, his expression changed. That withdrawn, cautious look that she had grown to hate so much had returned. Even as she tried to find her voice, he said sharply, "Would you prefer to wait for one of the crew to return, Miss Farnley?"

After taking a deep breath, she suggested in a bemused voice, "I. . .I could wade through the water myself."

A flash of laughter momentarily swept away his reserve. "And horrify, even offend, the seaman? It's me or one of them, I'm afraid."

Then he was grave again and held out his hand.

She stared down at it, her eyes once again staring at those scars. How could she not have noticed them before? Perhaps because the worst marks were usually concealed by the long sleeves that she suddenly realized he had worn even on the hottest days.

Then she gave a quick laugh before reaching out her own hands to have them clasped in his strong grip. "Oh, yes, Adam Stevens, I do trust you."

He looked at her strangely, but the next moment he had swung her up in his arms.

What did his past matter? If anything, it was a relief to know the reason for that deep sadness, that haunted expression she had seen sometimes in his eyes. And in some even deeper part of her, perhaps she was not really surprised after all. Certainly a good man would do as Adam had done, but all along she had wondered why he would go to so much trouble on his friend's behalf if he had not deeply understood all John endured as a convict.

He was still Adam, the man she had grown to like and admire so much for his intelligence, his sense of humor, his gentle courtesy, his faith in and devotion to God that seemed so natural to him, as well as his devotion to his friends, Timothy and John.

He was still the man she had given her heart to.

Automatically her own arms clutched at him, going up around his neck and clinging even tighter as he shifted her weight while trying to get his balance in the water swirling up to his knees.

"Oh, my dear, I'm afraid your skirt should have been caught up first. It will be wet."

His voice sounded a little hoarse, even slightly breathless. She looked up at his face and their gazes caught and held. There was an expression in his that brought the blood racing to her cheeks.

Hastily she looked away and tightened her grip on him with one hand while she hauled at her skirt with the other. After a brief struggle, she said with a forced laugh, "There, it is tucked up as best I can, and if it gets wet it will soon dry in this heat. I should have worn a dress with less fullness."

He started slowly through the water, and she grabbed for him again as his foot slipped in the sand. She held herself stiffly at first, feeling shy and awkward. And then, somehow the warmth of his body through his fine linen and the swish of the water as he slowly waded through it added to the wonder of at last setting foot on this strange continent he had told her so much about.

After what seemed an eternity, he at last swung her down to firm, wet sand. She wondered if it was wishful thinking that made her think that his hands lingered a few moments longer than necessary after she had gained her footing. Was he as reluctant to lose contact as she?

Not daring to look at him, she handed him his shoes, and he muttered something inaudible and hurried ahead to where William and Beth were already anxiously searching for their luggage in the huge pile on the dry, soft sand.

She stared after him and then slowly smiled a little gleefully. He too had felt the tension between them. The dark tide of red that had stained his face had not merely been from her slight weight!

Kate looked around and then jumped. Not too far from her, several dark-skinned men, women, and small children peered at her. The adults were standing motionless, staring at the invaders to their shores. She backed away and hurried to join the others.

"Those people, Adam, they are watching us so strangely."

He looked up at her and then back at the natives briefly. "Nothing to worry about, I was told. Apparently they camp at freshwater lagoons about half a mile away. Sometimes they fight among themselves, but otherwise they have not caused too much trouble. Ah, this looks like one of your bags, Kate."

By the time they had claimed all their belongings, all available transport had left along the winding track toward Adelaide. It would be dark soon, they were informed by the ship's crew, and they would have to stay the night.

The men were upset, and when they joined the others in a rough storage shed, Adam looked around at their primitive surroundings and said with considerable concern, "I'm not at all sure another night on board would not have been preferable to the conditions in this hot place." He swatted another hungry mosquito. "I am extremely sorry we could not arrange transport into Adelaide before nightfall."

Beth answered cheerfully, "Oh, I am too relieved that the ground is not heaving and rolling to be worried about a few bites."

Kate saw him smile approvingly at her sister's weary, pale face as he said, "You put me to shame, Mrs. Garrett, my dear."

Beth's face lit up at his response, and Adam looked surprised at the extent of her delight at his approval. His smile widened, and then he suddenly looked directly at Kate.

She smiled at him gently, acknowledging the remorse in his eyes that a smile from him had brought such pleasure to Beth.

As Beth bent over awkwardly, he quickly reached down to help her arrange a makeshift bed for her small son. He smiled even wider at Beth and was rewarded by her shy blush and the added brightness to her smile.

"Now, are you sure you and Harold are comfortable enough there?" he asked cheerfully. "I do wish I had been able to obtain some more water for you, but there seems to be none at all here unless we intrude upon the natives camped around the freshwater lagoon. Apparently the lack of good water here was one of the main reasons it was decided to establish the main settlement inland on the Torrens River."

Beth beamed at him, assured him cheerfully she would manage, and then busied herself settling the small boy to sleep.

Kate frowned. Several times she had wondered about Adam's coldness toward Beth, but when she had ventured to mention it, he had looked at her with that annoying, blank way he had, merely raising one of his thick eyebrows and refusing to answer. It worried her now even more. Obviously John Martin must have told him something about his friendship with Beth that had angered Adam greatly. But surely there had been nothing but friendliness between John and Beth.

"You were right, Miss Farnley," he said softly a little while later. "I did not realize my attitude toward Mrs. Garrett was adding so much to her distress and unhappiness. Surely being with child these difficult months she has deserved my pity, not my censure."

She stared at him, again wondering uneasily what on earth Beth could have done to earn his reproach. Before she could ask him outright, he added, "I have just remembered what I told you earlier today about John and forgiveness. It seems there is much for me to learn about forgiveness that he has already put into practice." Then he moved swiftly away.

🦋

With the relentless insect population, the hot night, and the lack of water in the December heat, there was little sleep for any of them that first night. As soon as it was light, Adam and William joined some of the other male passengers to set out on foot for the township.

When at last Adam and William returned with a large dray, both men looked grim. "It is worse than we expected," Adam said briefly.

There were very few spare rooms in the village spreading out along the river Torrens. The influx from their ship had filled every available place. Building materials were very basic and still hard to come by despite the wooden frames for houses that had been brought out on each ship. The number of dwellings could not keep up with the flood of emigrants.

After a fruitless search, they had at last managed to borrow tents and the bare essentials. A family in one house had offered a couple of beds which the men had urged Beth and Kate to take, but the sisters had looked at each other for one long moment, grinned in agreement, and then insisted that they not be separated from the men.

As soon as Adam and William had helped the others all they could, William suggested Kate and Adam go for a walk and investigate all possibilities of getting a ship to continue their journey. The two met with no success. They were told that the previous year only nine ships had arrived in South Australian waters.

One official shrugged and said, "Sorry, Sir. It could be in a couple weeks, six weeks, or with these weather conditions, as long as several months before another ship arrives en route to Sydney."

"It seems as though we have no choice but to make the most of conditions here until a ship does arrive," Adam said grimly as they at last started walking back to tell William and Beth.

"Oh, Adam, what are we going to do? We must get to Sydney as quickly as we can," Kate burst out. "There's something I have not told you."

"Adam? By all that's wonderful, is that you, Adam Stevens?" The loud roar came from a group of men they were passing on the dusty road.

Adam stopped and swung around. A tall, broad-shouldered man in rough country clothes started toward him, an equally tall youth just behind him.

Adam stared unbelievingly as the man stopped in front of him, removed the large-brimmed, dusty hat shading his face, and swept him a low, mocking bow. "Well, a fine gentleman you are this day, Mr. Stevens, Sir!" He laughed as he straightened his back and then thrust out his hand.

Adam's hand went out in greeting, and then he also welcomed the beaming younger man. "Will Gordon? What the. . .and Jim! Whatever are you doing here?" he asked in a rather dazed voice.

There was another hearty laugh. "Exactly what I was thinkin' meself, like. The last time I saw you was trailing behind that mob of sheep you'd just bought from me. . .why, it must be well almost two years ago now. Heard you were making a good go of the new place and then that you'd suddenly got up and off last year to Old England. And who's this beautiful young woman?"

He slapped his hat against his dirty trousers and roared again. "Now, don't tell me this pretty young lady is your wife, that you've gone and got married behind our backs, like?"

Adam's face suddenly went brick red. He opened his mouth and closed it as though he had suddenly lost his voice.

Kate felt the heat flood into her own cheeks but forced a laugh and thrust out her own hand to have it enveloped and enthusiastically pumped. "Mr. Gordon, is it? No, no, never fear; Adam is still a bachelor. I'm Kate Farnley. We are just good friends and have traveled out together from London."

Adam choked, and Will Gordon's eyes twinkled merrily. "Just good friends, eh? You're far too slow then, my friend, if you haven't snapped up this beauty yet. Hopefully my son Jim here won't be so foolish when he's a few years older."

Kate shook hands with the suddenly red-faced Jim and beamed at them both. She liked this Mr. Gordon. Besides, she suddenly found herself wholeheartedly agreeing with him!

She raised her chin and looked fully at Adam and saw he was still bereft of words. His lips had tightened, and as she saw the look in his eyes change, she took pity on him, even as she wondered at the pain there.

"We only arrived yesterday, Mr. Gordon," she said swiftly, giving Adam time to recover. "We have been rather stranded here by the captain of our ship who has decided not to complete the journey to Sydney."

"And we have just been informed it will be some weeks before we are likely

get passage in another," Adam said abruptly. "But tell me, what are you doing
ere so far from Bathurst?"

Will scratched his head and then replaced his hat at a jaunty angle. "Well, it's
wo years now since Sir Thomas Mitchell explored and found the Lachlan River
as a tributary of the Murrumbidgee. He also found that it flowed into the
Murray the same as the Darling does and that the mighty Murray entered the
outhern Ocean instead of some great inland sea."

He paused and ran a large paw over his face and then glanced swiftly at Kate,
ho was listening in fascinated silence. "Well, Mitchell traveled along to Port
hillip and then north on a different route back to Sydney. He was very enthusi-
stic about the country round Port Phillip. They reckon there's now more than
ve hundred people livin' there, and they are calling the new town Melbourne. So,
e thought we'd go have a look-see."

He paused again and glanced at his son, *almost warningly,* Kate suddenly
ought.

"But then," he continued swiftly, "we changed our minds, like, and came to
e what the fuss was here in this very newest settlement."

He turned and waved the group of men he had been with closer. "Come on,
ou blokes, and meet these folks just arrived from the home country."

Kate found her hand pumped up and down by a Bob Brown and his wife,
dy. Then a tall, red-haired man blushed a fiery red as Will Gordon introduced
im simply as Bluey. They were obviously old acquaintances of Adam and
reeted him enthusiastically with much backslapping. The last man, an aborig-
e, stood a little behind the others, staring at her from black, expressionless
yes.

"And this bloke here comes from the Lake Macquarie area up near New-
astle, north of Sydney," Will Gordon added hastily for Kate's benefit. "Only been
orkin' for us a few months before we left home. We call him Jackie because he
as some outlandish name none of us can pronounce. He's a good stockman,
specially with horses, and we brought him in case we ran into any of his kin,"
Will Gordon said.

The aborigine was dressed the same as the other men, including the broad-
rimmed, dusty stockman's hat. Kate noticed that Adam treated him exactly the
ame as the others, so she also held out her hand. There was a brief hesitation
efore a black hand slowly came out and then shook hers firmly.

She wondered how old he was. He seemed to be only a youth, but she knew
he could be wrong. She smiled at him and said gently, "What is your real name,
ackie?"

For a moment he did not answer, just watched her from those dark, fathom-
ess eyes. When she thought he was not going to speak, he said what sounded like
wo words slowly in deep guttural tones.

Adam repeated slowly, "Gindhanha Guudha. Why, I think that is Wiradjuri for 'laughing child.' Are you from the Wiradjuri tribe?"

A fleeting expression that could have been surprise touched the stockman['s] face before it returned to its expressionless state. He nodded briefly and sai[d] "Yeah, Boss, I reckon from Wiradjuri."

Will Gordon was staring from Adam to his stockman. "Well, I'm blowe[d] you've just said more words then I've heard you say in one sentence the whole tri[p] And fancy you understandin' his lingo, Adam. Reckon you've had a lot to do wit[h] those western tribes round your station. But, Jackie, I thought you was Awabak[al] from the Lake Macquarie area."

Jackie hesitated again. Then he grinned. His dark eyes sparkled as he sai[d] slowly in a heavily accented voice, "I live Newcastle, but not Awabakal. Wiradjuri[,]" he said proudly.

Kate noticed Adam frown slightly at him, looking thoughtful, but he said n[o] more to the man before turning once again to Mr. Gordon and asking which rou[te] they had taken.

"We traveled overland from home to Goulburn, then down to the Murra[y] River and straight across to here," he was told. "I've been trying to find where t[he] best place would be to get another property."

"Overland! You've come overland!"

Young Jim grinned widely at Adam's amazement. "Sure, and why not? An[d] we're not the first who have made the journey either, we discovered. Everywhe[re] those brave explorer blokes go, settlers follow. It's been a mighty grand adventure[,]" he said eagerly. "We just piled what we could on a dray. Only lost one horse an[d] had little contact with the natives."

He paused and grinned slowly. "But now we reckon the land be no bett[er,] even worse in some places, than around Bathurst and even out your way ne[ar] Wellington. So we think we'll stay in the area we know, after all. It's closer to t[he] markets also. We'll be leaving as soon as we finish stocking up supplies for th[e] journey home."

Kate looked from one man to the other and then at Adam. "Adam, do yo[u] think. . .is it possible. . . ?"

They stared at each other. Her heart sank as he quickly shook his head. "Kat[e,] it must be at least a thousand-mile journey, and you can have no idea of the con[-] ditions. Why, it is still summer, probably the hottest month of the year, and. . [."] He stopped, closed his eyes for a moment, and agitatedly ran his hand throug[h] his hair.

"Adam, I was just about to tell you why it is urgent that we waste no tim[e] reaching John."

There must have been something in her voice that brought his head up. Sh[e] looked from him to his friends, who were watching them curiously. Her eyes lin[-] gered for a moment on the native stockman. He was watching them from beneat[h] his dark hat with a stillness about him that intrigued her.

She looked back at Adam and lowered her voice. "The last time I met the lawyers, I was told that Percival had flown into an absolute fury when told about John's claims and made all kinds of threats against him."

"I know."

"You know! You. . .and you never mentioned it?"

"Neither did you," he said shortly. "When you did not say anything, I was not sure whether you knew, and then I reasoned you already had enough to worry about anyway."

She looked at him steadily. "Do you also know that when Mr. Blanders, Father's lawyer, came to bid us farewell at the ship he hurriedly warned me that he had just heard that Percival had already sailed on a ship bound for Sydney a few weeks before us? Mr. Blanders was very worried."

Surprise and sudden anxiety flooded Adam's steady gaze. "No, I did not know that," he said sharply.

She hesitated, glanced quickly at the group of men around Mr. Gordon and Jim who had withdrawn a little distance, and then added swiftly, "He seemed to feel there was a need to. . .to warn John and keep him safe."

"Why didn't you tell me?"

Again she hesitated. "I. . .he. . .Percival is my cousin. I have known him all my life, and I did not want to think of what they. . .they think he may be capable of. Oh, Adam, I just think we should not delay at all in finding John and warning him. Being a. . .a convict he is so. . .so extra vulnerable."

They stared at each other.

"Now then, you two wouldn't be talkin' about John Martin, would you?" Mr. Gordon had turned around from a low discussion with his son. He tipped his hat to the back of his head and exchanged a frowning glance with young Jim.

"Yes," Adam said briefly. "Miss Farnley here thinks she may be related to him. It is a connection only recently discovered, and it is urgent that we find out."

Keen gray eyes swept over Kate. "Reckon there is a resemblance at that. The same blue eyes, even the way you look directly at a man." Mr. Gordon nodded slowly. "And I reckon the young lady is right, Adam."

"What do you mean?" Adam said tersely.

"Well," the older man drawled, "apparently not long after you sailed for England, John Martin sought refuge at our place. He was beat up bad. It were only awhile before we left on our travels, but it seemed he'd been posted as an escaped convict, and the troopers were out after him. When I saw him last, he was hightailin' it back to Stevens Downs only a few steps ahead of them. He should be all right because Elizabeth Waverley was with him, but before we left, we hadn't heard if he made it."

Kate felt faint. She swayed, and Adam's hand reached out to steady her.

"John, an escaped convict? But. . .but what will they do to him if. . .if they catch him?"

Before Adam or his father could stop him, young Jim said thoughtfully, "If the troopers don't shoot him, he could be hung or sent to some rotten place like Norfolk Island or Van Dieman's Land."

Kate stared from one grim face to the other. She had heard dreadful stories about the harsh treatment of convicts in those places.

Mr. Gordon nodded solemnly again. "So, I reckon the young lady's right. According to John, a Lieutenant Edwards, who had badly mistreated him aboard ship had ambushed him, burned his papers, and given John the impression he was determined to have him hung. He thought all he could do was return to where he had been assigned to work, Stevens Downs."

He scowled. "We all liked that young man." He paused and then drawled what Adam was already frantically thinking. "Guess you'd be best not to waste any time getting back home, Adam, my friend, if you want to help John Martin. Especially as he was assigned to you."

Chapter 7

Y ou must leave without delay," William said grimly, "and we will just trust
God to give you safe passage."

"But what about you three?" Kate said, turning to look at her sister. "Are
you sure you will be all right?" Beth's baby would undoubtedly be born within the
next month, making it necessary for her sister and her family to be left behind. Mr.
Gordon had warned them the journey could take any time between six to nine weeks.

"And that is if everything goes smoothly, mind," he had added a trifle grimly,
eyeing Kate's slim body with perturbation. He obviously had doubts about this
gently reared, English lady's stamina.

Kate opened her mouth, but before she could force words past the huge lump
that seemed to have settled in her throat, Beth intervened, a suddenly fully mature
Beth, who smiled gently at her husband and the pale, grim Adam before taking
Kate's arm and moving a short distance away from the two men.

"I'll be fine, Kate, Love. God is our refuge and strength, and we are all in His
hands," she said softly. "There is much ministry He has for William and me to do
here." Lovingly she reached up and touched Kate's cheek with the back of her hand.
"We will all trust Him to protect and give us His loving care—no matter what."

Kate stared at her younger sister, who suddenly seemed so much older than
herself in wisdom and faith. "I have to go, Beth," she whispered desperately.

"I know, Love, I know," Beth murmured softly. There was a woman's understanding in her eyes. She looked swiftly back at Adam and then at William. There
was a light, a peace on her face Kate had never seen before.

"And I do understand it is not just because of John. I must stay, and you must
go—with Adam," Beth added firmly. "Believe me, I know how it is."

Kate stared at her dumbly. Beth knew. Knew that her sister was in love with
Adam, probably had known even before she had acknowledged it herself. There
was no censure in Beth's face, just acceptance of a woman's love, a woman's pain.
But would there still be no censure if she knew Adam had been a convict?

Then they were embracing each other, and as they held each other tightly for
a long moment, Beth whispered ever so softly, "No matter what objections he
makes, what obstacles he throws up, no matter what anyone says, don't let this
man get away!"

They stared at each other for a long moment through damp eyes. Then at long
last, Beth's lips twitched and her eyes danced. She added naughtily, "Whatever
would Father say?"

Despite the pang that swept through her, Kate's smile blossomed to a chuckle at the reminder of their old nanny's favorite saying. "Years ago, he would probably have applauded our courage and pioneer spirit, but then. . ."

Her smile disappeared, and she faltered to a stop as she thought suddenly of the young man their father must have been when he had fallen so deeply in love with a Spanish señorita and married her, not caring what his aristocratic family would think.

Beth nodded, her expression suddenly bleak. "He did change these last couple of years, though, didn't he?"

It had been their father's own attitude to herself that Kate was thinking of, but she said swiftly, "He loved your mother very much."

"Yes, I know." Beth was silent for a moment and then said strangely, "Kate, when you find John, would you tell him. . . ?" She took a deep breath and finished in a rush, "Please, don't ask me why, but tell him I am truly sorry for. . .for everything, and I hope and pray everything works out for him."

There was no time for any more private words, because there was so much to do before dark. Adam had enlisted William's help in looking after the remainder of their things and arranging for the rest of his equipment to be shipped on the first available vessel.

The Gordons were keen to get away early the next morning, and Adam had worked hard to arrange for horses and supplies. There were only a very few horses in the colony as yet, but they managed to buy from a hollow-eyed, desperately poor young couple.

Will Gordon muttered to Kate, "Trust that Adam to pay far more than any horse is worth." Then he shrugged. "But if that isn't just like the man!"

Kate beamed at him with delight. He gave her a wry, quizzical look in return that brought the heat to her cheeks. She also knew Adam had quietly mentioned the young couple to William and that William and Beth would start their work in this small colony with the needy couple.

Kate found out that the dray mentioned by Jim was simply a large cart drawn by two horses. "Anything bigger and heavier would have held us up, made the trip longer," she was told.

Kate and Adam had been assured that the horse-drawn cart could easily take their belongings and food as well as the barrels for water and sufficient supplies to last many weeks.

"As long as you bring the very bare essentials, Miss Kate," the friendly Will Gordon said sternly but still with that disconcerting twinkle in his eyes when he looked from Adam to herself.

There had been one last private word with Will Gordon before he had left them to return to his own camp that night. For once the twinkle had been absent. "I'll be sending some clothes for you to wear, Miss, and make sure you put them on no matter what anyone else says, you hear?"

She had been consumed with curiosity until Jim had arrived and thrust a bundle into her arms before smiling his shy grin and striding away. With something between horror, excitement, and amusement, she unwrapped two pairs of men's trousers and a wide-brimmed hat. To her added amusement, the trousers fit very well, and before sunrise the next morning, she presented herself to Beth with only a slight blush staining her cheeks.

Beth's eyes widened. "Kate, you can't wear those!"

"Of course I can," she responded brightly. "It seems that I will have to ride most of the way, and obviously Mr. Gordon has decided there is no way I can ride sidesaddle for that distance. I only brought the one divided skirt, and even its skirt is rather full and could be a real nuisance in rough terrain. Besides," she grinned impishly as she looked down at herself, "I think I rather like them."

By the way Adam's eyes flared and the way he stared speechlessly at her for a long moment, she thought he did also. Somewhat to her chagrin he made no comment—just nodded abrupt approval and busied himself with their horses. Apparently he had known beforehand about the trousers, because he had already put an ordinary saddle on her rather spirited but sturdy horse.

Beth, William, and even young Harold waved to them until they were out of sight. Kate brushed a few tears away surreptitiously, hoping Adam had not seen them. She was suddenly aware it could be a long time before she saw their dear faces again.

🦋

But Adam had seen, and although he longed to offer her comfort, he knew he dare not. The only chaperone Kate had was Judy Brown, who was responsible for all their meals, and he knew that he had to exercise all the restraint he could call upon not to give any hint of his increasing love for Kate or compromise her in any way. When this was all ended, she still would be the daughter of the late Lord Farnley with a reputation to guard carefully if she was to have any prosperous and happy future.

That first night when they at last stopped to set up camp, Adam, Will, and Jim were well satisfied with the ground they had covered. They had hoped to cover from twenty to twenty-five miles a day, and Adam knew Will Gordon was very relieved that Kate had kept up well, proving to be as competent a rider as she had assured them.

There had been a courageous, stubborn tilt to her chin the day before when she had told them she had practically been born in the saddle. There had also been such a look of determination at the slightest hint of leaving her behind that it had made him want to gather her up in his arms and keep her safe against all the dangers that could ever be. Instead, he had turned away without a word and tried to forget the dangers she would encounter.

As he dismounted beneath a towering gum tree, he looked across at Kate and saw her suddenly reel as she stepped away from her horse. He rushed to support her, angry with himself that he had not called a halt sooner. No matter how strong she was, this had been a grueling first day for all of them.

"I. . .feel like my legs are made of. . .jelly," she gasped.

He was horrified at the exhausted, gray tinge on her face, but without a word, he helped her to a fallen log, carefully searching the area to make sure it was not the home of some undesirable creatures of the bush.

"Stay there while we make camp," he ordered, and was relieved when she nodded and closed her eyes. Worry filled his heart because he knew she was so weary it would have been impossible for her to do anything else, and there were many more days and weeks to go.

When the men were caring for the horses together, he managed to have a quiet word with Will Gordon about taking it easier the next day.

Will shook his head. "We have to push through this country as fast as we can. I was told that the natives east of Adelaide and along the Murray are gradually becoming more unfriendly."

Adam looked swiftly around at the shadows of the bush. "You think they could attack us? Why didn't you tell me, Man!" he exploded. "I would never have let Miss Farnley come with us, no matter what she said."

"Now, now, I wouldn't have come meself if I thought the danger was too bad. But they have been starting to take some stock from the settlers at the edges of the town, and most owners can't understand that the natives don't see any reason why they shouldn't kill a sheep or bullock here and there to eat. After all, the animals are eating the grass on their lands. From what I've been told, I reckon there'll be bad bloodshed if things don't improve," Will said grimly.

He hesitated and then added, "And you might as well know that along the Murray River, I've heard tell a few things about the way the drovers and drifters have been treating the natives, especially their women. Their men can't be expected to stand for that too long. I'm not really expecting any trouble, but we'll certainly be setting a watch every night."

Nothing disturbed their rest that first night, and Adam was relieved that Kate, despite walking stiffly at first, seemed to have recovered considerably by the time they mounted their horses again at first light. She was obviously enraptured by her first sight of a mob of kangaroos grazing in the cool morning and pelted him with questions about other Australian animals they could encounter.

He did not want her to be unduly alarmed, but he should have known her quick intelligence would soon spot their watchful eyes during the day as they searched the bush for any sign of the original inhabitants of the land.

"What's wrong, Adam?" she asked during a moment when they were sitting by themselves after supper the next evening. "You men have been very careful to keep your rifles in your hands all day, and I noticed that Mr. Gordon has set you men to take it in turn to guard us each night."

He looked at her steadily and then sighed. It was best she knew so she would take care. He repeated all that Will had told him, adding quietly, "I won't let anything happen to you, my dear Kate, if it is humanly possible."

Kate watched the shadow that crossed his face before he looked away. Suddenly she longed to reach out to him, to hold him tightly, but she only allowed herself to touch his hand as she said simply, "I know you will, Adam. And, Adam. . ." She waited until he looked inquiringly up at her. "Beth reminded me we are in God's hands. Nothing will happen to us that He will not permit."

He turned his hand over and clasped her fingers convulsively. "I could not bear it if you were hurt. . .if you were. . ."

"Hush," she comforted him, holding his hand in both of hers. "Of course you could, as I would have to if anything happened to you. God would bear it with us, and even if we were to die, we would just go to be with Him," she added with a little smile.

They stared into each other's eyes for a long moment before reluctantly letting their hands drop and looking away.

As Kate stared across the campfire, she noticed the dark figure of Jackie not very far away in the shadows, sitting cross-legged and motionless, staring into the fire. Suddenly she wondered how much of their conversation he had heard and understood.

All the next day, a warm glow encompassed Kate despite her aching body. Adam still avoided her glance, but a deep well inside her was singing. He cared for her. She even thought he might love her.

That night as they all relaxed around the campfire, Bob Brown produced a battered tin whistle. Kate thoroughly enjoyed the ditties that were heartily roared out. Even Jackie seemed to enjoy these white men's songs, a rare smile crossing his face as he looked from one to the other.

Then Bob looked at his wife and started very softly to play something else. She smiled and nodded, and then to Kate's surprise and delight sang in a clear, beautiful voice a song of Old England that brought tears to the eye and a lump in the throat.

"That was very beautiful, Judy. Thank you," Kate said with a choked voice.

Judy nodded and stared consideringly at Kate. Then, while the others were still murmuring their appreciation, she started singing again. Soon nearly all of them were joining her in the words, "Guide me, O Thou great Jehovah, pilgrim through this barren land."

Kate sang along with the rest. Their voices were subdued to start with but rose in exultation of the God who cared enough to guide and lead them on their journey, and "to bid my anxious fears subside."

Even as their voices rang out into the silent bush, Kate knew that whenever she again sang that hymn, she would remember the vast starry heavens above, the dying glow of the fire, and the shining faces reflected in its light. God was very near, and afterward she slept through the night as a child secure in her Father's arms.

The days and then the weeks slipped by and began to blur into times when they rode carefully through heavily timbered country, times when they took turns to ride in the cart to rest the horses, times when mobs of kangaroos bounded away from their intrusion into their grazing land, times when they had to find the safest place to cross flowing rivers and trickling creeks, and times when they camped and enjoyed more singing.

Kate discovered that although Judy Brown presented a rough exterior, she was really very shy, and it was not until after that first night's singing that she relaxed with Kate, and the two women became friends. It was just as well, because they had to share much together, including the camp cooking, which Kate insisted on helping with. Then of course there was their bathing, with each woman taking turns to stand guard with a rifle in hand while the other washed in a small basin or, on a couple occasions, immersed herself in a cool stream.

Will Gordon continued to be very pleased with the time they were making, saying that if they could keep it up, the journey would only take six to seven weeks.

The men reported a few times that they had seen evidence that aborigines were in the area they traversed, but none were spotted. For some time they had kept fairly close to the mighty Murray River, but the day came when they started heading northeast. The sun beat down on them from a merciless blue sky as they traveled as swiftly as their tired horses allowed across seemingly endless plains. Only twice did they meet up with fellow travelers who told them that farther north it was very dry and to be careful to fill their water barrels whenever possible.

Kate was fascinated by the spirals of red dust that they occasionally saw sweep over the dried-out grasses. Judy called them "willy-willies," and they were not at all pleasant when they whirled around them, the grit and dirt getting into eyes and mouths of humans and horses alike.

Despite her broad-brimmed hat, Kate became sunburned, and then her skin turned a golden brown. One day as Adam reined his horse to a walk beside her, he mourned, "Your English peaches and cream have gone. Why, you are as brown as a berry. I don't know what Beth will say."

Her laugh rang out, and she studied her brown hand. "Oh, Beth will probably get as brown as a berry too, especially after the baby is born." Her smile disappeared. "She may have even had the baby by now. I do hope and pray everything goes well with her," she murmured softly but not so low that Adam did not hear.

"I'm sure it will," he said quickly. "I had a quiet word with a Dr. Woodforde and asked him to keep a very close eye on her."

"Oh, that was kind of you, Adam. Dr. Woodforde? Oh, I think I did hear someone on the ship mention that a colonial surgeon had been appointed to the colony."

"That was Dr. Thomas Cotter, I believe. There are at least two doctors there, so I am sure she will have every care."

Kate smiled at him gently. He grinned across at her and then looked over her shoulder. His expression altered. That morning the grassy plains had given way to low, rolling hills with scattered trees and low scrub.

"Kate, aborigines only a hundred yards away. There, watching us from those trees. Dig in your heels." His voice was sharp.

She gaped at him and swung around. Several aborigines were standing motionless, watching them from the shadows cast by a tall gum tree. Some held long spears.

"Kate!"

Adam slapped the rump of her tired horse, and it took off in a canter. She was relieved to hear Adam following close behind her.

It was Bob and Judy Brown's turn in the cart. They had been walking their horses a little behind the cart, with the others strung out in front of it. Bob heard the clatter of their horses, looked back, and then shook the reins of the two horses pulling the cart so the animals were running swiftly by the time Adam and Kate drew level with him.

"A large number of aborigines were standing watching us from among those trees!" Adam shouted. "We'd better make sure we stay together and alert the others."

Kate risked a look behind them and saw nothing, but she was relieved when they drew level with the others. They all drew rein, turned, and looked back.

"A big group of natives were watching us from those trees," Adam reported tersely.

"Didn't you see them, Jackie?" Mr. Gordon asked sternly. "Why didn't you warn us?"

Jackie's eyes returned from searching out the shadows of the trees. He tilted back his large-brimmed hat and shrugged. His eyes darted from one white face to another.

"I sure seed them okay, all right, and picaninnies. This country Wiradjuri country, Boss; but them fella's Wembawemba, sure 'nough."

"Picaninnies?" a wide-eyed Kate whispered to Adam.

"Children," he murmured, his eyes still looking back, searching to see if they had been followed.

Will Gordon was frowning. "Wembawemba people. But didn't you tell us on our way south they were the tribes along the Murray? Isn't this too far north for them?"

Jackie nodded vigorously. "It very dry there," he said abruptly. He darted a quick look at both women and then scowled fiercely, his eyes returning to sweep over the countryside. "Sure 'nough we camp long way from here tonight."

He turned and started his horse quickly forward once more. The others looked at each other.

At last, Bob Brown drawled quietly, "Jackie is Wiradjuri. I'd say them two tribes ain't speakin'."

Adam looked toward the west at the sun now close to the distant horizon. "Then we'd better do as he said and put as much space as we can between us and the Wembawemba before dark."

The horses were weary from their weeks of traveling. It seemed cruel to push them as hard as they did the next hour or so. When darkness fell and they at last drew rein beside a small creek, the horses' sides were heaving, froth blowing from around their bits.

"Where's Jackie disappeared to? I wondered when I employed him in Bathurst if we could trust him." Will Gordon looked around and was grim-faced as he turned to Adam and Kate. "There's something going on here he's not telling. I'd much rather we slept in the open tonight, and we'd better make sure we keep a good watch on our horses and supplies."

There was no singing that night, and the fire blazed brightly. Only the bare minimum was unloaded from the cart in case they had to make a rapid departure. For a long time, Kate could not sleep. She only realized she must have dozed off when she woke to a strange sound drifting across the land.

She sat bolt upright and looked fearfully around. Two dark shadows she quickly recognized to be Adam and Will were standing well away from the light of the still-burning fire and peering into the distance. Even as she scrambled to her feet, the others joined them. It was a hot night, even warmer than usual, but Kate shivered as she walked quickly across to stand beside Adam.

Adam turned swiftly and slipped an arm around her shoulders.

"What is it?" she faltered. "What's that sound?"

"Will says some kind of corroboree, the natives' dance," Adam whispered. "Listen."

On the still night air came the eerie sound of chanting, singing, and sticks being beaten against sticks. Somehow it was a mournful sound, a sound as old as time itself.

"Well, I reckon at least we know where they are," Jim said quietly.

His father grunted agreement and then asked, "Anyone seen Jackie at all yet?"

Kate noticed a movement in the shadows nearby, and she gasped in fright. Adam swung her around and put his body in front of her as a tall, dark figure moved lightly forward.

🦋

"Jackie here, *gabaa*," a guttural voice murmured.

Adam stiffened. He did not like that. The native stockman had used the aboriginal word for white man almost insolently. And he had discarded his shirt and hat. "Where have you been?" Adam asked angrily. "Are the Wembawemba going to attack us?"

"*Wirraay*."

Adam relaxed slightly. "Good."

"You understand what he said?" barked Will.

"He said no," Adam answered shortly, still watching Jackie.

"Them Wembawemba *wirraay marrambang.*"

Adam shook his head. "Sorry, Jackie, I only know a few words of your language."

There was silence. In only slightly accented English, Jackie said mockingly, "And you are to be commended for that, Sir. Not many white men have made the effort you must have to learn our words."

Adam heard Kate gasp in surprise, but he found himself unexpectedly relaxing. He had known for days that there was something very different about this aborigine.

Jackie gave a low chuckle. "So, I know many of yours, white man, from the mission school. I said, Mr. Stevens, that those aborigines are without much goodness. However, I do not think you need worry. There is sickness among them as often happens when they have contact with white men. They are just resting on their return home to the south and now mourning their dead."

Chapter 8

No one moved or spoke. Kate stared in astonishment and then a little apprehensively at the others, wondering how they would take Jackie's deception.

Will Gordon had been staring at his stockman with his mouth open. Suddenly he let out a roar of laughter. He moved forward and slapped Jackie's broad shoulder. "For cryin' out loud! You bin holdin' out on us. Hardly ever speaks so we don't know how much he understands and now. . .speaks English better than many Englishmen."

Bluey called out in his dry drawl, "Next thing, reckon you'll want him to teach you how to talk proper, Boss."

Everyone was grinning, and the tension dissolved. Jackie did not smile; he just looked from one to the other with his dark, watchful eyes. Kate thought he might be pleased, but then he nodded and shrugged off the large hand on his body.

She saw Adam's eyes narrow and wondered what he was thinking.

🦋

Adam was wondering what kind of upbringing this young aborigine had been given. He had practically no accent and so must have been reared among whites as a child. It was doubtful if he had even reached twenty years yet.

Jackie continued to look at them each in turn. Then suddenly he grinned cheekily before turning and disappearing into the darkness again without a word.

They stared after him, and after a few more laughing comments, the others dispersed.

"He said there was sickness. . . ."

Adam turned toward Kate and sighed at her wide, compassionate eyes. He knew what she was going to add even as she went on.

"Shouldn't we try to help them, Adam?"

"You are a nice white woman, Miss Farnley," a low voice said from the darkness, "but there is very little you can do for my people when they get measles. Many of them have died already, and now it seems no one new has the sickness. Some more will die. Some will live."

There was a faint rustle, the soft pad of feet retreating—then silence.

Adam had heard her gasp at the stark statement and saw her hand go to her mouth.

"Unfortunately Jackie is right, my dear," he said wearily at last. "The aborigines have no resistance to our diseases. Many of them have died from our most common illnesses. Even if we had medicines, there would be little any of us could do except pray for them."

❦

Later the next morning, with the subdued team well on their way, Kate managed to coax Jackie to ride beside her and tell her about himself. He was very reluctant at first, but she managed to get a rather sad picture of a boy growing into adulthood lost between two cultures.

Apparently, when he had been a very small boy, Jackie's mother had taken him to a white couple near Lake Macquarie. They had been trying to improve the spiritual and physical well-being of the aborigines in the area.

"She was sick. They were good people and looked after her, but she died. I can barely remember her, and they could only guess why she had gone to them and not her own people," Jackie said without expression. "More recently I've found out that she was ostracized by the other aboriginal women because my father was not of their clan. He was Wiradjuri. I never found out how they met or why he was not there. He may even have stolen her away from her people, and she may later have escaped back to the coast."

He was silent for awhile and then said softly, "Since coming here, I have found it very easy to learn the Wiradjuri language, which makes me think my father must have been there with his words when I was too young to remember him."

Or you are a very clever young man, was Kate's immediate thought. They let their horses pick their way through the low grass in silence, and then Kate said softly, "It must have been hard growing up away from your own people."

He studied her for a long moment and at last said, "After my mother died those good white people fed, clothed, and taught me, even loved me in their own way. But it was hard being a black boy growing up with whites, especially when my father was of the Wiradjuri people from beyond the mountains. As Mr. Gordon told you, the people where I grew up are the Awabakal."

He was silent for some time but at last said, "No aborigines ever came forward to claim me, even if at least they, unlike the whites, did understand how sad it made me that I barely knew my people's ways. I have come west to learn my father's language and try to find some news of him or his family."

That night, Kate told Adam what Jackie had said. "Apparently," she concluded, "he behaved as he has and hasn't told anyone at the Gordons' because everywhere else he's been, no one would employ an aborigine who had obviously been so well educated. They always said they could not trust him. Other aborigines also ostracized him once his upbringing was discovered. It is so unfair," she finished fiercely.

After a long moment, Adam said sadly, "Too many parents think they know what is best for their children, when all the children really want is to know, no matter what circumstances they may be reared in, that they are wanted and loved."

Kate looked at him and turned quickly away. "That is true whether you live in an English lord's home or in a native wurley, as Jackie said their bush homes are called."

Adam was silent and still. At last she heard him sigh and then scramble to his feet. She lifted her head but could not see his expression before he turned and walked away from the firelight and into the darkness of the bush.

The next morning Jackie reported that the natives had disappeared, probably heading south away from them. Several times after that day, Jackie reported that aborigines were in their immediate area. But they were rarely seen, seeming only too happy to keep well away from the heavily armed, large number of white men, fading rapidly away into the bush at their approach.

One evening, just after the sun had set and they had traversed a long flat stretch of country, they reached the line of trees they had rightly thought must follow the banks of a stream and with dismay found quite a large camp of aborigines already there.

Because it would be dark very quickly after the sun disappeared below the distant, western horizon—something Kate was still getting used to in this country—Jackie immediately became their spokesman and approached the men, who had quickly gathered their spears and stood silently studying them. After a lengthy discussion he returned, able to report that the old man who was their leader, or *"gaiyanaiyung"* as Jackie called him, was happy for them to camp a little farther upstream.

After Jackie had helped them all in their usual tasks of setting up camp, collecting firewood, erecting the tent for the two women and the bedrolls in and under the dray for the rest of them, he disappeared.

"They are Wiradjuri, and it's my guess he would be trying to find his father's people," murmured Adam to Kate as they sat alone for a few rare moments after their evening meal while the others were busy clearing up. "He was certainly speaking Wiradjuri, and although I only know a few of their words, I heard him say their word for father."

Kate said wearily, "As long as they let us sleep undisturbed, I don't really care anymore."

🦋

Adam stared anxiously at her white face. Very rarely had she admitted to being tired, and to do so tonight meant she was exhausted. Like all of them, her clothes were filthy dirty and becoming tattered. They had rarely stayed long enough near running water to have the luxury of washing their clothes.

Her cheekbones were more visible, her eyes more sunken. With a little shock, he suddenly realized how much weight she had lost these last few grueling weeks. And after the sea voyage, she had been thin enough to start with.

She started to rise to go and help Judy clean their rough, basic cooking utensils in which they had boiled the last of the meat from the kangaroo the men had managed to shoot the day before. Adam knew that she did not like the strong-flavored meat, despite the skill Judy had developed over the years of disguising its taste with her herbs and spices. He had refrained from expressing his concern at the small amount he knew Kate had forced down.

Adam hesitated and then said gently, "You're exhausted, Katie, my love. Judy won't mind doing it all tonight. Look, Bob has gone to help her. Let us rest here for awhile. There's something we need to talk about."

She looked at him inquiringly but relaxed again on the blanket spread on the ground. "That's the very first time you've called me that," she whispered.

He raised an eyebrow in question. The first week of their journey he had at last relented about using her first name because she had become Kate to everyone else.

She responded softly, "My love."

He stiffened, and then after a long silence he smiled at her. "I always call you that to myself," he murmured.

She smiled back, and they looked at each other for a long moment. He suddenly moved closer and took her hand.

They were silent, content just to be together until she said dreamily, "This is nice, isn't it? We haven't had much time just by ourselves."

Her hand seemed so small and fragile in his, and Adam longed to pull her closer, to wrap his arms around her as he had dreamed each evening of doing. Instead, he sat still, savoring the moment until at last he reluctantly spoke, sorry to have to spoil the moment between them.

"Kate, we are fairly close now to the Gordons' property near Bathurst, but Will has offered to accompany us on to Stevens Downs. I agreed to that this morning, but you are worn-out, and I think perhaps we should go to Bathurst where you can recover. I could travel on and bring John back to you."

He hoped she would not ask why they had made that decision. Jackie had told the men that he knew more and more aborigines throughout the country were angry at the invasion of their lands. Many whites had not listened or understood about the sacred grounds. Too many forbidden areas had been violated, their hunting grounds damaged. Their people were suffering, and the realization was sinking in that they were being pushed farther west, away from their traditional tribal areas, with no sign of the white man's thirst for grazing and farmland abating.

Besides, for some strange reason, as each day had passed this last week, something was telling Adam that it was urgent he get to John. The more concerned he had become, the more he had been praying for direction. The answer had been strong. They had to reach John as quickly as possible.

So he and Will had discussed splitting up, but in the end they decided that it would be much safer for all eight of them to stay together. Although Adam knew he had been very careful to deal as fairly as he could with the local tribes who wandered over his grazing land, he had been away a long time, and he knew things could have changed. There was also an increase in the number of holdups from bushrangers, usually escaped convicts or desperate men wanted by the police. It was not worth the risk.

"How far are we from Bathurst?"

At her quiet question, Adam turned from staring into the leaping flames of the campfire. "About ninety miles, Will and Jim think," he answered softly. "But it is harder going in places as we head east into the mountains. We would be fortunate to make our twenty miles a day with the cart on the narrow trails."

"And to your home?"

A pang shot through Adam. Home? Was Stevens Downs really his home? Certainly in England's green countryside and through its cold he had longed for the sunlit plains of Stevens Downs. Perhaps he had not been there long enough for it to seem like home. He had worked too hard in the heat and the dust, the flies and the primitive conditions for it to be a real home.

Maybe after he had lived there a few more years, after he had built a decent homestead, after he had a wife waiting for him each night after a hard day. . .

"Adam?" Kate was watching him, her brow slightly creased with a frown.

Suddenly he knew, as never before, that home would always be where this courageous, loving woman was. He swallowed to try and dislodge the lump that seemed to be squeezing his vocal cords, but his voice was still hoarse as he said at last, "Oh, Stevens Downs is farther north, about double the distance from here to Bathurst."

She was silent for a long moment. He was content to watch her thinking about what he had said and waited patiently for her response.

"Then you would have to travel east over these mountains, and then cross them again to. . .no, it would take too long, far too long!"

She was silent for a moment, searching his face, and then burst out, "Oh, Adam, these last few days I have had such strange forebodings. After all this time, Percival must surely have found John. Lately I have not been able to stop thinking of them. I think God is telling us to hurry."

"You have felt it too," he exclaimed.

They stared at each other in wonder, and then she said hurriedly, "At first, a few days ago when I found my thoughts constantly going to John, I just thought it must be because we were getting closer. But then, every time I thought of him, I thought of Percival, and. . .and, oh, I have been getting more and more worried and praying harder each day that God will keep John safe."

"Me too," Adam said simply. He hesitated and said a little diffidently, "Kate, we have not yet prayed together. Would you mind. . . ?"

"Oh, yes, please, Adam," she said fervently.

Their hands joined tightly together, and it seemed so natural to pray together. They took turns praying, simply talking to God as their heavenly Father. To Him who loved them they poured out their hearts, their concern, their pleas for John's safety and their own.

🦋

Neither saw the dark shadow that approached them through the trees, that stood watching as they prayed out loud. Then, as they were saying their "Amens," he pulled his dusty hat down more firmly over his tight black curls before slipping slowly back into the bush as if he were one with the night.

Jackie respected and liked all these white men he had traveled with on such a long journey. But especially did he like and admire this red-haired woman who never failed to smile at him and thank him even at the end of a hard day's riding. And this white man was different from so many others. He had cared enough to learn some of the Wiradjuri language.

Jackie silently moved away, wondering about these two people who were always kind to him, treated him as an equal, and now had prayed to their God just the same as the two white people had who had taken him into their home and treated him like their own son.

He sighed, feeling confused. He had been taught about the white man's God for so many years. But he had learned also that there were very few like his foster parents who really believed in Him, who seemed to think very much about their God at all unless they were in dire straits. They never seemed to let Him make any difference in their lives.

Since he had struck out on his own, he had been learning much about his own people's beliefs, about their Dreaming and regard for the land. They had a depth of spirituality that appealed to him immensely, that reached out to his lonely heart.

But. . .he still envied the peace and happiness that their God had seemed to bring to that man and woman as they talked to Him.

🦋

The farther north the group traveled the next few days, the drier the countryside became. In some places, especially on the black soil plains, large cracks in the ground meant they had to be extra careful their horses did not stumble. Any grasses that had survived the searing heat and lack of rain were merely stubble that crumbled under the horses' hooves.

Then there were acres of bare dirt among drooping, even dying, clumps of trees. Whenever a hot, dry wind sprang up, red or black dust covered everyone in clouds.

It seemed to Kate that with each mile Adam's face became a little more grim and drawn. Then one night, the creek they camped beside was bone-dry. Jackie showed them how and where to dig until water to drink seeped into the sandy hole. The next morning there was barely enough for them to water the horses, certainly not enough to wash in.

Kate rode silently beside Adam for a long time after they left the campsite. She was worried. What if they could find no water this day either? The barrels on the cart for just such an emergency were almost empty.

Their horses' hooves kicked up dust with every step. Only a few scattered clumps of dead grass had survived on the vast plain they started across. On the northern horizon was a faint smudge that danced in the shimmering haze. It grew in size very slowly as they advanced.

"It's the gum trees along the Macquarie River," Adam told her abruptly in answer to her soft query.

After another long silence, Kate plucked up the courage to ask, "How much longer before we reach your station, Adam?"

"We've been on Stevens Downs for the last few hours. The buildings are under those gum trees in the distance, not far from the riverbanks."

His voice was expressionless. Kate's eyes widened in surprise and also immense relief. So this was their last day. Why had he not said anything? Then she looked at the parched earth and had her answer.

After another long pause she said quietly, "It's very dry."

"Yes."

There was so much pain and anger in his sharp, solitary word that she was silenced. The rest of their party were strung out in a long line behind them. They were all exhausted, the horses thin and weary. She knew Adam's friends would be far more aware than she how devastating this drought must be.

They walked their horses without speaking for some time before Adam at last broke the silence. She could hear the anguish in his voice as he said, "I didn't want you to see it like this. The last time I was out here it was a sea of grass, and several thousand fat sheep grazed. It looks as though there has not been a drop of rain since I left."

"Where. . . ?" Kate swallowed and asked huskily, "Where would all the sheep be now then?"

"If they are still alive, hopefully on pastures nearer the river and the homestead," Adam replied grimly.

Kate thought of that dry creek bed and others they had crossed. She bit her lip. Adam had told her once that even rivers in this strange country could become dry, or even just a series of water holes. If the river was also dry. . .

She glanced at his pale face and watched as his dark eyes swept around the heartbreaking landscape. Suddenly he turned his horse and cantered to the right.

Without thinking she followed, then stopped in horror at what he was walking his horse among—the carcasses of several dead sheep. The stench reached her even as she heard the hum of blowflies. Sickened, she spurred her horse some distance away before stopping and watching Adam.

He rode on a little farther before rejoining her. His hat was pulled so far down over his forehead she could no longer see his eyes.

"I'm. . .I'm sorry, Adam," she faltered.

He grunted and said abruptly, "At least there were only about half a dozen, probably the weakest of the flock. They had been shot, probably when moving the mob to the river. Hopefully that is a good sign that Timothy and John. . ."

He stopped abruptly, but Kate heard the strain in his voice and refrained from commenting. He suddenly kicked his horse into a slow canter, and she followed him, knowing that nothing she could say would ease his fears.

Could this drought mean the end of his dreams, even with his uncle's inheritance?

As she had already learned many times during the last few weeks, distances could be very deceptive, on the plains especially. It took much longer than she had expected; it was well past midday before they were close enough to see the buildings nestled among the trees.

Suddenly Adam gave a low, amazed whistle. "Why, John and Timothy have been busy putting up more buildings. Now I wonder. . ."

She glanced across at him and then peered at the small settlement. There were at least two dwellings made out of roughly cut timber with bark and logs for roofs. What looked like one large shed was next to some fenced yards some distance from the houses.

Adam suddenly kicked his horse into a canter. She hesitated but then stopped and waited for the others. It would be best for him to meet his friends first before they all descended on them. Will and Jackie also seemed to think it was good manners and soon reined their horses into a slow walk beside her.

But when Adam pulled his running horse to a stop in front of one of the huts, they were close enough to see a woman leave the larger building next to it and advance a few steps toward him. They all saw what she had in her hands at the same time.

"What in the. . . ?"

Will gave a shout and kicked his tired horse into a startled gallop. Kate did also, and soon they were all flying across the ground to where a small, stout woman had a rifle leveled at Adam's back.

Chapter 9

Will gave an even louder shout of warning.

Adam swung around and saw the woman advancing on him with the rifle held steadily in front of her. Kate saw him staring at her in amazement.

As the rest of the travelers rushed nearer, the woman took a couple steps back and yelled in a firm voice, "Keep back, or this bloke gets it."

They pulled to a plunging stop, but Kate noticed that Will had taken his rifle from its saddle sheath and held it out of sight of the woman.

"Now, who are you, and what do you want?" the woman called loudly.

"What I want is for you to stop being ridiculous and put that gun away, Madam. By the look of you I'd say you must be Mrs. Hardy. Trust Timothy to have such a suspicious woman for a wife!"

To Kate's surprise, she heard laughter in Adam's loud voice. Almost simultaneously, a mighty roar came from the doorway of the hut. "Adam? It's you, Adam Stevens? Oh, God be praised. He's brought you home safe and sound, Man!"

Adam leaped from his horse. Ignoring the woman, he pushed past her and bounded up the steps toward the small, thin man who had appeared in the doorway.

"Timothy, you old rogue, what a welcome! To set your missus onto me with a—Tim!"

As Kate heard his voice change, she saw the small man slump against the doorpost. Adam's arms went out and caught him as he started to topple over.

Kate jumped from her horse, tossed the reins to Will, and raced forward.

"Oh, Timothy, I told you to stay on that bed," the woman wailed, then raced up the steps as Adam helped Timothy into the house.

When Kate burst through the doorway, Adam and the woman were just easing Timothy onto a chair. The woman looked up at her with a scowl, but then she stared. A look of astonishment swept over her face. Her gaze moved disapprovingly over Kate from her tangled, filthy hair under her dusty, wide-brimmed hat to her tattered trousers and worn riding boots.

"You're a woman!" she exclaimed in a horrified voice.

Kate ignored her. The travelers they had met on their trip had prepared her for people's reactions to her appearance.

"What's wrong?" she asked breathlessly, and then because she could not help herself, she looked frantically around the small room and asked unsteadily, "Where's John?"

"Nothing's wrong except I am a stupid fool who's gone and let a horse throw me on my head," a disgruntled voice answered her a little faintly. "And John's away."

"Away!"

Adam caught Kate's eye, and she subsided, suddenly realizing how foolish she was being. John could be anywhere on the property. But every moment since she had known they were on Stevens Downs, the thought of seeing him had been foremost in her mind.

"Well, it seems as though you are Mr. Stevens, what has been so kind to my Timothy. But who are you, dressed as a man and all, may I ask?"

The woman was not stout beneath her loose skirt; she was pregnant, Kate realized with a little shock. Her pretty face was pale and strained, her golden hair coiled neatly around her head, but she was standing aggressively with her fists on her hips, staring from Adam to Kate with shocked disapproval on her face.

Adam looked over at Kate and smiled. It was a tender smile, and Kate's heart almost stopped beating at the depth of pride in his dark eyes. Despite her looking as disreputable as any of William Garrett's down-and-outs in London, this fine man was proud of her!

"Kate, come and meet my very good friend, Mr. Timothy Hardy, and this woman, who undoubtedly fits the never-ending descriptions he gave John and me, must be his wife. This is Miss Kate Farnley, Timothy, and. . ." He turned and bowed deeply to the woman. "Mrs. Hardy. Ma'am, you can be none other, although how you come to be here at all in Australia I fail to understand."

Timothy ignored him. He was gaping strangely at Kate. "Miss Farnley?" He looked at Adam and said urgently, "Is it true then? Is she. . .can she be. . . ?"

His voice faded away, and while he was groping for words, Adam nodded abruptly and said, "Yes, but not now, Mate."

Timothy subsided. After staring at Kate for another long moment, he suddenly realized his wife was still staring in silent amazement and considerable consternation from one to the other.

He gave a faint chuckle. "Molly, my love," he chided gently, "you have not yet made your curtsy. This is Miss Farnley, an. . .an acquaintance of our John's from fair England. This gentleman is our employer and friend, Mr. Adam Stevens. And you've just held him up with one of his own rifles, you foolish woman!"

His wife stared at him. Then a vivid blush crept into her cheeks as she turned to Adam. She swept them both a slight, yet nevertheless dignified, curtsy but held her head high as she said, "I'm sure sorry, Mr. Stevens, but with the trouble we've had. . ." Her voice shook suddenly. She stopped abruptly and put a hand to her mouth for a moment.

Kate could see she was trembling, holding herself stiffly as though trying to maintain control. Something was badly wrong here.

Mrs. Hardy took a deep breath and added flatly, "I'm sure you will understand I was taking no chances."

"Trouble?"

Timothy nodded at Adam's sharp question. "Yes, trouble," he said shortly. Then he unconsciously copied his friend's previous words, saying with a forced smile, "But not now. We'll tell you about it later. You both look exhausted. After you've rested a bit and been fed, there is much to tell."

"Is John all right?"

The words burst from Kate forcefully, and they all looked at her. Then Timothy and his wife exchanged a look that worried her even more.

"Does this trouble have something to do with him?" she persisted.

"Yes, it does, Miss Farnley," Timothy said quietly, "but you are exhausted. I think we should not worry you with this until—"

Adam interrupted him. "We have been exhausted for days, Timothy. Another few minutes do not matter, but we must know about John. Have you seen or heard of a man called Percival Farnley?"

Timothy looked at him steadily. "No, not that Percival John has told us about, but a few days ago a message was brought from Waverley Station that a Lord Farnley had arrived there. He was very anxious that John go to see him as soon as possible because he had news of great importance to impart to him. John and Elizabeth left yesterday morning."

"But. . .but Lord Farnley is Percival."

At Kate's sharp words, Timothy and his wife stared at her and then at Adam. Timothy's pale face went even whiter. "But surely. . ." He faltered. "John thought it was. . .it was. . ." He stopped and chewed on his lip, darting a quick look at Kate and then his wife.

Kate looked helplessly at Adam. He shook his head slightly. This was not the time to go into lengthy explanations, and she was not sure how much these two knew about John's affairs, especially Mrs. Hardy.

Adam ran a hand through his hair. "You said John and Elizabeth left yesterday? Do you mean Elizabeth Waverley has been here?"

"I do mean that Elizabeth, but she is now called Elizabeth Martin."

"Martin? Do you mean she and John. . .?" Adam's voice faded away. He was staring at Timothy in utter astonishment. "But the last we heard he had been posted as an escaped convict. How on earth—?" He stopped abruptly and shook his head. "I think you might be right after all, my friend," he said at last in a dazed voice. "Perhaps we should hear all this after we have eaten and rested a little."

"Are you trying to tell us that John is married to this. . .this Elizabeth person?"

Kate could hear the mild hysteria and horror she was feeling in her voice. Adam had told her a little about Elizabeth Waverley. She was the daughter of a convict who, through sheer hard work and determination, had become a wealthy landowner. George Waverley had been Adam's benefactor, first employing him and then leaving Stevens Downs to Adam in his will. And this woman, daughter of a convict, had married an English peer?

Mrs. Hardy apparently also recognized how close Kate was to losing her self-control and was suddenly all action.

"There now, you poor dear, do sit down. You do look so weary and white," she said in a soothing voice, even as she bustled over to a large stove and adjusted a large black kettle. "Of course Mr. Martin has married Miss Waverley, almost twelve months ago now. A fine woman she is, and a happier pair I've rarely seen. But there," she added hastily after another look at Kate's face, "it can certainly wait to tell until after you have at least had a cup of tea."

Kate suddenly felt dizzy. She must have swayed, for Adam leaped forward and put his arm around her waist before leading her to a chair. She leaned into his dear, strong body, suddenly wishing wearily she would always be able to do so when life became so difficult.

"You are right, Mrs. Hardy," she heard Adam saying through a haze of exhaustion. "It seems much has happened in the twelve months while I have been away, but we do need at least a drink straightaway."

He made sure Kate was seated, sank down himself on a chair, and then turned to Timothy. "But how are things here, Timothy?" he asked tensely. "It seems the seasons have been poor since I left. Have we lost the flock?"

"No, no," Timothy said quickly. For a moment he looked stricken, and then he said sadly, "Not all the sheep, but some—far more than we should have, I am afraid, Adam. We've tried. Worked as hard as we could, but they are still getting weaker and weaker. And—"

A loud voice hailed them from outside. Adam straightened. Never had Kate admired him as much as when he said steadily, "I am being selfish and thoughtless. Our friends also need sustenance before we talk. They probably also need to be reassured that this savage woman with a gun has not harmed us."

A smile that did not reach his eyes curved his lips before he turned and went back outside. In the silence that had descended in the room, they heard him answering Will's anxious questions and then giving instructions where they could water the horses and set up camp.

"The poor man," Molly Hardy whispered, "to come home to this."

She exchanged a look with her husband. Kate looked at them sharply. There was something else wrong here besides the welfare of the sheep. Her fear grew. She wanted to ask again where John was but bit her lip. She needed Adam here for that. Wearily she leaned back and closed her eyes. Surely another few moments could make little difference.

After a short while, Adam rejoined them. Molly quickly set out cups of steaming tea and thick slices of fresh bread and meat. "There now," she said comfortingly. "You help yourselves. I just want to check on young Tim, and then I'll go and see if there is anything your friends need."

There were several minutes of strained silence after she had bustled out. Then at last Adam sighed, put down his cup, and began asking Timothy questions about the station.

"We had a real good wool clip last year," Timothy told him, his eyes alight with pride and satisfaction. "It were a great sight, seeing those bales of wool off to Sydney piled high on that long wagon pulled by a bullock team. Brought a good price too, it did. And we had quite a good lambing season, considering. Even the dingoes and aborigines did not kill more than a handful."

"No problems with the aborigines, then, Timothy?"

Adam's voice was even, but something in it made Kate's eyes go swiftly to his face. She could see the tension in him as Timothy said quite cheerfully, "Very little. Your policy of us all getting to know as much as we could about their customs and language, as well as respecting their sacred sites, sure has paid off. There are a few hot young heads among them, but their elders keep them pretty well in control. We give them some flour and, as long as we let them have a sheep when the hunting is poor, they seem okay."

Why didn't Adam ask Timothy about John? Was he afraid something may have stirred up the aborigines, and John. . . ?

But Adam had relaxed a little, and Timothy had started to tell them briefly about the months without rain, the merciless sun drying up the creeks and grasses across the run. Although they had moved the sheep to pastures as close to the river as they could, even that land was drying out and becoming a dust bowl.

"The river's also getting very low," Timothy said finally. "At last we had to agree to Elizabeth's suggestion that we take them to her place, even though Waverley is so far from here. Being closer to the mountains, they've had some rain and still have quite good conditions. It was that or risk losing the lot."

Adam looked surprised and then thoughtful. Timothy had paused for breath and was watching him anxiously. "We really had no choice, Adam. This is a harsh land out here. I think we have also been carrying more sheep per acre than the country can sustain," he said quietly at last. "There's more to tell, but. . ." He stopped and looked at Kate.

Adam nodded abruptly. "I have no doubt at all that you have both been very good stewards while the master was away." He smiled gently at the relieved look on Timothy's face.

Kate looked from one to the other, realizing as never before how much trust Adam had put in the two men to look after his affairs. Then it hit her. Because of their kinship in Christ, they were far more than master and servants.

Adam glanced across at Kate and caught her staring at him. She smiled lovingly at him. He looked startled for a moment, and then a tide of red swept over his face before he swiftly turned back to Timothy and said a little unevenly, "Perhaps you'd better tell us about Elizabeth and John."

Adam paused and then said to Kate, "I've told you some of that business on board their ship when John and Timothy both met Elizabeth."

"Yes," murmured Kate. She looked down at her hands, feeling thoroughly embarrassed by her fleeting lack of self-control. "You said she nursed them both and was one of the finest of the currency lasses, the women born and bred in Australia, and quite different from the English sterling, or something." She did not add she had felt a slight twinge of jealousy at the admiring way he had spoken of that Elizabeth!

"Well, what I did not tell you was that Timothy and I both knew that John had fallen in love with her."

Kate stared up at him. Something of what she was feeling must have been mirrored on her face because Adam said shortly, "I know that the majority of the transported convicts were the scum of English prisons, even if there are some like Timothy here who were arrested because their political views were different from their peers. But many also were good men who only needed a chance to make a better life. George Waverley was such a man. He married a woman of impeccable reputation, and his daughter is a lovely woman. John is a very fortunate man."

Kate swallowed, ashamed of the training of a lifetime in a society that looked only on people's station in life and that had made her momentarily question a person's worth.

But before she could say a word, Adam added stiffly, "What was even more important, as it turned out, the surgeon on board the ship found out she loved John also. He had become her guardian on her father's death and took his duties toward her very seriously. As far as he was concerned, any hint of a relationship with a convict serving a lifetime sentence for murder was completely out of the question."

"You knew about that?" Timothy asked sharply, and then he slowly smiled as Adam nodded a bit sheepishly. "Of course you must have. After all, because of your friendship with her late father and what you owed him, you would have been the natural person for Dr. Richmond to ask to employ me after he got my ticket-of-leave arranged, and also to have John assigned to you so he would not end up on one of the life-threatening convict assignments."

"I don't think we can ever thank you and Dr. Richmond enough for what you have done for Timothy and John," Molly Hardy's soft, tearful voice said from behind them. "Things could have ended up so badly for them."

Timothy peered up anxiously at her. Molly nodded and smiled back at him with so much love that a pang of envy shot through Kate. How she would love to have Adam look at her like that and be free to let him see her love for him.

Adam looked a bit embarrassed at the admiration and grateful thanks in both faces. He said huskily, "But they gave me far more than I ever could them."

At Molly's questioning look he added simply, "They told me about Jesus Christ, about God's love for even a man like me, and brought me to a living hope and new life in Christ."

Molly beamed and nodded. Then she frowned and said severely, "But you men had absolutely no right keeping hidden from Miss Elizabeth where the man she loved was."

"How did she find out?"

Timothy laughed softly at Adam's question. "That wonderful woman sent money and arranged for Molly to come out here to be with me. You remember she met Molly and Timmy that day the ship sailed from England? Well, in her letter back to Elizabeth, Molly naturally mentioned where John and I were."

Adam laughed also. "As simple as that?" Then his smile disappeared. "Will Gordon told us about John being ambushed by that old enemy of yours from the ship. That must have been the same time your wife arrived. What happened with that business?"

Timothy looked across at Kate a little uneasily. "It seems that Lieutenant Edwards was friends with. . .with Percival Farnley."

Kate and Adam both straightened.

Molly Hardy sat down and said compassionately, "You'd better tell them everything, Timothy."

Timothy looked across at Adam and Kate, hesitated only a moment, and then briefly started to tell them of the events of twelve months before. In something of a weary daze, Kate watched and listened while Timothy told first of all how it had come about that the bighearted Elizabeth Waverley—no, Martin— had arranged and paid for his wife and son to join him.

So at least this woman who had married John was not without some money, as well as having inherited her father's property. Kate stiffened. That thought had been unworthy of her, especially in light of the obvious affection the others had for Elizabeth. The Lord certainly needed to teach her a lot more about accepting a person like Elizabeth for who she was and not for her background!

"Molly and young Tim arrived not long after you left for England," Timothy was saying. "Molly's letters were held up somewhere, and we only had them after you left. John and I barely made it in time to meet their ship. Your ships must have passed at sea."

Kate saw Molly nod briefly. Timothy beamed back at her and continued hurriedly. "We accidentally met Elizabeth on the wharf that day. She too had just heard that their ship had arrived and come to meet it." He gave a mischievous chuckle. "John could barely take his eyes off her."

Then he sobered and told of the ambush later that night when John's papers had been stolen and he had disappeared and been posted as an escaped convict.

"But," he finished with deep satisfaction in his voice, "God worked it all out for good, because Elizabeth's guardian, that Dr. Richmond, changed his mind about John. It turned out the doctor is very involved in the moves to abolish the transportation of convicts here, as well as for New South Wales to have our own government. So, he has much influence in high places and fixed it all up. Got John his ticket-of-leave, and they were married quick smart. Since then they have been living here with us. The shepherds are in our old hut."

He looked a little anxiously at Adam. "I sure hope you don't mind that Elizabeth insisted on using some of her money to build a house for us?"

Adam was looking as dazed as Kate was feeling. John married! It was obvious that this Elizabeth was thought of very highly by both men. She looked around the cozy but rough and basic room. How would someone used to living in conditions such as this fit into the role of the mistress of Fleetwood?

"I don't mind in the least she was happy to make you more comfortable." Adam laughed and pushed his hand through his hair. "But how you've brought all the building material here and have done so much in such a short time does surprise me."

"It were that new Mrs. Martin." Molly Hardy was grinning as she spoke. "She had her folk organized as quick as a wink after they were married. We arrived here with wagons and bullock teams you wouldn't believe. Quite a few of her servants stayed for months until we were set up real good." She surveyed her domain proudly, but her smile faltered as she met Kate's gaze.

It was obvious she still disapproved of a woman dressed in men's clothes and traveling in their company. With an inward smile, Kate suddenly realized Molly did not know that Judy Brown had been with them, and that Judy had carried out her chaperone job so well there had been precious little time spent alone with Adam.

"And you said John and Elizabeth left yesterday?" Adam asked.

Timothy frowned and continued his story rapidly. Two men had arrived from Waverley saying that Lord Farnley claimed to have vital information of a particular advantage to John and was waiting for him at Waverley.

Molly snorted. "I never liked them men from the moment they set foot on the place. Their eyes was all wrong," she added cryptically.

Timothy frowned and added a little impatiently, "John was in a real state to meet his. . .this Lord Farnley. Elizabeth had already convinced us to move the sheep, and we were bringing them together in one big mob, except for a hundred or so in a fenced paddock near the creek.

"This seemed a heaven-sent opportunity to have two extra men to help with the drive. Old Bill could stay and help us out, while our other experienced shepherd, Joe, as well as Mirrang, one of Waverley's aboriginal stockman keen to get back to his family, could help drove them. That way, once John was sure they could manage without them, he and Elizabeth could go ahead to Waverley. By the time the sheep arrived, they would have been able to move some of their stock to make room for yours.

"Tim. . ." Timothy faltered, cleared his throat, and said, "Our Timmy was keen to go with them. He made friends with some youngun's when we stayed at Waverley. Reckon it's been lonely for him without any other kids." He paused again and then smiled proudly at his wife. "All along, John had refused to let me and Molly go because she is too close to her time, but we were happy to let Tim go with them."

"Tim?" asked Kate blankly. "Your son? But you mentioned him before as being somewhere here. He didn't go?"

Molly and Timothy's faces were solemn. Timothy's frown had deepened.

"Our son, Miss Farnley," Molly said softly. "Yes, he did go, but he—"

"Mother," a hoarse young voice called out from somewhere in the house. "Are you there, Mother?"

Molly and Adam both jumped to their feet.

"He's awake at last," Molly exclaimed and disappeared from the room. They heard her calling reassuringly, "I'm coming, Timmy, Dear."

"What's wrong, Timothy?" Adam asked urgently. "I know you only have the one boy, and I thought you said he had gone with John. What's he doing back here?"

"That's some of the trouble Molly was mentioning, and why she held that gun on you, Adam. It seems that those two men must have jumped John as soon as it got dark two nights ago."

Adam gave a startled exclamation, and Kate froze.

"When they left here," Timothy continued grimly, "as I said, John was hoping the men would prove competent enough to leave with the sheep while he went on with Elizabeth. But according to Tim, it very quickly became apparent that, despite their claims, they knew absolutely nothing about sheep. John was furious. Tim heard him tell Elizabeth he did not trust them and that they were too arrogant and hard to handle to leave with Joe. So he sent Tim, and Mirrang as well, off with Elizabeth. Then. . ."

Timothy swiped a furious hand across his eyes. His voice rose angrily, and he said rapidly, "After everyone had prepared for sleeping, Tim slipped away into the bushes for a few moments. He heard a large commotion and yelling back near the camp. He raced back. John was swinging a club of wood, trying to hold off the two guys. He saw Tim and yelled at him to run, which he apparently did with one of them chasing after him."

Timothy paused, swallowed, and then continued in a choked voice. "Somehow our small son managed to hide in the dark up a tree. He stayed there until he heard horses moving off and crept back. His horse had been taken too. Tim. . .the lad arrived back here at midday. Walked all day in the heat, he did, and him not even eleven years old."

Kate sat frozen, staring at Timothy.

"And John?" Adam's voice was barely above a whisper. "Where's John?" In a stronger voice he asked, "Did he. . .is he all right, Man?"

"We don't know." Timothy faltered in a hoarse voice. "Tim couldn't say. You know how big-built and strong John is, but. . ."

He swallowed and continued rapidly, "But Molly and me think if he was all right he would have tried to find Tim. The sheep. . .Tim said they were scattering with no one to mind them. So, unless John was somewhere rounding them up. . . Tim said he was too scared the men would hear him so he didn't call out for John. The only thing he could think of to do was hightail it back here."

He choked and rubbed angrily at his eyes. "And I'm glad he's home. How he found his way safely, only our dear Lord who watches over our children knows."

Before he could speak again, a small voice said from behind them, "I'm so sorry about the sheep, Father, but I had to come and get you to go and make sure Mr. Martin is all right."

Chapter 10

I do wish I could go with you," Timothy said fretfully.

"By the look of you, you wouldn't last past the home paddock," Adam replied grimly as he swung up into the saddle. "I'm just glad you had already rounded up so many horses before that snake made your horse shy and put you out of action. Our horses are exhausted, and we would have had to wait until morning at least to even use them to go look for fresh ones."

It felt good to be back on Rowan, his favorite horse, again, and Adam was thankful that John had not taken it with him. Now, as never before, he understood George Waverley's wisdom of years ago in insisting he have such a string of top-class horses.

He looked across at Kate, already mounted on another of his horses, and frowned. She was very pale but sitting relaxed in her saddle, talking quietly to Molly. He knew she was still very tired, even though she had rested the last hour while the fresh horses for them all had been saddled up and their saddlebags filled with as many supplies as they could carry.

Despite all he had said to persuade her to stay, she had just looked at him from her deep blue, tragic eyes and said quietly, "I am not giving up now. God was warning us. He is still in control and will care for. . .for all of us."

Timothy had privately told Adam more about John being ambushed. He had already heard most of it from the Gordons, but they had not been aware of the death of Lieutenant Edwards. By the man's dying words it had been obvious that he had been a friend of Percival Farnley, who had been the instigator of Edwards's vendetta against John.

Adam had not told Kate, reluctant to add to her anxiety, as well as her pain about what her family had done to John. Although none of them had put it into words, he knew that she also was praying John was still alive.

"The first time I ever let a horse throw me, and now this has happened," Timothy was saying in frustrated tones, causing Adam to force his gaze away from Kate.

Adam looked down at his friend sitting on an old chair he had insisted they drag out to the house's lean-to so he could at least say good-bye. A slight, affectionate smile crossed Adam's face. "You would still have to stay with your wife and son, Timothy. Besides. . .you can still do the most important thing for us."

Timothy cocked an eyebrow at him, and then his frown cleared. "I've already been doing that, and the praying's been mighty hard." He hesitated briefly and looked over at Kate. "She does her share of praying too?" he asked softly.

Adam's smile broadened at Timothy's not-so-subtle way of finding out if Kate was a true believer. "Yes, I reckon since we left England she's become even more of a prayer than me," he murmured as softly.

Timothy beamed knowingly. "And according to my Molly, she thinks the world of you, Adam. If I'm not mistaken, you love her too, Man."

Adam stilled. The smile left his face. "Timothy. . ." He took a deep breath. "There hasn't been a chance to tell you what happened in England, but I think you already realize John's claims are being proved, and Kate. . .Kate is John's sister."

Timothy nodded. "Sure, and I already knew that as soon as you introduced her."

"And as John's sister and the daughter of Lord Farnley, she is not for the likes of me," Adam added curtly.

Timothy's eyes widened. "She does not know you were a convict?"

"No."

Even as he spoke, he had a flash of doubt. He stared at Kate again. She had never mentioned his past. Indeed, she had shown very little curiosity about how he had come to go to Australia. Even during the hours they had ridden side by side these last weeks, she had not questioned him.

As though sensing the intensity of his gaze, she turned her head and looked at him. And smiled.

His throat tightened, but he smiled back. Their glances clung for a long moment before she turned back to Molly.

He shook his head as though to clear it. Helplessly, he looked back at Timothy, who was watching him with his wise eyes. "Even if by some wonderful chance she. . .she does care, the fact remains that her family are aristocrats with a proud heritage. She deserves much more than a man whose family have been in trade. Even if I had never been falsely convicted of fraud and taken the punishment that should have been my brother's, I would be unacceptable."

"In God's eyes, all men are equal," Timothy flashed back.

Adam gave a harsh laugh. "But not in society's eyes. It could be very lonely for her over the years."

Timothy opened his mouth to protest further, but Adam shook his horse's reins, as he had so often tried to shake off his love for Kate, and walked his horse forward.

When he had control of his voice he called out, "Everyone ready to move out?"

Will Gordon squinted at him a little strangely but nodded.

He cleared his throat again and said loudly, "Then let's get under way. I want to try and make Wellington tonight. Even if it's after dark, the moon should be bright enough. Someone there in the village may have seen or heard something."

In a few minutes they had called their good-byes to the Hardys and were galloping hard along the track heading southeast. The cart and packhorses had been abandoned so they could travel faster.

Adam was moved that they had all refused to stay behind, even Judy Brown. The men were well-armed, and all carried what they could in their saddlebags. They would not have even the basic comforts they had enjoyed the last few weeks, but it could not be helped if they were to catch up with John, or at least try and confront Percival Farnley before he could leave the area.

At places they had to walk the horses carefully. The dry ground had opened as though appealing for the rain to come and soak into its depths. But they ran their horses as fast as they safely could while it was light, then walked them along the track through the bush until they arrived at Wellington.

Adam roused the local owner of the small inn, who was notorious for knowing everything that happened in the district. But he had heard nothing except that much farther along the Macquarie River there was a mob of scattered sheep and no one had yet seen the drovers.

Adam's mouth tightened. "I've had some trouble with the men who went with the sheep," he said briefly. "I'd appreciate it if you would keep an eye out for them."

He gave the man brief descriptions of them before rejoining the others. Seeing the drooping figures of Kate and Judy, he said abruptly, "There are two beds here the man can let you two have for the night."

The two women looked at each other and then shook their heads. They had become firm friends during their journey, the differences in their social standing of no consequence as they had shared the hardships together. Kate knew she had earned Judy's respect by not complaining and always doing her share of the chores, and she certainly had admired Judy's competence in the bush, her strength, and her loyal, friendly manner.

"It will be faster if we all camp together and get a few hours rest. Then you won't have to come back for us, and we can move out as soon as it's light enough," Kate said with a strained, weary smile.

They camped near the river, and long before the sun touched the eastern sky with pink light heralding the new day, they were in the saddle again. The sun was already reminding them how hot it would be later on when, only a few miles farther along the river, they came upon the first bunch of sheep with the Stevens Downs' distinctive markings. Timothy had estimated there had been at least three thousand in the drive, and now they would be widely scattered.

Even after they discovered where the men had camped, there was still no sign of the horses, not even the packhorses that would have been hobbled for the night. But there were signs of the struggle Tim had witnessed. The ground and grass had been churned up in a wide area around the remains of the campfire. It was near its white ashes that Adam found the large lump of wood with ominous dark stains on one end.

Adam was grim. Hopefully it was John's attacker's blood, not his. He quickly put it down, hoping Kate had not seen it.

Fortunately, the camp had been made on the banks of the Macquarie River. At least there was some feed here, but there would be losses. The sheep were thin, and if they had wandered too far from the grasses on the banks and their water supply, they would quickly die in this heat.

But John's welfare was Adam's first priority.

After a brief consultation, the decision was made for Jim, Bluey, Bob, and Judy to stay behind. Two could start rounding up the sheep while the other two rode back to Wellington for supplies. Then they were to allow the sheep to graze and fatten some before continuing the drive very slowly to Waverley.

Adam wanted to take Judy with them as well, but she would not hear of being separated from her husband. Adam looked at Kate helplessly.

"Even the four of them may not be enough to get all the sheep, will they, Adam?" she asked calmly, and he was forced to nod in agreement. "Will, Jackie, and the two of us must be enough for what we have to do. Besides," she added impatiently, "it was perfectly ridiculous in the first place to think I needed Judy as a chaperone!"

Was it? If only she knew how many times he had wanted to kiss her, to pour out his heart to her. He was still for a moment. Something flashed between them as they stared at each other. Then he swung away, not daring to voice his wish that she would stay with Judy. By the warning in her eyes and her tight lips, he knew that she would never consider it.

"Jackie," he called out, "think you can track my friend for us?"

Jackie had barely said a word since they had left the station, just at times encouraging his horse in soft murmurs and watching them all with his black eyes. He had been poking around the edges of the deserted campsite until Adam hailed him.

He ambled over to Adam and hesitated before answering him slowly in his soft voice. "There is much I do not know, but since being at Bathurst one of my local blokes has been teaching me what most aborigines know almost since birth." There was no resentment or bitterness in his voice, and he immediately pointed in two directions. "Three horses went that way, and one without a rider that way."

For the first time since bidding farewell to the Hardys, a grim, relieved smile touched Adam's face. "Right, Jackie," he said briefly. "Hopefully the riderless horse is Tim's pony. Bob and Jim can try and find him as well as the packhorses if they have not been taken."

He paused and looked at Kate quietly listening to them. "That probably means John is with them, which means they do not intend to harm him, just escort him to your cousin," he said with some relief.

"Not yet, anyway," Kate said steadily. "Percival would want to gloat first. That's the kind of person he is."

Adam stared back at her before at last looking away and saying gruffly, "At least if he sustained any injuries, John was well enough to stay on a horse."

The trail left by the horses followed the river some distance and then led away from the river and into more rugged terrain. Then about midday, they lost some time when the trail disappeared after entering a creek.

"Three went in this side; only two came out and then went back in the river," Jackie told them shortly. "You wait here."

About to protest, Adam held his peace. Too many of them could destroy the signs Jackie was looking for. They dismounted and rested their horses while Jackie disappeared upstream.

Adam was getting impatient by the time Jackie reappeared. His heart sank when the aborigine shook his head.

"They must have gone downstream," he said briefly, "back the way we've already come. We can all go as long as you keep back and don't obliterate any tracks."

They followed behind Jackie as he walked slowly beside his horse down the center of the stream. His eyes darted from side to side, trying to find where the horse had left the water. Several times he searched the banks closely, until at last he gave a shout and pointed to some low, smooth rocks at the edge of the water under some bushes. Adam raced across and stared at the small broken twigs on the bushes where something had brushed past.

"Only one horse left here, Mr. Stevens. The others kept going. Do we follow it or keep searching?"

Adam stared down at the solitary hoofmark Jackie pointed out. Was it John's horse? Had he somehow gotten away from the others? Had he after all not been a captive but been followed by the others and here waded his horse through the water to throw his pursuers off? Should they follow this lone horseman or look for the other two?

He looked across at Kate. She looked steadfastly back at him, her eyes showing her confidence in him to make the right decision. He thought of Timothy's prayers and Kate's belief in God's power to keep John safe.

"What do you think, Jackie? Was my friend on this horse?"

"Yes," he said simply. "Otherwise why travel so far down the river and try to hide his trail on these rocks?"

"Of course." Adam smiled faintly and was rewarded by an answering smile. "We follow it."

Jackie rode slowly ahead of them. A couple hours later he was some distance from them when he stopped in a small gully surrounded by boulders. As he dismounted, he waved to them to wait and started searching in a wide circle. At last he beckoned to Adam.

"The other two joined the trail farther back there. Here a horse fell down. Look." Jackie pointed to two strong saplings. "Rope marks."

Adam could see nothing until the dark finger pointed to a couple of small threads obviously from a rope.

"And see this?" The grass was flattened and dug up in a wide area, but Jackie was pointing to a small rock.

Adam bent over and touched the dark stain. He looked quickly up at Jackie's suddenly grim face as Jackie said, "Reckon that's blood, all right, and there's more over there. Could be when the horse was brought down with the rope, but I don't think so."

Adam's heart sank. Even if this was not John's blood, he was a convict with a ticket-of-leave that could so very easily be taken away from him for any accusations of disturbing the peace or the slightest misconduct. Even if a new trial became possible because of the family lawyer's activities, it could go against him.

Jackie hadn't finished. He had continued circling the area and called out, "Ha, two horses here." Adam quickly joined him. Jackie continued his observations. "Walking very close together. Like they are tied together even. And to the side only one horse."

He grinned suddenly up at Adam. "Mine thinkit you 'em fwend okay, Boss," he said in his old guttural voice. "He beat 'em bad blokes orright. Your friend orright smart bloke for white fella."

Adam stared at him. Relief swept through him at the light of admiration for John on Jackie's face. For a moment he closed his eyes and gave silent thanks.

Then he grinned back at Jackie. "Too late for all that broken English lingo, Mate. Thank you, Jackie," he said sincerely, his smile disappearing. "Now," he added briskly, "any idea just where they are headed?"

Still smiling, Jackie tilted his wide-brimmed hat back. "Well, I reckon they are headed back to the road that leads right into Bathurst as well as to the turnoff to Waverley. I'd say your friend led them here to ambush them in this small gully."

Adam's smiled flashed broadly in response. "John's forcing them to go to Waverley?"

"You're pretty bright, for a white fella."

Adam suddenly laughed out loud, turned, and ran back to the others who were waiting by their horses. "Let's go, everyone. Looks like John must have everything under control. They are heading straight for Waverley."

He smiled gently at Kate's white, anxious face and quickly explained. "Seems one of them is herding the other two ahead of him. John is taking his cousin's bully boys to face up with him."

Kate didn't smile. "But does John know it's only Percival waiting for him and not. . .not Father? And, oh, Adam, what he must be thinking!"

At her hoarse whisper, Adam moved closer. He reached up and tenderly brushed a streak of dust from her cheek just for the sheer delight of touching her. He smiled reassuringly. "If John has been able to handle these two men, I think he can certainly handle his cousin. I had no trouble doing that, and John's bigger than me."

"Percival scares me," she said simply. "He may not have the physical strength you have, but don't ever underestimate him, Adam."

Somehow the free hand that was not holding her horse had found its way into his strong grip. He lifted it to his lips and kissed the back of her knuckles comfortingly before letting her go.

"I won't," he promised, "and you are smart enough to be up to any of his tricks for all of us."

He moved away and looked at Will, who had been close enough to hear their conversation and was watching them with a frowning face. Affection filled him for the man who had carefully refrained from asking questions about their urgency in traveling overland. He at least deserved to know the whole story, and he suddenly resolved, with Kate and John's permission, to tell him at the earliest opportunity.

But now he hesitated as Will waited silently and then said, "It's a long story; we'll explain another time. Enough to say that Kate's cousin is at Waverley and means serious harm to John Martin. Let's be off. We've made good time, and Jackie thinks we are only half a day behind them."

Despite the desperate need to push on, the horses had to be rested. So, after traveling at least thirty miles a day, they were forced to make camp for the next two nights. Each morning they got under way again at first light, but shortly after sunrise the second day, Jackie galloped back swiftly to Adam.

"Reckon your friend's got company following him beside ourselves," he said briefly. At Adam's frown, he drawled slowly, "Several men wearing no shoes."

Adam stiffened. "Aborigines?" he asked sharply. "How many?"

Jackie shrugged. "They don't leave as clear a track as white men or horses. Maybe six, ten."

Adam drew in a sharp breath and was silent for a long moment. "Jackie," he said hesitantly at last, wondering how much he should trust the aborigine, "do you think the aborigines in this area are restless enough to attack?"

Jackie hesitated also and then shrugged. "The Wiradjuri men are angry that the women they lend to white men are dying from their loathsome diseases, especially out in your area around Wellington. If they are from around here, perhaps not. I know they are upset about intrusions onto their sacred grounds, but generally the whites around here have been decent to them."

He hesitated again. "I think they are from the Bathurst region," he said slowly at last.

"How do you know that?"

Jackie shrugged again at his sharp response but this time just smiled and did not answer.

After a moment Adam said quietly, "I'll warn Will and the others, but don't say anything to Kate yet. She has enough worries."

They pushed their tired horses even harder. Several hours later, Adam reined in and waited for the others to join him. As much as the last weeks had toughened up Kate, she looked thoroughly exhausted.

Though he felt defeated, Adam said crisply, "Right, Jackie says he thinks they can be not more than half an hour in front. We have now reached the southernmost boundary of Waverley. There's a shepherd's hut not far away. We rest there." He saw the protest forming on Kate's lips and added bluntly, "It won't help John for you to collapse so that we have to look after you. Besides, we have been pushing our horses hard today. They need to rest too."

❦

Kate stared at him helplessly. She knew he was right. During the past hour she had only just managed to fight off feelings of faintness that had swept over her. She swallowed and dropped her head away from his anxious gaze.

At last she lifted her head and returned his look for a long moment. Then she shrugged helplessly. A smile lightened the frown in his eyes briefly before he turned his horse to walk beside hers.

"Adam, you and the others have had your rifles resting across your saddles the last couple hours like you did west of Adelaide," she said quietly some moments later. "What's wrong? Does Jackie know something you have not told me?"

Adam was silent and then made a sound that was part groan, part snort of laughter. "You don't miss much, do you, Kate Farnley?"

So there was something. She waited.

It was a long minute before he said quietly, "Jackie picked up signs that a party of aborigines are between us and John and his companions. He thinks they are trailing them."

"Natives! Why—?"

"Listen!" Adam stopped dead and sat motionless.

A moment later she too heard the sharp, distant sound his quick ears had picked up. "Oh, Adam—"

His raised hand stopped her. The echoing report of a gun again reached them. Jackie had disappeared, but Will quickly joined them.

"Where's it coming from, Adam?" Will asked abruptly.

"Sounds like the hut," he replied tersely.

Both men kicked their horses into motion. Without thinking, Kate started to follow them, but Adam called back in a low voice, "Stay here out of sight. You're not armed."

In only a few moments the sound of their horses had gradually ceased. The silence of the bush settled around Kate. A magpie warbled. There were some scratching noises in the bushes behind her. She suddenly remembered what Adam had just been telling her about the aborigines and looked fearfully around. A large lizard Adam had told her was a goanna raced up a tree. Kate relaxed.

A distant crack of a rifle disturbed the silence.

Perhaps someone in the hut was fighting off an attack by the natives. In that case, it could be as dangerous staying here as keeping up with the men. She shivered and rode her horse deeper into the trees and thick scrub at the side of the track before cautiously moving ahead.

There was more gunfire. Then silence.

She stopped again and waited for what seemed like hours but was only a matter of minutes. No other sounds disturbed the hush that had settled around her.

Surely Adam would come back for her as soon as he could.

If he could.

She waited a little longer, her nerves stretched until she could not stand the inaction any longer. She dismounted, tied her horse to a tree, and started forward in the direction the men had taken. Several times she had the incredibly eerie sensation that she was being watched.

"Only nerves," she muttered after one quick survey of the bush around her. But she crept forward as quietly as she could, peering constantly around as she went.

Then at last she heard raised, angry voices. Even more carefully she edged her way forward, trying to use the bush as shelter from any eyes, watching her feet as Jackie had once shown her, careful not to walk on noisy leaves or sticks, nor to brush noisily against any bushes.

The voices grew louder. There was no mistaking Percival Farnley's furious, high-pitched voice.

After a moment, she knelt down and crawled forward on her hands and knees until at last she could see from the shelter of a thick shrub where the voices were coming from.

"Percival Farnley, I might have known it was you," a loud, contemptuous voice rang out angrily. "You obviously found out your friend Lieutenant Edwards is dead, having failed to rid you of me. So I take it you have come to do your own dirty work this time. But before you kill me like I strongly suspect you killed poor Jock Macallister, perhaps you could tell me why Lord Farnley is here and how you think you can get away with this."

Kate stared at the scenario before her.

A rough bark shack sat in a large clearing in the bush. Immediately she knew it must be the shepherd's hut Adam had mentioned. And someone had been trying to fight off an attack.

But it was not aborigines who had been fighting. This was between foolish white men. The body of one man was lying sprawled in the dirt. For one horrible moment Kate thought it was Adam. But then there was a movement to her right.

Adam and Will marched into sight. She opened her mouth to call out a warning to them, but then she saw it was too late. Their hands were raised in the air above their heads, and a rough man appeared behind them, prodding them forward with his rifle.

They had been captured.

Frantically she looked back toward the clearing. A man stood there, also a prisoner in front of a rifle. She had seen him a couple of times before at Fleetwood. A black-haired man. A tall and powerfully built man.

The man holding his gun on him was still on his horse. He did not at all fit into this rough Australian bush setting. Even though his highly polished boots were thickly coated with dirt and his riding jacket a little the worse for wear, Percival Farnley was as correctly dressed as if he had been out galloping across the green meadows of Fleetwood.

And the black-haired man staring so disdainfully at him, his arms on his hips, was undoubtedly John Martin.

Her brother. John Martin.

Chapter 11

A clever trick, don't you think?" Percival was boasting. "I thought you'd come running to meet Lord Farnley. Well, I've got news for you," he snarled. "I'm Lord Farnley now, my dear cousin John, and I intend to stay just that. Your father was buried in the church graveyard these many weeks ago!"

Kate saw John's head rear back. His face was dead-white. She bit down hard on her lip to prevent her calling out to him. In that moment, she knew that he had lost hope his Bible and letters would ever be used to help him.

And that was the moment Adam and Will marched into the clearing. John swung around and gaped at them. So did Percival. He stared at Adam for a long moment, and then as recognition dawned gave a startled, furious exclamation. Then he carefully maneuvered his horse sideways, not for a moment taking his eyes from John as the second man forced Adam and Will over to join them.

Percival stared at Adam and spluttered, "You! What. . .how. . .you're here!"

Will stopped and stared from Percival to Adam, but Adam ignored them all. He continued on until he stopped directly in front of John. Neither man spoke or smiled for a moment.

Then Kate saw Adam suddenly tilt his wide-brimmed hat back on his head at a rakish angle. "Hello, Mate. Sorry we didn't see this blighter before he saw us," she heard his drawling voice say. "Having another spot of bother, I see?"

John reached up and tilted his hat back in the same position. "Yeah, Mate, just a spot," he mimicked Adam in his slightly accented voice, reminding Kate a little painfully of his Spanish origins. Her eyes clung to him as he drawled, "Glad you could join me but wish you'd managed it when I was in better company. But now I know you are home, it explains him. He's one bloke I hoped never to see again."

He nodded carelessly toward Percival without looking at him and then grinned at Adam and shot out his hand. Adam gripped it tightly, smiled back at him, and then cuffed him lightly on the arm. Their affection for each other was obvious.

Kate stared in astonishment at them and then at the gaping Percival. It was obvious he was a little bewildered but also getting more angry by the moment. Surely they realized how dangerous their captors were, and yet both men were taking it all so lightly.

Or were they?

John nodded toward Will, who had merely glanced at them before continuing to tensely watch the two armed men. "And good to see you again too, Mr. Gordon. Sorry you've been—"

"Be quiet, you. . .you. . . ," Percival screamed furiously. "This is not some picnic you're on. How dare you ignore me!"

There was silence. Kate held her breath as John and Adam slowly turned around and surveyed the man now waving his rifle dangerously from one to the other. He was literally shaking with rage, his face a fiery red.

Adam shrugged as though he were of no account and turned his head again toward John. "I suppose I should apologize, John, but I find I simply cannot like this cousin of yours. Now your sister, Kate, she is someone you can be very proud of. She—"

A rifle roared. Dirt shot up in a puff near his foot.

"Don't move, or I swear I'll shoot you down like a dog!" screamed Percival. "Now will you listen to me? I have some things to say to you before I kill you. And how dare you mention that woman! His sister! When I've dealt with you, it will be her turn next. She. . ."

He continued screaming at them in his falsetto voice, and that was the moment that Kate first knew anyone was near her.

A large hand suddenly slid across her mouth. Before she could struggle, it swiftly turned her head, and she saw Jackie. One finger was held up to his lips. She immediately subsided, only to tense again as a dark shadow joined him. Then there were others, crawling through the underbrush, sliding from bush to bush.

Suddenly she realized Jackie had removed his clothes and looked just like the tribal aborigines they had encountered down south; in fact, just like his present companions. He held several long spears, as she suddenly saw they all did. He beckoned her to follow him, pointing away from the clearing.

Kate hesitated only a moment but then stubbornly shook her head. He stared at her for a moment. Then he shrugged and pointed to a thick bush, indicating for her to hide under it.

She started to shake her head again, but this time Jackie not only gestured strongly but grabbed her by the arm and very slowly pushed her down, still very careful not to make a sound.

All the time, she was aware that Percival had been screaming and cursing. At last he fell silent. No one spoke. She peered from under her bush and saw that Percival's companion was staring at him with a fierce scowl. The three friends were watching them both closely. She saw Adam look swiftly around the edge of the clearing and then back at Percival. Adam was still standing seemingly relaxed, but Kate knew him well enough to see that he was actually very tense, every sense alert.

🦋

Adam was wondering where on earth Jackie had disappeared to. Fervently he hoped that Kate had stayed behind even after that barrage of shots the bloke had let loose around him and Will. Adam swiftly searched the bush and then stared hard again at the man he had last seen leaving the study at Fleetwood with a bloodied nose.

He was waving his rifle around so furiously that Adam thought they were likely in danger of it going off accidentally. Then Adam considered the man who had so cleverly captured himself and Will. He was scowling at the man on horseback, but his guns were still trained on the three of them, and he had already demonstrated he was a good shot.

Adam was angry with himself. He should have had more sense than to approach the hut directly. The man had been waiting for them, obviously having heard their horses crashing through the bush in the hurry to make sure John was safe. He had let off a warning shot that had whistled past their ears, then others, giving them no option but to throw down their rifles and dismount. Adam scowled. Goodness knew where their horses were now.

There was a brief pause in the hysterical screaming.

"Now just a moment, Boss," the man with the other rifle said, but Percival turned on him, swore again, and shouted, "I told you to call me Lord Farnley!"

There was a tense silence. Then the man said angrily, "Well, Lord Farnley or whatever other fancy name you might think you have, I just want to know what you intend me to do now. Just bring the man to you, you said. Use force if we had to, you said, but it would not be necessary because he would be keen to come back with us. But you said nothing about him having a missus, or that a kid would cause problems too, or that—"

"But you did *not* bring him to me, did you?" Percival said furiously. "He had captured *you*. . .you two useless idiots! It was just as well I was here and well hidden when you arrived."

"An easy job it was, you told me and me mate," the man persisted angrily. "Just tell him this Lord Farnley was very anxious to see him and he would come running, you said. Well, you was wrong. His boss's sheep was more important than meeting any English lord. It would have taken weeks at the rate they was travelin'. We couldn't wait no more so we grabbed him, but he. . .he. . ."

His voice rose higher. "First he gives me a wallop on the head. Then there's me mate shot by you while you was swinging your gun around so crazy, and now we have three of them to deal with. You never said nothin' about killing anybody. So, tell me, Lord Fancy-pants Farnley, what are we going to. . . ?"

His voice trailed off. He was staring beyond the three men, his red, angry face slowly turning dead-white.

Adam and his companions spun around. Half hidden by the foliage of the bush, a circle of aborigines was slowly advancing. As the man yelled a warning, they stopped, standing perfectly still.

Quickly Adam turned in a circle. Dark-skinned warriors, their faces grim, were silently standing up from behind bushes and stepping forward until they were completely surrounded. There were far more than the half dozen Jackie had estimated.

Each held a spear ready in their spear-throwers, their *woomeras*, Adam realized in a daze.

"What the. . . ?" Percival's voice was frightened.

Adam saw his rifle come up and shouted, "Don't shoot! Whatever you do, don't shoot. There are too many of them."

Frantically he wondered where Kate was. Had they captured her? Killed her? He had been worried about the aborigines attacking them. But here, on Waverley?

An aborigine to his right loudly spat out a few guttural words. Adam froze for a moment and then turned very slowly toward the speaker. He stared at the tall, almost naked aborigine.

The native was staring directly back at him. He spoke again, a little impatiently but more slowly this time. And suddenly the words were familiar, words Adam remembered Jackie trying weeks ago to teach him. In fact. . .

He stared more closely across the clearing. Then he knew. It was Jackie, and if he had understood correctly, Jackie had just asked him if he wanted the bad men killed.

Relief swept through him.

Then he shook his head quickly. "No!" he called back fast in the Wiradjuri language. He knew how badly it would go for the aboriginal tribes in the area if they dared to spear a white man—even a bad white man. There would be fear among the settlers, the soldiers could be called out as had happened over the years, and possibly many aborigines would be shot as had occurred in other places.

"What. . .what did he say?" Percival Farnley's voice was barely more than a whisper. His horse shied restlessly. Adam could see the rifle in his hands was shaking with the violence of the man's fear.

John answered him sharply. "He wanted to know whether they should kill you and the other man with the gun."

Adam glanced at him. John was staring with a frown at an aborigine several feet away from Jackie.

Moving a little closer to John, Adam hissed, "Glad you've been learning the lingo, my friend. Know any of them?"

"Yes, Mirrang, one of Elizabeth's men."

Adam relaxed slightly. "And the one who spoke is a friend." He thought of the times he had seen Jackie giving him strange looks, watching him. "Or at least I hope he is," he muttered.

Then he remembered how good and kind the Waverleys and Gordons had always been to the natives and relaxed a little more. He thought frantically, but before he could speak again, Jackie rattled off a few more words. This time they sounded much angrier, but this time Adam did not understand what he had said. He glanced at John, and for a fleeting moment saw a glint of a hastily concealed grin.

"That friend of yours has a sense of humor," John murmured. "Wants to know when we decide in our own sweet time what we want them to do not to forget to tell him—or something to that effect."

Adam called out to the two men still staring with white faces, and swinging their rifles around the circle of natives. "You had better both put down your rifles or they will throw their spears. And I think somehow they will aim for the armed white men first up."

Percival's hired man dropped his gun instantly. Adam held his breath as Percival stared at John.

"Good afternoon, Cousin Percival."

The woman's voice rang out in the tense silence, and all eyes swung toward Kate as she strolled slowly into the open. Her head was held regally as though she were entering her own drawing room at Fleetwood.

Adam held his breath. Then it surged back in a great tide as love and pride for her courage swept through him. At his side, he heard John gasp. He was staring at Kate with dazed eyes. Then he looked swiftly at Adam, and the sudden wild hope in his blazing eyes made Adam tremble in sympathy.

"Don't move, Kate," Adam called out urgently as Percival's gun swept up.

To his immense relief she stopped.

After one swift glance at him, she kept her eyes on her cousin. "You are really being very tiresome and foolish, Percy," she said in a calm, reasonable voice. "The lawyers checking out that John is my brother know you have come here, and you cannot possibly get away with this. Put down that stupid gun. You know that shooting us will achieve absolutely nothing."

Percival Farnley stared at her speechlessly. Then he laughed. The laugh sent shivers down Adam's spine.

"But then, you don't know that I have already killed someone, do you, my dear Katie? So a few more killings don't really matter, do they? A hangman's noose does not care whether it is for killing Jock Macallister or for killing all of you."

His lips twisted in a ghastly parody of a smile as he swung back toward John. "If it were not for Penny, that daughter of his, never believing you had killed her father, if the woman had not developed a conscience after her vengeful mother died, she would never have taken Martin's bundle straight to your father. And then your stupid father told me he had that pathetic proof you had raved about during the trial."

He smiled that dreadful smile again. "But at least finding out he had a son did your old man in. The shock and pain of that and what had happened to you finished him," he gloated sickeningly. "Of course, the few words from me saying if he ever claimed you as his son I would kill you, may have helped."

Suddenly his voice started to rise again as he turned back to Kate. "Then you and that sister of yours had to be there, didn't you? Your servants were always poking their noses in before he died. Every time I may have had a chance to look for those letters, you or they were there. Even that day of the funeral, you turned up before I could find them. And it was you who found them!"

His furious, high-pitched voice stopped.

No one moved. They were frozen in silent comprehension. Percival Farnley had committed the crime that John had been arrested and found guilty of. Percival all along had schemed and lied so that an innocent man had been convicted and sent to Australia in chains for the term of his natural life.

In horrified, stunned silence, they watched Percival swing his horse around in a tight circle, staring at the threatening natives before focusing again on John. The sudden hatred in his eyes as he glared at his cousin was dreadful to see.

Then, without a word, his rifle came up.

"Percy, no!"

As Kate screamed, Adam flung himself forward. The gun roared at the same time, and he felt something hit him, knocking him to the ground.

As he fell, he heard Kate scream again. There was a clatter of a horse's hooves. Men shouted. Then the pain was suddenly excruciating, and blackness blotted out everything else.

Chapter 12

K ate was barely aware of the horse that plunged under a hard, cruel spur and then took off wildly. She vaguely heard Jackie and Wirrang yelling furiously. She did not see the aborigines reluctantly lower their spears and then scatter before the plunging horse.

Racing across the clearing, her whole attention was focused on the man on the ground. The man she loved.

John and Will had already rolled him over by the time she reached them.

"Adam," she panted. "Oh, Adam! Is he. . . ?"

"Hit in the right shoulder," Will said briefly. "Must have clipped the bone to send him down like that. Bullet's gone right through, but he's bleedin' bad."

John had already stripped off his own shirt and was forming a thick pad with it. "Here, Miss. . .Miss. . ." He looked directly at her for the first time and said in a strangled voice, "Miss Farnley. . .Kate?"

"Give me that." Will impatiently snatched the shirt from him. "Time for greetings later when we've stopped this bleeding. Here, Kate, hold this tightly to Adam's wound while we get him into the hut and out of this hot sun."

Kate looked up through tear-glazed eyes at John. She had seen him at Fleet-wood from a distance many times, but only once or twice close up, and that had been when all her energy and attention had been on Beth and on her mother's illness.

This was her brother.

Now she understood what Adam had seen in the family portraits. Despite his dark olive complexion and that mop of black curls, his eyes were the Farnley eyes, making her own and Percival's look pale blue in comparison to the brilliance of his.

Just like their father.

"Hello. Hello, John." Her voice was trembling. She bit hard on her lip. "I. . .I've come a long way to find you."

Their gazes clung for a long moment, and then she looked away, all her attention again on the man she loved.

When Adam was at last lying on a crude stretcher in the shack's only room, John said a little breathlessly, "I'll have a look, but I doubt there's anything to use as bandages here."

He was right, but without a word, Kate turned her back and began tearing the bottom of her own shirt. When she turned around, John was bent over Adam, his bare, tanned back exposed to her startled gaze.

She caught her breath. His back was crisscrossed with raised scars from the flogging on board the ship ordered by that friend of Percival's.

This reminder of all he had suffered was too much. A sob caught in her throat. He spun around, saw she had been looking at his back, and stared in dismay at the tears running down her face.

"Oh, John, I am sorry, so very, very sorry," she managed to say.

"No time for tears, now, Lassie," Will's urgent voice said sharply. "Adam's still bleeding."

John had colored up a little. He smiled gently at her and then turned to help Will roll Adam over and pad the exit wound before tying both pressure wads in place with the makeshift bandage.

When at last they had done all they could, they watched anxiously to see if the red stain would start to seep through the thick wads of material.

After a few moments, Will sighed with relief and said slowly, "Looks as though it has missed the lungs as well as any major blood vessel."

"The bloke who has been shot has a bullet in his leg, so he won't be making a nuisance of himself, but what do you want us to do with that other bad man?"

They all looked toward the doorway. Jackie stood there. As they stared, the aborigine, still dressed simply in a loincloth, said slowly in his precise English, "Sorry to interrupt, but the fancy man got away on his horse, and the other one's still scared witless by the savages, who are gleefully prodding him with their spears." He allowed himself a faint smile.

John was staring at him in astonishment, and then another aborigine appeared beside him. "You want us catchem udder plurry man on horse, Boss?" he asked urgently.

John stopped staring at Jackie and said swiftly, "Yes, Mirrang, I think you had better find the man on the horse, but make sure you do not harm him. And if he's still got his gun, be very careful. There's been enough injuries for one day," he added grimly and looked back down at his friend.

"We'll have to take both of the other men to Bathurst once we get Adam to Waverley and let the police look after them. Just make sure you tie them up well," Will said abruptly. A faint grin twitched his lips. "And you'd better not frighten him to death anymore, either. Do you have our horses safe?"

Jackie grinned, nodded, and silently disappeared after Wirrang.

John was staring in amazement after the aborigine who had spoken such polished English.

Will smiled grimly at him. "Don't ask." Then he stood up, and as he moved toward the door, he growled, "I'd better go take a look at what those men are up to."

Adam stirred as he disappeared, and then gave a faint groan. Kate had slipped her hand around his, and his fingers flexed and then tightened on hers.

As Adam slowly opened his eyes, John crouched down beside Kate. Under his breath he said, "I was hoping he would stay unconscious until we got him to

Waverley." As Adam looked at him and then at Kate, John added in a voice rough with emotion, "Welcome back, Mate, even if you are a prize madman for jumping in front of me like that."

Adam had been staring into Kate's eyes and turned his head slowly toward John. "You had not had a chance to talk to your sister yet, John," he whispered.

Kate looked swiftly at John. He was staring at her, and slowly a wave of dark red touched his high, darkly tanned cheekbones.

"My sister?" he murmured. "You know for sure?" He swallowed and whispered, "Are you truly my sister?"

Emotion squeezed her throat. Kate nodded, her eyes clinging to the blue eyes so like their father's. She pulled her hand from Adam's and held it out toward him. As John's hand slowly closed around hers, she opened her mouth to speak, but suddenly her mouth was dry. No words would come. Her other hand reached out, and she held his between both of hers.

She swallowed, tried to clear her throat, and at last managed to say in a shaking voice, "I am so very pleased to meet you, my dear brother John."

John's grip on her tightened. Emotion filled his face, his eyes. He opened his voice to say something, but there was a sudden commotion outside and his head snapped up.

He was on his feet and heading for the door as a woman's voice called out frantically, "John? Where are you, John? Oh, John, my darling, are you safe?"

As he disappeared, Kate stared after him. Then she looked down at Adam. His eyes were once again closed and his lips tightened as a spasm of pain shot through him.

"Adam," she faltered softly. "Thank you, Adam."

He opened his eyes, raised his head slightly, and stared up at her. "I love you, Kate," he said clearly, and then his head fell back again.

"Adam!"

He loved her. This man did love her.

He did not respond to her whisper, and she called his name once more. But he had fainted again. She checked his wound swiftly, saw that blood had seeped through the pad, and raced to the door.

"John, Will!" she called frantically. "Adam's wound is still bleeding, and he's unconscious again."

John let go of the woman who was clinging to him and strode toward Kate. The woman followed, staring curiously. Dimly Kate knew she must be Elizabeth, John's wife, and that there were several men dismounting from their horses and talking rapidly with Will. She ignored them all and rushed back to Adam, her heart rising up in a desperate prayer that he would get well.

She never ceased praying during the long, difficult hours that followed, getting Adam back to the Waverley homestead. He had regained consciousness again, and although he was in a great deal of pain, he insisted on riding his horse all the way to the homestead. John did not argue with him. Instead, he climbed up behind Adam and supported him all the way.

Kate was thoroughly exhausted by the time they stopped outside a large, beautiful sandstone house set among tall gum trees and rolling hills. It was Elizabeth who helped her inside, her gentle hands that helped wash off the dirt and grime in a luxurious hot bath and then bundled her into a comfortable nightgown. It was her soft, soothing voice that constantly assured Kate that others were attending to Adam, that he would be fine, and all Kate had to worry about was eating a few mouthfuls of the thick hot soup and then sleeping.

And sleep Kate did. When at last she woke, the sun was low in the western sky. For a moment she lay without moving, enjoying the feeling of the soft pillow and mattress, the clean, fresh linen after so many months of the ship's narrow bunk, the wooden floor of the dray, and the last two nights on hard ground. Then the last traces of sleep vanished as she remembered Adam.

She flung the bedclothes back and sprang up, only to immediately feel so dizzy she had to plonk down again on the side of the bed. Breathing deeply, she closed her eyes tightly for several moments. When she opened them, the room had stopped swaying, and she tried standing once again.

The room tilted, and she clutched the bedpost. After a moment the dizziness disappeared, and she looked cautiously around the large room. It was luxuriously decorated, the furnishings expensive and stylish. The bed she had been sleeping in was a four-poster with beautiful, fine white lace draped around it. On a nearby chair, an elegant dressing gown had been left for her.

Thankfully, she moved cautiously over to it and put it on. She looked down at her bare feet, and then shrugged before slowly walking barefoot from the room and starting down the long corridor outside.

She heard voices coming from a room and paused. Before she could investigate, the door was flung open, and John appeared.

A delighted smile softened his face when he saw her. "Hello, Kate, my dear." Over his shoulder he called, "Elizabeth, Kate's awake at last."

He reached out and took her hand as his wife appeared beside him. In response to the desperate entreaty Kate knew he must see in her eyes, he said quickly, "Adam is fine. He's been awake for some time now and more anxious about you than himself," he added with a low chuckle.

Kate relaxed and smiled shyly at him with relief. Then she looked at Elizabeth. "You. . .you have been so kind," she faltered.

Elizabeth smiled understandingly and then whisked her back to her room to lend her one of her own cool, elegant frocks. During the time that followed, Kate felt she was moving in a dream. After partaking of a refreshing cup of hot tea in a delicate, bone china cup, she was helped to dress by a shy young maid who then brushed and artfully arranged her auburn hair.

As Elizabeth reentered the room after a soft knock, Kate was staring at herself in the mirror, a little dazed to once again be looking at the image of Miss Farnley, the woman who had in another time, a different world, been so elegantly dressed and groomed.

"Oh, Kate, you are so very beautiful," sighed Elizabeth. "That blue dress never looked half as good when I wore it. Now, if you are ready, there is a very impatient young man threatening John with all kinds of things if he does not see you at once!"

After all she and Adam had faced together, Kate felt ridiculously shy when she entered the large bedroom where a scowling Adam was sitting up in bed, propped against a pile of pillows. He stared at her with a stunned look of admiration that seemed to have stricken him dumb.

John rose from a chair and said cheerfully, "See, here she is, Adam, all safe and well as promised. Now perhaps you will stop snarling at us all."

Elizabeth gave a bright laugh. "And perhaps if Miss Farnley agrees to have some breakfast in here with you, you might at last eat something as well." She pulled a cord and, when a neatly dressed servant arrived, gave rapid instructions.

All the time, Adam and Kate had not taken their eyes off each other, earnestly trying to make sure that after all they had been through, they were all right. He was very pale, his face drawn with pain. His shoulder had been dressed with clean linen, and a sling was supporting his arm.

Kate found her voice first and asked in faltering tones, "Is your wound very painful?"

Adam swallowed and said in a dazed voice, "Only a very little if I move my arm around too much. You. . .you are so very beautiful, Kate. . .Miss Farnley."

Kate stared at him and then suddenly gritted her teeth. "If you dare. . .if you dare start that nonsense again, I'll. . .I'll. . ."

She was lost for words, incredibly hurt that he should think of refusing to call her by her name after all they had been through together. It meant a lack of intimacy and placed a distance between them again she could not bear to think about.

John stirred, and she looked swiftly at him just in time to see him trying to hide a smile. His eyes twinkled at her.

"Boss, looks like you've met your match at last," he drawled softly.

I hope so, oh, I do hope so. Startled at her wanton thought, Kate stared at John and then back at Adam. Sudden heat swept through her at the wondering look on his face. Confused, she looked hastily away and then thankfully subsided in the chair Elizabeth had just set for her near the bed.

There was a tense silence until John cleared his throat and said hesitantly, "Kate, Adam has just told us what has happened, about the Bible and letters, the way you found them and have given them to the lawyers, your courage in coming here to find me."

Elizabeth moved to stand beside him. Their hands met, and they smiled at each other lovingly.

"I. . .we can hardly believe it all." John took a deep, shaky breath. "And now, with so many witnesses to Percival Farnley's confession, Adam thinks there should be no problem with the authorities in sorting my unjust conviction out."

Kate's heart was full. She looked from one face to another. Tears had filled Elizabeth's eyes while she watched John speaking. "I told you God would work it all out for us, John, my darling," she whispered, and then she went to him and they held each other tightly.

Kate turned away, deeply stirred by the obvious depth of the love they had for each other. And as she stared at Adam, she realized how envious she was of them both. Despite all the trauma and difficulties they had experienced, they were together, married, able to share life with all its ups and downs.

Adam was watching them also. Then he looked at her. In his eyes was a deep pain, a haunting sadness. He stared into her eyes for one breathless moment before he looked swiftly away, sinking his head back on the pillows wearily and then closing his eyes tightly.

Kate longed to have the right to reach out to him as Elizabeth just had to John, to nestle so confidently into his arms, to feel them wrap lovingly around her. She started to raise her hand to reach out to him, but then it dropped back into her lap.

Now was not the right time. He was obviously still in pain, no matter what he had said. There was a touch of feverish color on his cheeks. But one day. . .perhaps one day there could be a future for them together after all.

Perhaps.

Her lips firmed. She loved him too. Except for Beth and her mother, there had been little love in her life. *There is no "perhaps" about it,* she seethed. Somehow she just had to find a way to convince him they could have a future together. Somehow she had to be able to convince him that his being a convicted criminal was in his past. Whatever he had done deserving of such punishment had now been paid for. Besides, it had all happened before he had become a Christian, before he had started trying to let Christ control his life.

Somehow she had to convince him she belonged with him, that she loved him enough to share whatever their loving God had for them both in the future.

Chapter 13

"Y ou love Adam, don't you?"

Kate jumped. At Elizabeth's soft question she had almost dropped the dainty china cup in her hands. She stared across at the beautiful, kind-hearted woman who was her sister-in-law. To her delight, they had very quickly become relaxed together and were well on the way to becoming good friends.

"You don't really need to answer that, Kate, my dear." Elizabeth smiled at her. "It is so obvious to both John and myself every time you look at Adam."

Kate very carefully put down her cup with only a slight rattle against its matching saucer. After a long moment, she plucked up the courage to ask the question that she had been wondering about for the last three days, ever since that first afternoon in Adam's bedchamber.

"Do you. . . ?" She lifted a dainty lace handkerchief to her suddenly trembling lips before continuing. "Do you think it has been obvious to Adam as well? Do you think he knows how I feel about him?"

Compassion filled Elizabeth's eyes. She nodded abruptly and then with a touch of anger said conversationally, "He would have to be stupid not to, despite the slight fever he has had. But then, don't you think men are the stupidest creatures God ever made? And aren't we just as stupid loving them like we do?"

Suddenly Kate's spirits lifted. "Oh, Elizabeth, I do like you so much. I am so pleased John found you."

A delicate blush swept into Elizabeth's cheeks. She beamed at Kate, and there was relief in her eyes as she said, "You will never know how happy that makes me, Kate, Dear. I have always wanted a sister, and now I suddenly have two."

She looked down and fidgeted with a fold of her skirt. "I was so worried in case you thought I was not good enough for John now that he. . .he will be a lord and everything."

All doubt of Elizabeth's ability to fill that role had fled the very first day spent in her sister-in-law's company. Kate smiled at her. "You have been running this beautiful homestead and this huge property extremely well from all Adam and John have told me. Even those years your father insisted you spend in England at finishing school has been a remarkable preparation for the role of mistress of Fleetwood."

A shadow crossed Elizabeth's face. "But my father was a convict, and John will have a great deal to live down because of his past and upbringing. Will they accept him at Fleetwood, do you think?"

Kate gave a short laugh. "Believe me, after the threat of my cousin taking over and all the dreadful things he would have been free to do, they will welcome you both with open arms. But are you sure you want to make your home there?"

The blush returned to Elizabeth's face. "Ever since we have been married, we have played a game. One I am sure John doubted could ever possibly be more than a game. But it was never a game to me," she added a little fiercely. "I had to hope John would be able to prove his innocence, at least be able to prove who he was. We have sometimes pretended we were Lord and Lady Farnley and talked over all the decisions we would have to make. We—"

She stopped abruptly as, with only a very hasty knock on the door, a wide-eyed servant rushed into the room. "Madam, there's a mob of aborigines approaching the house. Mr. Martin said for you both to come at once."

The two women looked at each. For the last two days, search parties had been out looking for Percival. His horse had been found with its saddle twisted around on its back, but there had been no trace of its rider. No one had even reported seeing the aborigines who had also followed him into the bush.

The two women quickly joined John on the wide, shady veranda that surrounded the house, protecting it from the sun. He was staring down the dirt track that sloped away from the house. Several dark-skinned men were walking toward them.

As the two women reached him, John shaded his eyes against the glare of the midday sun. "They are carrying something," he said slowly, then added more urgently, "Elizabeth, I think you had better take Kate back into the house, after all, and wait for me there."

Even as he spoke, the aborigines were close enough for Kate to see what they were carrying. It was a man's body, still dressed in what had once been an immaculate, dark blue riding outfit, far too hot for an Australian summer in the bush. And by the way he was being carried, it was apparent to all three that he must be dead.

One of the aborigines suddenly quickened his stride and stepped ahead of his companions.

"No, John," Kate said in a constricted, low voice. "That's Jackie. I have to know where they found him and what happened."

"It would be best if Kate hears now," Adam's voice said from behind them, "or it will only prolong it all."

They swung around to see him in the doorway, leaning heavily against the door. John sprang forward and took his friend's weight, muttering words that were barely audible about stubborn, blithering idiots who get out of bed.

❦

"Weaker than I thought," Adam gasped, his eyes on Kate's white, suddenly drawn face.

There was no way he could have stayed in bed once he had peered out his bedroom window and realized what was happening.

There was little Jackie could tell them. The group had followed the trail Percival had left, but he had pushed his horse hard, and it had taken them until the day before to find him. By then it had been too late.

"Snakebite," Jackie said briefly. "Two pairs of fang marks on his leg just above those fancy riding boots of his. I reckon his horse threw him and hurt him so he could not get up." He looked at Kate. "I am sorry, Miss Kate, but I think that your faith in your God will help you see that this is all for the best."

"Thank. . .thank you, Jackie, for all you have done for us," Kate murmured. She turned and looked helplessly at Adam.

His heart went out to her. No matter what the man had been, Percival Farnley had been a member of her family, a part of her life as long as she could remember. Adam would have given anything he could to have prevented the pain and sadness in her beautiful face.

"Adam?" Slow tears were starting down her pale cheeks.

"I'm here, Katie, Love," he whispered.

He opened his arms, and then she was kneeling beside him, his good arm holding her gently, his face buried in her fragrant, shining hair. She stayed there while John went to meet the aborigines and give them swift instructions and thanks for all they had done. Then with a sigh she stood up and, without looking back, went into the house.

❧

Several weeks later, Adam stood staring out across the blue waters of Sydney Harbor. The hot summer days had long since given way to the crisp, glorious weather of the Southern Hemisphere's autumn. Here there was not the blaze of autumn leaves as in England, but there were still some trees between the house and the water's edge whose leaves had prepared for the cold winter months and were now drifting slowly down to the earth.

"So, here you are, Adam," John's happy voice said from behind him. "We were wondering where you had got to."

Adam turned and forced a smile. His friend presented a very different appearance from the way he had looked all those weeks ago at Waverley. Much had happened. There had been an inquest into Percival's death, a hearing about his confession, and only the week before, all the papers had been finalized and John became a free man. Weeks ago his wife had insisted he be outfitted with clothes befitting his station in life as the new Lord Farnley, convinced his claim to his inheritance was probably already established.

"We have managed to book berths on a ship leaving for England tomorrow." John's face was radiant, but Adam's heart grew even heavier. Not only John and Elizabeth were leaving. Soon she would be gone—his love, his life.

He forced a smile. "My goodness, that was very quick work. Does Elizabeth think she will be ready in that short time?"

"Elizabeth was ready weeks ago," that lady said as she entered the room in a swirl of petticoats. Exuberantly she danced across the room, flung her arms around Adam, and kissed his cheek.

He emerged from her embrace with a genuine laugh. "Control this wife of yours, Lord Farnley!"

John twirled an imaginary mustache and said in a booming voice, "Control yourself, Wife!"

They all laughed, including Kate, who had entered behind Elizabeth. Adam's face sobered. He looked tenderly at her smiling face. "I do pity those poor servants at Fleetwood. They will not know what to make of this madcap of a new mistress. Just as well you will be there to protect them."

Kate removed her bonnet with a flourish, shook out her auburn curls, and then looked him straight in the face as she said lightly, "Oh, they will have to look out for themselves. But it seems to me John is more than capable of controlling my dear sister-in-law without me there. I'm going to be too busy continuing with her good work with the staff at Waverley."

John and Elizabeth froze, watching Adam's shocked face as he suddenly comprehended what Kate had just said. Kate grinned at Elizabeth and John, ignored Adam, and moved across the room to sink gracefully into a chair. She gave a relieved sigh and asked blithely, "Do you think there is any chance you could organize some refreshments for me from the inn's kitchens, Elizabeth? I'm famished."

No one spoke for a moment, and then Elizabeth went into action. "Oh, I am starving as well." She grabbed her husband's arm and started tugging him to the door. "Do come on, John, and use those handsome good looks of yours to bamboozle some poor woman into feeding us."

"But I. . .Adam. . . ," he spluttered helplessly. Elizabeth whisked him from the room.

Kate laughed. "I'm not quite sure who controls who in that relationship."

Adam stared at her. Her hands were trembling, and he could see by the high spot of color on each cheekbone that she was not as composed as she wanted him to think.

"Kate, I understood you were traveling with Elizabeth and John back to England to facilitate all that has to be done, as well as calling in at Adelaide to see Beth and the new baby."

"Oh, I changed my mind," Kate said lightly without looking at him. "There is so much to do with that schooling, church, and health program Elizabeth started with the aborigines and assigned servants on Waverley that we agreed it was imperative it not be interrupted at this stage."

"Kate."

"Even though Jackie has agreed to help, it still requires someone to oversee everything, and you will be so busy managing both properties, that—"

"Katie!"

She stopped twisting her hands in her lap and slowly raised her head. She looked at him and said with only the faintest tremor in her voice, "No matter what you say or do, Adam, I have decided. I am staying in New South Wales. Of course, I would prefer to stay as your wife, but since it seems as though I am destined to remain a spinster for the rest of my life, I prefer to do it here than back in England where I would eventually become such a burden to John and Elizabeth in my latter years."

Despite the tumult of his feelings, he said in a dazed voice, "You, a burden?" He straightened, swallowed, and said with a touch of anger, "But you are a very beautiful woman, an heiress in your own right with an impeccable aristocratic family background. Men will flock to ask you to marry them. It is ridiculous to think you will never marry!"

"Is it, Adam?"

She tilted her chin stubbornly and looked at him with an expression he had learned never to underestimate.

"I had one season in London and vowed never to have another. The constant round of senseless, selfish pleasure did not appeal to me in the slightest. And now with a brother who was never acknowledged by his father and was transported as a convict, a cousin who was a murderer, as well as my exploits these last few months, do you think many society hostesses would receive me or many men want to marry me?"

"But surely. . . ," he protested, despite the pain that swept through him at the thought of her as another man's wife.

Kate was not finished. She stood up. "Besides," she said quietly, "what man would ever even look at, let alone marry, a woman who has irretrievably lost her heart to another man and who could never love anyone else if she lives to be a hundred?"

❧

Kate did not know how much longer her trembling legs could hold her up, but she had been at too much of a disadvantage with him towering over her. Her whole future—her whole life—depended on these next few moments.

Adam had never ceased to be his pleasant, courteous self toward her, but since the day Percival had been brought back to Waverley he had withdrawn from her completely. At first her hurt and then anger at his intransigent attitude had made her want to go as far from him as the fifteen thousand miles of ocean could take her.

But then she had acknowledged that never to see his smile, never to see the tender look in his eyes that he had been unable to prevent, was more than she could bear. At least if she stayed here she would still see him sometimes know if he was sick or injured.

Adam held her gaze for a long moment, and she had to force back the threatening tears at the anguish on his face. Then he turned away and moved abruptly across to stare out through the window across the harbor.

"You do not even know my background, how I came to be in Australia," he said harshly.

"Oh, yes, I do."

He swung around and stared at her. Anger darkened his eyes. "John told you I was transported? I did not think he would."

"No, it was Will Gordon, actually."

Adam's eyebrows shot up. "When. . .when did he tell you?"

"Oh, I've known for sure ever since that first day after we left Adelaide." She added softly, "I saw the scars on your wrists and ankles that day you carried me to shore."

Adam closed his eyes. She moved swiftly across the room and reached out and laid her hand on his arm. "Even before he told me, I had already decided whatever you had done had been before your new life and hope in Christ," she said matter-of-factly, "and that it made no difference to the fact that I loved you."

His hand came up and took hers from his arm. He held it tightly in both of his and then raised it to his lips. "If I had not loved you from that first week at Fleetwood, that alone would cause me to love you. As it is. . ."

He drew a deep breath and looked speechlessly into her eyes, and she nearly cried out at the wealth of love in his.

Instead, she quickly snatched her hands away and said breathlessly, "I. . .I'm afraid I also pestered John unmercifully until he told me about. . .about your brother and how he let you take the blame for what he had done, stealing money from your uncle, altering the account books.

"He. . .he told me that it was probably because you too had been wrongfully convicted, even though you pleaded guilty to doing it because your brother was so young and had just been married, that you had listened to his own story and been prepared to believe him. And, oh, Adam, it was a brave thing to do, but it was foolish too. You were only twenty, and to suffer what you have in his place. . ."

She paused for breath and then whispered tearfully, "If I had not loved you before, how could I not love you when I found out what a wonderful man you are?"

His grip on her hand tightened. "Katie, Katie, you. . .is it possible, my love?" he said in a tortured voice.

"Adam, my darling. . . ," she choked as the blaze of love on his face increased. "Adam, I have been learning these past months so much about God and His ways. Do. . .do you think the God of love that He is would have bestowed on us this love for each other that He has if He did not want us to be married? For I am convinced that the depth of love I have for you could only be possible if it came from Him."

An arrested look flashed into his eyes. "I too have often thought that the way I love you could only have come from Him."

They stared at each other, hope flaring to glorious, wonderful life.

"If. . .if we did not marry and rear a family to know the Lord and to love and serve Him, we would be living in disobedience, would we not?"

She nodded dumbly.

He took a deep breath. Still holding her hands in both of his, he suddenly knelt down on the floor and looked up at her. "Kate Farnley, I will love you with this God-given love forever. Will you marry me?"

His romantic action drove the last tear from her eyes. She laughed delightedly and exclaimed, "Yes! Oh, yes, please, Mr. Stevens. It would be my very great pleasure and honor!"

He did not move. He simply stared up at her wonderingly, as though this were some wonderful dream. Then she tugged impatiently on his hands, and they were in each other's arms.

Neither heard the door to the inn parlor open or knew that Elizabeth and John peered into the room. The couple closed the door silently and slipped back across the corridor to their own room. There they beamed and then hugged each other tightly before kissing enthusiastically.

"Well, you were right after all," John said admiringly when he came up for air. "It's just as well we left our booking options open for that ship leaving later on. It means I can give my new sister away at her wedding."

Elizabeth tilted her head on one side. "Oh, I'm not sure about that. I think Adam will want you for his best man."

"Best man? No, no, Timothy can do that." John suddenly chuckled. "And I doubt if Adam has even had time to tell Kate that Timothy is going to manage Stevens Downs and that Adam is buying Waverley from you. At least, if you are still certain about that, my love."

She nodded vehemently and said lovingly, "I want so much to see your inheritance. Waverley was Father's dream, not mine. As long as anytime I need to smell the eucalyptus again we can visit here, I will be more than happy."

John hugged and kissed her again. Then he looked at her thoughtfully. "I wonder. . ."

"Of course he did," Elizabeth said blithely.

He grinned at this evidence that his wife could read his mind. "You really think Adam offered to buy Waverley just in case there was the remotest chance one delicately bred English lady would consider living in that comfortable house and milder climate rather than that hut in the outback?"

"I certainly do. In fact, I think it was a real blow to him a few days ago when she up and announced she was returning to England with us!"

John threw up his hands. "Women? How do you know these things?"

Her eyes danced. She opened her mouth, but the door behind them burst open and a radiant Kate called, "Elizabeth, John, we are going to get married."

They turned to express their delight, and later the four of them stood and together reverently gave thanks to their heavenly Father who had kept them, who would always help them to forgive what was humanly speaking unforgivable, and whose strength would be made perfect in their weaknesses.

LOVE IN THE GREAT SOUTHLAND

To my dear mother, Gladys Pedler (nee Telfer)
and the Pedler and Telfer pioneers of South Australia

Many thanks to my family researchers
and the information in their books
Pedlers of Australia 1838-1986
and *From the Borders to the Bush—
A Telfer Family History.*

Where the Telfer and Pedler names have been used,
these are my ancestors, and the incidents are based on actual events.

Thanks also to my darling husband Ray
who wrote William's poems, "I Love You, Beth" and "My Three Loves."
I have also used sections from one of his marriage services.
And of course, he has kindly given me his personal permission to use them all!

Prologue

England, April 1835

The public gallery in the courtroom was hot, stifling. The crowd squeezed in around her were restless, excited, yelling out curses on the white-faced prisoner now standing in the dock. She stared at the tall, handsome figure, not taking her eyes for a moment from this man she had befriended just a few months ago—a lonely man, a strong man, but a gentle one.

The judge's gavel thundered again and again. The crowd around her subsided. Their stillness frightened her even more. She looked apprehensively around, but no one was paying her heavily veiled person any attention. Every eye was avidly fixed on Judge Wedgewood.

"John Martin, you have just been found guilty of the felonious slaying of Lord Farnley's gamekeeper, Jock Macallister."

An excited buzz swept through the crowd. Her tears that had been so very close spilled over. A desperate sob whelled up and tore past her throat.

It was not true. It could not be true. He had often said how much he admired old Jock, had spoken so affectionately about him during their stolen moments together. Surely he would not, could not, have killed old Jock?

Suddenly she realized several heads had swung toward her, trying to peer through her veil, wondering who this strange woman was who seemed to have some sympathy for the felon. Her hand held the heavy veil to her lips, stifling the next sob that was threatening.

"Do you have anything to say before I pronounce your sentence?"

At the judge's ponderous words, her eyes swung back to the man in the dock. She froze, hardly daring to breathe. His eyes seemed to be looking straight at her. But no, they moved on as though desperately searching for just one friendly face. His shoulders suddenly went back. He stood stiffly, even as he had that last day when she. . .they. . .

"As God is my witness, I declare once more that I am not guilty!"

She believed him. Who could not believe that ringing, slightly accented voice that had spoken such tender, comforting words to her when she had needed them so much? Her mind blocked out the exchange between him and the judge, fleeing from the pain in him, from the oppressive heat of the crowded place, the smell of sweating, excited humanity. And suddenly she was back in the green meadow at Fleetwood, in his arms, letting his firm lips touch hers until. . .

Another hushed murmur brought her attention sharply back to the scene she had been staring at with unseeing eyes.

The judge had something in his hands. A black cap. She stared at it with increasing horror and jumped when the judge called out in his loud voice that reached to every inch of this courtroom.

"Prisoner at the bar! Have you anything to urge why sentence of death should not be passed upon you?"

What was he saying? What was he saying?

Her gaze clung to John Martin. Surely now he would tell them. . .tell them. . .

He was staring pleadingly, desperately down at someone in a row at the front of the courtroom. Then a slight frown, almost a puzzled look, briefly crossed that handsome face before he once more looked steadily across at the judge.

She leaned forward, trying to see who he had been staring at. Percival Farnley. Astonishment touched her. What was Percy doing here?

She drew back quickly. He must not see her. He would tell William for sure—perhaps even Father, and he was already so upset about Mother.

"I have said all I can, Your Honor, except to declare once again my complete innocence and pray that one day the guilty man will be found."

The prisoner's voice was so calm, so steady. Relief swept through her. Yes. . . surely now they must believe him.

But the judge. . .what was he saying?

"It is in my power to sentence you to hang by the neck until you are dead for such a heinous crime."

"Oh, no, no, not that!" She was on her feet; her voice so long silenced ringing out. Pleading. Nausea swept over her. Vaguely she knew John was again looking in her direction, searching for her. And she had failed him.

Percival Farnley was looking right at her, an evil, gloating smile twisting his lips. But she no longer cared. She felt so ill. Nausea had been creeping over her in waves. She had to get out of here now. . .away. . .

The judge was still speaking, pronouncing sentence, his words drifting to her as she frantically pushed her way through the crowd. "Mercy on you. . . transported. . .the great southland of Australia. . .term of your natural life."

He would not hang. He would live.

Thankfulness swept through her. Then the nausea welled up, fiercer than ever. John would exist for a lifetime in hopelessness. . .in a living hell. . . .

It was her last thought as she started to retch and then was violently, shamefully sick.

Chapter 1

South Australia—late February 1838

I t was a strange time and place to make the discovery that she loved her husband. Loved him. . .and not just as any dutiful Christian wife should—even in an arranged marriage.

She loved William. Loved him deeply. Loved him passionately. Loved him so much she would die if he never learned to love her a fraction as much.

Beth drew in a sudden gasp of air as though her lungs had been too long deprived.

"Are you all right, Mrs. Garrett?"

She turned and looked blankly at the curious face of the woman sitting beside her on the uncomfortable plank of wood that served as a pew. Beth blinked, nodded, and forced a smile she hoped was reassuring before turning back to stare once more at William.

At someone else's wedding I discover I love my husband?

Tears blurred the scene in front of her. There should be moonlight, music playing, roses. There were none of those. The morning sun was already very hot; not even a violin had been found for this wedding, and there were certainly no roses, only masses of eucalyptus gum leaves, with their own peculiar fragrance, heaped in makeshift containers.

"Today is a beautiful highlight in your lives."

Beth started. *Oh, yes! It is, it is. But only if. . .*

The Reverend William Garrett was staring earnestly down at the young couple he had just pronounced husband and wife. With a swift movement he raised that strong, handsome head and looked around the small gathering of wedding guests crammed into the roughly built bark and mud house surrounded by dense bush. His glance lingered on the sweet face of his young wife.

Beth stared at him, devouring him with her eyes. She was oblivious to the primitive surroundings. William's glance lingered on her own face for far too short a moment. Their gazes caught and clung. Something flashed in the dark depths of his eyes before he looked quickly away, back to the bride and groom in front of him.

She had known him, been such good friends with him since she was a child and he a tall, gangly youth. Ever since that first day they had met. . .

What a fool I've been! she thought passionately and then realized she was trembling quite violently.

She looked swiftly around, wondering if she had spoken the words out loud. Mrs. Young was still watching her with a slight frown. Beth nodded at her and then looked quickly away, taking another deep, careful breath.

Certainly she had always loved William in some way, but never with this heart-wrenching, soul-twisting love, this intense longing to be the recipient of his sole attention. She had intensely admired him ever since she had been that apprehensive, shy little girl meeting him that very first day her new stepfather, Lord Farnley, had taken her and her mother home with him to live at Fleetwood. After he had been introduced as Lord Farnley's ward, the son of his deceased cousin, William had suddenly smiled at her so sweetly, so reassuringly, that she had suddenly known she could be happy after all in this new, unexpected life.

Of course, her new stepsister had also been there, but at first poor Kate, closer to her own age than William, had been naturally resentful of a new mother and sister being thrust upon her without any prior warning by her thoughtless father and only a bare twelve months after the death of her own beloved mother.

During those first traumatic weeks of settling into a new opulent lifestyle on the prosperous estate, it had been William who had taken Beth under his wing, so much so it had set the pattern for the years that followed.

When he had been away studying for the ministry, she had missed him every day. Even then he had still been her champion, still the one person above all others she could call on in time of need.

Except that once.

That time when he had been desperately studying and taking his final examinations. That time her mother had become seriously ill and Beth had been barred from the sickroom and left to her own devices. That time she had, out of sheer loneliness and unhappiness, made another friend, which had been a very unwise choice.

Beth shuddered.

How selfish and spoiled she had been, bemoaning her solitary days when everyone's attention was being given to the mistress of Fleetwood. She had been very young, but at least her selfishness had not caused her to intrude on William's life and study. It was small comfort.

Certainly at that time it had been carefully kept from her how ill her mother really was, but she had been lonely, feeling sadly misused and isolated when she had wanted so desperately to help nurse her mother, to be needed.

And that was when she had first met the gamekeeper's handsome young assistant. John Martin, the intense young man with that slight, Spanish accent and his intriguing stories of another land, had fascinated her. He had been lonely too, and because she knew her stepfather would not have countenanced her friendship with one of his farm laborers, it had been rather exciting meeting him secretly.

A wry smile tilted her lips. She had been just sixteen and thought she was falling in love with John Martin.

Love?

That had not been love. This was love. This heart-wrenching feeling of tenderness, this need to always be near William, to touch him, and when he was away, that feeling that she was incomplete—that was love. To have him need her, to have those puzzling, undefinable barriers between them dissolve. . .

"Within the ceremony of marriage, you have made your commitment to each other in the sight of God and before witnesses. You are about to make a new life together. This life will be something entirely new to each of you."

William's rich tones washed over her. A deep longing to start anew with him filled her, to live over again the last couple years and more.

She automatically moved her position a little to ease a sudden twinge in her back, only to suddenly still again. The volume of his voice was increasing in a passionate way she had never heard before in one of his wedding sermons.

"You will face new dimensions of love and joy. There will continue to be new challenges and new opportunities to appreciate God's grace in your lives."

Why, William was now looking at her again but so. . .so strangely. For one long moment, Beth's gaze clung to his before he swiftly looked away and down at the young couple starting out on their own great adventure.

New dimensions of love. The words hammered their way deep into Beth's heart and soul. They expressed so clearly the confused feelings that were sweeping through her. New dimensions. . . But then that meant love had been there all along, that now its boundaries were merely changing, expanding.

A delicious shiver swept through her. Of course she had always loved him—but certainly not like this, not with this consuming passion.

She saw William swallow and clear his throat as though searching for some control. She studied his face intently. It was a face so familiar and yet suddenly not at all really known to her. He was certainly tanned by the months on board ship and the harsh, hot sun of this new Southland. His cheeks were leaner; his strong jaw seemed more pronounced, as did the lines on his face.

She had noticed only this morning that there seemed to be an added tenseness in him but had put it down to today's special responsibilities, perhaps even the nearness of being a father once again and worry for her in these new, primitive surroundings.

The muscle in her back was aching again from sitting so long, and one hand went to the swell of her body where their second child lay nestled. Only a couple weeks more and their little family would no longer be just the two of them and little Harold.

Her husband. Her son. Her family. Thankfulness and praise welled up in her.

William's face softened, changing so swiftly from that solemn, earnest expression as he smiled so gently, so lovingly down at the couple before him. Once again Beth forgot any momentary physical discomfort as a surge of emotion horribly like envy swept through her.

How long has it been since he smiled at me, really smiled at me with that devastating dimple in his cheek, those gleaming brown eyes twinkling so brightly? she thought sadly.

If only he would smile at her anywhere near as lovingly as he just had to the blushing young bride and her proud yet bashful young groom. Not even on their own wedding day had he smiled at her like that.

She shuddered and closed her eyes.

But then their wedding had been arranged, orchestrated by Lord Farnley, even to the actual ceremony being held beside her mother's bed. It had been such a rushed affair, only a few days after William had returned home as a fully ordained minister at last, with the news of an appointment to a church in London.

And the day he had arrived home had been the very day her father had told her at last just how ill her mother was. The doctors had given up hope weeks before, and now it was a matter of days, hours. Without waiting for her to recover from the shock of the confirmation of what she had already suspected, Lord Farnley had coldly informed her of her mother's dearest wish—to see her daughter happily married.

"I know you are still young, but it is the very last thing you can do for her," Lord Farnley had informed Beth in that icy, controlled voice that she had hated and dreaded so much, knowing he was trying only to be strong for the wife he loved.

And as she had so many times in the past, she had turned to William, and he had not failed her. He had been so pale, so stiff and formal, kindly pretending, informing her that he had her stepfather's permission to pay his addresses to her. Not then, or since, had either of them ever mentioned that their marriage had been arranged by Lord Farnley.

Beth frowned. It had not been until several days after their wedding that she had realized the Reverend William Garrett was a different man from her old lighthearted playmate and mentor. Indeed, William had changed so much that she had been forced to the conclusion that being an ordained man of the cloth had made him more aware of his responsibilities to society and the church he served and thus made him more austere, more dignified.

She had thought that they would become so much closer as a married couple. Instead it seemed as though being married had raised some insurmountable barrier between them. Of course, so quickly after their wedding, she had been devastated by her mother's death; and soon after that, she had been sick and tired with a difficult pregnancy.

She had often thought it had been no wonder the old, fun-loving William she had known had retreated more and more from a sick watering pot of a wife who had so quickly lost her shape as well as her temper.

After Harold had arrived, she had so hoped having a child would bring them closer together. Instead it had seemed to only increase the distance, that strange barrier between them. Certainly William was a good father in so many ways, but he still withheld himself from enjoying his son, even from spending too much time with him.

But then, these last few months on board ship crossing the fifteen thousand miles of ocean between England and South Australia, she had seen the way he had opened up with Kate and their new friend, Adam Stevens. But as much as he had seemed to be his old self with them, he had been even more reserved with herself, even more so with Harold, until she had gone from bewilderment to anger, and now to deep pain and a resolve to find out why.

But since they had been virtually stranded here in this new colony more than a month ago, instead of being able to sail on to New South Wales as they had planned, there had been so little real time alone together. They had been so desperately busy trying to organize their permanent accommodations before the baby arrived.

We've done it, she thought with satisfaction. *We've moved into our own home at last, no longer roughing it in that tent in the Youngs' clearing so close to their crowded one.*

After their momentous decision to settle here for at least a couple years, they had bought their ten acres permitted by the emigration commissioner. They had been blessed in that it had already been owned by one family who had started clearing the land and had half-built the primitive stone dwelling before the husband and sole provider of that family had died. The grieving wife had quickly sold it to raise the fare to return to familiar England and relatives.

William had been working so hard to finish the sturdy house. It was still primitive and lacked many of the comforts they had taken for granted in England, but for the first time in many months they were in their own home.

Perhaps now she would be able to persuade William to talk, to really talk to her about what was troubling him. She knew it was going to take a good deal of courage to confront him. In truth, after Kate and Adam had left on their journey overland to New South Wales, she had been plain scared to start talking to William about their relationship in case it only made everything worse. Night and day she had been praying for strength, for the right words.

She had insisted on accompanying him today, despite the frowns she knew could be directed at her by those who disapproved of her going out-of-doors in her advanced condition. When Mrs. Young had told her their oldest daughter, Bessie, would be more than happy to mind Harold with the Youngs' own children, she had grasped the opportunity.

It had only been a relatively short drive in the old cart, at the moment their only mode of transport. The track here had been almost nonexistent, weaving in and around trees, and the jolting over the rough ground had been much worse than she had anticipated. But the chance to share in this, his very first service in their new home, had been too enticing. She was determined to prove to him she could be a good minister's wife even in this primitive place on the outskirts of

Adelaide if he decided to minister here.

And then as the wedding ceremony had commenced, she had realized how long it had been since she had been able to simply indulge herself in watching him, listening to him. It had been so many months since he had preached. On board ship the captain had not been at all sympathetic to church services, so they had met informally for prayer and reading Scripture.

She had been so filled with happiness watching and listening as the vows had been made by the young couple. William's beautiful voice had sent delicious shivers through her. She was so proud of him. It had been absolute bliss until. . .until she had realized. . .now knew. . .

Tears burned at the back of her eyes as desolation filled her. There had been times in the beginning when William had told her lightly that of course he loved her. But he had not been so gallant for months now. In fact, ever since Harold had been born he had been different. And suddenly, she passionately, quite desperately, longed for him to not just mouth the words of love but mean them!

"I would like you to reflect on the meaning of marriage," William's deep tones rumbled, drawing her wayward thoughts back to the wedding ceremony. With some shame she realized she had missed some of his message and forced herself to pay attention so she could comment knowledgeably about it afterward as a good minister's wife should.

"It may be easy to enjoy the event, but sometimes it is more difficult to appreciate the reality behind the event." Once again the Reverend Garrett raised his head, slowly this time, and looked directly at his wife. "Marriage is a commitment to love," he added softly. "But what is love?"

Beth stiffened. William had always been very, very serious about commitment. What was he saying? And why was he looking at her so intently?

"In the first book of Corinthians in the Holy Scriptures, chapter thirteen is known as the Love Chapter. Wherever the word *charity* appears, I am going to take the liberty of substituting the word *love,* which is its true meaning." The slightest of smiles lightened his face once again before he looked away from her and down at the small, well-used Bible in his hand.

He started to read the familiar words she had heard him quote numerous times before at weddings. Never before had he used the word *love*. At first she thought that was what made him seem different from all the other times he had read this passage. But suddenly she realized it was far more than that. For a fleeting moment she thought she might be mistaken—that it must be because of her newly discovered love that she thought he was different. But then she knew it was not just her.

William was different. There was an added emphasis on each word, his voice rising louder with a growing passion as he quoted, "Love suffereth long, and is kind; love envieth not. . . ."

He paused and once again looked directly across at her. She hardly heard the next few verses that he quoted from memory, his eyes never leaving hers. It seemed as though there were only the two of them present. A tremor swept through her.

William paused for a long moment, but his gaze never wavered from his wife. No one moved. In the utter stillness, the final verse was spoken softly, with a depth of reverence that had even more impact than his triumphant, ringing tones.

"And now abideth faith, hope, love, these three." He stopped again, swallowed, and then almost whispered, "But the greatest of these is love."

Still no one stirred.

A moment longer William stared at Beth. How his heart was aching. He could see her wide, startled eyes, the blush that was rising in her beautiful face.

The young bridegroom gave a nervous little cough. William pulled himself together and glanced swiftly around. A wave of restlessness had started to rustle through the wedding guests. Wondering looks were being exchanged. A couple of folks were glancing from him to Beth, and he took a deep breath and rather abruptly concluded the service with a brief prayer.

When the newly married couple were at last receiving the felicitations of their family and friends, William started toward Beth. He had only taken a step when the bride's father stepped in front of him and held out his hand.

"Reverend, a great service, a great service. We are so pleased you agreed to do this for us here at home and for going to all the trouble you did to clear it with the authorities, like." The man beamed, and William felt the coins being thrust into his hand. Before he could protest, the man had turned his back and was moving back to the bridal party.

William hesitated. He had absolutely no need of this assisted emigrant's hard-earned money, but he knew that the man's pride would be hurt if he refused it. And it would also make people wonder about this strange minister who refused remuneration for his services! He had no desire to be seen to flaunt his and Beth's prosperity.

He shrugged and slipped the money into his pocket, knowing there would be other opportunities to help this poor family. Slowly, almost reluctantly, he turned away and started again toward where Beth had been seated. But she had gone.

It had been very hot in the crowded building. Sudden anxiety for her in her delicate condition made him quicken his pace, pushing his way as fast and politely as he could past those who would liked to have engaged him in conversation.

Beth was sitting by herself in the shade on the stump of an old gum tree and was vigorously fanning herself. He paused for a moment, studying this woman he had been married to now for so long, and yet whom it seemed he had always loved. Heavy with child, his child, she was more beautiful than ever to him.

But she was so young, so small and frail-looking. The gown she was wearing had long, fitted sleeves that seemed to emphasize the slenderness of her arms. She had still not completely recovered from the stresses of the long sea voyage, and he was worried about her. This morning she had been so pale, seeming more fragile then ever. He had not wanted her to come, but she had been so adamant that he had found himself weakly yielding when she had turned those incredibly beautiful blue eyes on him and stated indignantly, "Miss your very first service here in the Great Southland? Never, Sir!"

He had smiled slightly. Ever since their wedding, she had made up her mind to be "the best minister's wife ever," as she had earnestly told him. He did not feel like smiling now. Perhaps one day she might realize he just wanted her to be herself, not fill some role others put her in.

As always, she had paid careful attention to her toilet. Despite his urgings that the layers of petticoats in the full skirt were not suitable for this hot weather, she had insisted on dressing in one of the fashionable gowns she had brought from London.

She heard his steps on the rough gravel track and looked up at him. A strange, unfamiliar look flashed across her pale face. Then, as he halted a little distance from her, she frowned and moved uncomfortably.

Suddenly he wished she was again the twelve year old who had hero-worshiped him, who would have bounced up and hugged him, hung on his arm, who would have told him how wonderful the service had been, how wonderful he had been.

Instead, her frown increased and she asked sharply, "What was that all about, William?"

Chapter 2

Williams's hands clenched. Had he been so obvious? All he had been able to think of all through the wretched service had been how much he had wanted Beth to look at him at their own wedding with even a small amount of the worshipful adoration that this young bride had shown for her bridegroom. Instead, Beth had been extremely pale as she had stood beside him in that sad sickroom, repeating her vows in a trembling whisper. He had never been able to forget that dreadful, blind look in her eyes.

He moved closer and held out both hands to her. "What do you mean?" he heard himself murmur, and even to his own ears his voice sounded stilted. In a louder voice he said, "Come, we must get you out of this heat."

She did not stir. Her beautiful blue eyes surveyed him intently. "You. . .you were staring at me so strangely during the service."

"Was I?" he forced himself to say lightly.

"Yes," she said shortly. "People were looking at us. Some still are. It is most embarrassing."

"Then I suggest you let me help you to your feet so we may smile at these 'people' and then be on our way."

❧

Beth studied him carefully. To her dismay, he was avoiding her eyes, standing there with his hands still held out. Reluctantly she reached up and let him take a firm grip so he could haul her ungainly body upright.

"I can manage," she said through gritted teeth. But then, as she let him help her to her feet, she felt that muscle in her back clench once again and for a moment was glad of his support. He steadied her and then released her quickly and turned away.

She caught her breath and stared at his broad back. He was never so careless of her. It was almost as though he could not bear to touch her. The familiar stab of pain shot through her, but with it was mingled anger and frustration.

Her chin went up. With a rustle of her skirts she moved as swiftly after him as her body would allow. No way was she going to let him cause her to be the recipient of more curious looks.

She latched onto his arm and gave it a fierce little tug. He turned toward her, and she fiercely hated that raised eyebrow.

Raising her chin a little higher, she said angrily, "William, I will not, cannot stand this attitude of yours one more moment, and I demand—"

"Oh, Reverend Garrett, such a beautiful service. I swear your words brought me to tears."

Beth stopped abruptly. William looked relieved at the interruption. Gritting her teeth, she watched the polite smile move his lips as he turned around and graciously, if humbly, acknowledged the woman's flattering comments.

The lady's eyes swept a little enviously over Beth's elegant dress and bonnet. "But your dear wife," she simpered, "surely so close to your time. . .is it really very wise of you, my dear, especially in this heat?"

Beth fought back the hot words on her tongue. It would never do for a minister's wife to say, "Stop ogling my husband, Madam! He might be the most handsome man in the colony, but he belongs to me. He's mine!"

The sudden wave of possessiveness shook her, and she was immediately ashamed. It was a moment before she could murmur a polite response.

To her relief, William said hastily but firmly, "Just so, Madam, and I must not keep my wife standing any longer," before bowing again and continuing slowly over to where they had been forced to leave their horse and cart some distance away in the shade of some tall gum trees.

She waited tensely for him to comment on her furious outburst. But there were still too many people around, and she realized as he nodded or called out cheerful greetings to all and sundry, this was not the time to renew her attack.

After the silence between them had grown too long, Beth sought a little frantically for a topic of conversation and then blurted out, "I wonder if Kate and Adam have met up with John Martin yet."

The arm under her hand stiffened. She glanced up at him, and her heart dropped. Once again that steely look of reserve had settled on his face.

"It is extremely unlikely," he said abruptly. "Adam said even if all went well, the journey would take several weeks, and then it would depend upon where Martin was on the vast property."

"Oh, yes, of course," she murmured swiftly. Recovering quickly, she tried again. "Such a shame they missed out on your first formal duty as a minister here in this new colony. I do declare your wedding services get better with each one."

"Thank you, Beth." To her relief, although his tenseness did not disappear completely, he smiled briefly and then paused as he raised his hat in response to a greeting from a couple who had traveled out on the *Royal Duke* with them from England.

"No word yet from your sister and Mr. Stevens?" one of the women asked. Beth held her breath for a moment and stole a swift glance at William as the stupid woman rattled on. "Such a brave young couple, traveling all that way through the wilderness to Mr. Stevens's station in New South Wales, when only explorers and a few intrepid souls have been all that way overland from here before," she gushed.

"Yes, it was very unfortunate our captain on the *Royal Duke* refused to continue our journey to its completion in Sydney," William responded stiffly.

"However, I doubt very much if they would have arrived yet at Mr. Stevens's sheep property."

Beth glanced at him. And that was something else that puzzled and amazed her. Why did he hate talking about Kate's determination to find John Martin? Why had he refused to discuss any of that with her?

Ever since Adam Stevens and Kate's amazing disclosures about John Martin, William had always cut her off abruptly when she had wanted to discuss it all with him, stating that Lord Farnley's supposed son by a previously unknown marriage to a Spanish woman during the Napoleonic Wars had nothing to do with him. Which, of course, was patently untrue.

Besides the whole business being the catalyst that brought them from England to this new colony, the death of Beth's stepfather had led to them both inheriting a surprising amount of money from his estate. William's forethought in bringing sufficient funds with them so they could purchase property had been most fortunate.

Neither of them had realized just how wealthy his lordship had been, and his nephew Sir Percival Farnley, who for many years had thought himself heir to the title and entailed estate, had been furious at not being left more money in the will, and of course even more furious when the existence of another claimant to his inheritance had been discovered.

Beth's mind snapped back to the present and the persistent woman who had traveled with them on the *Royal Duke*. Somehow Beth managed to smile, to respond appropriately, ignoring the avid curiosity in the woman's eyes as she glanced from Beth to William and back. William murmured something politely, and suddenly Beth wanted to kick him, to scream, to do anything that would stop him from treating her as formally as he did everyone else.

Always he was so polite, so correct in his address to her. Just as he was now to these people who were practically strangers. She was his wife, the mother of his children. But sometimes she wondered if they were still even friends.

In the past, only at night in the privacy of their bedroom had something of the old, loving, lighthearted boy she had grown up with returned. But to her increasing pain and bewilderment, even those delightful times together had not occurred for many months now, not since Lord Farnley's funeral and Adam Stevens's intrusion into their lives.

In fact, she thought wearily as she leaned heavily on William's arm, *the last two years has been nothing but turmoil. First, I lost William's constant presence and support; then there was Mother's illness, my foolish friendship with John, and the grimness of our wedding day when it should have been so happy.*

Suddenly Beth felt drained of energy. Her mother had died only a few weeks after the wedding, and there had been no chance of getting used to married life before the early discomforts of being with child had prostrated her.

Then had come the discovery of John Martin's arrest for murder and the dreadful day he had been sentenced. Transportation to Australia for life. She had never really believed her charming young friend could possibly have done such a foul deed.

That horrible period had at the time seemed endless. Even the wonder and delight of becoming a mother had been tarnished. Harold had arrived weeks early. The constant, special care of such a tiny baby had consumed so much of her time there had hardly been a chance to prove to William and his new congregation she could be a good minister's wife, be of some use to him in his onerous tasks as a clergyman.

As though all that had not been enough, Lord Farnley had collapsed. There had been the hasty, long journey back to Fleetwood from London, and then the very day of his funeral, Adam Stevens had arrived with his information about John Martin.

There was so much about her friendship with John that she had never mentioned to a soul, not even Kate. And certainly she had been too ashamed to breathe a word to William. Perhaps if he had not been so changed, perhaps if he had not shown such determined lack of inclination to talk about John Martin and the whole sad business, she might have plucked up the courage. But as it was, she had been so fearful that he was already disappointed in his wife, in her lack of ability to help him in that parish in London with the impoverished people he had been trying so hard to care for both physically and spiritually.

The muscle in her back suddenly spasmed once more, this time so long and so painfully, Beth held her breath. And then she knew.

"Beth?"

William's sharp, suddenly anxious voice reached her through the wave of pain. She felt his arm go around her waist, and she thankfully leaned on him.

"Oh dear, oh dear, is she all right, Reverend Garrett?"

The pain eased, and Beth straightened but stayed close within William's grasp. She started to smile, and then her smile broadened as she saw William's eyes widen in comprehension and then his face go very pale.

"Yes, I'm perfectly all right," she swiftly reassured them both, and then chuckled mischievously. "Well, as all right as a mother-to-be at this stage can be. But I am afraid I have to ask you to excuse us, Madam. We need to make certain arrangements for the imminent arrival of our baby."

A groan burst from William. Before she could protest, he swept her up in his arms and hurried the remaining distance to the cart.

"Why didn't I insist on hiring a proper carriage?" he muttered angrily as he lifted her carefully to the hard, exposed seat.

She had loved being held so close to his strong body and gurgled happily. "Because there are very few way out—" She stopped abruptly, and her teasing smile disappeared as another, stronger pain swept through her.

🦋

William prayed silently all the way home. He should have known better. He should never have yielded to her reproachful eyes when he had said she should stay safely home. Having her share this first special time after so many barren months not ministering, seeing her delight in having a real occasion for which to dress up and then the delightful prospect of having her all to himself on the journey to and fro had just been too much temptation.

Those few miles along that narrow, bumpy road through the bush were the longest he had ever traveled. Never had he been so glad to see the house come into view. And yet. . .

"I haven't even finished the house properly yet," he muttered grimly and then hoped Beth had not heard him.

She had but only gasped, "No matter. I've been prepared for ages. Didn't want to be caught out as with Harold's. . ."

Another pain caught her breath. William glanced swiftly at her, but she was holding her stomach, her eyes closed and her face twisted in pain. He urged the horses to go faster still, but not too fast so he could avoid the worst bumps to save jolting her around.

He had wanted to build more rooms so badly, but so far there had only been time to finish a couple of bedrooms so they could at least move from the tent on the Youngs' property. All that could be said for their home was that it was dry and kept the rain out! Poor Lucy, so far their only servant, was still sleeping on a cot in the only other room, the detached kitchen.

The pains were coming much faster and stronger. As he hauled on the reins, he started roaring for Lucy to fetch Mrs. Young, praying she would have left the wedding early herself to tend to her own large family.

He was so afraid for Beth, this small woman, still hardly more than a child herself.

" 'What time I am afraid, I will trust in thee,' " he quoted over and over, wondering as he prayed through the long hours that followed if the author of that Fifty-sixth Psalm had ever felt like this for someone he loved.

🦋

Immense gratitude to a great and merciful God filled William with awe. He stared down at the red, rumpled face of the newborn baby cradled closely to Beth. Tears started to burn the back of his weary eyes. This was his son, flesh of his flesh.

"Would. . .would you like to hold him?"

His eyes lifted to Beth's pale, exhausted face. She was watching him with a curious expression.

"I—" His voice was choked. He swallowed rapidly and tried again. "I didn't mean to disturb you. Mrs. Young insisted you need to rest, but she did say it would be all right to take a peep at you both. I. . .I'm sorry. I just. . ." He drew a deep, much-needed breath.

A gleam of humor flashed into her blue eyes. "You just wanted to see your new son. By the look of you, I think nurses should insist fathers rest also. Do sit down before you fall down, William, my dear."

He only vaguely heard the mild exasperation in her soft voice, but he did sink onto the chair beside her bed, thankful to be off legs that trembled as they had only twice before, when she had been shyly waiting for him that first night and the day when Harold had been born.

Beth lifted the carefully wrapped bundle and handed it to him. "Meet your son, William," she said gently.

Without a word, he stared at her for a moment and then reached out to take her precious gift.

Father. He was a father.

His eyes returned to the sleeping baby. Even as he watched, his son's eyes flickered and opened. The baby's face started to screw up as though to protest being disturbed once again in this crazy new world. One tiny fist slipped out of the covers and waved around aimlessly. William tentatively put out a finger and the tiny fist closed around it. The baby seemed to think better of making a fuss, yawned, and settled to slumber again.

"He. . .he's so tiny," William whispered reverently.

"Not as small as Harold was, but then he is not quite as early," Beth said wearily. "But Mrs. Young did say that with two babies arriving early like this, we had better be extra careful if we have another one. It could be too early and too tiny."

William looked up at Beth sharply, but she was resting back on the pillows again with her eyes closed.

"He looks so much like Harold did," she added softly, and there was no mistaking the satisfaction in her voice.

William stilled. He looked quickly down and studied the tiny scrap, not daring to push the wraps back so he could have a better look. He closed his eyes and clenched his teeth.

Harold.

"Well, don't you agree?" Beth added a little hesitantly after a long moment, and he knew he had let the silence stretch too long.

She was looking at him with a slight frown on her face. He forced a smile and said as lightly as he could, "Well, if you mean all red and scrawny, I'd have to agree."

"William! I'll have you know none of our babies would ever look so horrible! They are beautiful." Beth reached out and gently traced a finger across the tiny cheek still marked by his rough passage into this world. She pushed the cover back from the tiny head and said proudly, "See, he has just the same mop of black hair Harold did. If anything, it's longer and thicker. And his ears stick out from his head just like yours do."

She was right. He certainly did look like Harold had. William stared and then inwardly sighed. But then, didn't most babies have dark hair and look alike just after they were born?

"Well, he must take after some distant relative, certainly not me or his beautiful fair mother," he said as lightly as he could.

"Oh, I don't know," she said idly, still touching the dark head. "Kate told me once she remembers your hair being a much darker color than it is now."

"She does?" Even he could hear the sharp note in his voice. Beth looked up at him, and he glanced down again and said as casually as he could, "Well, I don't remember ever being as dark as Harold." And then, because he did not think he could take any more comparisons, he added swiftly, "We never did decide on another boy's name if our daughter did not arrive."

Beth's face lightened. She gave an unexpected, unladylike snort. "You may not have thought beyond a daughter's name, but I most certainly have."

He looked up swiftly.

She suddenly smiled at him gently. "We gave Harold my stepfather's name because it pleased him so much and helped lift his sadness after Mother died. This young man shall have his own father's name. But I have always thought that to have the father's name the same only causes confusion in time, so what about James William?"

🦋

Beth held her breath, watching William carefully. He had never made any comment about Harold's name, but there had been times she had wondered if he had regretted her choice. And it had been her choice, because he had seemed almost indifferent at the time. In fact, he was already paying more attention to this baby then he ever had to Harold those first few weeks.

To her utter dismay, his eyes filled with moisture, and as she stared at him, one solitary tear made its way down his rough, unshaven cheek.

Deeply shaken and moved, she impulsively touched his hand and murmured, "I love you, William."

His face stilled. A tiny fire blazed deep in his dark eyes so briefly, that afterward she thought she must have imagined it. Then his eyes were hidden as he looked down once more at the baby, before at last smiling gently and reaching for her hand. "And I love you, too, Elizabeth Garrett," he murmured softly.

Beth searched his face and felt a wave of disappointment. Even so had they spoken to each other several times over the years before he had left Fleetwood. It had always been said lightly after some childish prank, his way of letting her know she was forgiven. But this time she could not laugh.

She opened her mouth and then decided this was not the right time—when she still looked so pathetically unattractive and was so exhausted—to tell him the true nature of her love.

His strong fingers closed so tightly around hers she winced. "My father's name was James," he murmured.

She swallowed on the lump in her throat. "Yes, I know," she whispered and felt her own eyes fill with tears of pity for him as they had before when he had first told her why he had come to live at Fleetwood.

Beth knew William could hardly remember his father, cousin to Lord Farnley, who had gone beside her stepfather to fight Napoleon and never returned. His mother had survived until she had instilled in her young son all she could about a personal faith in Christ and then thankfully given him up into the safe guardianship of Harold Farnley before succumbing to a lengthy illness.

Concern for Beth filled William's face. He let her go and stood up quickly. "I was warned not to stay long. You need to sleep. Shall I put. . . ?" He paused and looked down at the baby in his arms with such a wondering, loving expression on his face that she wanted to reach out and hold them both tightly to her. "Shall I put James William into his crib, or do you want him back on the bed with you?"

"Farva?"

The soft murmur came from the open doorway where a small, tear-streaked face peered through the early morning light. "Harwol come?"

"Harold, what are you doing here?" William's voice was sharp, and the baby in his arms moved abruptly. He lowered his voice and added in a softer voice, "I thought I told you to stay with Lucy until I came to fetch you."

Beth opened her mouth and then closed it abruptly. Several times during the hours just past, Mrs. Young had assured her William was minding Harold with every care and attention while Lucy had been helping them. But then, he had never failed in kindness to his son; he just always seemed to hold himself strangely aloof from him.

"He is trying to say 'Father' and 'Harold,' " she murmured with a teasing smile. "Someone been teaching him, I wonder?"

William actually looked a little sheepish but made a fast recovery. "He is a very bright little fellow, and he was upset at not being allowed near his beloved mother," he replied swiftly.

Her smile widened, but she watched William carefully as he hesitated for a brief moment before looking inquiringly at her. She nodded slightly, and William handed the sleeping baby back to her before going over to the door and swinging Harold up in his arms.

He sat down once more on the chair close to her and put Harold on his knees. "I told you when you woke up we would have a little baby for you. This is your baby brother, and his name is. . .is James William."

His voice cracked slightly, but it was gentle and his face full of understanding of a very small boy's impatience and curiosity as Harold stared with big dark eyes at the small bundle in Beth's arms.

Beth's heart was full. She looked at each face, the man she loved so much, the sleeping baby, and their firstborn who would always hold a special place in her heart. Surely God was good, and as Kate had so many times reminded her through their uncomfortable sea voyage, He would give strength in times of weakness.

It was only a few minutes before William and Harold reluctantly left Beth to her much-needed rest. After the door had closed behind them, she felt happier than she had for a long, long time. Thoughtfully she watched the still gently rocking, small crib William had placed James so gingerly in. He had surprised her with it only a few days before. Apparently he had not been able to buy one and so had spent a lot of time making it himself. At least that explained why she had seen so little of him in the evenings.

Then she frowned slightly. Already he seemed more taken with this baby than he had ever been with Harold when he was as small. Perhaps, like her, he was becoming more used to the idea of being a parent. But then, something about William had changed.

Exhaustion made her close her eyes, but then they flew open. She still did not know why William had behaved so strangely toward her during that wedding service. Somehow, she had to find the right words to ask him without widening the distance between them.

And above all, somehow she had to convince him she truly loved him, had to remove that wall between them until they were truly one forever.

Chapter 3

Beth surveyed her domain with considerable pride and satisfaction. Once again she marveled at the determination and industry William had exhibited in obtaining the builders and materials to finish their small stone-and-clay house during the six months since James's birth. The last of its extensions was now complete.

Lucy had proved to be an absolute treasure, even if she was so young, but they could still do with more help. Isabel Young gave what advice and help she could, but the running of the household and their little family was Beth's sole responsibility. For someone who had always been surrounded by servants, even in the house in London, she was satisfied they were coping as well as they could in a land where so many things they had taken for granted in the Old Country were just not available.

Although it still grieved her, that invisible wall between her and William had not seemed as high or unbridgeable since the birth of James. William included both children equally in his cuddles and attention, and these last months Harold had thrived under his father's extra attention.

Somehow, autumn and then the colder days had slipped by so peacefully and busily that she had not dared to mention William's strange behavior at the wedding. As for her own love for him, it continued to be a bittersweet joy mingled with such pain and fear of his rejection that she had never ventured again to tell him.

When the time was right she would tell William that she loved him. As she looked around the cheerful room, a stab of fear touched her. She had prayed so fervently about it all, but still the fear of damaging their fragile new relationship had stopped her. After James's birth, when the days became colder, William had determined that they had to let Lucy have her own room instead of the drafty, still-unfinished kitchen. They'd assembled the crib and little Harold's bed in their bedroom, and the four of them had crowded in. But as each month had passed and William had made no move to share his love with Beth, her frustration, disappointment—and then fear—had increased.

Perhaps now. . . She took a deep breath. Perhaps now that the other bedrooms were finished and Harold and James had their own room. . .perhaps now William would pull her close again in the privacy of their room, in their own large bed. As he used to.

She shook off the thought with some difficulty and continued to study the room, looking for ways she could increase its elegance and perhaps help them forget on cozy nights around the fire how different this new life was and how far it was from all that was familiar and comfortable.

She sighed. Despite her efforts, this room was certainly a long, long way from the elegance and space of Fleetwood, or even of the smaller house they had occupied in London with its adequate number of servants. But Beth felt tremendous pride in this home that she and William were creating from nothing in this strange land.

It had taken her long hours, but at last she had finished sewing the curtains and, with Isabel Young's help, had been able to hang them. They certainly added that touch of color needed to brighten up the small drawing room.

She walked across to plump up a matching fat cushion on the couch and then moved over to the fireplace. Using the poker, she stirred up the glowing embers before placing another piece of wood on them. In another few days it would officially be spring. Spring in September. She gave another little sigh. Would she ever get used to this strange upside-down southern land?

Already the days were warming up, but today there had been a chill wind, and the night promised to be very cold. It still seemed strange that winter had come and almost gone without one snowflake. Standing back, she watched as the flames flickered and then began to lap around the timber.

It was a rare, quiet moment. Lucy was in the kitchen, the large room detached from this main part of the building in case, despite all their precautions, the kitchen fire used for cooking somehow got out of control. James was sound asleep, and Isabel had taken Harold with her back to her cottage to play with her own children, assuring Beth that Bessie would keep an eye on him. The two women had become good friends since Isabel had acted as midwife at James's birth.

"Now, my dear," she had admonished Beth before whisking herself and Harold away, "you make sure you rest while you have the chance before James starts making a fuss for his next feed. You are still far too thin and tired. Been going too hard at getting this place to rights, you have," she had scolded gently.

Beth smiled slightly. She knew she was still not quite up to full strength because of a bad cold and nasty cough this past week, and she should really rest as instructed. But she had taken no more then two steps toward the inviting couch when she heard swift steps in the short corridor outside.

"Beth! Are you there, Beth?"

William burst into the room. His face was lit with a smile, instantly dispelling the fears that his urgent tones had aroused. He waved a thick envelope at her.

"Oh, William, is it from Kate?"

The weeks and then the months had slipped by with no word from her half sister. Their original concern about the travelers being able to reach John Martin and give him the good news that his parentage and inheritance had been proven and that their lawyers believed it should be possible for him to have a retrial by his peers at the House of Lords had been superseded by fear that Kate and her party might not have reached their destination safely at all.

"What does she say? Are they in Sydney? When are they returning? Did they find John Martin safe and well?"

William winced inwardly at the last question but smiled at his wife and said with forced cheerfulness, "I have no more idea then you yet, Sweetheart. We can read it together."

He watched the delight flash across her face. She said with a beaming smile, "How just like you not to read it first yourself so we can share it together."

Feeling an instant hypocrite, he hastily said, "It is addressed to us both."

He could not admit to her that he had not read the letter because he was so reluctant to once again be reminded of John Martin's impact on all their lives. The atmosphere between them had not been as tense or distant since James had been born. But then, they had both been so busy, with no real time to spend just on themselves.

He forced a smile at her, pulling her down to sit beside him as he handed her the letter. "Why don't you read it aloud for both of us?" he asked a little huskily, inhaling with delight the delicate perfume that always surrounded her. It reminded him of a fragrant English spring garden in bloom.

She started reading the letter out loud and then stopped abruptly. He stifled a smile. He should have known she would get carried away and race her eyes over the missive so much faster than reading out loud permitted.

She gave a startled exclamation, and he froze. Then, as his eyes never left her expressive face, he found himself praying fervently. . .praying for her as well as for grace and acceptance for himself.

At last she lifted dazed, wide eyes to his face. "Married!" she burst out. "They are married!"

For a brief moment, his heart stood still, hope raised that John Martin was safely married and even more removed from Beth.

Then reason kicked in. He was not sure about the liberties allowed convicts, even assigned convicts such as Martin, but he did think it unlikely that someone with a life sentence who had served just over twelve months would be permitted to marry. Especially when he lived on a lonely sheep farm—no, station, Adam had called Stevens Downs—and was unlikely to meet any women, especially one willing to marry a convict.

Beth's eyes had returned to continue scanning the closely written sheets. "They are not going to live way out west on his station, but at someplace called Waverley which is only a few days ride west of Sydney! A few days ride. . . !"

Light dawned. "Beth," William interrupted carefully, "are Kate and Adam married?"

"Yes, yes, and deliriously happy, she claims."

He swallowed a sudden sharp pang of envy and said softly, "I'm so glad for them."

She was still swiftly reading the letter, and a wry smile twisted his lips. From the moment she had first been able to read, she had always become carried away with any missive. How many times in the years he was away from Fleetwood had he pictured her just so devouring the letters he had written to her almost every week. Her replies had been spasmodic, but usually they spilled out a torrent of woes in a young girl's life. Perhaps that was one more reason why her failure to confide in him something so important had eaten into him so deeply.

"If you have finished with that first sheet, do you think I could now peruse it?" he murmured gently.

"Hmm. . ." She absently passed the beginning of the letter to him, still muttering occasionally with surprise. Then, before he had a chance to read more than the first few lines, she gave another sharp exclamation.

Her hand closed convulsively, the page in her hand rustling as it closed around it. She stared up at him again. This time her eyes were filled with horror. Even as he reached urgently to enfold her in his arms, her eyes filled with tears that slowly started down her face.

"What is it? Is it. . .is it John Martin?"

He gathered her closely to him. She put her head against his chest and gave a sob. He relaxed slightly as she shook her head, but then tensed again as she said sadly, "No, no. It's Cousin Percival."

"Percival Farnley?"

"Yes. He. . .he. . . Kate says he's dead."

"Dead! But how. . . ? I know they were afraid he meant harm to John Martin ever since they discovered he had left England before us. That was why, when we could not be sure when a ship might arrive, they had to travel overland to warn him, but—"

"He tried to kill them—John, Adam, even Kate. Oh, how dreadful it must have been. She. . .she says he was completely crazed. But. . .but they escaped with help from some aborigines. Then Percy was thrown by his horse, and they believe he died from snakebite."

Beth pulled away and handed him the letter. "I am afraid you have married into a scandalous family, William," she added with another sob.

Swiftly he read the letter and then slowly looked up at Beth. In a strangled voice William said, "He was the murderer. Percival murdered your father's gamekeeper and then framed John Martin. He. . .Martin. . .has been completely exonerated and plans to return to Fleetwood to claim it and the title."

She was staring off into space. He wasn't even sure she had heard him. A lace handkerchief was being folded and unfolded by her trembling fingers. There was a faraway look on her face, as though she had gone away from him in her spirit.

"That's why he was there," she whispered. "Why he was smiling just so, pleased. . ."

"Why who was where?" Her words barely registered, and he hardly knew what he had said himself. He was furious with her. Why could she not forget the man?

The anger that seemed to have been churning deep within him for a long time suddenly surfaced out of control. "So your old friend is innocent. In fact, according to Kate he will soon be Lord Farnley!" he snarled.

She jumped at his loud, angry voice and gaped at him. "My. . .my old friend?" she faltered.

🦋

Beth stared at William. His face was transformed, a sneer twisting his lips, and his eyes. . . She had never seen such fury in anyone's face before.

"Or should I have said your old *lover* will soon be Lord Farnley?"

"William!"

She sat frozen, staring at him in horror. He knew. Knew about John.

"Lover?"

Surely that was taking it too far, though? Her mouth was dry. She moistened her lips and at last said in a strained, dazed voice, "You. . .you know? How. . . what. . .how do you know?"

"I've always known," he snapped coldly. "Despite all your attempts at appearing so innocent, I've always known."

She shrank back. Utter astonishment and pain flooded through her. Never before had William spoken to her as though he hated her.

Even while she craved for him to love her in that special way a man should love his wife, always she had thought of him as a man who loved. He loved God, loved his family, his friends, even loved the unlovely she had seen others shrink from. Whenever she thought of God's love for her, she had always thought it must be a marvelous love, a love beyond description if it was greater than William's love and tenderness for those around him.

Then he closed his eyes tightly. While she was still trying to find her voice, trying to find the right words to answer this new William, he passed his hand over his face and looked at her. The anger had gone, but the dreadful sadness in them was even worse. Something in her heart broke there and then.

"Oh, William," she managed to whisper at last, "I'm sorry, sorry for being so stupid, but I was so lonely, unhappy."

He raised his hand and she stopped abruptly. "There is no need to apologize," he said hoarsely. "With God's help I forgave you a long time ago." He stopped and swallowed. After a moment he muttered, "Or at least I thought I had."

She could not bear the anguish in his face any longer. Springing to her feet she made for the door, anxious to escape so she could give way to the tears starting to well up in her throat. His hand shot out and halted her. She winced, and the grip on her arm loosened slightly.

"Don't go, Beth. Please. I have to know what you are going to do."

The urgency in his voice brought her head up. She swallowed, desperately fighting for control. "Do?" she said in a stifled, confused voice. "Do about what?"

He gave her arm an impatient little shake. "Please, Beth, I have to know what you are going to do about Harold," he said rapidly. "Are you going to tell him?"

Utter astonishment filled Beth. She stared at him blankly. "Tell who what? Harold? And what has Harold to do with this?"

It was as though he had not heard her. His face was dead-white, and he continued speaking in such an agonized voice that her confusion and wonderment grew.

"I fought hard to stop myself from loving him, but he is a wonderful little chap. He's twined himself so deeply around my heart I can never give him up. Never. He—" William broke off as a commotion erupted somewhere in the house.

In the kitchen, Lucy's voice screamed. A door slammed, and then light, running feet headed nearer. Simultaneously, Beth and William started toward the door, but before they reached it Mrs. Young's oldest daughter had flung it open and stood holding onto the doorpost, desperately fighting for breath.

Instant terror filled Beth. "Bessie! What is it? Is it. . .Harold?"

She nodded and gasped, "Mother said. . .come quick."

Beth was halfway along the narrow, mile-long track to their neighbor's property before she realized William was just behind her. She stumbled, and his hand steadied her. "Careful, Beth," he cautioned. "Hurting yourself will not help."

Isabel Young ran to meet them. Her white, tear-streaked face brought a moan past Beth's lips.

"Where is he?" William snapped.

"I. . .oh, that's the trouble. I don't know," Mrs. Young panted in a harsh whisper.

"You don't know!" Beth stared frantically around, searching for the little body she had been sure must be lying ill or injured, or. . .or even worse.

"Oh, Reverend Garrett, Beth, I'm so sorry. Bessie says she only turned her back for a moment, and he was gone. We've been out looking for him this past fifteen minutes or more, and there's just no sign of him. I sent her on to fetch you while I came to see if he had returned here."

"Gone! What do you mean, gone?" William's voice was sharp.

Beth took a step forward, but William's strong clasp on her hand tightened. She looked frantically around. Whereas they had money to employ builders, the Youngs were forced to do their own work, and so their house was still only half-built in a clearing in the bush. Their temporary home, still the tent lent to them by the emigration commissioner, was a little distance away, surrounded by crates containing their belongings, waiting to go into their new house.

"Where was he last?" William asked sharply, his voice hoarse.

Mrs. Young pointed with a trembling hand to the far side of the clearing. "They. . .they were gathering some sticks for the fire. Bessie says she told him to wait while she went in a little farther to get a big branch that was on the ground, but when she returned he was gone. She swears she could not have been out of his sight and was only gone a couple minutes. At first she thought he was just playing hide-and-seek," the poor woman faltered guiltily.

"She left him alone?" Beth's voice rose hysterically. She had heard dreadful stories on board ship of people lost in the wild Australian bush. And a small child lost. . .their child. . .Harold. . .

"Steady, Beth!" William's arm went around her shoulders, holding her. "You've gone right into the bush there?"

Isabel nodded wearily. "We've called and searched all around until we decided we needed more help. Lizzie is still out searching. Robert left this morning to get more building supplies, but he is due home any moment."

Tight-lipped, William removed his arm from Beth and strode forward. "Show us where you've already searched," he called back over his shoulder.

❧

Oh, God, this can't be happening, he prayed as they spread out and moved swiftly through the bush, calling out, searching desperately, knowing it was late afternoon already and in a few hours would be dark and freezing cold.

I know I've found it so hard not to love him too much, but please, give me another chance to hold him, to love him unconditionally no matter what pain may be mine eventually, he prayed.

❧

Beth felt as though this must be a nightmare from which she would wake up any moment. She plunged recklessly through the bush, not feeling the branches that whipped her face, her legs. She searched and searched, screaming out her child's name until her voice was hoarse. No little voice answered.

William's voice, some distance away, kept roaring out Harold's name long after her own gave out. Her heart was pounding, her breath coming in short gasps. Time had begun to blur. She had no idea how long they had been searching when she stumbled against the root of a tree and paused, leaning her hand against rough bark, trying to catch her breath.

There was a rustle in the short grass near her feet.

She gave a small scream and jumped back. A thick, striped lizard over a foot long scuttled a few feet away. It stopped, on full alert, as it surveyed the intruder. A blue tongue flickered in and out, and she relaxed slightly.

There had been a similar lizard around their own yard, and they had been warned its powerful jaws could inflict a vicelike painful bite, but usually it did not break the skin unless lacerations were caused when it was forcibly made to let go. She shuddered and gave it a wide berth, moving swiftly on, but now eyeing the ground more carefully as the shadows deepened.

Memory of Percival's fate made her trembling increase. There were far more dangerous reptiles than lizards here. And Harold was such a little boy.

"Oh, my son," she moaned out loud, "where are you?"

She knew men and women from the immediate district had joined the search, but now she could no longer hear their voices. Sunset was fast approaching. Soon it would be dark, cold.

"Harold," she forced past dry lips once more and then stood still, holding her breath, listening, praying, hoping to hear his lisping little voice call out "Muvva."

Only the noises of the bush answered her. A breeze had sprung up, softly whispering through the branches of the short scrub. A magpie warbled, and then there was silence.

She took another step forward and then paused. Surely the breeze would not make the branches of that thick bush wave like that. Even as she started forward, the branches parted and a dark-skinned figure stepped forward.

Beth froze, ready to flee. Stories had started to circulate through the colony about aborigines harassing settlers living in the bush on the outskirts of the settled areas. Then, as the aborigine pushed past the bush in her way, Beth realized it was a woman. There was a movement behind the aborigine, and a small, frightened little dark face peered out from behind her.

The woman was naked except for a tattered, dirty skirt that hung almost to the ground. Obviously she had been in contact with white people who had been generous with their cast-off clothes, or she had stolen the skirt from some poor woman's clothesline.

The aborigine gestured and said something in her guttural language.

"I. . .I'm sorry, I don't understand," Beth whispered.

She took a step forward. The woman tensed, looking as though she would flee. Beth stopped. "Please," she said in a louder voice. "My son, he's lost."

The two mothers from such different cultures stared at each other for a long moment.

Beth tried again. She pointed to herself and then rocked her arms, pantomiming the cradling of a baby. The small child ventured once again from behind his mother. He was about the same size as Harold. Beth pointed to him and then to her own chest again.

"My baby, my son," she said desperately, "lost." Tears started to trickle down her cheeks.

The woman's face softened. She hesitated, still watchful; then she shrugged and gestured to Beth to come closer. "*Kawai!*" she said in a demanding voice. Without waiting to see if Beth obeyed, she turned and made off amongst the trees.

Should she follow? As Beth was desperately trying to make up her mind, she heard a distant shout. This time it was her own name being called. William sounded angry, frightened.

She opened her mouth to answer him, but the strange woman had paused and turned back. She said something softly, then put her hand over her mouth and shook her head. Suddenly she held her thin brown arms across her chest and rocked them as Beth had done.

Hope leaped into Beth's heart, and she started after her. The woman turned and loped off through the trees again. Beth followed swiftly, feeling clumsy as she stumbled where the woman glided so fast over the ground in her bare feet.

A few minutes later the woman stopped and pointed. Very breathless, Beth came up to her, peering anxiously ahead.

"Wakowako," the woman said abruptly. A flow of other words followed, but Beth had rushed forward toward the small figure lying so still on the ground.

"Harold! Oh, Darling!"

Kneeling down she examined him swiftly. There was a cut on his forehead, and blood had trickled down over his eyes. He did not stir as she anxiously picked him up and cradled him in her arms.

The woman spoke again, this time very slowly and hesitantly, *"Wakowako. . . child. . .head."* She pointed, and Beth saw an exposed root and then the rock with a slight smear of blood on it.

"Thank you, oh, thank you," she managed, despite the tears streaming down her face.

The woman flashed a smile and then shrugged and turned away, gesturing to her own wide-eyed child to follow her.

"Wait," Beth called. "Please wait."

The woman stopped and tilted her head inquiringly.

Beth looked desperately around her. She had no idea where she was, having lost all sense of direction. Suddenly she realized why William had been calling her. She had been crazy blundering off the way she had. Now, she too was lost, and she had the added burden of carrying her small, unconscious son.

Chapter 4

B eth followed the aboriginal woman, trusting her for some reason she found it hard to explain later to William. When she at last recognized a familiar old, gnarled gum tree, she was totally exhausted and could only gasp silently with relief.

The woman stopped and pointed in the direction of their new home. Beth nodded, too breathless and exhausted to respond or wonder how the woman knew. The aborigine shrugged and turned to start back the way they had come.

Beth made a tremendous effort and gasped, "Thank. . .you. . ." But the woman simply vanished as silently as she had appeared, her own small boy taking one last, long look at Harold before obeying his mother's sharp command and running after her. The bush swallowed them up, and they were gone.

Gasping for breath, Beth forced one foot after the other. The precious burden in her arms must not be dropped. She was nearly there. She turned the last bend. A baby was crying.

With James in her arms, Lucy was pacing back and forth outside the front door, anxiously peering up the track toward the Youngs'. She saw Beth. A relieved look swept over her face, and she ran toward Beth, James crying even harder.

Beth felt numb. She didn't even feel remorse that her baby was so distressed, no doubt from hunger. Faintness swept through her. She must have swayed, for Lucy made a distressed sound as she reached them and said, "Oh, Miz Garrett, do put him down before you fall down."

Then Beth was sitting on the hard ground, muscles aching, fighting for breath, fighting her whirling head. Vaguely she knew Lucy put James down on the grass near her and took Harold from her vicelike grasp just as she fell back.

"Is he. . .is he. . .?" Lucy's fearful words stopped suddenly. In a relieved voice she added, "Why, he was only asleep. Look, he's waking up."

With a tremendous effort, Beth lifted her head. She knew it had been more than mere sleep.

A small voice started to murmur, "Muvva? Farva? Where my Muvva?"

"Here. . .Darling," she managed to gasp thankfully. "Mother's here." She struggled to sit up, but when she had managed to do so and had pushed away the persistent, descending haze for a moment, she saw he was still again.

William. She needed him. Everything would be all right when William came.

"Get. . .William. . . ," she managed to say with another spurt of energy, and then the haze gave way to blackness.

273

Never had William known such fear. He frantically pushed through the bush in the direction he had last heard Beth cry out Harold's name in that hoarse, frantic voice. Several times he had called her after he had realized far too much time had passed since they had made voice contact with each other.

He paused, called her name again, and then waited in breathless stillness for any sound that would indicate where she was. His short, rasping breaths seemed to keep pace with the silent plea flowing constantly from him. *Please, God. Please, God. Keep them safe. Help me find them.*

A feeling of helplessness filled him. Harold lost. Now Beth. What to do? Which way to go?

Slowly his breathing eased, and suddenly he had an overwhelming need to kneel in the dirt. As he fell to the ground, it was as though his whole being swept out in search of the Lord he had committed his will and his life to, his lips putting into hoarse words what had been tormenting his soul since Bessie had interrupted them.

"Oh, Father, I thought in my arrogance that I was so noble forgiving Beth, marrying her, not saying a word of condemnation to her for pretending Harold is my son," he gasped out loud. "But it was still all there in my heart. I have harbored it there. Forgive me my angry words to her. They. . .they showed me my sinful heart. Please forgive. . .forgive me."

He was silent for a moment, and then in a torrent of words he added, "Your Word says love is kind, does not envy, does not boast, is not proud, is not rude, is not self-seeking, is not. . .is not easily angered, keeps no record of wrongs. . .

"Oh, Father, I've fallen so short of all those things, and yet I claim to love her, to love You. Forgive. . ." He groaned in an agony of spirit. "You are faithful and just. Your Word says You have promised to forgive my sins if I confess them.

"Oh, Father, I shouted at her, was so angry, so unkind, and now she is lost and hurting, and I have not told her how sorry I am, how much I love her! Oh, Father, please forgive me. Cleanse me from all unrighteousness as You promised. I want to love as You love. Perhaps then I can someday be of some value to You again in the ministry I believed You called me to."

He fell silent. Gradually his shuddering, his groaning eased. A breeze sprang up. Slowly increasing in strength, it tossed the branches over his head to and fro. It was cold against the wetness on his cheeks, and at last he stirred and opened his eyes. For a moment he thought someone was beside him. He glanced swiftly around, but no one was there. Still, a sense of peace swept over him.

Raising his head, he stared heavenward and sighed. "Thank You, Lord," he whispered humbly.

A few moments later he was on his feet and with a strangely lighter heart started back through the bush in the direction from which he had come. Nothing had changed. Harold and now Beth were still missing, but his panic and fear were gone. God was in control.

A distant clanging noise echoed faintly through the trees. He caught his breath and began to run. It was the prearranged signal Robert Young had devised to announce if a searcher found any trace of Harold.

To William's surprise, he suddenly burst out of the bush onto the track between the two properties. For a moment he hesitated. He was closer to home than the Youngs'. Some impulse made him turn and head away from the clamor of someone hitting a pipe against the old metal bucket Robert had stuck up on a post.

And then he saw them. The three most precious people in his life lying on the ground near the house. His heart stopped. Then he heard the angry, healthy wail of a baby. Beth moved. She started to sit up, and then he was beside her.

"It's all right, Beth. I'm here." His arm went around her, his eyes swiftly searching from one precious face to the other, ensuring they were safe, determining what injuries there were.

"William." There was utter relief in her harsh whisper. She relaxed against him for a moment, and then she stiffened. "Harold. . .is he. . . ?" An increasing edge of hysteria colored her voice, and he quickly soothed her.

"He's fine," he assured her automatically, but it was not until he had released her and reached out to touch the filthy, bloodstained little face with his trembling hand that he knew for sure that Harold was indeed fine. The little boy stirred and opened his eyes. He blinked and then focused on him.

"Farva," he said faintly. As William reached to gather the precious little body into his arms, big tears filled the dark brown eyes. His little hand went up to his head. "Hurts, Farva."

Overwhelming love and thankfulness filled William. With his eyes closed tightly to stop his own tears from falling, he gently hugged the slight body. "Poor Harold," he soothed lovingly. "Did you fall over, Son?"

The little head tucked against his neck nodded slightly.

"And what about Mother? Did she fall over too?"

The little head lifted and followed his father's anxious gaze across to Beth. She was watching them both silently. Tears had started to run down her face, making pale channels through the dirt and scratches on her cheeks.

James had fallen silent, but just then he stirred and started to let his indignation at being so long neglected made known again in no uncertain terms. He had kicked his covers off, and his plump little legs and arms pumped the air frantically.

"James crying? Muvva crying? They fall over?"

Before William could answer the anxious little question, there was the sound of pounding feet. As Beth reached out to pick up the baby, several people burst around the bend, Robert Young leading them, closely followed by Lucy. He stopped dead, then walked swiftly forward as Lucy darted around him to pick up and soothe James.

William stood up and called out swiftly, "All seems well." Relieved smiles replaced anxious frowns as he continued quickly, "A bump on the head and exhaustion, I think. Beth?"

"Oh, Reverend, I didn't want to leave them," panted Lucy, rocking the baby swiftly. "But she keeled over like, and. . .and insisted I find you."

Beth said faintly, "You are a good girl, Lucy. You did exactly as I asked you to." She looked up at William and said in a stronger voice, "And I did not fall over; I just ran out of breath." She took a quivering breath and asked anxiously, "Is Harold really all right? He has a cut on his head and was unconscious when I found him, and. . ."

Isabel Young swiftly examined the small boy, who was still clinging to William. She nodded reassuringly, and Beth relaxed at last.

"Where was he? How did you find him?" a desperate little voice asked.

Beth's smile was forced, but a wave of love for her swept through William as she said reassuringly to young Bessie, "I didn't really find him. We were all looking for him in the wrong directions. I think he must have run across your yard and gone into the bush the opposite place we thought he must have. If she. . .she hadn't fetched me. . ."

She looked toward the bush where the woman had disappeared and said in a wondering voice, "There was an aboriginal woman and her child. She took me to Harold. He. . .he had fallen and hit his head on a rock. Then when I realized I didn't. . ." She gulped and looked pleadingly up at William. "I didn't know which direction was home, so she brought me here."

Exclamations of wonder filled the air. Someone said they had seen a small camp of aborigines several miles back in the bush near a creek.

Then William said firmly, "We have much to thank her for, but we must get you both—" A slight smile touched his pale face as he raised his voice over James's increasing bellow. "We must get all three of you looked after now."

Eager hands helped Beth to her feet and urged her toward the house. A sudden cheer went up from the other neighbors and friends who had also just arrived on the scene and saw their search was over.

At the bottom steps, William turned and surveyed the small crowd helplessly. What could he say to people like these who had left their urgent tasks so selflessly to help?

"Thank you, every one of you," he called out in a loud voice. He swallowed, and a brief hush descended. Feet shuffled in the dirt. Something suddenly moved him to say, "Tomorrow is the Lord's Day. If any of you would like to return here, perhaps you might like me to lead a church service for you?"

There was dead silence. William stared helplessly from one surprised face to another. Would they be offended? Had he been presumptuous making such an offer?

Several of the men and women looked at each other, and then someone called back eagerly, "You mean that, Parson, Sir? We haven't been able to get into town to any services for weeks."

William assured them earnestly that he did. "It's the very least I can do for all your help," he added eagerly. "And I can assure you I'll prepare the best sermon I ever have. Not too long, though," he hastened to assure them.

There were a few friendly chuckles, a time was set, and excited chatter marked their departure.

While Beth tried to feed and settle James, William insisted on bathing Harold himself, despite Lucy's protests. "You go and prepare something for us all to eat," he ordered her firmly.

Knowing Beth would not want to let Harold out of her sight just yet, he dragged the large tub into their bedroom where she was resting on the bed while she attended the baby's needs. He did let Lucy bring hot water from her large kettle, but he gently removed Harold's clothes himself, quickly examining him for any other injuries before lifting him into the soothing water.

"Just a few scratches on his legs and the cut and bump on his head, I think," he hastily reassured Beth.

She nodded briefly and relaxed.

Suddenly there was tension between them. The angry words he had flung at her before Bessie had interrupted hung again in the air. William found himself avoiding her eyes as he dried the now-fretful Harold and then persuaded them both to eat a few mouthfuls of the nourishing supper Lucy brought in. He hesitated only briefly before carrying the small boy over to lie beside Beth.

That was his place, where he should be sleeping every night, but he had been so unsure of his welcome he had not been there for so many long, lonely nights.

"If you prefer, he can sleep near me tonight," he said gruffly. "But I think if he wakes up he will want to see you first."

"And whose fault is that when you spend so little time with him?"

William froze. Slowly he raised his head. There was a decided, militant sparkle in her beautiful blue eyes. She gazed at him steadily. He chose to ignore the condemnation and query in her gaze.

Instead, he said quietly, "I can never tell you how sorry I am for the way I spoke to you before. Please forgive me, Beth."

To his relief her expression softened, but then, to his consternation it hardened again.

"I have absolutely no idea what you were talking about, what you were so angry about, William Garrett. Surely what happened with John. . ." She stopped, an arrested look on her face. "How did you know about him, about my knowing him before?" she demanded.

He hesitated, looked from her to Harold, who at that moment gave an immense yawn and snuggled closer to his mother's warmth.

"We cannot discuss this now," he said curtly, "and I have a service to prepare for tomorrow. Perhaps after everyone has gone we will get a chance to talk."

"We most definitely will," she declared with a trace of anger. "Oh, yes, William, we most definitely will make a chance to talk. Our talk is months—many months—overdue. I have questions, and I expect an answer to every one of them. I need answers, lots of them, and this time nothing is going to stop me from getting them!"

He stared at her blankly for a moment. Beth held his gaze with some difficulty but determined not to look away first. For a moment he looked bewildered, and then to her utter relief, he nodded abruptly and without another word strode from the room.

Exhaustion swiftly claimed Beth, giving her no time to think, to dwell on that strange, angry scene after reading Kate's letter. But it was still dark when Harold woke her up, his little body shaking with sobs.

Alarmed, she turned up the lamp, noting William's bed was empty but glad he had left the light. Quickly she checked the bandage over the cut on Harold's head, which had proved to be relatively minor, despite the amount of blood that had covered his face and hair. She drew him into her arms, murmuring soothing words, rocking him gently until the crying started to ease at last to a few hiccuped sobs.

"Is he all right?"

She looked up swiftly at the soft whisper. William was standing beside the bed, staring anxiously down at Harold.

"Farva!"

The small boy wriggled strongly. When she let him go, he flung himself at William, then clung fiercely as his father's strong arms closed around him.

Beth stared at them. "I think you were wrong," she murmured tearfully as Harold at last gave a few more quivering sighs, then relaxed and snuggled against his father's chest as William sat down on the bed beside her, holding him close. "He feels safer with his father."

William gave a shaken laugh that was almost a groan. She knew him well enough to know he was attempting to deliberately lighten the moment when he gave another, much lighter chuckle and said chidingly, "But surely it's the mother's prerogative to get up for the children in the middle of the night, so I hope this does not mean a sign of things to come."

For some inexplicable reason Beth's spirits lifted. "And I most definitely think every son should prefer his father to look after him, especially in the middle of the night," she added swiftly, settling back comfortably onto her pillow.

"Well, fathers—especially ministers of such a high and lofty calling—are the breadwinners," he intoned in pious, lofty tones, "and have many other, far more onerous, serious, er. . .dignified responsibilities and. . .and should not be laughed at by their wives!"

By this time, Beth had succumbed to giggling, suddenly feeling lighthearted, free to tease him for the first time in many, many long days. "Of course, William, most certainly, William," she managed in a worshipful, humble voice, and then spoiled it with another irrepressible giggle.

William's mouth twitched, but he continued in his best pompous voice, intoning softly but mournfully, "Such levity, Madam, especially in the minister's wife, is not to be tolerated. She should demonstrate sober piety and good works at all times, especially when it means letting her good husband sleep!"

"What about her bad husband?"

William stared in mock horror at her laughing face. And then he too succumbed and laughed out loud, immediately trying to stifle his deep laugh to a choked gurgle of amusement as the dozing Harold stirred in protest at being disturbed.

"Oh, Beth, you are such a darling woman," he whispered softly, earnestly, and then he was suddenly still, staring at her with an expression on his face that made her catch her breath, driving away her amusement and replacing it with a bewildering array of emotions.

Desperately striving to maintain the good feeling that had sprung up between them so unexpectedly, she murmured back, "Well, Reverend William, to overcome our problem, I think you should share this parenting and stay with us for the rest of the night."

She swallowed rapidly, fighting the urge to beg him fervently to stay, desperately frightened he would rebuff this tentative reaching out to him.

"So, if Harold wakes up from a nightmare again, you will be there for him of course," she added swiftly and with a catch in her voice at the light that sparkled at her from his suddenly intent eyes.

Without a word, he stood and leaned over her, putting Harold gently down beside her. He murmured a protest, and William's large hand stroked the black curls back from the bandage on his head. To Beth's immense relief he whispered, "It's all right, Son. I'm not going anywhere, I'll be with you. . .with both of you, in just a moment."

Only then did Beth realize he was still dressed in his day clothes and had not been to bed at all. He had been watching over his family. Watching over her. Over Harold.

"William. . ." Her voice choked, but she managed to smile at him.

Something flared in his eyes. He bent down again. "I will be back in a moment," he assured her firmly. With that he hesitated for the briefest moment.

Then she felt his mouth brush her lips gently. Instinctively she moved closer, reaching up for his lips. She heard the soft intake of his quick breath. He gave a muffled groan, and then he was kissing her with a passion, a desperation she had never known. Then it was over, far too quickly. He straightened and was gone.

With a pounding heart, she waited for his return and only relaxed at last with a soft sigh when, after what seemed an eternity, he returned, strode around to the other side of the bed, and climbed in beside Harold.

She turned to face him in the wide, four-poster bed that he had built with his own hands. "Thank you, William," she said softly.

A hand reached across Harold. She placed her own in it, and he squeezed it gently. For a long moment he held it in his soft grasp. Then in a husky voice, he whispered back, "Good night, my darling wife," before letting her tingling hand go.

His darling wife.

For a long time, Beth lay staring into the darkness. A slight smile tilted her lips. William had joked with her as he had years ago before their marriage. Not until now had she realized just how badly she had missed the old easy communication between them. Since he had asked her to marry him, there had been something—a reserve in him, perhaps a deep inner fear in her of saying and doing the wrong thing with this new William—that had stopped her from teasing him as she had always taken such delight in doing.

But tonight he had been different somehow. And that despite the strange encounter after reading Kate's letter.

She stopped smiling.

She would not think about that now. William had once again joked with her. He was once again in her bed, even if their child was between them.

Something deep inside her relaxed for the first time since they had left England. At last her eyelids drifted closed. Her heart lifted in a silent prayer of thanks and praise.

Tomorrow they would talk. Tomorrow everything would be beautiful and right.

Chapter 5

William woke slowly. As exhausted as he had felt, he had not been able to relax while lying so close to Beth, and it had been hours before sheer exhaustion had made him sleep. For a moment he was disoriented. There was a golden cloud in front of his eyes. Some parts of it were brushing his face with soft, silky strands. He brought up his hand to brush it aside, then froze. It was hair. Beth's beautiful, golden hair.

He was where he had so longed to be these last weary months, beside her in their bed.

She was lying facing him, her long eyelashes shielding him from the force of her sky blue eyes. Her long hair had not been confined in its usual nightcap and was drifting in glorious confusion over the bedclothes. He reached out toward her and then stilled.

Harold. He was no longer there.

William sat up swiftly and looked around. The door was open, and he relaxed as he heard first Harold's distant, childish voice chattering away in his own mainly incomprehensible language and then Lucy's soft murmur. William's eyes turned to study Beth. She was lying so still, her face mostly hidden by her hair. He could see she was still rather pale, yet a bright pink glowed high on her cheekbones.

It was not often he was able to study her unobserved. A sharp pang went through him at the hollows in her cheeks and the faint line on her forehead. She had been so young when they had been married, barely out of the schoolroom, and was still just twenty years of age. His look intensified, searching for the child who had captured his heart so many years ago with her sad, frightened eyes, who, despite her fears, had tilted her chin and set her lips as though ready to take on whatever unpleasant new future she might have at Fleetwood.

Beth had never been lacking in courage, neither the child nor the woman she now was. Their journey across fifteen thousand miles of ocean with a small boy and another baby on the way had shown how much courage she possessed. And then, only weeks after their arrival here in South Australia, William had declared his enthusiasm for staying indefinitely in this exciting new settlement where there were still very few clergy to give spiritual guidance and help.

"There were apparently many Christians in the very first company of emigrants, especially on board the *Duke of York*," he remembered telling Beth eagerly. "By some reports it was almost a floating church and Sunday school. But most leadership has been from laypeople, not ordained ministers.

"Divine services have been held regularly right from the day of the first arrivals, even before the governor arrived. I've talked with the appointed colonial chaplain, Reverend Howard. He told me he used a sail to erect a tent in Adelaide for the very first needs of the church. And despite all the other pressing requirements of the colony, the foundations of Trinity Church were laid within days of our own arrival."

William had paused for breath. Beth had been smiling gently at him, but there had been no mistaking her intense interest, and he had gone on to tell her that there was much for a minister of the gospel to do in this new land. He had heard of several other groups of Christians of various persuasions meeting together without shepherds.

"Oh, Beth," he had enthused, "there is a spiritual hunger here, so many sheep without a shepherd, and I believe this may be where God would have us serve Him."

Beth had tilted her head thoughtfully, studying him with an expression he could not quite fathom. Then she said quietly, "I agree; there is much to do here for God, and if that is what you believe God wants us to do, it will be fine with me."

He had loved her even more then. But still, he had not dared to tell her that the circumstances surrounding their marriage had played havoc with his effectiveness as a minister at the church in London. He had known it, and the church authorities there had seemed almost relieved when he had resigned. But now, his old zeal and love for preaching the Word and serving God and the church had returned, as well as a burning desire to tell all who would listen of God's love that caused Him to send His salvation, His joy, in His Son, Jesus Christ.

So William had swallowed, longing to draw Beth into his arms and kiss her senseless. Instead, he had been so stupid. She had been bearing his child, he had told himself, and it was not the time. Like an idiot he had just smiled and moved quickly away before he had yielded to the temptation of taking her into his arms, plundering her soft, red lips. Having that wedding to perform not long afterward had weakened him even further.

Now he feasted his eyes on her. She was more beautiful than she had ever been, had matured into the most beautiful woman he had ever seen. No wonder other men appreciated her beauty, her charm.

He closed his eyes tightly. *Lord, teach me to love until there is no envy.*

Without looking again at the tempting vision, he carefully rose so as not to disturb her slumber. He had work to do. Besides, it was unfair to cause her more stress on top of yesterday. Not daring to look back, he hastened from the room.

To his dismay, it was later than he had hoped. After swiftly cleaning and then dressing in his best clerical clothes, there was only time to quickly hug and kiss Harold and drink the cup of tea Lucy insisted on pouring for him. Then he shut himself in the small room he had commandeered as a study to finish working on his sermon and service.

For one breathless moment, Beth had thought William might reach across the bed for her.

He had sat so motionless, and then she had heard the slight rustle of the bedclothes as he had moved. Her eyes had flown open, but he was already on his way to the door, his back stiff and straight. Not once did he look back.

Her mouth had opened to call out to him, but then she remembered it was Sunday and he had the church service to prepare for. Their time was not now. Would it ever be? Her lips tightened. It most certainly would!

Ever since Harold had disturbed her several minutes before by his little hands patting her face and then crawling over her to get out of bed and find Lucy, she had lain there watching William. She doubted he had managed much sleep that night if even Harold had not woken him.

He had been so upset yesterday before Bessie had interrupted them. She had thought about that, trying to fathom what he had been so disturbed about. It had been something in Kate's letter.

With a swift, indrawn breath, a dreadful thought came. But she quickly dismissed it, the sudden fear, the anger, more than she could bear this morning. It was simply impossible William could think such a thing of her. He must have meant something else.

She sighed deeply. She should have called him back. Asked him.

Disappointment swept through her in waves, followed by anger and disgust at her cowardice in closing her eyes the moment he had stirred and leaving them closed, hoping, praying he would lean over and pull her into his arms and kiss her properly.

She should have reached over and kissed him!

She smiled slightly, picturing his surprise, and suddenly wondered how he would have responded. Her smile disappeared and she shivered. She would not have been able to stand it if he had repulsed her.

With another weary sigh, she climbed out of bed, wincing at stiff, overused muscles from the day before. The cuts and scratches on her legs felt very sore, and she knew she should have attended to them more last night than simply giving them that quick wash. One cut looked very red around the edges, and with a sigh, she washed the dried blood away again, wrapping a makeshift bandage around it. There was no time to fuss over her aches and pains. There was much to be done before the service.

Suddenly she wished William had not invited all those people here today, and still more, that Lucy and Mrs. Young had not suggested it would be a nice gesture to give everyone a picnic lunch after the service.

More delay in having their talk.

Harold, with the resilience of a small child, had recovered from his adventure, despite the bruise and cut on his forehead. When she had finished dressing and walked into the kitchen, he greeted his mother with a beaming smile, while he continued playing with the piece of dough Lucy had given him.

Beth bent down swiftly to hug him and plant a kiss on his sticky face. She removed the now-gray lump despite his protests and cleaned his hands on a damp cloth. Sitting him on her knee, she looked him steadily in the face and said in her sternest voice, "Harold, you must never, never go by yourself into the bush like you did yesterday. Not ever again."

He stared at her, and then his bottom lip quivered.

Her voice softening, she added quickly, "Mother and Father could not find you, and we were very frightened." Her hand went out and touched the fresh bandage on his head. "You were all alone when you hurt yourself." A shudder shook her at what could have happened if the aboriginal woman had not found him, and she hugged him tightly.

Harold pulled away and smiled a little tentatively at her. "Harwol not alone."

Beth hesitated. Just how much did a little boy not yet three understand? "Bessie told you to wait for her. When you ran away by yourself you were alone. You must never do that again."

His face lit up and he shook his head vigorously. "Not alone. Black boy ver."

She stilled. Taking a deep breath, she asked carefully, "You went with the black boy, the aborigine?"

His head went up and down. "Nice boy. We play runnin' an' hidin'."

Beth moistened her lips and then asked softly, "Was his mother there too?"

He dropped his eyes and kicked his legs to and fro without answering her. "Harold?"

He shook his head slowly and then peeped up at her. "His muvva come an' ver', ver' cwoss. She. . .she not nice. She yelled at us. I wunned away, and she chased me."

Beth drew in a swift breath. He must have run after the little aboriginal boy, and his mother had found them. Perhaps she had even been nearby or close enough when they had been calling out Harold's name. Perhaps she had been worried what the men would do to them if they thought her son had enticed Harold into the bush. No wonder she had not wanted Beth to call out to William.

"Oooh, Miz Garrett, that awful aborigine made him get lost!"

She had forgotten Lucy. "Lucy, that woman probably saved his life," she snapped. "She could have just left him there and not bothered to find me."

Harold's little body tensed. Taking a deep breath, Beth said quietly, "I think her son must have been as naughty as Harold. Perhaps he had even run off from her to watch the children at the Youngs' place. We wondered how Harold could have been where he was and thought he must have run around in a big circle through the scrub."

Beth paused and then added thoughtfully, "But he must have run right across the clearing from where they were looking for kindling and raced into the bush there after the other boy. No wonder Bessie could not find him, why he disappeared so quickly."

After a moment, she added, "The boy's mother must have found them some time later and yelled like many mothers would. Perhaps she had been frightened because her son had disappeared too. I suspect Harold ran off and she tried to stop him, but he tripped and hit his head."

Lucy, her eyes wide, opened her mouth, but Beth said with a glare, "I am so thankful the woman didn't just desert him and run off, and I do not want you to say a word to anyone about this—anyone, do you hear? I'll tell Reverend Garrett myself after the service. I'm sure we have nothing to worry about with that woman."

Lucy nodded reluctantly but said, "I've heard some dreadful things about what aborigines have done, been really big nuisances to settlers like us away some from Adelaide. But now we have a new police force—"

"And I've heard some dreadful things done by whites to aborigines," Beth interrupted swiftly. She shook her head at Lucy, glancing significantly at the big-eyed Harold. "Now, no more of this. We have too much to do for this picnic after the service."

Beth helped as much as she could, mixing the flour to make dough for the bush dampers and peeling more vegetables given to them by the Youngs. But eventually she had to attend to James's needs and dress both children and herself in their best Sunday clothes, leaving Lucy to place the dampers to cook in the hot coals of the fireplace and finish adding the vegetables to the huge pot of soup already hanging over the fire.

By midmorning, Beth was feeling very weary and was still stiff and sore. When William joined her to welcome the early arrivals for the church service, he also looked pale and drained.

Only a few families gathered together, but because they would not fit in the house, they sat on improvised seats or sprawled on the grass or ground near the house. There was no cold breeze as there had been the day before. A perfectly clear blue sky shone on them, and before the service commenced, several even sought the shade of the tall gum trees nearby.

❦

William felt more nervous than he had since the first service at which he had ever led and preached. For far too long before that wedding service the day James had been born, he had dreaded getting up and preaching. But God had dealt with him that day, given him a passion for sharing the Word. Certainly there had been times of talking about spiritual things to different folk at various times. However, there had been no opportunity to lead a service since that day, let alone be responsible for the sermon.

And to his deep regret, there had been so little time to prepare this one. Last night he had found some old sermon notes and started going over them. But they had not been about what was on his heart, so he had quickly roughed out notes for a completely new sermon, spending as much time in prayer over it as he could. Despite scant sleep, William felt invigorated, eager to preach for the first time in many long months.

And the Lord's presence seemed so wondrously close all through the service. To the unexpected accompaniment of Robert Young's small concertina, they sang a few old hymns with gusto. He heard Beth's pure soprano voice soaring with the others and, catching her gaze, beamed at her. His gaze traveled to their two sons. James was in her arms, and he was pleased to see she had let Bessie sit beside her to help look after Harold.

His gaze kept wandering back to the precious small boy, and when he led them in prayer, it seemed as if all creation held its breath as his fervent words of thanks and praise for God's protection the day before soared heavenward. When he finished, there was a murmur of earnest "Amens." The women, including Beth, had to resort to using handkerchiefs, while there was considerable self-conscious clearing of throats by some of the men.

Then, even William felt the added fervor and conviction in his voice as he preached about God's gift of His only beloved Son, who had willingly died on a cruel cross for each one of them. He spoke wonderingly of the Father's faithfulness, His providence and loving care, His desire to have constant fellowship—unbroken by sin—with those He loved.

Only then did the forceful words waver, his voice soften in awe, as he described God's wondrous grace, His willingness to forgive His children's sin that would keep them separated from enjoying the reality of the love He filled them with, making it possible for them to love each other as He wanted them to.

🦋

Beth listened in awestruck stillness. Never had she heard William preach like this. A deep yearning began somewhere deep within her to know God even a little like William spoke of him.

The message was couched in simple, understandable words. At the wedding she had been so consumed with her own shattering discovery that she had later remembered only a few fragments of the message on the Love Chapter.

William had always preached a good sermon. His learned utterings had always been received well by his congregations, but none had ever listened as intently as this small group of people in the Australian bush.

Beth glanced around at their absorbed faces with pride. And then she was swept up again in the torrent of words, the glow on William's face, his shining conviction that what he was saying was irrefutable truth from the Bible, God's Word.

"God loves me. God loves you. He so loved us, He gave His Son to die for me, for you. Forgiveness is there if we ask. . . . We can forgive others only if we are first forgiven. . . ."

The reality hit Beth as never before. God could forgive her all her sins, all her stupid mistakes, what she should have done and had not. He loved her not because she had proved herself good enough and worked hard enough to earn His love and forgiveness, but because His very nature was love. She simply needed to accept His free gift of love, of Jesus, of life. She did not have to strive, just believe and receive. . . .

After they had sung one final hymn and William had closed in prayer, the women started to bustle around preparing their picnic lunch. The older children, like Bessie Young, kept an extra-close eye on the small children and babies, while the men drifted together, yarning about the different events occurring in the colony.

South Australia's first governor, Sir John Hindmarsh, had sailed for England in July. There was great speculation over who would replace him.

"Just as well Hindmarsh has gone," someone snorted. "He's been a constant source of conflict since the beginning when he disagreed strongly with the surveyor, Colonel Light, about the site for Adelaide. If the colonists had not held that mass meeting and backed up Light, Adelaide may have been built closer to Holdfast Bay."

William thought about the long, hot trek into Adelaide that first day and wondered how it may have been if Hindmarsh had prevailed, but he kept silent. As they had found out, it was certainly a long way from good freshwater, and there were other problems.

"Since then he was far too often in disagreement with the colonization commission," another man contributed. "I know he may be a tough naval officer who fought at the battles of the Nile and Trafalgar, but Hindmarsh should not have begun suspending public officers the way he did."

There were a few murmurs of agreement, but then Robert Young said with a worried frown, "I just hope he is not right about this area not being suitable for our city of Adelaide, though. The biggest problem here is no good source of freshwater. Many of the wells we have sunk are no good. Where water has been found, it is often far too brackish for use. I doubt if the Torrens River is large enough to sustain any large population.

"There are already about four thousand inhabitants in the place, with more ships arriving every few weeks. But to my way of thinking, there will be far too little land under cultivation to feed everyone if we don't watch out. Seems to me too many have been too concerned with putting up buildings and not clearing and planting crops."

There were strong words of agreement, but some argued that the women and children needed a good roof over their heads as their first priority. William knew many of them were already desperately trying to clear their small acreages enough to get crops in. He listened carefully, hoping to understand the pressing concerns of these families he had endeavored to minister to that morning.

Robert added solemnly, "As we all know, the river is very low just now. In fact, I have been told last summer was much drier than the previous two years. Hear tell the drought is very bad throughout New South Wales and right down to Melbourne. Crops and stock losses have already been severe."

William felt a sudden trace of fear for Adam, who had so quickly become a good friend. And Kate—she had said very little about their journey in her letter. Perhaps the drought had made their overland sojourn even more of a hazard than had been expected?

The letter.

But he must not think of that now. He forced himself to listen to the conversations around him. Only as he learned to know and understand these people would he be able to exercise any kind of pastoral care.

"Well, it is a shame the big Murray River is not closer, that's for sure, but if we were any farther west over Gulf Spencer at Port Lincoln, where some first thought the capital should be, we'd be even farther away from the rest of the settlements and any help we might need," a grizzled old man was drawling. "Especially now that Charles Bonney and Joseph Hawdon have pioneered the first overland cattle route from Goulburn River, just south of the Murray, to Adelaide."

"What a sight that was!" William managed a genuine smile. "Apparently they only lost four of those long-horned cattle."

"You saw them arrive, Rev?"

With an effort of will, William pushed aside his own problems and smiled inwardly at the casual mode of address. The barriers had certainly come down, thanks mainly to Harold's adventure. This was proving to be a great opportunity to get to know the men in the area. From now on, perhaps the naturally reserved, independent settlers would feel more free to call on him for help in spiritual matters.

He grinned at the eager young man and nodded. "I did ride out and see them—and the few sheep they had, as well. First week in April it was when they arrived. Took them nearly twelve weeks, they reckon. But what a sight was Joseph Hawdon. I happened to be in Adelaide the day he walked in. His filthy cabbage-tree hat had those broad black ribbons I'm sure you've all heard about."

There were a few nods and chuckles.

"He was booted and spurred," William continued, "his stock whip in his hand and a filthy clay pipe in his mouth."

"Well," drawled the older man, "reckon he might a run out of 'bacca, though."

There was a general laugh, which William joined in, although some knew his stand against the smoking of tobacco.

"Well," Robert Young said firmly, "now they've proved it can be done, I am sure we can expect many more animals brought over from the east in ever larger numbers. But my money's on sheep, not cattle."

William ignored the gambling reference and said thoughtfully, "A friend of ours, Adam Stevens, agrees with you. He has thousands of sheep in the outback, hundreds of miles west of Sydney. He thinks sheep seem to suit the drier areas better than cattle."

"That's the friend of your sister-in-law who went overland with her, isn't it?" Robert asked curiously.

William nodded abruptly.

"Brave young couple, brave young couple to—" Robert broke off and suddenly slapped his hand against his thigh.

"That reminds me, William. Meant to tell you yesterday, but in all the excitement. . ." He smiled and then continued lightly, "In Adelaide I happened to mention to someone you had bought the Inghams out. When a bloke heard your name, he said he was sure that was who some man was trying to find. Reckoned he had just arrived from Sydney aboard a ship that was taking some more supplies on board before continuing on to England. Apparently was most anxious to find you before they leave."

William tensed. "Did they say what he looked like?" he asked sharply.

Robert shook his head. "Sorry, Friend, didn't think to ask, but they did say he claimed to be some new lord on his way back to England." He chuckled. "They thought that was a bit of a suspicious tale because he had a slight foreign accent like no real English aristocrat would have. They said it was most strange, because he was certainly dressed like one would expect a lord to dress."

"Please, Reverend Garrett," Lucy's excited voice said behind them. "Miz Garrett said to tell you we was ready to eat, and if you would say the blessing, please."

William silently led the men over to join the women and children. His voice did not quiver as he raised his voice so all could hear and thanked God for providing their food and for those who had worked so hard to prepare it.

A cold wind had sprung up, but it was not the cold that made his hands tremble as Beth approached him with his bowl of soup and some damper. Although his lips had stilled, silently and fervently he was still praying. . .praying for them both, for Harold.

John Martin. He was here.

And now William would have to rely on God's faithfulness to help him meet the man, to help him cope with all that could happen now that John was Lord Farnley, a wealthy man and owner of Fleetwood.

Chapter 6

The people did not linger long after the picnic lunch. While the September days were lengthening, there were still many chores to be done before night fell. As they said farewell, several expressed their thanks for the church service.

The old grizzled farmer said gruffly, "A right powerful sermon, Reverend, right powerful," before tramping off after his wife and passel of children.

After everyone had gone, Beth turned to her husband and said seriously, "I agree, William, that was without a doubt the best sermon you have ever preached."

He had swung Harold up to sit on his shoulders so he could better see to wave good-bye to the Young family, the last to leave. Somewhat to her surprise, at her words William swung around and stared at her. A touch of color rose into his tanned cheeks, and then he smiled slightly. "But you always have praised my sermons, Beth," he murmured.

"No, I mean it," Beth said earnestly. "Perhaps what happened to Harold yesterday made me realize as never before how much it must have cost God to not just lose His Son, but to give Him up."

She looked away from the intense way William was looking at her. It had never been as easy for her to talk about God as it was for William.

A little hesitantly she said, "There was also something special about having the service here."

She looked up at the towering gums. Several wattle trees were already in golden bloom, their glory beautiful amid the many and varied shades of green foliage. For a moment Beth and William were silent, listening to the twittering of the birds.

She smiled suddenly. "Even when that bird, a kookaburra, they called it, I think, started laughing in the middle of singing that hymn, it did not jar. It seemed to be fitting somehow—a raucous laugh, to be sure, but a happy sound. I love the beautiful cathedrals back home, but here. . . God was so close in a strange kind of way," she burst out and then dared to glance at him to see if he understood her foolishness.

He was staring thoughtfully at her and was silent for so long, she felt embarrassment steal over her. William's faith in God and his obvious love for the Scriptures and his ministry had always awed her, even made her feel somehow inadequate.

All her life she had been taken to church. It was as much a habit of her

290

everyday week as eating and sleeping. She even said her prayers during the week, but it had never really meant to her what it seemed to mean to William—or her stepsister, Kate, come to that. There was a glow about William sometimes after he had spent time alone in his study, where if she entered quietly, she would often find him on his knees.

She had always admired William's desire to become a minister. It had been obvious to her he believed God had called him into the ministry and that it was not just pious words he had uttered when telling his guardian why he had made his choice of study. When Lord Farnley had at first expressed his disappointment that William had no higher ambitions, Beth had supported William, even though she had secretly never really understood the extent of his passion for the things of God. But after today's sermon, she understood better.

Harold had been quite content to sit on his father's shoulders watching the distant figures, his tiny hands clinging to William's head. A brightly colored parrot suddenly screeched and swooped over their heads. Harold chortled with delight and drummed his heels on William's chest.

William tightened his grip on the little legs to protect himself. "Ouch! Gently, gently, young man!" He pretended to bite at the little ankles and growled like a puppy. Harold squealed with delight. "Your mother is filling my ears with sweet praise, and you kick me. Now what is one to think of that, huh?" he teased, tickling the little legs.

More often than not, Harold managed to discard his little shoes, but this day, due no doubt to Bessie's diligence, they were still on his feet. One suddenly came off in William's hand.

"What's this, what's this, then?" he cried playfully, ripping off the little knitted sock Beth had so carefully made with her own hands. "I think it's someone's foot, Mother! Oh dear."

He stopped and examined the little foot carefully and then quickly exposed the other foot also. "Beth," he said, suddenly serious, "these shoes are much too tight. They've left marks. Look," he commanded.

Beth had been enjoying their antics, that secret place inside her rejoicing at the light of love on William's face as he played with his son. The reserve that he had for so long shown with Harold seemed to be gone completely now.

Obediently she came closer and looked. "My, my," she said lightly, "our boy has grown. We need to do some shopping." She stopped and added a little anxiously, "So many things here are hard to find. Do you know anyone who might sell small shoes for little boys?"

William thought for a moment and then smiled cheerfully. "As a matter of fact I think I do. I met a certain William Pedler in town last week. Apparently he arrived with his brother Joseph and their young families aboard the *Royal Admiral* only a couple weeks after we landed at Holdfast Bay."

Beth frowned. "The poor dears. I hope they did not have to spend their first night in South Australia like we did in that place they called a storage shed."

William's smile slipped a little, and she knew he was remembering the anxiety, the fear, that dreadful night. They had just been informed by the captain that he was sorry, but he was not going to risk his ship sailing through Bass Strait between the mainland and Van Dieman's Land because of the reports of heavy seas and more bad storms expected up the east coast to Sydney.

They had thought they would only be disembarking briefly while the ship was repaired and loaded with fresh supplies. Instead, Adam Stevens and William had had to supervise the unloading of all Adam's cargo as well as their baggage. Longboats had taken them from the ship to as close as they could get to the beach. Despite their protests, all the passengers' belongings and cargo from the ship had been dumped in a huge heap on the fine, white sand just above the high-water mark and left to their owners to find and sort out.

One of the crew had carried Harold from the boat, while William had been so tender, so carefully holding her, as he had waded through the shallow water to the sand. *Not trusting me to any other arms,* she had fancifully thought. His concern for her had eased some of her hurt of his avoidance of her during the journey, but afterward, his reserve had returned more than ever. One day she had bitterly decided that he had just been concerned that no harm would come to their unborn child. Perhaps unfairly, she admitted now.

Never over all the years had she been able to fault William's protection and care of her. And that care had been extended to Harold, even if she had often felt it came from a sense of duty and not fatherly love and attention. But now, for whatever reason, he had changed. Perhaps Harold's misadventure had made William realize just how precious the boy was, how much he loved him after all.

But no, he had said such a frightening thing to her just before Bessie had interrupted them. Beth rubbed her head. It had been aching off and on ever since she had woke up, and now the pain was returning once more, making it hard to think.

The whole thing had her completely puzzled. William had always been someone she had thought cared overmuch about his fellowman. Surely it would be natural for that loving nature to have welcomed and loved his own child.

Suddenly she realized William had spoken to her again. She blinked and said rapidly, "I'm sorry, I was just remembering our first night ashore."

He stared at her a moment. "I was just telling you that the Pedlers had it even worse than we did," he said in a slightly husky voice. "A very cold wind blew, even though it was the twentieth of January. Apparently one of the women—Elizabeth, I think they said—slept in a large cask with three of her youngest children, but their eight-year-old boy had to stretch out on the spars on the side of a tent made of old sails."

He stopped abruptly. She thought she saw a flash of sadness in his eyes before he bent and put Harold down, saying gently, "Go and see if James is still asleep, little one, then stay with Lucy."

Harold's mouth drooped. Suddenly he put his hands on his hips, looked his father straight in the eye, and said belligerently, "No."

Beth stared at him in horror. She looked at William's stunned face and then quickly away, trying hard not to laugh. This was by no means the first time she had seen this type of rebellion from their usually angelic son and had had to deal with it, but she wondered curiously how William would handle this open defiance.

After a moment, when neither father nor son had said anything, she dared to glance at them.

William had put his hands on his hips and was staring steadily back at the rebellious, sturdy little figure in front of him. "I beg your pardon, Harold?" he said icily.

Harold glared back at him. Even more so did he look like his father. Her heart melted toward them both.

For another long moment the small figure hesitated. Then he dropped his eyes and his hands. One foot started to draw a small pattern in the dirt. "Want. . . wanta play wiv you, Farva," he said pleadingly.

Beth felt the smile stretch her face despite her efforts. William glanced at her swiftly before she could control her mirth. He looked pleased, helpless, and indignant all at the same time.

"I would like to play more, too, Harold," he said firmly after a moment, "but not now, especially with a little boy who just spoke to his father like that."

The brown eyes looked up at him and swelled with tears. Beth felt her own heart melt and was not in the least surprised when William kneeled down in the dirt and hugged Harold swiftly.

"But you won't do that again, will you, Harold?" he said gently. The little head shook in abashed agreement. Then his arms went up and hugged William back. "That's a good boy. We might be able to play later before bedtime, but now you must do what I said. Run in and stay with Lucy, please. I need to talk to Mother."

The little face only brightened a little, and Beth held her breath, half expecting further defiance. To her relief he gave in. She watched the small figure turn and trudge slowly to the house. When he had disappeared, she turned and peeped at William. He was studying her thoughtfully.

"Enjoyed that, did you, Mother?"

She stared at him uncertainly and then saw the twinkle in his eyes. Relieved, she smiled back. "No, I did not particularly enjoy seeing a son defy his father like that. But I did enjoy. . . Oh, William, he looked so much like you!"

All trace of amusement was wiped from his face in a flash.

Puzzled, she lost her own smile and said urgently, "What is it? Why do you look like that, William?"

He stared at her a moment longer and then closed his eyes. Alarmed, she stepped forward and put her hand on his arm.

"William?"

His eyes flew open. He put his hand over hers; the other went to her shoulder, holding her steady. "Beth, you really do believe Harold looks like me, don't you?" he bit out huskily. "I so want to believe he looks like me."

Utterly bewildered, she said slowly, "I have always believed it to be so."

Suddenly she knew his question had an importance to him that was beyond her understanding. Unless. . .

A little too quickly she added, "There is not a great physical likeness, although I have often noticed his smile is so much like yours. It lights. . .it lights up your whole face. Kind of starts in the depths of your brown eyes and then spreads all over your face. But his little mannerisms are becoming more and more like yours every day. I don't know how many times over the years I have seen you stand just so, your hands on your hips, your legs apart. . ." She faltered to a stop. His hands had tightened convulsively on her.

He was staring at her, searching her with such intensity that the fear which had not been far from her ever since he had acted so strangely yesterday began to increase alarmingly. The pain in her head started to throb. His fingers tightened even more and she winced.

Seemingly oblivious to her discomfort, he said urgently, "Beth, I know how weary you must be, but there is something we must talk about without further delay, and something I should tell you Robert Young said earlier." He swallowed and to her relief let go of her. Looking around he added, "Let's sit over there on that log. I don't want to risk Lucy hearing us."

She followed him and let him seat her with his usual, unconscious courtesy. Then he dropped onto the grass at her feet. Unable to say a word for the fear that now filled her, she waited.

"From what Robert said, I think John Martin is here looking for us."

She stared at him. Of all the things he wanted to talk about, this was the last thing she would have thought of.

"John is here, in South Australia?" she exclaimed with sudden delight. "But so soon after Kate's letter! Are you sure, William?" she asked eagerly.

Not looking at her, he pulled a long, narrow leaf off some grass near his feet and started to fold it over and over. Suddenly she realized his hands were shaking.

His obvious distress gave her courage. "William, please talk to me," she cried out. "What is it? Was it something. . .something in Kate's letter? I have been puzzled all day what you were so upset about before Bessie interrupted us. It's something to do with Harold, is it not?"

He raised his eyes and looked at her. The depth of sadness and misery in them frightened her even more. "I wish you had told me right at the beginning, Beth."

"Told you? Told you what?"

❦

William stared at her. Utter bewilderment was her only expression. There was not the slightest sign of guilt.

He frowned suddenly. He thought he had learned every expression on her face over the years. Was there any chance her stepfather could have been mistaken after all? At first he had been so sure Lord Farnley was wrong, that somehow, whoever had told him had been nothing more than a malicious liar. But when he had found out it had been Percival, heir of Fleetwood. . .

Percival Farnley.

He drew in a sudden quick breath. Kate had said it had been Percival Farnley who had committed murder, had tried to kill them, who had lied. . .

For the first time in almost three years, hope burned in him again. "Beth, Beth, I have to know. . .is Harold my son?" he blurted out desperately and jumped to his feet.

She stared up at him blankly. He could see she was trying to comprehend his question. He knew when the implication of what he was asking suddenly hit her. Her eyes widened and every drop of color drained from her face.

She sprang to her feet. Her mouth opened and then closed as though she could not speak. Absolute horror filled her eyes.

"You. . .you. . .how dare you. . .dare you ask. . .such a dreadful thing!" she whispered at last.

William knew he had his answer. He also knew he had just made the most dreadful mistake any husband could make.

"You gave him the name John for his second name," he added in a daze, at long last bringing into the open what had perhaps convinced him the most, hurt him the most.

"John?" Her voice sounded as though it came from a great distance. "It was my own father's. . .my father's. . ."

"Beth. . ."

🦋

His choked, horrified whisper barely registered with Beth.

Trembling violently, she started shaking her head from side to side in violent negation that he could even think such a horrible thing of her. Fear was replaced by a sudden dreadful anger all mixed up with unbearable pain of heart and body.

Through a thick haze she saw William's hand go out to her. She raised her hand and struck out at it. She missed, but she whirled around and strode off, not caring where she went, just knowing she had to get away from him.

Then she felt his hands grasp her shoulders. He was trying to stop her, turning her around. Suddenly she was hitting out at him, slashing at his face, his chest, anywhere her fists could land until at last he managed to wrap his arms so tightly around her she could not move.

"Beth, stop it, Beth. Stop it! Oh, be still, my darling; you don't know what it's been like," he panted desperately. "These past years thinking, praying, hoping he was wrong. . ."

His words barely penetrated. Her head was aching so, and suddenly every last ounce of energy drained from her. Her legs threatened to give way, and she leaned against him, hardly knowing she did so. Vaguely she knew he gave a tremendous groan. Then she felt his arms swing her up, clutching her to him.

For a moment he held her; then he gave a sharp exclamation and started swiftly toward the house. He stopped just as suddenly. A noise reached her then. Horses' hooves, the rattle of harness, wheels crunching on the rough stones of the road.

She started to struggle again, and his grip tightened. She lashed out, this time catching him full across his face. His head twisted sideways, and he gave an angry, "No! Behave yourself, Beth!"

Then a loud voice called out, " 'Ere, 'ere there, what's this, then? What you be doin' with that lady, Sir?"

Beth forced her eyes open. She looked straight up into William's contorted face. She stared at him, and when he looked down at her, she said in a harsh voice that sounded nothing like her own, "Put me down, please."

"Beth, I. . ."

"Better do like the lady says, Mister," another voice interrupted sharply and with authority. "Put her down at once."

The last time she had heard those deep tones with the slight Spanish accent had been in another time. Another place. In a crowded, stifling courtroom.

She gave a startled exclamation. The arms holding her tightened and then slowly let her go, putting her on her feet but still supporting her as she straightened.

"Oh," that voice spoke again. This time there was a trace of amusement. "Sorry, Reverend, er, Garrett, is it? Didn't see your clerical getup. Oh!"

The voice changed again as Beth raised her head and looked at him. She swallowed several times until she found her voice. Then she took a trembling step forward. William's hands dropped away.

"Hello, John," she said in a slightly hysterical voice. "You have perfect timing." She swung back a little wildly toward William. "William, I believe you never did meet the man you have obviously heard so much about."

Her head was throbbing very badly now, but she started to laugh and suddenly couldn't stop. The tears came then, even as she cried out wildly, almost incoherently, "Reverend William Garrett, I'd like to introduce you to my old friend. . .no, no, with what you believe, he could not just be that, could he? My dear husband, meet my old lover, John Martin!"

Then Beth, who had never fainted before in her life, for the second time in two days slipped into merciful oblivion.

Chapter 7

John Martin sprang forward to catch Beth, but William was before him, grabbing her as she started to sway and sweeping her up once more into his arms.

"Oh, God," he groaned out loud in a desperate prayer, "what have I done?"

"John, is that Beth and William?" an anxious woman's voice asked sharply.

William looked blindly up from Beth's still form toward the small carriage that had ground to a halt, its driver still trying to quiet the two horses. A woman was rapidly descending from it, and John Martin hastened to assist her.

"Yes, my dear, it is at last," William heard him say quickly, "but it seems we have appeared at an inopportune time."

He heard no more, too intent on carrying his precious burden to the house, yelling for Lucy to bring some water, putting Beth down on the couch in the front room, helplessly smoothing a few wayward strands of hair back from her pale forehead, patting her hands, calling in a tortured, panting voice, "Beth, I'm so sorry, so sorry, Beth. . . ."

He was hardly aware that the two strangers had followed him until a gentle woman's voice said firmly, "Sir, she is stirring. Let me attend to her, please."

But he refused to move until two large, strong hands took him by the arms and firmly pushed him aside. "Best leave her to Elizabeth, Reverend Garrett. She is very good with sickness."

William stilled. He looked down at the hands still holding him. They were the hands of a man who had spent much time working in the merciless sun. They were deeply tanned. A twisted scar marred the surface of one. The faintest edge of other scars at the wrists disappeared beneath the well-cut sleeves of a dark coat.

Adam Stevens had similar scars. Scars from cruel manacles that had rubbed tender skin raw. Convict's scars. The hands let him go, and William shut his eyes tightly for a moment. It was so easy to preach about it, to exhort others to do it, but. . .

Jesus, Jesus, he prayed silently, desperately, *this is the man who has haunted me night and day for so many long months. Help me, help me.*

Slowly he raised his eyes. John was a big man, taller even than himself. He was as he had been described to him by Lord Farnley when he had asked if William had seen him at all around Fleetwood. Very Spanish in appearance, olive skin now tanned even darker, hair. . .hair that had been so much a part of the nightmare that had been William's every time he had looked at Harold's dark curls. But this man's hair was black, a definite black.

Realization stabbed at him that while Harold's head of curls was very dark, it was not like this, not like a raven's wing of gleaming, shining black.

His absorbed gaze lowered and encountered startling blue eyes.

"They should be brown eyes," he thought in a daze, and only realized he had spoken aloud when those eyes suddenly brightened with astonishment and then gleamed with some amusement.

John Martin said a little stiffly, "So I was repeatedly told while I was a child. Something of an aberration, I always thought, until I met my. . .my father, Lord Farnley."

Speechless, William stared at him. The man was right. His eyes were uncannily like his guardian's had been, a strong trait handed down from generation to generation of Farnleys.

Then Beth gave a slight moan and drew William's sole attention once again. The strange woman had swiftly loosened his wife's clothes, fanned her, and was now lifting her head to help her swallow a few mouthfuls of the water the hand-wringing Lucy had brought.

He suddenly became aware that something was tugging at his trousers. He glanced down and straight into Harold's frightened little face.

"Muvva fall down?" he whispered fearfully.

William dropped down to his level and drew him to his chest, hugging him tightly. This beautiful child he had failed miserably to keep from loving with all his heart in case it was ripped from him if John Martin claimed his son, this small child he loved so fiercely, was truly his son. His flesh-and-blood son!

"Did she fall over?"

William looked up blankly at the woman. What had John Martin called her? Elizabeth? "No, no," he choked out, trying to reassure her frowning face. "She. . . she had a bad shock, and on top of one yesterday. . ."

"Muvva?"

Harold wriggled, trying to push his father's arms away. William let him go and swung around as the small figure hurtled toward his mother and her outstretched hand.

Beth was watching them. The blankness in her eyes suddenly alarmed him even more than her outburst of anger had. Her arms closed around Harold, but it seemed to William she barely knew what she was doing as she softly murmured faint words to reassure the boy and then sent him off to Lucy.

"I think she should go to her room. She would be far more comfortable on a bed and probably just needs a good sleep," the woman's firm tones said.

William looked at the speaker. She was scowling at him. "Who are you?" he asked bluntly.

There was a slight movement behind him. "Beth certainly had a novel way of introducing the two of us." The laughter had disappeared completely from the man's blue eyes. They were watchful, studying William intently. Then they were directed at the woman, and a tender light filled them. He stretched out a hand. She put hers in it and raised her head proudly.

"May I present my wife, Lady Farnley?" John Martin said very formally. "Elizabeth, meet Reverend Garrett and his wife, Beth, who is Kate's, and now also my, stepsister."

A brilliant blush rose in his wife's face. She looked at John with considerable confusion, but there was no mistaking her pride and love for him. She looked back at William and suddenly swept him a curtsy that would have been acceptable in any fashionable drawing room. She murmured politely, "Reverend Garrett, Mrs. Garrett," and then spoiled all her dignity and gracious airs by allowing her eyes to dance and barely controlling a gurgle of laughter.

John Martin's face broke into a tender, indulgent smile. It transformed him, suddenly making him look much younger and giving some indication of how his experiences the last few years had prematurely aged him.

"You must forgive us, William; my new status in life was only confirmed by mail that arrived as we were leaving Sydney. Everything has happened so fast these last weeks, and we have really had little chance to become used to. . .to. . ." He paused, his face becoming solemn again. "To my new title."

He was married? His claims had been proven? He was in truth Lord Farnley's son and heir? And now also then, Beth's stepbrother, even as Kate was her stepsister while being John Martin's half sister?

William stared from one to the other and then swung his astonished gaze to Beth. She was surveying Elizabeth and John with nothing more than mild curiosity. That blankness in her eyes suddenly frightened him immensely. "Kate did not say anything about you being married," he said sharply, still not looking away from Beth.

"Did she not?" There was impatience now in John's polite voice. "But I would still expect you to greet Elizabeth as my wife—and Lady Farnley," he added with a sudden snap in his voice.

With a tremendous effort, William pulled his gaze from Beth. He looked at John Martin a little vaguely. Those black eyebrows were lifted haughtily, and a stern look had replaced the twinkling eyes. Even so had another Lord Farnley looked at him after some youthful misdemeanor.

A sharp pang smote him. Like father, like son.

John's frown deepened at his continued lack of response. With great effort, William tried to pull himself together. Standing to attention, he gave a formal bow.

"I. . .we are very pleased to meet you, both. I trust your journey here was not too unpleasant? I only heard a couple hours ago. . ." He stopped. Was it really that short a time? His look darted back to Beth. Clearing his throat he said in a stilted voice, "I was only told after our church service this morning that someone was looking for us."

John suddenly relaxed and smiled amicably. "I've been making inquiries everywhere, hoping to find you while our ship is here. We did not think of you moving to the outer edges of the Adelaide district as you have."

Elizabeth said impatiently, "Yes, yes, I'm sure we have time for all this later. John, Mrs. Garrett—Beth—needs her bed. Right now." She too had followed William's gaze and was also watching Beth with a concerned frown.

William started forward, but stopped dead, rooted to the spot when Beth jumped and then shrank back and turned her head away.

"I. . .I. . .can manage," she whispered in a cracked voice.

He could not move as Elizabeth helped her sit up. Beth attempted to stand. She swayed and would have fallen. William instinctively took a step forward, his hand out, but she shrank away again and this time raised her head.

The blankness was gone. Her eyes were wild, filled with anguish as she panted, "No. No. . .don't touch me. Don't touch me. . .never again!"

For a moment no one moved; then Beth sank back onto the edge of the couch. She was shaking violently. Elizabeth raised shocked eyes to her husband. Some silent communication passed between them, and he moved swiftly forward and picked Beth up. Straightening, he asked grimly, "Where is her bedroom?"

Still William could not move. Lucy had returned moments before, and it was she who said in a trembling whisper, "This way, Sir." They moved in procession from the room, Elizabeth hesitating for a brief moment before shrugging and following swiftly after them.

Not until Harold ran to his side did William move. With a tremendous effort he tried to soothe the anxious little questions when his own were filling his heart and soul with something close to despair.

Desperately his heart reached out to the One who had alone been his source of strength and love for so long. *Help her, Father. Help her understand. Help her forgive me, even if she can never love me as I want her to.*

The touch of cool sheets barely registered to Beth. She looked up at John Martin as he laid her down. His face was a blur. She wiped the back of her hand across her eyes, and he came into focus. Still the same handsome face she had known, but now more deeply lined, showing the ravages of the last few years.

"John. . . ," she said in a wondering, trembling little voice. "You. . .you're here. You're really here."

"Hello, Beth," he said gently. "Hush now. There will be time to talk later. You rest now. Elizabeth will look after you."

Then he was gone. He would be able to tell William. . .tell William the truth about their friendship.

But why bother now? Nothing mattered. William had been thinking such dreadful things about her. . .about Harold. Her feverish, confused mind was a jumble of thoughts. She was suddenly fiercely glad she had never quite plucked up the courage to expose her heart to him since her discovery during that wedding service, even though that love had continued to grow. It would be too, too humiliating if he knew how much she loved him.

He did not love her, could not love her. How could any man love her, thinking what he did?

William. . .especially the Reverend Garrett. . .could never love a woman he thought such a dreadful, immoral woman, a liar of the most shocking proportions, she thought hysterically.

Why, more than once in London she had heard him praying for some immoral woman, heard him preach to those poor, unfortunate women from the gutter, heard how he would try to persuade them to turn from their wicked ways, heard him quote a verse that for some reason had stuck in her mind.

What had it been? A proverb. She had it marked in her Bible.

"My Bible," she muttered and tried to sit up. "I want my Bible."

The pain in her head stabbed sharply. Vaguely she knew the strange woman was still in the bedroom. The back of a hand touched her forehead and the stranger. . .no, she wasn't a stranger. Had not John said something. . . ? Ah, yes, his wife. It was his wife who was there with her, who was saying briskly, "As I thought, she has a fever."

"My Bible," Beth insisted.

"Yes, yes," the voice soothed. "I'll get it for you just as soon as you are more comfortable."

Beth subsided. She closed eyes that were burning now and was vaguely aware of the woman's firm voice saying, "Where are her night things?"

Lucy's trembling voice said, "Right. . .right here, Ma'am."

Somewhere James was starting to cry. Like he did when it was time for her to feed him.

"James," Beth said faintly and tried to struggle up. That awful pain jabbed her head again. Her head whirled, and then a soft, gentle voice was shushing her, telling her they would look after the baby. Lucy would go that moment. All she had to do was rest, sleep.

She looked up searchingly and with an effort focused on the stranger. The gentle but capable hands removing her clothes stilled. This was John Martin's wife—Elizabeth, he had called her. She was watching Beth with a peculiar expression on her beautiful face. They studied each other for a long moment.

Then suddenly, Beth's eyesight blurred once more. "I'm. . .I'm so. . .sorry. . . so sorry. . . ."

A gentle finger touched her cheek, wiped away a solitary tear making its slow way down. "Hush now. Like John said, we can talk later, when you've recovered."

Obediently, she let hands do what they would with her. Docilely she swallowed something vile Elizabeth held to her lips. But she had been trying to remember. . . .

"My Bible," she panted urgently.

"Yes, yes," the gentle voice soothed her. "It is here beside your bed, but later—"

"No, no! Must know the verse. . .must know. . . ," she whispered frantically. There was a brief silence. Once more she strove to sit up.

"No, don't move," the voice said urgently. "I have your Bible. Which verse is it? I can read it for you, if you like."

Beth tried to think. Which verse? William quoted it. "Proverbs," she gasped. "There should be a book token there." Pages rustled. "I marked the verse. . . ."

"This looks like it. Now, you have a mark beside Proverbs chapter 12 and verse 4," Elizabeth said softly. "It is about a virtuous woman. Is that the one?"

"Yes, yes. 'A virtuous woman is a crown to her husband: but. . .' I can't remember the rest," Beth whispered desperately. "I can't remember. . . ."

There was silence. Then Elizabeth said softly, slowly, "It says, 'but she that maketh ashamed is as rottenness in his bones.' Now, do relax, my dear," she added swiftly. "Whatever has happened, you are ill and must sleep."

Beth was still. Suddenly she muttered, "Maketh ashamed. . .rottenness. . . no, no!"

The pain in her head was mercifully easing at last. She had to think. . .think. . . God's gift of sleep at last claimed her.

🦋

William heard John Martin reenter the room and raised his head from its comforting place against Harold's soft curls. The child was sitting on his knees being distracted by his father's pocket watch, while the man had been staring into space, stricken, unable to move, unable to pray, hardly believing what Beth had said, how for the first time ever she had not wanted him near her.

"Is she all right?" he asked hoarsely.

"Elizabeth is seeing to her," the new Lord Farnley said shortly. "She says Beth has a fever."

"A fever!"

"Yes, but I think there is more than that, don't you?" There was a steely look in those bright, expressive eyes.

William stared at him and then shuddered and closed his eyes. They were silent a long moment, and then Lucy rushed into the room.

She paused, wringing her hands. "Sir, the lady, says to. . .to make some tea and to mind the children as I always do," she appealed to William in a frightened rush.

William put Harold down and with an effort said, "Yes, yes, you go about your tasks. Perhaps you could arrange some. . .some refreshments for our guests."

She bobbed, took Harold by the hand, and after another curious glance at the fashionably dressed stranger hurried away with the reluctant boy.

John said shortly, "I must speak to our coachman and pay his fee. It is satisfactory to bring our bags in?"

"Yes, yes, of course," William said in a choked voice. "I am sorry. You must of course stay the night. We. . .I. . .we will sort out a room for you," and then felt foolish as John merely nodded before disappearing.

William stared at the closed door. Then with a groan of anguish he sank down onto the nearest chair, buried his head in his hands, thinking of all that had happened, praying desperately. He had hurt Beth beyond belief. Gone was his hope of ever winning her love. Would she ever be able to forgive him?

Lord Farnley had been so devastated that day he had drawn William into his study the moment the young man had entered Fleetwood after an absence of too many months doing that very last frantically busy term at college. William's only desire had been to find Beth, to tell her how sorry he was her mother was so desperately ill, how sorry no one had told him so he could have at least written to her, telling her he was praying for them all as he always did.

At first he could not believe what his old guardian had been telling him, had in fact been furious! Beth, his sweet Beth, seen meeting a man many times in secret? His Beth seen kissing this man, a common farm workman? His Beth more than probably doing far worse with this worthless seducer? His Beth with. . .with child. . .ruined. . .

Impossible!

He had wanted to laugh in the older man's face, but then horror had filled him. There was no mistaking the man's depth of anguish, his dreadful disappointment in his stepdaughter, and his frantic desire to keep the scandal from his dying wife at all costs.

And then William had remembered that Lord Farnley had always shown special affection for the beautiful, fair daughter of his wife, even more, it had seemed at times, than for his own flesh-and-blood daughter, Kate. Whatever the old lord had been told about Beth, William had been forced to believe it was true.

At the time Lord Farnley had refused to tell William the name of the chief informer, merely assuring him vehemently it was not someone who would repeat idle, malicious gossip without proof, and had only done so in an attempt to preserve the good name of the family. It had only been later, after Harold's birth, that Lord Farnley had told William the informer had been his nephew, Percival Farnley.

Even though William had still not been able to really believe the worst of the information, he privately agreed that Beth might have been compromised by her actions, which he personally could see as nothing more than a sixteen year old's foolishness. So he had said nothing against Lord Farnley's earnest plea to marry her. After all, had not this been the burning wish of his heart since those last summer holidays at home when the girl who had been his old playmate and friend had suddenly been transformed into the most unbelievably sweet and beautiful woman he had ever seen?

He groaned out loud, then started as a hand touched his shoulder briefly. "I just saw Elizabeth, and she says Beth has at last fallen asleep," John's voice said softly.

William rose and took a hasty step forward.

"She also said she thinks it would be best for you not to, ah, not to disturb them for awhile," John added hastily.

William stared bitterly at the other man. "You mean, don't risk upsetting Beth again." His voice cracked and he turned away. Striding to the small window, he blindly stared out. It looked out on that part of the front yard where he had held the church service.

After a long silence he muttered, "I was foolish. It was too soon after yesterday's traumas."

"Yesterday's traumas?"

William barely heard the quiet words. He stood for another long moment, wishing he had suggested the following Sunday for the service. It had seemed fitting to want to give thanks immediately. But he had been selfish, keen to preach, to lead a service again, not thinking of his wife. It had been too much for her after the ordeal of the day before.

And then today he had blurted out his long-held fear in an unforgivable way. Perhaps if he had brought it all out into the open before, it might not have erupted like a volcano. For the last six months the evidence had been there before his eyes. There was no doubt James looked so much like Harold, and deep in his heart he had known the truth. Foolishly, he had still needed her to set his heart at rest after all the agonizing he had been through.

He should have trusted God more. He should have been more sensitive to His leading. He should have remembered that Beth had been slow to recover from James's birth. The long sea journey had deprived her of health and vigor. Living in those primitive conditions in that tent, even sleeping in that crowded bedroom throughout the cold winter had not been as restful as it should have been.

Then after the baby's arrival, he had been too busy to help her as he should. He had been trying desperately to get the house ready for them to move into as quickly as possible, and afterward, he had been busy clearing the ground, trying to start at least a small vegetable patch because fresh food was so hard to come by.

And of course, as soon as they had moved, Beth had gone into a whirl of activity to furnish the house, to make it a real home with what was available. The only help he had been able to get to come and live with them so far had been Lucy, an inexperienced young woman, kind and willing as she was. People prepared to be servants were few. Some had even grumbled that allowing convicts to live here might not be such a bad idea after all.

He had often thanked God for the Young family, but it was all still a far cry from the care Beth had received when Harold arrived in their comfortable apartment in London. Kate had been there to attend her, with plenty of servants. At the last moment, the nurse employed to go on the ship with them had fallen ill, leaving no time to find a replacement.

Now with James, there were two young children to care for, and despite all the help he had been able to give her himself, there was still far too much for Beth to do.

"What happened yesterday, William?" John asked softly again.

William turned around slowly. "Harold was lost in the bush. We had to search several hours for him," he said abruptly, reluctant to remember that terrible fear that they would not find the small boy by nightfall, perhaps not find him at all until it was too late.

John drew in a whistling breath through his teeth. "And Beth searched also? That's why she has those cuts on her legs," he murmured.

"On her legs? She said nothing about. . .I was unaware she had cuts there, only the small scratches on her face," he said sharply, and then immediately felt the natural reserve a husband should at this betrayal that he had not seen his wife's legs.

"Elizabeth told me they are quite nasty and red and no doubt have contributed to the fever."

Something like relief touched John's voice, and William stared at him blankly. Then his eyes narrowed, and he raised his chin and said indignantly, "I can assure you I have never laid a finger on her. In fact, it was Beth who found Harold."

"William," John said with horror in his voice, "I never thought for a moment you had caused them—perhaps someone else, but not you, especially when you intimated something had happened. Adam spoke so very highly of your faith and love of Christ. I could never believe you would hurt anyone, let alone your wife!"

William relaxed slightly. Belatedly remembering his manners, he gestured for John to be seated. He hesitated taking his own seat, still wanting to make sure that Beth was all right.

John noticed his glance toward the door and said sympathetically, "You would be best to leave her to Elizabeth." A slight, faraway look came to his face, and then he smiled slightly as William looked at him. "I can assure you from personal experience that she is an excellent nurse and will know just what is needed."

William remembered suddenly that one of the stories Adam had told them about John had been his severe illness on board ship and the care given to him by a woman, the daughter of a man he had worked for.

He cleared his throat. "We are so far. . .there are only two doctors in the colony. But I will fetch one if. . .if. . ." He faltered.

"Elizabeth will know whether we should send for one," John replied firmly, settling himself even further into the soft chair.

William looked at him. How did one behave, what did one say to this man he had heard so much about, the man he had thought he had much reason to hate? Beth's old lover.

Chapter 8

Whether John sensed William's discomfort or not, he made it easier for his host by asking, "Have you really decided to settle here in South Australia? And are you turning from the ministry to farming?"

William sat down opposite John and said with an effort, "We have almost decided to stay, but my continuing officially in the ministry will depend on the church authorities and my superiors. There is much need here," he finished simply, "for shepherds of God's flock as well as for farmers."

John looked around the small room and at the rough furnishings. "This is much more comfortable already than the home Elizabeth shared with me on Adam's property for many months," he murmured softly.

Curiosity stirred in William. "Adam told me how you and your convict friend showed the difference a personal devotion to Christ made in your lives so clear during those months you were working for him at Stevens Downs that he too could not but come to believe in the Savior," he said impulsively.

John looked surprised and then embarrassed. He threw his hands out in a self-deprecating gesture. "The Holy Spirit had already been doing His work in Adam's life long before we met him. Elizabeth's mother was apparently a wonderful Christian woman."

"Your. . .your mother-in-law?"

"Yes, but she died several years ago, as did Elizabeth's father awhile back. I deeply regret never meeting the Waverleys."

"The Waverleys? Your wife was a Waverley? I do remember they were the people who. . .who looked after Adam for several years."

John held his glance with a solemn look and then drawled, "You mean the master he was assigned to by those in charge of convicts, as I was, with my friend Timothy Hardy to Adam."

William stared at him. "I apologize," he said stiffly. "It was not my intention to remind you of something I am convinced you would much rather forget."

John looked thoughtful for a moment; then he said quietly, "There is much I do not like dwelling on, of course, yet I do rejoice in the knowledge that during all that happened to me, God never ceased to prove His love and faithfulness to me."

He cleared his throat and added steadily, "When Elizabeth convinced me I could marry her, even though I only had my ticket-of-leave then through the petitioning of a powerful friend of hers, our marriage was an act of faith in Him, in

His promise to work all things out for good to them that love Him. We believed our love for each other was a precious gift from Him. It was a step of faith that I have never regretted." His voice choked, and he stopped abruptly. There was a wonderful light in his eyes.

William stared at him, remembering what Adam had privately confided to him about the harsh treatment convicts received and the cruel, unjust flogging in particular that John had endured so unjustly. He had also been challenged by the testimony Adam had given of the convicts learning to forgive, something he knew they would need to be ready to do again and again as the bad memories returned time after time.

"It has worked out for good," William repeated softly, and then in a stronger voice, he said sadly, "I have preached on that verse in Romans several times. By faith I believe it to be true, but now. . .now. . .when there is so much pain, it is so hard to hang on to that promise!"

John was silent, and then he said quietly, "If there is any way I can help you, I most certainly will." When William remained silent, he added hesitantly, "I do not want you to feel you must speak of what pains you, and it is obvious Beth was ill when she introduced us the way she did, but I. . .we. . ."

He paused, and still William did not, could not move.

"Beth was right the first time. We were never lovers, only ever friends except for one kiss."

William looked up sharply at that.

"Don't look at me like that, Man," John said swiftly. "I swear to you it is the truth. How often when I was in that foul prison did I think of those beautiful, stolen hours spent with a very young, innocent girl not long out of the school-room. I was lonely, very lonely, wondering what to do, how to present myself to Lord Farnley as the son he had long thought had died with my mother, fearing he would not acknowledge me. Beth was very beautiful but also so desperately unhappy, confused—missing you."

William's eyes widened.

"Oh, yes." John smiled tightly. "It seemed as though you came into every conversation. It was 'William said this' or 'William said that.' And I started to feel quite jealous of your place in her affections. That very last day we met before. . . before I found old Jock Macallister murdered, she was talking on and on about you coming home the very next day. It annoyed me immensely. She was in a very happy mood, the happiest I had ever seen her, despite her worry over her mother's illness."

He swallowed but continued steadily. "I had become very fond of her, even thought perhaps we might start to love each other. I am still somewhat ashamed of taking advantage of her; she was so young, although afterward. . ." He paused and hurried on. "I lost my head and kissed her, kissed her quite passionately that day, I'm afraid. So much so, it frightened the life out of her, and she ran straight off home."

William suddenly felt quite ferocious. This man had kissed Beth, his Beth!

"Oh, there is really no need to look at me like that, Man," John said with more than a trace of impatience. "We were never lovers! I never even saw her after that until today. I was arrested within the hour and hauled off to prison."

Lucy knocked on the door, and William was relieved to be able to turn his attention to offering his guest refreshments. After they were alone again, William said in a stilted voice, "I do thank you for confiding what you have, but I would be pleased if we talked of something else now."

"Of course, of course," John said swiftly. "Perhaps you would not mind telling me something about the adventure your son had yesterday."

Rather to his surprise, William found himself telling John quite comfortably about the events of the last couple days, even about the aborigine's part in finding Harold. John was very interested in all that he said, asking questions about the Youngs, and then especially about the aborigines in the area. On that subject, William had to admit to an appalling lack of knowledge.

"I feel very sorry for the aborigines," John said gravely. "As well as being dispossessed of their lands, their numbers have been sadly depleted by our diseases, which they have no resistance to."

William frowned. "Someone yesterday mentioned that their numbers are not great in the Adelaide plains, only a few hundred as far as anyone knows. The scars of smallpox are apparently on many of them. From what has been ascertained and from what they claim, the disease spread here from contact with the eastern tribes, and a great many died some years ago before the first settlers arrived. They are retreating to the fringes of the settlement."

"And as more emigrants arrive, those fringes ever move farther out."

Both men were silent, and then John said proudly, "Elizabeth has long had a real burden for the plight of the aborigines in her property's area. In fact, she is absolutely thrilled that Kate and Adam are more than happy to continue her work among them at Waverley."

"Work among them?" William said thoughtfully. "Would you tell me what she has been doing?"

Enthusiastically, John started explaining the details of the health and education programs that Elizabeth had begun, as well as the attempts to teach them about Jesus Christ. But he had barely started when Elizabeth came into the room hastily, her face grave.

William sprang to his feet. "Beth. . . ?"

"She slept for only a brief time, and now she is very restless," Elizabeth said quickly. "I have only the barest amount of medicines with me, and I think perhaps a doctor should be sent for."

William stood stunned, and John said quickly, "It is as you thought then. William, I took the liberty of asking the man who brought us here to find a doctor on his return and ask him to attend us."

Without a word, William rushed from the room. Beth was lying very still when he sank down beside her bed, but several moments later she began muttering and tossing to and fro in the bed as though having a nightmare.

"Harold!" she suddenly called out clearly. "Harold, where are you?" Her voice faded again into unintelligible groans.

William took her restless hands, holding them to his face. "Harold is safe, Beth. He is safe in his bed."

Her restless movements stilled, and she relaxed. Suddenly her eyes flew open and she called out, "William, William?"

"I'm here, Beth. . . ." His voice choked, but then he said steadily, "I'll always be here, Beth."

Her thin hands suddenly clenched his, but then she relaxed and was still again.

How long William sat beside her he did not know. While Elizabeth and Lucy cared for her other needs, constantly sponging her hot body, changing the hot sheets, in a desperate attempt to lower her temperature, it was only his hands that calmed her feverish restlessness, his voice that soothed her feverish fears.

That fact eased the ache in his heart just a little. The light faded from the room, candles were lit, and then there was the welcome bustle at last of the doctor's arrival. When William eagerly looked up he was very pleased to see it was Dr. Thomas Cotter, the officially appointed colonial surgeon who had arrived in the settlement at its very beginning.

William looked with some awe toward John, who smiled briefly and murmured, "I told the coachman to make sure he brought only the very best doctor in Adelaide." *And no doubt paid him accordingly,* William realized, and he managed to smile his thanks back.

Even though the doctor was such an important person, William politely but adamantly refused to leave the room while he examined Beth. He had already seen the red, angry cuts that Elizabeth had bathed, treated with foments to try and draw the poison, and he had felt the pain of them as his own. He should have been more discerning, more aware that the mother would care for her babies first, not worry about cleansing her own wounds properly.

After a series of sharp questions, Dr. Cotter gave his patient a thorough examination. After considering the inflamed cuts, he held a strange, narrow, cylindrical instrument to Beth's chest, listening carefully with his ear at the other end.

William looked at him with some surprise. He had heard of this way of listening to the internal chest and abdominal sounds and was glad this doctor in a colony so far from England at least had such modern equipment.

When at last the doctor had finished, he stood back with a frown on his face, watching his patient. She called out again for Harold and William as she had so many countless times the last hour, and again William hastened to soothe her.

When she was quiet again, he looked helplessly up at the doctor, filled with guilt and anguish.

Dr. Cotter smiled at him and said reassuringly, "She certainly has a bad infection, but she has been given just the right care immediately. If we can keep this fever down, she should do quite well." He looked with approval at Elizabeth's concerned face. "Her lungs seem quite clear, but tell me. . ." He paused and then asked gravely, "Has she had a bad shock of some kind?"

There was silence. The doctor looked from one to the other, and then at William.

"Shock? Unfortunately she has had several in the last two days," William said briefly.

He knew what the doctor was saying and closed his eyes briefly. His reaction to Kate's letter had undoubtedly shocked her. The whole episode with Harold had badly shocked her as well as exhausted her. Then he had so stupidly blurted out his question when she must already have had the poison from her infected legs burning up her body. Even John and Elizabeth's arrival had been a shock. It had all been too much for Beth, and was as much the cause of her fever as the infection.

"Right," the doctor was saying briskly to Elizabeth. "Normally I would advocate putting her whole body in a cool bath to bring down her fever, but it may be too much for her, another shock to her already overstretched mind and body. Keep bathing her as you have been doing. I have salves for her legs, medicine to help the fever, but above all. . ."

His last words were directed toward William, his voice and face stern. "She must be protected from anything that will disturb her mind. No more upsets; even the slightest may hinder her complete recovery."

No one moved. Then William looked down at Beth's deathly pale features and vowed, "I will see to that; you can be assured, Doctor. No more upsets."

He was grimly determined it would be so but was not even sure how that could be prevented, especially when Beth once again knew what was happening around her.

❦

It was dark when Beth woke. Only the faint light of a single candle flickered in the room. Vaguely she wondered why she had not blown it out before getting into bed. Then she remembered. William had asked her that dreadful question.

Before she could move, she was aware that somewhere close by in the room a low voice was murmuring very softly. William's voice.

She froze. How dare he be in her bedroom after what he had asked her, after what he had thought about Harold! She started to sit up, but just then his voice rose, and she stilled. He was speaking to someone. She strained to listen. Why. . . why, he was praying! She strained to hear.

"O Lord Jesus, please let me know Your will about this. Make it plain. Am I wrong in believing You have work for me to do for You here? Show me clearly, I pray. And for Beth. . ."

She started on hearing her own name. "William," she said loudly.

To her surprise her mouth was very dry, her voice hardly more than a cracked whisper. She swallowed, moistened her lips, and tried again in a louder voice.

"William, please go and do your praying in your own room."

There was utter stillness, and then he appeared beside her. His form was shadowy, and she could not see his face clearly.

"You're awake!"

"Of course, I'm awake," she said crossly. "Who could help waking up with you praying out loud like that?"

His hand reached out and touched her forehead. She lifted her hand to push it away and was astonished that her arm felt so heavy. Then his strong fingers caught hers, and he spoke in such a choked voice she wondered if he were sick.

"I've been doing a lot of praying in here the last couple of days, and this is the first time it has disturbed you."

She frowned. Vague images of people prodding and poking her, forcing her to drink horrible-tasting things came to her mind. "I've been ill," she said faintly.

His hand tightened on hers. "Yes, Beth, my darling," he said quietly, "you have been very ill, but your fever has eased now."

He let her go, and suddenly she wanted to cling to him, but he was moving toward the door. "I promised Elizabeth faithfully that I would let her know the moment you were awake," he said, and then he disappeared.

Elizabeth? She thought carefully. There had been a woman in that dream-world that must have not been dreams after all, but fever, sickness.

Then there was a rustle of silk and soft, rapid footsteps. Beth blinked in the sudden extra light and stared up at the woman's face.

"Oh," she said in that scratchy, harsh voice which seemed all she could manage, "you are John's wife."

There was a soft, pleased laugh. "Yes, that is perfectly right, and I am very pleased you are so much better at last."

Beth started to feel agitated. There was something she had to ask John to tell William.

"William," she panted and tried to sit up.

Pain stabbed her in the leg, and only then did she realize it was heavily bandaged.

"William!" she cried out in a panic.

"I'm here, Beth," his quiet voice said.

Sudden fear welled up in her. Irrational fear, but she did not want to talk to him.

"No, no, go away, go away," she cried out.

Then she realized she was crying, great wrenching sobs. Elizabeth was there, soothing her, coaxing her to drink more of her horrible drinks. But William had gone, and she felt empty, alone as she never had before, until once more the sedative took over and she slept.

Chapter 9

Beth felt so tired. She found it hard to be interested in what was going on around her. At regular intervals she obediently swallowed the tasty broths and then the more solid foods Elizabeth permitted her. And in between she slept and slept.

She fed James as regularly as she could, although because of the state of her health she was being forced to wean him far too early. This should have worried her more than it did, but thinking about it just seemed too much effort. Harold was brought to her for only brief periods when she asked to see him, but once assured both children were well, she was only too happy for them to leave so Mother could have her sleep.

She was astonished how much strength she had lost after only a couple days in bed.

When she mentioned this to Elizabeth, she looked thoughtful for a moment and then said quietly, "Beth, Dear, I think your tiredness is far more than the result of an infected leg. The sea voyage must have been very trying for you. From what I can understand, you have been working extremely hard since you arrived here, and I doubt if you even allowed your body sufficient rest after James was born. You have exhausted yourself, and now your body is letting you know it."

She hesitated as though she would like to say more but smiled instead and added softly, "Just rest and sleep as much as you want for the moment."

Beth was forced to agree with this woman who had so quickly become such a good friend. Physically she was exhausted, but she realized this was more a weariness of her soul and spirit.

The fever had disappeared altogether after those first dreadful, dream-filled nights and days. The doctor permitted her to stand as soon as the fever had abated and the red streaks up her legs had disappeared. Humbly she had accepted the doctor's mild scold at permitting them to become so infected without seeking attention.

That first day out of bed her legs trembled violently, but as the days passed and she was gradually allowed to be up in a chair for longer periods, she still refused to leave her room. She could not explain the feeling of panic that came every time she thought of doing so.

John visited her very briefly each day when Elizabeth was with her, but Beth did not know what to say to him. There was so much that should be said, perhaps needed to be said, but when she had tried, hesitantly mentioning Fleetwood, he had immediately put her off, patting her hand and saying there was no need to talk about all that just yet. With considerable relief, she had subsided.

Not once did William enter the bedroom, and not once did she mention his name. Many times she heard his voice in the house, his even tread pause outside her room. She would close her eyes, hold her breath, hoping he would enter, afraid he might. Her confusion about him distressed her greatly. She wanted to see him quite desperately one moment and hated him fiercely the next.

And so the days drifted by. For the most part, she simply sat and stared through the window of her bedroom at the leaves of the tall gum tree that gave the house shade. Although spring had officially arrived, it had turned very cold, and the fire in the bedroom was kept burning. Beth often shivered, but not always from the wintry chill.

Day after day Beth just could not be bothered getting out of her nightclothes. Elizabeth eventually insisted she dress each day. One morning after Beth had reluctantly dressed herself, not really caring how she looked, she finished forcing down a few mouthfuls of a late breakfast just as Elizabeth breezed into her bedroom after a brief knock.

She greeted Beth cheerfully and then said, "Good, you are already up and finished your breakfast. You have some visitors."

Beth stared at her. "Some visitors? I really don't think. . ."

"And they have called many times inquiring most anxiously after you," Elizabeth said brightly as though Beth had not spoken. "I am afraid today I just have not had the heart to say no to them once again. A Mrs. Young and her daughter Bessie have walked quite some distance in the freezing wind to visit you. And William and John have gone into town today. Now, you have not yet brushed your hair? That will never do, or your friends will think you are sadly neglected."

William was not at home. She would not risk meeting him.

Beth tried a feeble protest, but almost before she knew it, she had been fussed over, tidied, and was being escorted from the room.

She was still not at all strong but was astonished at the gasp of horror Mrs. Young gave as soon as she saw her leaning on Elizabeth's arm and blurted out, "Oh, my dear, how thin you have become in such a brief time!"

Elizabeth gave a short, significant cough as she led Beth to a chair.

The good woman recovered herself immediately, saying with a beaming smile as she hastened forward to kiss Beth's cheek, "But it is so good to see you are on the mend, and you will soon have some color back in those pretty cheeks, for sure. We have all been so concerned for you and so pleased your stepbrother and his wife arrived at the right time to help care for you."

Her stepbrother. Of course, John was her stepbrother.

Beth looked across at Elizabeth suddenly and saw she was watching her with an anxious expression deep in her eyes. Suddenly she realized how much she had taken for granted all that this woman had done for her since she had collapsed.

She smiled mistily at Elizabeth and said earnestly, "No one could be more fortunate in her sister, Isabel."

Elizabeth stared and then beamed happily back at her. "And I have been an only child and am so very pleased to have a sister since I married John. In fact, two sisters," she said with a delighted laugh.

Bessie shyly greeted Beth and said fervently, "I am so glad you are better, Mrs. Garrett."

Beth looked at the young girl dressed in her very best dress and smiled gently at her. "Elizabeth tells me you have been a great help with both the boys, Bessie, Dear."

Big tears filled the girl's eyes. "I've felt so bad about Harold," she whispered.

Beth sat up a little straighter. "Oh, Bessie, surely you are not still blaming yourself for his escapade, are you?" she exclaimed.

"There, didn't I keep telling you Mrs. Garrett was not angry with you?" Mrs. Young said with satisfaction. "The foolish child has been fretting herself silly."

For the first time, Beth noticed the black circles beneath the girl's eyes and her drawn face. "Oh, Bessie, my dear, dear girl," she said earnestly. "Not for a moment did either his father or I blame you. We know how quick he can be, how naughty at times. It is very good of you even to mind him for us as well as you have."

Relief swept across the girl's face, but the tears started in earnest. Beth stood and moved swiftly toward her. Crouching down beside the girl's chair, she put her arms out and hugged the thin young body, letting her sob on her shoulder a few moments before saying in a bracing tone, "Now do stop crying, or whatever will Harold think if he finds his friend like this?" She thought of something and added slowly, "He will think you have fallen down and hurt yourself, as he did when I first became sick."

She stood up and looked quickly at Elizabeth, who was watching her with a worried frown, and suddenly Beth realized how much Elizabeth had sheltered her from thinking in any detail about that horrible day.

"I think we could all do with some tea, don't you, Elizabeth?" she said softly with a gentle smile and then quickly sat down again because her legs had started to tremble.

Elizabeth was still and then slowly smiled back a little tremulously. Her eyes gleamed suspiciously, but she said brightly, "I took the liberty beforehand of asking Lucy to bring us some. Ha, I think this must be her now."

She whirled from her chair to hold the door wide for a flushed Lucy, who almost tripped in her eagerness to enter the room with her heavily laden tray. She beamed at Beth excitedly, and again Beth realized how much these good people cared for her.

They were also very thoughtful, chatting lightly about local gossip and not lingering over their refreshments. Mrs. Young rose and said their good-byes firmly. "We must not tire you too much on our first visit," she added briskly before kissing Beth's cheek, bidding Bessie make her curtsy, and taking her daughter swiftly away.

Beth looked after them and then slowly turned to Elizabeth. "Thank you," she said simply.

Elizabeth flushed slightly but did not pretend she did not know what she was being thanked for. "You have been in danger of slipping into a serious decline," she said gently, "and we have been at our wits' end to know the best thing to do," she added bluntly. "Especially when you have not even shown much interest in your children or. . ." She hesitated and then added resolutely, "Or your husband."

Beth stared at her. Bitterness stabbed her, and ignoring the reference to Harold and James, she said fiercely, "And I do not see that he has shown very much interest in his wife!"

Shock registered on Elizabeth's face, and she cried out, "Oh, how could you say so? William never left your side the whole time you were delirious. He was the only one who could soothe you. We could not even persuade him to lie down on his bed for a couple hours sleep. He insisted on a mattress beside your bed. It was only after you woke properly and cried out at him to go away that he has not dared to approach you, except I suspect he has crept into your room when you have been sound asleep to assure himself you were improving, and all because—" She stopped abruptly, her hand going to her mouth.

Warmth was swelling, growing inside Beth, dispelling the chill that seemed to have been her constant companion ever since she had woke from her first natural sleep and William had not been there.

"I told him to go away?" she gasped in horror. "Surely not," she wailed suddenly. "I so wanted his arms around me, but when he did not come I thought he had such a disgust of me that. . .that. . ."

Elizabeth stared at her and then exclaimed, "Of course. How stupid we are. I should have known you were still not in your right senses."

Beth stared at her in horror. She opened her mouth and snapped it shut at the sound of horses outside. Both women stiffened.

"I. . .I must go to my room," Beth stammered in sudden fright.

"I think it is too late for that," murmured Elizabeth, just a little triumphantly. She jumped to her feet and darted toward the door as heavy footsteps approached. John's laughing voice rang out. Elizabeth said something inaudible to Beth.

Beth tried to stand, but she heard William's voice say heartily, "Tea in the drawing room? Very good. That road was very dusty." Her legs were suddenly trembling so much she sank down weakly again just as William strode into the room.

He stopped dead. "Beth," he cried in a glad voice, "my dear, you are up!"

He took a few more eager strides toward her and then stopped once more. She nearly cried out as the happy, welcoming smile disappeared abruptly and his face lost its color. He drew himself up and gave her a slight bow. "I must apologize,

Madam, I was unaware you were in here," he said in an expressionless voice and immediately turned to leave.

"William!" she cried out breathlessly.

He spun around, an anxious look on his face. "You are well. Do you need something?" he asked sharply.

She stared at him. If her appearance had shocked Mrs. Young, his drawn, thin face and deeply sunken eyes equally shocked her. "You. . .William, you look dreadful!" she whispered.

A cold look wiped out his obvious concern for her. "Then I will relieve you of having to endure my appearance," he bit out and once more started to leave the room.

"Please," she called out frantically. "Have you been ill also? Are you quite well? Is that why you have not been to see me?"

He stopped once more and stood very still, watching her carefully. "I have not been to see you because you became so distressed, and then. . .then you told me to go away."

Her eyes widened. "No, no," she whispered. "I could never tell you that."

The sudden hope that flashed into his eyes brought tears close to her eyes. "You also told me earlier that day you could not bear me to touch you."

There was such pain in his voice that the tears spilled over, and immediately he was crouching beside her chair. "No, no, Beth you must not upset yourself. The doctor expressly forbade it," he murmured urgently.

"And you think that not seeing you all these long dreary days has not upset me?" she protested angrily.

He looked taken aback and said swiftly, "He said you were already under too much stress and must have no further upsets or he would not be responsible for the consequences. I thought. . .you said. . ."

Furiously she swiped at the tears rolling down her cheeks, and to William's obvious astonishment actually snorted. "And obviously he has only been attending gently nurtured society ladies, not a pioneer minister's wife and mother!"

That earned her an abrupt laugh, and she felt a large handkerchief being thrust into her hands. "But Beth," he said softly, "until you married me you *were* a gently nurtured society girl."

She used the handkerchief effectively and straightened. For a moment she glared at him and then slowly subsided. She looked down at the handkerchief and started twisting it.

"I've changed, William," she whispered in a choked voice. There was no answer and she looked up swiftly, surprising a sadness on his face that smote her deeply.

His lips moved in that lopsided smile that had always made her want to do whatever was necessary to make him smile properly. "Not too much from my dearest friend of so many years, I trust," he murmured.

Was she still his dearest friend then? Even though he had thought such horrible things about her?

Beth nearly blurted out the questions, but a sudden fear that he would only be prevaricating if he said of course she was his dearest friend stopped her from speaking. She knew that she would never be able to go along with such a lie. A deep pang clutched her. But she would settle for friendship, if that was all he could offer.

After a long moment, she took a deep breath and cocked her head to one side. "Well, I hope I've changed enough that if the Youngs had an orchard like the one at the Macallisters' place I'd not want to climb a tree and pelt you with rotten peaches anymore," she said in a serious voice.

Then she grinned suddenly and was very gratified that the sadness from his dark eyes disappeared. The dark chocolate-rich eyes lit instead with that glorious smile that seemed merely a reflection of a greater light that was always within him.

Then they were both chuckling at the memory of their youthful escapade that had brought the full wrath of Jock Macallister upon them both and a complaint to Lord Farnley about his ward and his new daughter. If tears were not far behind her laughter, that would remain her secret alone.

"Trouble was, not all of those peaches were rotten, Mrs. Garrett, Ma'am!"

"And Mr. Macallister had just arrived to pick the last of the crop for his good wife to make her preserves!" Beth chuckled again, and then her smile faded. "He was a good man, Jock Macallister."

"Aye, that he was," said a deep, somber voice from the doorway.

William stood up hastily, looking a little confused at being discovered with his arms around his wife's waist.

"Hello, John," Beth said a little shyly. She watched John advance into the room with his wife on his arm.

He smiled slightly at them both, but there was a shadow on his face, and she wished fervently he had not been reminded of old Jock's tragic death and its consequences. But before she could say so, he said quickly, "I'm very sorry to interrupt you both, but has William told you yet that unfortunately today is our last full day with you?"

"Oh, no," Beth cried out. "Elizabeth, you never said."

"I did not know," she said with a scowl. "John and William left early this morning to do business in town and ensure our ship was still scheduled to leave when we had been told, only to discover the captain wishes to leave earlier than originally planned. I thought we had at least another two days here."

Beth looked at them both and then helplessly back at William. "We. . .we have not talked about any. . .any of the past yet."

He smiled gently at her. "John and I have spoken a little about what happened."

Frustration surged through her and she cried out, "But I have not! And every time I have mentioned Fleetwood, John and Elizabeth both have refused to talk about it!"

William looked suddenly worried. "Beth, you must not distress yourself so. Dr. Cotter especially said you must not be allowed to get upset."

She gritted her teeth. "And you think that not talking about the past does not upset me? That knowing these last three years and more that my self-absorption, my self-pitying, my cowardice meant a good friend was in dire need and I did nothing—did not even know—has not upset me? And when I did eventually find out he had been accused of something dreadful, something I knew he could not possibly have done, that I did nothing has not upset me?"

She turned to John. He had gone a little pale and was very still. Passionately she cried out, "It has lain on my heart like a heavy stone. You told me I was the only real friend you had in all of England. I believed you, and yet I failed you miserably. You had even kissed me, and I never sent you a word of sympathy, of friendship! And then I found out you are my own stepbrother! And I am so ashamed, so ashamed! Do you think that has not upset me?"

William sucked in a quick breath, and John stood as though he had been turned to stone.

It was Elizabeth who rushed forward and threw her arms around Beth's tense figure. "There, there, I am sure you had many reasons why you did not contact John. Have I not been telling you ever since we got here, John, that Beth is not the kind of person to have turned her back on you the way you thought she had?"

John still did not move. Beth was dry-eyed, her face flushed as she stared at him above Elizabeth's head.

Then she dared to look at William.

He seemed dazed. "Is that why you insisted on coming with Kate and Adam all the way to Australia to find John, Beth?" he asked urgently.

She felt bewildered for a moment. She looked from him back to John and knew suddenly what he had thought. At the very least she would want Harold to meet his natural father!

Anger stirred in her and she said shortly, "Well, it most certainly was not for the reason it seems you may have thought!"

He looked stricken.

She suddenly could not bear his pain and looked again at Elizabeth. Beth thought back to that day at Fleetwood over twelve months before. Adam Stevens and Kate had just found John's lost papers that proved a son had been born to Lord Farnley's Spanish bride in Spain and that he had not died with his mother as the grief-stricken soldier had been told by her vengeful relatives.

"I am not sure what was the main reason. I knew I had to accompany Kate," she said slowly. "Guilt at my neglect of John was certainly one of the reasons, but there were others. I shared Kate's need to do what Father had wanted to do just before he died, to find his son and let him claim his rightful inheritance. It was the very last thing we could do for him and Fleetwood. We both knew it would have been so quickly brought to rack and ruin by Percy's mismanagement.

"To at least right that wrong for John seemed to be another essential reason, but then, at the forefront of my mind was that we perhaps could do something to change John's conviction, or at the very least ensure his life as a convict was endurable."

John gave a sharp exclamation, and she added swiftly, "Of course, then the lawyers said if your claim to be a peer of the realm was proven you could then ask for a retrial by your peers at the House of Lords."

"And that has not been necessary, because of Percival Farnley's confession," Elizabeth said swiftly.

"Yes, thank God," Beth said thankfully.

She looked at John, but he was looking at Elizabeth. She shook her head at him slightly, and Beth wondered what the silent messages passing between them meant.

Beth gave a wry smile and added hurriedly, "Another reason was Kate. I knew from that very first day how attracted she was to Adam Stevens. We knew nothing of him, and I was not absolutely sure we could trust him as much as she said we could. To my way of thinking, she needed a chaperone, or at least someone close to her if things went wrong out here. Of course, when I realized I was pregnant, I. . .I nearly did not go."

She stopped, bit her lip hard to stop its sudden quiver, took a deep breath, and said slowly, "But the main reason was you, William. You seemed so eager yourself to come to this new country."

William simply stared at her and, without taking his eyes off her, sank down onto the nearest chair.

"I. . .we. . .don't you remember we prayed about this together, William?" One of the rare times they ever had. She pushed the thought away and added swiftly, "It was only afterward that I started feeling ill in the mornings and suspected I was having another baby. You had said you believed it was what God wanted us to do," she finished simply. "So after that, I knew even being pregnant would not stop us coming here."

"You. . .you came because in the end it was what you thought I wanted to do?"

She looked swiftly away from the dawning look of wonder on his face. Shyly she said, "When you believe something is God's will, nothing stops you from doing it, William. I knew we had to go."

No one spoke. At last John moved for the first time since her initial outburst. He came right up to Beth and crouched down until he was at her eye level.

"Beth," he asked quietly, "why did you not at least agree to testify that I was with you that morning Jock was killed?"

Her eyes widened. "Testify? Agree to testify? Whatever do you mean?"

Elizabeth said sharply, "John, is this really necessary, especially now?"

It was William who answered. "Yes, Elizabeth, I believe it is," he said wearily. "As Beth said, we have not talked about the events in England yet, and you are leaving tomorrow. If there is anything at all that John needs to know, it should be asked now. I. . .we. . .Beth and I have proved that it is important to ask questions and not think we know the answers."

John frowned, looking from him to Beth curiously. He hesitated as if to ask what he meant, and Beth was relieved when instead he said, "William has told us that Kate told you in her letter about Percival Farnley's part in my misfortune, but now I am wondering if we have yet to realize the extent of his mischief." He hesitated, swallowed, and looked again at Elizabeth.

She came to his rescue, saying swiftly, "When I first met John on board ship, I found out that besides being devastated about his wrongful conviction for Jock's death, he was very bitter. He believed you had completely ignored his letters and his urgent messages to come forward and swear in court that you had been with him in the upper meadow and that he could not possibly have been in the woods when Jock was killed."

Beth gasped and her hand went out to John. "But I received no word from you! Not a word! And when I found out you had been imprisoned for weeks, that made me very sad. Besides," she frowned thoughtfully, and then looked pleadingly across at William, "were we not told Jock was killed the very day you came home from college, William?"

William nodded silent agreement, and she cried out, "Don't you see, John? That was the day after we. . .our last meeting."

They stared at each other. "Oh, John," she said with a sob, "I swear I never received any word from you of any kind, and whoever told you they had given me any lied horribly."

"Percy." William's tone was flat, expressionless. "It was he who informed your father that the murderer of his gamekeeper had been apprehended. He also told him in my presence that he need not concern himself about the matter any further, that as your mother was so ill he would act as his uncle's deputy."

Wordlessly, John looked at William and then back at Beth. He looked stunned.

"Oh, John, John, don't you see?" Beth pleaded. Tears started rolling down her cheeks in a torrent. "Percival was just making sure you would be convicted. Please, please believe I did not even know you had been arrested until the very day before your sentencing by that horrible judge! I only just made it to that dreadful courtroom a little while before he. . .he. . . I thought he was going to hang you!" She was shaking badly by the time she finished speaking.

William strode forward. "That's enough. No more now. This is too soon."

He swept Beth up into his arms, and it was heaven to hear his strong voice protecting her, feel his familiar arms around her, holding her safely as he strode toward her bedroom.

Instinctively she clung to him, turned her head into his shoulder, and let the tears flow. They washed away the memory of that day so soon after her mother's funeral when she had managed to elude William and make her way to where the trial was being held.

"Oh, William, William, it was dreadful," she sobbed.

"Hush now," he whispered, "hush now," and went to put her on her bed. But she clung to him even tighter, so he sat on the bed, cradling her body in his arms, rocking her silently until her storm of tears had abated.

When she was still, he continued to silently hold her until at last she stirred, opened her eyes, looked up into his face, and asked huskily, "Do you remember that afternoon I arrived back at Fleetwood so ill a few weeks after we were married?"

Their gazes locked. William answered in a steady voice, "That evening I called the doctor so urgently, and he told me you were suffering from nothing more than many women suffer in the early months of expecting a baby."

She nodded. "I had just returned from the trial."

His arms tightened convulsively around her.

She continued in a rush, relieved that at last she could talk to him about those dark days that had haunted her for so long. "The evening before Mother had died. I had needed to get away from. . .from the house. I wandered down to the stables. Tom, our old groom, told me about the trial. I was shocked beyond measure, horrified. Not for a moment could I believe the young man I thought I had gotten to know so well and who had spoken so affectionately of Jock Macallister could have killed him.

"Tom was very upset and worried. He had known John and I had been friendly, and he was still trying to come to grips with the fact that he had not done anything to stop me from associating with a murderer. But as we talked, he at last expressed his doubts about John's guilt. In the end I persuaded him to drive me to the trial.

"But we were too late. John had already been declared guilty. I had gone there. . .oh, I'm not sure now just why I went, what I thought I might be able to do at such a late stage," she said wearily. "But I had started feeling so ill by the time we got there. I thought it was only travel sickness, but the heat. . .that horrible crowd wanting blood! As the minutes passed, I became worse. In fact, I was violently sick just outside the courthouse."

"I know."

She jerked upright. "You. . .you knew! But Tom promised me faithfully—"

"It wasn't Tom," he interrupted. "It was your dear cousin making more mischief. He took great delight in telling me he had seen you there, and that was just one more reason why. . ."

He stopped and pushed her onto the bed, saying a little desperately, "Beth, I refuse to talk about this anymore now. You are as white as a ghost." She opened her mouth, but he said sternly without looking at her, "If you have a relapse, I am not sure that I will be able to look Dr. Cotter in the eye. He already does not think I can be much of a husband because I let my wife get in such a state."

To Beth's dismay, William's face had assumed that expressionless mask she had grown to detest and dread. It was more and more apparent that too many things had happened all those years ago that she had not been aware of.

Suddenly the desire to reach up and pull his face down, to touch his lips with her own as she had so delighted to do after they had been first married, almost overwhelmed her. But it had been so long now since they had kissed as lovers. Too long. Fear of his rejection made her close her eyes tightly, clench her hands together to stop them from reaching out to him, clinging to him longer.

She felt him pull up the blankets over her in swift, jerky movements. Then she felt the unexpected, soft touch of his firm lips on her brow, but by the time her eyes had flown open he had already turned away.

By the rigid set of his shoulders as he made for the door without once looking back, she knew she would be wasting her voice trying to tell him he was wrong not to talk it all out now, wrong not to grasp the opportunity to get rid of the poison that had caused so much heartbreak.

She had to know—needed to know—all that had happened, all he was thinking. Otherwise, she was dreadfully afraid that any chance for them to have a healthy, happy marriage would be gone forever.

Chapter 10

Although she did remain in bed for some time after William left the room, Beth's turmoil of mind was not conducive to having the rest he had commanded.

Her mind went over and over all that had been said. Her heart cried out, *O God, O God, what should I do? Help me!* At last, with grim determination, she rose, tidied herself swiftly, and made for the new addition to the house where she knew Elizabeth and John had their room.

"Beth! You should still be resting," Elizabeth exclaimed when she opened the door in answer to Beth's knock.

"Is John with you?" When Elizabeth hesitated, she said pleadingly, "I will be able to rest after you both leave, but I do need to speak to you both now."

Before Elizabeth could speak, John's voice said from behind her, "Let her come in, Elizabeth. You said yourself how much better she has been today, and we do have such little time left."

However, to her disgust, they firmly insisted she sit propped up by pillows on their bed, pushing aside their belongings they had obviously been packing to make room for her. When they had stopped fussing at last, they sat silently watching her, waiting for her to say what was on her mind, and suddenly Beth was bereft of all the words that had been bubbling up in her as she had made her way to see them.

At last she sat forward and said hesitantly, "John, you. . . William did not give you a chance to say anything after I. . .after I. . ."

Understanding suddenly softened his face. He said softly, "Oh, Beth, are you worrying whether or not I believe you never received those messages from me?"

She nodded miserably, and Elizabeth gave a small murmur of protest. John smiled at her gently and then looked compassionately back at Beth. "Be assured I. . .we do most certainly believe you," he said gently. "Elizabeth and I have been talking about it all. It is obvious that somehow Percy must have found out who I was."

His face hardened as he continued. "Perhaps I had not hidden my father's letters to my mother as well as I thought I had when I was staying at the Macallisters. Their daughter Penny sometimes cleaned out my room. We think she may have found them and read enough to at least tell Percival."

"Tell Percy?" Beth asked with a puzzled frown. "But why would she do that? I was not even aware she knew him, and he was always so above himself he hardly spoke to the servants at Fleetwood, let alone speak to a gamekeeper's daughter."

John gave a dry laugh. "But then, the servants at Fleetwood were not as beautiful as young Penny Macallister."

Beth's eyes widened. "Oh."

"And from what you have said," Elizabeth added, "she would have been glad to get back at the most handsome man in the county for not taking any notice of her, especially when he started showing any interest in another woman."

John grinned at her. "Perhaps," he conceded, then became grave again. "Percival Farnley told us that it was Penny who had taken my packet of papers and given them to my. . .my father, so she must have removed them from beneath the loose floorboard in my room before my lawyers looked for them when I was trying to prove my identity."

"Or," Beth said slowly, "her mother may have. She was apparently convinced you had killed her husband and became very bitter. But at least when her mother died, Penny did the decent thing and took the papers to Father."

"If they looked for them at all," Elizabeth said in a thoughtful voice.

They both looked at her, wondering what she meant. Comprehension dawned on John first. "You think the lawyers only told Judge Wedgewood the papers could not be found, further proving me a liar?" he asked sharply.

"Well, you did tell me once it had been Percy who had been so kind to you from the start, telling you he was acting on Lord Farnley's behalf, that he did not doubt for a moment that you were innocent. And wasn't it he who employed the lawyers for you in the first place?"

John swept his hand through his black hair in a gesture that brought back vivid memories to Beth of a boy and girl innocently enjoying themselves in a flower-strewn meadow. Pain lashed through her. The boy was long gone—and she? There were some days she could hardly believe she had ever been young.

"So this is where you are?" a furious voice said from the open doorway.

"Oops!" John muttered, and Elizabeth stifled a smile.

Beth looked at William's angry, white face with trepidation. But she lifted her chin gamely and said steadily, "There were things I had to know."

"But surely—"

"Oh, come and sit down with us, William, and stop babying her," Elizabeth interrupted impatiently.

Beth glanced at her with some surprise. Until that moment, she had only seen Elizabeth as the embodiment of patience.

William hesitated, and Beth said coaxingly, "Please, William, I did rest for awhile, but we do need to find out what happened when Jock was killed, and also all about Kate and Adam."

John looked from William back to Beth and said gently, "William and I have spent a lot of time together while you have been ill. He can tell you some other time what I have already told him about my good friend Adam and your. . .*our* sister's adventures."

He gave an incredulous laugh, his eyes sparkling brightly. "Oh, you don't know how good it is to say that, to know I do have a loving family. All my life, the only relatives I thought I had were a taciturn, hateful grandfather and uncles and cousins who made my life an absolute torment because of my English ancestry."

"So all you told me about living with your Spanish relatives was true, John?" Beth asked quietly. "Even to your looking for your English father?"

Compassion filled his eyes. "I never lied to you, Beth; I just never told you who my father was and that I was only there working at Fleetwood to try and find out what kind of man he was and how best to approach him."

She surveyed him thoughtfully and then smiled slightly. "And also befriending me to ask me all those questions about him."

He colored slightly and gave a light, apologetic grimace.

"There is one thing you have never told me." William interrupted their exchange a little harshly. "Do you have any idea why Percy killed old Jock?"

John's expression hardened to flint. He glanced at Elizabeth and then Beth before saying, "Shall we just leave it that we think Jock may have challenged him belligerently about his relationship with his daughter, who, after all, was even younger than Beth. Percy would have considered that an insult, a challenge to his position as the future Lord Farnley. I think that had become an obsession with him, especially if we are right in thinking he knew or guessed who I was."

He stopped and then added thoughtfully, "I wonder if his father, my uncle, knew about the marriage to my mother. He would certainly have told his son, and when I arrived with my Spanish complexion and the family's unmistakable blue eyes. . . That was why I made sure I never actually met my father."

He shrugged sadly. "I don't suppose now we will ever know, but whatever did happen, Kate and I both agree that Percy must have been mentally unstable even then. As I told you, he was absolutely insane when he confronted us that day. . . that day. . ."

He stopped abruptly, and it was Elizabeth who said firmly, "And we have decided not to talk about that horrible day anymore. It just makes it harder for us. . . ." She drew a deep breath and continued. "Harder for me, at least, to forgive Percy as God wants me to for all he did and tried to do."

Beth looked at her curiously. Forgive a man like Percival Farnley? A murderer, a man who had been responsible for so much misery? Was that possible? She glanced across at William. He was nodding slightly in understanding and looking sympathetically at Elizabeth and John as though he fully acknowledged what she was saying.

He turned and caught her watching him. His face stiffened, and he said at once, "Well, Beth, is that all you need to know right at this moment? I went to your room to find you and tell you Lucy has food ready for us. She has set a place for you and will be very disappointed if you do not put in an appearance in the dining room."

She stared at him. She desperately wanted to ask if he had mentioned anything to their guests about his misapprehension of her and John's relationship. Something of her thoughts must have appeared in her face, for his eyes narrowed, and he shook his head ever so slightly as he stood up quickly and held out his hand commandingly to her. "Come on, Mrs. Garrett, it's time you took your seat at our table with our guests."

She hesitated and then gave in gracefully, accepting his hand and letting him lead the way to their luncheon.

The rest of the day flew by. Beth deeply regretted the amount of time she had wasted hiding away in her room as the four of them spent the remainder of their time together creating bonds of love and friendship that she knew would last through time and distance.

It thrilled her to see that John and William had so obviously become good friends. John was very different from the intense, sometimes bitter young man she had befriended years before. Despite all he had been through, he had an inner peace and joy that she envied, and rather to her surprise, could not but help feel a twinge of jealousy at the way the other three spoke so easily and naturally about their faith in Christ.

It had never been easy for her to talk about church and religion, but the others had a common rapport that made her realize how little she and William really discussed spiritual things outside of church affairs. As she watched and listened, she suddenly felt a deep hunger to somehow also find this personal relationship with God.

The next morning, William was to drive Elizabeth and John to their ship. Beth deeply regretted not yet being strong enough to survive the drive to Port Adelaide where their ship was waiting, even though the new carriage William had purchased was well-sprung and so different from the old cart that had carried her that Sunday when James had been in such a hurry to arrive.

They left early, and after last hugs and fond farewells, Beth waved good-bye until they disappeared from sight. With tears in her eyes, she wondered if she would ever see them again. From several things William had said the evening before, she knew that he was becoming more and more committed to staying in South Australia, and she was not at all sure how she felt about that now.

It was almost dark by the time she heard the carriage returning. Throughout the day, although she still had to take regular periods of rest, she had once again taken up the reins of ordering her household. But the more she realized all that would need to be done, the more concerned she became. As the children grew older and their demands increased, how would she manage properly with just Lucy to help? Single, unattached women with no family were not permitted to settle here, and as they had discovered when trying to find servants, those who were part of a family already had more than enough to do helping their own.

As the hours had passed and William had not returned, Beth's agitation about how they would be able to relate without the buffer of Elizabeth and John increased. Would the old barriers still be there? Despite her fears, her heart leaped with relief and pleasure when she heard his familiar step and voice at long last. She hurried to meet him, then stopped in surprise at the sight of his companions.

William came toward her, a beaming smile on his face. "How do you like my surprise, Beth?" He waved his hands toward the two women standing in the hallway. "Please come and meet Mrs. MacGregor, our new housekeeper, and Miss Fisher, our nurse for the children."

"William!" Beth exclaimed with delight.

Stepping past him she shook both women by the hand. They looked surprised and then gratified at her sincere welcome. Mrs. MacGregor was a rather stout, middle-aged woman and answered in a soft, Scottish voice. Miss Fisher was considerably older than Beth but still blushed as she murmured in response and bobbed a shy curtsy.

"But how. . . ? Where have you come from?" Beth laughed at the amazement on each face as they looked at each other. "Oh, I am so sorry; it is just that we have tried and tried to get someone willing to come out here and work. I am so pleased, and I do hope you will be happy with us," she added a little more subdued, suddenly realizing this might not be the most mature way for the mistress of the house to welcome the servants!

After they had been assigned a room in the addition to the house only vacated that morning by Elizabeth and John, Beth left them to their unpacking and bustled off to get Lucy to prepare supper for them. But Lucy greeted her with a beaming smile and the information that the situation was all under control because the Reverend had let her into the secret before he had left that morning.

"Said he interviewed them yesterday when he was in town with Lord Farnley. That's why I was so insistent I did out those rooms today and not tomorrow, Ma'am," she beamed. "Reverend Garrett had ordered me to already, like."

"Oh, did he just?" Beth said with a smile and hurried to find the miscreant.

All thought of any constraint between them was gone as she rushed into his study babbling out, "Oh, William, they both seem so nice. However did you find them, you clever, clever man?"

Without thinking, she rushed up to him, and it seemed so perfectly natural when his arms came out for her to fling herself into them. His arms closed around her as they had so many times over the years, and with a sigh of pleasure she hugged him enthusiastically.

Then she pushed back slightly to look up into his face, still bubbling over with delight and relief, saying, "I realized today as never before how much more work there is now, especially with the house so much bigger and James showing us it will not be long at all before he is on the move, and now you have solved our problems, and. . ."

She stilled. He was looking down at her in bemusement, as though she was not real, a figment of his imagination. And the past was there between them again. She started to pull back, but his arms tightened convulsively, not letting her go.

"Oh, Beth, Beth," he choked and rested his head against hers. "It has been so long, so long since you came into my arms like that."

It was the feel of his big, strong body trembling against her that dissolved all her stiffness. Her body melted against his, pressing even closer, reveling in his touch, the familiar fragrance of him. Then he pulled back just enough to search out her lips, and she lifted her own to meet his with a sigh of relief.

The kiss seemed to go on forever, time meaning nothing as two hearts strove toward each other.

"Farva? You home now?"

There was a squeal of delight, and a little body barreled into them.

Beth winced as he jarred her still-tender leg. William let her go and grabbed at his small son. "Oops, there, don't hurt Mother's sore leg, you young fiend."

He swung Harold up into his arms, returned his enthusiastic hug, and then looked at Beth from dark, glowing eyes. His whole face was alight with that smile she loved so much and which had been missing for so long.

"A man should go away all day every day for a welcome like this when he gets home," he said in a husky, delighted voice.

Beth felt the heat mount up in her face. "Don't you dare!" she threatened, and then, despite her effort to control it, her voice cracked as she said, "I don't want you away for a moment longer than you have to be, and. . .and I don't think my heart. . .my heart could stand it either."

It was his turn to color up, but wordlessly he reached out and brought her up against him again, Harold squeezed in between them. His embrace lasted far too short a moment for her, because Harold squealed with delight and flung an arm around each of their necks and hugged them enthusiastically.

At the same time, Lucy's happy voice said primly from behind them, "If you please, supper is ready."

A laugh rumbled through William's chest, and he whispered in Beth's ear, "If we want fewer interruptions, it is even more a blessing to now have a housekeeper who may hopefully be a little more successful in training Lucy to be more circumspect in interrupting the master and mistress of the house at such moments!"

He let her go, and she looked at him reproachfully, feeling incredibly embarrassed as she saw their new housekeeper peering curiously over Lucy's shoulder.

William watched her red face with delight and grinned unrepentantly. She flashed him a look that made him laugh out loud.

She drew herself up and, with her nose in the air as befitting the stepdaughter of a lord, said regally, "Thank you, Lucy," as though what Mrs. MacGregor had just seen was something she could either like or get used to.

Despite Beth's invitation to join them, Mrs. MacGregor insisted in her soft Scottish voice they would take their meals with Lucy in the kitchen. She calmly bore both the just-arrived nurse and Lucy off so firmly that William looked at Beth and laughed.

"Her husband died earlier this year and left her practically destitute. Only her married daughter came out from Scotland with them, and she told me straight out she preferred to work for strangers for money than be an unpaid skivvy for her lazy daughter. Miss Fisher expressed similar sentiments about her brother's brood."

As he escorted her to the dining room, he added reverently, "As He has promised, the Lord has met our needs once more."

Beth smilingly agreed and immediately thought of that even deeper need she had. Was William right? It seemed to work for him. God did seem to answer his prayers, but could she dare to tell Him her desires? As she smiled and enjoyed their meal, thankful the constraint between them was not as she had feared it might be, she wondered if God could possibly make William return her love, care for her even a fraction as much as she loved him.

🦋

After the household had settled for the night, William sat for a long time outside in the darkness. Beth had already murmured her good night and slipped away to her room. He had been uncertain what else to say to her.

Would she welcome him if he dared to join her?

He had felt a tremendous wave of relief when John and Elizabeth had told him Beth had not even known she had pushed him away, rejected him so cruelly when she had been ill. But all day he had been wondering if it had only been the fever speaking. Had it been that only in her delirium was she able to voice her true feelings toward him?

If she rebuffed him now, it would hurt so very, very much. More than he dared think about. He did not want to put her in the position of asking him to leave. It could harm the very tentative green shoots of a new, deeper relationship that he longed for with her.

In the end, she had looked so pale and weary, he had let her go to her room with only a brief kiss good night on her cheek. *There would be another day, another time,* he had tried to tell himself.

But now he was feeling so lonely, wondering what he should do. It was a warm evening, and he studied the bright stars as he often liked to do, trying to find the constellation that had been pointed out to him as the Southern Cross.

"Well, Lord," he murmured, still looking up toward the twinkling canopy of stars, "thank You for this good day. Thank You for leading me to our two badly needed servants. Thank You for the time with John and Elizabeth. Thank You that he is such a fine brother in Christ it was easy to love him after all. Thank You for his faith in You and the mutual fellowship in You that he and I enjoyed so much."

He paused and dropped his head. "And now, Lord, please. . .please give me wisdom about what to do, what to say to Beth."

He was still for another long moment, and then with a heartfelt groan he spoke quickly, his voice rising in his pain. "I know I should never have married her the way I did. I am so very sorry for not seeking Your will back then, for not talking to her before about the whole mess. But we are husband and wife. It is done, and now how do we go back to what we had before? Does she want to still be my wife? How can I. . . ?"

There was a movement behind him, and he swung sharply around.

A soft, trembling voice said out of the darkness, "Why don't you just ask her, William?"

He sprang to his feet. And was struck dumb.

In the dim light of the lamp she held, he could see she was wearing nothing but a silky nightdress. She was very still, and then at long last, while he was still trying to find his voice, she took a slow, hesitant step forward. A gentle breeze lifted the gossamer-like folds of fabric around her ankles and bare feet. They came alive, shimmering and dancing in the flickering light.

Suddenly he remembered. They were the same enticing nightclothes she had worn that very first night. Their wedding night.

"Elizabeth said. . .she said. . .oh, William, I am so sorry I was so horrible and nasty to you when I was sick. I did not mean it, William. How could I possibly not want my old friend and protector near me?"

He heard the tears in her voice, and his heart trembled even more. He opened his mouth, but the words were tumbling from her as though she was afraid she might lose her courage.

"I have been so lonely in bed all by myself. Oh, William, it has been so for many, many months. Now you know. . .you know that what you thought wasn't so. . .can you bear to share it with me again?"

There was a pleading in her soft, almost incoherent whisper that broke his heart, that kept him speechless even as he stepped forward and enfolded her in his arms.

She held herself rigidly for a moment, until with a shuddering sigh she at last melted against him as she had a few hours before. And he knew his lonely bed would be so no longer.

🦋

As Beth felt William's arms holding her close, she sighed with the most profound relief. She had been so scared, so afraid as she had waited for him, hoping against hope that he would come to her.

But she knew him well enough to know how hurt he would have been when he had heard her ban him from her sickroom, even if she had been delirious at the time. What he would have thought, his pain and humiliation in front of John and

Elizabeth, had been haunting her dreadfully.

At last she had known this was all she could do to try and make up to him for the dreadful anguish Elizabeth had told her he had been through. But, as she felt his arms close around her, as she held him close, as he carried her to their bedroom, she knew this was only the beginning of sorting out all that was between them.

He kissed her gently, tenderly said he loved her as he had told her so many times before. But as before, she knew it was still only the love he had felt for her since she had been a child.

Long after he had fallen asleep she stared wistfully into the darkness above their bed. She was happier, more at peace than she had been for a long time. And yet she wished fervently that there could be more. More than respect and friendship. More than the shared love of her childhood days.

She wished he could love her as she loved him—with that once-in-a-lifetime, God-given love between a man and woman.

Chapter 11

As the days and then the months slipped by, the household settled down. Mrs. MacGregor and Miss Fisher proved to be the treasures William and Beth had hoped. Harold and James took to their nurse straightaway.

Beth, used to the servants at Fleetwood and their London church house, was amazed but absolutely delighted with Mrs. MacGregor. That resourceful, hard-working woman willingly turned her hand to anything that needed doing, from cleaning and laundry to even helping in the large vegetable garden, declaring she loved the excuse to be outdoors. Lucy bloomed as a cook under the experienced woman's tutelage.

Henry Wild, a strange, silent little man, was added to the household. He claimed to have been working for some years in New South Wales, but William suspected at least some of those years may have been as a convict.

However, he had looked William straight in the eye with a fierce look of pride mixed with such desperate hope that William had given him a job, and not for a moment had he regretted the decision. Henry rarely spoke about himself but proved to know a great deal about farming and worked for long hours in the fields—or paddocks, as the Garretts were told was the more popular term. Things progressed so well, William even bought adjoining acreage lots as they were released.

William had at last managed to purchase a couple more horses—a scarce commodity in South Australia—to help with the plowing. Poultry was added to the farmyard as well as a couple extra cows. Harold took great pride in helping to feed the "hickins" and find their nests where the eggs were laid. Some fences of rough branches and scrub had been erected to keep the animals away from the vegetable garden, and more were under construction around the small wheat crop William had managed to plant earlier in the year with help from Robert Young.

Life was so hectic, there were times when William and Beth marveled at how some assisted emigrants managed with no money to hire help and purchase items that made life easier. As a result, once their more urgent needs had been met, Henry found himself several times working side by side with William on neighboring properties, taking their horse and plow to turn over virgin ground and clear stumps, fencing, even helping to build the primitive wattle and daub huts, which was all many settlers could afford.

And of course the women were there also. Sometimes Mrs. MacGregor and Lucy even swung a hoe or digging fork to help establish a vegetable garden for a new, often bewildered and overworked settler's wife. More than once some poor sick woman or new mother would find her piles of laundry done or find baskets of prepared food left to tide the family over.

Although it was essential for William to take care of the immediate and future physical well-being of those in his household, he believed more than ever that he was called to be a minister of the gospel. Each day immediately after breakfast, he insisted that everyone gather for prayer and a short reading of the Scriptures.

Henry had at first strongly resisted, but when he discovered his continuing employment depended on his attendance, he had sat glowering through each session. To William's gratification and Beth's relief, Henry's attitude was gradually softening, even to the extent of voluntarily starting to attend the church services. People of all persuasions enjoyed the fellowship, teaching from the Scriptures, and worship. Somewhat to William's bemusement, there were Primitive Methodists, Wesleyans, Scotch Baptists, Presbyterians, Congregationalists, and others. Of course it did lead to some interesting debates at times, which William enjoyed immensely.

At the insistence of the community, William continued to organize the services each month, although as the numbers increased Beth had suggested they should be held more often. She even ventured to suggest that some building be erected to hold them in.

"More and more settlers are moving into this area," she had argued after the last meeting, "and none of us like having to travel every other Sunday all the way to the services in the center of Adelaide. If the numbers keep increasing, that old sail shelter will never do on days of bad weather, even for these sturdy, faithful people."

But the last week or so, William had gradually become more concerned about Beth, and this last day or so his concern had increased. For weeks after Elizabeth and John had left, she had seemed happier than she had for a long time. Occasionally he thought he saw a fleeting look of sadness in her eyes he could not understand. As soon as she realized he was watching her, she would smile at him so quickly that he decided he must be mistaken.

They had gradually reverted to the easy friendship they had known for so many years before their marriage, and if he longed sometimes quite desperately for there to be more, he managed to hide it. Or he hoped he had.

In those first few weeks his hopes had been high that she might grow to love him as he had prayed she would ever since she had been sixteen. But gradually that hope was once again fading, and now he realized how much she had again lost her sparkle. She was quieter, her smile coming less spontaneously, and sometimes he had caught her staring into the distance with a strange look on her face he could not fathom.

Of course, spring in this great southland had proven much warmer then those spring days in Yorkshire, where the snow would ever so slowly melt away and allow the daffodils to poke their heads up. Now in early December, the days had become very dry and hot, reminding them that in this upside-down country, Christmas would be celebrated in the heat of summer.

Beth had very quickly regained her full strength, organizing the household and family affairs efficiently, supporting him fully with the church services and other areas of ministry. More demands were coming for him to visit individuals for spiritual counseling, and William knew God had provided Henry at just the right time to free him up to minister to those in need.

But he had been reluctant to put more pressure on Beth. The folk who came to the services had got into the habit of sharing a picnic lunch together. Since that first service they now always brought their own food, but he knew it inevitably did mean extra work for Beth and their servants, even though he did his utmost to help, especially if the weather turned nasty and everyone had to cram indoors.

He tried to think of anything that may have upset her. Mrs. MacGregor and Miss Fisher were working out very well, so it was not them. The children were thriving. Beth always greeted him just as warmly as ever when he returned home after being away all day.

More of his time was being taken up visiting those in need. On many occasions Beth joined him on those visits and displayed a sensitivity and caring that soon made her a very welcome guest indeed. Never did they go empty-handed. Whether it be fresh vegetables, a pot of soup for a family with a sick mother, or something as simple as a batch of scones to share with busy parents over a quick cup of tea, it always seemed to be the appropriate thing to ease his way, to help break down any barriers so he could minister to other, deeper needs of the mind and heart.

Sometimes he even wondered if Beth was not trying just a little too hard to be a good minister's wife. And then one day he received news he had been waiting anxiously for.

"Beth, how would you like a few hours in Adelaide with me?" he asked her that evening. "We will leave the children with Miss Fisher. I am sure there is much we must need to purchase in preparation for Christmas."

To his concern, a look of dismay touched her face briefly. She usually jumped at any chance for one of their rare outings to the shops.

But then to his immense relief, she said, "There are quite a few things we need, including some special gifts for Christmas." She frowned and added quickly, "In fact, Miss Fisher told me today we simply must have more material for clothes for the boys. They are both growing so fast. It was then I told her William Pedler made those beautiful little shoes for Harold, and she became very keen to have her own replaced by him. I ended up promising her she could have tomorrow off."

He felt annoyed and knew it sounded in his voice as he said shortly, "It would have been best to have mentioned it to me first. I'm afraid tomorrow is the only day I can spare. We start to harvest our meager crop of wheat any day now. Miss Fisher will have to go another time."

Beth scowled at him and opened her mouth to argue. To his relief she changed her mind and smiled reluctantly before saying feelingly, "As long as you are the one to tell her so. I hate to disappoint her. She was so excited."

Early the next morning, Beth sat beside William as he tooled the carriage down the rough and narrow track toward the main road to Adelaide. Despite her discomfort, she felt a thrill of pleasure to know they would be spending the whole day by themselves. There was a suppressed air of excitement about William, and she was delighted that he, too, was so looking forward to their day together. He had braved Miss Fisher's displeasure and even refused Henry's offer to drive the carriage.

"I still don't know why you insisted on bringing this huge thing instead of our smaller one," Beth grumbled mildly as the carriage lurched and creaked its way onto the slightly wider but still rough main road.

"But think how many more parcels it will hold, my dear wife," William answered lightly.

A pang shot through Beth at his light endearment, but she grinned up at him. "More like to hold more bags of seeds for your precious garden," she teased.

He grinned back at her and turned his attention back to the two eager, fresh horses now trotting swiftly along the wider road that wound down from the foothills where they had their property. They chatted casually about various things until the dwelling places were closer together and more areas of bush had been cleared and the land cultivated.

Looking around at the few tired-looking wheat paddocks they sped past, William frowned as he said briefly, "It is still very dry here despite the rain we had a couple weeks ago. Even drier than where we are closer to the mountains."

"Mrs. MacGregor said her daughter told her when she visited her yesterday that they heard from some new arrivals that the drought in New South Wales was so severe that the governor of New South Wales, Sir George Gipps, had called the nation to prayer," Beth said softly.

"Yes," William said slowly, "she told me also. Apparently he proclaimed last November 2 a day of fasting and humiliation throughout the whole land, right down to Melbourne."

Beth was silent. She saw William glance at her, and she turned and watched his face as she said slowly, "Did she also tell you that within two days heavy rain began to fall?"

"Yes, she did."

He smiled at her, and after a moment she smiled back, but then said softly, a little shyly, "God does care, doesn't He?"

"Oh, yes," William said fervently, "and I am so thankful He cares just as much about the small things as the big ones in our lives."

She hesitated, wishing she could speak as easily about Almighty God as William could, wondering if this was the moment she should ask him the question that had been troubling her so in recent months. Why did she not have anywhere near the same closeness with God that he had? She had worked so hard trying to be good, especially these last months.

All she had been assured of was that at the very least she was a virtuous woman as the verse in Proverbs urged her to be. She loved William so much she would be a "crown to her husband" and not "rottenness in his bones" if it killed her!

But despite all her efforts, God did not always seem real to her. During their short visit, it had been so very obvious that Elizabeth and John also had that something extra in their relationship with God that William had. There had been times Beth had listened quietly as the three had talked about Jesus and spiritual matters as though He were so real He was in the room with them. Why did she not have that same easy relationship with God they seemed to have?

Once again she hesitated too long. The traffic had increased a great deal, too much for them to engage in a serious discussion, and William had to concentrate as he drove through the increasingly congested streets to the heart of the city. After a few moments, William pulled the carriage to a stop, and Beth was pleased to see they were outside the shoemaker's premises in Leigh Street.

As William fixed the brake, a young lad raced out to hold the horses' heads for him.

"Why, thank you kindly, young William the Fourth," he said teasingly to the boy, who grinned and informed him cheerfully in his Cornish accent that he was welcome and his father was at home.

William helped Beth down, saying with the twinkle she loved so much, "Come on, my dearest, this young man's father, William the Third, has been busy on an order for me. I'm glad they are so fond of the name 'William.' It shows very good taste indeed."

As soon as they were out of earshot he murmured, "But I am still very glad we have not burdened our sons like that! Now, we'll have to be quick with this errand, as I have an appointment in Emigration Square very soon."

She glanced at him curiously, wondering again about his suppressed air of excitement and whom the appointment could be with. Surely he was not contemplating hiring more help, as she knew he had already organized help from the locals for the harvest in another week or so when their few acres of wheat were completely ready.

Mrs. Elizabeth Pedler greeted them cheerfully as they entered the small workshop at the front of their primitive mud hut. Beth remembered the story of Mrs. Pedler's first harsh night at Holdfast Bay, and as she looked at the woman's pale, tired-looking face, she knew the Pedlers' fifth child would arrive the following year.

Mrs. Pedler confirmed Beth's assessment with a grimace as she saw her guest's comprehensive glance. "Next May or June," she said bluntly, adding proudly, "and the first Pedler born here in South Australia." She smiled briefly. "I do hope

William has finished your work boots, Reverend Garrett. He is very excited because his brother Thomas has decided to join him and his other two brothers, Joseph and James, out here. A decision rather forced on him, I'm afraid, because he has faced very strong opposition to the new machinery he installed at his shoe-making business in Falmouth." She gave a wry smile and added, "The usual story—the people objecting to losing their jobs destroy the business."

William smiled easily as she sent her solemn little son Darius to find his father. "I am sure his shoemaking skills will be put to very good use out here. By the way, I have heard that your brother-in-law Joseph is involved in digging wells. I would be very much obliged if you would tell him I have decided to add another one to our property."

Beth stared at William, a little peeved that he had not mentioned this to her beforehand. In the beginning they had discussed everything to do with their new home.

"I thought too many wells in our area contained water that was too brackish," she commented later as they walked toward Emigration Square.

"I thought of trying again in the paddock right next to the house," he said in such an absentminded voice that she glanced at him sharply. He was peering around at the passing crowd eagerly, as though searching for a familiar face.

"Just who are we meeting here, William?" she asked curiously, glancing around herself.

Several feet away, a tall woman wearing a very modish bonnet stood with her back to them. She was also looking around at the crowd. Beth's glance lingered for a moment on the very pretty bonnet, and then something about the woman reminded her of Kate. The woman turned her head and stared straight at her.

For a moment Beth thought she was dreaming. Then the woman's face lit up in a radiant, familiar smile. It was Kate!

Her hand tucked into William's elbow tightened convulsively. Even as he swung around, she gave a breathless gasp and then was flying toward Kate, into her arms to laugh and cry and exclaim over and over at seeing her dearly loved sister again.

Chapter 12

B ut how. . .when. . .what are you doing here?" Beth exclaimed between hugs and tears of delight.

"We came by ship, which anchored yesterday, and we are here because Kate could not bear another moment without seeing her sister," a deep, amused voice said from behind her.

Adam Stevens was shaking a radiant William's hand. Kate disentangled herself from Beth's arms and held out her hand to Adam. For a fleeting moment, Beth had an image of John doing a similar thing to Elizabeth. The Farnley blue eyes were flashing with the same excitement and pride as Kate said with a loving smile, "Beth, I believe you received my letter with our news?"

Impulsively, Beth stepped forward and flung her arms around Adam. She gave him a swift kiss on the cheek and then stood back and beamed at them. "Oh, I was so very pleased for you both, but how dared you get married without me, Kate!"

She gave Kate a cheeky grin and added, "Let me tell you, I was not over-surprised. I saw on board ship how it was with both of you, and I am so very glad you have realized you were meant for each other."

Adam stared at her, and then he looked quickly at Kate. "So you were right. Beth does not miss much."

Kate laughed at him and then held out her hand to William. "And how is my favorite brother-in-law? Still trying to keep this minx in order, I hope?" Her smile died a little, and she glanced quickly from him to Beth. "I do hope you are fully recovered now, Beth, my dear," she added a little anxiously. "Elizabeth and John were very worried about you."

"They wrote to you?" Beth felt something like disappointment, which was entirely stupid, of course. For one moment she had thought William must have asked them to come as a special treat for her on their first Christmas in Australia.

But then Adam chuckled and said indulgently, "Getting John's letter was bad enough for Kate, but when William's letter arrived there was no stopping her from agreeing to his pleading to spend Christmas with you."

Suddenly Beth's heart was singing again. She beamed at William, delighted to see the telltale touch of color stain his face. "And I suppose you let poor Miss Fisher into the secret of your surprise and that was why she was so amazingly complacent about you imperiously delaying her day off!"

The use of the large carriage was also explained when they loaded it with the huge amount of baggage and boxes that had accompanied the two travelers.

"No, no, we have not come to stay any longer than a little while into the new year," laughed Kate as she saw Beth surveying all their belongings with considerable awe. "But it will soon be Christmas," she teased, "and I know how much you have always enjoyed opening presents, Beth, Darling."

Beth felt the smallest trace of irritation. That had certainly been true when she had been younger. Now she enjoyed giving even more than opening her own presents—had, in fact, for the last three years. Would Kate and William never stop thinking of her as a child? Feeling dreadfully guilty at the thought, she gave Kate an extra hug in silent apology for being so ungrateful.

Beth certainly did thoroughly enjoy the weeks leading up to Christmas. The days took on an excitement that she could never quite remember being as intense at Fleetwood. There were moments of nostalgia—as when the men brought in some pieces of green leaves and tied them in strategic places, claiming they were as close to mistletoe as they could find amid the eucalyptus trees. But although the leaves produced the same sneaked kisses and although the huge plum pudding carried in by a beaming Lucy on Christmas Day was from the same recipe Kate had had the cook use at Fleetwood, it was still not the same, still not at all like Christmas without the snow and cold of England.

Yet there was a closeness between the colonists that gathered for the early morning Christmas Day service that Beth could not remember among the folk on the estate in Yorkshire. Here there was so little of the class distinction that had inevitably been part of past celebrations of the Savior's birth.

She and William smiled at each other in understanding as at one stage they saw Adam and Henry in deep conversation. Both were ex-convicts, although Beth strongly suspected Henry's sentence had been for crimes he had committed, whereas Adam had told William about his taking the blame and punishment for his younger, weaker brother's embezzlement of family money.

There was no doubt in either William or Beth's mind that Adam and Kate were blissfully happy together. They spoke eagerly of their new home at Waverley over the huge mountain range west of Sydney and of their good friends the Hardy family, now managing Adam's other sheep property, Stevens Downs, a few hundred miles farther west. They told of the limited success they were having in getting to know the language and ways of the local aborigines and their attempts to care for them.

Both Adam and Kate were extremely interested in Beth's account of the aboriginal woman who had helped her find Harold.

"And you say you have not seen any sign of aborigines near here since?" Kate asked Beth with some disappointment.

Before she could answer, William said swiftly, "As a matter of fact, I was told only the other day that they seem to have returned and have established a small camp in the hills near the water hole several miles back."

"Why, William," Beth said with excitement, "perhaps we can go and find that woman and her child after all."

William looked cautious. "Perhaps," he said flatly, "but only if we make sure it is safe to do so."

"And perhaps she may not want to be found," Kate said quietly. "They are usually very independent and self-reliant unless good-meaning white people mess them up."

Adam looked grim and said shortly, "The local people in our area have been given too much alcohol by unthinking settlers, and it is breaking our hearts to see what this is doing to many fine aborigines."

"But Jackie is standing out against it," Kate said with a fond smile, and then she had to tell them about the aborigine reared and educated by white missionaries in the Hunter Valley who had helped them so much when they had been in danger from Percival Farnley.

"I heard that some men have recently been brought to trial for murdering aborigines at Myall Creek, west of Tamworth in northwest New South Wales," William said gravely.

Kate shuddered. "That massacre of twenty-five men, women, and children in June was absolutely appalling, although apparently it is by no means the first time aborigines have been killed with virtually no action taken against their murderers by the authorities."

"And even sadder was the fact that this particular group was peaceful and had not caused any of the troubles others had. Unfortunately they were the only ones the vengeful stockmen could find," Adam said grimly. Then he added slowly, "Of course, in all fairness to the white people on isolated stations, they were becoming completely demoralized and scared out of their wits by the constant harassment and attacks by some aborigines. They were further upset because the promised mounted police were suddenly called away to other troubled areas. But there can never be any real excuse for killing innocent aborigines like that," he concluded sadly.

"The report said some squatters in particular are very opposed to the trial of the men responsible and are raising money for their defense," William said quietly, looking curiously at Adam. "I heard that the station superintendent who reported it to the government and acted as a witness at the trial lost his job because of it."

Adam shrugged. "Well, I am not one of those squatters, but the argument has certainly divided the country. The men were acquitted at their trial, but last we heard a new trial has been set, and I doubt they will escape the hangman this time round."

He hesitated before adding slowly, "As I said, I can sympathize a little with those in areas where the aborigines have been causing trouble. Some have had their workers at outstations, both men and women, killed. And the number of stock being killed by the aborigines has risen sharply. Quite a few seem to prefer taking sheep and cattle for food rather than hunting for kangaroos, especially during periods of drought."

Adam sighed. "There is no easy answer, but the problem is that it is still not right to allow any man to take the law into his own hands like those men did. Innocent people may die. It is not just and is certainly not allowed under British law."

William looked at Beth with a worried frown. "It is all beginning to happen here too, Beth, on a lesser scale, perhaps, but that is why I want you to always be very careful."

She smiled at him and nodded reassuringly before changing the subject.

❧

With the mixed delights of Christmas behind them, the new year of 1839 commenced with sweltering heat. There were only a few brief thunderstorms, and any moisture quickly dried up. Fortunately the well sunk by Joseph Pedler had yielded a reasonable supply of freshwater, but taking Adam's strong advice, they were very careful not to waste a drop of the precious water they had.

Beth and William took their guests around the new settlement as much as they could and were surprised themselves at the way the number of assisted emigrants were flooding in. Several people were eager to tell them about the German refugees who had arrived in December. They were especially sympathetic toward them when they found out they were Lutherans who had escaped from Prussia and the religious persecution of King Friedrich Wilhelm the Third. Apparently Captain Dirk Hahn of the frigate *Zebra*, on which they had traveled, was so impressed with his passengers that he went out of his way to see them settled on land they could farm.

William had been quiet and thoughtful for some time afterward, and Beth had smiled to herself. She knew it would not be long before he found some way of meeting and offering help to fellow believers who had suffered so much.

Then one day they were introduced to another newly arrived family in the long, rough buildings at Emigration Square. They were about the same age as Adam and Kate, a little older than Beth and William. Francis Telfer was a shepherd from near Dumfries in Scotland. He and his wife, Jean, and their three young children aged six years and younger had arrived on the *Prince George* on Boxing Day, right after Christmas.

When they wearily, and sometimes with tears, recounted some of what they had experienced, the two couples were reminded vividly of their own unpleasant journey just twelve months before.

Less than four weeks after their application to emigrate, the Telfers had only been given twenty-six days notice that they had been accepted and were due to sail from London the beginning of September. The conditions on board ship had been very crowded, and that combined with the heat and the roll of the ship in turbulent waters had proved too much for their baby boy, John, born just three months before their departure.

"We committed his soul to the Lord and his tiny body to the ocean depths and sailed on," Francis told them gruffly.

Jean gave a small, stifled sob, and Beth was relieved that, as they were leaving, friends the Telfers had made on board ship arrived to help with the children. Dinah Flavel was the same age Beth had been when she had married William but took immediate, capable care of the three small children.

Beth hugged her two healthy sons even tighter that evening after they arrived home, and she shed a few tears as William held her close and he said softly, "That poor woman. I fear for her."

Beth did not ask what he meant. She too had quickly noted how frail Jean Telfer had been. She could hardly have recovered from the weakness of childbirth before going through the mental and physical strain of leaving her home. It was to be hoped that the cramped conditions on the ship, the death of her baby, and their arrival with no comforts or conveniences in the midsummer heat would not prove too much for her.

Far too swiftly, Adam and Kate's time with them was drawing to a close. Yet as much as she would have liked to have them nearer, in some strange way, Beth knew that her own roots were growing deeper into this place she could so easily now call home.

Kate and Beth had, of course, had several long, private discussions. Beth shuddered, and they both shed tears over Percival Farnley and what he had done to John and so nearly done to them all that dreadful, final day in the bush on Waverley.

They all rejoiced together when a letter unexpectedly arrived from their lawyers telling them that despite the initial shock and wariness of the people at Fleetwood, John and Elizabeth were quickly winning the majority over with their love and management of the estate. The letter was full of praise for both John and Elizabeth, and the considerable relief of the lawyers that John had at last agreed to be known as John Farnley brought smiles to their faces as well.

Then one day, Beth at last told Kate something that her mother had told her about her new stepfather, insisting she never mention it to Kate.

Kate stared at her in disbelief. "You knew Father had been married before he married my mother? Married to someone when he had served with Wellington in Spain? But why did neither he nor my mother ever mention it to me?"

"I do not know," Beth said quietly, "except. . ."

She stopped, reluctant to continue, but after a moment Kate gave a sigh and said sadly what Beth was thinking, "Because it hurt too much to talk about the loss of his first love and their baby son. He never loved my mother like he did yours. And I think he was so unloving toward me because in his own strange way he was still grieving for the son he had never seen and whom he thought had died with his wife. Perhaps it would have been different if I had been another long-desired son."

Beth thought of the anguish on William's face when he thought there might be a chance he would lose claim to Harold, the joy on his face when James had been born. "Poor Father," she whispered.

Beth thought long and hard about telling Kate what William and her father had believed about her and John's relationship, even about Harold. In the end, Beth knew it was still eating into her so much she had to speak of it to someone. She knew she could trust Kate not to mention it to William if she asked her not to, and after the men had gone outside early the morning before Kate and Adam were due to leave, Beth told her stepsister everything.

Kate sat in stunned silence for a long time, staring at Beth with horror. "Now I know why Elizabeth was so concerned about you," she said at last, and when Beth still did not raise her head from staring down at her tightly clenched hands, she whispered, "And how desperately William must have loved you to marry you while believing what Father told him was true."

At that Beth looked up swiftly and said wildly, "Loved me? Loved me! It was Father he loved. Father he wanted to help for all he had done for him over the years."

"Rubbish."

Beth gaped at her, and Kate shook her head at her in disgust. "Really, Beth, certainly you are still very young, even though the mother of two, but when will you grow some sense? William has loved you ever since he first laid eyes on you. And when he returned for your sixteenth birthday, he simply devoured you with his eyes! Even Father commented on it to me."

When Beth continued to gaze at her from dazed eyes, Kate snorted. "Perhaps you think William is a soft touch, lets other people get away with what he has let you get away with over the years. If that is the case, you have not seen him dealing with disobedient servants like I have. Always very firm, very kind, but not giving an inch when he believed he was in the right."

Beth thought of the way he had once dismissed one of their London servants for stealing. Certainly he had tried to help the man when he had been discovered the first time, but he had shown no hint of weakness when he had dismissed him after he had stolen again. Suddenly she remembered other incidents. The way he dealt with unrepentant sinners was always kind, even gentle when necessary, but always very firm. Over and over, William had proven that although he was gentle, he was a strong man in body and spirit.

"And," Kate continued with a decided glint in her eyes, "if you think for one moment he is the sort of soft, spineless man who would marry anyone he did not want to marry, no matter if the queen demanded it of him, well," she concluded with an expressive sweep of her hands, "you are just crazy, my dear. Even now, anyone can tell his face simply lights up whenever you come into a room."

Beth went around in a daze for the rest of the day. Was Kate. . .could Kate possibly be right?

She found herself hardly able to take her eyes off William when they sat down with Adam and Kate for their last evening meal together. She beamed at him when he asked her anxiously if she was feeling all right, simply because she had stared at him without moving when he asked her to pass him the salt. She had been remembering the times in the privacy of their room when he had whispered he loved her, thinking, hoping that if Kate was right, he must have, after all, meant those words the way she wanted him to.

Kate gave a gurgling, choked-off laugh and, to Adam's obvious surprise and bemusement, covered it up quickly by launching into some humorous tale of an event involving Jackie and a new chum at Waverley. It turned into a rather involved story of Jackie pretending not to understand a word of English, stringing the poor man along until Adam had been forced to intervene.

Adam took up the story, dryly saying, "Of course, Jackie takes no notice of me whatsoever in that particular area. He just nods in agreement with what I say, grins, and strides away. No doubt he will continue to play his trick on each new white man he meets, backed up, of course, by the rest of our station hands, who think it is a huge joke."

To Beth's frustration no one made any move to go to bed early, and she was forced to stay up with all of them very late that night. Beth was disappointed when William tugged her into the curve of his body but promptly went to sleep, not giving her a chance to talk to him. In the morning when she woke, he had already gone to help Henry harness the horses to take Kate and Adam to Port Adelaide.

Kate was disgustingly and naughtily amused at Beth's frustration at not being able to talk to William. "Serves you right," she muttered with a heartless chuckle on the way into breakfast, and then laughed out loud at Beth's reproachful look. "I cannot believe you have been married all this time and not known your own husband loves you as much as he does."

"But then you have not realized how often he has treated me the same as he did when we were children," she burst out in a desperate whisper. As she uttered those words, Beth suddenly knew she was wrong. He had many, many times treated her very much like a woman.

She felt the heat mount up in her face and grinned weakly at Kate when she laughed out loud at her blush. But Kate's amusement quickly changed to concern when Miss Fisher informed them at breakfast that both Harold and James had woke with a slight fever. "Oh dear," she said, "does that mean you cannot come down to the port to see us off?"

After quickly ascertaining the children were not really ill but decidedly off-color and miserable, Beth swallowed her own disappointment and said with a brave shrug and attempted smile, "It seems I am never fated to be able to wave our family off shipside."

"I could stay with the boys, and you could go, Beth," William said anxiously.

He looked so upset for her that Beth stared at him for a moment and then looked suddenly across at Kate. Her stepsister gave her a knowing "I told you so" look, which made Beth suddenly blush a fiery red once again.

"Beth, are you also not feeling well?" William asked in a worried voice. "You look very flushed."

"No, no," she stammered quickly. "I'm fine except for feeling nauseated most mornings," she added without thinking. She jumped to her feet and swiftly followed after Miss Fisher, who had already hurried away again to be with her charges.

For a moment, no one in the room moved. William had half risen from his chair to go after Beth as she exited the room, but then with a stunned look on his face he sank back into his chair.

Kate gave a wobbly laugh that was almost a sob and said with feeling, "William, I think you may now know the reason Beth has been so pale at times the last few weeks. Believe me, I know how she feels!"

It was Adam's turn to stare at his wife with a puzzled frown. Kate smiled brilliantly at him and jumped to her feet. "Come with me, my darling," she whispered. "There is something I should tell you. Something I was waiting to tell you when we got back to Waverley, but now I find I will burst if I cannot share it with you this minute!"

William stood politely as they left the room, but he ignored Adam's questioning glance, hardly comprehending what Kate meant until a sudden joyful shout of, "Kate, my darling wife!" rang back from the hallway. William smiled for a moment, sharing Adam's wonder and delight at the prospect of being a father in a few months' time.

Then his face creased again in its worried frown. If Beth were pregnant again, why had she not yet told him? A thrill of delight swept through him at the thought of another small baby for them to share, to love. Perhaps a girl this time with golden curls and blue eyes like her beautiful mother.

But then his delight was overshadowed once more by his question. Was Beth, could Beth possibly be worried about what he would say, what he would think? Were the circumstances surrounding Harold's birth still weighing on her mind when he thought they had at long last been laid to rest?

Chapter 13

Beth waved until the carriage disappeared around the bend. She waited then, cuddling the miserable, teething James in one arm and reaching to hold Harold's little hand tightly, until at last the understanding Catherine Fisher whisked both children away, leaving Beth to wipe at her tears. The carriage appeared again, for a few far-too-brief moments, where the narrow road traveled up the crest of a small hill before once again rolling out of sight.

They were gone, and despite her and William's plans of visiting Adam and Kate at Waverley one day, Beth knew that journey could be a long time in the future.

Before they had bought their property, she and William had both agreed that they would stay in South Australia until the boys were older and it would be safer for them to travel. They were seeing every day how much need there was in this new land for a minister of the gospel.

The decision not to risk traveling with the small children had been confirmed to Beth once again after meeting the Telfers and being reminded of how dangerous even a sea voyage to Sydney could be. And now. . .now there would be another baby to consider.

Once again, she thought of telling William about the baby. She would do so this evening, along with other things she needed to tell him, to ask him! She thrilled at the thought of convincing him of her love for him. Although, now she knew there was really no need to ask him to confirm his love, and she castigated herself for ever doubting someone of his integrity.

Her lips twitched in a rueful smile. She would still need all the strength and patience God could give her once he knew about the baby. Once again she would be fussed over until the Reverend Garrett drove her crazy!

He had paid such detailed attention to her every comfort on the other two occasions she had suffered from the sickness in the mornings that she had decided to put off telling him as long as she could. It had always just seemed one more way William made her feel too young. She, a mother of two children, just hated being treated like a child, even if at times she did act like a foolish one, she acknowledged with a grimace.

But ever since she had talked to Kate, she had looked at William's care of her with new eyes. Always she had bemoaned her short height and slight, fair frame, longing to be tall and strong like Kate. And in all honesty, she had to admit that her seemingly frail appearance did give William every excuse to treat her gently.

But had he really treated her like a child when he had agreed to their long journey to Australia, to their buying their own ten acres and making their home so far from the security of England and any family?

Beth turned and surveyed her domain with sudden pride and satisfaction as never before. Their large, white, stone house with its bark- and brush-covered roof gleamed in the sun. A separate kitchen had been built next to it to protect the main house against kitchen fires. William had stated only a few days ago that their next project should be to replace the roof of the house with neat shingles.

The stables down the slight slope, well away from the house, had been extended, and a couple rooms had been made to give Henry the comfortable accommodation away from the house that the independent loner had said he strongly preferred. The improvements to the cow and poultry sheds and the yards to confine their three horses and two cows had been finished with the expert help of Adam in recent weeks. The large, fenced vegetable garden was between the stables and the house and, to their delight, was now starting to yield produce over and above their own needs so that they could sell or even give it away.

Beth smiled slightly, thinking about the inevitable upheaval that would occur while the roof was being replaced. She started toward the house with a light step. William would always accomplish what he decided should be done. He always had, and he always would.

The sound of a fast-running horse made her pause and swing around. Bob Young came into sight. His grave face worried her, even before he called out to her as he pulled his plunging horse to a stop.

"Hello there, Mrs. Garrett. Is William home?"

"He has just left to take our guests to their ship. The boys are not very well, and I stayed behind. What's wrong?" she asked sharply when he frowned.

He pointed beyond their property to the east and the rolling hills that gradually became steeper and covered with heavy forest to the horizon. Beth shielded her eyes from the morning sun and saw what she first thought was a low cloud. And then she knew.

"A bush fire!"

"Word came it must have started up during the night," he said briefly. "So far it is no real threat, but we are concerned it may spread quickly if the wind increases, and that is very likely." He looked toward the cow yards. "Is Henry still milking?"

"No, he has driven Mrs. MacGregor and Lucy into Adelaide. We needed several things, including supplies for our medicine cupboard," she explained briefly. "They left early so they could be home to do the milking tonight and prepare our evening meal."

Bob tipped his wide-brimmed hat back on his head and wiped the heavy film of perspiration from his forehead. "My whole family has already left."

Beth suddenly held her breath. He thought it was that serious?

"Bessie is taking the younger ones to safety closer to town, and the others have gone to fight the fire," he was saying briefly. "Perhaps when Henry returns, you would not mind if he checked on our place?"

He hesitated and then added solemnly, "And tell Henry and your husband you would be best to keep the horses close by, even harnessed. Just in case, Mrs. Garrett."

He was gone before his final words had registered. Beth gave a frightened gasp and looked toward the hills. Surely the fire was too far away to be a real threat to them? Even as she looked, it seemed the cloud of smoke beyond the ridge of mountains was spreading wider, getting thicker.

She turned and ran inside.

When she had briefly told Miss Fisher what Bob had said, the lady turned pale. "I've heard dreadful stories of bush fires," she gasped and wrung her hands. "My brother even had to help fight one last year on the property he was working on."

"Good," Beth said briskly. "That means, I am sure, that he told you something of what they had to do."

Miss Fisher hesitated and then drew herself up and nodded. "I remember him saying that one of the problems was that the wind carried burning leaves and branches, often starting up fires wherever they landed miles away from the fire front."

Her voice faltered, and she bit her lip before continuing in a steadier voice. "We need water, plenty of water, blankets, bags, anything we can keep damp, anything we can use to beat out fire. Perhaps. . ." She gulped. "Perhaps we may even be able to wet the roof, although if the sun stays hot it will dry it out quickly."

She hesitated again, then said in a voice that trembled just the slightest, "And do you think perhaps we should pack a few things just. . .just in case?"

Sudden fear swept through Beth. She sent up an urgent prayer. For a moment she stared at Miss Fisher and then at last shook her head and said slowly. "No, not yet. The fire is still on the other side of the ridge. We'll get the water first. It is very still outside, so I don't think there is any danger at the moment from wind-driven embers, but we had better do what we can. Besides, everyone will be out fighting it, so it may not even reach us."

She stopped. No matter what she thought, Bob Young was a levelheaded man. The risk of the fire reaching this far must be bad for all the Youngs to have left.

James started crying in the nursery, and they heard Harold's little patter as he talked to his brother.

The two women stared at each other silently. Beth saw her own fear reflected in Miss Fisher's eyes. They had no horses to help them flee. And they had two small boys to carry.

"We had best do all we can," Beth whispered at last, "just in case. And we will trust in God to look after us all."

She stepped forward, and the two women hugged each other. Catherine Fisher had always insisted on the formalities between mistress and servant, but all barriers were down now. They were merely two frightened women alone in a suddenly hostile environment.

Swiftly they organized themselves, taking turns watching the boys and drawing water from the new well to fill every container they could find. They collected as many items as they could think of that would beat out flames, and as they worked, both women kept glancing toward the east.

It was midday when they saw flames suddenly appear along the distant ridge, and to their horror, almost simultaneously the light easterly breeze increased considerably in strength. They could smell the smoke, and they watched as a few pieces of black leaves and ash flew into the yard.

"Do you think we should leave along the road and try to reach the river?" Beth panted after they had carried the last heavy bucket of water to the shade of the house.

"My brother said that the fires can swing around, can start up ahead of one from the flying embers and. . .and the heat drains all the air so you can hardly breathe." Catherine Fisher gave a frightened sob. "There is so much bush each side, the track is so narrow, and we would be far too slow. Besides, are you sure you know where the river is? What if we got lost?"

Beth stared at the bush and knew Catherine was right. Her memory of being lost in the bush, stumbling through it while trying to find Harold had never left her. She looked around and was suddenly very, very glad William had insisted all the tall trees surrounding the house had been cleared in a wide circle. The intense heat of the past days had dried out the low bush, and the grass crackled under their feet.

"There is only one more thing we can do besides watching out for burning embers," she said sharply and raced to where the tools were kept.

They desperately raked as much of the twigs and dry grass as they could in a wide circle away from the house, and then set to with forks and spade digging up the ground to form some kind of firebreak. The ground was rock hard. Their hands soon blistered, and Beth had to agree at last that they were only wasting their energy.

All they could do was pour as much water on the roof of the house as they could and take turns keeping watch. And they prayed as they had all day.

When the first red-hot embers started falling, Beth went to gather what she could in the house and put it in the safest place. Where that might be she was not sure, she acknowledged grimly, but there were some things she would keep on her body.

She slumped wearily for a moment in the chair at William's desk before opening the drawer where she knew he kept their important personal papers. As she hurriedly slipped them into a large leather satchel, Beth spied some sheets of paper with William's scrawl on them. They were partly tucked under the large blotter on top of the desk.

No doubt important notes for his next sermon. She picked them up swiftly. She was wrong. Her own name caught her eye: "I Love You, Beth."

A poem followed. It was the title of a love poem. Poetry. William had written a poem. A poem about her. Beth.

She stared at it, then started to read. . . .

I love you as birds love to fly
*   As desert flowers long for rain.*
I love you and my soul doth cry
*   For you to love me again.*

I loved you, but then I failed you
*   When my mind was reeling from fears.*
I loved you for remaining true
*   And turning my life with your tears.*

I love you for being my wife
*   You are, I know, God's gift to me.*
I love you, faithful in the strife
*   Caused by my own stupidities.*

I love you, with love more than mine
*   With a passion enriched by trust.*
I love you, Beth, with joy divine
*   Because our God did first love us.*

I love you, my sweet gentle Beth
*   With heartfelt longing, great pain.*
I love you, O beautiful Beth
*   And pray you'll embrace me again.*

It was the last few words, scrawled fiercely, the pencil almost piercing the paper, that brought the tears:

*   O God, how I love her! Forgive me. Cover me! Help her to forgive me.*
O God, how I love her!

She sat, stunned. Then, her hand trembling, she turned over the second sheet of paper. The title at the top declared it to be "My Three Loves."

Swiftly she read:

I love the Lord because He first loved me. His love is giving, my love is responding. His love is dying, my love is in living. His love is unchanging, my love is trembling. I love the Lord because He first loved me.

In brackets he had scribbled 1 John 4:19. Beth had heard him quote that verse many times, but she stared at the words in wonder and then at last smiled mistily. She already knew this was how William loved his Lord. And his next love she also knew.

I love the Church because Christ gave Her Life. Betrothed Bride of Christ. Salvation's centerpiece. Through Her is Christ proclaimed. In Her, He is glorified. With Her He shall reign through all eternity—because Christ gave Her Life.

And then Beth caught her breath as she read the next line. . .and the next:

I love my wife because God gave her to me. A Grace gift to me to love, to cherish in all circumstances. She is wife and lover, my friend and coworker, mother to our children because God gave her to me.

This was how the Reverend William Garrett loved his wife. As a precious gift from God. And she had dared to doubt his love!

Beth turned quickly back to that first precious page and was still staring at William's scrawl, trying to take in his beautiful words, when Catherine Fisher started screaming.

Chapter 14

William was eager to get back to Beth. Although she had been obviously distracted by the departure of Adam and Kate, as well as by the boys' slight fever, she had been unbelievably loving toward him all morning. And then there was her condition. . .

There had been all kinds of delays when they had arrived at Port Adelaide. It had taken much longer than they had expected to unload their baggage and ensure it was safely taken out to the ship. Other passengers had also decided to arrive early, and there had been long queues waiting in the hot sun for the longboats making several trips out to the ship at anchor offshore.

Eventually it had been Adam and Kate's turn. William had felt sad watching Adam and Kate disappear across the now-choppy waves of the gulf. The wind from the east had strengthened several hours before, and he knew it augured well for the commencement of their journey.

He had promised that one day his family would pay a return visit, even perhaps consider ministering at a church somewhere closer to them in New South Wales. But all of that required finding out what God wanted them to do, and at that Kate and Adam had smiled in perfect understanding, even if Kate had said fervently, "I'll certainly be having a few words to say to Him about it, though."

William wasted no time hitching up the horses and starting off. It was only after he had left the sandhills and the smell of the sea that he smelled the smoke. Uneasy, he stopped at the next rise and scanned the horizon. Only then did he see the distant gray wall of smoke. Relieved that it seemed well to the north of their area, he shook the reins and clucked to the horses to move off again, but with every mile the smoke became thicker and covered more of the sky. It seemed to be ominously close to their area.

With sudden fear, William remembered that Beth had insisted she and the nurse would manage perfectly well for a few hours while Henry took the other two women into town. He shook the reins and used the whip to start the horses running as they had never run pulling the carriage before. The farther he traveled along the main road, the more people he met, their wagons piled up with all they could carry.

Not too far from the turnoff to their area, William suddenly recognized the cart pulled over to the side of the road and the girl standing on the seat peering back up the main road.

He pulled up swiftly, and Bessie Young turned her frightened, tear-streaked face toward him. "Oh, Mr. Williams, Mr. Williams, have you seen Ma and Pa?" she screamed.

He managed to calm her enough for her to sob out that she and her siblings had been there for hours, expecting anytime to see her parents. "They all went to stop the fire spreading over the ridge, Sir," she cried. "Pa told me to take the youngun's and wait for them here on this wide road nearer to town. Just in case the fire got as far as our place. And now no one has been able to tell me any more than that it was heading directly toward us."

"You have been a very good girl, and you should perhaps go on closer to Adelaide now. Go to the church. I am sure there will be people there who will help you," William managed to say as calmly as he could, adding urgently, "Have you seen anybody from my place?"

"No, no, but Pa was going over there to get you to help them as we left this morning."

"This morning! When. . .Bessie, what time did your father send you off?"

When he heard the answer, William's heart pounded. His whole being was one prayer as he raced along the narrow track. Bob Young must only just have missed him! Each mile the panting, heaving horses drew closer, the smoke settled around him. The wind had dropped. Perhaps it would swing back. Perhaps the fire had missed them.

But as he topped the last rise, he groaned out loud. He was too late. The stables were blazing. From his viewpoint it looked like flames were shooting up from the house roof.

From that last hill to the house, the bush on each side of the track was still smoldering from the fire that had raced to devour and then sped on to search and claim more fuel in its relentless fury.

The horses' nostrils were flaring, their eyes showing their fear. William had difficulty controlling them as he forced them along through the smoke and heat, the smell of fire, until they at last stood trembling and snorting in the burned-out clearing surrounding the house. The stables had been consumed, the cow shed was still burning, and most of the fences were smouldering piles of ashes. Badly burned domestic and bush animals would have to be found, some to care for, others to put out of their misery.

But William hardly noticed or thought of them now. "Beth! Beth!" he croaked.

He was coughing, his eyes streaming from the smoke as he automatically tied up the frightened horses. Frantically he raced toward the house. Flames were shooting out from the windows of the kitchen. The roof caved in with a roar.

A section of the house nearest to the kitchen had just caught fire. Blackened figures formed a chain from the well to pass buckets of water to throw at the fire in a desperate fight against the enemy.

A small figure was up on the roof of the main house, frantically trying to put out a small fire that had just started. Someone else joined him, risking life and limb in a desperate attempt to save the whole house from going up.

One of the blackened figures near the kitchen gave a shout. William saw it was Robert Young and quickly joined him. "Beth, the boys," he gasped. "Are they safe?"

Robert shook his head. The soot-covered woman beside him panted desperately, "We don't know, but don't you dare say she is not safe somewhere, Bob Young! All our dear ones just have to be safe!"

And William realized it was Isabel Young, her legs clothed in an old pair of trousers, her hair tightly wrapped in an old scarf.

"I passed Bessie on the main road. They were very frightened but all safe. I sent them on into Adelaide," William said swiftly, relief sweeping through him. "Henry must have returned in time to get Beth."

Robert shook his head again. He grabbed the next bucket as he nodded toward the roof and panted breathlessly, "That's Henry. . .up on the roof. Only arrived a few minutes ago himself. Said. . .turned back. . .fire across the road. . .took your housekeeper and Lucy to safety. . .when he saw. . ."

But William had already gone. He raced around the house until he was as close as he could get to the frantically working little man above him and yelled, "Henry!"

A sudden gust of wind blew. It lifted some burning thatch from the kitchen, and sparks landed beside the small figure. Like a flash he jumped on them, desperately trying to extinguish the small flame before it could spread.

William saw the ladder Henry had dragged up to climb to the roof and was beside him as the last smoldering piece was sent hurtling down to the ground.

"A close one, Boss." Henry smiled at him grimly but was flicking his hand, and William knew he must have burned himself. "The whole roof would have been long gone if it had not been so damp on this side."

A fit of coughing from the smoke choked William again, and before he had recovered enough to speak, Henry was saying urgently, "I'm so sorry I didn't get back in time. They had all gone. The fire. . .they must have tried to run away through the bush. I'm. . .I'm sorry. . . ."

William stared at him, trying to take in what he was saying. Then a large tear trembled on the small man's rugged face, perhaps the first tear in a lifetime of harshness.

And William knew what he was saying. Miss Fisher, Beth, Harold, James. . . they could never have survived the intense heat, the smoke, the flames of the fire as it raced from treetop to treetop, consuming all in its path.

"No. . .no," William whispered. "I won't. . .I can't believe. . . Oh, no!"

A faint, exhausted cheer went up from the people in the yard. The flames were dying down. The plowed ground of the vegetable paddock, even the pitifully small firebreak near the house, had slowed the fire until they had arrived. The barrels, the buckets, the kettles, even the kitchen saucepans filled with water had given the firefighters a head start, and now they had won the battle to save the house.

Even as they cheered, the strong wind was easing, changing direction, now more friend then foe. Later they would find that in the vagaries of a bush fire, it had somehow completely missed the Youngs' small property so close by.

Henry gave a deep, shuddering sigh. "We've won," he said with no sound of victory in his voice.

William was crouched with his head bowed, his strong shoulders shaking. "Oh, no, she. . .they. . .mean more than life to me. No. . .no," he said over and over in shock.

A firm hand landed on his shoulder. He ignored it, and then it shook him hard. Henry's shaking, wondering voice whispered, "Look. . .look, Boss. Through the smoke."

William raised his head and stared blindly at Henry. Then he looked numbly where the man's hand was pointing.

Two figures were moving like shadows through the smoke. They slowly stumbled into sight, dodging around burning tree stumps, disappearing into pockets of smoke, but getting ever closer until Henry and William's straining eyes could see them more clearly.

William had stiffened and stared, his eyes hardly daring to believe. And then he moved. Across the roof. Down the ladder. And running. . .and running. . .

Henry gave a great shout. The exhausted people on the ground looked up at him. At his pointing hand. They turned. A gasp went up as a tall, black man grasping the wrist of a short, slight figure stumbled into view.

Another tall, desperately racing man had nearly reached them. The aborigine gave a grunt and let go of the woman. She gave a faint cry before she flung herself forward and was enclosed in strong, loving arms.

Only a few noticed the black man gaze for a moment toward the group of people near the house. But none noticed him slip silently away, back through the burned-out bush and into the gray wall of smoke. All eyes were on the couple standing as one.

"Oh, William, William, you're safe!"

Words were beyond him. She was safe! All he could do was hold her to his shaking, gasping body, and then push her back to look into her eyes with a desperate question in his own.

"We are all safe," Beth told him swiftly, her words tumbling over, trying to reassure him. "Harold, James, Catherine. The aboriginal woman and her man came and made us all go with them to the river, to a wide water hole. They came racing up to the house and frightened Catherine badly at first.

"We did not want to go. But the woman screamed over and over that word I told you about, 'Kawai.' The man grabbed up Harold, even prodded us with his spear until we were running and running. We. . .we did not realize the fire was so close, coming so fast," she panted. "We made it into the water just in time. Oh, it was dreadful! We never realized. . .it came so fast. I could never believe the fury of it, the heat. It was so hard to breathe. We crouched up to our necks in the water in the middle of a huge water hole while the fire burned all around us."

She gave a loud sob and started to shake. "We. . .the boys. . .would not have survived that heat here. Catherine. . .she. . .has stayed with the boys, the woman, and their son because the smoke is still so dense, while I. . .I. . .I had to make sure you were safe!"

He was holding her again so tightly she could not speak, could hardly breathe. Nothing mattered but that she was safe. Together they would rebuild what was lost in the fire. Together they would love and serve their God in this great southland.

And at last he found his voice. "I thought I had lost you," he groaned, and he knew she felt his tears against her face. "Oh, Beth, I love you more than life."

A shuddering sigh swept through Beth. "I know, my darling William, I know," she whispered.

Her hands were soothing him, wiping away the moisture that still flowed down his strong, smoke-stained face, and at last he drew one more deep breath and slowly raised his head to devour her filthy, soot- and smoke-blackened face with his eyes. Some of her hair was singed, making him realize how close the danger had been.

🦋

"And I love you more than life itself, my husband," she whispered at long last, knowing now the words to use to convince him.

The brilliance of the light that flashed into William's eyes and spread across his face awed Beth. She knew that their love would last through the years. Because what William had written had been so true.

Their love for each other had been given by the very source of love. They loved because God in Christ had first loved them. Their love for each other was a precious gift of sheer grace from the God who is love. And this kind of love would never fade, just grow richer and deeper.

Later there would be hours of talking, as they should have talked over the years. He would tell her about being so nervous when he asked to speak to Lord Farnley privately, intending to ask for her hand in marriage. Instead, he found himself being rushed into that appalling arranged wedding and then feeling dreadfully guilty about the whole affair because he believed she had been pressured into it. He would confess the jealousy, the hatred he had fought not to have toward John, until he had been able to allow God to love John through him, even before he knew the truth.

She would tell him that she now knew how selfish and immature she had been when they married, how childishly foolish. They would laugh joyfully together that as he had been marrying two strangers, she had finally realized the true nature of her love. He would admit that he had come so close that same day to damaging their reputation by publicly hauling her into his arms and kissing her senseless beneath the tall gum tree!

She would share with him that she had realized it was her nature and upbringing that made her feel shy about talking publicly about deep spiritual issues, yet her own trust and love for God had grown over the years. And he would kiss her again with a loving groan when she informed him emphatically that this was due mainly to the Christian life he lived before her each day.

Shyly she would ask the question that had puzzled her for months. How had he not known on their wedding night there had been no other lover? She would delight in the tide of color that swept into his face as he briefly muttered that it had been because he himself had been totally innocent and could not judge the matter. And she knew that it had been because of his incredible gentleness and care of her that night as well.

He would tell her that despite the temptations he had faced when men upheld standards for women they did not keep for themselves, it had been easy for him to resist because of his love for her and his determination to obey God's Word.

But that was all still to come. None of it mattered at this glorious moment. Now they were smiling radiantly at each other, and Beth put it all into words.

"Because God loved us first, we love," she whispered tenderly. "He gave you to me, me to you, 'Grace gifts' to love and cherish in all circumstances, for all eternity."

And in the end, the telling and the knowing was as simple as that.

Note from the Author

In 1840, transportation of convicts to New South Wales ceased. But just as it ended in the east of Australia, it began in the west. It was not until January 10, 1868, that the last convict ship to Australia landed at Fremantle, eighty years to the month since the First Fleet dropped anchor in Sydney Cove to colonize the Great Southland.

South Australia is the only state that never had convicts transported to its shores to help establish the settlement. Adelaide has often been called "The City of Churches."

The early pioneers faced many hardships. Although all other characters in this story are fictitious, where the Telfer and Pedler names have been used, the incidents are based on actual events.

The Pedlers and Telfers are perhaps typical of so many who had the courage to voluntarily leave their homes to try and establish better lives for their children. Jean Telfer died just twenty-six days after arriving in Adelaide. Her husband, Francis, married their shipboard friend Dinah Flavel in November 1839. In March 1844, at the age of twenty-three, Dinah also died. Three months after Dinah's death, Jean and Francis's twelve-year-old son, James, went missing, and his body was never found. Francis married again. John, the first child of this marriage to Margaret, was my mother's grandfather.

The Pedler family also had their share of tragedies. William the Third's brother Joseph died in 1845 of consumption, which may have developed in the damp conditions of a mine in Cornwall years before. I have discovered that he had a granddaughter who was called Mary Ellen Pedler, my own name!

William and his brother Thomas were shoemakers for some years and then farmers. The child born to Elizabeth Pedler in May 1839 was Nicholas, my father's grandfather.

Down through the decades, branches of both families moved to Eyre's Peninsula to pioneer farming around the Tumby Bay and Ungarra area. And then one day, two people who loved and served Jesus Christ, Les Pedler and Gladys Telfer, were married. They also inherited the pioneer spirit and in 1939 were among the first wheat growers on the Darling Downs in Queensland.

I am very proud to be their daughter, Mary.

GREAT
SOUTHLAND GOLD

For Lois Bentley,
a great sister-in-law, encourager, best friend,
and one who shares my love of reading those romance novels!

Chapter 1

New South Wales, 1843

S till no sign of your father, Tim?"

For a long moment there was no movement from the boy perched in the highest possible spot of the old gum tree. At last he shook his head, though he continued to stare out across the valley, searching the winding road that disappeared through the tall timber at the foot of the distant mountain. Adam knew how desperately the boy hoped to see the familiar horse and wagon carrying the man he had missed so much these last long months.

After a pause, Adam Stevens tried again. "Anything could have delayed him, Son," he called in an even louder voice. His voice was troubled, revealing his own anxiety. They had been expecting Timothy Hardy to arrive midmorning, at the latest by midday. But the sun was low in the west. Adam had been out in the back paddocks all day, and when he had returned a few moments ago, his anxious wife had met him at the homestead gate. Kate was deeply worried about Tim, who had climbed the tree hours ago and resisted all her pleas to come down.

Tim stirred slightly but never stopped watching that distant dirt track. It was a long moment before his quiet tones answered, "But Father would have allowed for that and set out even earlier than he had planned. He always camps somewhere so he can be here as early as possible. His letter said to expect him this morning. Besides, he knew I'd be waiting."

Adam's concern deepened. Tim was right. It was so unlike Timothy. After the tragedy of losing his wife and small daughter the year before, Timothy had found it especially hard to leave his beloved son at Waverley so the boy could finish his schooling. More than once, Adam's lonely old friend had arrived a day or so earlier than expected. And because of all that had happened, Adam had been making plans that he was eager to surprise his friend with this evening.

"Well, what if we grab a couple of horses and go meet him?" Adam forced his voice to sound cheerful.

That did bring an eager response. "Oh, Sir, could we?"

There was a rustle of leaves, and Adam watched with some relief as Tim made short work of reaching the ground. He was nowhere near as tall as Adam, but Adam knew that Tim's father would be astonished at the way the lad had grown these last few months.

"Yes, I don't see why not." He didn't give a hint how weary the hard day's work had made him; he just placed his hand on the boy's shoulder and turned toward the house. "But we'd better tell Kate first. We'll get her to put together some food and water for us. If anything, we can have a picnic tea in the bush with your father," he finished with a grin.

There was no answering smile from Tim. He paced silently beside Adam for several yards before he at last took a deep breath and blurted out, "Something's happened to Father, Mr. Stevens. I–I woke up early this morning, was praying and reading the Bible like I always do, when. . ." He paused.

Adam glanced at him and noticed color creeping into his cheeks. He looked quickly away, wondering why Tim was suddenly feeling embarrassed.

The last two years, Tim had stayed with the Stevenses so he could go to the small school Kate had started years ago for the station children and any aborigines who could be persuaded to attend. During that time, they had always encouraged Tim to continue the habit of having personal devotions each morning as his father and mother had taught him. Like his parents, Tim had never been shy about his faith in God, and Adam and Kate had enjoyed many discussions with him about spiritual things.

Even when Timothy senior had been in his convict chains on board that transport ship to Australia all those years ago, he had never hesitated to talk about his Savior and Lord, Jesus Christ, no matter how many times he had suffered physical as well as verbal abuse from the other convicts. Because of his unjust treatment when trying to stop a convict riot on board ship, Timothy was granted the deeply longed-for ticket-of-leave. Despite all the restrictions still on him until his ten years were served, that piece of paper allowed him to choose his employer and actually be paid for work. He had gladly chosen Adam as his boss.

Adam had been a bitter, angry man in those days. He too had known what it was to be a convict but had met Timothy Hardy not long after becoming an emancipist, the name given to those in Australia who had finished their prison term but chosen to stay and make new lives for themselves. Adam knew Timothy had suffered far more in his first few months than Adam had his whole term and, at the time, had marveled that the small, gentle man's attitude was so different from his own. Timothy had joined an organization in England trying to right unjust laws. Foolishly he had let himself be swept up in a riot that ended in his arrest and transportation. Despite all he had endured, Timothy's life had wonderfully demonstrated God's forgiveness and the peace and quiet joy that a personal relationship with God gave.

To his own surprise, Adam had found himself prepared to listen to Bible readings and discussions around the lonely campfires in the bush. At last he too had believed it was all true, accepted Christ as his own personal Savior, and found his life transformed from darkness to light. There was simply no other way to describe it all. He still often marveled in sheer wonder at his life now compared to what it had been.

Adam glanced briefly at the set face of Tim. According to Kate, the boy had seemed unusually tense all day, showing none of the excitement he usually exhibited each time his father was able to make the long journey southeast from Stevens Downs. And Tim had more reason than usual to be looking forward to his father's return. Kate had taught Tim all she could in their little school. Now he was to return home with his father for good, or at least until Kate could persuade Timothy to let them help give the bright, intelligent lad a chance at further education—perhaps in a good boarding school in Sydney. Hopefully Adam's new plans would help Timothy make those dreams possible.

Nearing the gate to the homestead, Adam asked quietly, "What happened during your devotional time, Tim?"

Tim stopped. He looked down at his boots, scuffing one of them in the dirt. Adam waited patiently until the boy at last looked up, searching Adam's face anxiously. "You'll think it's all my imagination," he said rapidly, "but I. . .it suddenly seemed as though God was telling me to pray for Father. I felt really anxious for him all of a sudden, and since then. . ."

A horse whinnied a short distance away. Tim and Adam turned as a deep, guttural voice said, "Me reckon you wantum horses like, Boss?"

Adam looked with considerable exasperation at the solemn face of a tall aborigine slouched on the back of a large black horse. Then he saw that the man was holding the reins of three other horses—two saddled and one a packhorse.

Tim gasped, and Adam said swiftly, "Jackie, how many times do I have to tell you to cut out that false native talk?"

This was an old joke between them, the European-raised-and-educated aborigine reverting to "blackfellow" talk, especially to fool white strangers who were stupid enough to think themselves superior. But for once, there was no brief gleam of teeth as usually happened when Adam chided him. Jackie eased the wide-brimmed cattleman's hat back off his dark forehead and stared silently back.

Adam tensed, studying the expressionless face. Jackie knew something. It never ceased to amaze him how aborigines discovered things long before white people did, but Adam had learned long ago never to underestimate Jackie.

"Mr. Stevens, please, can Jackie come too?" Tim's voice held a shrill note of urgency.

Adam glanced at Tim and then back at Jackie and the horses. "Seems to me he's already decided that," he said as lightly as he could.

A faint glimmer of amusement briefly touched the black eyes. "Reckon that Missus already packum food and dem blankets for three, like," he drawled.

Adam put his hands on his hips and glared in mock anger at his old friend. "I don't know, Tim. Do you really think we should take a no-good aboriginal black-fellow along with us who tries to fool white folk with his attempts at English?"

To Adam's relief, the boy relaxed a little, and a slight smile crossed his pale face. Tim reached for the black mare that had been unofficially his ever since he had come to live with the Stevens family and patted the long nose that nudged him. "Guess you shouldn't be too hard on Jackie, Sir. After all, he has to be such a good example of an educated blackfellow when he helps Mrs. Kate at school that he probably needs a chance to be himself."

Although this was part of the same old joke between them, this time something flashed across Jackie's face. It was gone in an instant, but Adam knew that Jackie often felt the pain of being caught between two worlds. He had never been fully accepted by his own people because of his upbringing by well-meaning missionaries after the death of his mother and was rarely accepted by white people—usually only those who knew him well, loved and respected him.

Jackie straightened in his saddle. Adam wasn't in the least surprised when he said in the polished, educated accent of an upper-crust Englishman, "That is enough cheek out of you, my young man. And no more nonsense if you want to share any of this food and camping gear. Now, do you intend to stay here chatting instead of being on our way before dark?"

Only then did Adam realize the horses already had full saddlebags and blankets. He stepped forward and took his horse's reins from Jackie. "Kate?"

Jackie nodded. "I was going with a couple of the men, if you were any later getting home."

They stared at each other in silent communication. Jackie was an excellent blacktracker. Aborigines were noted for their ability to track animals and people over the most difficult terrain. Their feats since early settlement had never ceased to amaze the unskilled "white fellas." Now, and not for the first time by any means, Adam was glad that over the years Jackie had been sought out by police and folk from across a wide area to help find people lost in the bush or criminals seeking to escape the law.

Tension filled the air. Tim was already in his saddle. Without another word Adam mounted swiftly. Only then did he see the rifle resting in its leather holster. He always carried a revolver at his waist in case he came across badly injured stock that needed to be put down or any of a number of dangers that lurked in the bush, but if Jackie thought they might need rifles as well, it was an ominous sign.

Kate was waiting a little wistfully for them near the gate. Adam knew that if she did not have the responsibility of their two small children, nothing would have stopped her going with them. He bent quickly for her kiss. She told him softly that she had instructed Jackie to pack enough supplies in case they had to travel all the way to Stevens Downs. Grim-faced, he stared at her for a long moment.

Glancing at Tim, Kate called out an encouraging word. Then she looked back at Adam steadily. "We'll be fine here," she murmured at last. "I just hope Jackie's information is wrong. Take as long as you need, but I'll be waiting."

Adam nodded briefly, then turned his horse, and the trio set off down the stony road in a clatter of hooves. Near the gum tree he glanced back. Kate was still watching. She waved until a bend in the road took her out of sight. Adam knew she would be busy praying for them all as she waited, and especially for their old friend Timothy Hardy.

They kept the horses trotting along at a brisk pace until they reached the winding track usually taken to reach Stevens Downs. Adam was content to let Jackie lead the way, knowing the man's sharp eyes would see any trace of a recent traveler that the other two could easily miss.

Hours later, as the brief twilight gave way to darkness, the three friends quietly set up camp on the dry creek bed at Lewis Ponds. They were sure that something had either happened to prevent Timothy Hardy from starting out or that he was sick or injured somewhere on the trail.

Jackie finished attending to the horses and then disappeared into the shadows of the bush. Adam left Tim to roll out their blankets while he started a small fire and poured some water into a blackened billycan and set it to boil.

"Sir, do you think Father could have gone the long way round on the main road from Wellington through Blackman's Swamp, even gone on to Bathurst before. . .before heading for Waverley?"

Adam's heart ached at the sound of the exhausted, trembling voice. Reluctantly he shook his head. "He could have, I guess, but he never has before—always taken you with him if he needed to go near the villages."

Low, pain-filled tones asked the inevitable question. "He. . .he still has a couple years of his sentence to go. No one would have. . .would have demanded he show them his ticket-of-leave, would they? And if he had lost it?"

"I'm sure that would be no problem, Tim," Adam reassured the boy. "Except for the authorities who renew his ticket each year, I doubt if many people out here even remember he was transported to Australia. He is very highly thought of in the whole district as my trusted manager of Stevens Downs." He paused and added, "I still think it's simply that he's had a horse go lame or sick on him. And you know as well as I do how well he cares for his animals."

❦

Tim stared at Adam for a long moment. Then he looked into the deepening shadows of the surrounding bush. He knew as well as the older man the dangers in the harsh Australian bush, so different from England. During the long hours that afternoon, he had already accepted the fact that his father's plan to bring a small dray to carry home Tim's possessions would mean a much slower journey. But Tim also knew his father would have made allowance for that.

He heaved a sigh. At least his father had not intended to ride, so his horse couldn't have thrown him. But something—a snake, a startled kangaroo, any number of things—could have startled the cart horses, making them bolt. His biggest fear was that his father was lying sick or injured somewhere.

Mother had always fussed over his father whenever he had even the slightest cold. Tim knew his father's health had never been the same since his ordeal in prison and on that horrible convict ship when he had been flogged. And Tim sensed that his father hadn't fully recovered from losing Mother and Tim's small sister, Jane, from the fever last year. Tim was convinced that only faith in a God of love and mercy had kept his father sane.

During that dreadful time, Tim himself had begun to doubt that God really cared about them. All that had happened to his family these last few years would surely make anyone wonder. But he had certainly been praying today.

Tim's thoughts stayed with him throughout the evening as he sat by the campfire and then later as he struggled to fall asleep under his blanket. He also wondered where Jackie had disappeared to and why he had led them so far east of the main route to Wellington. Adam had told him that this often happened with Jackie out in the bush, but the man's absence added to Tim's unease.

The next morning, Jackie reappeared and quietly informed them that Tim's father had been last seen a long way off his usual route, near the Turon River, a few miles from where it joined the Macquarie.

Adam stared at him in the faint, predawn light. Tim knew Adam had learned a long time ago not to ask Jackie how he gained information. They had not seen a soul since they'd left Waverley, but aborigines could easily be watching them.

Tim looked from Jackie's somber face to Adam's puzzled one. "What would Father be doing over there? It's a longer way from our usual track than here at Lewis Ponds Creek."

"I don't know," Adam replied quietly. "But we had better head that way. Let's hope Jackie can find the trail there."

They made it to the Turon River and followed its winding path east through the hills and scrub until it was once again too dark to go farther in the rugged country. After another restless night on the hard ground, the silent trio set off at first light. Tim had stopped praying by then.

They found the remains of the small camp first. The dray was gone, along with the horses. Some of Timothy's meager personal belongings were scattered on the ground.

The hills rose quite steeply a little way back from the creek, and Jackie swiftly led them in that direction. When they reached an area of fallen rocks, he lost Timothy's trail.

"Spread out and walk around the edge of this," Jackie said wearily. "Keep an eye out for any tracks leading away from this stony ground."

It was Tim who found his father.

After searching the area allotted to him, he desperately plunged a little deeper into the bush and rounded a large boulder.

Tim froze. A still, slight figure lay sprawled on the ground. Rushing forward, for one horrible moment Tim thought there was no life in the still body.

"Father!" His voice was barely a harsh whisper.

Tim swallowed, tried to moisten his dry mouth, and reached out to gently touch the gray face. His heart leaped as the closed eyelashes flickered and a soft groan escaped through his father's cracked, swollen lips.

Tim grabbed his water bottle, but his shaking hand spilled the water on the still face before it splashed onto those lips. The eyelashes flickered again, and then the eyes opened. Tim's father stared into space for a brief moment before his eyelids drooped again.

"Father, oh, dear Father, it's Tim. We've found you."

He suddenly remembered his companions and screamed out their names.

"Tim?" The murmur from his father was so soft, Tim barely heard it. He reached out and lovingly wiped away the water he had spilled on the dirt-streaked face. Only then did he realize the dirt was mingled with dried blood.

"Yes, it's Tim, Father," he choked out, fighting the tears that had begun to clog his throat. "And Adam and Jackie are near."

The eyes were searching, searching. His father moved his hand slightly toward him. Tim grasped it and held the callused, work-worn hand gently to his chest. His father clutched at him weakly and struggled to speak.

"Here, Father, have some water."

This time a couple mouthfuls were painfully, slowly swallowed.

"No. . .no more. Something must tell you. . .find. . .find Molly's box. . . ."

The voice was slightly stronger, but Tim still had to lean close to the barely moving lips.

"Find. . .the gold. . .love you. . .all for you. . .but. . .wrong. . .wrong. . . God would have. . ."

The dull eyes closed once more, and the hand the boy held went slack. A sob tore from Tim. At the sound of the boy's agony, the slack hand tightened slightly.

The lips moved soundlessly. Timothy made one last effort and managed to whisper, "Jesus. . .more. . .more. . .precious than. . .gold. Jesus. . ." The wounded man fought to draw another shallow breath. His eyes looked up one last time. Tim saw them focus on him and fill with love. His father's eyes remained open, but gradually something went from them.

"Father? *Father!*"

Tim heard a rush of feet on the ground behind him, but he dared not take his eyes from his father's face. Adam bent over them, closed the empty eyes, and said in a choked voice, "I'm so sorry, Tim. Your father's gone to be with Jesus."

Chapter 2

New South Wales, 1850

The wily bullock was determined to get away from the whip-cracking man on the back of the black horse. It plowed through the low scrub, twisting and turning around the scattered gum trees. The narrow creek and the steep, rock-strewn hill beyond that presented no deterrent.

Tim Hardy reluctantly hauled on the reins of his weary horse and watched the bullock disappear. It wasn't worth risking his horse's legs over one stubborn bull. Blackie didn't seem to disagree. He willingly slowed to a walk, and when the reins remained slack, stopped altogether. Once the horse's sides had stopped heaving, Blackie lowered his head to nibble at a tempting green shoot.

Frowning, Tim studied his surroundings. He had been out camping for several days with the stockmen from Waverley Station, trying to round up cattle that had strayed a long way off the property. He hadn't realized how far into the scrub he had pursued the bullock after it had broken away from the small mob of cattle. Now he wasn't quite sure where he was.

He listened intently. No sounds of men or cattle traveled on the light breeze. Even the trees around him barely rustled. A bird chirped nearby, a magpie warbled from a tall gum tree, and then a distant crow added its harsh cry to the sounds of the bush—sounds Tim had missed during those long, weary years of study in Sydney. Only a few times had he managed to sneak away from his books and lecturers to explore the bush that lined most of Port Jackson.

Tim set his horse in motion to the edge of the trickling water and paused to let Blackie have a short drink before slowly following the creek. It ran only a short distance before it flowed into a wider river that rippled over small, smooth pebbles. He frowned again as Blackie carefully picked his way along the bank. Something about this area felt familiar, but Tim very much doubted if he had come this way before—certainly not during the past year since he'd returned from Sydney and begun looking after Waverley for Adam.

The river narrowed as it curved around a pile of small boulders. The bank stood higher and the water ran faster and deeper. In the distance to the east, hills rose more steeply.

Tim hesitated. It was long after midday, and he still had to find his way back to the others. But it was more sensible to follow a river when he wasn't sure where he was. Getting lost in the Australian bush was not a pleasant experience, even though this was spring and not as hot as full summertime. Of course he knew how to survive if he were lost. His father and Adam had made sure of that.

He shrugged. It was a pleasant spot, with numerous golden wattle trees and flowering gums. Tim still had that nagging feeling he had been here before. He gave in to his curiosity and the lure of the quiet bush. Turning his horse, he tried to find an easier way along the riverbank. The farther Tim went beside the river, the more he was certain he had been here before. The hills had become steeper, but the valley had gradually widened. Several large boulders stood out among the thick scrub on the hills on the other side of the river.

Only once before, a long time ago, had he ever traveled in this direction from Waverley. He shrugged off the thought and concentrated on walking his horse safely over some particularly rough ground. A moment later he came to a place where the river was shallow once more, spreading out over a wider, flatter stretch of heavily pebbled soil. A good place to camp.

Tim froze. He had not realized how far north they had traveled. He did know this place. It was where they had found his father's wrecked campsite all those years ago.

Since those first few weeks after his father's death, he had refused to let the memories of that dreadful day surface. They were too painful, too much a reminder that he was alone, despite Adam and Kate taking him into their own home and treating him like a son.

Here there was no escape.

He stared around, trying to pinpoint where he had searched, where he had so desperately run from his father's few scattered belongings.

He still had so many unanswered questions from that tragic day. Tim had desperately tried to work out what his father had been attempting to tell him. To his surprise, his mother's keepsake box had not been in its usual place at Stevens Downs. Adam had assured him that it had not been among his father's things at the campsite. Jackie had even led a group of men back to make a thorough search. They could only conclude that whoever had wrecked the camp must have stolen the box along with the dray and horses.

Adam had told Tim much later that Jackie believed Tim's father had camped beside that river before—perhaps made it a regular stop on his journeys from Stevens Downs to Waverley and back. But why? The site was far from the direct route to Wellington. What had been the attraction of this isolated place so far from even a lonely shepherd's hut? If it had not been for Jackie's blacktracking skills, they might never have found him.

What had been important enough to cause Timothy Hardy to behave so uncharacteristically?

For a long time his father's last words had haunted Tim. Were they delirious ramblings? Tim had never told anyone of his father's words about gold and Jesus. At first he had been too numb; later he had tried to forget the horrors of that dreadful day. But now, in this place, the memories would not be denied.

Tim had decided that his father's dying wish had been to impress on him how important Jesus Christ was. But then, Tim had always known the love his father had for his Lord. Nothing had ever taken priority over that love, not even his wife and children.

Tim examined the site with adult eyes. Could his father have been trying to tell him something else as well, something about real gold?

In recent years, especially since the gold rushes in America, there had been more rumors about large deposits of gold being found in Australia. But that was all they seemed, rumors. No one had come forward to claim the reward the government was offering to anyone finding payable gold deposits.

Slowly Tim dismounted. He tethered Blackie and reluctantly made his way in the direction he had taken that day of heartbreak. He walked for several moments but paused, thinking he had heard a faint sound foreign to the call of the bush birds. He listened intently. For a moment all was still. Then he heard it again. A bright, cheery whistle.

Tim looked back. He had come quite a distance from his horse and suddenly wished he had brought his rifle with him. This area was very isolated, and over the years reports had circulated of cattle thieves and bushrangers hiding up in the hills.

Well, whoever it was seemed to have no fear of being discovered. For another moment he hesitated, then started forward as quietly as he could.

The whistle stopped abruptly, cut short in the middle of a very familiar Irish ditty.

♥

Patricia inspected the bottom of her prospector's pan closely. For one brief moment she had thought. . .

Her lips twitched in a wry grin. She had heard stories of wishful men back home in California imagining they saw the yellow color that would fulfill their dreams of wealth and glory. And a little of the real stuff would certainly finance this venture!

She shrugged and used Andy's small trowel to fill the dish with more mud and water from the riverbed. After all, there wasn't much else to do while she waited for him to return from his search for the old shepherd's hut they had been told was somewhere in this area. He seemed doubtful they had even found the right river. Certainly they had found no trace of Danny during all their travels west of Sydney.

She sighed, wondering if they would ever find him. Her lips firmed. They simply had to. So much depended on it—her father's health, their whole future.

Patricia absentmindedly swung the shallow dish, using the technique Andy had taught her on his gold claim in California last year. Always hope remained that when all the dirt was washed away a few yellow specks might settle in the bottom. At least it passed the time on a perfect day, and besides, each week they continued their search, she found herself falling more in love with this bush and its golden wattle trees and cheerful bird life.

Hopefully they would stay longer in this small valley. After that dreadful voyage across the vast Pacific Ocean, there had been all the hustle and bustle in Sydney as they got outfitted with their horses, dray, and camping gear. Neither Patricia nor Andy had realized how rough the terrain would be through the rugged Blue Mountains and the Bathurst area. It had taken them days longer to travel that far than they had expected. By then, she'd needed a good rest, as had their horses.

But at Bathurst, Patricia and Andy had heard news of a young man who fit Danny's description, so they had pushed on. Rumor had it he had been working with some shepherds on property a good distance to the northeast, near the Turon River. At the thought of the man they so desperately wanted to find, a shadow touched Patricia's heart, but she thrust it determinedly aside as she had many times before. The bush was so peaceful, and washing for gold so soothing, although it would certainly be a miracle if she found any color.

Grinning at herself, Patricia started whistling again.

She stirred the pan and then swung it carefully. Gradually the muddy water disappeared, leaving only a few small, heavier pebbles in the bottom of the dish. Something yellow flashed in the sunlight.

Patricia caught her breath. It couldn't be.

Her hands started to tremble slightly as she carefully filled the dish with water and repeated the process. There was no mistake.

Trying to dampen her rising excitement, Patricia muttered, "Of course, it's probably just what the old-timers called fool's gold." She grabbed the large bandanna in the pocket of her trousers and carefully tipped the pan's contents onto the dark material.

What if the rumors Danny had heard in the California goldfields that had sent him chasing out here to Australia were right? Perhaps it had not just been an excuse he had used to leave America. His last letter had mentioned an Australian called Hargraves who claimed that the country they were mining in California was very similar to where he had once worked in these central tablelands of New South Wales.

Feverishly, she started washing another pan of dirt. Even more gold remained from that lot.

Footsteps crunched on gravel a small distance behind her. Hurriedly, Patricia finished emptying the pan's contents onto the small pile in the bandanna and wrapped it up. Was Andy in for one big surprise!

As she straightened and started to swing around, she called out excitedly, "Andy, Danny probably is here somewhere. You'll never guess in a million years what I've—"

It wasn't Andy.

A man stood a little distance from her. His wide-brimmed hat sat low over his forehead, and she could barely see his eyes. His clothes were filthy, with several large tears on his shirt, and he looked as though shaving was not his favorite occupation. All in all, he looked so tough and rough she would have never let him near the house when back home alone.

As she gaped at him, he started walking toward her.

Patricia quickly dropped the pan and thrust the bandanna into her trouser pocket. For a moment she held her ground, but the man was scowling, his face so grim she backed away a few paces. Then she paused, remembering the gun Andy had insisted she always carry in the bush. Every sense on alert, she let her hand rest on the handle of the revolver at her waist.

The man stopped also. He stared at the gun for a long moment and then glanced around briefly before his gaze came to rest on her face once more. "Sorry, I'm not Andy. Tim Hardy's the name." He paused and added slowly, "And who might you be, young man?"

Young man? Good. She managed to control her sudden grin and called back in as deep a voice as she could manage, "Howdy, Tim. The name's Pat."

He tilted his head to one side as though a little puzzled by that faint Irish lilt in her speech, but then he started toward her once more. Suddenly she panicked. Had he been watching her for long? Had he seen her excitement?

"Stay right where you are, Mister," she said as sternly as she could.

He stopped and stared, then lifted his lean brown hand to shift his hat farther back on his head. His face was as covered in dirt as the rest of him, but he was younger than she had first thought. His amber eyes glanced down once more to where her hand rested on her six-shooter. His lips twitched. "And if I don't, you're going to shoot me, right?"

She tilted up her chin. "If I need to, yes."

His lips widened, and white teeth flashed as he laughed briefly. "Not very friendly of you, Pat, my lad."

The smile transformed his face, and something in Patricia eased a little.

Not moving his gaze from hers, he started forward slowly. She stood her ground. His lips straightened, but as he came closer she could see amusement still sparkling in those light brown eyes. She began to back away, but anger started to rise over any fear. He was treating her like a naughty child.

Patricia stopped dead and reached for her gun. Pointing it steadily at him, she said firmly, "Not another step, Tim."

He did stop at that. All trace of amusement was wiped from his face. "Didn't your parents ever teach you it's extremely rude to point guns at strangers with no provocation?" he snapped.

"On the contrary, Pa made sure I knew how to defend myself almost as soon as I could walk," she retorted.

"A shame he didn't teach you some manners as well," he shot at her angrily. "What are you doing here?"

"None of your business."

He glared at her and then searched the area once more as if to see if she were alone. His gaze settled on the low cliff a little distance away. Sudden emotion she could not understand flared across his face. Beneath his dark tan, his face lost color. His lips tightened to a thin line.

Slowly Tim's gaze returned to her face. She thought she caught a glimpse of pain and grief in his eyes before they swiftly filled with suspicion and anger. He suddenly seemed more worn, much older.

"Anything that happens in this particular spot is very much my business," he said harshly. "Where's your camp?"

She remained silent, puzzled at the sudden change from friendly to hostile. But then, not many people enjoyed being held off at the point of a gun.

He took an angry stride closer, and she froze. "I'll. . .I'll shoot you if I have to!"

Her voice had risen, and she despised the tremble in it. To her relief, he paused. For a brief moment Patricia thought the expression in his eyes softened slightly as he studied her.

He suddenly looked behind her. "Okay, Mate, you can grab him now."

Patricia swung around. As she realized she had been fooled by one of the oldest tricks, Tim's hand grabbed the wrist of her hand that held the gun. In the same movement his other arm looped around her waist and flung her down to the ground. He banged her hand against a rock. The pain made her scream. Instead of releasing its hold, her finger tightened on the trigger. The crack of the gun made her go still.

Tim roared with pain.

Patricia dropped the revolver, crying out, "Oh, no, oh, no, don't tell me I've killed him."

An astonished voice cried out near her ear. "You've shot me!"

"I'm. . .oh dear, I'm so sorry."

"You'd better be!" he roared.

He didn't need to keep such a strong grip on her wrists or hold her down with his body as he squirmed to look at the damage. Fright kept her motionless. What would he do in retaliation?

Silence hung in the air.

"Lucky for you, young man, I think it's just a flesh wound."

Young man? He still thought. . .

Her first reaction was relief. But he was still sprawled all over her, and there had been just enough amusement in the cool tones to infuriate her. She gave a huge heave and managed to partly dislodge him. Her fist connected with his face even as his hands grabbed at her shirt. The top buttons went flying.

He gasped. Horror filled his face. "What the—?"

A loud crack rang in their ears. A bullet hit the ground near them.
They both froze.

"Reckon you'd better get away from her if you don't want the next bullet in your hide," Andy's voice yelled furiously from behind them.

Chapter 3

Without moving off the lithe body pressed into the ground under him, Tim swung his head around. A tall man was rushing down the riverbank. The stranger held two revolvers that were aimed right at Tim.

This could not be happening. In a daze, Tim stared back at the unmistakable feminine curves under him. Two green eyes sparked fury and embarrassment at him. Heat flooded his face, and he snatched his hands from her softness.

Not fast enough for the gunman.

Something cold pressed hard against Tim's back, and the man roared, "Get off her! Now! And get those hands in the air where I can see them. Move!"

The body under Tim tried to heave him off. The gun barrel eased only slightly from his spine.

Tim moved.

"You all right, Girl?"

Gimlet green eyes never left Tim as he scrambled to his feet. Pain knifed through his leg. Some stubborn, indignant streak he hadn't realized he possessed made him bite back a groan of pain and keep his hands lowered but well in sight.

"Of course I'm all right," the "girl" snapped breathlessly.

Tim could not keep himself from turning his head from the two guns trained on him and watching her scramble to her feet. She clutched the shirt across her chest. Her face remained almost as red as her fiery hair. The wide-brimmed hat had fallen off, and it seemed that her head of curls danced gold in the sunlight.

Now that he wasn't concentrating on a gun in her hand, Tim wondered how he could ever have mistaken her beautiful face for that of a boy. As she fumbled to close up her shirt, he opened his mouth to apologize, but that stubborn streak made him snap it shut and glare from her back to the gray-haired man still staring at him with narrowed, dangerous eyes set in a weathered face. If anyone should apologize, it wasn't Tim Hardy!

"Oh, Andy! Put those guns away. Can't you see he's unarmed? It was my gun that went off. Sometimes I think you must want to be back in Nevada with your gunslinger friends."

Tim's eyes widened. Nevada? Wasn't that somewhere in America? But their accents sounded more like the old Irishman who worked at Waverley.

The black holes of the two gun barrels did not waver.

Tim remained stubbornly silent. He looked back at the girl—no, woman would be more accurate. The color had left her face, leaving it pale and strained.

She was holding the hand he had slammed onto the ground. Regret swept through him. He had been taught to be gentle, to care for women, but he had not been gentle with her.

Tim gritted his teeth and managed to say calmly, "Pity you hadn't realized I was unarmed, *Pat*, before you drew your gun on me."

Patricia stared at the young man, still feeling dazed that her gun had actually gone off. "Well. . .I. . .you startled me. I thought. . ." Andy flashed a look at her, and she stopped. She would never hear the end of this from him.

"What happened?" her uncle asked, still in that hard, cold voice that chilled her. His eyes were fixed on the young man as he added, "And it had better be a good answer."

"To start with, I didn't know the person who pulled a gun on me for no reason whatsoever was a. . .a *woman!*"

Patricia tilted her chin but avoided Tim's accusing glare. She swallowed a couple times before at last muttering, "He. . .he came out of nowhere. I heard footsteps and thought it was you. He startled me and. . .and I didn't want him too close." She didn't think it wise to mention the yellow grains that had so absorbed her attention she had not realized anyone had been approaching. "Oh, do put those guns away, Andy," she added impatiently.

The guns' barrels lowered slightly. Her uncle was still scowling. He didn't take his eyes from Tim as he said, "And so you tried to hold him off with your gun. I heard it go off. Did he attack you?"

"No, I didn't attack him—her!" Tim yelled. "At least not until she pulled that stupid gun. For some strange reason, I just don't like a gun pointed at me for *no* reason."

Patricia noticed Andy's lips twitch slightly, and she relaxed a little. But the faint trace of amusement seemed to infuriate Tim.

He roared, "The gun went off when I tried to make her drop it. I thought he—she—was about to attack me. I swear I didn't know she wasn't a boy until I felt. . .saw. . ."

It was not a wise reminder. Andy stiffened. The guns leveled once more.

Patricia didn't blame Tim for stopping abruptly. Andy was even scaring her. Only once before had she seen that expression on his face. That horrible day before he had gone out to find the Indian who had killed her mother.

She swung her gaze back to the furious young man. Heat rose in her face again. Never before had anyone touched her so intimately. What her uncle must have thought!

After a long pause, Tim added in a quieter, puzzled voice, "It's you two who are in the middle of nowhere. What are you doing way out here? It sounds as though you're a long way from home."

He looked around, searching the immediate area. Once more he stared for a long moment at some point beyond Patricia. Momentarily his expression changed, but before she could understand the expression on his face, it disappeared. He looked back at her and asked harshly, "Are you camped nearby?"

Patricia studied him and then looked at Andy. He was still watching Tim closely, but he glanced briefly at her and slowly lowered the revolvers to his side. To her considerable relief, he expertly slipped them back into the holsters low on his hips.

Very expertly. Patricia frowned.

From the moment just before they'd boarded the ship in California until that night after they'd left Sydney, Andy hadn't worn his guns. In the past she had often teased him that they made him look like a gunfighter. He had always replied with some joking comment, but now she wondered.

She had never actually seen Andy draw them before, nor had she seen him so riled, so hard and cold, except that horrible time after her mother. . . She slammed the thought shut once more. Not for the first time, she wondered about Andy's years as a cowboy in the plains of America before he settled on land in California with her mother and father. He seldom talked about his past. Perhaps he had really been a gunfighter after all.

"We might ask you the same thing." Andy's voice brought her attention back to the current situation. "What's your name?"

❧

Tim stared at the older man. "I'm Tim Hardy from Waverley Station," he answered curtly. Noting their blank looks, he added tersely, "It's a cattle and sheep property a few days' ride from here toward Bathurst. We've been rounding up stray cattle."

"We?" drawled the man the girl had called Andy.

Tim's leg had started to burn fiercely. "Me and three of our station hands," he snapped as he tried to ease his weight onto his good leg.

"You're bleeding!"

At the girl's dismayed cry, Tim looked down and saw that a dark stain had seeped through his trouser leg. As he moved, the wound stung, and he felt a warm trickle slide down his leg.

"Guess that's what happens when guns go off," he muttered angrily and glared at her. The pain stabbed him, and he swayed as he tried to balance on one leg.

The girl went white.

A strong hand grabbed his elbow, and Andy said with a slight Irish lilt, "Reckon you'd better sit down before you keel over." When Tim had been eased down to the ground, Andy added tersely, "Can't be too bad or there'd be a lot more blood."

Tim thought there seemed to be more than enough blood trickling down into his boot. He concentrated on not letting them see just how painful it was. He failed miserably when Andy touched his leg. A groan ripped from him, and Tim shut his eyes. But Andy paused and was a little more gentle as he briefly examined the wound.

"Yeah, reckon you're lucky," Andy concluded. "Looks like it's just a flesh wound."

Lucky? Tim opened his eyes to look straight into brilliant green ones filled with tears of remorse.

"I'm really, really sorry," she whispered.

Tim was struck dumb. *She has the most beautiful eyes I've ever seen.*

"You got your horse hereabouts?" Andy's sharp voice was an intrusion.

Tim blinked and looked away, straight into another set of green eyes. These were much paler, knowing. They narrowed and held a hint of temper as Andy glanced from Tim to the girl and back again.

It took Tim a moment to remember the question. "Quite some distance downstream," he muttered hoarsely.

Andy dragged out a large piece of rag and started to wrap it tightly around the wound that was dripping blood onto the ground. Tim shuddered and not simply from the increased pain. He had been taught to be very careful to put only clean linen on open wounds. But dirty or not, at least the rag might control the bleeding.

Andy frowned at his makeshift bandage. "Our camp and horses are upstream."

"I didn't hear you come past here on your way back to camp. Did you find—?" The girl's slightly surprised voice stopped abruptly.

Tim glanced up from examining his leg and saw the warning look the man was giving her.

Andy scowled when he saw Tim staring at him and said briskly, "You may only have a flesh wound, but it's deep, and it's still bleeding too much for you to try and walk that far." He glanced around, squinted at the sun low in the west, and heaved an annoyed sigh. "We'd best be moving our camp here for the—"

"No!"

Andy stared. He raised an eyebrow, and Tim realized how panicked he must have sounded. Swiftly he added, "I can't stay here. It. . .it's. . ." He hesitated and looked over toward the place he knew would haunt him until he died.

"There's bad memories here for me," Tim muttered at last and glanced at the girl.

She was watching him curiously. Andy snorted angrily. To Tim's immense relief, the girl said swiftly, "But we have our tent up and everything set out, Andy. And what about his horse? One of us will have to fetch it. Wouldn't it be much easier and faster for you to go and bring his horse back here while I wait with Mr. Hardy?"

"And that would be the stupidest thing I've heard you say yet," Andy exploded. "You felt threatened enough to pull a gun on him, and now you want me to leave you here alone with him?"

"And haven't we just decided my pulling a gun was unnecessary?" she retorted.

Her hands settled on her hips, and she and Andy glared at each other. Tim couldn't help admiring the sparks that flashed between the two.

"Besides," she added stubbornly, "I can hold my gun on him again if he tries anything."

"He'd better not try anything!" Andy roared.

Tim saw the threatening scowl leveled at him and knew that the man's roar was more for his benefit than the girl's.

"Unlike some people, I'm not stupid," Tim retorted sharply. "I'm already feeling what she can do when she's being stupid."

Andy glared at him, then looked at the defiant girl. Color rose in her pale cheeks, but she glared right back. He shrugged and then studied Tim again.

Unexpectedly Andy grinned, his eyes lighting up in sardonic amusement. "Well, if you think you'll be safe with her, guess I'll leave you two youngun's to be stupid together."

Tim opened his mouth and snapped it shut, staring after Andy as he loped swiftly away toward the bush lining the river. In a few moments the older man had disappeared from sight.

Upstream they would have to go right past where Father died.

Tim closed his eyes tightly.

The journey back to Waverley that dreadful day had passed in a daze, but he remembered Jackie quietly telling him all the signs showed that his father had tumbled down the rocks a few days before. Why his father had been in this isolated place or why he had risked climbing up that cliff had never been discovered. They had only been able to speculate that he might have been hiding from whomever had wrecked his camp.

The old familiar ache settled in Tim's heart. He tore his gaze away. The young woman was still watching him curiously.

"Why do you keep looking up there? Is that where something bad happened?"

He swallowed hard and nodded briefly. He averted his eyes, looking down at his leg. Blood had already started to seep through the rag.

"Whatever did I do to make you feel so threatened you drew your gun on me?" Tim asked, hoping she would not ask him any more questions. Although many questions had hovered in his mind about that black day, he had never been able to talk about it again, not even to Adam or Kate.

A shrewd look crossed the girl's face as she surveyed him. He moved restlessly. Something in the way she stared at him told him she'd guessed he didn't want to talk about the "bad" thing that had happened. A flash of sympathy touched her eyes, and she looked swiftly away, but not before he had seen her lips tighten and the pain that filled her face. She obviously had her own bad memories and understood about experiences too painful to talk about.

She stared for a long moment toward the place near the water where he had first seen her. A large tin plate of some kind rested on the ground as if she had dropped it when he had startled her. She must have been washing it or something. After a moment she glanced back at him, and Tim was surprised at the apprehension on her face before she looked back at the creek.

The silence lengthened. Her hands clenched into fists, and she stood so tensely that Tim felt his anger start to rise once more. No one had ever been afraid of him. He cleared his throat. "Would you consider me too threatening if I asked your name and what you are doing here?"

She jumped slightly at his loud, sarcastic voice and swung around. A strange expression filled her face as though her mind had been on something completely different. Then a look of apprehension returned. She bit her lip and crossed her arms in front of her, hugging herself as though she were getting cold.

"I'm. . .I'm sorry." She swallowed and added with an attempt at a smile, "I'm being very bad mannered, aren't I?"

"Bad mannered?" he exploded. "I would hope your parents would have clipped you in the ear for having such bad manners you'd aim a gun at a man for no reason!"

Her expression changed in a flash. All remorse gone, she glared back at him and opened her mouth, thought better of whatever she was going to say, and swallowed instead. "Yes, Pa would certainly have done just that," she muttered and then blurted out, "You. . .you are so pale. Your leg must be very painful."

He stared at her silently and waited.

"Patricia Casey," she said, abruptly answering his question. "And my uncle is Andy O'Donnell. We were hoping to. . .to meet up with. . ." She hesitated and then added, "With an old friend out this way, but I guess it's unlikely he's here."

Tim raised his eyebrows. "Very unlikely. As far as I know, even the nearest shepherd's hut is many miles from here."

Excitement flashed into those incredible eyes. "So there is a hut somewhere in this area," he thought he heard her murmur. He moved his leg slightly, and the pain made him grit his teeth.

After a deep breath, he said irritably, "Afraid I can't say it's been a pleasure to meet you, Patricia Casey."

Color swept into her face, and she bit her lip. She swung away, and he watched her long, angry strides as she went over and picked up the dish near the water's edge. As she straightened, she looked beyond him toward the trees and froze.

He glanced swiftly around but saw nothing. When he looked back at Patricia, she was racing toward him, her hand grabbing for that gun of hers once more.

"Natives," she gasped. "There. Two of them."

Tim looked swiftly in the direction of her pointing finger. In the dark shadows of the bush, two aborigines stood staring at them, as still as statues. Both were naked except for their loincloths. Both were carrying several long spears. Even more menacing was the way their bodies were painted with white clay and yellow ocher.

Ignoring the pain, Tim scrambled awkwardly to his feet. The two aborigines moved slowly out into the sunlight, and he sighed with relief. One of them was Jackie. So that was why Jackie had refused to go on the muster to help find the strays—aboriginal business.

Tim looked at Patricia to tell her, then paused. Once again she had whipped out that wretched gun. His gaze narrowed. If ever anyone needed to be taught a lesson. . .

Making a split decision, he ordered in a low voice, "Put that gun away."

She glance at him indecisively.

"Now!"

To his relief, she obeyed him. On the whole, there had not been strife between whites and blacks for some years in the Bathurst and Orange areas. But in the past, the military had been called out too many times to "teach the natives a lesson" using guns and death, so even Jackie would not be complacent about a gun being pointed at him.

Tim called out loudly, *"Wanjibaayn waajin."*

To his relief, Jackie paused and studied Patricia. He must have decided that she was indeed the "naughty white woman" Tim had called out. He said something to his companion and after a moment yelled back in rapid Wiradjuri.

Over the years Tim had learned much of the local aboriginal language from Jackie, but he understood it only if it was spoken slowly and clearly—something Jackie knew well. By speaking so quickly, Jackie was letting Tim know he too could play games. Tim had understood only two words that Jackie had spoken *"Guuwiyn"* meant "white man," and *"yaambul"* meant "nonsense or a lie."

Jackie's voice sounded threatening, and to Tim's dismay, Patricia once more held that gun. Hoping Jackie was close enough to hear, Tim said loudly, "Put your gun away, Patricia. They feel threatened."

She looked at him from wide, frightened eyes. "The. . .the savages back home paint themselves when they are on raiding parties," she gasped.

He relented. She was really scared. "They won't hurt us," he said swiftly. "They look like they are just passing through to a corroboree somewhere."

"Co. . .corrob. . . ?"

"A kind of native dance."

Jackie called out again, this time more slowly. Tim heard real anxiety in the man's voice as Jackie asked if Tim was all right or needed help. He must have noticed the rag on Tim's leg.

Tim relented, suddenly feeling foolish. "I'm okay, Jackie," he called back in English.

Jackie hesitated and then waved the handful of spears in his hand. The next moment both men had disappeared as quietly as they had come.

"They. . .they've gone," Patricia gasped. "Do you think they will come back when it gets dark?"

She was trembling badly. Tim regretted his impulse to punish her. "No, they won't be back," he assured her swiftly. "One of them works for us." He didn't think it necessary to tell her that he was almost certain the other aborigine was Mirrang, who had also worked at Waverley periodically over the years.

Those glorious eyes searched the bush and then turned on him. "You called him Jackie."

Feeling guilty, Tim nodded briefly and looked away.

She did not move. Tim risked a quick glance at her. To his relief, her color was slowly returning. She started putting her gun away, and he was relieved to see she had stopping shaking. He had probably been rather foolish to upset her when she had her finger on that trigger.

"And how well do you know this Jackie, I wonder?" she murmured. Suspicion had crept into her eyes. "I don't suppose by any chance you were trying to frighten me out of my wits?"

Respect filled him. She was so different from most of the girls who had tried to befriend him when he had been at college in Sydney. This was one very intelligent woman.

"Rather *stupid* of me." He could not stop the grin that twitched at his lips.

Temper flared for a moment in her face. "Guess you don't know my mother was killed by an Indian."

He was stunned to silence. No wonder she had reacted the way she had! "I'm sorry," he at last muttered weakly.

Patricia looked away. "A. . .a small number of Indians raided our first ranch." He saw her swallow several times, then draw a deep breath before adding softly, "It was a long time ago."

So she did have bad memories.

While Tim was trying to find the right words to say, she suddenly straightened her shoulders, looked back at him, and said steadily, "Guess this means we are even."

"Guess it does," he said seriously.

They stood eyeing each other in awkward silence. Then Tim imagined what Jackie must be thinking right now. His lips twitched and a soft chuckle burst from him. At the return of her frown, he said hurriedly, "I'm sure your Andy would agree."

Relief swept through him when a reluctant smile chased away her anger. "Well," she whispered conspiratorially, "let's not tell him."

They grinned at each other, then started to chuckle. The chuckles became roars of laughter until Tim moved his leg unwarily and his laugh turned to a groan. Carefully he slid back down to the ground.

The light died out of her face, and she sat down beside him. "But at least I didn't get a spear in my leg." Her face was full of regret. "I really am so sorry about hurting you."

He couldn't bear to see a shimmer of tears in those beautiful eyes that had so recently been lit with laughter. "There was never a moment's danger of that," he reassured her quickly. "I've known Jackie since I was a boy."

She was silent for a moment. "And I don't suppose he taught you to speak his language by any chance?" she asked mildly. "And you haven't taught him English by any chance?"

"Er, yes, he did teach me," Tim answered sheepishly, deciding to be honest with her. "But I didn't have to teach him English. He was adopted by white missionaries after his father disappeared and his mother died."

Patricia stared at him and then sprang to her feet, avoiding his gaze.

"I. . .I didn't understand more than a couple of words he said that first time," Tim rushed to say, hoping she would not retreat again. "But I think he either called me a nonsense white man or a lying one."

She muttered something that sounded like, "Both would be appropriate."

Regret swept through him. His mother and father would be so disappointed in him for being called a liar. "God hates liars," they had often told him.

Patricia picked up the dish she had dropped when she saw the aborigines. Without looking at Tim, she turned away, tossing over her shoulder, "I'm going for a walk. Perhaps I'll meet Andy coming back."

Tim opened his mouth to protest as she headed downstream but then snapped it closed. In a moment she had disappeared around an old gum tree that had fallen down the bank during some distant flood when this small trickle of water had been transformed into a swirling river of mud and debris.

The silence of the bush settled around Tim. He raised his eyes and looked toward the spot where he had held his dying father so long ago.

"Well, Father, I never thought I would be able to laugh here of all places," he murmured.

Suddenly he realized that the devastating anguish he used to feel when he thought of those last moments with his father was gone. Perhaps he should have had the courage to return here years ago as Adam and Kate had gently suggested.

A loud scream rang out. A woman's scream.

Patricia.

Ignoring the pain, Tim jumped to his feet as fast as he could. As he started forward, she scrambled over the fallen tree and rushed toward him.

"Ab. . .abo. . .aborigines," she panted frantically. "They've got Andy!"

Chapter 4

For a moment Tim stopped dead. There had been no serious trouble with the aborigines in the area for a long time. But there was always the chance. . . .

He'd thought Jackie had been going to some tribal ceremony, one of their dances, an initiation, perhaps something as simple as a ceremonial hunting party. But an aborigine raised by white people and eager for acceptance by his own people might agree to anything to achieve that. And if it were some special gathering of the tribes that Jackie was on his way to, there would be other aborigines from near and far to impress.

"Get those filthy spears away from me." Andy's roar carried clearly to both Tim and Patricia. "Give me back my guns, you. . .you limbs of Satan!"

Tim tried to hurry toward the source of the ruckus. Patricia had caught up with him, and he heard her gasp of horror as a strange procession came into sight. Two aborigines were herding Andy before them. To Tim's dismay, neither was Jackie. As Andy tried to turn around, one of them prodded him with a long spear. Andy roared again.

Another aborigine appeared. He was riding Blackie.

Tim breathed a sigh of relief as he recognized Jackie. Using his native tongue, the aborigine yelled out to Tim. Although the words came too fast for Tim to understand clearly, he knew Jackie was concerned that Andy was trying to steal Tim's horse.

"Jackie," Tim yelled back, "let him go! He isn't a horse thief. He was just getting Blackie for me because I've injured my leg."

Both natives with Andy stilled. They looked at each other and then at their captive. Tim breathed easier. Obviously they also understood what he had said. They lowered their spears, and Andy stumbled away from them toward Tim.

He stuttered in his fury. "You–you. . .these are friends of yours?"

Tim nodded helplessly and continued to limp slowly forward.

Andy roared again and advanced on him. "I should have shot you myself. You—" Speechless in his fury, he shook his fist at Tim as the distance between them narrowed.

One of Jackie's companions, whom Tim now recognized as Mirrang, raised the spear in his hand menacingly.

Patricia cried out.

Tim stopped dead. Not taking his eyes from the raised spear, he said sharply,

"Andy, don't move." Then he yelled out, "Mirrang, *marrambang!*"

Mirrang didn't move.

Andy stopped and swung toward the aborigine. When he saw the spear posed to throw, he froze. A breath of relief hissed through Tim's teeth.

Still Mirrang did not move.

Had he used the right word for "friend"? Tim's concern deepened. He didn't know the older aborigine very well, although Mirrang had worked on Waverley some years ago for Elizabeth Waverley, the woman who was married to John Martin and had sold the station to Adam and Kate.

"Jackie, please tell Mirrang that Andy's a friend."

Tim saw Jackie's lips move. Mirrang ignored him. Jackie spoke more sharply, and to Tim's immense relief, Mirrang slowly lowered the threatening spear.

No one moved.

"Jackie, give the white fella back his guns and let him have my horse."

Jackie stared at Tim and then took his time studying first Andy and then Patricia.

Tim waited. He had learned a long time ago to wait for Jackie.

"Reckon you one crazy boss-man," Jackie said at last in heavily accented English, a sign of how angry and disgusted he was.

Jackie dropped Blackie's reins, turned, and strode away. Realizing that Jackie had not given him his familiar salute with the spears, Tim did not look forward to the next time they met.

Mirrang stared from one white person to the next. He angrily shook his handful of spears and followed Jackie and the other aborigine into the bush.

Blackie tossed his head and turned to follow Jackie. Tim let out a piercing whistle and the horse swung round, tossing his head up and down. At Tim's second whistle, the horse started ambling toward him. Andy moved swiftly and grabbed Blackie's bridle. Tim was relieved to see the gun belt slung across the saddle.

A slight figure flew past Tim. Patricia flung herself into Andy's arms. "Andy, Andy, are you all right? I was so frightened."

The horse snorted and pulled back on its reins. Andy held them tightly but wrapped an arm around the shaking girl. "Easy there, Girl, of course I am. They crept up on me, jabbed me with their spears when I was busy trying to get the horse, but I doubt there's more than a scratch or so."

Tim reached them and started soothing Blackie. He felt absolutely wretched. If he had not started that nonsense with Jackie, Patricia would not be so shaken and pale, so different from the courageous young woman who had not hesitated to pull a gun on him.

"Oh, Andy, if anything had happened to you, how would I find Danny all by myself in this dreadful country?"

Andy glanced sharply at Tim. He murmured something to his niece. She let him go and looked at Tim. He kept rubbing Blackie's neck, pretending he had not noticed. Whatever their business with this Danny, it was not his concern. Shame swept through him. He wanted nothing more than to get up on Blackie and leave, but the pain in his leg was considerably worse. He suspected the wound had started to bleed more since he had put weight on it.

Reluctantly Tim called out, "Mr. O'Donnell, I'm afraid I'm going to need your help getting up in the saddle. The sooner I can get this leg tended to, the better."

Andy took his time strapping his gun belt to his waist before marching up to Tim. "And I'm thinking that once you're on that horse, you'd best be on your way and about your own business, Mister. We've had enough trouble for one day."

Before Tim could reply, Patricia cried out, "But he's injured. We have to—"

"We don't have to do anything, Pat," her uncle replied sternly. "And we don't owe him anything. If he hadn't jumped you, his leg wouldn't have stopped that bullet."

"But I pulled a gun on him first," she pleaded. "You've already said we were both at fault. It will be dark soon, and his men will be too far away for him to reach. Besides," she added swiftly, "he did rescue you from those aborigines. What if they come back?"

Tim stared at Patricia in astonishment. He had frightened her so badly that she had pulled a gun on him. He'd jumped on her, hurt her hand, and allowed her to be scared to death. And after all that, she was pleading for him? What sort of woman was this?

A woman just like Mother.

The thought slammed into him. His father had once laughingly told Tim to make sure he found a wife "just like your mother." Molly Hardy had blushed and scolded her husband, but Tim had never forgotten. He had adored his mother. She had been a woman with a great sense of humor, an immense capacity to love, and an even greater faith in God. His mother had loved her husband and children fiercely, joyfully caring for them in the very best way she could.

It had taken great courage and love for her to forgive her husband for letting himself become embroiled in political unrest the way he had. When he had been arrested with other rioters, she had fought for him. When that had failed to stop his transportation to Australia, without hesitation she had packed Tim's and her own bags and followed her husband across those fifteen thousand miles of ocean from England. It had been Elizabeth Waverley, a passenger who had befriended Timothy on board ship, who had paid their fare.

And now Patricia—this courageous, compassionate young woman who shared his own sense of the ridiculous—reminded Tim of that mother.

Andy O'Donnell was still hesitating as Patricia pleaded, "I'm sure he'd be able to tell us the best and easiest way to get to Wellington, or Orange even, from here. At least let us attend to his wound properly first."

❧

Andy just stared at her. Patricia wasn't quite sure just why she was so anxious to help Tim Hardy. Certainly she had an obligation to make sure the wound she had inflicted was cared for, but something else had happened to her when they had laughed together. She had felt that she'd found a friend. And friends had been very scarce in recent years.

Their ranch had been primitive and isolated. Danny and her mother had always been her best friends. After Patricia's mother had been killed, her father had changed radically, becoming harsh and unreasonable. Her brother had finally given up trying to work with him, packed his bags, and gone to join the army and fight the war with Mexico. The day the news had reached them that he had been reported missing and was believed killed, her father had changed even more, blaming himself bitterly for the deaths of both his wife and his only son.

And then last year. . . Patricia shuddered and tried to push aside the memories. The joy. The pain. The California gold rush had been the last straw. It had turned her world upside down.

Patricia pushed away those memories and watched Tim calm his horse. Here was someone who shared her sense of humor, someone like herself who had not thought twice about tackling a person holding a gun on him. This last year she had met so many men with bold glances who had made her cringe and be very wary of her femininity. His embarrassment and confusion when he had realized she wasn't a young man had touched something deep inside her. But what really intrigued her about Tim Hardy were the flashes of sadness that occasionally darkened his strong face, making him look so vulnerable.

Tim looked at her uncle. "If you give me a leg up, I'll be on my way." His chin was set at a stubborn angle that matched his brisk words.

Patricia looked pleadingly at Andy.

He stared at her with his hands on his hips, gave a snort, and stepped forward. "Hold the horse, Pat, while I heave this bloke up."

When she did not move, he sighed and said, "All right. We'll let him camp with us tonight, and we'll see what happens tomorrow."

She smiled at Andy affectionately before moving to help. Her uncle presented a tough image to the world, but she knew what a compassionate man he could be to those he cared about.

Tim was gray, and perspiration beaded his forehead by the time he swung up onto the saddle. As they started off, Patricia saw him grit his teeth when Blackie scrambled up the low bank. She watched him carefully, but he kept his head down as they followed the river upstream.

When they passed the place Tim had seemed disturbed by, Patricia looked around, searching the area for some clue as to why it affected him. Then, near the slope of stones and dirt that looked as though it must have slid down the hillside some time ago, she saw something on a large old gum tree that made her catch her breath.

She glanced at the two men. Tim still had his head down. Andy was as close to him and the horse as the narrow track would permit. As she opened her mouth to draw their attention to the roughly constructed cross, Tim swayed in the saddle, and Andy reached up to steady him.

She quickened her own pace. Time enough to mention what she had seen when Tim had been attended to. No doubt he already knew what was there in any event, and that's why he kept his head down. Her heart went out to him in understanding. Some dreadful tragedy had happened in this place, and Tim still carried its mark.

When they stopped at their camp, Tim swayed forward onto the horse's neck. The black horse moved restlessly. Patricia called out and rushed forward. Andy was already reaching for him.

Tim gasped, "Sorry. . .feel sick."

Although Tim was not a particularly tall man, his size was such that both Patricia and Andy were panting by the time they had eased him from the saddle and half-carried him to their tent.

Dazed eyes gazed briefly up at them from his pale face. "Sorry," he gasped again before his head fell back and he passed out.

Patricia gave a little distressed cry, but Andy murmured compassionately, "Ah, the poor lad. Just as well he's out of it while we get this boot off and. . ." He paused and added a little more urgently, "No wonder he's fainted. This is full of blood. Silly young fool—brave but foolish."

He glanced up at his niece and frowned at her. "Now, now, no more tears, Pat, me dear. From what you've both said, the gun went off accidentally. Get some fresh water while I get this boot off. We'll hopefully have this cleaned up properly by the time he comes to."

They almost succeeded in doing just that. Tim stirred as Patricia finished wrapping his freshly dressed leg in the piece of clean linen ripped from the only petticoat she had in her kit. She had been shocked at just how bad the wound was.

As Tim groaned and tried to sit up, Andy said softly, "Quiet, Boy, we are almost finished. I'm afraid you've lost quite a bit of blood. You can have some water in a moment. We'll have a fire going in no time and get some food into you too. Hopefully you'll be feeling much better soon."

Although Tim managed to drink some tea made in the blackened can, he ate very little. At first Tim refused, but eventually Andy managed to persuade him to drink some rum. "We brought it for medicinal purposes," the older man insisted. "Afraid it's all we've got to take the edge off your pain and help you get some sleep, Son. We used some to wash out the wound, but it will probably do more good inside you."

Tim stared from Andy to Patricia and muttered something that sounded like, "Hope you aren't watching, Mother." Then he spluttered and choked as he downed the fiery spirits. Whether it was from the rum or from sheer exhaustion, he finally fell asleep, much to Patricia's relief.

Andy chuckled. "Not often you meet a young man who is not at all used to alcohol," he mused.

"Danny wasn't before. . ." She bit her lip.

Andy finished her thought gently. "A lot of things didn't happen before your dear mother, my sister, died." He sighed and added bracingly, "We had better get something to eat ourselves. If I'm not mistaken, we may be in for a restless night with this lad."

Unfortunately he was right. Tim tossed and turned most of the night, giving them little rest. Although the bleeding seemed to have stopped, by morning his cheeks were a little flushed.

"We've got to get you to your home for proper medical care," Patricia said firmly after very carefully bathing and redressing the red-looking wound.

"Home," he muttered. A strange look filled his eyes. Pain. A great loneliness. Then he scowled and closed his eyes once more.

When Tim didn't move for several minutes, Patricia reluctantly left him to find Andy. He shook his head over the idea of leaving. "I suppose we could try him lying down in the dray, but you know how rough it was getting here through the scrub. It's probably a long way to his place, and he has lost too much blood to risk starting up the bleeding all over again from the jolting he'd get."

"But he needs a doctor!"

Andy grimaced. "Wouldn't be the first bullet wound I've doctored, me darlin'."

With that, she had to be content.

As the morning wore on, Tim became pale, losing the flush in his cheeks. Although Patricia and Andy knew he was still in pain, Tim point-blank refused to drink any more rum, and they were both immensely relieved when at last he dozed off.

Andy stared down at Tim's still body for a long moment before moving away. He tilted his wide-brimmed hat onto the back of his head. "Might as well not waste time here. It's almost midday, but I think I'll head downstream and see if there's any trace of that shepherd or his hut. Might be a track leading from the creek."

He looked at Patricia's doubtful face and added abruptly, "That man in Bathurst seemed quite definite that someone answering Danny's description went to this region with the old shepherd. I'll take the black horse. Ours was limping a little yesterday and should be rested."

Patricia hesitated, glancing uncertainly toward Tim.

"Reckon he owes us that much," Andy drawled.

The young man's horse was certainly younger and fitter than the saddle horse they had purchased in Sydney. Andy's chin was set at the angle Patricia recognized from of old. She shrugged, knowing he had hated riding their sluggish old horse and would never listen to her protests about needing to ask permission.

When Andy tried to mount Blackie, the horse objected strongly, but Andy was a skilled horseman and swiftly brought the snorting horse under control before riding off.

"What's he doing with Blackie?"

Patricia spun around. Tim was at the entrance of the tent. Even as she rushed to prevent him from taking another step, he sat down in the dirt with a groan.

"You mustn't move! You might start the bleeding—oh dear. You have already."

Tim resisted her efforts to make him go back to his makeshift bed, so she fussed over him, dragging the folded blankets under his leg to keep it elevated as Andy had shown her. To her dismay, Tim's cheeks were flushed once more. She touched his forehead with the back of her hand. "Now you have the beginnings of a fever. Please do lie still. Andy's only gone to try and find someone we were told was around here someplace. You don't need to worry about your horse. My uncle is good with horses."

"It's not the horse I'm worried about. It's your uncle. Blackie doesn't like some people riding him and can be very difficult."

Uneasily, Patricia looked down at Tim. "But that native. . .your friend was riding him."

Tim made a sound between a laugh and a groan. "Jackie knows Blackie better than I do. He was a foal from my old horse, and Jackie's helped me care for him since he was born."

Patricia gnawed on her lip uncertainly. "My uncle should be able to manage him. He is very experienced with horses." She saw the question in Tim's eyes and added swiftly to change the subject, "Are you sure not even a shepherd lives near here at times?"

"Land around here does belong to a Mr. Richards, and farther still there's a Mr. Suttor who runs cattle," Tim answered. "I'm not sure just where their boundaries are. But no one lives here. I've never heard of so much as a shepherd's hut in this immediate area. This part of the country is very isolated."

"We were told in Bathurst there was a shepherd living somewhere along the Turon River," Patricia explained, gratified to have steered the conversation away from any personal questions about her and Andy.

Tim stared at her doubtfully and then murmured gently, "This is certainly the Turon, but it runs through quite a large area before it flows into the Macquarie. It's also very difficult country to be searching for anyone."

Patricia could see the questions forming in his eyes again, so she added hurriedly, "Don't talk now. You must rest. I'll get you another drink."

When she returned, Tim was lying with his eyes closed. The feverish spots of color on each cheek had returned. She knew his leg must be paining him, but he again refused any rum.

"My mother and father never allowed alcohol in our home," he murmured.

"Sounds like mine," Patricia blurted out with a wistful smile. "We did keep a bottle strictly for medicine, but Ma always claimed alcohol was too often the devil's tool to take men's willpower from doing what God wanted them to do."

Tim's eyes widened. "That sounds like something my father would have said."

His eyes clouded with pain, and Patricia sensed that this reaction was from a far deeper wound than the one her bullet had caused. Hoping to take his mind off such sad memories, she asked, "How come you have an aborigine you claim as a friend?"

"Jackie?" Tim was silent for a long moment and then said slowly, "I've known him ever since I was a boy living on Stevens Downs. He was working then for the Gordons, neighbors to the Waverleys."

He was silent once more, and she prompted him by inquiring, "Stevens Downs?"

Tim was so still that she thought he must have dozed off. Then he murmured, "It's a beautiful place—flat fertile plains as far as the eye can see. Stevens Downs is a large sheep station out past Wellington, and my family's first home in Australia. My father worked there from the time he was transported until he—"

"Transported!"

The eyes he turned on her horrified face were fierce with pride. "Yes, transported. My father was shipped off to a penal colony to serve a ten-year sentence for participating in rioting and destruction of property. He had been foolish enough to want to make a better life for his wife and son, but he trusted the wrong people. They merely used him for their own political agenda. Timothy Hardy was a convict, but he was the most courageous, honest, and humble man you could ever meet. He was also the most loving and faithful Christian anyone could be. He was also. . .also the most wonderful father. . . ." His voice choked and he flung an arm up across his eyes.

Was. That said it all. She recognized Tim's pain as the mirror of her sorrow whenever she thought of her beautiful Irish mother with the fiery hair and temper and love enough for the whole wide world.

"My mother was also loving and faithful. She tried to teach us about. . .about being a good Christian," she murmured sadly. Distressed to see Tim so upset, Patricia instinctively reached out and touched him, stroking his head, his hand, trying to find the right word to offer him comfort. He tensed and flung her hand off.

At Patricia's little gasp of dismay, Tim looked regretful. "Sorry," he murmured huskily. "It's this place. My father died not far from here. It has thrown me off balance, I'm afraid. It. . .it's the first time I've mentioned Father to anyone since Adam, Kate, and their two children departed for England, leaving me in charge of Waverley."

His voice faded away. Tim stared into space, and Patricia thought she had never seen such pain or emptiness on anyone's face before.

The cross. It must have been there that his father had died.

Patricia swallowed and said quickly, "Then let's talk about something else.

Tell me about this Adam and Kate or perhaps this Waverley."

He looked at her, and she added a little desperately, "No, no. Blackie. Tell me about your horse."

He studied her face and then to her relief smiled slightly. "All right, let's talk about Blackie. He was born on Waverley while I was studying in Sydney. He is the foal from one of my father's horses."

Her eyes widened. "You went to school in Sydney?"

He scowled. "Yes, and I hated it, but Kate and Adam insisted that it was what my father had wanted and been planning for me—a decent education."

Kate and Adam again. She would dearly love to know more about them but said instead, "My mother taught us as best she could, but I would have loved to have gone to a school with other children. After. . .after the Indian raid, Pa moved us to another ranch in a safer area, but there was no more chance for formal schooling."

Patricia's face was wistful, and Tim judged her more beautiful than ever. He thought of his own mother, the indomitable Molly Hardy.

"My mother taught me to read and write too," he murmured softly, "but after she died, Father insisted I go to Kate's school for the station hands' children at Waverley." He saw Patricia glance at him a little apprehensively and added swiftly, "She and my little sister, Jane, died from a fever a few years before Father died. I've lived with Kate and Adam ever since."

Her eyes widened in dismay and then filled with compassion.

Tim studied her carefully. What was it about this woman's soft, expressive face that made him want to talk about his family for the first time in such a long, long time? "Tell me about your family, Patricia," he requested softly.

She glanced at Tim and then away, staring toward the campfire. "We lived in Ireland when I was little," she said at long last. "Andy is my mother's brother. He went to America before I was born but from time to time sent glowing letters home to my mother and father about the opportunities there. In the end, they decided life was far too hard in Ireland and sailed to New York."

Patricia gave a short laugh. "If anything, life was harder in the big city for most Irish immigrants than the troubles they had left behind in beautiful Ireland. By then Andy was a cowboy. Eventually we managed to track him down and moved west to join him. The plan was to grab some land and set up a ranch together. We eventually ended up in California."

Tim watched the play of emotions on her face as she fell silent. He had heard stories of the hardships the pioneers in America had encountered as they had pushed the frontier farther west. Obviously some of her memories were far from pleasant.

"Were you there when the gold was discovered?" he prompted softly.

She turned her head swiftly and stared at him. He frowned. For a moment he thought he saw something like fear in her eyes, but why would she be afraid?

Glancing away, she said briefly, "Yes, but we lived some distance away. Our ranch was pretty well established before then. Andy and Pa had been very successful raising horses as well as cattle. The horses sold well to the army."

Her voice caught on a little gasp. She looked up at him, studying his face for a long moment. At last she added quietly, "Times were very difficult after Ma died. Some of the men we employed joined the army, and then just after the war with Mexico finished, others headed off to try their luck on the goldfields."

She paused, staring into the distance. Her shoulders were hunched, her voice strained and low when she added harshly, "I've seen only too well how the thought of discovering gold and riches—more than an ordinary man could make in a lifetime—can turn the most sane of men crazy."

The old chestnut horse gave a long whinny. They turned and saw the horse staring in the direction Andy had disappeared earlier, her ears pricked forward. Then they both heard the answering call of a horse and the clatter of hooves.

"Sounds like your uncle's back," Tim said abruptly. He moved restlessly, trying to peer into the bush.

Patricia scrambled to her feet. She was frowning. "But it's not that long since he left. Andy said—oh, no!" She ran toward the black horse that had come into sight.

Tim heaved himself painfully forward until he could see. Blackie was walking slowly along the creek toward them. He shied away from Patricia as she approached, tossed his head, and started trotting away. She stopped. Tim let out a piercing whistle and saw Blackie pause and swing around, searching for him. He whistled again, and Blackie took a few steps forward, tossing his head up and down. Tim frowned. Blackie was very nervous.

He heard Patricia's soft, crooning voice as she started edging toward the horse. After several attempts, she managed to grab Blackie's reins, and following a brief tussle, she led the horse back to the camp. As she neared, Tim could see Patricia was pale, battling to keep her voice calm in order to reassure the horse.

"Blackie probably just got away from Andy," he said swiftly.

"No," she croaked. "Andy's too experienced a horseman to let one toss him off or to fail to secure one properly."

"Blackie can be pretty unpredictable, but something has certainly frightened him. He's trembling," Tim said slowly, wondering if the hot-tempered Irishman could have harmed the horse. He dismissed the thought immediately. Andy had shown his affection and care for animals, even the big old cart horse.

"Would. . .would the aborigines. . .?"

"No, they will be long gone," Tim reassured the white-faced woman, hoping fervently he was right.

Patricia stared at him. Then she turned, swiftly unsaddling Blackie before tying him up near the other horses. She strode into the tent. When she reappeared, her revolver was once more strapped to her waist and a rifle rested in her hand.

The resolve on her grim face increased Tim's alarm. Before he could speak, she hurried off in the direction from which Blackie had come.

Tim bit off words of caution. Admiration for Patricia's courage and determination warred with his concern for her. Perhaps it had been their shared memories of godly, praying mothers, perhaps his horrible feeling of helplessness. Whatever the reason, as she disappeared from sight, he did something he had not done for far too long.

"Oh, God," Tim pleaded, "keep her safe. Help her find her uncle, and bring them back. And please. . ." He paused as his wretched shivering started to subside and the fever once more began heating up his body. "Please," he whispered, "this is no time for me to be sick and leave her to cope alone. Please heal me! Don't let me get any worse."

There was nothing left to do but crawl back inside the tent to his rough bed and wait.

Chapter 5

Patricia found Andy beside the river, not far from the old landslide and the area where Tim had not wanted to camp.

She heaved a sigh of relief when she first saw her uncle, but her anxiety increased as she raced closer. He made no effort to stand, remaining seated while holding his right arm tightly against his body with his other hand. The face he turned toward her was lined with pain.

"Andy," she gasped breathlessly as she reached him, "what happened?"

He nodded his head toward the cliff behind him and said through gritted teeth, "Thought I'd go and have a look at that."

Patricia stared up the sharp pile of dirt and rocks to where the neat cross had been nailed to the white bark of the old gum tree. "So you saw it too," she said sharply.

He nodded. "Wanted to see what was carved on it."

She hesitated, but it was for Tim to tell Andy about his father if he wanted to. Crouching down beside her uncle, she studied him anxiously.

"You fell from up there? Are you hurt bad?"

"Stupid horse shied at a snake just as I was getting off him."

"A snake!"

Andy saw her glance swiftly around and snorted. "A black one and long gone."

"And Blackie threw you!"

Andy reared his head proudly and glared at her. "He did nothing of the sort! I fell. And no," he added more forcefully and even less truthfully, "I'm not hurt bad. The reins somehow twisted around my arm. Almost wrenched my arm off when the horse jumped back."

She gave an exclamation of distress. "You could have landed on the snake. Here, let me help you up."

Andy groaned and then snapped, "Why do you think I'm still sitting here? Can't stand on my leg. Landed on the side of my foot."

Patricia stared at him speechlessly.

"Don't think anything's broken," he added swiftly. "If you give me a shoulder to lean on, reckon I can make it."

After swiftly examining him, Patricia concluded that while he hadn't broken any bones, he had certainly given the muscles of his ankle, shoulder, and arm a battering. She helped him up, and the two slowly worked their way back to Tim.

Patricia and Andy were thoroughly exhausted when they at last stumbled into camp. A very worried Tim Hardy managed to limp forward a few steps to meet them, but Patricia noted the perspiration on his face and the brightly flushed cheeks that stood in sharp contrast to the paleness of the rest of his face.

There was no choice but to let him help them. She gasped out how Andy had come to grief, omitting any mention of the memorial cross. Once Andy was lying down, she almost fell down herself. She gratefully accepted the cup of water Tim gave her. Andy already had a cup to his lips, and she hoped his wasn't mere water. He too needed the only painkiller they had.

The thought almost made her panic. Alone in the Australian bush, she was now responsible for two injured men. Even as she stared at Tim, he swayed, then sank down onto the ground beside them, shivering violently.

"Oh, Tim," she cried, "your leg. . ."

Through chattering teeth he mumbled, "Sorry, Pat. Afraid I'm not going to be much more help to either of you for awhile. I did manage to keep the fire going."

Once she had persuaded Tim to lie back down in the tent, Patricia attended to Andy, grateful that Tim had placed water on the campfire to heat. She put hot packs on Andy's shoulder and ankle and was immensely relieved when gradually, with the help of a few more swallows of rum, the gray, pinched look started to fade from his wrinkled face.

Patricia got little sleep that night. She sponged Tim down when the fever swept through him and piled the blankets on when he started to shiver. Andy also spent a painful night despite her attempts to ease the pain with rags soaked in hot water. Both men tried several times to persuade Patricia to seek her own bed. Both men failed.

🦋

At last when soft snores came from Andy's pile of blankets, Tim pretended to be asleep. To his relief, Patricia curled up on her own bedding. He heard her sigh of relief and almost immediately knew she was asleep. After a few moments he raised his head cautiously to make sure she had pulled a blanket over herself, only to see that Andy also had raised his head slightly to peer at Patricia. The two men stared at each other over her sleeping body. Andy's white teeth gleamed in the faint light from the campfire for a moment. Tim grinned in response and then relaxed.

Sheer exhaustion made Tim doze off and on. When he was awake, he heard Andy tossing with discomfort. But whenever Patricia stirred, only gentle snores came from both men. When the long night was at last over, both men paid for their deceit. Andy's muscles were stiff and sore, and Tim's fever was worse. They spent another miserable day.

Patricia cared for them as best she could with the pitiful supplies she had. That night, Tim's fever was no better, and in the light of the new day, his wound looked even worse. Andy forced himself to move around, trying to loosen his strained muscles despite Patricia's white-faced protests.

When Patricia finally left for the creek to get more water, Tim discovered why Andy had not been content to rest. "We've got to get out of here," Andy told him abruptly as soon as she was out of sight. "Pat's exhausted, our food supplies are running low, and you need that leg seen to in better surroundings. It's going bad."

Tim regarded him. He knew Andy had started to respect him for the way he tried to spare Patricia as much as possible. "Why have you dragged a young woman like Pat out into this wilderness, Andy?" Tim asked abruptly. "And without adequate supplies?"

Anger flashed across the older man's face. "None of your business. We had enough supplies for two people," he snapped. "And it would have lasted much longer if I'd been able to get out these last few days and go hunting."

"Hunting?" Tim's eyes narrowed. "And what would you have been hunting out here?"

At Tim's sharp tones, Andy stiffened. "Well, it wouldn't have been your precious cattle, that's for sure," he snapped. "And for your information she has dragged me here, not the other way around."

"To look for someone called Danny?"

Andy glared at him. "As I said, that's none of your business!" He swallowed, glanced toward the creek, and added hurriedly, "Look, we've got to persuade her we are well enough to tackle the trip to that place you come from unless there's somewhere closer."

"Waverley is the only place for many miles. And I'm well enough." Tim's brave words were belied by the perspiration dripping from his flushed face.

Andy's grin flashed. "Neither of us are, but we've got to get her to a place where she has help and can rest." Worry creased his brow. "Will there be others at your place who could take over your care? She's been living on nerves for too long as it is, and if I'm not careful, she's going to collapse."

Tim thought of the beautiful stone homestead that Elizabeth Waverley's father had built his wife and only daughter. Since they had bought it, Adam and Kate had made it even more comfortable, extending the gardens and orchards, employing more staff. It was indeed a home, a place to relax. Patricia would be able to rest there.

His lips tightened as he remembered the only drawback to the place. Mrs. Wadding. From the start he had not been sure if his new housekeeper and cook would fit in at Waverley. There had been little choice but to employ the woman temporarily after dear, comfortable old Mrs. Cook had been forced to leave abruptly to care for her seriously ill daughter back in Sydney. Since the transportation of convicts had ceased, servants were becoming harder and harder to find, especially so far from Sydney.

Tim had tried to convince himself how fortunate he had been that Mrs. Wadding was in Bathurst looking for work the very day he had driven Kate's old housekeeper there to help her on her way. Certainly, the woman had been all eagerness to please at first and obviously surprised and even awed by the grandeur of Waverley. She seemed capable enough, but a few times Tim suspected she was far too hard on the girls who helped in the house. They had so quickly lost their smiling faces and cheerful greetings, and the stockmen began to avoid going to the homestead.

When Mrs. Wadding had discovered Tim was not the son of the owner, that his father had been merely a convict, her attitude toward him had changed, often bordering on insolence. The pleasant atmosphere he had always taken for granted at Waverley rapidly deteriorated. He had been only too glad to join the other men in looking for the cattle, but he knew that if Mrs. Cook did not return soon, he would be forced to go to Bathurst and find a replacement for Mrs. Wadding. Kate and Adam would be coming home soon, and the last thing he wanted was for them to return to such an unhappy household.

"Right," Tim said decisively, "we'll go this morning. Between us we should cope."

Relief lit up Andy's face. "Sure we'll cope. We're excellent actors, although I think you need to work on your snoring," he noted, his eyes twinkling. "Besides, between the two of us, don't we have three good hands and two good legs? Although yours might be a bit feeble awhile yet."

Tim grinned. "I'd better work on getting stronger then."

Andy chuckled in appreciation, and soon both men were laughing out loud. Tim found himself liking Andy immensely.

"Right then," Andy said cheerfully. "Let's start breaking camp before she gets back."

Between them, they managed to roll up the bedding and get some of the tent ropes untied.

"Stop! What are you doing?" Panic laced Patricia's voice. She dropped the water container and rushed toward Andy, who was trying to undo the last rope.

"It's time we moved on," Andy said briefly, but he glanced at Tim before scowling at her. "Tim needs more help than we can get him here, and we are fast running out of food."

Patricia put her hands on her hips and glanced from Andy to Tim, who had just managed to finish tying up a bundle Andy had dragged to him. He straightened and swayed. Abruptly, he fell back down. There was no need to act. The little he had attempted had exhausted him.

"Tim's still too sick," she cried out. "And what happened to all that 'live off the land' talk of yours?"

"Can't hold a rifle well enough," Andy muttered, "and with this bad leg, I couldn't get near enough to get a kangaroo in the sights anyway."

Tim tried to smile at her as he gasped breathlessly, "Just. . .bit weak. Been in bed. . .too long."

"And you should still be in bed," she cried out, rushing over to him. "Andy, look at him!"

Tim started to push himself up from the ground but fell back with a disgusted groan. "Sorry, Mate," he mumbled to Andy. "More lessons will have to wait. Done all. . .can for a bit."

Andy used the piece of wood he had selected from the pile of firewood as a crutch and limped painfully over to them. "Then we'll make a bed in the dray for us to share."

Patricia looked from one to the other.

"We have to get out of here, Patty dear," Andy said quietly, "or we'll all get weaker without enough to eat. We can take it slowly, but we have to start moving."

Patricia stared at her uncle. "You only call me that when. . . You're very serious, aren't you?"

Andy nodded silently.

"I–I could try and trap or shoot something myself," she faltered.

Tim shook his head. "Isn't much wildlife in the immediate area," he said. "I agree with your uncle. It would be much better to go to Waverley. On the way we might even meet some of the stockmen. They should have arrived home already with the cattle and discovered I hadn't made it back. They. . .they wouldn't look for me here."

Because I never come to this place where the memory of Father's death still haunts me.

Patricia stared at Tim and then back at Andy. "Right," she said reluctantly. Andy started to bend down to pick up the bedding, and she added hastily, "Only as long as you let me do the heavy bits and you men rest when you should."

She grabbed the bundle from Andy and hefted it into the cart. Swiftly she spread the bedding out to form a rough bed. When she turned around, she thought she caught Andy winking at Tim, but their smiles quickly disappeared and Andy started slowly back to the tent. She stared after him suspiciously, but she felt too pleased that the men were getting along to pursue the matter.

"I'm packing my own gear," she called out rapidly, "as well as the cooking things. That way I'll know where everything is when we stop next."

Only when she picked up the pan that she usually cooked on but that she had used to pan the riverbed did she remember the gold dust. She had hidden it carefully in the battered old bag that held her few pieces of clothing.

Patricia hesitated, wondering if she should show it to Andy. A small amount, it was probably only what the miners called "fool's gold" anyway. She shrugged. Getting help for Tim and Andy was far more important. But she looked around, taking careful note of the hills that rose a little way back from the creek, looking for landmarks to help them find this creek again. Perhaps when they found Danny, they might be able to come back and explore this region. And they could use that cross on the tree to make sure they were in the right place.

Despite her protests, both men helped her more than she considered wise. Tim had to rest frequently, but it took all three to harness the horse to the cart and tie the chestnut and Blackie to the back of it.

Two Irish tempers exploded when Patricia refused to let Andy drive the cart. At first Tim was alarmed by their fiery words, but at last he shrugged and closed his eyes, glad to rest on his makeshift bed in the cart until the battle was over. When Patricia won the day by jumping up and sitting in the driver's seat, completely ignoring her spluttering uncle, Tim chuckled softly at them.

At last they were on their way. As the dray jolted slowly over the rough ground, Tim grabbed his leg, his teeth clenched from pain. He had tried to give them directions to Waverley, and he fervently hoped they found the road before he succumbed to the pain and his worsening fever.

Three excruciating days passed as they made their way to Tim's home. His infection had refused to go away, and he knew Patricia was desperately worried about the state of his leg by the time the Waverley homestead came into view, nestled in its setting of pine trees and tall gums.

Through a haze of pain and weakness, Tim heard Patricia's sharp exclamation. "Is. . .is that really Waverley?" she gasped. "Why, it's beautiful!" Astonishment and something like awe sounded in her voice.

"Yes," Tim managed weakly, "but it's still not Stevens Downs."

He saw Patricia glance at him sharply. Had he told her about his old home, about the horizon that stretched for miles without a hill in sight? As much as he loved Waverley, those never-ending plains had always called to something deep inside him, something he wasn't even sure he understood.

The last stretch to the house was not as rough as the bush track, but not far from the house, a wheel hit a rut in the side of the road. Pain slashed through Tim's leg. He could not stop the groan that slipped past his lips.

"Careful, Girl. You went off the road there," Andy admonished sharply. "Here, let me take over this last bit or you'll land us in that ditch. You're exhausted."

After that, things were confused for Tim. He thought he must have passed out for several minutes. He came to when he heard a woman screaming, "Oh, you wicked, wicked people! What have you done to poor Mr. Hardy? You've killed him!"

Tim groaned. "Be quiet, you stupid woman," he started to mutter, but his voice was drowned out by Andy's voice saying that very thing.

"Good man," he whispered approvingly and let the darkness descend.

The next few days were a blur. There were strident tones and rough hands until he heard Andy's roar once more. Then to his relief, she was there. Her hands were gentle, easing the pain in his leg, her tones soothing him to rest.

And then her voice raised in fury roused him. She was ordering someone to get out. He forced his eyes open and peered curiously at a red-faced, plump man retreating before her. Mrs. Wadding screeched again, but the sound was shut out as the door slammed.

"Pat?" he croaked.

"Yes, Tim, I'm here," her voice whispered.

"Don't. . .go. . . ."

"I'm not going anywhere," she said in a choked voice and then vehemently added, "And neither are you!"

He wondered vaguely where she thought he might go, but then her face loomed closer. Soft lips touched his forehead. Comforted, he smiled and went to sleep.

Patricia wiped furiously at the tears streaming down her face as she collapsed into the chair beside Tim's bed. She shuddered as she heard more shouting and screaming from somewhere in the house. Then she identified the thud of the big cedar front door followed by the rattle of horse and carriage.

A few moments later, Andy limped into the room. His face was red with anger, his eyes fiery.

"Has the doctor gone?" she whispered.

"Yes, and good riddance to him," he said in controlled tones.

Patricia gave a broken laugh. "Poor Tim. He told me housekeepers are very hard to come by out here. I don't know what he is going to think about us upsetting his so much. She was furious enough when we banned her from Tim's bedroom after he became so agitated every time she came near him. Now she is utterly scandalized, certain we are letting Tim. . .letting Tim. . ." She choked on a sob, unable to put into words what the woman had screamed as Andy had bundled the pompous, incompetent doctor from the house.

Andy drew her head against his comforting shoulder. "But we know we are doing nothing less than saving that young man from a fool," he stated vehemently. "When Tim comes to, if he's anything like the young man I'm thinkin' he is, he'll agree with our decision." His Irish accent had increased, indicating just how upset he was.

"Oh, Andy dear! What if we're wrong? What if. . . ?"

"We aren't wrong," he interrupted her anguished whisper, adding with grim determination, "but we've got much work to do to prove it. Let's get started."

Two days passed before Patricia knew they had won the battle to keep Tim Hardy alive after refusing to allow the doctor to amputate his leg.

Andy found Patricia in her bedroom, sobbing her heart out with sheer relief. She raised a beaming face to him. "Oh, Andy, he's going to be all right. He spoke quite lucidly to me, and now he's sleeping more soundly than he has since. . .since. . . I've been so afraid we made the wrong decision not letting that doctor. . ." She stopped, not able to voice the horrible recommendation the doctor had made.

Andy hugged her and let her cry all over him until her tears dried up at last.

A few more days passed before Tim was well enough to be told about the doctor and to be informed that his housekeeper was not speaking to either Patricia or Andy, refusing even to cook for them or let the maids clean their rooms.

At first Tim was furious. "And you didn't make her leave with the doctor?" he exclaimed.

Andy chuckled. "Can't say I wasn't tempted! She will never know how close she came to being tied up and bundled into that buggy with him."

Tim looked from Andy's defiant face to Patricia's apprehensive one, and his scowl lifted. He grinned at them. "Pity you didn't. They could have driven each other crazy all the way to Bathurst. What stopped you?"

"We couldn't look after this place as well as care for you," Andy said bluntly. Tim looked at Patricia's exhausted face with concern, and Andy added swiftly, "Afraid I also didn't have the authority if—"

He stopped abruptly, and Patricia knew that deep down Andy had also been afraid Tim might have died.

"It would have been good riddance," Tim said weakly.

He reached out and took Patricia's hand, holding it as tightly as he could. Looking into her tear-filled eyes, he whispered a fervent thank-you. He looked over at Andy and smiled gratefully.

Then he turned back and smiled so tenderly at her that Patricia knew her heart was in grave danger. No matter how often she told herself she did not know Tim well enough, her heart risked giving itself to the thin, pale man she had prayed and wept over until they had won him back from the very gates of death.

Chapter 6

Tim remained thin and weak for some time, but Andy and Patricia were amazed by how rapidly his general health improved. He insisted on getting out of bed long before Patricia thought he was ready to do so. Certainly he did not stay up very long those first couple times, but each day he steadily improved until he only needed to rest for an hour or so each day. After that first morning they had talked to Tim, Patricia found herself gently but firmly banned from Tim's bedroom until he was dressed.

When she protested, Andy dropped into the exaggerated Irish brogue he liked to adopt at times. "Now, me darlin', it's a very proper young man, it is." He paused, his eyes twinkling mischievously, before adding, "Tim is already embarrassed enough you have been so intimately caring for him all this time. And he doesn't want to give that there sour Mrs. Wadding any more juicy bits of scandal." The smile disappeared, and he became very much the stern, protective uncle. "Nor does he want to risk damaging your reputation!"

She gaped at Andy. Did she have any reputation left? According to one of Mrs. Wadding's tirades, Patricia was nothing more than a "hussy dressed in men's clothes, and no better than she should be!" Patricia had been thankful Andy had not heard that particular session with the housekeeper, or Mrs. Wadding might have found herself summarily dispatched back to Bathurst after all. And Patricia had acknowledged to herself that she was far too exhausted to take over the running of the large house as well as supervise the food for the stockmen's quarters.

Once she was not so consumed with Tim's hour-by-hour care, Patricia made it her business to sort out her and Andy's clothes and bedding. Despite the scorn directed her way by Mrs. Wadding, she washed and cleaned their things, glad to get rid of the dust from their travels and camping. Andy grumbled at his niece's burst of energy but helped lift the heavy buckets of hot water and baskets of laundry for her when Mrs. Wadding made sure the other servants were too busy to help. Patricia disdained accepting assistance, but because bouts of deep weariness swept over her from time to time, she was secretly glad of Andy's help.

The days, and then the weeks slipped by. Except for Mrs. Wadding's unpleasantness, Patricia found herself relaxing in the peace of Waverley.

Andy soon became restless and often wandered down to the stables or sheds, chatting with any station hand around. The men out with Tim had not arrived back until several days after Tim was well on the road to recovery. The drought conditions provided little feed for the herd and slowed the return to Waverley.

Apparently only one man had made a brief search for Tim, the conclusion being reached that Tim had returned to Waverley by himself.

Andy had shaken his head at their slackness and lack of care, but he enjoyed discussing with the stockmen the differences between running a ranch in America and the Australian cattle and sheep station. As his injuries healed, there were soon plenty of tasks around the place he willingly helped out with.

Although they had discovered Jackie was Tim's main offsider, he still did not put in an appearance. When Patricia mentioned that to Tim, he merely shrugged and said with resignation that Jackie would get back from his walkabout when he was ready. It could be weeks—even months—before Jackie's aboriginal business was completed.

Patricia and Tim spent many hours sitting quietly together, reading, and playing games. At first they sat in Tim's bedroom, but as he improved, they graduated to the parlor or study. Once he was well enough, he insisted on going outside, long before Patricia thought he should.

"Four walls have always stifled me," he explained, giving an endearing smile to his petite nurse.

She stared at him doubtfully. Certainly his cheeks were filling out again. Plenty of healthy color now brightened the lean face tanned and wrinkled by hours spent in the outdoors. Her heart stirred again. It was a handsome face, a strong face with steady, thoughtful amber eyes. The light brown hair, now needing a trim, had the most beguiling wave in it. That lock of hair had fallen across his forehead again. So many times she had smoothed it back when he was ill.

In the end she agreed to let Tim sit on the veranda. Eventually she allowed him to take a small walk in the garden, leaning on her arm and an old walking stick. Those walks gradually became longer as Tim's strength returned.

A little diffidently at first, but with increasing confidence, Patricia and Timothy talked about many things that they had never shared with anyone else. They told each other stories about their parents, the adventures of sailing and settling in a new country, the lessons about God and faith their parents had tried to teach them.

❦

After a few weeks, Tim found himself telling Patricia about that dark day his father had died. It had not been something Tim had intended or planned to share with her. They had been sitting on the veranda watching the sun display its glorious colors as it sank beneath the horizon of undulating hills. Their friendship had developed to the point that telling her seemed natural.

Patricia watched Tim's face, listening silently as he poured out his heart to her. As he started to describe those last moments he had held his father, Tim faltered and stopped.

Tears filled her eyes. She simply reached out and held his hands tightly in her own. Then she quietly told him about the time her mother had been shot by that first arrow launched before any of them had been aware of the small group of Indians creeping up on their small farm. Fortunately both Andy and her father had been home and had quickly fought off the Indians, but it had taken several days and nights before her mother had finally succumbed to her wound. After that, her father and Andy had sold up, moving to a more settled area where the Indians were friendlier.

Somehow, in that quiet corner of the garden under a massive flowering peach tree, it seemed perfectly natural for Tim to put his arm around Patricia. Pink petals gently floated down and settled on the white daisies at their feet. When she finished speaking, they were still for a few moments, her head resting on his shoulder.

At last she sighed and started to sit up, saying quietly, "Well, it was a long time ago now for both of us, and life has gone on since then."

Tim softly smoothed back a stray piece of hair from her beautiful face.

She turned impulsively toward him. "I haven't mentioned Danny yet. He. . ."

Tim hardly heard what she said. He was watching her, staring into her expressive eyes that never ceased to fascinate him. She paused. A look of startled surprise, of awareness, filled her face. Her adorable lips, so close to his, opened slightly. A deep flush spread across her face.

She was absolutely irresistible.

They were so close he only had to move those last few inches. Gently, ever so gently, they explored each other's lips. They withdrew, exchanged a look of startled wonder, and then kissed again. Tim's arms slipped around her. Her hands reached behind his neck to hold him closer to her.

It was bliss.

It was sheer heaven.

"Mr. Hardy! Miss! How could you?" The screech froze them.

They tore apart.

Mrs. Wadding was staring at them in absolute horror. "I knew it," she screeched, "taking advantage of a poor ill man!"

Tim swallowed, feeling the heat flood into his face. He glanced at Patricia. Her fingers were on those luscious lips he had just tasted. Her face was white as a sheet. But her eyes were looking behind Mrs. Wadding, staring at her uncle as he came running toward them across the lawn.

"What is it? What's wrong?" Andy barked.

"That wicked, wicked girl," wailed Mrs. Wadding. "She's been. . .been. . .oh, the shame of her! And you such a Christian gentleman, Mr. Hardy!"

Tim came to his senses. Fury took over from his first anguish at having the wonderful moment torn to pieces. "Mrs. Wadding," he roared, "that is enough! Be quiet, Woman!"

Something in his face made the woman take a step back. She opened her mouth, but Tim was not finished.

"If you say one more word. . .one word," he spluttered, "I will put you on a horse and have you off Waverley in the next moment."

She stood there. Her gaze darted from Tim to a glowering Andy. She tossed her head and stomped away.

"What's going on here?"

Patricia was still staring at Tim in bemusement. At Andy's abrupt question, she turned to confront her uncle.

Tim started to say, "Sir, I'm afraid—"

"It is absolutely none of your business, Andy!" Patricia interrupted fiercely.

Andy stared at her. His gaze dropped to her lips. Scarlet flooded into her face, but she tilted her chin and stared back at him with haughty challenge.

Tim felt a flood of relief as Andy relaxed. He thought a twinkle briefly flickered in Andy's eyes, but then his expression hardened again as he turned to Tim.

"Anything that happens to you is very much my business, Patty darling, especially when your own father is so far away from here," Andy murmured softly. His gaze became menacing as he looked at Tim with much the expression Tim had seen when they first met over the barrels of Andy's two revolvers. "You do understand that, don't you, Mr. Hardy?"

Tim stared back at the man angrily for a long moment. He nodded ever so slightly. "I believe your niece is very privileged to have you to care what happens to her, Sir," he said crisply.

He glanced at Patricia, who watched them with apprehension. Tim smiled at her gently, comfortingly, before turning back to Andy O'Donnell. Tim looked at him steadily. The men had become quite good friends, but he knew that Andy would not put anything above his niece's welfare. "I can assure you that I will do everything in my power to see that nothing happens to her," Tim stated firmly.

Patricia gave an embarrassed moan, turned, and fled.

Tim took a step toward her, then stopped. His head high, he turned back to Andy, who was watching the fleeing woman thoughtfully.

When he looked back at Tim, the two men studied each other for a long moment.

"See that you keep that promise, Lad," Andy murmured before striding after his niece.

Tim deeply regretted that things remained strained between Patricia and himself for several days. He realized how much talking to her about his father had helped melt away a lot of his pain and sense of loss. Tim hoped she too had been helped, but there were times after the strain had eased at last, that he knew she was holding back from him, holding him at a distance, especially when any mention of their families came up.

🦋

Patricia was so thankful when she and Tim at last regained their old easy friendship. She wanted to tell him about Danny; she came so close to doing so, but

Danny's very life might depend on her keeping his secret. And she had promised him so faithfully not to say a word to anyone. She had already broken that promise when she had told Andy.

As the days flew past, Tim and Patricia, in unspoken agreement, refused to let the sadness and wounds each carried deep in their souls to surface, so as not to disturb the fragile relationship developing between them. And if there were moments when Patricia longed for Tim to kiss her again, she gave no sign of it.

Just sitting in each other's presence in the evenings and quietly reading together was a delight the two lonely young people savored. A few times they slipped into discussions about faith and what they had been taught about the Bible, God, and how to experience a meaningful relationship with Him.

At other times, Patricia persuaded Tim to tell her more about his father. She was fascinated by his stories, including how young Tim had fallen into the Thames River trying to reach his father as the convicts were being loaded onto their transport ship and how the boy had been rescued by the convict John Martin. On the journey to Australia, Tim's father had been a faithful witness for his Lord to the other convicts. But only one listened to him—the same John Martin. John, a convicted murderer, had often protected the frailer Timothy from the persecution of the other convicts, and eventually John had come to a personal faith in Christ that had transformed him from an angry, despairing young man to a man at peace and with the certain hope that God had his future in His control.

Even more fascinating to Patricia was the story of how Elizabeth Waverley, a passenger returning to Australia, had befriended both convicts on board the ship, believed John's pleas of his innocence, and fallen deeply in love with him. She told Adam Stevens about the two men. Adam had been a convict assigned to Elizabeth's father, who was himself an ex-convict. Adam had worked so faithfully on Waverley for Elizabeth's family that he had been left Stevens Downs in her rich father's will. For Elizabeth's sake, Adam had employed Timothy and had had John assigned to him, never dreaming that he would become so caught up in the lives of the two convicts. Adam, too, had come to believe John Martin's story that he was innocent of the murder he had been convicted of and that he was the rightful heir of a member of the English aristocracy.

"This Kate of yours, Adam's wife, is John Martin's sister, the daughter of a lord?" Patricia gasped at that part of Tim's story.

Tim nodded, his eyes twinkling at her awe. "Adam traveled to England and met Kate. Together they brought Kate and John's wicked cousin's schemes to naught, proving that he was the real murderer all along. John Martin is now my Lord Farnley, and Elizabeth Waverley is Lady Farnley," he added in impressive tones.

Patricia gaped at him. He laughed and told her more, of how stubbornly Kate had ignored all Adam's scruples about a man convicted of fraud marrying an earl's daughter until Adam could no longer resist their deep love for each other.

As enjoyable as these conversations were, however, the time Patricia spent with Tim was kept fairly brief, and it was usually Patricia who cut the sessions short. A certain look would cross Tim's face that told her he expected her to tell him more about her family in return for his own stories. She felt desolate, longing to be able to share with him, but not daring to. She hated pushing Tim away when he so naturally wanted to know everything about her as their affection for each other grew.

A couple times Patricia caught an expression of concern in her uncle's eyes when she and Tim were talking or laughing together. Although it had upset her at the time, the little talk Andy had given her after that episode in the garden made far too much sense. She was glad Andy had held his peace since, not putting into words what she knew only too well to be true. Her home and responsibilities were a long way from this quiet valley in New South Wales.

And there was still Danny.

As Tim became stronger, he gradually became busier with running the property. Patricia deliberately spent less time with him. She became quieter, more withdrawn.

Andy went searching for her one day when he knew Tim was busy catching up on the paperwork that had been accumulating. Patricia was sitting in the shade of the veranda, staring out across the homestead garden toward the west. She glanced up at Andy as his boots clumped toward her and swiftly wiped a hand across her wet cheeks.

Her uncle sank down on one of the chairs near her and took her hand. They stared out across the paddocks. It had been a hot day, a foretaste of the summer almost upon them.

After a long silence, she sighed and said softly, "It's time to go, isn't it?"

Andy squeezed her hand understandingly before letting it go. "Yes," he said abruptly, "long past time." After a pause he added, "The stockman arrived back from Bathurst a little while ago."

Something in his voice brought her sad gaze back to him. At the look on his face, she exclaimed, "Danny?"

Andy nodded. "The stockman brought word that a few weeks back someone called Sean McMurtrie had been asking all kinds of questions about any stories of gold being found in the Bathurst, Wellington, area. They think he headed west."

"That was the name Danny used in California. What we were told by that other old man must be true. He headed out this way to try to find gold."

Patricia closed her eyes, waiting for the rush of excitement that should come at the confirmation that Danny was indeed in this part of New South Wales.

It didn't come. Instead she fought threatening tears at the thought of saying good-bye to this place that had become a haven. And then there was the young man with light brown hair still bleached by the relentless sun of this land. The young man with that light in his amber eyes that warmed her through and through, who had become so much more than an acquaintance.

"We should leave tomorrow morning, me darlin'."

She slowly stood up, brushing down the skirt of one of the old-fashioned dresses Tim had insisted weeks ago she borrow from an old trunk. When she had murmured her regret at only bringing one skirt from their luggage left in Sydney, he had told Andy to haul the trunk out of a cupboard in a storeroom. It had only taken a few stitches to make a couple fit her perfectly and a careful clean and press before she could wear them. She had been well rewarded by the glow in Tim's eyes as he looked at her. For the first time, she had felt truly beautiful.

"I'll go and pack." Her voice was steady, and she did not look at Andy as she asked quietly, "Have you told Tim?"

"I thought you might like to do that yourself," Andy said a trifle huskily.

"Yes. Thank you. He. . .he's busy now. I'll tell him after tea."

Instead of heading straight to her room, she hesitated for a moment and then hurried down the steps and out into the sunshine for one last look around the garden. It was a blaze of late spring color. Waverley employed a gardener to make sure it was well kept, especially in the dry seasons.

Tears blurred her eyes as she walked aimlessly. At last she reached the gate that opened out onto the road they would take the next morning. She leaned on it, her shoulders hunched, her head bowed.

❧

Tim was never sure what drew his attention away from his books to look out the wide study windows. Watching Patricia walking down the path was far more pleasant than studying his accounts. She had looked absolutely beautiful at breakfast that morning, and he had suddenly realized nothing would make him happier than to be greeted by her smiling face every morning for the rest of his life.

She paused at the gate, staring out across the dry, dusty paddocks, then bowed her head. He frowned. Something was wrong. She looked unhappy, a very picture of misery. Had Mrs. Wadding upset her again? He knew Patricia took care to hide from him the many mean and petty things the spiteful housekeeper had subjected her to. Despite his inability to go to Bathurst himself, he should have rid Waverley of that woman weeks ago.

Tim jumped up and made his way out of the study, only to be waylaid by Mrs. Wadding with vicious complaints about not having her supply order filled correctly by the luckless stockman who had been to Bathurst. Without giving Tim a chance to respond, she raved on, listing other misdemeanors committed by the two servant girls.

Then she was foolish enough to start in on Patricia and Andy. "No-hopers, the pair of them," she spat out. "Threw poor Dr. Mint out, they did. Refused to let him treat you. It's a miracle you survived. And now throwing herself at you. . .well. . ."

"Quiet, Woman!"

Tim's roar stunned Mrs. Wadding to silence. Only once before had Tim raised his voice to her. He had not mentioned that incident again, but she had severely underestimated him if she thought he had forgotten.

Tim drew himself up and fixed her with an angry glare. "I should have done this that day you so rudely intruded on our privacy in the garden," he ground out. "Seeing you are so dissatisfied with all you have to put up with at Waverley, I believe it is past time we parted company, Mrs. Wadding. Have your bags packed by tomorrow morning, and I will arrange for you to be driven to Bathurst."

Her mouth dropped open, and she went pale. "But you need me. You—"

"You are sadly mistaken, Madam. We certainly do not need your constant carping and poisonous tongue and will manage much better without you."

Fury swept over her narrow face. "I suppose you think that harpy of yours will be able to—"

"That is enough, Mrs. Wadding!" Tim turned his back on the spluttering woman and limped from the house.

Patricia no longer stood at the gate. It hung slightly open, unusual for a woman reared where shutting gates was taught from the time her first steps were taken.

Nevertheless, Tim went around the garden, hoping to find her. Unsuccessful, he returned to the gate and wondered in which direction she might have gone. It took a few minutes before he saw her standing a long way down the driveway, peering up into the branches of the tall gum tree.

He hesitated. His strength was increasing every day, but he had not yet ventured quite so far from the house. A pang went through him. He knew that tree only too well and the steep rise on which it stood.

❦

Walking swiftly up the hill had somehow eased the sharp ache in Patricia's heart. She was sure this was the tree from which Tim had watched the road for his father. It was certainly the tallest one on that rise. As she paused beneath it, she heard a faint mew and looked up. A small kitten crouched on a high branch.

The small animal provided a welcome distraction from her somber thoughts. She called to it, trying to coax it down. It started toward her, then ran out onto a thin limb above her head that bent alarmingly underneath the kitten's weight. Terrified, the animal clung to its precarious perch. The branch swayed up and down, and Patricia expected it to come crashing to the ground at any moment. The kitten mewed frantically.

"Oh, you stupid creature," she sighed. "I suppose you want me to rescue you?"

Patricia had climbed many trees with Danny when they were young. But it had been awhile. This one looked relatively easy. She shrugged, hitched up her skirt, and started up. She could not help thinking of the young Tim sitting in the tree, searching the horizon for a father who never came.

She was quite a long way off the ground when Tim's voice called out breathlessly, "Patricia, whatever are you doing up there?"

She froze and then looked down. He stood directly beneath her, one hand resting on the trunk of the tree.

"There. . .there's a kitten. . . ."

"She'll find her own way down."

Patricia peered around the branch she was clinging to. Sure enough, the kitten had already reached the relative safety of a strong branch just above her. She hesitated, unwilling to retreat without the wretched creature.

"Pat, Darling, do come down out of there!" Tim called anxiously.

Darling? He had been so reserved, as proper as any gentleman could be, since that unforgettable moment in the garden. She had thought he must have regretted it, when she had wanted only to repeat it again and again and—

She gave a little gasp, her breath quickening. And now Tim had called her. . .

Eagerly she started back down the tree, leaving the kitten to its own fate.

Afterward, Patricia could never say what happened for sure. Perhaps the skirt she so seldom wore was her downfall; perhaps it had been her reaction to Tim's endearment. One moment she was several feet from safety; the next her foot slipped and she went crashing down.

She screamed. Tim cried out and sprang forward. She hit him with enough force to send him flat on his back with her in a tangle of petticoats on top of him. For a moment she lay there, the breath knocked from her, then realized Tim had not moved.

"Tim, your leg!" she cried in dismay, rolling off him.

He lay motionless, blood trickling from where his head had hit the sharp edge of a protruding rock.

"Oh, no! Not again," she moaned.

Once more her foolishness had brought injury to Tim Hardy.

Chapter 7

There, I think he's waking up at last."

Tim wished the man would go away and let him sleep. He was too weary to wake up. He tried to tell him to go away, to let him sleep. All that seemed to want to come out of his mouth was a dry croak. Pain shot through his head.

Someone gave a low, choked sound. He wasn't sure if it was a sob or a chuckle. Soft lips touched his forehead, his cheek.

A woman's voice spoke softly. "But you've had more than enough sleep these last few days, my dear, dear Tim. It is time to wake up now so you can have some broth."

Broth? He hated broth. Tim frowned. The woman sounded anxious. What was she doing in his bedroom? And surely he knew that voice with the Irish lilt, whose lips were so gentle, so loving.

With effort, he opened his eyelids. He was rewarded by the sight of a sweet face and green eyes that sparkled with tears as she smiled down at him.

"Patricia?" he croaked, trying to sit up. A sharp pain pierced the back of his head even as gentle hands reached to prevent him. His head whirling, he fell back on the soft pillow.

"You must lie still," Patricia said urgently.

Tim stared up at her. "You. . .you shot me and. . .and. . ."

She stared and then nodded slowly. The tears started trickling down her face as she whispered, "You'll never forget that, will you?"

He stared at her, trying to remember.

"That time you lost a lot of blood, had a bad fever, but now. . ." Her voice choked and trailed to a stop.

He tried to move a hand up to her. Patricia mustn't cry.

At his attempt to move, the pain throbbed again in his shoulder, his head. He closed his eyes, fighting to remember. Images started seeping through him. His leg had been on fire. He had been in the back of a dray. No, no, that had been before. There had been some woman screeching.

"Mrs. Wadding. . .she. . ."

The man's voice said firmly, "She won't be troubling you anymore."

"Andy?"

"Yes, it's me, Lad."

Tim tried to remember. There had been something about a gunshot, then a

412

doctor. No, no, it had been a. . .a tree. . . .

His head filled with pain. Someone gave a muffled sob. Tim frowned and opened his eyes, squinting around. He was in his own comfortable room at Waverley.

A gruff voice said abruptly, "And how many times do I have to tell you to stop feelin' so guilty, me darlin'?"

Tim turned his head a little too swiftly, and Andy's scowling face swam into view.

"That last time this idiot lost a lot of blood because of his own foolishness over those aborigines and even more because of his stubbornness in not telling us. And this last was pure and simply an accident." Andy stopped as he saw Tim looking at him. "Come on now, Lad," he added in a softer voice that belied his scowl, "let's get a couple more pillows under you so you can get some food into you."

"Not. . .not broth."

"Oh dear, and after all the trouble that has been taken to kill the hen and pluck it and cook it," another woman's voice said lightly from near the doorway.

Patricia gave a start and stepped back from his bed.

For a moment Tim thought he must still be crazy from the fever. . .no. . .this time he had hit his head.

"Kate?" he managed, staring at the face that should have been fifteen thousand miles away. He shut his eyes. He must be hallucinating.

From behind her another voice, a very familiar drawl, said loudly, "Well, it's about time you came to and welcomed us home, Tim Hardy."

"Adam?" He jerked his head around, lifting it up to peer toward the doorway. He fell back with a groan from the pain.

"I told you he wasn't well enough yet for you to surprise him," Patricia said crossly, and then her voice lost its sharp edge as she turned back to her patient. "You really mustn't move too quickly just yet, Tim," she admonished him. "Here, have a sip of water."

A gentle hand lifted his head and a cup was held to his dry lips. Suddenly he knew it had been Patricia's hands that he had felt through the haze of pain, her lilting voice that had soothed him during the dark night. Or had there been more than one?

It took an effort to swallow, but the water did relieve his dry mouth and help clear his head a little.

And it was Adam and Kate beaming down at him.

"You're home!"

"Yes, only in the last hour, and only to find you've turned the place upside down," Kate said with a smile. She bent down to kiss him, and he saw the caring and concern in her eyes that had warmed his lonely and motherless heart so many times over the years. "And we've brought visitors who are very anxious to see you."

"I really don't think you should bother him too much just yet," that voice with the attractive lilt said sharply. "He has been very ill and was still not fully recovered before. . .before. . ."

"Yes, so we discovered the moment we arrived!" Adam's voice was filled with fury as he glared across the bed at Patricia and Andy.

"Not. . .not her fault," Tim managed.

"Not according to Jackie and that wretched housekeeper who still hasn't stopped screeching about—"

Adam stopped abruptly as Kate raised an urgent hand. "I thought I said you could only come in here if you didn't disturb him about what has happened."

Patricia moved abruptly, shrinking closer to her uncle, who was glaring back at Adam Stevens. For a moment Tim thought she looked frightened, but then she straightened, tilting her chin and gazing steadily back at Adam.

Tim looked from her to his old friends, still hardly believing that after all those lonely months they had returned from England. Relief swept through him. Everything would be all right at Waverley now that they were here to take charge once more. It had been a huge responsibility.

"Why, Kate. . .Adam. . .you're really home!" he stammered again, holding out his hand. "But how. . .why didn't you let me know? I could have met your ship."

Kate took his hand, saying softly, "We wanted to surprise you, Tim dear. We were in such a rush to get here, we've even left the children in Sydney with friends. But you've surprised us instead. Now, don't try and talk just yet. I'm so sorry you haven't been well, but I'm sure you will be up and about very soon."

She glared at her husband. "And if you can't be trusted not to upset him, you may leave, Mr. Stevens, and not be allowed back here until he can cope with your bossiness."

Tim found himself starting to smile despite his throbbing head. Kate only called her husband that when she was cross with him.

"No," he muttered, "too good to see you again."

That earned him another quick kiss from Kate. "And it is so good to see you too, my dear boy. But we can all talk more when you are a little stronger." She turned to Patricia and said dismissively, "I'll attend to him now, Miss Casey. You must be tired."

Tim frowned. There had been a sharp note in Kate's voice that he did not like at all.

Patricia, her head still raised, stared at Kate. Then, before he could protest, Patricia turned and strode from the room. Tim frowned, only then realizing she was wearing her trousers once more.

He looked swiftly toward Andy. The man was scowling savagely at Kate and Adam. Andy opened his mouth and then snapped it shut before following his niece without a glance at Tim.

"I'll see you later when this dragon says you can have visitors," Adam said heartily. A little too heartily.

As the door shut behind him, exhaustion filled Tim. He was ashamed at the feeling of relief the quietness gave. Eagerly he accepted a cup of water from Kate and then endured her fussing with his pillows. Suddenly he remembered other hands ministering to him, coaxing him to swallow some vile drink, bathing his burning face with cool water.

"How long have I been ill?" he muttered urgently.

"Apparently your last injury happened a couple of days ago," Kate said briskly. "Now don't worry about anything until—"

"My last injury. . .a couple of days ago!" Horror swept through Tim as he started to remember more clearly. "The tree. I fell. Patricia, she. . .she. . .was she hurt?" he asked urgently.

Kate made a sound that sounded like a well-bred snort. "Don't worry about that young woman. I have no doubt she can look after herself."

Tim stared at her. What did she mean? What was wrong with Patricia?

He thought hard. The tree had been afterward. His head was aching so much, he couldn't think straight. A faint memory of raised voices came to him. Patricia had been shouting at someone, ordering him from the room.

"She. . .she made the doctor leave," he muttered, still rather confused at what had happened when.

"She did, did she?" There was stern disapproval in Kate's voice.

"He. . .wanted to bleed me. She. . .she told him I'd already lost too much blood. And. . .and there was something else. Oh, yes, he wanted to cut off my leg, but she wouldn't let him." He rubbed a hand to his forehead.

Kate's frown disappeared. She gasped in horror. "Your leg. . .she. . . Well, good for her!"

Kate was silent. After a moment, Tim thought she muttered something that sounded like, "At least she had sense enough for that." Then she added brightly, "I left orders for Mrs. Wadding to prepare some broth for you as soon as you were awake enough to eat. Now if you are comfortable, I'll go and. . .oh!"

"I had already taken the liberty of seeing to the cooking myself, Mrs. Stevens."

Relief swept through Tim at the familiar voice. He raised his head as swiftly as he dared. "Patricia?"

She was looking defiantly at Kate as she came closer. Her eyes were large in her pale face. They turned and searched his face keenly. A relieved smile transformed her.

"You're really better," she said simply. "I'm glad."

He reached out his hand. Disappointment swept through him as she ignored it and looked away. Only then did he see the tray she was carrying as she placed it on a table next to the bed. When she turned back, he held out his hand again. She looked at it and then slowly reached out and clasped it in hers.

"It's not the chicken broth, just some nourishing vegetable soup I've had simmering all day in hopes you'd be well enough at last to manage some," she murmured softly, her eyes down.

He held her hand as tightly as he could. Relief and weariness swept through him in equal measure. "You will stay until we can talk? And Andy?"

Uncertainty filled her face. For the first time, Tim realized just how exhausted Patricia looked. Black circles ringed red-streaked eyes, and she was very pale and drawn.

She bit her lip, glancing briefly toward Kate. "We. . .we should be on our way now that you have your folk to look after you," she murmured.

Kate cleared her throat and said in a stilted voice, "It was very good of you to prepare the food for Tim, Miss. . .Miss Casey." Her gaze swept over Patricia's clothes, and her expression tightened. She added coldly, "If Tim wants you to stay, of course you must, but I can take over his care now."

There was no mistaking the dismissal in the older woman's firm voice. Patricia stood her ground a moment longer, but then her head drooped and she turned and left the room.

Tim wanted to protest, but his head was worse. Other parts of his body felt battered as well. Exhaustion and pain were sweeping through him, blurring his thoughts even more. It was all he could do to swallow a few mouthfuls of the delicious soup Kate fed him. To his relief, it was far better than the broth his mother and then Kate had forced on him the few times he had been ill when he was a child.

He moved. Pain jolted through his leg as well as his head. His leg. It had been his leg that had bled so much, been infected. And he had fallen under that tree. No, no. . .Patricia had fallen out of the tree. On top of him.

"Are you sure Pat is all right?" he asked urgently. "She fell out of the tree."

"Pat?" Kate said forcefully and then added in a hard voice, "So Jackie told us. Mrs. Wadding also informed us, amongst a lot of other stuff, that Miss Casey fell on top of you."

He peered up at her, disturbed by her tone. "Jackie? Good, he's back. But is Pat okay?"

She smiled at him and said in a quieter voice, "As far as I'm aware, that young lady is fine. Now, don't worry about anything. Just go back to sleep."

Tim was only too thankful to try and relax. He was glad Kate simply gave him a dose of medicine to dull the pain before telling him once more to get some sleep.

Tim obediently closed his eyes, but he couldn't rest. Anxiety swept through him. Kate was so cold toward Patricia. Adam had glared furiously at both Pat and Andy.

And Adam had started to say something about Jackie.

He reached out and grabbed Kate's arm. "Don't let Adam do anything foolish about Pat and Andy until I've talked to him," he muttered urgently as he felt the medication start to take effect.

She was still for a moment.

"Please, Kate, my fault too," he managed to say.

She nodded abruptly. "All right, Tim. Now don't worry about anything except having that sleep."

❦

"And I'm telling you, Mister, only a fool jumps a woman holding a gun on him. He's lucky I didn't shoot and ask questions later! He was asking to be shot, and a lot worse than he was."

Hearing her uncle's furious tones, Patricia caught her breath in dismay. She rushed into the large, well-stocked library and study where she and Tim had spent so many pleasant hours. A red-faced, furious Andy O'Donnell stood in front of an equally angry stranger who towered over him.

"I tell you it was his fault he made Patricia feel threatened enough to pull a gun on him to start with! What else was a frightened young woman—?"

Guilt swept through Patricia. Andy broke off, and both men stared at her as she hurried between them.

"Oh, Andy, pray do hush; you will disturb Tim."

"A little late for your solicitations, isn't it, Madam?"

"Andy!" Patricia grabbed her uncle's arm as he started to step around her.

"Why, you. . .you. . .after all she's done!" Andy snarled.

"Standing up to that quack, hardly a wink of sleep for days, nights. . ." He bit his lip tightly. At last, through gritted teeth he told Patricia, "After all your sleepless nights and our care of that young rascal, this. . .this gentleman is talking about having you arrested for malicious injury!"

Patricia's hand tightened on Andy's arm for support as the blood drained from her head. Arrested? For hurting the man she loved, the man for whom she would die rather than see be hurt? If she went to prison, Danny might never be found. And her poor father. . .

As she stared dumbly at the stranger, the room started to tilt alarmingly. Vaguely she noted what fine clothes he was wearing. Mr. Stevens had said something to Tim about visitors. Important visitors by the looks of this one.

Someone moved forward. A lady's voice said quietly, "Now calm down, both of you. I'm sure there's no need to involve the police in any of this. John, can't you see the poor girl's exhausted? And from what we've been told, her fatigue is the result of her devoted care for Tim."

Patricia had managed to hide from Andy how badly shaken and bruised she herself had been from the fall out of the tree. Now, as she turned her head cautiously to stare at yet another stranger, the room continued to move alarmingly.

There was a wealth of compassion in this woman's kind eyes.

Whoever she was, the stranger was right. Patricia was exhausted. At first, sheer relief had swept through her when the capable Kate Stevens had arrived a couple of hours ago. Patricia had been so afraid there should have been something else they could have been doing for Tim. It would have been pointless sending to Bathurst for the doctor again after they had refused his choice of treatment for Tim the first time.

She had spent other sleepless nights caring for someone she loved—her dear mother during the horrible time before her death. But this situation had been so different. Despite all her uncle's attempts at reassurance, she had felt the heavy responsibility of knowing she had caused Tim Hardy's injuries.

She—who had seen on the American frontier what guns could do, who always had hated guns—she, Patricia Casey, had shot someone. She had fallen out of a tree. Knocked Tim unconscious. She knew he had not fully recovered from the infected wound. Ever since they had carried Tim's unconscious body once more into the house, she'd felt that horrible, heartbreaking dread that he would never wake up.

Once more, the tears were not far away. But these tears were different. For days and nights, perhaps even years, these tears had been suppressed, never able to be released because it would mean she was no longer in control. Patricia fought desperately to hold them back. But she started to shake. The tears filled her eyes, rolled down her cheeks.

The tremendous strain had lasted for far too long. Her mother's death. Her brother being swallowed up by the army and the worry for his safety during the Mexican wars. Then he had been posted missing, believed killed. Andy had been lured off to the goldfields. Many of their cowboys had also gone. As her father slipped into depression, more work had fallen on her shoulders. Above all, only she had known the truth about Danny.

And through it all, that other horrible fear had ever been creeping closer. Talking to Tim and being reminded of some of her mother's teachings about God had been sweet, had held back that fear. Until she had fallen from that tree, for a few precious days she had even begun to wonder if God could possibly love her as her mother had always insisted—if the things Tim had talked about could be true.

But now, in her sorrow and exhaustion, the fear was back. Darker than ever. God had deserted Patricia Casey.

He never answered her prayers.

Not once in all those dreadful hours trying to save her mother from her injuries. Not once through the years since Mother had died. Not once when Patricia had been unable to stop her brother and father from fighting so bitterly. Not when her brother had run away to the army.

For a little while she had hoped it had been God answering the desperate prayers wrenched from her that had saved Tim's life. But there had been no sense of God's presence. Deep down she knew Tim could quite easily have recovered without divine intervention.

Patricia Casey was all alone.

And now this.

The loving and caring God her mother and Tim's parents had believed in might be true for good people like them. But for some reason He had turned His back on the Casey family, on Patricia Casey especially. Despite her prayers over the years, there seemed no hope of help from Him.

She had caused injury to an innocent man, a good man, a man she loved with all her heart. When he had been unconscious again these last couple of days, she had been so frightened he was going to die. But even then she had found she could not pray. Patricia was quite convinced God had stopped listening to her prayers.

Surely He must hate her now.

And now Tim Hardy's employer and their friends all the way from England, rich and important people, were blaming her that Tim had come so close to losing his life. Tim had told her about Kate and Adam Stevens. And had the woman called this man John? Surely he couldn't be that old friend of Tim's father, the English lord he had spoken so fondly of?

Whoever they were, they loved Tim. They hated her.

And they were right to do so. She had nearly cost Tim Hardy his life. Twice.

The shaking grew worse. She moaned. A sob ripped from her. The tears flowed, a veritable torrent of them. The room began to whirl more violently. Vaguely she realized the big man called John was moving toward her. But next to her, Andy gave a cry of concern. She felt his arms go around her, supporting her as she fought to speak.

"I–I am so. . .so truly. . .sorry. I. . ."

That strange woman's voice cried out as the room spun even faster. Patricia crumpled.

Chapter 8

Tim woke slowly from a deep and dreamless sleep. Early morning sunlight was seeping into the room through the small space between the drawn curtains. He glanced swiftly around. No slight figure was curled into the comfortable armchair near the window.

Disappointment touched him. Only then did he realize how many times in his few conscious moments when his fever had been raging and more recently since he had hit his head he had been comforted by the small, red-haired woman's mere presence as well as by her capable hands.

His lips curled in a smile as he thought about her. Patricia. The most beautiful woman he had ever met, with her sun-kissed curls, her sparkling eyes—who had made him angrier than he had ever been before with a woman. Who made him laugh with her wry sense of humor. Who made him stop and think about his relationship with Jesus Christ again. Who made him willing to think and even talk so freely about faith, about precious memories of his mother, his father. And there was still so much to tell her about his father, his last few puzzling words.

But Kate had tended to him since virtually chasing Patricia from the room. When he had last been awake sometime the previous evening, she had refused to allow him to see anyone or even talk, especially about Patricia or Andy. She had just fed him more soup, murmuring soothingly that all was well now that they were home. Before he could protest, she had quietly left the room, and as the pain in his head eased, sheer exhaustion had made him fall asleep.

Patricia. No doubt she was exhausted from looking after him day and night. He should be glad that she could rest and let Kate and Adam assume the work she had been doing. But he missed her.

Then he remembered the harsh words from Adam in this room. He frowned. That would have upset Patricia and no doubt roused Andy's quick temper.

Even though Adam and Kate were home, he wasn't so sure all was well. Adam had been furious, furious with Patricia and that gruff uncle of hers, who had nevertheless cared for Tim as gently as a father.

Why had Adam been so angry?

Mrs. Wadding. No doubt she had filled Kate's and Adam's ears with her spite. And hadn't someone mentioned Jackie?

A sense of urgency touched Tim.

He sat forward and moved his head cautiously. To his immense relief, his body's protest against the motion lasted briefly, encouraging him to swing his legs out of bed. The effort that simple action took surprised him. Perhaps he shouldn't attempt to walk unaided after all.

A small jug of water rested on the small table next to him. Eagerly he reached to remove the dainty throwover and pour himself a drink, but his hand was surprisingly shaky and he only succeeded in knocking over the jug.

Tim gave a loud, exasperated exclamation. As he grabbed at a small towel and tried to mop up the water spreading rapidly over the bedclothes, someone entered the room. Without looking up, he said in an irritated voice, "Do be careful where you walk, Kate. I'm afraid there's water everywhere. Sorry."

A man's voice replied with a trace of amusement, "Oh, I'm sure Kate won't mind in the least, young Tim. She'll be so relieved you are awake, and if I'm not mistaken, much improved."

Tim had abandoned his efforts as soon as the man started speaking. He stared at the very tall, well-built stranger standing just inside the room. Then he frowned. Surely he knew him, those dark blue eyes set beneath thick black eyebrows. His voice, too, was familiar—that slight accent.

Amusement sparkled on the man's face, mingled with a trace of disappointment. "So, you don't remember me. Oh, well, it has been a long time, Tim lad. You were but a boy, and I have many gray hairs now and—"

"John. John Martin!"

Something flashed into the dark eyes, a hint of past pain.

Tim felt his face warm and added hurriedly, "Oh, Sir, I do beg your pardon. I–I meant Farnley. I did not mean to remind you. . . . Oh dear, I mean—"

He stopped abruptly and drew a deep breath. One hand raked through his tousled hair. With an effort, he pulled himself together and bowed his head formally. "Please accept my sincere apologies, my Lord Farnley. I fear the bump on my head has not only addled my brains but my good manners as well."

To his immense relief, John grinned at him. He advanced closer to the bed, saying cheerfully, "Well said, my dear boy."

That certainly was the old John Martin Tim remembered from when he was a boy, his father's first and dearest friend in this new land so many miles from their homeland.

John added quietly, "You were right the first time. John will do. It is such a relief to be away for awhile from being 'my lord this' and 'my lord that.' Oh, it is good to see you again, Tim."

Tim eagerly grasped John's proffered hand. But John did not stop there. His arms went around Tim and hugged him.

Tim's eyes grew moist. This man brought so many sad and sweet memories of Tim's mother and father. Not only had he once rescued Tim from a watery grave in the river Thames at great risk to his own life from his heavy convict's shackles, but he had also saved Tim's father's life on board the ship that had conveyed them both to their years of punishment in New South Wales.

John stood back and studied him. "And now it is my turn to apologize," he murmured a trifle ruefully. "You are certainly no longer the small, indomitable boy your father never could stop boasting about. From all I've heard about you, he would be even more proud of the man you've become. And I am sorrier than ever now that this is the first time I have been back here in all these years."

Tim's throat tightened with emotion. "He. . .my father was most appreciative of the way you wrote to him, kept contact with him over the years since you. . . since you. . ." Tim hesitated, not sure if it was wise to remind this man of those dreadful years before he had been able to prove his innocence and his claim to be John Farnley, the rightful heir of his father's title and lands.

"Since I was able to throw off my convict clothes and put on robes suitable to wear before the queen?" John finished softly. He glanced down at his well-dressed person before looking thoughtfully back at Tim. "I can tell you it does not begin to compare to the sheer delight of being clothed in the righteousness of Christ so I can dare come into Almighty God's presence. And it was your dear father who led me to Jesus Christ."

Emotion made it nigh impossible for Tim to speak. In a similar, matter-of-fact way, his father had often mentioned aspects of his faith in Christ.

Tim swallowed rapidly and managed at last to say in a trembling voice, "You. . .you wrote that to my father once. He. . .he was so very happy that your faith was prevailing despite your change in circumstances."

Tim wondered just how the transition from convict to member of the privileged aristocracy had affected this man's faith. It would not have been easy to maintain the simple beliefs his father had espoused.

"And your faith, Tim? Has your trust in God prevailed despite all that has happened to you and those you love?"

Tim stiffened. He averted his gaze and moistened suddenly dry lips. Once again he was reminded of his father's directness when he was concerned about another's spiritual welfare. Suddenly Tim felt deeply ashamed. Would his father really be proud of the man he was now, a man who had let his childhood faith wither so badly?

After a long pause, he looked up slowly. "It. . .it has taken a hammering, Sir."

John watched him keenly. There was no censure, only compassion and understanding in his eyes. "Perhaps that is understandable. I was so sorry to hear about your mother and little sister, and then for your father to. . ." He stopped.

Sadness filled John's eyes, and Tim looked away, afraid of his own emotions.

"And pray, my dear brother, what are you doing in here disturbing my patient?" Kate Stevens stood in the doorway. Mock indignation crossed her face as she surveyed them both.

John swung toward her and a smile chased away his grief. "Brother," he said slowly. "No matter how many times you call me that, you can have no idea how happy it makes me feel."

A slight blush rose in her cheeks, and she smiled back at him warmly. "We lived far too many years not knowing each other, my dear."

Tim looked at them a little curiously. So, even though John was now happily married to Elizabeth, even though he had children of his own, the man still took great delight in being acknowledged as Kate's brother. It made no difference they were really only half brother and sister; they were still family. Of course, with John's history, it was understandable that having a loving family was so all important to Lord John Farnley.

Once Tim had heard his mother and father discussing how horrible John Martin's upbringing in Spain must have been. From birth he had been wrongly taught that he was illegitimate, the son of an English soldier who had seduced his innocent Spanish mother. She had died in childbirth, and he had been reared by his Spanish relatives in an atmosphere of hate and hardship. Not until he reached adulthood and his bitter Spanish grandfather died was John Martin told the truth about his parents' true love and marriage.

Sadly, John's search for his father had led him to being the target of his malicious English cousin. That cousin had thought to prevent John being declared heir to what he had always considered his own heritage. It had not been until Adam Stevens had befriended John and with Kate's help proven his innocence that John had been set free to enjoy his inheritance and, more importantly, the wonder of his own loving family.

Now Tim no longer had a family. No matter how hard Adam and Kate had tried to make him part of their family, they had never been able to make up for the loss of the special bond he had enjoyed with his parents and for such a brief time with his small sister, Jane.

Kate moved closer and surveyed with a slight frown the wet bedding and the puddle of water spreading over the floor.

Tim fought back the old pain and managed to smile at her apologetically. "I'm sorry. Afraid I was rather clumsy."

She studied him carefully and then beamed. "Well, it seems you are much improved this morning. And this won't take long to clean up." She turned back to John. "Unfortunately the staff are in turmoil with our unexpected arrival, so, seeing you are here, John, you can help me get Tim up for a time while we change his sheets."

Tim stared at them. Certainly John was her brother, but to commandeer Lord Farnley's help like any servant. . .

Before Tim could voice his protest, John said cheerfully, "Most certainly, and perhaps I could help him bathe and shave as well. He'll feel more like his old self." He smiled at Tim's bemused face with a twinkle in his bright eyes. "Now, where might we find your dressing gown?"

Kate already had the garment in her hands, but as she placed it on the bed, Tim asked, "Patricia and Andy, are they still here?"

Kate and John looked at each other quickly.

"Adam hasn't sent them away, has he?" Tim asked in alarm.

"No, he didn't have to." John's voice was a trifle grim.

Tim stiffened. "Kate?"

"When we went to call them for breakfast this morning, they had gone. They must have sneaked away during the night," Kate said reluctantly. "No one claims to have seen them, although. . ." She frowned and added quickly, "They must have decided to continue their search for this Sean person they came all the way from America to find. But then we discovered—" She stopped abruptly, but Tim hardly noticed.

"Gone!" He was astonished at the depth of his dismay, the sense of loss. Something about Patricia Casey had stirred emotions he had not realized he had. She had seemed so strong, so independent, and yet vulnerable.

At Tim's dismayed exclamation, John said ruefully, "Yes, and it seems it might be my fault. My wife has forcefully told me that it is. I'm afraid I let that man Andy get under my skin, and I came on a bit too strong."

Kate snorted. "A bit too strong? You were talking about calling the police and having his niece arrested. Now," she added decisively, "they've gone, so let's forget about that pair and—"

"No, we can't forget about that pair," Tim burst out. "Pat saved my life."

John's dark eyebrows rose. "Pat?"

At the sudden speculative look his father's friend gave him, Tim felt heat touch his face. He looked steadily back at John and said carefully, "At first that's all she told me her name was." He hesitated for a moment, wondering just what Andy and his niece had said. "She wanted me to call her Patricia after she. . . afterward," he finished quickly.

"After she shot you, you mean?"

Tim looked quickly at Kate's stern face. "She told you about that?"

Kate shook her head. "Before we had alighted from the carriage, a very worried Jackie rushed over and told us you were unconscious once more. He had apparently arrived back here not long before us and received some hysterical story from the stupid housekeeper. For some—"

"The housekeeper? Is that woman still here?" Tim interrupted urgently.

"Why, yes," Kate replied abruptly. "We'll come to her in a minute. As I was saying, for some reason, Jackie was angry with himself, as though perhaps he could have prevented your being shot."

Kate searched his face. When Tim remained silent, she continued thoughtfully, "But then Jackie clammed up and wouldn't say another word, except that the doctor had been dismissed by Miss Casey despite Mrs. Wadding's strongest protests about your severe infection from a badly neglected bullet wound."

Tim frowned. "But I told you about my leg."

Kate nodded.

Jackie. Tim realized he owed the man a huge apology. And what must Jackie be thinking about Pat? Dear Pat.

Tim forced his thoughts back to Jackie and breathed a short sigh of relief that the aborigine had decided it best not to mention Tim's childish behavior. But Jackie certainly had no need to feel any guilt. Feeling confused, Tim stared from John to Kate.

John started to scowl and added briefly, "Miss Casey insisted she had shot you after her uncle at first tried to take the blame—if he is really her uncle. According to Mrs. Wadding, Miss Casey never calls him 'Uncle.'"

Tim gaped. That thought and its implications had not for one moment entered his mind. Suddenly he was angry with Lord John Farnley, with Kate Stevens, with all these adults who were failing to realize what a special person Patricia Casey was. Certainly she had tried to deceive him at first, but what else would a young woman do if confronted by a strange man when alone in the bush?

He thought of the indomitable girl who had not hesitated to draw a gun on him, the tender touch of her hands as she dressed his wound, the warmth of her smile while trying to hide the worry for him in her beautiful green eyes. A woman who was so courageous and special she had reminded him of Molly Hardy. A woman he had kissed. The one woman in the whole world he longed to kiss again. To hold close. To never let go.

Then he remembered the white-faced, exhausted woman he had last seen standing up to Kate so steadfastly. That Patricia Casey must have been very afraid to have run away in the middle of the night. What had gone so horribly wrong?

Mrs. Wadding. She must have told her version of events to them all, including Jackie. Tim should have sent her packing when she had first started to disrupt the peace and harmony of Waverley.

The growing anger in Tim exploded.

"If—of course he's her uncle! Whatever that...that horrible woman may have told you," he said furiously. "And after all they have done for me, you had no right to frighten them so much they took off like that. They could have left me alone in the bush if they had wanted to instead of bringing me safely back to Waverley. Besides, it was an accident and as much my fault as hers. Even Andy went for us both for being so stupid! They are my friends, my very dear friends!"

John and Kate stared at Tim and then looked at each other.

"If you feel like that, then it's just as well Adam and Jackie have chased after them, even if it was for retribution." Kate stopped and then added swiftly, "We think they are probably heading toward Sydney."

Relief flooded through Tim. Adam would find them.

"We are most annoyed with Jackie," Kate added abruptly, her voice rising. "Apparently he saw them sneaking away just before first light and did nothing to stop them. He did not say a word about it to us until he realized we were anxious about them. But why ever he thought we'd have given them—"

She stopped and bit her lip on the angry words.

Tim stared at her. She had used the word *retribution*. Alarm swept through him. Something else was going on here. "Given them? Given them what?" he snapped, looking from one to the other.

Kate shrugged, avoiding Tim's gaze. "Oh, they helped themselves to some supplies." She glanced briefly at John and added firmly, "Now, let's get you up. I think you seem well enough to get dressed after all."

"Before I do, there is one thing I want you to promise to do," Tim said. As Kate looked at him he added angrily, "Send Mrs. Wadding packing, and don't let me catch a glimpse of her again."

Kate smiled slightly. "That is one thing that will give me great pleasure—if Adam hasn't already gotten rid of her. He couldn't stand her screeching."

As he submitted to John and Kate's help, Tim thought anxiously about Patricia and Andy. Even if they had helped themselves to supplies, he was relieved that at least they would have food to tide them over. And Adam was a compassionate man. With Jackie's help he would find the two Irish Americans, ensure Patricia and Andy were safe, and perhaps even coax them back to Waverley.

Another thought caused Tim to frown. "Did you say they wanted to find someone called Sean? Are you sure it wasn't a man called Danny?"

John replied, "I'm sure it was Sean—Sean McMurtrie."

Tim stared at him and then turned swiftly away, not wanting to raise any more doubts about Pat. Who was this man they had come so far to find? Was his real name Danny, or were there two men? Obviously their search was important to Pat and Andy since they had let it take them all the way to that isolated camp beside the Turon River.

Tim thought long and hard, trying to remember more of what they had talked about, especially before he had become so ill.

In all the hours they had spent together, why had Patricia never directly mentioned the man they were looking for? And what would this Sean, or Danny, be doing out there anyway?

Suddenly he doubted if Adam was right that they would go back to Sydney, unless they had given up their search. Why would they give up now?

Tim drew in a swift breath as he remembered just where they had been camped, where they had been looking for that shepherd's hut. It had been a beautiful place, that creek meandering along the gully surrounded by those eucalyptus-covered hills with the flowering wattle dotted among them. Perhaps his father had thought so too. Perhaps that was why he had camped there. Perhaps. . .

Resolve settled on Tim. Whatever happened with Patricia and her uncle, he would return there. And soon. He was a man now, not a terrified fifteen year old.

It was time to put the past behind him.

Chapter 9

B y the time Patricia and Andy had driven the few miles down the long road from the homestead to the high wooden archway denoting the entrance to Waverley Station, the sky in the east had lightened. Soon, weak sunlight would start peeping through the tall timber and scattered scrub on the rolling hills.

Patricia was hardly aware that Andy turned onto the main road heading toward Bathurst and Sydney instead of taking the rough track they had traveled with Tim. Her heart was sore. The last time she'd seen Waverley's neatly painted sign, she had been so thankful they had been able to follow Tim's mumbled directions, so thankful they could get help for him.

"You don't have to worry about Tim anymore," Andy said gruffly. He cleared his throat. "That young man certainly has plenty of help now and doesn't need you any longer."

That had been made only too clear when Kate Stevens had turned Patricia away from Tim's room. Pat shuddered as she thought of the scene that had preceded her faint. It had only lasted a few moments, and she had fought off all but Andy's strong arms. But she had not been able to resist the warmth and tender care of the woman she thought someone had called Elizabeth. Apparently, neither had Andy. Despite Patricia's protests that she could walk, he had carried her to her bedroom, placing her carefully on the bed. At first he had angrily resisted help from the woman who had followed them.

"Now, Sir, relative or not, you know it is not proper for you to be in Miss Casey's bedroom. I will help her," the woman had said very firmly. When he still didn't move, she had added more gently, "From what I have been told, she must be exhausted from caring for Tim. I'm sure she is only in need of a good sleep."

Feeling she could not take any more confrontation, Patricia had raised her head and whispered, "Please, Andy. I'll be fine. And you need rest too."

Andy had stared at her with narrowed eyes, then back at the woman holding the door for him to leave. He muttered something under his breath that made the woman's eyes flash, but to Patricia's relief he turned and left without another word.

Not even her own mother could have more tenderly wiped Patricia's tear-streaked face and helped her prepare for bed. She had been tucked in, even kissed gently on the forehead with a murmured, "God bless." Then the woman had said, "Try not to worry. The Lord is in control. Just sleep now."

Patricia must have fallen into an exhausted sleep almost before the woman had left the room. And Patricia still wasn't sure who she was—a friend of Tim? The wife of that angry man Andy had been arguing with?

Tim Hardy's friends obviously thought the world of him, were very protective of him. Patricia knew that Kate and Adam Stevens were the owners of Waverley and must have just returned from England. Patricia tensed and her eyes widened. John? Elizabeth? Could they possibly be the English aristocrats Tim had told her about? They had also come from England, and by the excitement of the old staff at Waverley, they were important and well-known.

Patricia opened her mouth to ask Andy, but he had slowed the horse and was turning them into the bush.

"Andy, where are you. . . ?" The wheels jolted into a hole hidden in the deep shadows, and she hung onto the sides tightly to keep from being flung out of her seat. "Andy!"

He ignored her, peering ahead, steering the horse more carefully, deeper into the bush. She had to hold on as they were jolted from side to side. To her relief, after a few minutes, they jerked to a stop.

Andy handed the reins to her and muttered, "Won't be a moment." He jumped down, and she was still trying to steady the horse when Andy disappeared behind them.

The minutes passed, and Patricia became more agitated by Andy's absence. She was about to get out of the dray and tie up the horse to go looking for him when he appeared at last, breathing fast as though he had been running. Swiftly, he climbed up to sit beside her, and without a word, he took the reins once more.

"I was about to come looking for you," she said shortly.

He looked at her. For a moment she saw indecision in his eyes, but then he smiled crookedly and murmured, "Sure glad you didn't. Now, do you want your turn?"

She stared at him and felt the color rush into her face as she realized why he must have needed privacy. Folding her hands, she stared straight ahead and said primly, "No, thank you. I went to the outhouse before we left."

He grunted and shook the reins. The horse ambled forward once more, but after jolting along for a time, the bush became denser among tall gum trees. At last Andy gave a sigh, and they stopped.

"Guess I'm going to have to scout ahead for the best way," he muttered. "You'll have to drive. Think you can manage?"

Without waiting for her response, he handed the reins to Patricia and unhitched the saddled horse tied to the back of the dray. A weak beam of sunlight shone on the horse as Patricia turned to look. She gave a sharp exclamation.

"That's Blackie, Tim's horse!"

She had been in a deep sleep when Andy had woken her earlier that morning. It had still been dark, but he'd insisted they had to make an early start. "Never did stay a moment longer where I wasn't wanted," was all he'd said. She had been too sleepy to think clearly, too dazed and heavyhearted to protest.

Andy had their loaded dray waiting a little distance from the house, already harnessed to the big cart horse that had pulled it so faithfully all the way from Sydney. He had flung Patricia's few belongings in the back of the dray before swiftly tying the other horse to the back. Still in a daze of misery at leaving Waverley, she had not even looked at the horse.

Now Andy ignored her cry until he was in the saddle, Blackie tossing his head and snorting. As Andy expertly gentled the horse, he said casually, "It's an exchange for our chestnut. It hasn't recovered from that sprained leg. And don't worry, I've been riding Blackie at Waverley for Tim."

Before she could question him further, he rode ahead, calling back over his shoulder, "Mind you, follow carefully now."

For a moment Patricia sat still. She had already noticed the extra bags of supplies in the back. The Stevenses had certainly been generous but to let them have Blackie as well. . .

But then, she decided sadly, to lend the horse showed how anxious the Stevenses had been to have their guests depart, and Tim certainly would not be able to ride for some time. Even without the injury to his head and the bruises on his back and sides where she had landed on him, his almost-healed leg would make riding impossible for awhile.

Patricia sighed and urged the horse to follow Andy. As they continued on their way, the terrain became more rugged and hilly. She gritted her teeth, concentrating on controlling the horse. After awhile, they came out onto some kind of overgrown track, which was at least an improvement over forcing a new way through the bush. She was glad when Andy at last climbed back beside her and took over the driving.

It took awhile for Patricia to realize they were no longer heading toward Bathurst but were instead following a northeast route. It might be the track they had followed with Tim, but she was too tired to care much anymore. At least this change meant that Andy had decided to try to follow the last lead they had been given about Danny.

She'd never seen Andy so grim-faced. When they stopped at long last to rest and water the horses, he thrust a water bottle at her, followed by some bread and cheese. Patricia was thirsty, but after only a few mouthfuls of food, she could eat no more.

Andy, too, looked exhausted. His face was pale and strained. But he insisted they move on after only the briefest stop.

Patricia had started to take for granted they were going back to where Tim had stumbled over them, but after awhile Andy swung west. She thought of protesting, of telling him about the gold dust she had panned. But what did finding a few grains of gold—if it were gold—really matter anymore?

Even as she hesitated, Andy broke his long silence, saying quietly, "I promised to help you find Danny, Pat, but this has to be our last attempt to track him down. We'll make discreet inquiries in the village at Orange, even go on farther west to that place called Wellington. If there are no more leads for a red-haired, heavily freckled man with an accent similar to our own and calling himself Sean McMurtrie, then we return to Sydney and take the first ship back home."

Although his voice was low, his decisive tones and stern demeanor kept her from arguing. Tears filled her eyes. She brushed them angrily aside. In her heart she had already said good-bye to Tim Hardy.

"Patricia?"

Andy's voice had sharpened. Rarely did he ever call her by her full name when they were alone. She nodded, not able to trust her voice. He was silent, but after a moment she heard him give a deep sigh before slapping the reins to urge the horse to a trot.

They crossed a few dry creek beds and then managed to find a crossing over a much wider river that fortunately had knee-deep water. It was very rough in many places. Sometimes Andy climbed onto Blackie to try to find a better way through the steep gullies for the dray. Several times they had to backtrack and try a different route.

Patricia didn't dare question the tight-lipped Andy O'Donnell. A measure of his tension was the two guns he wore for the first time since they'd arrived at Waverley. It saddened her to see them. They seemed to change Andy in a way she did not like.

Throughout the day, she had thought about the threat made to have them arrested. Andy had confirmed that the man who had made the threat was indeed Lord Farnley, but Patricia was not terribly worried about the matter. She trusted Tim to put it right. He had always said the gunshot was an accident and had even teased her about it until he had seen how upset the reminder of it made her. But then again, Andy had always claimed with an Irishman's conviction that one could never trust the English aristocracy.

Patricia had never seen her uncle quite like this, so angry, so grim. And she was still weary, sad at leaving Waverley without a word of farewell, even though Andy had assured her he had done and said all that was necessary. The thought that he could not possibly have said all to Tim Hardy that she wanted to had been forced back to the secret place deep within her where so much other sorrow was stored.

It seemed like the well of grief just kept getting fuller, deeper. Her mother. Her father. Danny disappearing the way he had. The change in Andy. And now Tim Hardy.

Patricia sat up a little straighter. Her lips settled in a tight, firm line. Those moments with Tim, that kiss, and her dreams had been a fantasy. There could be no future for the son of an English convict living in Australia and the daughter of Irish immigrants living in America.

She tried to brush the thoughts away, to concentrate on guiding the horse so he would not break a leg or tip the dray over on the uneven ground. But thoughts of the young man with the twinkling warm amber eyes who had strolled toward her across the sand on the Turon River, who had kissed her so tenderly with love and passion in his eyes would not be easily dismissed.

And Patricia had plenty of time for thinking. Their progress was slow, much too slow for Andy, who refused to stop until the sun had set. She could tell he was on edge as he carefully chose a sheltered place to set up camp. But he was very gentle with her, insisting she rest while he looked after the horses and prepared a meal. She was glad to let him do so, although he must have been more exhausted than she was.

Once again, she forced some food past her lips—food that had not required a fire, she noted with some surprise. But it was a passing thought, gone long before they had finished their brief meal. Swaying with exhaustion, she obediently crawled under the dray and onto the pile of bedding Andy had prepared for her. As was his custom, he would bed down a little distance away. In a few moments she was sound asleep.

When Andy shook Patricia awake, faint light in the eastern sky was just beginning to disperse the darkness. He already had the horses ready but looked as though he had not slept much, if at all.

That night they again camped in thick bush. Andy let Patricia clear a safe area and gather sufficient wood to light a fire long enough to heat water for a hot drink, but he insisted on dousing it as the evening shadows deepened. She nearly rebelled, longing for a hot water wash rather than the cold water he pulled from a creek for her. But he turned away from her glare so decisively that she remained silent. Had something happened at Waverley that he had not told her about?

Still feeling the effects of the sleepless nights and days caring for Tim, as well as the exhausting days of travel, Patricia fell asleep while still thinking about it all. But some hours later she awoke. Light from the full moon showed Andy sound asleep a little distance from her. Something moved just beyond him. It was a measure of how deeply Andy slept that he did not stir when a couple kangaroos hopped into the small circle of moonlight not far from him.

Patricia was enthralled. Several times, especially in the evening or early morning, she had seen the strange animals moving swiftly through the bush, but she had never seen them so close before. The kangaroos straightened, resting on their strong back legs and long, thick tails. Standing perfectly still, only their ears twitched back, forward, to the sides. Something moved on the nearest animal. To Patricia's delight a tiny head peeped out into the moonlight from its mother's pouch.

One of the two horses tethered a little distance away moved, jingling the hobbles. The kangaroos took flight, crashing their way through the bush.

Andy was on his feet in a flash. To Patricia's dismay, she saw the glint of moonlight on the rifle in his hands as he swung it up, glaring around him.

For a moment she could not move, but then she lowered her head cautiously, not once taking her eyes from her uncle. As far as she knew, Andy had never slept with his rifle beside him, at least not here in Australia. Something was definitely wrong to make him so on edge.

A moment later, he lowered the rifle. He muttered something and stared toward her. Suddenly he seemed menacing, not at all like the uncle who in recent months had been like a father to her.

She dared not move, thankful she was in the dark shadows under the trees. Hopefully he could not see her. She tried to shake off the feeling, to call out to him, but then she heard him swear softly, viciously, before returning to his bedding.

Andy never swore. At least not in her presence. Stunned, she slowly lay down and stared up at the starry sky. Had he simply reacted instinctively to being woken from a sound sleep? Yet the more she thought about the last few days, the more she realized Andy was acting as though they were under a threat of some kind.

Until now, she had been too weary and depressed to think clearly about their departure from Waverley. But her senses were wide awake at last. Frantically, she examined what had happened from the moment Andy had woken her that night.

So they did not disturb anyone, he had insisted she move quietly as they packed her few things and crept from the house. There had been that moment when one of the horses had snorted as they approached. Andy had tensed and then hurried her even faster. It seemed now as though they had been sneaking away from Waverley, not wanting anyone to know they were leaving.

They had only traveled that very short distance on the main road before turning back into the bush. While she had been waiting for him, had Andy gone to erase any sign of where they had turned off? If he thought someone might be following them, he would do just that. He had shown her many such tricks over the years—ways to hide a trail he had learned from the Indians and experienced frontier men. And he had been a little too cautious about where they camped, each morning obliterating as many signs of their campsite as possible.

How foolish and blind she had been. They were running away. Hiding.

Why? Had Lord Farnley or Adam Stevens really sent for the police? What had been said after she had gone to her room?

She thought about Kate Stevens and the woman called Elizabeth. She dared not let herself think about Tim. Certainly the men had been angry and upset enough, but Andy knew Tim would put things right. And if Andy were really afraid of her being arrested, why were they going so close to Orange? Did he think the only police in the area were at Bathurst?

When they had been making inquiries about Danny at an inn on the road near Bathurst, Andy had left her to watch the horses while he went inside. She had started chatting to a friendly old man. He had proudly told her he came from Orange, explaining that it had been called Blackman's Swamp until just four years back.

"Called after a bloke named John Blackman," the old man had said, grinning at her from around the pipe dangling from his lips. "Not them pesky blackfellas that ran rampart here with their fierce tribal wars. Our Blackman became chief constable at Bathurst. But the name did confuse some." He chuckled. "Might be the real reason we're called Orange, although the official reason is it's on account of the explorer Mitchell, what discovered this neck of the woods, worked for that there prince of Orange or somethin'.."

Patricia had smiled back, wanting to ask more about the aborigines but listening patiently as the man continued his rambling history lesson. It had only been four years since the plan for the village had been approved by the government. The first sale of surveyed allotments had been held less than two years before. The first public building had been a watch house, the Methodists had erected a small brick building, there had been several slab huts built, but not much land had been sold, he had informed her a trifle gloomily.

A watch house. That meant there was a police presence in Orange. Suddenly Patricia wondered if she had ever mentioned that to Andy—as she still had not mentioned the gold dust hidden among her few clothes.

She bit her lip and shrugged. After all, it was only a small amount of gold. But would Andy think that, or would that feverish glint come into his eyes as she had seen it in California before he had taken off to the goldfields? That look had been in her brother's eyes too, and even in her heartbroken father's eyes the last time she'd seen him. Perhaps Andy had a right to know, to decide if they should go back to the Turon River to search for the precious metal while they were here.

There was little sleep for Patricia the rest of the night. She was up and dressed long before Andy stirred in the chilly morning. She watched him as he rose and stretched. He stilled when he noticed she had lit the fire and steam was starting to rise from the water heating over it.

"I thought I told you not to light a fire," he said angrily, heading toward the fire.

She moved swiftly to stand in front of him. "And why would that be, Andy O'Donnell?"

He stopped.

"Afraid someone might be chasing after us?"

They stared at each other. Andy studied her defiant face and at last nodded. "That too, but more because it has been too dry and we wouldn't like to start one of those bush fires we've been warned about, would we now?"

Patricia felt uncertain. She looked around. They had camped close to the trees. The undergrowth certainly was very dry. "We could have camped beside that creek farther back," she said sharply.

Andy shrugged and then sighed. "Yes, we could have. And then we would also have been easier to find."

She closed her eyes and whispered hoarsely, "We are really hiding. They sent someone to the authorities?"

Andy was silent, and her eyelids flew open. He looked uncertain. "I don't know for sure," he admitted defensively, but then added bitterly, his Irish accent suddenly very strong, "but you saw how that English lord fellow was attacking us. Our people learned a long time ago not to trust the English, especially their aristocrats!"

"Our people," she whispered. "You. . .you mean the Irish?"

"Yes, the Irish," he roared. "Your own flesh and blood. Your own grandfather transported, here to this very colony, falsely betrayed by an English lord who pretended to be his friend while plotting to take his land, our home. My. . . my father. . ." His voice cracked. He turned away but not before she saw the anguish on his face.

Patricia dimly remembered overhearing her mother once saying something to her brother about forgiving those who had disrupted their family. But Andy had bitterly retorted that it was very well for her to talk about forgiveness; it had all happened when she was too small to remember. Patricia knew her grandfather had died when her mother was very small, her grandmother soon afterward. The two children had been reared by a distant relative. But there her mother had always stopped, leaving Patricia to guess at their difficult life, which Andy had eventually escaped after his sister had been safely married. Obviously Andy had been old enough to remember.

Andy stood with his back to her, his shoulders hunched slightly. She moved swiftly and stood behind him, putting her hand gently on his shoulder.

"I'm sorry, Andy," she murmured. "Ma. . .Ma never talked much about anyone in her family but you, and then just that you were reared by relatives until you migrated to America."

He turned swiftly and tugged her into his arms. "And you are all I have left of family now," he said fiercely. "I'll do anything to protect you."

Not until then had Patricia ever appreciated the love this man held for her. She hugged him back and said earnestly, "I know you will, Andy dear. I love you, and I am so privileged, so thankful to have you look out for me, help me. But. . ." She drew a deep breath and let him go. Taking a step back, she added gently, "But I am an adult now. Don't you think you should have told me we were running away?"

"I didn't think you were in any fit state," he said harshly. "You scared the life out of me when you fainted. But even before that I could see how fond you were getting of that young fella."

Her eyes widened. She opened her mouth, but he waved his hand and added impatiently, "Oh, I know you didn't realize it yourself at first. I wanted to get you away before you did, even before those people arrived back home. What hope could there ever be of a future for you with someone like Tim Hardy, especially when you have your home so far away?"

His words only expressed what Patricia had been trying to convince herself of. She looked away.

"Then, before they had so much as met us," Andy continued, indignation and anger making his voice rise again, "they believed that nonsense Jackie and then Mrs. Wadding filled their heads with. That. . .that Lord Farnley was so furious! He was going to have you arrested, even though his wife was so nice to you afterward."

Patricia stared at him doubtfully. "But. . .but Lady Farnley was lovely to me. Said 'God bless' to me. Assured me that He had everything in control. She. . .she even kissed me."

Andy's eyes widened in surprise and then narrowed.

"Andy, you were too angry to think straight. Probably more angry at being confronted by an English lord than anything else." His eyes flashed fire, but she added swiftly, "I am sure they are decent and fair people. Tim told me the Stevenses—the Farnleys, too, for that matter—are very strong Christians. It is obvious how much they all love Tim. And remember, he told us he was only the son of a convict. Lady Farnley did not have to put me to bed herself. Would most English aristocrats, at least like you have known, do that to a stranger rather than order a servant to do so?"

He looked uncertain, and she continued relentlessly. "I think you are wrong, Andy. These people are different; they care. I am sure she at least would not have let the police be involved, especially after we looked after Tim so well. Besides, as soon as he could, Tim would tell them what really happened."

Patricia took a deep breath and then said pleadingly, "I think we should go back to Waverley and try to put things right."

Andy's face paled. He opened his mouth, closed it again, and swallowed. He looked from her across to where Blackie was searching for some green shoots in the dry grass. Patricia's heart plunged even farther.

"This last day I've known I—I had the temper on me for sure." Andy swallowed again. "We can't go back," he whispered hoarsely, "because now they would certainly arrest us, but for thieving, perhaps even horse theft."

"Blackie?" She stared at him with increasing horror. "You. . .you stole Blackie?"

For a moment Andy did not move. Then he nodded, flashing her one swift glance before looking away. "I lost me temper," he muttered again, and she saw the shame that filled him at what he had let his temper do.

Patricia swayed. They may have been entitled to help themselves to some provisions until they had reached a town where they could buy their own, but this. . .

They had stolen Tim Hardy's horse! Tim loved that horse. He had told her many stories about Blackie as a colt, about adventures they had shared together. Even if Tim could have forgiven her all the physical suffering she had caused, there was no excuse for stealing his horse.

That knowledge was bad enough. But it was the other thought that came racing through her mind that made a low moan slip from her lips. *Tim Hardy will most surely hate me now.*

"I am not a horse thief!" Andy roared, punctuating each word by slapping a clenched fist against his other hand.

Patricia looked up at him for a long moment. "If that is so, then it is time the horse you borrowed was returned," she said for what seemed the hundredth time. "Unfortunately the food we have eaten is another matter. Perhaps we could send some payment for it."

He looked away, staring off through the trees at the cultivated paddock that informed them Orange Township was not far away. She did not stir, returning her gaze to the defiantly blazing campfire and the vegetables cooking on it, not even glancing up when at last he stomped away.

They had been arguing ever since he'd told her about Blackie. Now the sun was high in the sky, but she had refused point-blank to move one step until Andy promised to return Blackie to Waverley.

At first, she'd wanted to simply turn around and go back. Although deep down she believed the people at Waverley would never do so, she had reluctantly accepted the possibility that they just might have Andy, at least, arrested. Besides, he had adamantly declared there was no way he would go back near that English lord. She had just as stubbornly insisted that the least they could do was return Tim's horse.

A snort from Blackie and a shuffle of sound made her look over her shoulder. She sprang to her feet. Andy was swinging up into the saddle. He stared at her, his lips in a tight, angry line. As she opened her mouth, he pulled on the reins and kicked the horse into motion.

"Andy," she called, but Blackie broke into a brisk trot and Andy was gone in the direction of the Orange village.

Relief mixed with trepidation. Was he going for supplies and information about Danny as he had originally planned, or would he return Blackie? She looked at the solid but slow old cart horse and bit her lip. Should she follow him? She could not leave all their belongings here. It would mean driving the horse and dray by herself into town and then hoping to find Andy.

Reluctantly she decided it would be best to stay put. She would serve them both well by allowing Andy time alone so his anger could fade.

"But you could have at least let me give you a note of apology to post," she muttered and then moved slowly to douse the fire and wait anxiously for Andy to return.

Then a horrible thought struck her. She had not warned Andy about the watch house at Orange or of the possible law enforcement officers who might be there.

Chapter 10

Tim stared from the grim-faced Adam Stevens to the scowling John Farnley. "What do you mean, there's no sign of them? Couldn't Jackie track them?"

It was the third day since Patricia and her uncle had disappeared. Adam had just returned alone from Bathurst. He tossed his dusty, wide-brimmed hat on the floor of the veranda beside Tim's chair and wearily sank down onto an old canvas chair. Staring out across the dry paddocks toward the distant, tree-covered line of hills, he said curtly, "We didn't try to track them at first. We went too quickly, hoping to catch up with them before they reached Bathurst. Had not been there long when Jackie went all native, as he can. Rattled off a few aboriginal words or, when I got really annoyed with him, stared from that expressionless face of his without a word."

John quietly asked, "What happened to upset him this time?"

Adam scowled. "The usual, I'm afraid. But for some reason ever since we arrived home, he's seemed upset with Tim as much as with himself for letting Tim get sick." He fixed Tim with a glare. "You wouldn't like to tell me why, I suppose?"

Tim hesitated, knowing how wrong he had been to use Jackie in that crazy way. To his shame he knew it had been a childish attempt to impress a beautiful woman. A woman who had just humiliated him by shooting him!

Now that same Patricia Casey's absence from his life left him feeling as though some vital part of him were missing. As wonderful as it had been to get to know John and Elizabeth as an adult and having Kate treat him like a son, Tim found himself listening for that lilting Irish accent, waiting for her brisk step, missing her saucy smile, her compassionate eyes.

Kate and Elizabeth joined them in a whirl of petticoats, forcing his attention back to the issue at hand. He swallowed, glad that the interruption caused by their arrival with a servant carrying a tray of refreshments made any response to Adam's question unnecessary.

Tim ignored Kate's frown when he waved away the cup of tea offered to him. Adam fell on his with relish, and Tim had to wait until he had swallowed several mouthfuls before prompting him to finish telling them what had happened.

Adam studied him long enough for Tim to begin feeling not much older than the young lad his father had left with them all those years ago. But he wasn't that same person anymore. He was a man, and it was time his old friend and mentor recognized that.

Tim raised his chin and stared back at Adam steadily.

Elizabeth came to his rescue. "Do tell us what happened. You said you saw or heard nothing of our young friend and her uncle?" she asked eagerly.

"Friend!" Adam snorted.

His wife interjected smoothly, "Yes. After what Tim has told us, we are most decided that Miss Casey and Mr. O'Donnell are indeed our friends. Despite what we have been told, their care of Tim has made that very evident. They dismissed that Dr. Mint not only because he wanted to bleed Tim, but because he wanted to amputate his leg! Oh, and by the way, I have sent that Mrs. Wadding packing. Tim had actually dismissed her just before he hurt his head."

Husband and wife exchanged a look that Tim had noticed many times over the years. Kate's head was raised, her eyes steady on Adam's. Whatever he saw in her face made Adam relax suddenly and smile so sweetly at her that a pang of envy whipped through Tim. Her smile in return was full of the understanding and love they shared for each other.

John muttered dryly, "And as their 'friends,' I have been told we should do all we can to help them."

"But of course," Elizabeth said matter-of-factly and sipped at her tea. "It is what Jesus would want us to do."

Adam suddenly gave a low chuckle. "So be it then."

A wave of love for these people swept through Tim. He and his family owed so much to them. Kate and Adam had always maintained they owed his father much more for the faith in God he had demonstrated and taught them. Yet their trust in God, their love for Him seemed to grow each year. Yet Tim knew their stories, knew that even in recent years they had suffered loss and disappointments. Life had not been easy for Elizabeth and John either. The stigma of John once being a convict still clung to them in England.

Shame hit Tim hard as he admitted to himself how he had allowed his own faith to shrivel in comparison to theirs. These four friends had learned to forgive, to leave the past in the hands of their loving heavenly Father. They were totally committed to living out their lives in a way honoring to Him.

Tim's heart swelled. Their change in attitude toward Patricia Casey and Andy O'Donnell was so typical of them, so typical of the way his own father and mother would have behaved.

So many times, he had been told the stories of his father's part in their coming to faith. Such had been the strength of his witness that he had brought John to faith. Then by the Christian life they had demonstrated, together they had won Adam to trust Jesus Christ. Elizabeth and Kate, too, had grown from having a shallow religious faith to experiencing a deep personal relationship with God in Christ.

All had not become smooth sailing after that. Only a couple years ago Tim had watched Adam and Kate grieve over the loss of a baby. He had seen their tears, their anguish. Until then, in his immaturity, he had thought Christians were not supposed to grieve as he had at the death of his father. He learned through watching Adam and Kate that grief was natural, and tears brought God's gift of healing.

Unlike Tim, the Stevenses had not let their terrible time of sadness separate them from God. Instead they had let the experience draw them closer to Him and to each other. Their trust in a loving and merciful God had never wavered. The voyage back to England had been undertaken to help the whole family during that time of grief.

And I have ruined their homecoming.

"Perhaps we had best forget about Patricia Casey and Adam O'Donnell," Tim said in a harsh voice.

Four pairs of eyes stared at him.

"They said they were here trying to find a man called Danny, or Sean something or other, so we should just let them get on about their business," he muttered.

"But they have made their business ours by what they did to you and for you," Kate commented quietly.

"I did it to myself by intruding on them in the first place!"

They were silent, the two couples exchanging glances.

"But you were so adamant we find them," John said gently, "and given the way they looked after you, I do believe we owe them at least the peace of mind that we intend them no harm." He paused and then added stiffly, "And I am afraid I did not behave at all as Christ would have me do when I lost my temper. That alone needs to be put right."

Tim stared at him and then at the others. Kate and Adam slowly nodded in agreement. Elizabeth smiled approvingly at her husband.

"We, too, were at fault," Kate murmured with regret.

Adam began to frown thoughtfully. "Sean, did you say, Tim? Do you remember the man's other name?"

Tim thought hard but at last shook his head. Despite all the hours they had spent together, except for that one time she had blurted out they had to find someone, Pat had always changed the subject when their conversations had swung to why she and Andy were in Australia. Not for the first time, Tim thought it strange that she had never talked about this person they wanted to find, never asked him if he had any knowledge of the man. Surely after they had become such good friends these past weeks she could have mentioned him!

Or had they only been friends from his perspective? he wondered a little bitterly. Perhaps that kiss had meant nothing to her. She had told him stories about an older brother, but Tim could not recall her mentioning his name. This man could be a brother, but he could just as easily be her husband or a lover. . . .

Pain lashed Tim's heart. Patricia's reticence was simple. She had not trusted him enough to tell him.

"I actually met a man at the inn in Bathurst called Sean," Adam said quietly. "Sean McMurtrie, it was. I noticed him first because he had an accent so similar to that girl. Even looked like her. I introduced myself and mentioned he looked very like a young woman called Patricia Casey I had recently met on my station and was looking for. He seemed startled but then laughed it off and hastily left, claiming he had an urgent appointment to keep."

"He looked like her!" Tim's heart suddenly lightened. Then he scowled. But her brother would have the same name, Casey.

Watching Tim closely, Adam said, "Yes, he looked very much like her."

"Then that settles it," Elizabeth exclaimed with a happy laugh. "We have to find them and, if for no other reason—" she paused and smiled lovingly at her husband, "—make sure they know the man may still be in the district. For them to travel all the way from America to find him, he must be very important to them."

Tim shut his eyes against the burning behind them, annoyed that his physical weakness still made it so hard to control his emotions. The love these people were demonstrating was overwhelming. To help someone else, no matter who they were or what they had done was as natural as breathing to these four. All because "Jesus would do so." A consuming desire filled him to have a similar relationship with God.

Kate stood up and began gathering their afternoon tea. "Right, gentlemen," she said brightly, "Elizabeth and I will see about a meal while you talk strategies."

Adam and John laughed out loud at her. "And then you two will come and tell us what you have decided," John said in a teasing voice.

The women looked at each other a shade ruefully before smiling back at them and retreating into the house.

The men were silent until John said quietly, "So if Patricia Casey and Andy O'Donnell were so keen to find this Sean McMurtrie, the only conclusions we can reach are that you missed them in Bathurst or they never went there at all. They may have gone north to where they were searching before. We need Jackie. Do you have any idea when he might condescend to return home?"

Adam shrugged. "Jackie took offense at something one of the aboriginal half-caste servants at the inn said to him. It must have been the last straw. That's when he went into his old routine of not speaking any English. The next morning he just drawled that he was 'goin' walkabout, Boss' and rode off. If you want to find them—or get Blackie back for that matter—that leaves us with the alternative of informing the authorities and—"

"No way," Tim interjected. "I've already told John if you report them to the police I'll deny everything. The bullet wound was my fault, and I gave Andy permission to ride my horse."

Adam looked at Tim with surprise. John's scowl deepened for a moment, but then that thoughtful, knowing look spread over his face.

"Let me finish," Adam responded. "I only mean we may need help to find them, not arrest them."

Feeling a little foolish, Tim turned hastily away but not before he saw the twinkle dawn in John's eyes as it had several times during the last few days whenever there had been any mention of Patricia or her uncle. He suddenly realized how much he had talked about her. The heat started to climb into his face.

He avoided looking at John as Adam continued calmly, "I didn't mean to tell the police any more than that we need to find them to give them an urgent message. I was going to add, perhaps we might be able to find that Sean McMurtrie for them. He may have some idea where they could be."

Tim started up out of his chair. He grabbed the crude wooden crutch John had fashioned for him.

"It's certainly good to see you up and about, Tim," Adam added smoothly, "but do take it easy. I can tell that Kate is still worried about you and—"

"And he's improving rapidly each day. He's surprised everyone by the way he is so rapidly regaining his strength," John interrupted, "especially if his temper is anything to go by when the women start fussing over him too much." He grinned cheerfully at Tim.

Tim felt the heat rise to his cheeks once more. Several times his anxiety about Patricia and Andy had made him grouchy, short-tempered. He had not been able to bear thinking of the possibility of never seeing Patricia again.

Before Tim could defend himself, John added meaningfully, "Adam, I think it's about time you and Kate realized that Timothy Hardy's beloved son is a man in his own right and not a boy to be mollycoddled."

Tim stared at John gratefully. He straightened. "Thank you, John," he said crisply, "and I would be most grateful if there is no more talk of police in this whole business. Andy is not a bad man. He is just very protective of his niece."

Tim remembered the look in the Irishman's eyes over the barrels of those two guns. Too protective? To the extent of harming anyone who threatened her in any way?

Then Tim remembered the soothing voice that had calmed him when he was feverish, the tender way Andy had helped his niece care for him. He added firmly, "We'll wait a few days and see if Jackie returns or sends us a message. By then I should be much stronger."

He saw alarm flash into Adam's face. Before the man could object, Tim added swiftly, "I'll decide what we will do after we hear from Jackie. In the meantime, I'm sure neither Patricia nor Andy will harm Blackie. They must have had a good reason for what they did, but when they realize a warrant has not been issued for their arrest, my guess is they will eventually return Blackie or at least let us know where he is."

He saw the doubt in both faces but was relieved when John and Adam nodded slowly in agreement.

Tim turned and awkwardly started to make his way inside, trying to ignore the throbbing in his leg and head that reminded him he would have to be patient for some time before. . .

He drew in a deep breath and stopped. Before he found the one woman he loved and longed to spend his life with.

Impulsively he swung around. Adam was still watching him, a slightly puzzled frown on his face. John was staring intently across the paddocks and the road to the house.

"It's only fair you both know." Tim drew himself up and said quietly, steadily, "Patricia Casey is the first young woman to ever remind me of my mother's indomitable spirit and loving heart. I intend to ask her to marry me and would be extremely happy if she could find her way clear to have me."

A picture of Patricia flashed straight to his heart, blotting out the surprise and then frown on Adam's face. Oh, how he wanted once more to see her beautiful lips start to curl into a smile that then reached her incredible green eyes, to light those eyes with mischief, with sparkling laughter, with that other fleeting expression he had never quite been able to understand. A sharp longing to find Pat so he could bathe in her beauty and warmth flooded through him.

"Tim," Adam began hesitantly, "you don't need my permission, but are you sure that—?"

"Gentlemen," John exclaimed as he stood to his feet, "we have visitors."

Something in his voice brought Adam to his feet as well.

Two horseman had just passed the tall gum tree lookout and had kicked their horses into a trot down the last slope to the homestead. The younger of the two men increased his lead on the other. His large hat bounced behind his head, revealing a face and fiery red hair that brought Tim swiftly forward.

As the stranger pulled his horse to a stop, he glared up at them with an urgent, grim expression.

Even before the man opened his mouth, Tim knew it was more imperative than ever that they find Pat and her uncle without delay.

❦

It was dark before Patricia heard a horse approaching. She grabbed the rifle Andy had left behind and slipped into the shadows away from the light of the fire.

"Patricia?"

She breathed a sigh of relief at the sound of Andy's voice and moved swiftly toward him. He rode into the light and dismounted from a chestnut horse.

"Thank you, Andy," she said softly. "Did you have any trouble?"

"No," he said shortly, "but I thought it safer to stable Blackie and send a note to Waverley for someone to collect him."

He started attending to the horse, finally leading it off to hobble and tether near the other one. She had expected him to still be angry with her and was not surprised when he did not speak to her until after he had eaten the food she silently dished up for him.

Speaking formally, he said, "Patricia, I have a terrible temper on me. I am really sorry I let it get out of control so that I have shamed you like a common criminal. Would you please accept my sincere apologies?"

She flew toward him and knelt at his side. "Oh, of course I do."

For a moment she felt the tension in his body as she put her arms tightly around him. She knew only too well what it was to have a temper. She also knew what an effort it had been for this proud man to humble himself by apologizing.

"I love you, Uncle Andy," she murmured and kissed his bristly cheek.

She felt his body relax, and then he hugged her back. "You haven't called me that for a long time," he murmured in a choked voice.

"Haven't I? How remiss of me, but it was you who forbade it. Said it made you feel too old," she whispered, tears choking her own voice. Giving him another hug, she sat back and said anxiously, "Did you hear any word about Danny?"

She didn't need to see the shake of his head to know the answer. If he'd had news, Andy would have been excited and told her immediately.

Andy sighed. "So, we go on to Wellington first thing in the morning. I didn't see any police, but there is a watch house in Orange. We must avoid the main road and follow the Bell River to its junction with the Macquarie at Wellington. The Turon also runs into the Macquarie." After a pause, he added softly, "You do realize this is our last chance?"

She nodded sadly. Only a miracle would help them find Danny.

That night, unable to sleep, she knelt on her blanket, and despite her fears that God did not listen to her, she prayed fervently for a miracle. Then she was still. At last, with tears streaming down her face, she whispered repeatedly, "I'm sorry, God, so very, very sorry."

In the cold light of day, she wondered why she had bothered. She didn't feel any different. Even if she had been wrong before, this last escapade must surely have turned God against her. There would be no miracles for Patricia Casey.

❦

Some of the country Andy and Patricia traversed over the next few days was even more steep and rugged, slowing their progress significantly. Then one evening when they had just come over a ridge, they started down a steep slope and were suddenly in the midst of a small flock of sheep. The animals dodged off in all directions. Two disgruntled shepherds shouted and then started after the scattered flock. Immediately Andy handed the reins to Patricia and jumped down to help.

At first the two men were very abrupt, but after Andy had helped round up the sheep, he successfully used his apologies and Irish charm to good effect. The two shepherds greeted Patricia politely, if a little warily. The one who had introduced himself as Billy seemed friendly enough, perhaps a shade too friendly. He smiled smoothly and professed himself very glad to see anyone so pretty to help relieve the monotony of droving sheep with only sheepdogs for company.

The other man studied her without speaking. She wished she could see his eyes, but his wide-brimmed hat was pulled low on his forehead. At last he nodded and in a cold, quiet voice said, "Ma'am."

Patricia was taken aback by the shepherds' rough, filthy clothes, their unshaven faces, and the coarse language. She wasn't sure what to think when Andy, hesitating only briefly, accepted their offer to share their campfire. While they shared some of their food with the two men, she remained quiet, listening to the men talk. Andy was adroit at parrying any curiosity about their own affairs while at the same time drawing the men out about their business.

Billy told them cheerfully that the station they had come from was so short of feed from the long stretch of dry weather that they were trying to fatten the sheep along the riverbank before taking them to markets at Wellington in a few weeks.

Although the quiet man his friend called Harry left most of the talking to Billy, it soon became apparent Harry was the leader. Patricia appreciated the fact that, unlike Billy, Harry at least removed his hat and washed his hands before eating. But as the evening wore on, she decided he was watching her too much. He seemed fascinated with her red curls. At first she only felt uncomfortable, but he kept staring at them until she began to feel a little belligerent. Always she had been self-conscious of her hair coloring, especially since she had cut it unfashionably short for this journey.

She stared back at Harry crossly, ready to tell him to stop being so rude, but he looked away and muttered, "Never seen hair quite like that before, and then two in a couple of weeks."

Patricia drew in a sharp breath. Andy swung around.

Before either could speak, the other drover, busy tidying away the remains of their meal, chuckled. "Reckon it looks much better on her than the young bloke, though. He had a lot of freckles too."

Patricia sat stunned. Before she or Andy could ask about Danny or mention his name, Harry drawled thoughtfully, "McMurtrie not only had hair like yours, but his accent was just like yours too, I reckon, Miss." He stopped suddenly and peered at her intently. "Now, like him, would you be originally from old Ireland, Miss?"

Before she could speak, Andy laughed. "Not for many years, I'm afraid."

The garrulous drover scratched his head and said slowly, "That bloke were a strange one. Said he'd heard talk of gold being found in this area and was askin' us about it."

He eyed Patricia and Andy keenly before adding, "Reckoned he'd been in someplace in America where he had worked on the goldfields in California near where the rush started a year or so back. Claimed to have overheard some big Australian bloke boastin' that in the Bathurst area was the same kinda rocks they was diggin' up and findin' gold in. He said he thought the bloke's name was Hargraves, but we'd never heard of him."

Patricia opened her mouth and then snapped it shut as Andy interjected, "Well, guess it would be like one of them fairy tales come true for a young bloke to find gold out here."

He stood up, stretched, and yawned as though not the least interested in the red-haired man or any stories about gold in Australia. His Irish brogue was even broader as he added casually, "Not sure what I'd be doin' with a lot of gold, though. A bit might be nice, but too much would be bringin' too many problems, I'm thinkin'. Now, it's been a long haul today. Guess it's time we got some sleep."

Patricia stared at Andy, incensed at his not questioning the men further. He shot her a warning glance. When she turned back to the men, she realized Harry was watching them intently. He stared at her, and for a moment the strange look in his eyes perturbed her. But then he smiled slightly, and she thought it must have just been the light from the campfire playing tricks.

"Yeah," Harry said softly, "I suppose it would be like a fairy tale—but a nice one at that. A man could do a lot of things, go a lot of places with money," he added wistfully. "But still. . ." He shrugged. "There've been tales over the last twenty to thirty years of gold being found in Australia from the mountains south even to here, but there's been no gold rush here like that bloke told us about where he come from."

Patricia stared at Harry, not liking the expression in his dark eyes one bit.

The drover's lips moved in a brief smile that did not reach those eyes. "I reckon there's a heap of gold waiting to be found right here by some lucky bloke. Why, only a few years ago someone in England wrote an article claiming he'd seen samples of gold from here and predicting that gold would be found in great quantities in Australia," the man murmured, still watching her.

Abruptly, Patricia turned away. Despite Harry's rough appearance, he was no ordinary workingman. And he certainly seemed interested in gold. As in California, the sparsely populated areas of New South Wales would contain men from all walks of life. Some would be simply trying out a different lifestyle, some trying to get a new start, but some would be trying to escape something in their past.

She winced and glanced at her uncle. She was sure that not only Danny was one of that latter group, but so also was Andy O'Donnell.

Harry was still speaking thoughtfully, his gaze on the fire that was gradually dying down. The shadows deepened on their faces. "Some think the governor then was scared of what effect a gold rush might have. There's rumors that over ten years back Sir George Gipps refused to let stories of gold finds made then be given publicity. But I knew old McGregor and know for a fact the rumors about him were true."

"McGregor?"

Harry glanced up at Patricia and Andy before looking away and adding slowly, "He was a shepherd working on a property near Wellington. Found gold not far from here a few years back. He's probably out there somewhere now trying to find more."

Harry laughed grimly and glanced up at Andy again, who was frowning. "Guess Gipps was right. Everyone would leave their humdrum lives and rush off to find gold and perhaps the everyday running of the country might come to a halt. But a lot of blokes have gone and joined the search in America anyway, so the powers that be are offering a reward for finding worthwhile gold in Australia."

Billy laughed. "And wouldn't you just love to find some of that lovely yellow stuff, Mate! You're always talking about going off to California. But perhaps you won't have to go that far with the rumors around here more recently. That young Sean fella sure pricked up his ears at your story of that bloke called Smith who's recently been claiming he's found gold. Won't say exactly where, of course, but rumors say he was prospectin' east of Orange. When we told him, he lit outa here real fast. Reckon he's already over there somewhere tryin' his luck."

Harry grunted and stood up. He scattered the hot coals and then busied himself pouring water on the fire, making sure every spark was out.

Andy shook his head ever so slightly at Patricia. She swallowed the words hot on her tongue and also stood, giving a forced laugh. "And I suppose you gentlemen egged him on in his foolishness. Oh, well, I'm to bed too. Good night, everyone."

But excitement kept her awake long into the night. She had to tell Andy about the gold.

The next morning, Andy was very quiet. He looked tired, as though he, too, had not slept well. She found out why after they had waved good-bye to their hosts.

"I'm not sure I trust those fellows, especially that quiet one," Andy said abruptly. "I decided seeing it was going to be dark in a few minutes, it would be best to camp with them than risk having them creep up on us."

Her eyes widened. "You stayed awake all night, didn't you?"

He nodded grimly.

"But you do think that was Danny they met?"

He nodded again. "I don't suppose there'd be too many men out here answering his description and with an accent like ours."

To Patricia's relief, Andy added wearily, "Looks like we go back southeast of here to where we were before at the Turon. That's twice we've heard he could be in that area. Let's just hope Danny hasn't left by now and is back in Sydney."

Chapter 11

The wattle trees lining the steep gully on the other side of the narrow Turon River were drooping in the heat of the afternoon. When she and Andy had first visited this place, Patricia had been enchanted by the golden balls of fluff that had so liberally covered the trees. Now only a few brown reminders of that splendor lay on the ground beneath the silver-leafed trees. But other bushes were starting to flower in the early summer heat. Wildflowers struggled to survive along the banks of the river as they competed with the native grasses for moisture.

Not once had it rained since they had left the Blue Mountains. Tim had mentioned that it had been unusually dry. Waverley needed rain so that its pastures would be green for the sheep and cattle, not to mention its acres of wheat that needed moisture for a good harvest.

Tim.

No matter how she tried to banish him from her mind, he kept invading her thoughts. Today especially, Patricia had been inundated with memories of Tim Hardy's quiet, deep tones telling her about that day his father had died near this very place, how she had held him to her, comforted him.

And now there was the cave and what she had just found in it.

Shivering, she forced her eyes away from the old landslide of rocks and dirt that she had scrambled over to reach the cave. Filling the camp water container first, she then scooped up water in her tin mug. She drank deeply of the cool, refreshing liquid, refilled the mug, and started back up the steep bank to the shade of a large old gum tree. She wiped perspiration from her face and eagerly drank more.

The days were becoming hotter. In the two days since she and Andy had set up camp here, the water level had dropped noticeably. And this was only late spring. By December it would be much worse.

Patricia looked thoughtfully down at the creek bed. Perhaps God had brought them back to this very river where she had met Tim Hardy for a purpose. The idea had crossed her mind several times that day. Mary Casey would have thought so, for she had always claimed not to believe in coincidences, only in God's leading. Especially if one prayed for Him to lead!

Patricia sighed. The bittersweet memory of her mother's faith died away, and the old ache flowed through her. Certainly she had reached rock bottom that night at Waverley. There was no doubt her thoughts and fears had been exaggerated then by sheer exhaustion and despair. But still, she had prayed for God to lead her more than once these last few years, these last few days especially, and until now she had thought her prayers were a waste of time.

Her prayers recently had been sheer acts of desperation. Deep down, she wondered if God didn't want to listen to her prayers, let alone answer them.

Yet Tim so obviously believed in prayer.

Well, for that matter so did she. It was just Patricia Casey's prayers she doubted God listened to.

She had prayed for Tim with all her heart that dreadful night when they had battled so hard to get his roaring fever down. He had certainly recovered.

But had God really heard her prayer, or would Tim have recovered anyway? And then, Patricia had prayed for a miracle to find Danny. Would God use rough men like those drovers? They were nothing like what she had always thought angels might be!

"Oh, God, if You are listening, if You do care what happens, could You please, please tell me what to do now?"

The prayer burst from her. Her loud words startled a magpie just above her, and it took off in a flutter of wings. Once more there was only the soft sounds of the breeze through the bush and the burble of the creek. Patricia leaned forward, clasped her hands around her battered trousers, and rested her head on her knees.

After a long moment she stirred and sighed wearily. There had been no blinding flash of wisdom, no sense of what she should do. And as for Tim Hardy. . .

She had tried so hard to push that young man into her past with all her other heartbreaks. But he refused to stay there.

Irritated with herself, Patricia took another long swallow of water. So many times she had promised herself she would not think of Tim, but it had been impossible, especially since they had set up camp on this stretch of the Turon.

And now this.

She still had not told Andy about the gold dust hidden among her possessions. Until they had returned here, the discovery had lost any importance to her. Yet somehow, they had come right back here to where she had found the gold.

Andy had left early again that morning, muttering something about hoping to find the shepherd's hut they had been told was somewhere in this vicinity. Each day, as soon as the sound of his horse's hoofbeats faded away, Patricia had not been able to resist panning for more gold. Until today, only a small amount had been added to her hoard, but this morning there had been more, much more.

In California that gold would have been worth many dollars, and it had been found in only a relatively few hours with her small pan. If she could find more gold, she could pay Andy something for this whole journey to Australia.

Each time the color of gold had shown in the bottom of her pan that morning, excitement had flown through her in waves. She had found herself feverishly washing more and more pans of dirt, knowing that many gold prospectors would have been incredibly excited at finding half as much gold as she had in such a short space of time. It might be that the whole area, the banks and hills, were well worth prospecting.

Then she had stilled. Why, she was no different from those men filled with gold fever, the men she had been so critical of. Suddenly ashamed, she had returned her pan, small spade, and the gold to camp. Then she had set out, determined to climb up the cliff to the cave still waiting to be explored. Andy had pointed it out the day they had set up camp. Neither of them had noticed it before, even though it was some way past where that cross still clung to the gum tree. Andy thought a fresh fall of rocks and earth might have revealed it.

Now, Patricia not only had to wonder what to do about her gold discovery but also about what she had discovered in the cave.

Again she wondered, had God been leading all along? She remembered Tim once saying something about "God working things out for good for those who loved Him."

It could certainly not have been God who had caused her to shoot Tim. That was clearly her own stupidity. But had God led them here for reasons other than simply finding Danny? The more she thought about it, the more bewildered she felt. How could it all possibly tie together?

Patricia made herself more comfortable against the trunk of the gnarled old gum tree and closed her eyes. She wondered if those drovers had finished taking their sheep to the property back out west they had claimed to come from. She frowned. There had been something about them, especially that quiet one, that had made her feel uneasy even before Andy had expressed his reservations. Had it just been their talk of gold?

Patricia shook her head. It had been a more personal wariness, a womanly one.

She wondered if, after listening to their stories, Andy had wanted to search for gold around here even more than he'd wanted to look for Danny. Perhaps the way Andy's eyes had gleamed at the talk of gold had been the real reason she had not yet told him about her find. She had seen what fever the thought of finding gold could bring to the sanest of men. Even her own stern father.

She shivered again. Now she knew what that gold fever felt like. Would she have reacted so crazily to Tim Hardy if she had not just found that gold? Would Tim Hardy get that same feverish look in his eyes at the thought of finding his own gold, of becoming rich?

With a sigh, Patricia tried once more to banish Tim from her mind, concentrating on thoughts of Danny. He should be her chief concern, not a man who had been a complete stranger only a few weeks ago.

And yet, she thought wistfully, *after only those first few days he seemed someone I could know so well.*

Tim had been so sweet worrying about causing her too much trouble, and yet so strong in the way he had coped with pain and illness.

Danny. She had to think of Danny.

She had never told Tim that Danny was her brother. Regret flooded through her. Would she ever have the chance to now?

She frowned, forcing her thoughts back to her brother. Surely if Danny had been in this area prospecting for gold, they would have come across him by now. Her heart had sunk a little further each day as Andy became more taciturn. She was surprised he had not insisted they return to Sydney long before this. Perhaps he would have if he still did not believe that Lord Farnley and his friends would have the police waiting for them.

But even Patricia's hope was fading fast. There simply was no sign of Danny. For days, she'd seen no sign of any living thing except the creatures of the wild. And this river basin, this whole country was so vast. The way they had picked up Danny's trail as soon as they had gotten off the ship in Sydney had been a miracle.

Miracles.

Had meeting those drovers been one of God's miracles? Her lips twisted wryly at the thought of those men being anyone's idea of a miracle. Her smile faded fast. The thought would not be banished. Was God helping them? Leading them?

"Are You, God?" she murmured. "Are You leading us as Ma said You would? Perhaps You know how desperately I need to find Danny. But You knew how desperately I wanted Ma to live, how desperately I want Pa to love me. Danny is all I have left. Are You even now leading Andy to find him?"

Wearily she moistened one corner of her filthy shirt with water and swiped it over her hot, sweaty face. It still seemed strange that in late November the days were becoming hotter instead of colder. Back home in the Northern Hemisphere, the trees in the mountains near their ranch would have almost finished carpeting the ground with their yellow and golden leaves. The animals in the wild would be energetically stocking up food and preparing for winter.

Patricia wondered sadly how her father was coping. Had he returned home? He had abruptly told her one day that he had decided to try his luck for awhile on the goldfields. The very next day he had packed up and left with little more than a muttered farewell. With a heavy heart at the change in her father, she had stood and watched until he was out of sight, only then allowing the tears to flow.

Then Andy had arrived and inevitably dragged out the whole story about Danny, how instead of being killed he was a deserter and had begged her not to tell their father. Several weeks before, she had received a letter from him telling her he was going to Australia to search for gold and a new life.

Many times since then she had wondered if her father had returned and found her note or had ever bothered to write to her. Had he found any gold?

A wry smile twisted her lips. As she had?

He certainly hadn't written to her before she and Andy had left the ranch. Probably Michael Casey never missed his daughter. Patricia swallowed, feeling the burn of tears prick her eyes.

She scrambled to her feet, picked up the water, and turned toward the track leading to their campsite set well back from the river. She set her shoulders.

Already she had decided that when she and Andy returned home, with or without Danny, she would make her father listen to her, talk to her.

She stilled. The sound of movement came from downstream.

Andy had expected to be away for hours. Of course, it could be cattle, even kangaroos. Yet. . .

The sound grew nearer. Hoofbeats clattered swiftly over the stones and sand beside the running water.

And she had left the rifle back at camp.

Ever since meeting the drovers, Andy had insisted she always have the rifle near at hand even though she resolutely refused to wear the revolver. She hated guns even more now but had obeyed Andy. If there were other men in the bush like those drovers. . . All day she had kept the rifle with her, but it had been too heavy to carry with the water barrel.

There was no time to make it to camp for the gun now. She looked around. Only a few tall gum trees stood nearby, little vegetation to hide in.

A horse snorted. She heard the swift click of hooves on the large, smooth rock not far from the outcropping she could see.

Patricia dived for a small bush, peering anxiously toward the bend in the river. A few moments later she breathed a sigh of relief as Andy came into view on the chestnut horse. She stood up and started scrambling down the slope toward him. As he rounded the bend, he kicked the horse into a sudden gallop along the straight stretch of sand past the track leading up to their camp. She opened her mouth to call out to him, when he saw her. Frantically he waved her back, gesturing with a finger to his lips for her to be quiet.

He pulled on the reins but only slowed the horse to a walk as he drew level with her. "Get out of sight," he commanded harshly in a voice that barely reached her. "Someone's following me." He urged the horse on toward the next bend in the river.

Patricia's heart leaped. Her thoughts flew to Tim. Had he guessed where to find them? There had never been any real doubt in her mind that Andy was wrong. Tim would never let the police be sent after them.

She hesitated.

As Andy disappeared, the clatter of more horses sounded on the rocks he had just crossed. Then Patricia made out the sound of voices.

Her heart thumping, she scrambled back up the track. She had almost reached the shelter of the bush when a voice called out. For a moment she thought it had called her name.

Could it possibly be Tim?

She twisted her head to look, stumbled on a rock, and fell sideways. The earth moved beneath her. An involuntary cry escaped, even as she felt the ground give way completely. Then she fell in a tumble of dirt and rocks, desperately trying to grab hold of anything to stop her descent.

Something hit her head.

She stopped fighting and let the tide take her where it would.

Someone was swearing. Another harsh voice said, "Quiet, you! She's not hurt much. Help me to get her out of sight. This is a golden opportunity."

Not sure if she had passed out for awhile or not, Patricia groaned as she felt someone grab her under the shoulders and start dragging her. Some relief came when other hands lifted her legs and her body left the ground. After a few minutes she was dumped down. Pain knifed through her back, her head. She groaned again.

"Get some water," that same harsh voice commanded.

"I ain't goin' back down there," another voice protested. "He'll be back. Won't let this little girlie far out of his sight. We'd better get out of here. He knows we're followin' him now anyways."

Patricia forced her eyes open. Dazed, she stared up into a face she recognized only too well. It was furious. Fear swept quickly over her as the anger on the bearded face changed to that look that made her flesh creep.

"What. . .what are you doing here?" she gasped.

Bold eyes swept over her disheveled body. She shrank back and started to push herself up, but her head spun too much.

"Why, Miss Casey, we were just riding along, minding our own business when you fell down right at our feet," the drover Harry smirked. Then hardness swept over his unshaven face. "And now you can help us find it."

"Find. . .find what?" She put a hand to where her head was stinging. It felt damp.

"The gold, of course."

He knew about the gold!

She lifted her eyes to his face. He was watching her intently. As she stared at him in astonishment, a faint gleam of excitement changed his expression.

He nodded slowly. "So I was right. You have been stashing gold away. Looks like we've found what we were looking for, Billy, Lad!" he added triumphantly.

Again Patricia tried to lever herself up but fell back with a low moan. She felt as though her body had. . .had fallen down the riverbank.

"Go get a drink for the little lady, Billy, and then she just might show her appreciation of your kindness by telling us where it is. Reckon we might even get our dray and set up camp here nice and close to the river."

Billy protested once more, but after a brief argument and a few more sharp words from Harry, the man disappeared. Patricia looked around her. They had carried her some distance back from the river into the thick bush not that far from where their camp was hidden.

She stared at the drover, the quiet one she had not liked at all. He was looking at her body in that way she feared and hated. And she was alone with him.

Trying hard not to let her voice shake, she said haltingly, "We. . .we haven't been stashing gold away."

"No? Then what is all that bright stuff that man of yours has been getting out of the river? He should have a nice pile now, surely enough for us to go and claim that reward from the government."

Andy had been finding gold? Shock held her still. All those days they had been here, he had been panning the river too? What about searching for Danny? Her heart sank. Perhaps he had given that up after all.

Harry grabbed her fiercely by the arm. Then he reached out his other hand and ran a filthy finger down her cheek and then her neck. She cringed, frightened even more by his scorching eyes.

"Reckon I might have some fun making you tell us at that," he muttered, then licked his lips.

"And I reckon not," a soft, deadly voice said from behind him.

Patricia gave a sob of thankfulness.

The drover grabbed for the rifle near his feet.

"No," Andy's voice whipped out. "I wouldn't touch that if you want to live."

The drover froze and stared at the two revolvers pointed at him. Andy had stepped from behind an old river gum.

"Get away from him, Patricia."

She obediently crawled a few feet away before starting to get to her feet. Dizziness swept through her, and she sank back to the ground. "I. . .hit my head," she gasped. "Be right in a moment."

"You've hurt her! I ought to shoot you right now!" Andy snarled in such ferocious tones, he even scared Patricia.

"No, no," she called out, "the riverbank gave way under me." She made another effort and this time regained her feet. "He. . .he said you had found gold, and he wanted me to tell them where you had hidden it."

Andy gave a mirthless laugh. "So I was right. Someone has been watching me the last few days."

"The last few days?" the drover snarled. "We only arrived this morning."

"We? There's more of you?"

Andy went on full alert, but he was too late. Patricia screamed, but the piece of wood in Billy's hand did its work.

Andy's finger hit the trigger, and one of his revolvers went off. The bullet plowed uselessly into the ground as he went sprawling.

And then lay horribly still.

Chapter 12

A ndy!"

Patricia started toward him, but Billy reached him first, and Harry grabbed her by the arms. She struggled, but he was too big, too strong. She had wrenched her shoulder as well, and her struggles only made the pain worse. Harry flung her to the ground. Pain knifed through her, and she went limp.

When she came to, she was lying on the ground, her head resting on Andy's lap. He was sitting propped against a tree. One large hand was smoothing her hair, but both his hands were tied. She groaned.

Relief echoed in his voice as he whispered, "Hush now, me darlin'. Just rest quiet for a few more minutes. Be worse than you really are—or I hope you are."

Worse than she was? A sharp pain knifed through her head. Every inch felt bruised and battered. Then she understood. Her ankles were tied, but her hands were free. She obediently closed her eyes.

Another voice snarled, "We ain't got more time to let 'er wake up properly. You tell us where that gold is, and then she can rest."

"Billy, Billy, where are your manners?" Harry's cold, quiet voice admonished mockingly. "Let's give the little lady a bit more time. Perhaps that drink? I'm sure very soon we can persuade them to tell us all," he added menacingly.

Patricia felt Andy tense. A hand roughly shook her shoulder. The moan that welled up in her was no fake. She opened her eyes. A cup was thrust into her hands. She almost dropped it, but Andy's hands were there.

"Can't you see she's hurt bad?" he snarled.

Billy hesitated but after a moment stomped back to his comrade. "Reckon you're right," he snarled. "She's still too crook—"

"Crook? You're the crooks," Andy snarled.

They both stared at him. For a moment they looked affronted, but then Billy began to chuckle. "Reckon we've just taught this bloke another Australian meaning to that word. Crook means sick, you idiot!"

His companion was not appeased. "Hmm, perhaps if we hurt her more, make her even more crook, her man will talk."

Andy stiffened and only relaxed slightly when Billy said vehemently, "I ain't hurtin' no woman, and neither are you."

Harry gave a low, laughing sneer.

"Have a drink, Darlin'," Andy said loudly, and then he added under his breath, "but make it like you're still out of it. Might get a chance to untie me."

454

He coaxed her until she managed to sip a few mouthfuls. She didn't have to pretend very much at first, but she did peer around as her head slowly stopped spinning. They were still in the small clearing surrounded by thick bush. The men were talking quietly around a campfire several feet away, and a small dray was a little distance away from them.

She looked up anxiously at Andy. A bruise and some scrapes marked his pale face where he must have hit the ground. "Are you hurt much?" she whispered.

He shook his head slightly. "And you?" he asked in a soft, tight voice. "Did they hurt you?"

"No, no," she said softly, and something in his eyes relaxed. "That track gave way. I have a few bumps and bruises. Except for my head, I should be fine. How long have we been here?"

Andy shrugged. "I don't know," he muttered with relief in his voice. His gaze returned to the two drovers. "When I came to, they had tied me up and already had a fire going. Must be a little while."

"What. . .what are we going to do, Andy?"

He shrugged, his eyes on their captors. "Get away somehow. Lie down again. Pretend to be sick, asleep."

She gave a realistic groan and rested her head back on his knee so her face was hidden from the other men. Her trembling fingers started working on the rope around Andy's wrists.

She whispered, "Is there really any gold stashed away, Andy?"

He stiffened. She glanced up. His lips were twisted slightly, but his eyes had darkened. "Quite a bit more than you have in that bandanna of yours," he admitted quietly.

She gasped.

"I found it when I was looking for more bandages for Tim and remembered you had been washing dirt here." He paused. A puzzled look with a touch of hurt flashed into his eyes. "Why didn't you tell me?"

"I. . .I don't know," she faltered. "I had just found it when Tim arrived that first day. That's the main reason I was so jumpy. Later, he was sick and. . ." She put her hands on his. "I–I guess I just forgot it for awhile and then—"

"Forgot!" He looked at her with amused affection. "So like your mother. Only someone like Mary could forget finding gold!"

"Hey, what you two doin'?" a voice asked threateningly.

Patricia froze. The men were walking toward them. Too late, she closed her eyes. Andy's ropes were tied so tightly, she had made no progress.

"Now, don't you go gettin' any ideas of untyin' him, Missy, or I'll have to tie you up too!"

"Oh, I don't think tying her up yet is an option. We'll just separate them," Harry said in a cold voice, so calm and matter-of-fact that Patricia felt suddenly very afraid. He added, "I think Miss Casey will be more than happy to behave once I've finished with her tonight."

"You touch her, and I'll kill you." Andy's voice was low and deadly.

"No, you won't," a familiar voice said furiously from behind them. "I'll reserve that pleasure for myself."

Patricia gasped and cried out, "Danny! Oh, Danny!"

Harry and Billy dove for their weapons. Two rifles thundered, kicking up dirt near their feet. They froze as three other men stepped from the shelter of the bush, surrounding them. A dark-skinned man also slipped from the deepening shadows, a long spear balanced, ready to throw. The other three men had their guns aimed at the two drovers. One was a weathered, gray-haired man whose rifle had roared at the same time Danny had fired. The other two Pat recognized as Lord Farnley and Adam Stevens.

A deep voice from behind Patricia said calmly, "Good shooting. But I think that will be enough for now."

Patricia started and peered up at the two men behind her. "Danny? Is that really you?" she whispered. "And. . .and Tim?" she said incredulously as her gaze shifted to the man standing beside Danny.

He hurriedly tossed his rifle down and crouched beside her. "Pat, have they hurt you?" he asked in a strained voice.

She stared at Tim, then turned her head once more toward Danny, and then to where the two drovers were being forced to lie on the ground. He was still there, that gray-haired man. He was helping Lord Farnley pull the two drovers' hands behind their backs, starting to tie them up. She shut her eyes tightly and opened them again, sure that the figure would have vanished—but he was still there.

Andy was also staring across the clearing. He gave a short, incredulous bark of laughter. "Well, I don't believe it!"

Gentle hands touched Patricia's shoulders, turning her around. She stared up at Tim, seeing the fear in his eyes. Danny had already cut the ropes on her ankles and was busy attending to Andy's.

"Pat, oh, my darling Pat, you must be all right." The urgency in Tim's voice increased. "There's blood on your head, your hands," he croaked.

She kept staring at him. Everything was happening too fast.

Tim ran his hands gently over her arms, her legs. "Where are you hurt?"

The touch of near panic in Tim's voice reached her at last. Still hardly daring to believe, she leaned forward. With a choked exclamation, Tim caught her in his arms and pillowed her against his chest.

"Careful there," Danny warned. "That's my sister you're touching."

Patricia didn't stir. Not even for Danny. She felt safety as she had never known before in Tim's tender embrace.

Someone gently pushed aside her dirty, blood-caked hair and lifted her head from its warm resting place. Someone touched the back of her head. She groaned and put her face back on its comfortable pillow.

"Careful, Man," a cool voice said. "She must have hit her head. Can't see much else wrong with her though except scratches."

She forced her eyes open. That horrible Lord Farnley was frowning at her.

"Oh, thank You, God!" Tim's dear familiar voice held a world of relief.

Patricia looked straight into his concerned amber eyes. The arms cradling her tightened. She closed her eyes. It must all be a mistake. She must have hit her head harder than she thought.

Another voice asked anxiously, "Are you hurt anywhere else, Patty? Those men. . .did they harm you?"

She opened her eyes and swiftly turned her head at the same time. Not a good idea. Pain slashed through her, and she fought back a groan.

The question had come from the gray-haired man who had been with Lord Farnley and Adam Stevens across the clearing. She gazed up at him, still wondering if she was dreaming. His lips smiled gently, lovingly at her in a way she had not seen for far too long.

"Pa?" she whispered.

Tears sparkled in his faded eyes. He crouched down. A gnarled hand reached out and touched her face as gently as a feather.

"Yeah, it's your stupid old pa at last."

It was. It really was. Relief, elation swept through her. And he was with Danny!

Her father cleared his throat. "I didn't stay on the goldfields," he confessed. "Must have just missed you by a couple of days. Besides your note, a letter was waiting." He swallowed and added gruffly, "Went straight off to see about a pardon for this idiot before hightailin' it to Bathurst. Deserting from the army, making you promise not to tell even me! Some stupid idea you both had I might be so noble as to turn in my own son!"

"No, no," Danny protested swiftly, "I–I was more ashamed of you thinking me a coward than that."

"You wrote to Pa!"

Danny hesitated. He twisted his hat in his hands and ran his fingers through the head of red curls so like her own. "Wasn't fair to let him think I was dead," he muttered, "especially once I was relatively safe here."

"And didn't I try and tell you that over and over?" she said with a flash of temper. She tried to scramble to her feet, but Tim's arms prevented her.

❧

Tim had been angry for days, but that anger intensified at what he perceived as thoughtless neglect of the woman he loved. Glaring at Patricia's father and brother, he barked, "Can't this all wait? Pat's been through a nasty ordeal."

Tim's anger at the two men had started the day they had ridden into Waverley, having followed Adam from Bathurst. Apparently after Adam had spoken to "Sean McMurtrie" in Bathurst, Danny had told his father, and they had followed Adam. "We guessed it could only have been that wonderful, protective sister of mine and Andy who the guy was looking for," Danny had explained gruffly. Only after they were reassured that no harm was intended to Patricia or Andy had Danny and Michael Casey been persuaded to tell their own story and then allowed to join the search party.

"Surely you can sort this all out when we've seen to your injuries, Pat," Tim now said in a carefully controlled voice. "Just stay where you are until we make sure. . . ." He faltered, at last losing the little self-control he had left. All he had been feeling over the past few days consumed him. In a strangled voice, he cried out desperately, "Pat, Darling, you frightened the life out of me!"

Tim cleared his throat. "I'll never to my dying day forget how I felt when Jackie appeared out of the bush with his tale of what he had seen happen to you. Then we heard a distant gunshot. I knew Andy must be somewhere, but it could have been your captors shooting and. . . Oh, I am so thankful to God that He brought us right here!"

Was that a glimpse of joy he'd detected in Pat's eyes when he first spoke? Now, of all things, unmistakable concern followed swiftly by anger darkened her face.

"Whatever are you doing here anyway, Tim Hardy? You are as white as a sheet. You shouldn't even be riding a horse yet! Your injuries. . .let me go!"

Tim gaped at her. Instead of letting her go, his grasp tightened. She had fallen, injured herself, been taken captive and tied up, just been reunited with her father and brother, and she was worried about *him?*

John Farnley started to smile. "I know what you mean about dear Molly Hardy now," he murmured to Tim.

Tim glanced up. Michael and Danny Casey were scowling, staring at John suspiciously. Although John had already made significant cracks in their prejudices, obviously it would take more than a few days for the two Irishmen to overcome their natural aversion and mistrust of an English lord.

Dismissing them all from his thoughts, Tim turned back to Patricia. He was oblivious to everything except the wonderful woman whose small, capable hands pushed at his arms, forcing him to let her go. Patricia stood up and swayed.

He reached for her again, but she groaned, "Don't touch me. Where's Andy?"

John gave a snort of laughter.

As Tim disobediently slipped an arm around Patricia to steady her, Tim glared at the man.

John swiftly turned his laugh into a cough, explaining, "Your uncle is fine. Adam's just tending to his injuries."

"Where is Andy? We've got to tell you. . ." Patricia's voice weakened. "So much to tell you, Tim, but Andy, he has to agree to. . ." She swayed.

Tim saw a look of sadness and regret touch the face of Michael Casey as his daughter searched for Andy. Tim glanced from John's curious expression back to the mild shock and indecision still on both Danny and Michael Casey's faces as they watched Patricia. He took a deep breath. Someone had to take charge here.

"Anything you have to tell us can wait, Pat," Tim said firmly. "You have to recover first."

"Recover? I'm. . .I'm fine." Patricia put a hand to her head. "I want to go to our camp. In the dray there's. . ." She stopped, looking toward Adam crouching beside her uncle.

Tim hesitated and then said grimly, "I'm only too happy for you to get as far away as possible from those two bushrangers."

"Bushrangers!"

"When Danny and I were making inquiries about you and Andy, we saw their wanted posters at the Bathurst police station," her father explained.

"You. . .you were making inquiries about us?" Pat asked in a dazed voice. "And bushrangers? Aren't they like highwaymen or something? But we thought they were drovers."

"Droving someone else's stock probably," Danny assessed.

Patricia looked from him to her father and back again. "How, when. . . ?" She paused, closed her eyes, and swayed.

"Not now. All explanations can wait," Tim said sharply. His mouth went dry as he remembered the fear and horror that had swept through him when Jackie had reported how she had fallen in that landslide, the way the men had carted her off.

Despite Patricia's protests, Tim swung her up into his arms and started off. He heard startled objections behind him, and then John's amused voice saying gently, "May I suggest you leave her to Tim's capable care? I would say they have a few things to sort out, don't you?"

A smile touched Tim's grim face. Just one more debt he owed his father's old friend.

Tim was breathless and trembling by the time he deposited Patricia on the ground near the dray. His shortness of breath was as much due to the feel of her soft body in his arms as to the exertion needed to traverse the slope and winding track.

Patricia stared up at him from her white, strained face with an expression in her eyes he could not decipher. "You. . .you came straight here. How did you know where our camp was?"

He hesitated a moment and then shrugged. She would know soon enough anyway. "Jackie and his people have been watching your movements since not long after Andy left Blackie at Orange. Jackie led us past here so we could get close before the bushrangers spotted us."

Her eyes widened in alarm, staring at something behind him.

He turned slowly and wasn't surprised to see Andy glaring at him ferociously. The man's hands rested warningly on his guns. Andy seemed to have more of a problem with Tim touching Patricia than either her father or brother!

459

Yet it was Andy who had ridden off with her in the dark and allowed her to be put in such danger. Andy O'Donnell definitely had not been Tim's favorite person these past days.

Tim glared right back at Andy. Then he turned and stooped to examine the bump on Patricia's head. "It's only a small cut, Pat, but I guess you will have a headache for awhile."

Without glancing back at him, Tim snapped, "Andy O'Donnell, if you think you can do anything besides wave guns around, how about getting something to help clean her up? She took a nasty tumble."

🦋

Andy didn't move. Patricia watched him over Tim's shoulder. She saw the indecision on his face but also something like admiration for a man who would ignore his guns like that. Then Andy's gaze swept the immediate area. Her glance followed his, and she saw her father and brother standing at the edge of the camp watching them.

Tim kept brushing dirt from her face and hair, his touch gentle. He stroked her face, and she felt his hands tremble. Then he stilled. With a deep sigh, he slowly stood and confronted her uncle. Only then did he notice the Casey men. He stiffened.

Tim turned back to Andy. "Look, contrary to what you might be thinking, until Jackie told us a couple of hours ago what had happened to you both, we were only on our way here to put your minds at rest, as well as reunite a family. But we'll talk about all of that later. Right now, you'd be better off getting a drink for Pat. . . Miss Casey," he corrected himself swiftly with a wry grin.

Andy ignored him. "You were saying you wanted to speak to me, Pat. But first, what really happened to you? How did those men get hold of you? Are you sure they didn't hurt you before I got there?" he asked ferociously.

Tim drew in a deep breath. He surveyed Pat with frantic eyes.

A deep voice behind them answered. "She fell when the ground gave way under her, O'Donnell, and Mirrang tells me they did not hurt her themselves."

Jackie stepped from the shelter of thick bushes. He ignored all of them, looking only at Tim, searching his face anxiously. Patricia stared at Jackie, seeing the aborigine's obvious concern for Tim change to anger as he studied Andy and then deliberately turned his back on her uncle.

Tim had told her many stories about Jackie. She knew Tim was as close to Jackie as the aborigine would let any white man be. Well-meaning white people had reared the orphaned boy until his longing to find his own people had made him go west. He had eventually ended up on Waverley. He was well regarded by most of the other station hands, but she had not seen him since that day weeks ago when he had been with the other aborigines.

Andy spun around, his hands once more going to the handles of his revolvers. Jackie continued to ignore him, instead studying Tim. "You still don't look too good, Tim," he said quietly.

Tim shrugged and asked impatiently, "Where did you get to, Jackie? We thought you would meet up with us last night. Today we waited a long time before coming on to. . ." He swallowed and then straightened his shoulders before finishing in a tight voice, "to that place where we found Father's camp."

"Sorry, Tim, I was watching this bloke." He nodded toward Andy.

Patricia's menfolk stared in fascination at the aborigine. Even though his clothes were the worse for wear and his beard and hair looked little different from other aborigines they had seen since arriving in Australia, his voice was cultured, his English perfect.

Patricia looked at Andy to see if he felt her own surprise. She frowned in sudden dismay. Was he ill? His face had lost almost all its color.

"Watching me?" Andy whispered.

Her concern increased. It wasn't illness. There was a trace of fear in Andy's voice.

Jackie merely stared at Andy impassively, all expression wiped from his face.

In a strangled voice Andy asked again, "You've been watching me?" Then he added sharply, "All day?"

Jackie shrugged. "And yesterday and the day before that."

If anything, Andy grew paler. He glanced at Patricia. A tide of red swept into his face. She frowned. That had been guilt and trepidation she'd seen on his face. Just what had he been doing that he had not wanted Jackie to see?

Suddenly she remembered. Andy had been panning for gold.

"Today I was supposed to meet up with the Waverley mob and lead them to you," Jackie continued, "but those bad men were watching you. I was concerned they would find Miss Casey too." As though Andy were the least of his concerns, Jackie turned and scowled at Tim. "But guess I left it too late. And I didn't expect to see you here as well. Miss Casey was right. You shouldn't be riding again so soon. We could have handled this."

"No doubt." Tim's voice was crisp. "But Miss Casey's welfare is my business."

Jackie stared at him a moment longer and then switched his attention to Patricia. "For many years I searched for my father's people, and I understood your need to find your brother, Miss Casey," he said with great dignity. "I saw you fall. You were fortunate not to be more seriously injured, Madam."

Patricia swallowed. "Thank. . .thank you." Her voice came out in a surprised squeak. Humor briefly touched the dark face, and she felt embarrassed heat sweep into her own. She looked away, putting a hand self-consciously to her face where it felt rather battered.

Tim crouched down again. Gently he pushed some strands of hair back from her cheek. She stared back at him.

"I'm really sorry for what happened at Waverley, Pat," Tim said softly. "They didn't mean to frighten you so badly. I want you to know I didn't blame you for either of those accidents, or. . ." His brief glance toward Andy was cool. "Or for anything else, come to that."

Patricia felt mesmerized by the way Tim touched her, the gentle expression on his face, the tenderness in his eyes. "I knew that," she said huskily.

Something flared in Tim's eyes, but then Jackie held out a cup to her with a sudden smile. As Tim took the cup from him, she smiled shyly back.

"Thank you, Jackie," she murmured. "Thank. . .thank you for everything."

He nodded and moved away.

Her eyes were drawn back to Tim's face. Her cold hand touched his warm fingers. The cup tilted, and he wrapped his hands over hers.

Someone shouted from a short distance away. Jackie melted back into the bush and a few moments later reappeared with Adam and John, leading their horses.

"Blackie," Pat murmured with relief.

Tim nodded and smiled. He hesitated, murmured, "Just rest now," and stood to meet his friends.

Tears filled Patricia's eyes as Tim reached the black horse. Blackie gave him a welcoming snicker and reached to push at his chest. The affection both had for each other was obvious. Tim patted Blackie as he engaged the others in a low conversation.

Patricia looked over at Andy. Relief mingled with regret registered on his face as he watched Tim and Blackie. Andy noticed her watching him and came swiftly to her.

"I'm glad Blackie made it to Waverley okay. He's some horse," he muttered. "Are you really okay, Girl?"

She nodded. "Andy, you. . .you should. . ."

He raised a hand and she stopped. "I know what I should do," he said briefly and started toward the three Waverley men, who were still talking quietly a little distance away.

Jackie, with the assistance of Danny and Michael, led the horses away. Patricia smiled. No doubt her family was very curious about this aborigine.

Patricia saw Andy reach the other men. As they turned toward him, she saw tension on Tim's face. He glanced briefly back at her and then scowled at Andy as the man began to speak. They were too far away for her to hear what Andy was saying, but she knew she should be there with him. She struggled to her feet. For a moment, dizziness returned, but she started toward the group of men, planting one foot carefully in front of the other.

Whatever Andy was saying had all three men staring at him intently. Not even Tim looked her way until she was close enough to hear Andy say, "And so, if you will forgive and forget this whole sorry mess and let us be on our way, I'll let you have the gold and show you where I found it."

She gasped. Andy swung around and stared tensely at her.

"Andy, haven't you realized yet what kind of people these are? They don't mean any harm to us," she cried indignantly. "And from what Tim has told me about their being Christians, they won't be bribed anyway!"

Andy snapped, "Who said anything about a bribe? We owe for our supplies as well as any inconvenience." Then he gave a hard laugh. "Anyway, I've never yet met a man who isn't interested in gold!"

"And I doubt you ever will," Adam said bluntly. A slight smile lit his eyes. "But there is a difference between an interest in gold—especially when it seems to be so close to where one lives—and the priority some folk give it. Many things are much more precious than gold."

Tim's head went up.

Suddenly Patricia remembered him telling her his father had whispered something about that, about Jesus being more precious than gold. Could it be possible. . . ?

"At the moment," Adam continued, "our main priority is to set up our camp here with yours before dark and let you both recover from your ordeal. Then we can have this talk about gold," he finished firmly, "and all that has happened."

He hesitated and looked at John. "I believe John also has something for Tim that perhaps should not wait until we are back at Waverley?"

Tim frowned, looking from one to the other as John grinned happily back at Adam and said, "Exactly what I was thinking, Mate, but later."

Patricia watched the confusion on Andy's face as he stared at them all.

"Come on, Andy," Adam said with a smile in his voice. "By now we'll need to rescue Jackie from two curious Irishmen. Jackie and Mirrang are going to stay at our trussed-up prisoners' camp to keep an eye on them for us until morning. Unfortunately it's too late now to take them to the police." His face darkened. "But tomorrow will be another story."

Chapter 13

That was the signal for all except Patricia to get busy. Despite her protests, she was made to watch as, in a remarkably short space of time, canvas shelters were erected and a neat camp set up. Patricia could not help smiling at the amazed looks the three Irishmen gave each other as they found themselves working side by side with Lord John Farnley. Obviously, he was no stranger to work or to setting up a camp. He helped gather firewood, started a roaring fire, and trudged up from the Turon River with buckets of water to heat so that Patricia and Andy could bathe away their ordeal.

John teasingly told the Irishmen to look out for Adam. "Now I warn you," he said, eyes twinkling, "don't let this bloke near the cooking pots. He's hopeless. You should have seen that first meal Timothy Hardy and I ever had with him around a campfire just west of the Blue Mountains." Then John proceeded to prepare a nourishing meal for them all.

Much later around the campfire, Patricia was pleased when Tim managed to get Adam and John to tell more stories about his father. Patricia could see by the look of delight on Adam's face that he realized the significance of Tim's eagerness to hear about Timothy Hardy. It was as though that deep well of pain Tim had kept hidden for so long was finally open to God's healing power. Even though Tim must have heard many times before the stories about how his father and John had first met Adam, he listened now with wonder and thoughtfulness, especially when the men described how Tim's father had so fervently shared his faith and helped them grow in their commitment to Christ.

Patricia was fascinated to hear Adam describe how he had taken the blame for his weaker brother's crime and then tell a little more of his own hardships until he had been assigned to George Waverley. Elizabeth's father had come from the dark slums of London and been deservedly imprisoned for his crimes; but after serving his sentence, he prospered as a pastoralist. He ended up treating Adam as he own son, even leaving the newly acquired Stevens Downs to him in his will. Not long after that, John Martin and Timothy Hardy had entered Adam's life.

Stories about Elizabeth as a young girl clearly delighted her husband. John reciprocated with stories about his own upbringing by his mother's family in Spain, his journey to England to find his father, and his new life with Elizabeth at the ancestral home of the Farnleys in far-off Yorkshire. John's voice deepened with affection as he told other stories about Tim's father. Inevitably the conversation turned again to how Timothy Hardy had shown first John and then Adam through his life and his knowledge of Scripture that a personal relationship with God was possible because of Jesus taking the punishment for their sins on the cross.

During this time, Patricia's father had been very quiet, but when John and Adam at last fell silent, staring into the fading campfire and remembering their dear friend, Michael Casey said softly, "My Mary used to talk like that about God."

Andy moved restlessly but didn't say anything.

It was Danny who whispered harshly, "But can God forgive a man who kills someone, especially a soldier who shoots a small child, even if it was unintentionally?"

Patricia saw the look of compassion on her father's face as he looked at his son. Hope flared. If Danny had been able to tell Pa everything, including his dreadful experience in the battle against the Mexican army at El Brazito, perhaps he was on the road to healing those hidden wounds in his soul.

She closed her eyes, remembering that morning when she had promised Danny to keep his secret. Perhaps if the letter telling them Danny had been reported missing, believed killed in action had arrived first and she had seen Pa's agony at the news, she would never have made that promise.

For when Danny had approached the house after her father had left for the day, she had not even recognized him until he spoke. There was little of the Danny she had known in the gray-faced, exhausted man who had stared at her from haunted eyes that had seen too much horror. After he had told her he was a deserter, she had promised not to tell Pa on the condition that Danny keep two promises. The first had been to never leave California without getting word to her somehow. That promise he had kept and was why she had followed him to Australia.

Patricia looked at her brother sadly. Remembering his clenched jaw and the denial covering his face when she had raced to her bedroom that day and returned with a familiar book, she doubted Danny had kept his other promise. But Patricia had said it anyway. "I want you to read this from cover to cover." She had cleared her throat and lovingly stroked the cover of their mother's well-used Bible.

At first Danny had refused, his face growing more bitter and angry. "You don't understand," he had said at last in a tortured voice. "I not only hate myself for running away, but my hands are stained by too much blood to even touch Ma's Bible!"

Patricia had waited in horrified silence, and at last Danny had whispered, "At Christmas we defeated a Mexican army at El Brazito. The very day Jesus was born, this little girl. . ."

Patricia shuddered at the memory of the horrors that had poured out of her brother. Somehow she had persuaded him to let her slip the precious book in his saddlebag.

"Yeah." Andy's cynical tones brought her back to the present. "And what about a gunfighter forced to kill some stupid man who wants to prove he can draw faster? And he only in that wild country because of what was done to his father!"

"Thought that had been eatin' at you all these years," Patricia's father muttered. He swallowed and added softly, "Mary told you and told you all you had to do was repent, like in throw those guns away and tell God how sorry you are and ask His forgiveness. Then He would help you forgive too."

Her eyes misty, Patricia looked at these three men she loved so much. "Tim has been telling me some things his parents taught him from the Bible, especially about forgiveness," she said softly. "I guess they must be what Ma believed too."

Adam and John glanced at each other and then looked at Tim with delight and affection. Considerable relief showed in Adam's face as he murmured, "You've found your way again."

Tim smiled at them a little self-consciously. Then quietly, with unmistakable conviction ringing in his voice, he said simply, "One of the things I remember Father telling me was from the letter the apostle Paul wrote to Timothy. Paul had been responsible for the death of many Christians before his own conversion to Christ. He called himself the 'chief of sinners,' so there is no doubt in my mind God can and will forgive every single thing—except not putting your trust in Christ's death, burial, and resurrection for us."

Joy shone from him as he added softly, "Because of Jesus, I am certain I'm going to see my dear father again."

Danny stared down at his tightly clenched hands. Patricia's heart ached for him. He had a long way to go before he could let God heal him of his grief, anger, and self-loathing. And she knew only too well that real, lasting peace and relief from all burdens could only come from the hands of God.

Andy stood up abruptly and strode off into the darkness.

Patricia stared anxiously after him. Tears had glistened in his eyes. She hesitated, wanting to go after him, but looked back in time to see Tim nodding at John. Immediately John stood and followed Andy.

Tim smiled at her and said softly, "John will be given what to say to help Andy." He paused and looked at Adam sadly. "I've had to do a lot of talking to God myself lately. When I let Father's death stop me from reading the Bible, praying, and having fellowship with other believers, I let my own faith slide badly. I've come to realize that instead of having my own faith in Christ, I was relying first on Father's faith and then yours. I've asked God's forgiveness, but Adam, I know how much my attitude these last few years has hurt and worried you and dear Kate, and I am so very sorry."

Adam beamed at him. "That dear wife of mine, as well as my perceptive old friend Elizabeth, have already assured me they were certain you were on the way back to a close relationship with Jesus."

Patricia was battling tears herself, feeling anguish for her family. She saw Adam look from Danny's tense figure to her before he added gently, "And now I think we've talked far too long. We all—especially Patricia, judging by her pale face—need a good sleep before our journey home tomorrow."

Patricia was delighted he had called her by her name and even more relieved when he smiled at her. She glanced at Tim. The look of disappointment and frustration on his face echoed her own. She longed to be alone with him, to talk about all that had happened, but Adam Stevens was right. She felt almost sick with exhaustion, and it was best to leave such conversations for a new day.

Before John and Andy returned and the others had even settled, Patricia fell into an exhausted sleep despite her aches and pains. But she woke before the sun peeped over the hills and tall gums. As she swiftly dressed, no one else stirred. She pulled on her thick coat and quietly left the campsite.

Tim watched Patricia until she was out of sight before stretching his stiff body and getting up. He had been longing to be alone with Pat. Glancing around, he was thankful no one else seemed awake. This was a good opportunity.

His mind had seethed long into the night, wondering how best to say all that was in his heart to the woman he loved. Yesterday had decided him. Despite all the difficulties that presented themselves with his lack of financial means and her family's demands on her, somehow there just had to be a future together for them.

If this was what God wanted for them both.

If Patricia loved him enough to work through the obstacles.

Tim had pretended to be asleep when John and Andy had at last returned the evening before, but John had given Tim a pat on the shoulder as he passed. When Tim had raised his head slightly, John's smile and thumbs-up sign made him sag with relief. Andy would be all right. That was one thing less to worry about.

Tim set those thoughts aside as he followed the path Patricia had taken out of the camp. He found her sitting on a rock near the water's edge. Behind her the water trickled gently over the riverbed that held even more of that precious metal men so hungered to find. She was studying the sloping cliff a little upstream and farther back from where their camp nestled.

A kookaburra in a high gum tree started laughing, giving warning of an intruder. Patricia turned her head swiftly and saw Tim. For a long moment, neither moved.

Then she gracefully uncurled, stood up, and held out her hand to him. "Why, Tim, I was just wishing you were here." Gladness rang in her voice, and he hurried to her.

Her words ran over each other in her eagerness to continue. "No, not wishing, I was praying God would send you. And He did! He answered my prayers again." Wonder filled her voice.

Tim gave a low laugh and said teasingly, "So I told you many times during those glorious hours we talked. God always hears and answers His children. It's only when my faith has been right down, when He hasn't given me quite the answers I've wanted, or when I've been away from Him that I thought He didn't hear me."

She nodded in agreement. "They were glorious hours for me too," she murmured a shade wistfully.

Patricia's smile made Tim catch his breath. Words he had not intended burst from him. "Marry me, Pat, my darling?"

Wonder filled her eyes, then a hint of shyness. Suddenly her whole face radiated such a wealth of feeling, it seemed perfectly natural for them to be in each others' arms. The kiss that followed left them breathless and trembling. The murmured words of love and commitment to each other that also followed left them in awe and wonder at the gift that was being given to them.

When they at last drew a little apart, Tim looked at Patricia and tried his best to be sensible when all sense seemed to have fled. He took a deep breath. "Oh, my darling, we have so much to discuss, to decide. I was going to talk first about where we might be able to live, what work I will be able to get. I am only a poor man and have nothing to offer you," he said in a concerned voice. "I don't know what your father will think."

"Perhaps you should be more worried about what Andy and his guns think!"

Tim shared a smile with her. "I'm sure the Lord's already sorting out your dear uncle," he retorted. Then he frowned. "But there is Danny. You love your brother so much you came all this way to find him, and it's obvious he still needs you. As wonderful as Adam and Kate have been, the fact remains that I only have the wages I earn working for them and no home of my own. From what you have said, your ranch is not big enough to support all of us and—"

Her husky laugh stopped him. "Why, Mr. Hardy, worrying about all this! I thought we had just decided the most important thing. You asked me to marry you, and I've said yes!"

Patricia's face sobered a little when Tim just kept staring at her. He was very serious about all these things he perceived to be problems. Patricia sighed. "I know only too well that men can get strange notions in their heads at times." She took a deep breath, and he thought he heard her murmur, "Here's where I stretch this newfound faith in You, Lord, even further still."

Decisively, she stated clearly, "If this is what God wants for us, we are going to be together, Tim dear. Nothing is going to stop us. Everything will work out."

He felt his tension begin to fade. "Yes," he said simply. Faith swept through him, around him, almost overwhelming him with excitement. "Oh, my darling, you are perfectly right! God is in control of every detail, isn't He?"

Patricia's eyes suddenly widened. "I forgot," she said with wonder in her voice and on her face. "I had actually forgotten until this moment the main reason why I've been praying God would bring you to me this morning." She started to chuckle joyously. "Why, discovering you love me as much as I love you drove it all from my head. And this is part of God's provision for us."

Tim stared at her in confusion.

Urgently she exclaimed, "There is something I must show you. Quickly."

Before Tim could speak, she had caught his hand and started tugging him upstream toward the cliff and that cave.

Tim loved the strong clasp of her hand in his and prayed again, as he had so many times since her disappearance, that somehow they could have a future together. Even though he was the son of a convict with no money of his own, and she with a family and home she loved so far away across the oceans, somehow God could work it all out.

He was so bemused by her, so full of all that had happened, that it was only when she stopped and looked at him sympathetically that he suddenly realized where they were.

"Tim, am I right in thinking this was where you told me you found your father?" she asked gently.

He stood very still. Suddenly he realized the deep anguish, the fear of this place that had haunted his dreams for so many years was gone. In this very place, Timothy Hardy had gone home to be with the Lord he loved, and one day they would be united where there was no more pain, no tears.

Tim looked up. His eyes widened. A hiss of surprised breath escaped him.

Patricia read his expression accurately. "You didn't know the cross was there? Then who. . . ?"

"I put it there."

They spun around. Jackie had slipped from the shadows cast by the weak, early morning sun now rising in all its splendor on a glorious summer's day. He smiled gently at their startled faces and said quietly, "I thought your father would have liked a cross above where he died to remind people of the One he always spoke of. He must have managed to drag himself quite a distance. His tracks showed he was injured in that landslide."

"Jackie. . . ," Tim whispered.

A dark finger pointed up to the piles of rock and dirt Patricia had scrambled over to the cave the morning before. "That slide was much bigger than the one you found yourself in yesterday, Miss Casey." Jackie paused and looked sadly at Tim. "All those years ago I thought it best to leave what I found in the cave."

A multitude of confusing emotions tore at Tim.

Patricia gasped.

Jackie nodded at her. "I returned yesterday and saw your tracks up there. I too looked and read what he wrote." He hesitated. "Perhaps I was wrong to leave it where Mr. Hardy had hidden it." He shrugged and watched the dawning of wonder, of comprehension and hope sweeping through Tim. "But at least now you are old enough, strong enough to know better what to do with his legacy as he would have wished."

Before either could gather their scattered wits, Jackie turned and disappeared silently and unobtrusively back into the bush in that timeless manner of his ancestors.

Tim found his voice. "Father. . .he had been up there? Can it. . .can it be Mother's box? The box Father insisted I find?" His voice rose in excited wonder as he stared at Patricia.

Patricia searched Tim's dazed eyes, trying to read what this discovery might mean to him. After all that John and Adam had said about Timothy Hardy last night and the wonder of the time she had spent in the Lord's presence that very morning, she now understood a little more the thinking behind that letter that Timothy Hardy had written to his son.

At last she nodded. "You. . .you never told me about any box, but there is one, a very old, metal box. I found it up there not long before those drovers came. It was only after I opened it and read the letter that I realized it must be something of your father's. The letter mentioned your name as well—"

Tim did not wait to hear more. Patricia watched him climb toward the cave until he had disappeared from her sight up the cliff. She hesitated but decided not to follow him. This moment belonged to Tim and his beloved father. He would find the box easily enough once his eyes became used to the darkness of the small cave.

It was not a very long wait, not as long as she had expected before Tim was striding slowly toward her, the box in his arms. By the time he reached where she had been waiting for him, praying for him, he was staggering a little under the weight of it.

Tim carefully, almost reverently, placed the box on the ground before staring from it to her. His eyes were filled with moisture, but Patricia knew she would never forget the expression of joy, of wonder in them as he sank to the ground.

She knelt down beside him. "You. . .you haven't opened it yet," she whispered, knowing with a sense of awe that he had wanted to share that moment with her.

He shook his head and then took a deep breath and very slowly opened the box. Silently he stared at its contents, several large, dirty bags, each one carefully tied at the top. And a large envelope.

It was the last he reached for, extracting the faded, yellow piece of paper it contained. He glanced up at Patricia one more time and then started to read. When he had finished, he was very still. He reached to untie one of the bags.

Sunlight reflected off gleaming yellow.

At long last Tim looked up, searching her face. He looked completely dazed, bewildered. Tears slowly trickled down his face. Patricia put her hand into his and clasped it tightly.

Hoarsely, he whispered, "You. . .you read Father's letter?"

She nodded apologetically. "I–I'm sorry," she whispered back. "I thought it might give me some idea of the owner, what it was doing there. It wasn't until the very end when he called you 'my dearest Tim,' that I realized the author must be your father."

He was silent, staring at her. Color started to wash back into his pale cheeks. He began to quote, "My dearest Tim, something has compelled me to write this letter. I know not why because this is my last time here, my last search for this gold and. . ." Tim choked, and he looked away.

Patricia waited for him to compose himself. She knew what he was thinking. God must have prompted Timothy Hardy to write that letter.

At last Tim murmured sadly, "He. . .he accidentally found gold here that first year after Mother died and came this way every time afterward when he made the trip to Waverley. Pa intended to collect his hoard when he returned that last time to take me home and. . .and hoped it would be enough to send me to Sydney, to give me a decent education, to give me the start in the world he never had. Enough!" Angrily he added, "And all the time Kate and Adam had already made provisions and now. . ."

His head swung swiftly around and excitement started to chase away the tears and any hint of sadness. "There probably isn't enough there," he began hesitantly, then his voice began to rise with his excitement, "just enough to buy a few merino sheep to start with, but. . .oh Pat, Darling, at least it will be a start for us."

"Tim," Patricia said a little nervously, "there's something I haven't told you. When you first saw me, the main reason I was so, so. . ."

His eyes twinkled briefly as he tried to help her faltering words. "So stupid as to shoot me?"

She didn't smile back, just nodded. "I–I had just been washing some river dirt and found gold. Andy didn't even know until later. Apparently when we were on the way to Waverley, he found it where I had hidden it."

Tim's eyes burned into her own. He opened his mouth to speak, but a voice hailed them. They both jumped to their feet. Impatience at the interruption covered their faces as they watched John walking toward them.

"I am sorry to interrupt you." A sympathetic smile touched them both but faded completely as he held out a large envelope to Tim. "I believe that before you two talk, you should know something, Tim. Adam picked this up in Bathurst. We were going to give it to you later, but guessing how things are with—"

He stopped, his eyes widening as he saw what was on the ground. "That's Molly's box! But I thought Adam said. . ." Brilliant eyes searched first Tim's face and then Patricia's. "You can tell me later," he said hurriedly. "I can see that I have indeed interrupted you at the wrong moment."

He hesitated and thrust the envelope at Tim. The touch of diffidence and unusual uncertainty in John made Tim stiffen in sudden apprehension. He took the envelope, staring from it back to his father's old friend.

"Open it, Tim, my dear fellow. Adam and I. . ." John cleared his throat and said swiftly, "We both know how much you always longed to go back to your old home. This was something we were planning to do for your father before he died. Afterwards, Adam thought it best. . . Well, anyway, we. . .we all love you and know this would please that great man, your dear father, who, in sharing his faith, gave us both the greatest gift in all the world, Jesus Christ."

Emotion thickened the tall man's voice, making his slight Spanish accent far more noticeable. He started to turn away and then paused, saying swiftly to Patricia, "And perhaps you should know that your father and brother have been talking to us about the possibility of staying on here in Australia instead of returning to California." His face lit with skeptical amusement. "At the moment they have joined with Andy in teaching us how to prospect for gold."

He moved off again, tossing over his shoulder, "There are more plans to help you both get a start, but we'll talk after you two have rejoined us. God be with you both!"

The two young people stared after him and then at each other. Tim looked down at the envelope. It just had his name on it and the words, "The trial of your faith, being much more precious than of gold that perisheth."

He caught his breath. "Patricia," he cried out, "these refer to the last words Father spoke to me, the words he had written in that letter in case, as he put it, 'anything should happen to me before I speak to you about the contents of this box.' And now this. . ." His hands were shaking as well as his voice.

"Open it, Tim." Patricia's soft voice was full of understanding at the turmoil he was going through.

❧

Tim looked at Pat, loving her deeply. She had lived near the California goldfields. She would know far better than he how many long hours Timothy Hardy must have spent along the Turon River washing pan after pan to find the alluvial gold he had so carefully hidden in the box for his son's future. She had read the letter that told of his father's deep love for him, the letter Timothy Hardy had written telling of his hopes, his dreams. She knew, too, the risks he had taken in this isolated place, the ultimate cost his father had paid for being so foolish as to put so much importance in mere gold.

The eyes of the woman Tim loved were full of compassion and a love that would last a lifetime. His heart leaped with thankfulness that he was not alone, that at this moment he had this wonderful woman with him.

God's timing was perfect.

Tim tore his eyes from her and ripped open the packet. After a few moments, he raised his face and stared blindly at Patricia.

Alarmed, she cried out, "Tim?" She took a step forward, and he felt her arms cradle him close. "It's all right, my darling Tim," she whispered soothingly. "Whatever it is, God is in control."

He gave a broken, bewildered gasp and held her tightly for one more blissful moment. "Oh, Patty, Patty darling, God is doing a marvelous job of being in control. These are. . ."

He took a deep breath and pulled away slightly to show her the papers. "These are the deeds of Stevens Downs and. . ." He gulped and added in a dazed voice, "Tell me, am I dreaming, or are they in my name?"

After a few moments, in a voice filled first with disbelief, then with wonder, Patricia read the accompanying note out loud.

Dear Tim,

Between the four of us, Adam, Kate, Elizabeth, and me, we have more wealth than we know what to do with. When he realized how much you still love Stevens Downs, Adam often bitterly regretted selling it. When recently it came up for sale again, we shared in buying Adam's old property back for you.

Patricia paused. Delight tinted her face.

Tim looked over her shoulder at the note. His arms slid around her, holding her to him as he finished reading the rest. A few more words had been added in Adam's handwriting.

As he read it out loud, he held Patricia close, smiling with joy at his friend and mentor's perception, his mischievous way of letting them know they all approved of Tim's choice of a life's partner.

If you have any doubts about accepting this expression of our love for you, Patricia and you may consider this as our wedding gift to you both!

Epilogue

I n 1851, Australia became engulfed by gold fever both in New South Wales and Victoria. On February 12 of that year, Edward Hargraves found a few specks of alluvial gold in Lewis Ponds Creek. He later claimed the amount was much greater, and this claim helped entitle him to be acknowledged as the first discoverer of payable gold in Australia. His partners, John Lister and William Tom, hotly disputed his claim for years, until in 1891 a select committee of the Legislative Assembly found in their favor.

In reality, on April 7, 1851, while Hargraves was away, William Tom went down to the Lewis Ponds Creek to get some water and noticed a glint. The heart-shaped nugget he picked up weighed about half an ounce. He and Lister quickly found several ounces of gold. The place was named Ophir. A report in the *Bathurst Free Press* on May 17 of that year told of the "complete mental madness that seemed to have seized almost every member of the community."

Although alluvial gold would be found all along the Turon River and provide Patricia's family means to start their new life in Australia, the newspaper's report of Tom and Lister's discovery failed to excite the residents of Waverley more than their own activities that week. Waverley homestead had been a hive of joyful industry for many days, and it sparkled from top to bottom. Not a stray leaf or dead blossom was allowed to mar the perfection of the garden where the late autumn roses still bloomed.

Adding to the excitement was the arrival from South Australia of the Reverend William Garrett and his wife, Beth, who was Kate and John's stepsister, with their family for the wedding. And of course, a few days before the special event, Tim, Adam, and John, along with Patricia's three menfolk, returned from working at Stevens Downs. At Harold Garrett's shout from his perch in the old gum tree, Elizabeth and Kate were not far behind Patricia as she rushed outside to greet the six men. William and Beth stood on the veranda with their arms unfashionably around each other's waists as they waited for the excited kisses and hugs to be finished between Adam and Kate, John and Elizabeth. The three couples all turned and beamed at the squeals of the bride-to-be as she was swung up and whirled around by an excited Tim Hardy.

But at last the great day had arrived.

Seeing Tim look so full of love and pride as Patricia came down the garden aisle on her father's arm, Lord John Farnley felt his heart ache that his old friends, Timothy and Molly Hardy, were not there to witness this moment. But then the glowing bride, her love for Tim shining in her brilliant eyes, clasped her bridegroom's hand, and the radiant young couple turned eagerly to face William Garrett.

Kate's eyes were moist, but it was Elizabeth who had the happy tears sliding down her cheeks as she witnessed the marriage ceremony. John slipped his hand into hers, and she clung tightly to him as they both remembered a dismal day when they had first seen each other and the boy Tim. The day when it had all begun beside a grim ship waiting to sail up the river Thames. They smiled at each other, their faces alight with joy.

Perhaps John summed it all up when he whispered, "God has blessed us so richly, and I know that Timothy Hardy would not have been at all surprised that the Lord he loved and trusted has worked it all out so very, very well."

A Letter to Our Readers

Dear Readers:

In order that we might better contribute to your reading enjoyment, we would appreciate your taking a few minutes to respond to the following questions. When completed, please return to the following: Fiction Editor, Barbour Publishing, Inc., P.O. Box 719, Uhrichsville, OH 44683.

1. Did you enjoy reading *Australian Outback?*
   - ❑ Very much—I would like to see more books like this.
   - ❑ Moderately—I would have enjoyed it more if _____
   _____
   _____

2. What influenced your decision to purchase this book?
   (Check those that apply.)
   - ❑ Cover   ❑ Back cover copy   ❑ Title   ❑ Price
   - ❑ Friends   ❑ Publicity   ❑ Other

3. Which story was your favorite?
   - ❑ *Faith in the Great Southland*   ❑ *Love in the Great Southland*
   - ❑ *Hope in the Great Southland*   ❑ *Great Southland Gold*

4. Please check your age range:
   - ❑ Under 18   ❑ 18–24   ❑ 25–34
   - ❑ 35–45   ❑ 46–55   ❑ Over 55

5. How many hours per week do you read? _____

Name _____

Occupation _____

Address _____

City _____ State _____ Zip _____

E-mail _____